I0583581

# THE DOOMSAYER JOURNEYS

# THE DOOMSAYER JOURNEYS

## The Complete Trilogy

### STEVE WETHERELL

Copyright © 2012-2019 by Steve Wetherell

Cover Design by Melissa McArthur

All rights reserved.

No part of this book may be reproduced in any form or by any electronic or mechanical means, including information storage and retrieval systems, without written permission from the author, except for the use of brief quotations in a book review. Any resemblance to any person or place, living or dead, is purely coincidental.

Praise for The Doomsayer
Journeys

*"Wetherell writes like a modern Douglas Adams with a darker, more fantastical bent. The Doomsayer Journeys is stiff upper lip, prim and proper madness – like a nice cup of tea spiked with malicious nanobots and mescaline."*

- Robert Brockway, *RX: A Tale of Electronegativity*

*"There's far too little good comic fantasy out there. Wetherell's Doomsayer series is not only consistently funny all the way through, but it's a fast-paced, world-is-at-stake adventure too. Any fan of the genre will want to read this."*

- Robert Bevan, *Critical Failures*

*"I'm just going to say I gave this novel five stars. Why? If my wife has to ask me to stop reading because my laughing is disturbing her Candy Crush game, congrats, your book just earned five stars."*

- Underground Book Reviews

*"The thing I really like about editing Steve is I don't have to. He's naturally funny, concise, and maniacal. The thing I don't like about editing Steve is that I go home, and visions of his twisted imagination haunt my fevered dreams all through the night. So, you know, life is all about trade-offs."*

- Brendan McGinley, *Man Cave Daily*

# The Last Volunteer

## BOOK ONE OF THE DOOMSAYER JOURNEYS

*Dedicated to my wife and kids, who do a marvelous job of putting up with me.*

*Dedicated also to Stone Cold Iain. Cheers, man.*

# Prologue

There are some who say the outcome of events within the universes can be predicted by a mathematical equation so complex that not even the most highly evolved life form could begin to comprehend it. They speculate that if we were better able to follow a breadcrumb trail of chemistry and physics, we could trace events back through endless oceans of randominity and land on a tranquil beach of predictability and purpose. A certainty principle. A master pattern.

There are others who would call it naïve, optimistic, and even arrogant to assume the universes could be dumbed down to a recognizable shape, and that all perceived patterns are imposed by tiny minds trying to humanize oblivion, that chaos and unpredictability are the very nature of existence.

Both points of view have their merits, and the ensuing discussion between enlightened intellects of opposing opinions would doubtlessly make for a thrilling party. However, seeing as we have little time for high bar tabs and likely fistfights, we will bypass the philosophical route and head straight for the truth. Which is to say, there *is* an equation out there that defies the logic of the broadest human mind. In fact, there are many, but the one that interests us now is a formula, which if correctly understood, and if the right tools were present, could very well predict the exact course of a raindrop through a river. More importantly, however, the equation could tell us why the raindrop fell and what it was thinking at the time...

But most importantly of all, this equation is the very reason the raindrop *exists*. It is called the Universal Theory, and once you get to know it, it is far friendlier than you might imagine. It prefers to be called Ted...

1

# Space, the Sentinel, and a Man Called Bip

Adjust your perspective to infinite. Now readjust to the averagely astronomical. And finally, set your sights on the merely gigantically enormous.

This is the planet Bersch, named ages ago after an astronomer who was enterprising enough to realize that no one had yet officially named the ground they were standing on. More practical people may have called their planet *Earth* or even *the ground*, but those people have little imagination.

Gigantically enormous is a particularly relevant term for this planet. Not on an ultraversal scale, or even on a universal scale, but as far as this particular solar system is concerned, Bersch is the big cheese. Burly planets swerve to avoid it and tiny moons hang in its orbit like barnacles on a warship. Even the resident gas giant is a touch intimidated.

If we concentrate and wait patiently, we can see a tiny twinkle of light curve around the planet's shoulder. Drift in closer and we can see that the light is reflected from a metal globe, a vessel of some kind, gliding along the blanket of stars like an ice skater's dream, hugging Bersch's exosphere like a shy child hugs its mother's legs.

A small plaque on the side of the vessel reads *S.S. Sentinel*.

Inside the globe it is dark, and cold too, with the kind of lifelessness that can only be found in lodgings abandoned by even the most molecular of tenants. From outside, dwarfed by the girth of Bersch, the vessel seemed tiny and toy-like. From the inside, however, perspective reveals that the *Sentinel* is verging on the cavernous. The long, wide decks are only partially illuminated by the soft, blue glow from the neighboring planet. The only noise is the calm hum of unseen machinery, a whispered lullaby for a slumbering starship.

On the inside wall on one of the many decks, staring out toward the vast vista of the galaxy, eight-foot-high pods stretch as far as the eye can see, their weighty, oval shapes tracking the curve of the globe's interior far into the distance. Each one emits a light into the gloom that, even though the pods are very close to us, seems to shine distantly through a thick fog. The only blemish on these otherwise smooth capsules is a small indentation that allows us to see inside. Inside this pod is a man. In the eerie stillness and translucent glow, he looks very peaceful...

Captain Finnegun dreamed. Technically, he shouldn't have been able to—the design of the chronostatic pod made the passing of centuries seem instantaneous to its occupants—but it is hard to contain a mind as broad and sharp as Captain Finnegun's.

He dreamed of penguins.

Slowly, but with an attitude toward urgency, a small light began to flick from red to green inside Finnegun's pod, harshly illuminating his clean-shaven face and giving him the appearance of a drunk in a disco. A gentle beeping noise began a soft but insistent monologue. It was the kind of beep that, while happy to be discreet at present, was promising to become a lot less patient and a lot more hostile if left unattended.

Years of the finest training had prepared Captain Finnegun for this exact moment. Even so, the first word he uttered as he awoke was a slightly confused, "Muh?"

With a suddenness seeming totally alien in the accustomed stillness, a green matrix of information began to scroll across the view port of Finnegun's pod, juddering and bleeping with urgent abandon. Blinking the weariness from his eyes, the captain began to process the situation, and with a growing sense of horror he realized that nothing was as it should be.

Like a layabout's nightmare, Captain Finnegun's alarm had gone off nearly a millennium too early.

IT MIGHT BE prudent to point out that countless light years away from Bersch and the *Sentinel*, in a very different time and place, a civilization was standing—somewhat reluctantly—on the cusp of a new era of peace and prosperity. The assembled world leaders were standing sheepishly, like a group of boys caught fighting by an irate mother, shuffling their feet and avoiding one another's gaze. They were waiting for a countdown that would change everything they had ever known.

Since the beginning of their planet's history, there had been an ever-increasing love of war. Nations had never been more content than when bombing the living hell out of other nations. Oodles of political time and money went into merely looking for *excuses* to have a war. War was good. Everyone knew where they stood with war. Even if it was usually in a bomb shelter.

Now, though, it was becoming evident that in order for them to save their entire planet from being blown to pieces or rendered uninhabitable by radiation, something was going to have to be done. The Hundred-Year Arms Race had left the richer countries with more nuclear warheads than libraries, and the crippling financial consequences had forced them to sell on excess nuclear arms to smaller countries. This had all seemed like a good idea at the time, until one day everybody had come to the uneasy realization that nearly every country in the world, regardless of affiliation or financial power, had a more or less even supply of nuclear weaponry.

The slow and horrible understanding that one paranoid dictator or one political misunderstanding could result in a war that, while lasting only a few days, could blow up the world several times over began to sink into everybody's consciousness. And, thus, a referendum was proposed. And then discussed, and then scrapped, and then re-proposed and eventually—after five years of cold sweats and sleepless nights—was signed by every king, queen, president, and prime minister on the planet. It was a testament to the general mentality of this planet's people that the first thing politicians could all fully agree on was that the prospective fiery death of the entire population was not a good thing.

And so the world's government representatives stood rather dejectedly in the viewing area of the planet's largest spaceport, waiting for the pleasant electronic voice to finish the countdown that would signal the beginning of the biggest arms armistice in history. Billions watched through live satellite images as a fleet of more than a thousand rockets began to take off one by one, each of them laden with nuclear warheads and other payloads of destruction.

A cheer went up from the collective military and media personnel who had been assigned to chaperone the event. A few of the world leaders wiped a tear or two from their eyes; whether from relief and happiness or from a deep sense of loss no one could tell.

Destined for outer space, the rockets would undergo a few years of very careful maneuvering in orbit until they formed what the media had dubbed a "Massive Ball of Death." Further years would be spent welding these nuclear arms together to form the biggest man-made space artefact in the planet's history—a cluster of devastating weaponry just over a quarter the size of the planet's moon. Then, when all the weapons were in one comparatively safe place, a drive thruster would begin the bomb heap's steady journey toward a neighboring sun, where it was predicted it would explode with a minimal amount of fuss.

Hooray! Global security had advanced to the stage where only weapons of acceptable amounts of destruction were allowed, and the populace celebrated, glad that their problem now belonged to the seemingly uninhabited folds of outer space.

It says something about this civilization's nature that a few months after the nuclear arms had been sent on their merry way and it was reported that the Massive Ball of Death was a substantial way off its intended course, no one really cared much.

NOW LET'S get back to Bersch...

This is the northernmost continent of Bersch, although some people are reluctant to call it a continent as they're not sure whether building a continent out of ice isn't somehow cheating. But it is a continent nonetheless, and it rests like a white toupee on the crown of the bulbous world. Those who bother to learn about this chilled wasteland call it the Ice Plains because it is quite plain and made out of ice. And snow. There is also a lot of snow.

But mainly ice.

Nobody comes here; not just because it is a nasty place, but because it's a nasty place that is a bother to get to. No, nobody but the most bizarre and blubbery of creatures would inhabit this frosted stretch of soul-destroying wasteland. Therefore, it is quite surprising to see, nestled between two enormous mountains and teetering on the edge of a vertical cliff face, a quaint and surprisingly not ice-covered village.

The village comprises of several dozen triangular houses, some thatched, some tiled, but all made from wood, bar a large dome on the side of the village closest to the cliff, which appears to be made entirely of snow. In contrast to the surrounding icy harshness, the area around the village is a stretch of lush green farmland and forest that climbs the sides of the mountains and stops abruptly near the cliff edge. Comfortably cuddled from the raging elements, the village is reminiscent of an inverted snow globe.

This is the community of Kaneq: an oasis of spring in an eternal winter.

Hovering above and around the village is the reason Kaneq hasn't been eaten by a glacier or snowed under in mere seconds. A haze of nearly transparent heat creates an effective greenhouse wall, keeping the harsher elements out and letting only the weak sunshine in. It's quite interesting to watch it in action. For instance, if you could follow the direction of a particularly cruel gale as it winds through the Ice Plain mountains, past Old Bachalack and the Patient Mother, you'd be surprised to see it disperse in a flash of warmth as it hit the almost invisible barrier of shimmering heat that surrounds Kaneq. So, too, if you looked up at a vengeful snowstorm plummeting angrily from the sky, you might be impressed to see it transform, with a barely audible fizzing noise, into a gentle summer rain.

And so, thanks to the heatshield, it was on a warm spring day that Bip Plunkerton stepped back to look at his accomplishment. He removed his small half-moon glasses to see if what he was looking at was indeed actually there and not just some terrible trick of the light. A familiar sense of general disappointment crept over him. He turned to his friend Michaelmas, who was gaping at Bip's handiwork and looking as though he was attempting to cry and laugh at the same time. The portly man walked around the construction, scratching and shaking his balding head in a mixture of amazement and disgust.

"My wife is going to kill me," he finally said.

"Sorry, Michaelmas," said Bip. "I don't know what went wrong."

"No, no. You never does, but I think I can give you a hint, right?" Michaelmas walked back to Bip and put a burly arm over his smaller friend's shoulders. "What I said, right, was, 'Bip, if'n you're needing some practice with that psyence of yours, why don'ts you do us a favor and turn that crumbled old garden shed of mine into a conservatory for the wife, yes?' And you says, 'No problem, Michaelmas, my friend, it's the least I can do what with you being such a good friend and all.'"

Bip opened his mouth to speak. He wasn't sure that was exactly how the conversation had gone. His potential protest, however, was cut short by Michaelmas's litany.

"'Grand,' I says, and I lets you work yer hocus pocus on me garden shed—which me old granpappy built with his bare hands I might remind you—and what I get is not a conservatory, is it?"

Bip shook his head. There was no denying it. It definitely wasn't a conservatory.

"No, Bip, it isn't," continued Michaelmas. "What you did, instead of turning my garden shed into a conservatory likes I asked, you turned my garden shed—and my entire house—*into a bloody igloo!*"

Bip nodded in dumb agreement. Where before had stood a

modest, hand-built, wooden house with a lovely thatched roof, now stood a rapidly melting igloo.

"Sorry, Michaelmas," he said. "I don't know how it happened."

"No, no you never does," said Michaelmas, running a hand across his suddenly tired-looking face. "I'm going to have a tough time explaining this one to the council. And then there's the wife." He groaned. There was always the wife.

Bip cleaned his glasses thoughtfully for a moment. "Well maybe I can try and—"

"Oh no!" interrupted Michaelmas. "No, no, no. Do me a favor and don't do me no more favors." He stopped and sighed, taking in the slump of Bip's shoulders and the defeat in his eye. "Look, mate, you've got talent and that's no lie, but you're going to need a hell of a lot of practice if'n you want to make your apprenticeship this year. The psyentists ain't just interested in talent—they need reliable men. Men who ain't suddenly going to turn their houses into igloos!"

"I know, I know," whined Bip. "I just don't know why this keeps happening to me. They're never going to let me be a psyentist if I can't even do a simple restructuring equation!" He kicked the igloo in frustration, resulting in a shower of ice.

"Tell you what, mate," said Michaelmas. "You bugger off and get some practice in, and I'll get a councilman or an elder to sort this out. I'll blame it on vandals or something."

Bip frowned. "What? Vandals turned your house into an igloo?"

"You got a better idea? No, vandals it was and vandals it shall be. A practical joke by some young upstart is what I'll tell 'em." He rubbed his moustache thoughtfully. "They've no reason not to believe me— stranger things have happened. Remember when Biron's cows tried to storm the town hall?"

Bip nodded in recollection. What had come to be known as the Great Bovine Rebellion had ended firstly in riots then mainly in steak. In a community where people often tampered with the very fabric of nature, phenomena such as super-intelligent livestock were a commonplace occurrence.

"Thanks, Michaelmas. If they find out I'm practicing psyence without proper supervision, they'll have my guts for garters," said Bip.

"No problem, lad, but if yer going to practice, then...erm...do it elsewhere, would you? I don't need no more home improvements if you get my drift."

Bip nodded and ambled off, leaving Michaelmas to stare at what had formerly been his house.

---

CAPTAIN FINNEGUN REVIEWED his crew in an emergency assembly on the foredeck of the *Sentinel*. Everyone was present, still bleary-eyed from the abrupt ejection from chronostatic sleep. Looking out over the crowd of nearly identical gray and yellow uniforms, Finnegun cleared his throat.

"Ladies and gentlemen," he began, rather lamely. "It appears that we have been activated far before our estimated crisis intervention deadline by what appears to be an unexpected crisis of our very own."

The crew began to murmur until a man to Finnegun's left hushed them to quiet. Finnegun continued. "The situation is as follows—a large spherical metal object of unknown origin has struck the ship. While there is no major damage to life support or the primary structure of the ship, we have, I regret to say, been knocked out of orbit—"

A harassed looking woman in the crowd raised her voice. "So we're hurtling out into space, then?"

"Not quite, no. Not really," said Finnegun. The crew let out a collective sigh of relief. "We are, in fact, hurtling toward the planet's surface." He gestured to the giant holo-screen behind him, where the planet Bersch waited like a blue and green fist. The crew gazed at their fate with carefully blank expressions. The fact that they didn't begin shouting and screaming in a general panic said a lot about their nature.

The same harassed woman floored another question. "Shouldn't we just use the maneuvering thrusters, then?" There was a more positive murmur of agreement from the crew.

"Ah, good question that, good observation," said Finnegun. "But I'm afraid that's the problem you see; the actual aforementioned metal sphere is, in fact, lodged in our main engine, causing...let's say...a bit of a mess in the fuel ducts. Any attempt to utilize the maneuvering thrusters, or any other means of propulsion for that matter, could very well result in our being blown to smithereens."

Once again, Finnegun surveyed the rows of expectant faces. There were some times when being a captain wasn't an easy job. At the moment, he was hard pressed to think of a time when it had ever been easy.

A technician put his hand up to speak. "No disrespect, sir, but… erm…you are Elite-Gifted, sir. Couldn't you just…I dunno…convince the metal object it doesn't want to be lodged in the engine?" he finished, carefully probing the electric fence of fate, hoping to avoid a nasty shock.

Captain Finnegun smiled broadly. "Very good," he said. "Very good indeed—a superb suggestion. Alas, it wouldn't work. The problem being, you see, that if we by any means removed the sphere, it would leave a dirty great hole in the ship that might cause us all to implode."

The expressions of the crew turned slightly blanker. The technician spoke again. "Is there any chance we could repair it?"

Captain Finnegun clapped his hands together. "You really are a keen one, aren't you? Repair it? Yes, of course, and you chaps are just the sorts to do it, aren't you? With your tools and your mechanical ingenuity and whatnot. But I have to ask, to be on the safe side, how long would you think it would take?"

"Weeerrrlll…" began the technician, rolling his eyes toward the ceiling in a manner common to all mechanics across the ultraverse. "Repairing the main engine and a hull breach? If I got all the lads involved and worked straight through, we could get it repaired in say…seven hours? Five if you wanted a rush job."

Finnegun whistled through his teeth. "That's a damn pity, damn pity," he said. "Because, you see, we have less than two hours before we hit the planet's surface."

The harassed woman looked thoughtful for several seconds before flooring another question. "Well that's a bit of a bugger, isn't it?" she asked.

There was a general murmur of agreement.

# 2

# Psyence, Hostility Advice and Things that go Bang.

Bip sighed. It was a sigh that was comforting in its familiarity. It was sigh of resignation despite ambition. It was a sigh of the eternal soul who, for the millionth time, has pushed a boulder up a hill only to watch, for the millionth time, the boulder roll back down again. It was a well-tailored and expertly delivered sigh that would make anyone present feel the immediate desire to ask Bip what was wrong, then possibly make him a cup of tea. But Bip was alone, and here—in a rather pleasant meadow where sheep grazed and cows plotted revenge—there was no kettle in which to make tea.

Bip was thinking about employment. It was a perfectly natural thing to get depressed about for a seventeen-year-old in Kaneq, with his schooling years behind him and a lifelong career ahead of him. Come the apprentice fair, those of age would be taken aside by Kaneq's employers and ushered into trades most suited to their abilities and ambitions. As far as Bip was concerned, there was only one job that suited him. He wanted to be a psyentist.

All the children of Kaneq had psyentific potential from birth, a gift passed down from the near-mythic ancestors who had founded the community centuries ago. Those who showed more knack than others were encouraged to develop their talents throughout their education, and those of a significant enough talent were more often than not taken on as apprentices to the council, or more rarely employed to assist the elders. Kaneq had a tiny population, only a few thousand, so those who had significant talent were recognized very quickly. Bip had not been recognized. He sighed deeply again.

There were plenty of other jobs in Kaneq, but most of them required skills, patience, or a level of effort that Bip just wasn't cut out for. The trouble with the Kaneq way of life was that there were plenty of jobs essential to the running of the village, but if you wanted to get paid for doing very little, then the options were quite limited. Hard work and diligence were required by all to ensure the smooth running of the isolated settlement, and there was no room for laziness.

Sadly, Bip wasn't particularly keen on a life of good-natured diligence. No. With his scrawny frame and his aversion to hard work, Bip felt he was far better suited to working in an academic position. More specifically, the position of apprentice psyentist.

He had only ever heard about what it was the psyentists actually did with their time. The exclusive group was very secretive about their activities, spending all of their working life in the great, snow-covered, dome-shaped building at the very edge of the village known to the town folk simply as the dome. However, he had heard rumors that most of an apprentice's time was spent either studying the legendary archives or maintaining the heatshield that prevented the community from becoming a pointy pile of snow. Bip marveled. That kind of quiet life enriched with non-challenging work was more than he could ever hope for. And people thought the psyentists were dull!

He desperately wanted to be a psyentist, but he was filled with nagging doubt. He knew he had talent—even compared to some of the journeymen, his potential was remarkable. It was quite a difficult thing to turn an entire house and garden shed into an igloo. But his talent was unreliable, often disastrously so.

With fresh resolve, Bip decided to continue his practice. Rolling up the sleeves of his baggy gray jumper, he lay belly-down on the soft grass and focused on a hapless daisy that happened to be the nearest target. Squinting hard, Bip tried to convince the flower that it needed to grow to double its current size. It was quite simple to reach the flower's essence; sensing the common energies at its core was the easiest part of the process. Tears of concentration blurred his vision as he gently persuaded the flower to grow. A daisy was a hard target, far more complex than, say, a brick, but Bip needed to develop his skill to a level where it would not fail to impress the council come the apprentice fair.

Bip concentrated.

*Concentrated…*

As far as daisies go, this one was fairly blameless and did not deserve to be accidentally blown into tiny hay-feverish powder. Bip sat back, a petal hanging rather sadly from the end of his nose. He sighed. There was a lot of work to be done if he ever wanted to be a psyentist…

THE *SENTINEL* BEGAN its slow but deadly plummet toward the surface of Bersch. Inside, the harassed-looking woman took the floor. Her name was Izzy, and she was a junior technician. The gray boilersuit-like uniform did very little for a figure that would politely be called curvy but would more accurately be called dumpy. She was young and harbored an adolescent aggression that most people of the crew's culture had to be specially trained for. Currently, she was standing with her fists balled at her sides in futile anger.

"So what you're saying, Captain, is that with all of our most skilled technicians and all of you Elite-Gifted, we get blown out of orbit by a bit of space-rock?"

Finnegun rubbed his eyes. Every member of the crew was highly trained in various specialized fields, and for the last twenty minutes, they had been feverishly conducting thought experiments as to how they could escape the rather urgent predicament they found themselves in. So far it had all been to no avail, and usually with such a high concentration of genius, twenty minutes of intense thought was enough to provide at least a few solutions. The fact of the matter was that nobody on the ship could devise a way out of the current situation because nobody on the ship had ever thought it possible *to be* in this situation. He decided to turn to what the crew always felt was the last resort.

"Handen Strike?" he said. The man to Finnegun's left, who had been standing stock still during the hubbub, turned to look at his captain. "Handen, would you be so good as to take the floor?"

Handen nodded and cleared his throat. Instantly, the attention of the room focused upon him. Those who knew anything about the culture or home worlds of Finnegun and his crew would be surprised to see Handen amongst their registry. He was neither technician nor Elite-Gifted, but to the crew of the ship, he was something far rarer and, in some ways, far more important. He was a hostilities advisor.

Other cultures may have referred to Handen as a chief of security or defense secretary, but hostilities advisor was more like a combination of field marshal, general, man-at-arms, and security guard. Handen had a very important job for the sole reason that he was unique among his comrades in his knowledge about the concept of violence, weaponry, and other general products of hostility.

The crew of the *Sentinel* could not fathom that there were intelligent beings who might, for any reason, want to cause them harm. This was because the crew were Clarions—a completely peaceful race, and also because of their unique gifts and superb technological abilities, an extremely advanced one. Unfortunately, the major gap in their otherwise outstanding intellects was the ability to recognize when someone was eyeing them up for a fight.

Throughout the history of the Clarions, many embarrassing and disastrous events had occurred due to the simple fact that they could not recognize potential for hostility in a situation, let alone deal with it. People like Handen were a rare breed on the home worlds, fewer than one in a thousand of the total population. Any signs of aggression in a Clarion child meant careful nurturing for selective training. Having nothing like a standing army, the sole reason for the continuation of the Clarion culture is that the hostility advisors have always been present to tell the them what a gun is and how to build a much bigger one than their enemies have.

If not for men like Handen, the Clarions would have spent their time scratching their heads in confusion as space pirates made off with their houses.

Handen spoke. The crew listened. "Precisely forty minutes ago, the *Sentinel* was struck by an external, almost certainly man-made object, resulting in the disruption of our orbital trajectory and the disabling of our ability to maneuver in any way. Unfortunately for us, the object has penetrated the one part of the ship that its collective crew cannot repair in an appropriate time period—"

Izzy interrupted, "No offense, Handen, but we know all this already."

Handen retorted with a cool gaze. Izzy began to feel a touch uncomfortable under his deadpan stare. Handen continued. "After studying the estimated trajectory of the object and collating the available evidence, I have come to the conclusion that the object originated from the surface of Bersch and is the direct result of a hostile action."

The crew began to murmur in shock. Handen waited for them to try to comprehend what he had just said. A technician raised her hand to speak. "I'm not quite following you…"

Handen sighed and punched in a code sequence on a small console attached to his wrist. Behind him, the huge holographic display flickered and changed. It showed a picture of a cannon on a beach and a gaudily colored ship bobbing merrily on the ocean.

"Observe," said Handen.

The crew watched with delighted interest as the cannon made an exciting booming sound and flashed a pretty color, giving birth to a ball of some kind. Their delight quickly faded as the newborn spherical object crushed the gaudy ship into pieces. The presentation had effectively highlighted the gravity of the situation. It was weapons-grade hostility in a nutshell, really.

Handen spoke while he still had the crew's horrified attention. "It appears we have underestimated the evolution of the people of Bersch. It appears they are at the stage of technological advancement where they can pinpoint the engine block of an orbital target with a ballast-style weapon. Unfortunately for us, it seems they have not yet evolved to the point where they can ask questions first."

Finnegun had been looking thoughtful throughout Handen's demonstration. "Surely, even if we have underestimated their rate of advancement that much, they are nowhere near a level of technology that would allow them to penetrate our shields?" he said.

Handen nodded. "I've consulted the Mother Tongue, and it's not picking up any readable signals, not even radio. With this in mind, it's probably safe to assume that the people of Bersch have nothing within their arsenal sophisticated enough to penetrate our shields, Captain," he said. "However, when the Sentinel is in its sleeper cycle, it drops and reconfigures its primary repellent field every seventy-two hours. I'm not sure if the people of Bersch are aware of this weakness, but the evidence is too grave to suggest coincidence. My opinion stands that we are victims of a well-formulated and malicious hostile attack from the planet's surface."

The crew gasped. Izzy looked as though she would burst into tears of frustration.

"But...why? Why would someone want to blow up that pretty ship? Let alone us?"

Again, Handen sighed, then took a sheet of paper from his notepad, screwed it into a ball, and launched it at Izzy's forehead. It made a satisfactory smacking sound. Izzy's eyes went wide in shock and fear.

"Why did you do that?"

"Because I can," replied Handen. It was the most basic demonstration of why hostility existed and what the consequences were, but Handen had found himself repeating it countless times during his service to the *Sentinel*. It was an example that tended to get the message across, if only for a short time.

Finnegun, who had also been staring in horror at Handen's destructive capabilities, shook himself and returned his focus to the matter at hand. "Do you suspect pan-dimensional influence?" he asked.

Handen thought for a moment. "The attack has all the hallmarks of adverse randominity, sir, but there are no readings to suggest any recent dimensional transgressions."

Finnegun frowned. "Hmm. Not the Discordance, then." He looked up, focusing his attention on the hostilities advisor. "What do you suggest we do, Handen?"

"With respect, Captain, retaliation would be futile. A waste of power. I suggest we use the Mother Tongue to send a message back to command central explaining our situation and then..." He swept the crew with his stony stare. "Then we prepare ourselves for a crash landing."

IT MIGHT or might not have pleased Handen to know that the large ball of metal lodged in his ship had been put there entirely by accident. It so happened that down on the planet's surface, Lord Draegul III—ruler of the Argustin Empire, supreme commander of the world's most feared and powerful army—was a bit of an enthusiast when it came to things that went *bang*. Indeed, it was this enthusiasm, shared by his father and grandfather before him, that had led to many of the military and territorial advancements of the Empire. Draegul's army possessed the most finely crafted swords as well as the sturdiest armor and a nightmarish array of siege weaponry, most of which was of his own innovation. It was one of these monstrous contraptions that currently commanded his attention.

The Research in Death Development Master stood nervously ringing his hands. The weapon known as the Giant's Middle Finger was technically of his devising. Draegul himself had commissioned it, requesting a weapon that with one shot could lay waste to a small castle as well as rudely offend his enemies. The Master had exceeded his own expectations and taken his knowledge of trajectory and dynamics to new levels in order to create what was, essentially, a really big trebuchet with a suggestively stylized launching arm.

Draegul had been pleased with the results and had spent a few wars merrily crushing (and offending) small villages and hamlets alike, but—as with most new toys—Draegul had soon grown bored with it and demanded a weapon that could lay waste to an entire *city* in one shot. The Research Master had spent many months pleading with Lord Draegul to reconsider—the Giant's Middle Finger (Mark 1) was already extremely dangerous to the operators as well as the victims, and anything of a greater scale was likely to be disastrous. But Lord Draegul had insisted, and there was nothing like Lord Draegul's insistence—which was usually coupled with the promise of agony—to focus the mind.

It had taken five years and enough gold to feed several small countries and had cost the lives of countless engineers and apprentices, but finally the Giant's Middle Finger (Mark 2) was locked, loaded, and pointed at the only safe target available—the sky.

Draegul bounced on his heels in anticipation, his dark features taken over by an eerily pleasant smile. He surveyed his new toy from the high tower of his palace—and "surveyed" was the word, as the weapon was over ten times the size of the original Mark 1 device. It was stood far outside the capital city's walls, lit against the night by countless torches and bonfires. Its wheels were blocked and bolstered with stone constructions the size of large houses. You could hear the strain and scream of miles of rope and pulley as it struggled against its payload—a gargantuan ball of pure iron the size of an uberbeast.

The Research Master had wisely made himself scarce. He knew all too well that the pent-up force of the monstrous weapon was unlikely to be purely directed at the sky. He had several nasty suspicions about the feasibility of the GMF's structural ability to withstand its own force, all of which he had voiced to Lord Draegul and all to no avail.

Draegul gazed up to the stars from beneath the long, thin fringes of his raven-colored hair. The stars had always annoyed him slightly, and although the night sky was merely a testing ground for his new weapon, he secretly hoped he might knock down a few of them, just to teach them a lesson.

"One day," Draegul whispered under his breath, "I'll rule everything I see. Including those glittering bastards." As he spoke, he began to hear echoes of encouraging whispers at the back of his mind...

He was brought back from his megalomaniacal musings by the discreet throat-clearing of a royal aide. He shook his head and tried to remember where he was and what he was doing. Ah, yes—he was on the palace balcony, preparing to address his subjects, who were gathered in the city's capital square, shuffling their feet and glancing around with a growing sense of unease. Draegul clapped his hands twice, indicating that he was prepared to begin his ceremonial address. He needn't have bothered with the gesture; the assembled crowd was already listening politely and attentively. This was mainly because anyone who didn't listen politely and attentively was promptly taken away and beaten by attentive yet extremely impolite royal guardsmen.

"My loyal subjects," shouted Draegul, his reedy voice amplified by a huge cone of metal. "Today we witness yet another triumph in the glorious reign of the Draegul succession." He raised his arms to the sky and basked in the nervous pattering of applause of the crowd below. "It is with great pride that I, Tragus Thomas Tomberry Draegul the Third, unveil a weapon fit to poke the eye of God, a weapon huge enough to compensate for my crippling emotional inadequacies, a weapon of such magnitude and horror that I probably shouldn't even use it..."

The crowd held their collective breath at the small glimmer of hope Draegul's sudden moment of sanity had presented.

"But I'm going to anyway," he finished, and the crowd chided themselves for their foolish optimism.

Draegul continued. "It is but one more rung in the golden ladder that is the immortality of the Draegul succession. May the Lord bless me and keep me. And some of the people I like as well. But not all of them." Lord Draegul sat back and enjoyed yet more nervous applause, and even some impromptu cheering from those members of the crowd closest to the watchful glare of the royal guardsmen.

Feeling happier than he had since he'd first pulled the legs from an insect, Lord Draegul lifted a silken handkerchief above his head, giving the signal to fire. The secondary watchtower received the signal and relayed it to the next watchtower, which, in turn, gave the order to fire to the trigger operator. Without hesitation the operator, picked solely for his idiocy, took his torch and set fire to the GMF's trigger rope. It was to the credit of the Research Master's genius that several thousand tons of tension caused by the deadly contraption was held back by a stretch of entwined rope no more than a meter thick.

There were a few minutes of suspicious quiet as the GMF's trigger rope began to burn. Some of the more realistically minded of the research and engineering team ran very quickly in various directions.

Without warning, the trigger rope snapped like the sound of a god smacking his forehead in frustration. There was a flurry of confused whipping sounds as a chain reaction of releasing ropes happened in a split of a second. A deep rumble began almost instantaneously.

Lord Draegul fought hard to keep the expression of manic glee from his face as the rumbling reached a thunderous crescendo. There was a sonic boom as the GMF's launching finger was released, flipping the bird to the entire world. No sooner had it done so than, succumbing to the massive conflicting forces of kinetic energy and friction, the entirety of the Giant's Middle Finger exploded with an earth-shattering bang and a cracking flash of brilliant white. Countless pieces of flaming shrapnel no larger than toothpicks zipped lethally for miles around, burning, impaling, and obliterating anything with the misfortune to get in the way. An almighty cloud of red-hot dust shot into the air and rolled slowly and menacingly toward the city, much to the horror of its occupants. The larger pieces of shrapnel that had launched at unimaginable speeds into the skies above began to pelt haphazardly into the ground, causing massive craters wherever they descended. Lord Draegul was oblivious to the apocalyptic destruction around him; the screams and thunder of his burning city proved no distraction to him. He was watching, with an expression of awful ecstasy, the glowing arc of the ballast's pure iron tip, successfully launched and burning a painfully bright white as it rocketed toward the stars like an angel who has just remembered he's left the kettle on. He wiped a tear from his eye as the ballistic ballast winked into nothingness, spanning a distance too far for him to follow. Then he laughed maniacally, as mad people are want to do in such situations.

Various cultures across the globe of Bersch looked up in awe at the reverse shooting star, and a lot of excited astronomers made a lot of inaccurate assumptions. Not by one was it predicted that the object was a rogue metal sphere that would spell doom for the *Sentinel* and the sleeping alien species that watched over them. In fact, the only accurate reading of the celestial anomaly was by a poorly educated astronomer called Harry Fudeperred who was rumored to have observed the gleaming arc and exclaimed, "Crap. This can't be good."

———————————————

3

Tuesday is a Good Day to Die

———————————————

Captain Finnegun adjusted his seat harness for what seemed like the hundredth time. Clarions were by nature a very calm and thoughtful people, but Finnegun couldn't help but be slightly unnerved by the prospect of an entire planet punching him in the face.

He looked about him. The ship's intellium hull had flawlessly transmuted into an arrowhead shape, all the better to combat the sudden turbulence of entering Bersch's atmosphere. Almost the entirety of the crew was assembled near the center of the arrow, strapped in tightly to their seats and focusing all their energies on maintaining the aerodynamic new shape of the *Sentinel*. Two engineers and an Elite-Gifted had volunteered to stay in the engine rooms in an attempt to divert shield and engine power to where it would count in free-fall. The plan was that as soon as they had escaped the lethal vacuum of space, they would remove the metal sphere from the engine block and see if the ship's descent could be slowed by one last burst of the maneuvering thrusters before the engine fell to pieces. Finnegun grimly suspected that the engine would explode before any of the thrusters could be utilized. He admired the bravery of the volunteers but couldn't help but regret that their sacrifice might ultimately be for naught. The *Sentinel* was never designed to plummet unpowered through the air.

He looked at Handen, who was seated to his left. The big man didn't take his eyes from the view screen, where the steadily expanding bulk of Bersch loomed menacingly.

"Twenty seconds until we enter the atmosphere, Captain," he stated matter-of-factly.

"Wonderful," muttered the captain. "And how is our angle of descent?"

"Not great," replied Handen, scanning over the rapidly scrolling charts of information on the holographic side monitor. "I think we can expect a bit of turbulence, actually. Ten seconds."

Finnegun sighed. In ten seconds, it appeared life was going to be terminally interesting. He spared a few moments contemplation for the message he had sent via light wave to the Clarion home system. The message had calmly detailed the *Sentinel's* dilemma and Finnegun's recommended course of action, along with a few messages from crew members who had used what might be the last moments of their existence to put their affairs in order. Captain Finnegun was a tad worried. He had sent the distress message via the most logical and efficient system of wormholes he could calculate, but even with his precise calculations, he wondered if his people would be in time to save the world. In the large stretch of infinity that stood between Bersch and the Clarion systems, there was a lot that could go wrong.

He looked around at the crew again. A few of them had tightly shut their eyes or were muttering rapidly under their breath. Finnegun had never been one for unnecessary drama, but now, with the prospect of total destruction rocketing toward them, he decided it might be time for a few heroic last words.

"What day is it?" he asked Handen, who looked briefly puzzled before answering.

"Tuesday."

"Ah," said Finnegun. "I suppose that's as good a day as any to die..."

And with that, the *Sentinel* entered the atmosphere of Bersch.

BIP GLANCED AROUND NERVOUSLY. The hubbub of the apprentice fair had always been a pleasant diversion when he was younger, but now, standing on a wooden platform with the other young men and women for the entire community to gawk at, Bip felt uneasy.

The people of Kaneq treated the apprentice fair as a holiday. Traditionally it lasted for four days, two for the choosing and allocation of apprentices, one day purely for a celebration of their new starts in life, and a final day to nurse the inevitable hangover. Becoming an apprentice was very much a coming-of-age ceremony for the youth of Kaneq.

The crowd mulled around the marketplace, which was far more active than usual, providing a brisk trade in cold beer and candied treats. The psyentists had taken extra care to ensure the filtered weather would be clement for the day. A warm, gentle breeze was textured with merry music from the various bards and bands, while bunting hung in the air, swaying as though dancing. An atmosphere of merriment and a tang of excitement made for a happy crowd, while the warm smells of roasting chestnuts and tart cider honeyed the air.

Bip looked around at the other potential apprentices. Many of them wore expressions of cocky self-assuredness, others looked vaguely anxious, and only one or two looked as petrified as Bip felt. A long, drawn-out yawn caught Bip's attention and he turned and looked into a familiar face. The face, green-hued and waxy, belonged to Bailey, an old classmate of Bip's who wanted nothing more than to apprentice in the fields of hospitality and distillery. The burly lad looked into Bip's eyes and belched quietly.

"I feel sick," he said.

"What's up with you?" said Bip with a frown. "Surely you can't be worried? You've spent your entire education learning about beer and beer-related activities."

"I'm not worried," muttered the larger youth, flicking his greasy fringe away from his eyes and pinching the bridge of his nose. "It's just that I've got a stinking hangover. Bit of last minute primary research the other day...and night..."

Bip sighed. *You have to admire such dedication to one's calling,* he thought.

A sudden trumpet blare announced the beginning of the ceremony, causing Bip to stumble and nearly fall from the podium. He turned his attention to the gaudily decorated stage of address, where the senior councilmen and various craft masters began to fill the vacant seats. When everyone had been seated, a second trumpet blare announced the arrival of the elders.

They filed in slowly and crookedly, uniformly ancient and hunched under their dark black robes of office and their flat-brimmed hats. On cursory examination, it was difficult to see the purpose the revered elders held in the community of Kaneq. They were generally referred to as the Keepers of the Ancient Wisdom, although what this ancient wisdom was, no one was entirely sure. Even so, the elders held a prominent place at all meetings and events of importance.

After what seemed like an age they were seated, and finally, with one last trumpet blare, Truggle, eldest of the elders, began his slow progress to the center of the stadium. He was far older-looking than the other elders, with a long, crooked nose and long, crooked beard that fought for dominance under his tufty-bald head.

He did not walk anywhere these days, his frail form instead supported by a chair modified with swiveling wheels on each leg. He steered and propelled the chair with an old broom, and this, coupled with the fact that the hem of Truggle's ceremonial robes obscured most of the wheeled chair, made him appear to be an ancient, gliding janitor.

The crowd hushed as Truggle prepared to give his traditional opening speech, which would signify the official beginning of the choosing. With a sound like a cat choking on a fishbone, he cleared his throat.

"Ladies and Gentlemen. Bloody hell, is it that time of year again? You know, it doesn't seem that long ago that I was down there with you lot, wondering what I'd be. And now, here am I, being what I would be regardless. Makes you wonder if there's any point in worrying about anything at all, seeing as things sort of just happen whether you like it or not. On the other hand, it's not as if you can just lie around in bed all day and hope for the best, can you? Or can you? Well, you can if you like, I suppose, I'm not your mum. Anyway..."

There was a long pause as Truggle sat in contemplative silence. Eventually he began to snore, and a kindly councilman wheeled the elder away from the stage. The assembled crowd began to applaud politely, this being one of the most coherent speeches Truggle had given in a long time.

Dunman, the chief councilman and closest thing Kaneq had to a leader, took the center of the Stadium of Address. He polished his small, round spectacles with a handkerchief and smoothed down his unnaturally smooth hair before he spoke in his awkward and wobbly voice.

"Ladies and Gentlemen, today we make futures not just for the individual, but for the community."

"*The community*," chorused the crowd, the line finely rehearsed over countless public events.

"You may begin," announced Dunman, and the crowd once again boiled into a busy throng. Immediately Bip spotted the senior psyentists who would likely be doing the choosing. Their long white robes and high collars stood out clearly in the surging crowd. As they began to approach the large podiums where the potentials waited, Bip puffed out his chest and smiled broadly.

"Cut that out," muttered Bailey. "You look like a nutter."

Bip sagged back into a more natural stance, looking as deflated as he felt. Suddenly, Bailey seemed to stiffen as a figure bustled through the crowd toward them. It was Michaelmas. With a flurry that was the closest the morose youth had ever reached to urgency, Bailey began to rake the hair out of his face and blink the sleep out of his eyes.

"Oi," he whispered to Bip. "It's the landlord from the Empty Goat!"

"What, you mean Michaelmas?" said Bip, perversely pleased by being on a first-name basis with one of Bailey's potential employers.

"You know him?" gasped the hungover hopeful. "Could you put in a good word?"

"I'll see what I can do," said Bip smugly (although he doubted how much he could sway the opinion of someone, friend or not, whose house he had turned into an igloo).

"Mornin', Bip," Michaelmas hailed him as he approached the boys. "You'll be pleased to know that the council have returned my house to normal and are keeping a sharp eye out for the vandals concerned." Michaelmas gave Bip a non-too-subtle wink before turning his attention to Bailey, who did his best to stand up straight without swaying from side to side.

"Now then, young Bailey." The rough-looking lad's eyes widened at being recognized. "Yeah tha's right, I've been keeping an eye on you, lad." Michaelmas grinned. "They tell me yer quite the expert on bar studies?"

Bailey tried to formulate an intelligent reply but only succeeded in making a modest grunting noise.

Michaelmas clapped the tall youth on the shoulder. "Come on then, my lad, you and I has lots to talk about!"

The two alcohol enthusiasts walked out into the crowd talking about the intricacies of both the consumption and brewing of fine booze. Bip watched them go with rising sadness. Bip, like many people on the right side of the bar, assumed that beer was beer and that was all there was to it. To hear Michaelmas and Bailey drivel on about matters of physics and biology seemed a touch absurd. Beer, he had always thought, went in one way and out of the other, taking a bit of your common sense with it. That there was expert logic and research behind the process seemed ludicrous. However, what really annoyed Bip was that, as silly as the whole affair seemed, Bailey looked likely to gain a life career in something he loved, while Bip was left standing on the podium in an ever-decreasing gaggle of youths.

His heart sank as he saw the senior psyentists pull a young girl from the crowd and walk off, chatting excitedly, not even glancing in his direction.

THE EMPTY GOAT thudded and vibrated to the beat of an energetic folk band. The air hung heavy with sweet smoke and the musky atmosphere of many people crowded into a relatively small space. Although the celebrations weren't supposed to begin until the following night, many of the potentials who had been chosen on the first day were starting early.

The center of the Empty Goat, normally filled with tables and chairs, had been cleared to make a serviceable dance floor in front of a stage made up of beer crates and planks. The band was playing a stomping beat, and the dancers whirled with no signs of slowing down. Amongst the merry-makers, well-wishers, and good-natured drunks, one face stood out as being terminally depressed. Bip sat in a darkened corner drinking from a tankard larger than his head.

Bailey and Michaelmas had taken the night off to "welcome Bailey to the family" and were getting roaring drunk on some of the Empty Goat's finer celebration ales. They shouted at one another in the manner of those too inebriated to realize they were shouting as they manhandled another barrel of beer from Michaelmas's personal collection over to Bip's table.

Bip was vaguely aware he had drunk far too much but was much too upset to care. He hadn't been picked. While various potentials were taken aside as willing apprentices to willing masters, Bip had been left standing like an idiot, the last on his podium, until Dunman had signaled the end of the first day of choosing. Despite Bip's initial urge to crawl into bed and cry, Bailey had persuaded him to join in the premature celebrations with the vain promise of finding solace at the bottom of a tankard. So far, all Bip had found at the bottom of the tankard was the reflection of his miserable face, and the desire to get another tankard.

"Cheer up!" yelled Bailey with annoying enthusiasm. "Anyone would think you hadn't been picked or something!"

"Well, I haven't, actually," said Bip, reproachfully.

"Oh...yeah...well, what I mean is...I mean to say..." Bailey looked confused for a moment. "I do beg your pardon, I appear to have lost all ability to articulate a cogent retort," he said, and turned his attention back to his beer.

"What he means," Michaelmas interjected, "is that there's still a whole other day of choosing left. Not everybody gets picked on the first day. It'll be all right!"

"But what if I don't get picked on the second day?" said Bip.

Michaelmas knitted his brow in concentration for a while. "Come to think of it," he said eventually, "I don't think that's ever happened."

"Then what if I'm the first?" Bip wailed. "I'll be a laughing stock!"

"Now, now, Bip," Michaelmas said, patting him reassuringly on the shoulder. "Even if you don'ts get picked—and that's a big *if*, mind you—the community'll take care of you."

"What, like some kind of charity case? I don't see how that's supposed to make me feel better. Even Derren Doonby got picked as an apprentice lumberjack, and he's much less qualified than I am!"

"Oi!" said Bailey, looking up from his tankard. "I won't hear a bad word said about Derren—he knows more about wood and trees than anyone I know, and I'm sure he'll make a great lumberjack!"

"But he's got no hands!" said Bip. "How is he supposed to hold an axe?"

"All right there, Bip, I knows yer upset, but bad-mouthing young Derren won't help anyone," scolded Michaelmas.

"Sorry," mumbled Bip. "I'm just…sorry."

"Look, I'll tell you what," said Michaelmas leaning over conspiratorially. "If the worst comes to the worst and nobody picks you, you could always come and work for me as a kitchen boy. I know it ain't much, but you could apprentice here for a few years while you practice your psyence, and then maybe you could reapply for another apprenticeship later on down the road."

"You'd do that? I mean, I know you've already more staff than you need," Bip said.

"Not a problem, me ol'mate. Yer pappy would have wanted it." Michaelmas sniffed and rubbed an emerging tear from his eye.

Bip shifted uncomfortably. When Michaelmas was drunk, he would often talk about Bip's father, who had left Kaneq thirteen years ago and never returned. Bip had never really known the man but was assured by his mother and the various village-folk that *had* known him that he was a great man with commendable psyentific talent.

"Great man, was your pappy," mumbled Michaelmas, gazing dreamy-eyed into a happy memory. "Did I ever tell you about the time when—"

"I'm sure you did, Michaelmas," Bip interrupted. "But I don't mind hearing it again."

---

CAPTAIN FINNEGUN OPENED his eyes again and, with a great deal of effort, managed to unclench his teeth. He looked over at Handen, who was still grimacing at the view screen. He turned to the screen himself and gasped.

A few minutes ago, but which had seemed like hours, they had entered Bersch's atmosphere, experiencing not so much turbulence as an extremely localized hurricane. While the *Sentinel* had been beaten about quite badly on its entry, the inner environmental functions had remained stable, meaning that the crew had been neither burnt to a crisp nor pressurized to the point of implosion.

Instead, they experienced an uneasy feeling of weightlessness as the ship fell toward Bersch at a faster rate than the gravity stabilizers could compensate for. The clouds had cleared from the view screen to reveal an endless blue void looming ominously below them as they headed toward one of Bersch's larger oceans. Finnegun, who had not seen any geographic detail first hand in several millennia, could not help but feel awed.

Handen checked their angle of descent. The modified shape of the *Sentinel* was dealing with the aerodynamics surprisingly well; they were falling rapidly but maintaining a sound forward trajectory. He quickly checked the short-range scanners for the nearest landmass.

"Captain," he said, "I've got a suitable landing site for us coming up. Virtually uninhabited, plenty of flat space, a few mountains, but—"

Finnegun interrupted. "Are there any alternative landing sites? Excluding the bottom of the sea, I mean."

"Well…" said Handen, checking the scanner screen. "No."

"Well, then, it seems that the decision of where to crash has been made for us. Engage manual controls."

Handen complied and pressed a short sequence of buttons on a nearby keypad. Outside, various flaps and shoots unbuckled from the flawless silver skin of the starship. In the cockpit, a joystick emerged in front of the captain's chair.

"Mr. Strike," Finnegun said. "I understand that as a hostilities advisor you are a man of some experience when it comes to quick reactions and so on?"

"Yes, sir."

"I wonder if you'd do us the honor of piloting the craft and attempting to avoid our seemingly inevitable destruction?"

"Yes, sir." Handen pressed another sequence of keys and the joystick retracted and reappeared in front of his seat. A targeting monitor showing the distance to the landing site and the ship's altitude and speed of descent closed over one of his eyes. The main view screen began to depict the landscape in a series of green and blue lines with various measurements and probability lines drawn here and there in red.

Finnegun turned back to the crew and watched their calm faces as they engaged in the various tasks assigned to them. As Handen began his attempt to glide the craft, the sound of rushing air began to permeate the hull. Finnegun thought briefly how eerie the sound was in the dead silence of the foredeck.

# 4

# Rejection, Penguins and the Truth about Everything

**B**ip tried to fight the feeling of overwhelming embarrassment that crawled over him like an army of spiders. It was quite difficult. He was once more on the podium with the other potentials, surrounded by the gawking crowds. The main difference was that this time, instead of being surrounded by comfortable numbers of people in the same situation, there were only three potentials left. Including him.

The second day of choosing had been an unglamorous affair, with the remaining potentials being plucked from the crop quickly and quietly while Bip stood feeling as stupid as he thought he looked. Not one psyentist had approached him. In fact, he hadn't even *seen* a psyentist all day.

Bip looked at his two companions on the podium. All that remained of the good and great had been selected early in the second day, and now Bip was left with "Half-Brick" Thompson and "Bogey" Betty Bogeyton. Bogey was a bright enough girl but had a rather disturbing odor of very old cabbage, which would saturate the senses if you spent too long around her. Half-Brick, however, was widely believed to be several baskets short of a picnic and had earned his nickname for famously being outwitted in a game of skill by half a brick. How this was actually possible no one knew, but the brick had won nevertheless. It wasn't long before a master tanner, whose sense of smell had long since given up, took Bogey aside for a new career. Bip was left standing with Half-Brick.

"I wants to be a farmer," said Half-Brick.

"Really," said Bip, expressing not one iota of interest.

"I wants to be a farmer and chase the penguins."

"That's good," said Bip. It was an essential job for an apprentice to chase the domesticated penguins of Kaneq, who were very extremely docile by nature and tended not to move around very much. If the penguins weren't chased sufficiently, they would become too fat and would be unable to move at all. And so the position of Penguin Chaser, while far from being dignified, at least warranted respect due to its necessity.

"I wants to shave the cows 'n all," added Half-Brick.

"That's good," said Bip. Shaving the domesticated Kaneqian snowcow of its ever-growing woolen coat was also an important job for an apprentice, providing materials for the looms and weavers and preventing the cows from becoming entangled in a giant ball of fluff.

*Even Half-Brick*, thought Bip, *who is clearly a danger to himself and those around him, is still more useful than me.* He sighed.

"I'd quite likes to be a cow," said Half-Brick.

"That's good," Bip said, and briefly contemplated a life of chasing penguins and shaving cows.

---

AT THE BACK of the crowd, two figures watched Bip from the shadows. One of them was hunched in a chair and smoked a long, rank pipe. The other wrung his hands and nervously smoothed his already smooth hair.

"I just don't see why we have to humiliate him like this."

"Leave him be," said the pipe smoker. "No point in giving him an apprenticeship. Not where he's going."

"Are you sure he's the right candidate? I mean, in a couple of years, he might make a good apprentice psyentist, but it seems unwise…"

"Don't you tell me what's unwise, my boy," hawked the figure through clouds of smoke. "I still remember you when you was knee-high to a penguin, and I was pretty damn wise back then too!"

"Sorry, Truggle, I forget myself. Just nerves, I suppose."

"That's all right, Dunman. These are nervous days…"

---

THE FARM MASTER circled Half-Brick and prodded him occasionally. He lifted the boy's lips to check his teeth and gave him a few more experimental prods before tipping back his flat cap of office and staring hard into Half-Brick's vacant eyes. Half-Brick stood rigidly, his face a picture of oblivion.

"I wonders if you can tell me, lad," said the farm master, "where you are at the moment?"

Half-Brick's face twisted into a rictus of concentration. "I'm ere, aren't I?" he concluded.

"Well, that's good enough for me," said the farm master. "Welcome aboard, my lad."

"What?" said Half-Brick, as he was led away to his new life.

Bip felt sick. He stood alone on the podium as the crowd began to dissipate. Suddenly a trumpet sounded, and Dunman waved to the crowd from the stadium of address.

"Thus we signal the end of the choosing," he said. "Let the celebrations begin!" There was a loud cheer from the crowd and a band began to play.

"Wait!" said Bip.

The crowd continued oblivious, gearing up for a celebration that would likely last all through the night and most of the following day.

"What about me?" wailed Bip. He searched desperately for Michaelmas in the crowd and finally located him at the back of the hubbub, where he was walking hurriedly away. "Michaelmas! Wait!" shouted Bip. Michaelmas lowered his head and continued to scutter away, clearly pretending not to have heard his friend. Tears of frustration began to well up in Bip's eyes and he balled his fists in the air. "Everybody wait!" he screamed, causing many people in the crowd to turn and watch the luckless potential with interest. He more or less had their complete attention.

It was his last resort, a trick he had been saving for a worst-case scenario such as this. A trick that couldn't fail to attract the attention of the psyentists. He concentrated all his will into bonding with the energies within the podium he stood upon and, with streams of sweat gliding down his face, persuaded the podium to rise into the air.

The theory of the process was relatively simple and was designed for showmanship rather than real effect. It was impossible to make the podium rise without making it lighter than air, therefore becoming a gas rather than a solid, and therefore no longer being a podium in the classic and relevant sense. Bip's trick was much simpler than levitation. He would convince the podium to redistribute its mass to its own center. The effect, Bip had planned, would be that as the podium grew smaller in its radius, the center (the part he was standing on) would be pushed into the air. Bip had been proud of the idea, and if it worked without a hitch, there would be no way for people to doubt his knack for psyence.

He concentrated hard…

*Concentrated…*

With a giant *whoosh* and a blinding flash that no one had been expecting, Bip's shoes caught fire. He blinked through his half-moon glasses in stupefied disbelief as he watched his burning shoes, then in a moment of horrified realization began a frenzied tap dance of panic. A lot of the crowd rushed to his aid, attempting to douse the flames with bottles and glasses of whatever they had been drinking. A lot of the crowd were too busy trying not to laugh. A lot more of the crowd couldn't help themselves and were laughing and hooting hysterically as Bip danced a crazed jig across the podium.

"What a thicko," said Half-Brick, shaking his head.

---

THE *SENTINEL* SOARED across an icy landscape, emitting a low roar as it inched closer and closer to impact.

Captain Finnegun watched the view screen with a growing sense of dread. In an attempt to kill some of the *Sentinel's* lethal speed, Handen had decelerated too much. Although they had safely reached the icy continent, they were a good hundred meters under their ideal angle of descent, and it looked likely they would catch the belly of the craft on a ragged pair of mountains before they reached their intended landing site. The only options were to attempt to decelerate more and risk a full-on collision with the mountains, or to find some way to regain the height they had lost. Finnegun watched a rearview monitor for a while, then calmly activated an intercom panel on his wrist.

"Officer Kanick," he said, "I wonder if perhaps this is the time for that little plan of yours?"

When the *Sentinel's* shape had been modified, the crew had moved the entire engine room, complete with breach, to the back end of the ship. Shortly before entering the atmosphere of Bersch, three of the crew had donned environment suits and redirected the repellent field to seal the rest of the ship off from the engine room. After doing this, they had harnessed their suits to the ship and safely dislodged the metal ballast from the hull, depressurizing the engine room and enabling them to begin repairs on the ravaged engine block. The intellium that served as the hull of the ship had begun to knit the breach into repair as soon as the obstruction had been removed, but the engine block and wiring were composed entirely of more common and stable materials, and they hadn't been able to make much progress in mending it. For the last few minutes, they had been grimly watching endless fields of ice rush beneath them through the slowly decreasing breach. The ground was beginning to look uncomfortably close.

Officer Kanick listened to his intercom. "Will do, Captain," he said, then turned to the engineers. "Well, chaps, looks like its plan B after all. Robinna, you ready the fuel flow. Christian, get ready with the warm-up ignition pistons."

The two engineers nodded.

"Wait for my mark," said Kanick, and looked at his wrist piece where a steady countdown marked their approaching doom. "I'd just like to say, chaps, all formalities aside, that it's been a damn pleasure working with you."

Robinna nodded, her flyaway blond hair clearly visible through her environment suit's domed helmet. "You too, Kanick," she said.

"Cheers, mate," said Christian, trying hard not to let his voice crack.

"Okay," said Kanick, with forced calm in his voice. "Fuel flow, go."

Robinna punched in a code sequence at a console, and various pieces of machinery began to whirr into life. At the hull breach, a severed tangle of pipes began to emit a clear gas with a loud *hussssss.*

"Warm-up ignition pistons, go," said Kanick. Christian hesitated for a moment, then punched in a code at his console. At the hull breach, a ton of obliterated wiring began to spark and smoke dangerously.

"I hope this works," said Kanick. And then his world went white.

Back on the foredeck, Finnegun clenched his fists as the mountains crawled quickly across the view screen. Impact was inevitable. Finnegun desperately tried to think of a course of action that, in the milliseconds available, might avoid the certainly fatal collision. Suddenly, a huge blast emitted from behind the vessel. Finnegun looked into the view screen with horror as the mountains flip-flopped upside down.

The explosion of the *Sentinel*'s engine block as the leaking hyperfuel ignited had been titanic in its power, instantly snuffing out the lives of Kanick, Robinna, and Christian. It was only because of the redirected repellent field that the entire ship was not destroyed. Instead, the mighty blast acted as a boost to the falling craft, sending it spinning slightly upward.

Finnegun, despite developing nausea, managed to keep his eyes on the view screen. The mountains were still upside down, but rather than being directly in front of them, they now appeared to be directly above them. As the craft span around to its upright position it was, of course, revealed that the mountains were directly below them. The plan had worked. They had avoided collision with the mountains.

"Thank you, Kanick," whispered the captain, as he watched the trail of flaming debris in the rearview monitor.

BIP SAT alone in the graveyard, listening to the slow tweet of some nameless songbird. He didn't view the graveyard with any sort of romantic morbidity; it was just that here amongst Kaneq's dead and gone he would be able to avoid the rest of the village.

His father was buried around here somewhere, he knew. At least, *technically* his father had been buried here, though his actual body had never been recovered. It was an assumed grave for an assumed death, taking the view that anybody who had been missing in the Ice Plains for as long as Bip's father was either dead or…well, they were most likely dead.

Bip tried to imagine what his father might say to him now, if he were alive, tried to imagine what words of advice he might have for his unemployable son. It was difficult. He had never really been old enough to understand the man, who had been just another friendly face in the sky who'd picked him up when he was upset and kissed his forehead at bedtime. He realized with some dismay that he couldn't even conjure up what his father had sounded like.

He sat on a tombstone and stared glumly at Old Bachalack and the Patient Mother, the two mountains that permanently framed Kaneq's skyline. They were unchanging and familiar and extremely definite, and for this reason, they were normally a comforting sight for Bip in times of uncertainty. Not today, though. Today he sat lost in thoughts of a bleak future.

He was shaken from his reverie by the sudden crack of a snapping twig behind him.

"It's a bugger, isn't it? Death, I mean," Truggle said, rowing his rickety wheeled chair up to Bip's side, his peanut-like head dappled with sunlight.

Bip was surprised. Though he had been around Truggle before, this was as lucid as he had ever seen the elder. "I'm not thinking about death," he replied.

"Bloody hell, I am," said Truggle. "You start to, you know, when you get to my age."

Bip's curiosity overtook his etiquette. "How old are you, exactly?"

Truggle counted on his fingers. "About...about a hundred and sixty?" he ventured. "You don't pay as much attention to your age when you hit triple digits."

"A hundred and sixty? That's...well, that's very...old," Bip finished lamely.

"Thanks very much," said Truggle, cheerfully. "I intend to live for a good few years yet, though, so don't look at me like I'm half dust already." He chuckled for a moment, then leaned over toward Bip with a conspiratorial air. "They think I'm senile, you know," he whispered. "A few toys lost in the attic. But then, what do they know, eh? Best to let them think I'm barmy—saves me having to listen to them, at least."

"You mean you pretend to be mad?" Bip said, shocked despite his melancholy.

"I'm a wise old fool," Truggle mumbled, a distracted smile playing across his withered lips. "And what they don't know can't hurt them."

"I think that's utterly immoral," said Bip.

"I think it's bloody brilliant. You hear things, you know, when people think you're barmy. You learn a lot about people."

Bip stared at the ground, trying to indicate politely that he didn't wish to talk any further. A few minutes passed. In the silence, the sound of distant music could be heard on the breeze.

"That was some trick, by the way. Setting your feet on fire, I mean," Truggel said, tapping his fingers reflectively on his broom. Bip winced and continued his examination of the floor. More moments of silence passed unchecked into the atmosphere.

"Did you come to visit your father's grave?" said Truggle finally.

"No," said Bip. "It just seems like a...a waste of time if there's no body in it."

"I always thought it was rather touching that the community made honorary graves for those who chose to venture out into the wilds," Truggle mused.

"My father didn't choose to leave," said Bip glumly. "He just went out to practice some heavy psyence and didn't come back. They said he must have just got lost in a snowstorm."

"Oh really? Is that what they say?" Truggle lit his rank pipe and took a few puffs. "Of course, what would they know?"

Bip looked at the ground for a while, then looked up at the sky. He turned to Truggle and looked into his watery gray eyes. "What?" he said.

"I wonder if it's time for you to learn the truth, my lad."

"The truth about what?" Bip replied.

Truggle blew a thin cloud of smoke, and for a moment, Bip saw a twinkle of intelligence in those old gray eyes that he had never noticed before. "The truth about everything," he said.

---

THE *SENTINEL* SCREAMED toward the ground, its repellent fields directed entirely around its underbelly and nose. Inside, Finnegun checked their velocity one last time and quickly worked out the probability of surviving such a crash. *It would be fifty per cent,* he thought, *if we weren't heading toward a cliff face and consequently a thousand-foot drop onto a massive lake of ice.*

With an unfathomable *boom*, the craft plunged into the snowy ground, its shielding causing gigantic clods of earth to be ploughed up in front of it. The momentum of the impact sent the vessel crashing through ice and snow toward the sheer cliff face at an alarming rate.

Within the foredeck, Finnegun closed his eyes once again as warning lights flashed and beeped in a rave of panic. *There is no way,* he thought, *that we can possibly slow down in time to avoid sliding over the cliff. Bugger.*

As a sense of finality washed over him, Finnegun opened one of his eyes, determined at least to face his fate head on. He was surprised to see that the landscape had changed slightly; where before there had been an empty expanse between the tobogganing ship and the cliff, there was now a gigantic, oddly shaped snow drift. Finnegun had just enough time to wonder where it had come from before the *Sentinel*, smashing clouds of ice into the air, collided with the mysterious snow drift with an odd suddenness and a sound that can only be described as a colossal *poff!*

*Well, that was odd,* thought Finnegun. And with that last thought, he blacked out.

Within its icy airbag, the craft gradually slowed and finally stopped, some way from the cliff edge, and began cooling with loud *tinging* noises. There was a long period of stunned silence.

---

*DARKNESS.*

A nagging sensation that he had something to be getting on with.
*More darkness.*

An awareness of cold. A problem in the chronostatic chamber. Not supposed to feel. Pain. Pain in his leg and neck.

*Darkness.*

"Captain?"

*Who, me?*

"Captain!"

*Five minutes, please.*

"Captain, wake up!"

"Muh?" said Finnegun, for the second time that day.

"We made it, sir," Handen said, shaking him. "We're alive!"

"Jolly good," said Finnegun, then groaned as his protesting body began airing a long list of complaints. "Oh dear," he said, wincing. "I think my leg is broken. How is everyone else?"

"We lost two more crew. Defty and Michaelmas. They were killed on impact, sir."

Finnegun nodded. There seemed little else he could do. "Are all the other crew in good shape?"

"A few casualties, Captain, mostly superficial."

"We made it, then?" said Finnegun, a smile spreading across his face for the first time in a few millennia.

"I wouldn't celebrate just yet, Captain," came a voice edged with familiar irritation. "We're buried under tons of snow, and making an exit could be a big problem without looking at a full damage report first. Whatever it was that stopped us going over that cliff has us trapped! And to top it all off, the power's down, and I doubt we have much oxygen left."

"Ah, Izzy." Finnegun smiled sleepily. "I've always admired your optimistic, can-do attitude."

He looked across at the access hatch, which, while open, merely opened onto tons of snow.

"Well, then," said Finnegun, shaking his groggy head, "I suggest that everyone gets into their environment suits and prepares to clear an exit—" He stopped abruptly and cocked his head toward the ceiling. There was an odd thumping sound, like the shuffling of gigantic feet. The crew fell silent as the noise grew louder. After quite some time, a flurry of snow began to cascade into the ship from the access hatch until a hollow was made near the exit. A weak light and a bitter wind swept into the foredeck. Completely against everyone's expectations, a penguin plummeted from the sky and landed with a bang on the ship's deck. It was followed by several others, which proceeded to wallow around in confusion, quacking with the attitude of an animal that has nothing better to do than quack. Finnegun tried to think when he had last seen penguins...

After a few minutes and several more confused penguins, a face dangled from the top of the hatch. A face that Finnegun found disturbingly familiar.

"All right?" said the face.

---

BOMBING THROUGH SPACE LIKE A BULLET, the Massive Ball of Death twinkled prettily in the light of a nearby sun. Countless years in the coldness of space had left the nuclear cluster dusted with ice, giving it the appearance of a huge and lethal snowball.

In a nearby galactic diner, situated on the third ring of the planet Xarghy'Putput, two Snx' Prtickas sat chewing merrily on Tch' Paknap. They had been hauling a payload of Chifk' kapow back to their home world of CnKTippkle, when they had stopped in the diner for a spot of lunch. FnIk'rrr stared dreamily out of the window, his head resting in one of his twelve hands, while Rrrrrrrrr continued to scoff his Tch' Paknap.

Suddenly FnIk'rrr's facial viewing mesh widened in shock as the Massive Ball of Death zoomed through his field of perception. He could see the enormous destructive potential of the man-made meteor and was alarmed that it was being allowed to roam unchecked through such a widely used transport sector. He tapped his twenty-six fingers nervously and considered telling Rrrrrrrrr about his disturbing discovery. Unfortunately, the Snx'Prticka's language was vastly impractical (as were their seventeen stomachs, their statically charged body hair, and the irrelevant trunks at the smalls of their backs). In the time it would have taken for FnIk'rrr to voice his alarm in the cumbersome Snx'Prticka dialect, the meteor would be long gone. It had taken them three hours merely to order their lunch.

FnIk'rrr tutted loudly through his vocal nostrils (which took several minutes) and once again wished that the Snx'Prticka species wasn't so crap.

The Massive Ball of Death continued to drift through space, accelerating slowly but surely as the gravitational pull of the nearby sun altered its direction by a few degrees.

# 5

# Kaneq: The Beginning and the End

"What?" spluttered Truggle as he flailed his arms and swiveled his head to and fro in confusion.

"I said wake up." Bip sighed. "You fell asleep."

"What? No, I didn't!" replied Truggle, blinking his eyes and yawning hugely.

"Yes, you did. You said something about the truth about everything and then you just fell asleep."

"Really?" muttered Truggle. "Curse my ancient head, I've gone and spoiled a perfectly good dramatic moment."

"Are we quite done here yet?" Bip said, tapping his foot impatiently. "Only I had the rest of the afternoon booked for moping around and such..."

"How long was I asleep?" interrupted Truggle.

"About five minutes?"

"Then we've no time to lose! Quick, lad, follow me!" With an elderly cackle, Truggle began rowing his wheelchair away at a surprising speed, his broom sweeping at the ground like the world's most enthusiastic janitor.

"Wait!" cried Bip. "What's happening? Where are we going? Tell me before you fall asleep again!"

BIP HEAVED for breath as he followed Truggle's chaotic path through the market square. The old man's erratic wheelchair steering, coupled with some well-targeted broom-prodding, was cutting a winding passage through the crowds of revelers. Bip tried his best to keep the rampaging elder in sight. He had never been particularly athletic, preferring slow comfortable paces, or better yet no pace at all, so the unplanned exercise of chasing down a madman's wheelchair was taking its toll on his underused lungs.

Bip had followed the old man's unpredictable chase from the cemetery, past the lumber camps, the farmlands, even the tanning houses and blacksmiths, until, nearly falling over from exhaustion, they had arrived at the market square. What annoyed Bip was that, without the diversions, the market square and the cemetery were only five minutes apart.

Bip had never seen a supermarket, so he had never seen a trolley with a wobbly wheel, and even if he had, he certainly would have never chased a rocket-powered one. Thus, Bip was unable to compare his recent experiences to anything in his personal frame of reference.

Without warning, Bip's stumbling took him into a clearing at the edge of the square where, sitting casually and smoking his long, foul pipe, was Truggle.

"What took you so long?" he chided. Thankfully, Bip's breathless reply was unintelligible to the old man's ears.

"Come along, lad," said the elder cheerfully. "We haven't far to go now."

"Where…are…we…go…ing?" Bip managed.

"Didn't I mention that part?" said Truggle.

"…o," wheezed Bip.

"I'm sure I did," mused Truggle.

"…" said Bip.

"Well, anyway, we're going into the Dome."

Bip choked mid-wheeze. The Dome was one of the few places in the community that was closed to the general public. Only the higher-ranking psyentists and councilmen were allowed access to the mysterious building on the outskirts of Kaneq... and the elders, of course. The contents of what was rumored to be Kaneq's oldest building were kept a deep secret. Even the most friendly and carefree of those who were allowed access would turn quiet and withdrawn if their friends enquired about the Dome's significance. Of all the chosen elite who were allowed access to the Dome, and all the worthy who were not, it seemed wrong for Bip to be invited to enter on the whim of someone who was quite possibly insane. Even so, as Truggle wheeled away, Bip could not help but follow, his curiosity overriding his sense of duty.

AFTER ONLY A FEW MINUTES' walk, following a surprisingly coherent and straightforward route set by Truggle, Bip found himself at one of the few portal points in Kaneq's heatshield. Far on the opposite side of the shimmering barrier, he could see the distant snowy mound of the Dome.

It was not considered wise to attempt to enter Kaneq by simply walking straight though the heatshield (unless you wanted a really, *really* deep tan), so exit and entrance points were set up sporadically for the few occasions when a citizen might want access to the rest of the Ice Plains. The dangers of going too close to the heatshield were stressed to Kaneqians from an early age, and its value for keeping the unwanted elements outside far outweighed the occasional fatality for those inside who would do anything for a laugh. As he approached the portal point, Bip could feel the uncomfortably hot temperature of the transparent heat wall, even though they were still some distance from it.

The two psyentists manning the portal point hesitated slightly when they saw Bip, but one nod from Truggle sent them immediately into action. They concentrated on the equation that would allow a thin gap to appear in the shield and grant access to the Dome. A faint shimmer and a loud fizzing noise were the only indication that part of the colossal force field was being drawn aside like a huge, boiling curtain. A third psyentist came up to Bip and offered him a very thick coat, fashioned from the woolly hide of the snowcow, with huge gloves and a tight hood sewn into the heavy fabric. Bip had a brief moment to wonder what the coat was for before an icy wind, the likes of which he had never experienced, blasted cruelly from the slowly appearing portal.

The Kaneqians deemed it a necessity that the community should experience at least some of the winter season. For a few months every year, a tolerable amount of ice and snow was allowed into the village. Bip, in his childhood, had thoroughly enjoyed building snowmen and chucking snowballs with the other kids in the brief winter spells. However, the season that lived just meters from the cozy embrace of the ever-burning heatshield was not a light-hearted reminder of the frivolities of winter's play. No. It was a harsh, slapping cold that tore into the bone and into the soul. Bip clutched at his body, shivering madly and immediately re-evaluating his decision to follow Truggle.

"A bit nippy, isn't it?" said Truggle. "I should wrap up if I were you."

Bip clambered into the cumbersome coat and relished the tiny relief it gave. They waited while an obliging psyentist tied some worn-out skis onto Truggle's wheelchair then ushered them out into the cold.

Bip looked around at the vast expanse of the Ice Plains and experienced an odd conflict of agoraphobia and claustrophobia. Having spent most of his life in the familiarity of the village, the unreachable horizons and towering mountains of the icy wilderness he now faced were intimidating to say the least, but the thick whirling of the constant snow seemed to muffle sound, vision, and distance, adding an uncomfortable sense of restriction to the cold panorama.

It was only a few short minutes' walk to the Dome, which Truggle spent merrily gliding through the snowdrifts, singing an old drinking song in a gruff tenor. The minutes were not so carefree for Bip, however, as he trudged pathetically through the overwhelming elements, blinking away the stinging ice that was continually thrown into his eyes. The moisture in the air forced him to remove his glasses, meaning that the white blindness around him was even more blurred than before. Bip gave a sigh of relief that turned to cold steam before him as they approached the Dome.

The building reminded Bip of the igloo he had turned Michaelmas's house into, though on a much larger scale. He briefly wondered how much effort it would take to make a mistake resulting in an igloo as large as the Dome. Then he wondered miserably if he was capable of making it.

Suddenly, Bip realized that the raging winds around him had calmed somewhat and that the temperature had warmed slightly.

"Another heatshield," called Truggle from ahead, by way of explanation. "Not a big one, mind. It keeps the entrance clear." He pointed to a large funnel in the snow that led downward and seemingly underneath the dome.

"Follow me!" he cried merrily, and slid down the funnel into an all-embracing darkness. Bip heard the slight echo of an old man's voice saying, "Wheeeee!"

Gulping back his doubts and considering the alternative of a harsh walk back to Kaneq, Bip slid down the funnel.

FROM SOME DISTANCE AWAY, a beast watched as Bip disappeared from view. It watched and thought about killing. The beast was a grubear, one of the most ferocious creatures to stalk the snowbound tundra of the Ice Plains. Standing nearly seven feet at the shoulder, the grubear's shaggy, white hide was crisscrossed with scars from territorial battles and the occasional challenging prey. It was old and tough, one of the most revered hunter-killers even amongst its own competitive kind, but for some reason, it had left its normal hunting territories, leaving them vulnerable to ambitious rivals. For days now, it had stalked an unspecific but all-consuming hunger, fueled by the strange nagging whisper in the back of its mind that had convinced it to give up its hard-won champion status and venture into unknown territory. Now, finally, the grubear had found the source of the unexplained need to kill. It stared hungrily at Bip's disappearing frame and listened briefly to the maddening whispers in its head. It knew what had to be done.

If the beast had not been so intent on the unusual messages it was receiving and had paid more attention to its innate ability to sense fluctuations in the surrounding magnetic field, it would certainly have detected the presence of the monster behind it. Unfortunately, even if the grubear had been able to detect the threat, it was massively outmatched. A fist the size of boulder slammed down onto the oblivious beast's back, snapping its spine, and instantly ending its life. The grubear stood stock still for a moment, then fell heavily to the ground. What had been a magnificent animal mere seconds ago was now just a lifeless carcass, splayed and broken in the snow. The assailant lifted its massive fist from the rapidly cooling corpse and absentmindedly rubbed its gory knuckles on its chest. Then it paused, tilted its huge, hairy head, and listened carefully to the incessant whispering at the back of its mind.

BIP BLINKED RAPIDLY, trying to adjust his eyes to the gloom. The slide down the funnel had been uneventful, starting rapidly then slowing smoothly to a halt in the room he now stood in. Peering into the darkness, Bip hoped for some clue as to the shape of the strange cavern. He took a step forward and was unnerved to hear his footstep echo with a metallic ring.

Without warning, an eerie glow began to illuminate the darkness around him. The light had a misty quality and emanated from no source Bip could locate. Soon the light was bright enough for him to get a grasp of his surroundings. He gasped. The room was the largest indoor space he had ever seen. The ceiling stretched too high into the darkness for him to see it, and the walls and floor seemed to merge into one cylindrical curve. More impressive than the sheer scale of the room was the fact that it seemed to be constructed entirely of a metallic substance. Metal was not uncommon in Kaneq, being used in everything from plumbing pipes to cutlery, but the mining and processing of the scarce metals in the surrounding Ice Plains was too costly a process to encourage a large demand. The Kaneqians, with their carefully controlled environment, were quite happy to construct most things from the more easily attainable wood sources within the perimeter of the heatshield. Bip had never seen much metal in one place before, and the room he found himself in now seemed horribly alien to his sensibilities.

"Welcome to the Dome," said Truggle, his cracked voice resonating harshly. Bip, who had been staring in awe at the ceiling, very nearly fell over in shock. It seemed that Truggle had come from nowhere.

"Come along, lad, we can't be standing around gawking all day." With that, Truggle wheeled his chair slightly backward, causing a disc of white light to appear on the floor. Bip stepped backward hesitantly.

"What is this place?" he breathed.

Truggle sucked thoughtfully at his gums. "Well, put it like this; you've seen the fishers who head down to the frozen lake now and then?"

"Yes."

"And you know that, sometimes, when the season is right, they go out into the sea on boats?"

Bip nodded. He had seen boats, but only as they were constructed, never afloat.

"Well, that's sort of what this is," said Truggle, gesturing to the walls around them. "This is a really, really big boat."

Bip frowned doubtfully.

"Trust me, that's the best way I can explain it. Now, come over here."

Bip started hesitantly toward the glowing area of floor.

"Come along—there's nothing to be afraid of," said Truggle.

For the second time that day, Bip took a leap of faith and stepped onto the quietly pulsating disc. He nearly screamed in terror as the disc suddenly plummeted downward. Truggle poked him reassuringly with his broom. "It's an elevator, lad. It's like a ladder but faster."

Bip nodded and tried to calm down, but his terror was not so easily dismissed as they fell into the unknown. Unlike the room they had come from, the corridor surrounding the elevator was oppressively close. It was hard to judge their rate of descent, although occasionally an odd glow would zip past them toward the ceiling at high speed. The only sound Bip could hear was the faint *swish* of the traveling disc moving through the air.

"Am I dreaming?" he whispered.

"What are you whispering for?" replied Truggle. "This place is huge! You can talk as loudly as you like!" He demonstrated by screaming in Bip's face.

"Don't you feel a little overwhelmed?" said Bip when the echoes had died down.

"Nah. You get used to it," said Truggle "You get used to pretty much everything when you're as old as I am."

As they descended, the tight corridor gave way rapidly until they were entering a room that, while not as big as the one they had come from, was still enormous by Bip's standards. He was slightly relieved, and a little surprised, to see that the room was filled with people, all of them hurrying back and forth from various tasks. The room was also filled with more metal contraptions, many of which twinkled with random lights or made the occasional whirring sound. Bip could see no purpose to the various metal boxes, but many of the people below seemed to be regarding them with great interest.

As the disc came to a smooth halt in the center of the room, Bip was surprised by how many of the people he recognized. Whether it was from the tavern or merely passing them in the street, the various faces of the Kaneqian elite were all familiar to Bip. Here, in this alien environment, he had expected to find something different from the everyday citizens of Kaneq.

"This is the archive," said Truggle. "This is where we keep the ancient wisdom, in case you've ever wondered."

"So it is true?" Bip gasped. "There is an ancient wisdom?"

"Well, not so much wisdom," mused Truggle, "but certainly information. Lots and lots of information. Some of it far too complex to tell us anything useful, but some of it...well, some of it very useful indeed."

"Where do you keep it all?" said Bip, craning his neck, searching the large but mostly empty room.

"In these metal boxes," Truggle said, banging one of the contraptions with his broom for emphasis. Bip was unimpressed; on the occasions when he had given any thought to the legendary "ancient wisdom" he had envisioned dusty tomes of rotting leather, stacked ceiling-high in some neglected catacomb. The flashing box, as pretty as it was, seemed a bit of a let-down.

"They're called computers," said Truggle. "They're sort of a big library in a little box. Well, more like lots of big libraries in a box, really. We don't fully understand how they work anymore. They're a relic of our ancestors, the founders."

"The founders?" Bip's prior disappointment dissipated dispassionately. Information about the pilgrims who had decided to build Kaneq in the middle of a desolate wasteland was vague at best, stating only that they had come from a far-off land to make a new home. Bip, like many other Kaneqians, had always been curious about why the founders had chosen to live in such isolation.

"The founders, yes," said Truggle, rubbing his hairy chin reflectively. "Yes, I suppose that's the best place to start. At the beginning, I mean." He rowed himself over to one of the computers, this one looking no different from the rest but for a contraption that resembled a large and intricate pair of goggles, which Truggle gestured for Bip to look into. Bip, figuring that he had gone along with everything else so far, looked into the goggles without hesitation.

"Now this might feel a bit funny..." said Truggle, and Bip felt his brain being sucked through his eyeballs.

---

*LIGHT. A million spectrums of multidimensional light. Solid light. Breathing light. Light that looked like sound. Sound that felt like light. A sense of time passing. Passing the wrong way. A feeling of incredible speed. Bip opened his eyes.*

---

CAPTAIN FINNEGUN OPENED HIS EYES. He wiped the sweat from his brow and surveyed the handiwork of the combined efforts of the *Sentinel*'s Elite-Gifted. What before had been a blizzard-soaked stretch of certain death had been transformed into merely miles of dead countryside. The heatshield equation, especially at this scale, was difficult to initiate but easy to maintain once established. Finnegun relaxed and turned his attention to other matters. He tried to take a step and stumbled slightly. It wasn't just the cold that made this new land hard going; owing to the planet's size and density, the gravity was stronger than he was used to. It would be a trial just walking around until his muscles adapted. He sighed. Another inconvenience in an already *very* inconvenient situation.

After the crash landing, they had decided to leave the *Sentinel* outside the perimeter of the heatshield, buried under the tons of snow, lest it attract the attention of any locals who might not appreciate extra-terrestrials in their back garden. Finnegun had thought the possibility of meeting anyone on the icy continent unlikely at best, but the stranger who had rescued the crew had insisted that they prepare for a long stay, and in turn, Handen had insisted on the various security procedures designed for this particular turn of events.

Finnegun allowed his mind to dwell on their odd rescuer for a while. The stranger had disappeared, rather mysteriously, soon after explaining that he thought it was extremely doubtful that the captain and his crew would be able to leave the ice continent in the near future. He had been right. Even now the engineers and technicians were trying to salvage any useful components from the *Sentinel*, but the main engine laid scattered in fragments on a mountaintop several miles away. There was no question that the crew would have to survive on the seemingly lifeless ice continent for quite a while. Erecting the heatshield had been a good start to the long process of bunking down in a hostile environment.

The captain thought back to the face of the stranger who had helped them in their time of need. His striking familiarity was still an intriguing mystery, and although Finnegun had formulated several conclusions as to the rescuer's origin, none of them were relevant to the situation at hand. He would file his suspicions away for later consideration.

Finnegun turned at the sound of approaching footsteps. It was Izzy, her flustered features looking more flustered than usual.

"It's bloody freezing out there," she grumbled, shaking the snow from her spiky head.

Finnegun allowed himself a small smile. "I would have thought that after so many millennia in stasis you would appreciate the feel of a real atmosphere again," he mused.

"A beach would have been nice," Izzy snapped, "but for preference anywhere but here would have been lovely."

"How's the salvage going?" said Finnegun

"We have most of the provisions, various tools, various materials we can recycle. Long term data storage is available for read only access, and probably will be for the foreseeable future. It's one of the few useful systems that relies on the secondary reserve batteries."

"Communications?"

"Down. We tried to bypass them to available power sources, but the danger of an overload is too great. The Mother Tongue survived intact, but without the appropriate amplification relays we've no hope of sending any more sub-space messages. Or even deep-space messages, for that matter."

"I wouldn't worry about it, Izzy; if the message was received, they will come for us. If not, they know where we are."

The two stood for a while, watching the rest of the Elite-Gifted as they began to cultivate the dead land within the heatshield, encouraging life wherever they could find it.

"I'm sorry about Kanick," said Finnegun, after a while. "I know you and he were—"

"He did what was...necessary," said Izzy, not looking up from the ground.

"Even so..." said Finnegun.

"Even so..." Izzy agreed.

The two Clarions stood awhile, gently steaming as the snow melted from their shoulders.

"We buried him along with Defty and Michaelmas," said Izzy, sighing heavily.

Finnegun nodded his approval. Though the remains of the three crew members who had given their lives for the survival of their shipmates had been evaporated along with the main engine, the honorary grave and ceremony was very typical of the Clarion people, who would treat and tend the graves as though they contained the mortal remains of their lost comrades.

Finnegun pretended not to notice as Izzy sniffed loudly and walked away. He would have liked to say something comforting, but there were many things to be done and there would be time to mourn later.

He thought again about the mysterious stranger who had helped them in their time of need. He thought about one of the various conclusions he had reached and took a laser pen from his top pocket. Bending down, grunting slightly with the unaccustomed effort, he picked up one of the smaller debris fragments of the ship's hull and began to burn a message into it with meticulous handwriting. It was possible that the information on the ship's computers would remain accessible for centuries to come, even without primary power, but sometimes it was best to put faith in more tangible and traditional forms of communication.

He began the letter with, "To whom it may concern…"

---

*TO WHOM IT MAY CONCERN…*

A long time ago, further back than the birth of the oldest sun, there were sides to pick. Two sides to the basic conflict. Before there was war, there was always order and chaos, and those who knew this chose their sides.

And the sides competed.

Many ages ago we, the Clarion people, looked to the stars and wondered if there was other life in the universe. We reached out nervously with signals and ships to discover if we were alone in existence and, in a moment that would define our history, we made Contact. Suddenly the universe was a more interesting place. Our reality had changed. Our existence had been redefined. We looked upon the stars and knew we were not alone. Soon, we had bridged our tiny solar system with a wondrous and intriguing intergalactic community of uncountable alien souls, and in doing so had opened our minds to information beyond our imagination…

It was then that we learned of the sides and the conflict, then that we learned of the Caretakers and the Discordance; those who defended order and those who actively sought chaos. It was then that we learnt of the Choice, something that all civilizations will eventually encounter. We were obligated to decide whether we believed order should be protected and nurtured in the ultraverse, or whether unfettered chaos is the natural and proper state of things, in which no life form has the right to interfere. Being what we were and believing what we did, we chose order, joining many other species and uniting in a common and simple goal: to protect less evolved life forms from the forces of adverse randominity, the shadows of those who would see order disrupted.

There were other factions across the ultraverse, other subgroups and divisions. There were the Indifferents, the Interferers, the Headstarters, the Optimists, the Harshliners, the Resounding Yessers, the Nearsayers, the Old Guards and the New Pop Fallacy and many, many more. But the alliance that dedicated itself purely to protecting order called themselves the Caretakers.

The Caretakers would use their powers and technology to watch over less developed species, keeping them safe from the harsh surprises of the ultraverse until they were better able to decide their own destiny, as we had so long ago. We took it upon ourselves to watch over worlds until they could make the Choice, and regardless of what they chose, we believe that to live long enough to realize this choice is the right of every civilization.

Now to the matter at hand...

It was the duty of the Clarions, and specifically the crew of the Sentinel, to ensure that the planet of Bersch reached an appropriate level of maturity without interference from hostile outside forces. Unfortunately, due to circumstances outside our expectations, the Sentinel is now unable to defend the planet of Bersch. In a thousand years' time, from this day, Bersch will be utterly destroyed by a powerful astral disaster.

It is my hope that Clarion reservists will arrive in time to intervene. Until then, the mission of the Sentinel remains the same: we must attempt to protect Bersch, or at the very least warn its inhabitants of the impending danger.

I am unsure how long my crew will be stranded, or how soon we will be able to warn the planet's inhabitants of their precarious situation. For now, we will remain, as always, Caretakers.


CAPTAIN JULIUS FINNEGUN. EG.
     The SS Sentinel

6

## Big Fat Responsibilities

**B**ip reeled and stumbled back from the goggles, the nauseating feeling of existing in two places making his head spin wildly. He reached out to steady himself and found only the floor for support.

It was too much information. Not only was there life outside Kaneq—he had always been led to expect as much—but life outside the planet, the *galaxy*!

Bip's vision spun erratically as he tried to process the unfathomable. The images he had seen had been real, he knew it as surely as he knew his legs existed, although he quickly reconsidered that analogy as his knees turned to jelly and he sprawled face-down on the cold metallic floor.

Caretakers, Order, the truth about everything... Bip screamed for a while then threw up before slipping into blissful unconsciousness.

"Just once," said Truggle, after the commotion had died down, "I wish they'd take it with a little more nonchalance."

*DARKNESS.*

A nagging sensation that he had something to be getting on with.

*These aren't my memories.*

*More darkness.*

An awareness of cold. A problem in the chronostatic chamber. Not supposed to feel.

*What's a chronostatic chamber?*

Pain. Pain in his leg and neck.

*These aren't my memories. There is no pain.*

*Darkness.*

"Bip?"

*Who, me?*

"Bip!"

*Five minutes, please.*

"Bip, wake up!"

"Muh?" said Bip, and wondered where he'd last heard the expression.

"It's all right, boy," said a familiar cracked voice. "I'm here."

"I had the strangest dreams," murmured Bip.

"Hah! No, not quite, lad. You had the strangest reality!"

Bip sat up suddenly and blinked rapidly as his eyes readjusted to the gloom. The first sight to greet him was the horrible grin of Truggle's withered face.

"Oh no," he muttered. "It was all real, wasn't it?"

"Hah! Well done, lad," said Truggle, his laugh snapping like a gun shot. "Usually people try to deny the inevitable for a touch longer, but I see you're ready to get on with things—"

Truggle was cut off by the sound of Bip throwing up again.

"Maybe not, then," he concluded. He fished around in his heavy robes for a while until he produced what looked like a piece of scrap metal. "I usually have a speech prepared to convince people that what they've seen is real, but I've found that this is a much easier way of getting the message across." He threw the piece of scrap metal at Bip's feet. It had eroded slightly with the years, but was still instantly recognizable to Bip as Captain Finnegun's message. Bip couldn't help but believe in its authenticity—he had, in effect, been there when it was written. He looked up at Truggle for an explanation.

"What you saw," Truggle began, "was something like a memory—a diary entry but with pictures and sounds and emotions. As I said, we're not sure how it works, but the important thing is that now you know the truth. You know the reason why every man, woman, and child in Kaneq is here."

"I did wonder," Bip croaked.

"But the question on your lips, I should imagine, is 'What on Bersch has this got to do with me?'"

Bip nodded, still too busy spitting away the taste of vomit to answer.

"Well, Bip," said Truggle, cheerfully, "I hate to be the bearer of big fat responsibilities, but you're going to save the world."

Bip nodded. Then he threw up again.

---

*CAPTAIN'S LOG. Day Fourteen.*

I am beginning to wonder if the stranger's assessment of our situation was really as bleak as he made it seem.

His exact words were, "I wouldn't expect to leave this place any time soon," though part of me hopes he was exaggerating. Of course, another part of me wonders how far a man who disappeared without a trace should be trusted.

However, these musings are not useful to our current dilemma.

The establishment of a temporary base on the ice continent is accelerating at a very satisfactory rate. The crew has managed to construct barracks from surplus materials salvaged from the ship's wreckage and the Elite-Gifted have managed to encourage the growth of various useful plants and foliage within the boundaries of the heatshield.

Although food stock is, at present, abundant, we consider it wise to prepare for all possibilities. To this end, Handen has suggested forming a "hunting and scavenging" party—though I daresay he is having great difficulty explaining the processes involved to the rest of the crew. Currently he is taking aside those with "hostility potential" for extensive training in "aggressive survival behavior." What this means I have no idea, but I trust Handen's judgment…

.  .  .

FINNEGUN PUT down the wrist console and tapped the stylus on his teeth. He was glad the technicians had been able to update data storage for minimal input functions. At least if their mission failed utterly, they would have a detailed log of their progress that might be useful to other Clarions who found themselves in similar situations. Also, though Finnegun didn't like to admit it, the log was good for his morale. It helped him to believe that soon there would be someone to read it. He turned as footsteps approached. It was Izzy, ready with her progress report.

"You'll be pleased to know we now have plumbing in the barracks." She smiled smugly.

"Fantastic," said Finnegun with a grin. "I was beginning to wonder if we'd smell this bad for the rest of our time here."

"I've been thinking," began Izzy, reproach evident in her usually confident voice, "about what we're going to call our temporary home."

Finnegun looked out at the colossal mountains they had narrowly avoided during their landing. "I thought 'Kanick' might be appropriate," he said.

"I thought so as well," said Izzy. "Thank you."

Finnegun continued to look at the mountains as Izzy walked away. Tomorrow he would talk to Handen about the progress made with his hunting party.

---

BIP SAT in his usual secluded table at the Empty Goat and thought hard. For the first time in quite a while he had something very hard to think about. In less than a year, the world would end. All his friends, family, and the people he didn't care much about but didn't want to see obliterated, would be…well, obliterated. In less than a year.

Bip pulled hard at his tankard of ale. He had no desire to get drunk, but a strong desire not to think.

He had been shocked by how many people knew about Bersch's impending disaster and the true purpose and origin of the Kaneqians.

That Dunman and Truggle were at the heart of the conspiracy hadn't been too surprising, but when he'd found out that Michaelmas and even his own mother were in on it, he'd been quite upset. He'd been even more upset to learn that he wasn't the first person chosen to "save the world." Since the crash landing, every generation had thrown up people who would venture into the wilderness in an attempt to reach civilization. As the community had settled and the original founders had grown old, the knowledge of Kaneq's true purpose had been entrusted to certain individuals who would pass it down the generations to the present day's inner circle of trustees. Thus, from every generation, a candidate was selected to leave the community and make the dangerous journey to find and make contact with other peoples. These candidates were rarely heard from again, the success or failure of their mission never disclosed.

Bip pulled hard at the tankard again. Selected candidates hardly ever refused the mission once they were told the truth, Truggle had told him. Bip could see why. Firstly, if the world is going to end and you're given a chance of saving it, there is a very strong moral obligation to comply, especially if it's the world you happen to be standing on at the time. Secondly, if you didn't at least try, you would get some very scathing looks from everybody when the world did end.

These reasons were all very well and good, but the clincher for Bip was when he'd learned that his father had been a previous candidate. He'd had a very long and tearful conversation with his mother and Michaelmas about the true fate of his father, after which he had been first outraged at being lied to, then later quietly proud. It had turned out that Bip's family line had a long history of selected candidates, dating back to the early volunteers. He had understood, eventually, why he had never been told the truth about his father. The knowledge of Bersch's appointment with annihilation was best kept from the general public, as people don't tend to sleep well if they think the planet is going to explode. He also understood why Michaelmas couldn't keep his promise about offering him work. There would, after all, not have been any point. As a sort of apology, the drinks were entirely on Michaelmas for the evening, of which Bip was taking full advantage.

The question that still bothered him a lot was why he had been picked instead of anyone else. Truggle had admitted that there were far more qualified candidates but professed his faith in Bip's psyentific potential and adaptability to new situations.

"Turning a house into an igloo," he had said, obviously having been informed of the botched home improvement by Michaelmas, "is no easy feat. There's definite potential in you, lad. You just need a bit of a kick in the bum."

Even this argument hadn't convinced Bip, who knew that if he were picking a savior of the planet, he would look a lot further afield than himself. Eventually Truggle had confessed, in a roundabout manner, that sometimes candidates were picked purely on gut instinct. This had not instilled Bip with confidence.

Truggle had attempted to reassure him, stating that he wouldn't be thrown into the wilderness unprepared and would be trained vigorously for a solid month. Bip, who had already made peace with his lack of physical motivation, winced hard at words like "trained" and "vigorously." He had winced harder when he had been introduced to his "personal trainer," a bear of a man called Rynford, whose square jaw, steely gaze, and amazingly intimidating moustache Bip had only ever seen lurking at the back of council meetings. Rynford was Kaneq's Huntmaster, and like all the hunters, he was surly, secretive, and had more muscle than could possibly be convenient. Bip had never got on with the hunters, who forsook the Kaneqian lifestyle of fairly docile contentment for a life of danger exploring the surrounding wilderness and scouting for possible hostile animal or monster activity. Rynford had taken one look at Bip and insisted that the training begin at dawn the next day, which had made Bip wince so hard his face had nearly fallen off.

Bip sighed his well-practiced, forlorn sigh. He had never wanted anything more than a quiet, easy life, but it seemed the universe was conspiring to make this a laughable impossibility. He emptied his tankard and was surprised to see it replaced almost immediately. He looked up into the broad face of Bailey, who was going through one of his rare phases of being neither drunk nor hungover.

"What's up with your face?" said Bailey. "You look like you've got the weight of the world on your shoulders."

Bip pulled hard on his new tankard. "Sod off, Bailey," he said.

---

BIP WAS EXHAUSTED. He was past exhausted. If he'd had any energy left, he would have invented whole new words for just how exhausted he was.

Dawn had been merely an hour ago, and already he wanted to go back to bed.

He had been sleeping, quite peacefully, when the first rays of morning sunshine had sidled through his curtains. Before he had even had time to acknowledge the new day, his bedroom door had crashed open and he had been lifted bodily from his bed and placed in a freezing cold shower in what had seemed like only a few blurred and terrible seconds. When he had finally recovered from the shock and got his bearings, he had looked up into the wide grin of Rynford.

"Time to get up," he had said. "We're going out for breakfast."

So far, "going out for breakfast" had consisted of an hour-long jog through the endless snowdrifts of the Ice Plains.

Bip panted, struggling against the weight of his insulating leathers and the quick pace of the athletic Huntmaster, whose flapping furs and long spear could be seen racing ahead through the constant blizzard. Bip's knees had long since turned to rubber, and he had begun to lag farther and farther behind Rynford—which was not encouraging as he had no idea where he was or, for that matter, *who* he was anymore. His whole body burned with effort, which seemed odd because various extremities were telling him it was very cold indeed. Freezing, actually. With a heaving sigh, Bip fell face-first into the snow and wondered if anyone would mind if he just fell asleep for a little while. He was jerked from his thoughts of slumber by the rough grip of Rynford, who hauled him from the ground and held him up easily by the collar.

"Aye, I think that'll do for a warmup, lad. Time for a bit of breakfast, I'm thinking."

Bip blinked rapidly and waited for his breath to steady before saying, "What are you on about, you muscle-headed madman? We're in the middle of nowhere!" At least, that was what he meant to say. What he actually said was, "Whu? *Cough cough…COUGH!*"

Rynford pointed to a patch of snow that looked pretty much like every other patch of snow. "Driftdiggers," he said, with a hint of smugness.

Bip looked confused for a moment before understanding slapped him with the fingers of doom. A driftdigger was a vicious breed of mammal, akin to a giant carnivorous gopher, whose main method of hunting was to burrow under prey and eat them from beneath while they were off balance. Bip had heard many deeply nasty campfire stories about encounters with driftdiggers; the fact that they were all based on fact was less than reassuring.

"We can't eat driftdiggers!" he wailed. "Driftdiggers eat people, not the other way around!"

"Nonsense!" Rynford snorted. "You can eat just about anything if you put your mind to it."

Bip was momentarily flabbergasted, unsure whether Rynford was deliberately ignoring reason or just trying to upset him. "The point I'm trying to make is, yeah? The message I'm trying to convey here is, right? We'll be killed. That really is the be-all and end-all of it. We'll be killed. Horribly."

"That's a very negative attitude, laddie, and besides…" Rynford turned a stern gaze to his young trainee. "Where you're going, chances are there are a few worse things than a glorified gopher."

Bip looked glumly at the ground while this harsh observation sank in.

"And anyway," continued Rynford, "there's good meat on one of them buggers."

Bip looked thoughtful for a moment. He was cold, and he was tired, but it was starting to dawn on him that he was also very, very hungry.

"So how do you go about killing a driftdigger, then?" he asked.

Rynford bent down and dug up a rock from under the snow. "Strength, skill, ingenuity, cunning, and…" he carefully weighed the ice-bound rock in his massive fists, "something to hit them with."

BIP WATCHED from afar as Rynford casually approached the driftdigger's lair, his spear held nonchalantly over one shoulder and the newly acquired rock concealed in one of his various leather satchels.

For a while, nothing seemed to happen. The endless whistle of the blizzard was the only sound. The rolling ocean of snow remained undisturbed by erupting monsters. Bip felt an awful twist in his guts as the snowdrift Rynford was approaching first shuddered and then, with a rumble and creak, collapsed. The deep rumbling continued as the ground between where the drift had been and Rynford began to shake and subside. It was clear that the driftdigger had sensed the Huntmaster's presence and was moving in for the kill.

Bip bit his knuckles in terror as Rynford stood stock still, his spear ready in hand, awaiting the onslaught of the beast. Bip couldn't help but think how small and inadequate the once-mighty Rynford seemed compared to the wave of menace that approached him. He wanted to call out but could not, could only watch helplessly as the driftdigger moved closer and closer until it was very nearly on top of the Huntmaster. Just when Bip had thought Rynford truly done for, the big man plunged his spear into the ground and vaulted his body high into the air, narrowly avoiding the erupting muzzle of the driftdigger. Time seemed to slow as the giant beast's head reared up in an explosion of ice to snatch the arcing hunter out of the sky with teeth liked razored tombstones. Bip even had time to see the wicked red glint in the creature's beady, ferret-like eyes, shining like a firework in the surrounding palette of white. But the monster's actions were halted unexpectedly. Just as the driftdigger seemed set to devour Rynford, it stopped suddenly, finding its jaws jammed open by the length of the Huntmaster's spear. Rynford, with an astonishing feat of muscular control, balanced calmly on the shaft of his spear, the sturdy piece of wood the only thing between him and the wet, gaping maw of the monster beneath him. Quickly but carefully, Rynford reached into a satchel and pulled out the rock he had picked up earlier. With little ceremony, threw it into the Driftdigger's throat. Then he ran along his spear and flipped gracefully from the creature's nose as it began to slowly choke to death.

Bip realized he was still biting his knuckles. He had drawn blood.

---

"AND THAT," Rynford said, "is how we get breakfast."

They had found shelter in one of the Ice Plains' many cubbies and caves and were enjoying some small relief from the cold provided by a fire Rynford had made. One of the useful benefits of a driftdigger's carcass was that the natural oils in its pelt were conveniently flammable, meaning that both trainer and trainee could reap the benefits of a warm, if stinky, fire.

Bip had been quietly nauseated when Rynford had taken out a long dagger and begun carving the useful meat from the defeated beast, bagging and burying what they couldn't carry and taking as much of the pelt as possible, which had a number of other uses in Kaneq, such as providing lamp oil and lubricants. When Rynford had carefully removed the slab-like front teeth, Bip had been confused.

"Personal collection," Rynford had explained. "I've nearly got enough to tile my house with."

Despite how queasy the butchery of the animal had made him, Bip couldn't help but salivate at the smell of the thin strips of meat that Rynford was now carefully roasting over the fire.

"Of course, driftdigger always tastes better with a fried egg," Rynford muttered distractedly as he handed Bip a lump of sizzling meat on the end of a stick. "There's nothing like a couple of fried eggs to make up a good breakfast."

Bip nodded dumbly and began munching on the cut of meat, finding great satisfaction in both the succulence and the warmth of the food. He chewed happily as warm juice trickled down his chin.

"So, then," said Rynford, after a while. "What are you killing for breakfast tomorrow?"

Bip paused mid-mouthful, his eyes widening. "Sorry?" he said.

"Well, I'm supposed to be training you, you know. Saving the world and all that, you remember? Today I showed you how to get breakfast in the wild—tomorrow I want to see how much you picked up."

For a long while Bip couldn't think of anything to say, still unsure whether or not the big Huntmaster was exercising his robust and sadistic sense of humor.

"I'm sorry, Rynford," he concluded finally. "I don't think I can do what you did."

"Oh, you mean all the back-flips and whatever? That's mainly just for show, laddie, you don't have to—"

"No, you don't understand," interrupted Bip. "I don't think I could kill anything. It just seems a bit...well, cruel, really."

Rynford stared for a while, a muscle in his cheek twitching rhythmically. Bip couldn't figure out whether the big man was angry or thoughtful and could only wait as the Huntmaster's trail of thought reached its conclusion. Finally, Rynford let out a short sigh before saying, "Look, lad. I don't want to seem pushy or anything, but I've got to prepare you for the worst. As far as I'm concerned, there is only one priority in the wilderness, one golden rule that every hunter should remember, and that is, don't get eaten."

Bip sat for a while. "I think I can remember that one," he said.

"No, no, lad. It might seem fairly obvious, but you'd be surprised by the number of people I tell that to who go out and get themselves eaten. They might die of exposure first, or starvation, or from falling off a cliff, but sooner or later something eats them. So here's what I do to get around it, see? If I think something's going to eat me, I eat it first." Rynford leaned back smugly. "Top o' the food chain, see? It's harder to eat something that's eating you right back. Law of the wild."

Bip thought for a while. "So what you're saying is, if I think something is going to eat me, I should eat it first?"

Rynford grinned widely. "Aye, that's right! It's a metaphor for the whole of aggressive survival behavior in one. There's beasties out there with more teeth than brain cells, and they're all just itching for an easy lunch. The defenseless are nothing but wafer-thin mints in the delicatessen of the wilderness. The trick is to grow your own teeth: cunning, intelligence, skill! The trick is to become the diner, not the dinner!"

"You mean it's a dog-eat-dog world, sort of thing?"

"Aye, I suppose. Though I'll eat pretty much anything, to tell you the truth."

---

FROM SOME DISTANCE AWAY, the monster watched the soft glow of the fire that was nearly lost in the brightness of the surrounding snow. It watched and thought about killing. The monster was a yeti, and with its masses of matted white hair, it blended quite easily into the landscape of the Ice Plains. It was often mistaken for a large hill, or sometimes a small mountain. This sometimes meant that, instead of wasting energy hunting, it could simply wait around all day for some unsuspecting creature to try to use it as shelter. It rested its weight on its giant fists and thought about the best way to kill the little man peoples who were currently eating the tooth beastie.

The yeti hadn't been intimidated by the larger man people's display of skill in killing the tooth beastie—the yeti could have dispatched it in half the time, and with a lot less showing-off involved to boot—but a gut feeling stayed the monster's urge to attack. Though the yeti wasn't the brightest of monsters, it had a wary sense of cunning that told it that attacking two of the man peoples might not be to its advantage. It had seen man peoples in action before and knew them to be swift, intelligent hunters who would retaliate in large numbers if openly threatened.

The yeti momentarily put a hand over its ears. The maddening whisper that was urging the monster to attack was becoming more persistent every day. It was starting to affect the creature's judgment. Part of the monster's animal brain wondered why it was taking such an interest in killing these particular man peoples, who had very little meat and were more trouble than they were worth. The constant whispering at the back of its mind scattered these thoughts, leaving the yeti with a simple and unquestionable desire to kill.

With one last glance over at the man peoples' position, the yeti lumbered off into the white. It was a patient beast and would return when the odds were more to its liking.

BIP STUMBLED into his room and stood briefly in the doorway, relishing being indoors. Then he staggered across the floor and landed in a heap on his bed. He was too cold and tired to run a bath, too exhausted to make any supper. Bip curled up under his duvet and moaned aloud.

He had thought that after the slaying of the driftdigger, the rest of his first training day might be a little less extreme. He had been proved horribly wrong. Rynford's boundless energy had allowed for only a short break after breakfast, after which they had taken another jog through the freezing cold to a short cliff face, where Rynford had taught Bip the benefit of "not falling to an icy grave" by forcing him to climb the slippery rocks with only a few daggers for support and a thin rope that Rynford held as his only insurance against a messy death. If that experience hadn't been traumatic enough, three hours of intense weapons training had left Bip a nervous wreck. Though the practice weapons were padded, and Bip had crammed as much of the training armor onto his body as possible, Rynford had still managed to beat him black and blue while demonstrating the finer points of "not being stabbed to death by something sharp." There had been some respite while Rynford had taken Bip through a few survival techniques, which mainly involved how to cook, wear, or otherwise recycle the animal you'd just killed. However, the relief had been short-lived, as the Huntmaster had decided to end the day by showing Bip some of the more interesting hand-to-hand combat techniques he had developed.

Bip had limped back to town in a daze, cold, wet, and exhausted beyond anything he had experienced in his life. Muscles that he had never known existed were aching ferociously, and his nose streamed a cold wave of snot. He curled up further still in his thick blankets and enjoyed the warmth and security of his bed. The ecstasy of relaxation was marred only by the looming realization that, at dawn the next day, the training would begin all over again.

# 7

# Handen Strike Vs. The End of the World

*Captain's log. Day Two Hundred and Sixty Three.*
Progress continues as normal. I have to say, as temporary as I believed the arrangements would be, Kanick is appearing more and more like a home rather than an outpost. While many of the crew still brood for civilization, a few have begun to settle down and make the most of the situation…even come to enjoy it.

I must confess I reside in the latter camp.

Supplies are still plentiful for the time being. Various projects and committees to ensure a more comfortable existence in Kanick are currently being undertaken, and people are content to busy themselves cultivating our base into a more homely environment.

Though I have come to terms with our being stranded, I cannot help but feel guilty that there is currently not much we can do to further our original mission to protect Bersch. It seems wrong to settle down and relax while a planet is unwittingly heading toward catastrophe. All we can do is wait…

FINNEGUN LOOKED up from his wrist console as Handen

approached. He took a brief moment to take in the scenery of Kanick, which still warmed him. The lush green village, surrounded by towering trees, was a far cry from the patch of lifeless snow they had originally crashed into. These days, life in Kanick was spent in individual housing rather than crammed together in barracks, and though Finnegun missed the camaraderie of those times, it was a relief to relax on the porch of his own private lodgings.

Handen stopped at the foot of Finnegun's porch and snapped a smart salute. Finnegun smiled briefly to himself. While the rest of the crew had grown relaxed and informal in their new community, Handen and his hunting party had retained the rigid military discipline of their station.

"At ease, Handen," said Finnegun, smiling wryly.

"Reporting from patrol, sir," said Handen.

"Ah, really? And how goes the hunting party?" said Finnegun.

"Excellent, sir. We've been pacifying the northern borders, sir. A large tribe of yetis had seen fit to take up residence by the heatshield, and so we dispersed them with a show of force. No casualties were sustained."

"Really? No casualties, eh? Hmm. Brilliant." Finnegun grinned nervously. The hunting party had flourished under Handen's strict and rigorous supervision, which had turned a group of men and women who previously would have had trouble with the concept of beating an egg into a team of skilled trackers, survivalists, and fighters. The hunting party had become close-knit, spending most of their time patrolling the Ice Plains and very little time in the security of the heatshield at all.

Though Finnegun understood the need for reconnaissance and security in the outlying regions of Kanick, he couldn't remember authorizing battle with a tribe of fifteen-foot monsters.

"These yetis," he said. "We couldn't have tried...reasoning with them?"

Handen's deadpan stare did not waver. "A messenger was sent to contact the yetis under a flag of negotiation, sir."

"And?"

"They ate the flag, sir, and tried to eat the messenger."

"Ah. So. No negotiations, then?"

"No, sir. They just tried to eat us, sir," said Handen. "You'd be surprised how many things out there want to eat us, sir," he concluded by way of explanation.

"Well," said Finnegun, at a loss for what to say. "Jolly good. Carry on, I suppose."

"Sir…" began Handen, and Finnegun bit his lip. This was a conversation he had seen coming for a long time.

When they had first landed on Bersch, Handen had been in his element, taking to crisis like a fish to water, but in the recent months, as the crew had settled down and the hunting party had reached an acceptable level of skill, Handen had become increasingly restless. Finnegun knew exactly what the Hostility Advisor was going to say.

"No, Handen," he said.

"Pardon, sir?" said Handen, feigning stupidity.

"You want to try to contact this planet's civilizations, Handen. Doubtless you have some dashingly intrepid quest in mind to save the world. Well, I'm sorry, but it's just impossible. We need you here."

"Julius, listen," Handen replied.

Finnegun stopped, stunned. That was the first time Handen had referred to him as anything other than "Sir" or "Captain."

Handen continued. "Things here are fine. The hunting party is taking care of itself. Kanick is more like a holiday camp than a survival outpost. I can't just sit here and wait for help. It's not in my nature."

Finnegun sighed. Handen was right, of course. The *Sentinel's* crew could ill afford to wait around and hope for the best. Not with the fate of the world at stake.

"What do you need?" he said, defeated.

"I've taken the liberty of drawing up a list of supplies. I'll also need the assistance of two of the more accomplished hunters."

"Done. Done. Take whatever you need. But who, may I ask, is going to be my Hostilities Advisor?"

"I thought Izzy was shaping up very nicely, sir."

Finnegun smiled. Thanks to Handen's hunting party, Izzy's temperament had finally found an environment in which to flourish, and it had flourished abundantly, the buds of petty tantrum growing into a tactical understanding of violence that rivaled even Handen's.

"An excellent choice, I'm sure. When did you wish to leave?"

"Tomorrow, sir. At dawn."

"Dawn? Why dawn?"

Handen shrugged. "It's how we do things in the hunting party, sir."

---

AS THE FIRST light of day struck a cold dagger into the gray of the pre-dawn wilderness, Handen stared out into the slowly revealing horizons. The hunting party had escorted the three volunteers to the ice floes, which led out into the seemingly endless ocean.

Anchored to a fairly stable chunk of floating ice was a sea vessel constructed from leftover debris from the crash landing. The metal ship was powered by a series of small outboard motors that ran on a makeshift fuel the Elite-Gifted had managed to cultivate from local vegetation. Handen had no idea whether the vessel would be adequate for their journey, largely because he had no idea where their journey would take them. Though they had mapped Bersch extensively before entering chronostatic hibernation, quite a few millennia had passed since then, and all Handen was certain of was that the next continent was several hundred miles to the south.

They had decided to call the vessel the *Sentinel II*, purely for the sake of sentiment.

Handen turned to the hunting party. They stood solemnly in a row, their furs and weapons grayly silhouetted against the ever-white background. He would miss them. He would miss the wilderness.

Over the passing months, Handen had found he had an affinity with the Ice Plains. They offered him challenge and adventure, the two things he craved above all else. He had been annoyed when he had first taken on the hunting party, their whinging and complaining spoiling the soundless peace of the open tundra, their naivety and lack of respect taking the excitement from the danger. Eventually, though, through his personal training and the endless pressure of the wilds, the crew had turned into true hunters and had become one with the wilderness.

While the rest of the crew had struggled to build their homes and lives in the boundaries of Kanick, Handen and his comrades had found their place on the open run of the Ice Plains. Now they stood silently. There was little need for words in the hunting party, who could often communicate all they needed with a look or a hand gesture, but Handen felt there were a few things that needed to be said. He turned to Izzy, who held his gaze.

"I'm not needed here anymore," said Handen.

"Debatable," replied Izzy, her face as deadpan and unreadable as the former Hostility Advisor's.

"You'll do fine. You'll all do fine."

"I think so."

Handen surveyed the beckoning horizon again. He signaled for the two volunteers to prepare the boat for cast off. He turned back to Izzy and shook her hand, holding on a little longer than the formality of the gesture allowed for."It's a big, wide world out there," he said, an uncharacteristic half-smile breaking his face.

"Good luck," she said.

"You too. All of you."

The *Sentinel II* sailed into the brightening sea. Handen stood on the bow, looking back at the slowly shrinking shapes of the hunting party, his family, and his home willowing into a blurred nothing. Then he turned around, compelled by the seductive pull of new horizons. He smiled.

———

TWENTY-THREE MONTHS LATER, an honorary grave was dug for Handen and the volunteers.

———

*KABLAAM!*

Anyone standing next to the Dome would have been surprised by the deep, ominous rumble in the ground and the clouds of snow and ice that were shaken from the normally and reliably static building. Thankfully, the only thing near the outside of the Dome that could have been surprised was a cluster of penguins. The penguins, not being masters of environmental awareness, continued to shuffle around in the manner of creatures with not much else to do but shuffle.

*KABLOOIE!!*

Elders and councilmen walking around the upper levels of the Dome paused briefly as the ground wobbled beneath them, regained their balance and continued about their business as though nothing had happened. They were all aware of what had been scheduled in the lower levels for today and were quite used to the floor shaking and the thunderous—

*KABLAMMY!!! sizzlesizzlesizzle...phhupt*

Bip unblocked his ears and slowly opened his eyes. The practice room near the bowels of the Dome was gloomy and dark and thickly quiet, but Bip's vision swam with blue and purple flashes from the frantic light show that had seared across his glasses, and his ears rang with the reverberations of the almighty booms that had accompanied it. Where there had been five of the grinning test dummies at the end of the room, there now stood two, looking lonely next to three ominous piles of dust and rubble.

Up on the gantry, overlooking the vast and nearly empty practice room, Truggle coughed through the thick smoke from his pipe while Dunman cleaned the steam from his glasses.

"I think," said Truggle, slowly, "that Bip has seen enough of your commendable talent for exploding things, Glimton. Perhaps if you went over some theory now?"

Glimton looked up at the gantry, a slightly manic grin still skewing his thin features, his dark, round goggles reflecting a wicked glint from the lamps that shone down from the high ceiling. "Sorry, Truggle," he called, merrily. "Just demonstrating the finer points of rapid molecular discombobulation."

"Yes, well, as much as I enjoy watching you obliterate straw dummies, we are here for the purpose of developing Bip's knack and not your own," replied Truggle.

Glimton scratched his egg-like head and turned to regard Bip as if he had only just noticed he was there. Bip had changed a little over the past fortnight. Rynford's intense training sessions had left the volunteer looking tired and drawn, but already there was a slight set to his scrawny shoulders and a bit of a spring in his normal shuffle. Rynford's unorthodox fitness regimes still left Bip feeling like he wanted to die, but when he'd caught a look at himself in the mirror one evening before going to bed, he had been pleased to notice if not any *actual* muscle then at least the promise of muscular development on his normally unremarkable physique.

While Rynford insisted that Bip had a long way to go before he was ready for the wilderness, he had admitted that his rate of progress for the first two weeks was very nearly at a minimal level of acceptableness. With this sterling stamp of approval, Truggle had suggested that Bip pay more attention to developing his psyentific knack, and he had been turned over to the teachings of Glimton, who, despite his penchant for blowing things up and his legendary arrogance, was the most able psyentist in Kaneq.

Glimton adjusted the high collar of his white coat and peered at Bip through his shaded goggles.

"Well, well, well, well, well," he began. "Haven't we come a long way? It seems that Rynford has got you using all your muscles except the ones in your head!" He snickered a light and annoying snicker. Bip, who had learnt a great deal of interesting things under Rynford's supervision, albeit most of them involving the killing and processing of animals, opened his mouth to protest.

"No, no. Don't speak," interrupted Glimton. "I should imagine you don't have anything worthwhile to say, anyhow. I, after all, have shaken hands with the very fibers of being, have waltzed with the microscopic intricacies of life, have skipped the light fantastic and moved on to higher things, whereas you..." He looked Bip up and down. "You are a pleb."

Bip looked uncertainly up at the gantry where Truggle and Dunman sat. Truggle gave an apologetic shrug. Glimton continued to speak, his high-pitched and clipped tones echoing grandiosely around the practice room as he paced up and down.

"Oh, you may have been impressed by Rynford's flip-flops and what-nots, and you may think it's awfully clever to chuck sharpened pieces of wood at dumb beasts, but I..." Glimton turned his full attention back to Bip. "I will show you how to see what a flower is thinking, how to change the shape of stone, how to manipulate the very air you breathe!" Glimton was suddenly uncomfortably close to Bip, his voice a low murmur. "I will show you how to unlock your birthright!"

Bip leaned back slightly and blinked, his perplexed face reflected in the blackness of Glimton's goggles. "Good?" he said.

Glimton's manic smile collapsed instantly. He turned away and began muttering to himself. "Good? Good, he says? I offer him the secrets of the universe and he says 'good'? I ought to replace his eyeballs with his other balls just to teach him some respect! Ingrate! Unenthusiastic, disrespectful, little..." He spun wildly from his mutterings and raised his clawed hand to the gantry in spectacularly dramatic rage, his reedy voice now booming with fury. "You waste my time, Truggle! You give me this and call it a student? You waste my time!!"

There was an uncomfortable silence as the echoes died away.

"Anyhow," said Glimton, his demeanor changing from boiling rage to indifferent cheerfulness in a split-second, "I suppose we'd better get on with things. Busy, busy, busy, yes? The sands of time wait for no one, hmm? Let's talk a little theory, shall we?"

Bip reeled, unsure how to deal with the sudden shift in temperamental weather. He opted to shut up and listen as Glimton began talking animatedly about psyence, cheerfully preaching theory as if he hadn't just threatened to radically alter Bip's anatomy. He attempted to concentrate, but part of him couldn't help wishing he were out on patrol with Rynford, who was at least predictably insane.

"Where was I? Where was I?" muttered Glimton. "Ah, yes! Instructions! Everything is, at its core, a set of instructions! Little bits of information, a trillion billion invisible scraps of data, that tell a thing not only what it is but also what it does! A rock is a rock is a rock— but even a rock knows, on some infinitesimally small level, that it *is* a *rock*! Do you understand!?"

Bip was uncomfortably aware that Glimton seemed to be getting over excited and wisely chose not to say anything. Instead, he smiled and nodded politely.

"Grins like an idiot," Glimton said scornfully, before continuing his lecture as though he had never interrupted himself. "So even the smallest and dullest of things are aware, on a level too far below what we understand as comprehension to recognize without looking very closely indeed, not just of what they are, but what they do! A rock knows to lie still and be hard! It's what it does! If it didn't, it would be a pretty useless rock, wouldn't you say? Ahahahaha!!"

Bip deemed it appropriate to give a polite chuckle. He also stepped back a little bit.

"Laughs like a girl," Glimton muttered angrily, before once again launching into his rant. "Instructions! The important thing to remember is that on the most microscopically microscopic of levels, all these instructions are written on the same paper! The same energy! They can all be beheld, and if understood, they can be persuaded to change! That is the process of the Knack, the secret of the Psyence, the legacy of our Ancestors! A rock is a rock is a rock—but it used to be magma, maybe, or sand, or part of a mountain, or even a star! Even the lowliest of pebbles, at its core, knows how to be a mountain! The smallest of seeds can dream of the towering oak! And these dreams can be seen in the instruction, can be read, can be understood—and can be altered!"

Bip stood and listened attentively. It was a vague and introductory lecture on the nature of the knack, usually reserved for children many years his junior, but he couldn't help but be awed by Glimton's passion and enthusiasm.

"Stands there listening like a…like a…like a *pleb*!" shouted Glimton, for no good reason. Then, so suddenly that Bip fell over, he blew up one of the few remaining test dummies. The dummy, writhing briefly under Glimton's outstretched finger, expanded radically before igniting into a ball of flame, showering flaming straw and cloth, its grinning head rocketing into the air and navigating a gentle arc before coming to rest between Bip's legs.

"Meep!" said Bip, too horrified to say anything useful.

"You see!?" screamed Glimton. "The Dummy already knows how to be a lots of different pieces, it remembers being molecular! It was just a matter of reminding it! With a vengeance!!!"

When the echoes died away, a polite coughing from the gantry broke the uncomfortable silence that always surrounds the unpredictably explosive.

"Glimton," said Truggle soothingly. "I believe you're getting a bit carried away again, yes?"

"Ahahahahaha," said Glimton. "Silly me. How embarrassing. So sorry. Very sorry." Glimton picked up the head of the straw dummy and addressed it.

"Are we sorry, Mr. Head?" said Glimton, and then, in quite a convincing act of ventriloquism, replied, "We certainly are, Mr. Glimton—we're very sorry!"

"Yes, that's right, Mr. Head! Very sorry indeed!"

"Boy howdy!"

"Ahahahaha!"

"Please don't hurt me, Mr. Glimton! I won't tell your secrets!"

"Silence, you ignorant troll!!" screamed Glimton, and obliterated Mr. Head in a wave of fire.

Bip, Dunman, and Truggle all stood with their mouths open in idiot disbelief—whether at the fate of Mr. Head or the continually revealing depths of Glimton's humongous eccentricities, no one could tell.

Glimton turned to face the gantry, the mask of psychotic rage ebbing from his features.

"And so ends today's lesson," he said. "Tomorrow we shall discuss the Persuasion of Physics, the Cajoling of Base Substances and the Exploding of Things I Have Lying Around. Good day." He turned and walked calmly out of the practice room.

Bip, in his utter confusion and terror, applauded nervously.

---

LATER, Bip sat with Truggle in the Empty Goat, a cup of hot, sweet tea clutched in his thin fingers.

"I know he's a little bit...odd," began Truggle.

"A little!?" cried Bip. "He's off his rocker, is what he is!"

"Well...yes," Truggle conceded. "But he's also the finest psyentific mind in the community."

Bip gulped his tea. "So you keep saying, but so far all I've learned is that a madman with the ability to explode things with his mind is not good company. And I'm pretty sure I already knew that, so I haven't really learned anything!"

"Nevertheless," sighed Truggle, "Glimton is the best chance we have of preparing your knack for the outside world, where I'm fairly sure that exploding straw dummies will be the least of your worries."

Bip shivered. He was beginning to have serious doubts about saving the world.

---

SEA SPRAYED over the prow of the *Sentinel II* as it ploughed effortlessly through the choppy ocean, its metal frame gleaming a brilliant orange in the setting sun, its sharp symmetry slicing smoothly through the oncoming waves. Over the rushing wind and the roar of the ocean, the sound of the ship's outboard motors could be heard burring steadily and confidently.

Handen was pleased. They had sailed for eight days straight without a single sign of bad weather or any other impediments. Supplies and fuel were still plentiful, and the *Sentinel II* was as in as good a condition as she had been when she had first been put together. Widge and Beggs, the two hunter volunteers, busied themselves checking over the engine stats and the short-range scanner they had managed to salvage from the original *Sentinel*. Their bustle was fruitless, though, as there had not been an inkling of incident since the ship had cast off.

Beggs yawned, ruffled her short, feathered hair, and relaxed a little in her console chair. Widge, however, maintained an iron vigil over his scanner display. Handen surveyed the reassuringly boring horizon through his view panel. It looked like smooth sailing all the way.

"Um…sir?" said Widge, not taking his eyes from the scanner.

Handen closed his eyes. He knew that any question that began with "um" was likely to be trouble. "What is it, Mr. Widge?" he said.

"There's something coming up on the short-range, sir—something big. I think it might be land."

"Land? Impossible, I would have…" Handen stopped. He looked out of his view panel again. What before had been an idyllic image of clear seas had now turned gray and murky. A thick fog had sprung from seemingly nowhere.

"Cut the engines," ordered Handen, and for the first time since the beginning of their journey, the hum of the outboard motors ceased.

The three sailors stiffened slightly. It was eerily quiet, and not just because of the lack of engine noise. There was no wind and no slap of waves. The *Sentinel II* didn't even rock slightly in the water.

"The scanner is still reading a large mass, sir. It has to be land—it's too big to be anything else."

Unease crept down Handen's spine like the fingers of some swamp-dwelling thing. "Widge, take the controls. Beggs, accompany me up on deck. Let's take a look around."

Before leaving the control bridge, Handen unthinkingly picked up some choice weapons and secured them about his person, adding a short sword, and a long bullwhip to the spear and dagger combination he usually preferred. The decision to pick up his weapons was a nearly unconscious act, a nervous habit rather than a planned defense.

Up on the deck, the thick, yellowish fog obscured any long-range view, making it difficult to tell if they were, indeed, approaching land. It also seemed to toy with the acoustics of the sailor's voices, making them seem hollow and distant.

"Look over here, sir," said Beggs, who had for some reason begun talking in a low whisper.

Handen looked over the ship's bow where Beggs had pointed and could not help but stare. The ocean was dead still, barely rippling as it came into contact with the *Sentinel II*. The water, as far as Handen could make out, was as dark and smooth as some black mirror, or a slab of onyx. Handen shivered, not sure whether it was merely the cold air that chilled him, though the thick fog let through no sea breeze.

"Land ho, sir!" cried the voice of Widge from the control bridge. Handen looked around wildly and saw that Widge was right. Through the thick fog, he could see the silhouette of what looked like a small island. All of a sudden, a low, rumbling moan seemed to saturate the surroundings, bellowing like the bending of iron or the ghosts of a thousand whales. Handen shivered again, first suspecting they had hit rock, then realizing that the *Sentinel II* still had not moved. The low moan sounded again, and the glass-still waters of the ocean began to ripple into steady, rhythmic waves. The island silhouette seemed to be getting closer, or bigger, and the low moan sounded again, louder this time. As it did, the seawater around them began to bubble, and the rhythm of the waves began to intensify. Clouds began to blacken the sky, and rain and thunder quickly joined the stormy chorus. There was a sound like a giant waterfall coming from the direction of the island.

Realization dawned a brand new day of terror in Haden's guts. "Start the engines," he muttered.

"Sir?"

"*Start the damn engines!*"

Before Widge could react, Handen's worst fears were confirmed—the silhouette *had* been getting closer and was also getting bigger. As the fog cleared and the sea began to boil madly, a colossal black fin was revealed, already towering above the boat, water cascading from it as it rose steadily through the fog.

"Incredible..." murmured Handen. Everything began to take on a dreamlike quality now that an intense fear paralyzed his senses and dulled his consciousness. Beside him, Beggs began to scream hoarsely.

The fin continued to rise, the resulting waves sending the *Sentinel II* sprawling backward. As the fin rose, the water around them seemed to darken still further, until the shoulders and head of some terrible force of nature arose from the depths. For a brief and giddying moment, Handen stared into an eye the size and color of a full moon. As water rained around him in a torrent and the vessel rocked manically, Handen stood face to face with a Kraken.

The incredible beast's head looked something like the skull of a dead fish, though a grimy, burnt black rather than white. Its huge, pupil-less eyes bulged over a mouth full of a thousand teeth like giant needles. From its cavernous throat, an ear-piercing screech shattered the gloom like a million fingers on glass. And still it continued to rise.

Handen stood stock still, frozen with a terror he had never experienced before, while beside him, Beggs was blue in the face from screaming.

Widge, with the slight illusion of safety the control deck offered him, recovered from his terror far more quickly than his comrades and prepared to initiate the vessel's weaponry. Though the *Sentinel II* had been built solely for exploration, it had still been constructed by hunters, and hunters especially knew the value of a good weapon to the explorer. Thus, at the prow of the ship, four heavy harpoon cannons stood poised and ready—though even Widge, through a cloud of panic, knew they wouldn't do much good against a target the size of the Kraken. Still, he punched the firing keys for all four harpoons and watched as the powerful cannons unleashed their payload into the neck of the rising leviathan.

Despite the size of the towering sea-creature, the harpoons, by a twist of chance, managed to hit the Kraken in one of its few weak areas. The beast reared up in pain, causing an enormous wave to wash over the hapless *Sentinel II,* slamming Handen and Beggs to the rear of the ship. The shock snapped Handen out of his terror trance.

"Start the engines! Start the engines!" he screamed, his voice barely audible over the angry screeches of the Kraken. Luckily, the same thought had occurred to Widge at the same time, and he quickly punched in the ignition sequence. The engines roared into life and began to move the *Sentinel II* away from the raging sea-monster. However, compared to their goliath adversary, the progress of the vessel seemed far too slow.

As the beast reared up to its full height, water cascading from its shoulders like so many rivers, Handen was surprised to see a smooth, human-like torso eclipse the setting sun, and even more surprised to see two scaly, finned, and heavily clawed arms rise to its throat and begin scratching the harpoons away from its gills. Seeing that the beast would soon recover from their meager assault, Handen knew that there was no way they could outrun the giant reach of a Kraken.

At this point, Beggs, whose survival instincts had finally surpassed her terror, prepared to equate an attack. Beggs had been Elite-Gifted before joining the hunting party and knew a wide range of aggressive equations. Screaming hysterically all the time, she began launching torrents of lightning at the chest of the sky-scraping horror. Handen watched as the Kraken screamed with rage, swatting at the energy bolts as they exploded about its torso. Beggs, her face contorted with a bizarre mix of terror and rage, looked almost a match for the titan as sparks crackled from her fingers and hair and her clothes flapped crazily in her own personal energy storm. Handen wished he could contribute somehow to their escape but knew, deep down, that even if he had had double the equating power of Beggs, they still would not be able to slow the beast sufficiently.

The Kraken, recovering from Beggs's onslaught, lifted a planet-like fist high into the sky and swung it down toward the *Sentinel II*. Beggs stopped her assault and looked up in dumb horror as the leviathan's fist plummeted toward them like a meteor strike.

*Well that's it then*, thought Handen's head as the world slowly began to eclipse. *We're dead.*

*Bugger that*, said his legs, and propelled the rest of him over the side of the ship. He began to swim madly for freedom as the Kraken's fist crashed into the *Sentinel II* behind him, obliterating it totally and sending out a tidal wave that rippled hugely from the point of impact. Handen held his breath and closed his eyes as he was lifted by the swell of the humongous wave. He had expected to be dragged under but, by a million to one chance, the wave lifted him to its peak, carrying him far from the reach of the Kraken. He flew through the air as the wave broke, narrowly missing hunks of burning wreckage from the *Sentinel II*, zipping and ripping in all directions, then was dumped unceremoniously into the brine.

Handen erupted from the choppy waters with a panicky splutter and was briefly tempted to sigh with relief but quickly realized the inappropriateness of such an action. He was far from out of danger yet. The Kraken, its opponent vanquished, dived back down to the deeper waters it had emerged from, letting out a victorious shriek as waves exploded around it. The undertow from the retreating monster began sucking down the floating debris—and Handen along with it.

*Great,* Handen had time to think, *so I miraculously avoid being crushed only to be drowned instead...*

However, a part of Handen much less cynical than his brain, which had kept him alive in situations where lesser men would have perished, began to search for a way out of this new predicament. As the tail of the Kraken submerged in the distance and Handen felt himself being pulled unstoppably downward, he happened to catch a glimpse of something that almost made him laugh out loud. Only a few feet away, circling endlessly amongst other miscellaneous debris from the *Sentinel II*, was a fragment of the ship that contained one of the outboard motors, running aimlessly at full power.

Handen briefly applauded the decision to make the vessel's motors independent of one another in case they had to lighten their load or construct a new vessel. Or, apparently, in case the ship was obliterated by an angry sea-monster. He was torn away from his self-congratulation by the rapid pull of the ocean beneath him.

The motor, burring only a few meters away, might as well have been on the other side of the world for all the progress Handen could make against the deadly undertow. He had one idea left, and it would be a one-shot, hit-or-miss action that would either save his life or merely accelerate his demise. Handen stopped struggling enough to reach for his bullwhip and, with a skillful flick of his wrist and a mighty crack, managed to snag the sturdy whip around the motor. He sagged with relief as he felt himself being pulled away from the sucking undercurrent and watched with fatigued interest as the unpowered debris was slowly pulled under. He spared a thought for

Widge and Beggs, his most trusted allies, and for the *Sentinel II*, which had suffered a fate worse than that of its predecessor.

Sighing heavily, he managed to secure the bullwhip around his shoulders. Then, with the tow of the motor keeping his head above water and the still-fresh horror swimming in his mind, he passed out in a dead faint.

8

## Interlude—Even Gods Need Someone to Complain to...

He was the spirit of the planet of Bersch. He was the sigh in the wind. He was the glint in the stream. He was known by a thousand names and faces: The Almighty, Krund, Great Heebie Jeebie, Torrac, and in one unusual religious case, he was even known as Molly From Next Door. Mostly, he was referred to as God, as that was not just his nature but also his job description.

Currently he was putting his feet up in a sunny, beautifully kept garden and having a natter with his old friend Ted.

God had chosen to adopt one of his more common appearances, that of an old man dressed in a white robe, with a long, flowing beard. He preferred this incarnation. There was something fundamentally relaxing about being an old man in a white robe. He took a long sip of his tea and began complaining again.

"It's not enough that grass continues to grow and that rivers continue to flow. They want bright lights and visions! Party tricks!" He spat the word "visions." "Pah! Since when was seeing believing? People only see what they want to see! And even if they did see me, they'd probably only be disappointed."

Ted nodded sympathetically, pushing his flat cap back on his head.

"It's the age of reason, I'm afraid. I've seen it before. It tends to get people confused a little," he said.

God tutted. "Age of reason, indeed. People would be a lot happier if they just stopped poking around in things and got on with their lives. Do you know I overheard some schmuck the other day saying that, if I truly existed, then why would I allow bad things to happen?"

Ted nodded again. He had heard that one a lot from other Gods.

God continued. "Oh, I could have given him such a slap! But it's the same with the other types as well. Something wonderful happens, 'Oh! 'Tis the will of God!' Something terrible happens and it's, 'Oh! 'Tis the will of God!' Honestly, sometimes I feel like just grabbing them and saying, 'Listen, you punk, if an earthquake happens, it's because of necessary environmental pressures, and if you find a fiver on the floor, it's because someone dropped it!'"

Ted nodded sympathetically and sipped at his tea. He was used to Gods getting a bit wound up. It's hard when everyone blames you for everything.

"I mean, you know me, Ted—I get on with things, I make sure things are happening like they're supposed to. Don't these people know how difficult evapotranspiration is? I don't have time for all this theological argumentative rubbish. We have a very nice set-up here on Bersch, and people should really just make the most of it and stop giving me hassle every time they hit their thumb with a hammer or whatever."

Ted nodded. He was glad to lend an ear whenever God was feeling a little irate, but there were more important things to talk about at present.

"You wanted to talk about the upcoming destruction of Bersch?" he said, politely cutting short God's rant.

"Oh, yes." God gave an embarrassed chuckle. "I do go on some-times, don't I?"

Ted waved a hand dismissively and poured God another cup of tea.

"Yes, where was I?" said God. "The Massive Ball of Death. I've tried some subtle warnings about it—you know, appearing in dreams and such—but mostly people just ignore it."

"The age of reason," laughed Ted.

"Don't get me started again!" God chuckled. "Anyway. I'm not sure that, even if the whole world was fully aware of the approaching disaster, they could do anything to stop it. I don't think they have the power. As you know, this is a little out of my jurisdiction, so...er...do you have anything in the cards?"

Ted carefully put down his teacup. "All I can say is that forces are in play, and right now things could go either way. This universe, we know, operates solely on the perceptions of Order and Chaos, and the balance therein. All I can tell you is that it's all a bit up in the air at the minute. It's fifty-fifty."

"And the Caretakers?" said God.

"They're doing their best, but the Discordance have given them a bit of a low blow this time. They're fighting dirtier than usual."

"I see. That's a pity," said God solemnly.

"Cheer up, God," said Ted. "If the worst comes to the worst, at least you won't have to worry about philosophers any more, will you?"

# 9

# Bip Plunkerton Vs. The End of the World

Huddled in the unceasing blizzard of the Ice Plains, the wild snowcow grazed dumbly on the thistle-like shrubs that grew sporadically across the wilderness. In comparison to the domesticated Kaneqian snowcow, the wild snowcow was leaner, had more prominent horns, and was often much angrier. This was probably because it didn't get regular haircuts and more often than not couldn't see very well.

The temper of this specific snowcow was particularly nasty, which was why it had strayed from the rest of its herd to dine by itself. In fact, the temper of this snowcow was so particularly nasty that when Bip—who had been sneaking up on it for some time—prodded it in the jacksy with a spear, it flew into a near-incoherent rage.

The snowcow whirled around and came face-to-face with Bip, whose terrified and apologetic grin did nothing to quell its nuclear irritation. Huffing a great cloud of steam from its nostrils, the snowcow charged.

Bip legged it, a constant litany of "Dammit, dammit, dammit, dammit!" giving rhythm to his breathing.

It had been his turn to get breakfast that morning, and the solitary snowcow, even though it dwarfed Bip by a good two feet, had seemed the most likely target. Running in his panic, though, pursued by several hundred pounds of sharpened bovine, Bip was beginning to have doubts about his choice.

Unexpectedly, Bip stood his ground and whirled around to face the onrush of the snowcow. The beast lowered its head, readying it horns for a swift and brutal impaling. At the last possible second, Bip rolled to his left. The charging cow missed him by inches. Momentarily confused by the absence of gore on its horns, it tried to brake and turn at the same time in a flurry of hoof and horn. In its fury, it had failed to notice that Bip had been standing only a few feet in front of a vertical cliff face. The great beast scrambled briefly before falling to its doom with a mournful "Mooooo!"

Bip stood panting, his heart hammering a crazy tattoo against his ribs.

"Well done, lad!" came the voice of Rynford from a safe observation point. "Now get that mess cleaned up and let's see what we can stick on the grill!"

<hr>

"THAT WAS a novel way of taking care of the snowcow, son. Personally, I would have just beaten it to death with a club, but each to his own, I suppose."

Rynford raised a chunk of roasted beef to his mouth and chomped hungrily. Fortunately, the impact of the snowcow at the bottom of the cliff had meant that Bip had to do very little to prepare the meat for eating. It was more a case of picking up the bite-sized bits.

They were eating in the shelter of their usual breakfast cave. Bip reflected that he had begun to enjoy these moments. Despite the daily terror, hardship, and flirtation with certain death, he had developed a sense of camaraderie with Rynford that he had come to anticipate and enjoy. The old Huntmaster had become something of a father figure to him. Or at least a crazy uncle figure. He often wished he could say the same about Glimton, who still hadn't ceased to shock and awe the young trainee with his unpredictable temper tantrums. These mood swings had not improved when, despite Glimton's constant screaming, Bip had failed to make any real progress with his psyentific knack. Bip remembered his last lesson, when Glimton, in an uncharacteristically calm mood, had tried to show him the benefits of meditating. They had sat cross-legged on the practice room floor, attempting to equate the Fire Dance, a basic exercise in molecular control.

"The Fire Dance is simple in its equating. Firstly, you have to visualize the components of your target. You must visualize the air molecules in front of you. See them swaying and colliding. See them dance," Glimton had said. Bip had attempted to visualize.

"And now that we can see them, we can make contact with their energy, we can communicate, we can see the equation. Now all we have to do is persuade the molecules to increase the tempo of the dance. Get them to jig. Faster and faster." Bip had concentrated, visualized the air molecules tap-dancing into a frenzy.

"As they dance," Glimton had continued, "they get warm. Now we have to encourage that heat, encourage the fire." Tiny sparks began to interlace and sway before Glimton's eyes. Then, with a soothing gentleness, a wave of fire had rippled softly in front of him, swaying with the currents of the air. "Visualize it, Bip. Make them dance." Bip had concentrated…

Concentrated…

*Concentrated…*

With a sound like a wet burp, a small puff of flame had appeared in front of Bip and landed in his crotch. He'd had no trouble visualizing dancing after that, as he hopped erratically around the room, his screams of panic mixing with Glimton's hysterical and merciless laughter…

"You all right there, lad?" said Rynford, shaking Bip from his gloomy thoughts. "You zoned out on me there for a bit."

"Sorry, Rynford. Just thinking is all."

"About the psyence thing again?"

"Yeah," said Bip glumly.

"I wouldn't worry about it too much, laddie. There've been plenty of volunteers who have ventured out with little or no knack. Fair enough, none of them have been seen again, but then again, none of the volunteers have been seen again anyway, so…" Rynford stopped when he saw the appalled look on Bip's face. "Er…sorry, lad. Not the most encouraging of words, I know. I tell you what." Rynford reached into one of his many satchels and pulled out something wrapped in oiled leather. "I was saving this for when you left, but you may as well have it now."

Bip unwrapped the leather and gasped appreciatively at what he saw inside. It was a Kaneqian sidesword. It was roughly two feet in length, with a delicately thin and wickedly sharp double-sided blade coming to a slight curve at the end. The workmanship on this particular blade was exquisite, with patterns of thorns embroidered all the way from the tip of the blade to the guard.

"Don't be put off by the girly designs," muttered Rynford, embarrassed. "They actually help the blood run off the blade."

Bip nodded and continued his examination of the sword. Kaneqians very rarely used swords, spears being more than adequate for their uncommon instances of combat, but the sidesword seemed perfect for Bip—light, manageable, and deadly even in the hands of an amateur. He stood and made a few experimental slashes with the sword. It made a pleasant swishing sound.

"I was going to give it to my son, if I ever had one," Rynford continued. "You know, just until he was old enough to carry a real weapon."

"It's brilliant, Rynford. Thanks. What's it called?"

"Called?" Rynford frowned. "It's called a sword, you bloody eejit."

"No, I mean, don't people usually give swords a name?"

"Fair enough. Um…I'll call this sword…Brian."

"Brian?" questioned Bip.

"Brian." Rynford nodded.

"Why Brian?"

"I dunno. Just always liked the sound of it. Nothing wrong with Brian," Rynford huffed defensively.

"No, no! Brian's fine. Very…serious sounding. I suppose."

He swished the sword through the air again, getting to grips with the restrictions of the hand guard and the balance of the blade.

"It's great."

"Well, I know you're not much good with a spear, so I thought maybe you'd get on better with this. I'll give you a few practice spars with it and see how you get on. After all, you're leaving soon. Can't go into the wide world without a weapon you feel comfortable with."

Bip nodded, suddenly knowing that he was going to miss Rynford terribly when he left. Of all of his few friends, even Michaelmas, Rynford had shared something unique and special with Bip. He had taught him to avoid being killed in nasty ways, and that warranted affection of a sort.

"But remember, lad," Rynford continued, "cunning, skill, ingenuity; these are our weapons! These are our teeth!"

———

BIP LAY AWAKE. It was his last evening before he set off into the unknown. He had spent the morning and afternoon with his mother and Michaelmas, neither of whom had said very much, but had sat gloomily, occasionally squeezing Bip's hand or telling him how proud they were. He had spent the evening with Bailey and his few friends, who still had no idea he was going, and had enjoyed a final drink in the Empty Goat. Bailey had been a little puzzled at Bip's goodbye, which had been a bit more emotional than even their level of drunkenness had called for.

It had been hard for Bip not to tell his friends what he was doing. It had been hard for him not to tell anyone. He had felt like standing on his roof and shouting into the night, "See you later, then. I'm off to save the world now. Don't wait up." But, of course, he couldn't. He could only disappear like a snowman in a blizzard, probably never to return. He had cried a little, he wasn't ashamed to say. He would miss his mother and Michaelmas and his friends. He would miss Truggle and Rynford, and even, to a certain extent, he would miss Glimton. Most of all, he would miss his trouble-free, simple Kaneqian existence, which until a few months ago had seemed like the whole world.

He didn't feel ready, of course. He wasn't sure that anyone could feel truly ready for the task ahead of him. His final assessments hadn't helped his confidence much either, with Rynford grudgingly admitting that Bip had reached an adequate level of survival skill, and Glimton refusing to admit that Bip had even an ounce of psyentific talent. Truggle had remained firm, though, insisting with an inexplicable confidence that Bip would more than shape up to the task in hand.

Truggle. He would miss Truggle. The strange old man he had always thought no more than a harmless, loony old duffer had turned out to be a keeper of fantastic secrets and terrible knowledge. Bip couldn't quite explain it, but ever since he'd first looked through those goggles and seen the true origins of Kaneq, he had felt like he had always known. Always known that the Dome, was, in fact, the long-beached vessel of his distant ancestors on the *Sentinel*. Always known that Kaneq had a deeper purpose. Truggle had called it genetic memory, though Bip preferred to think of it as spiritual inheritance, which while admittedly sounding a bit nebulous, was a little more warm and personal than Truggle's terminology.

Truggle. He'd had a final talk with Truggle about his upcoming journey. They had talked about the Clarions and their purpose, and the universal struggle between Order and Chaos. Then Truggle had talked about something called the Discordance, a race of beings that had devoted its allegiance to Chaos, with powers, Truggle had hinted, exceeding those of the Clarions.

"Deception," he had said. "Cunning, half-truths, and lies. Bad influence. These are the weapons of the Discordance. Be careful of those who would try to sap your will—these are the agents of adverse randomicity."

Finally, Truggle had taken him deep into the sublevels of the Dome, where in an unremarkable room at the end of an unremarkable corridor stood a huge iron obelisk. On it, stretching high toward the ceiling, were the names of every volunteer and the year they had left in. All the way from a chap named Handen, in year two, to the name of his father, in year nine hundred and eighty six. Bip's name, for better or worse, would be the final name added to the obelisk.

Bip had broken down. Standing before the weight of the massive obelisk, he felt a huge physical pressure on his shoulders and sank to his knees. The responsibility of taking on the mantle of a volunteer seemed too great. Truggle had left him for a while, to deal with his emotions.

Tomorrow, at dawn, his quest would begin. He would face unknown adversaries and unknown odds to warn a civilization he had never met that its doom was at hand.

He was more than a little nervous.

***

HANDEN STRIKE AWOKE and instantly began spluttering the lungful of seawater that clogged his throat. He retched for a while onto the rock he had been clinging to, then looked around. He was wedged in between two jagged rocks that seemed to appear from nowhere in the middle of the ocean. Farther down he could hear the splutter of the motor he was still attached to. He turned in the direction of the sound and saw the motor struggling weakly against another rock until, with a few defiant coughs, it died utterly, and the battered piece of debris it was attached to begin to sink. Even in his half-concussed confusion, Handen's almost automatic survival instincts gave him the presence of mind to unwrap the bullwhip from his shoulders. He watched help-lessly as it disappeared under the waves with the rest of the debris.

Still dizzy from confusion and half drowned from…well, water, Handen began to take in his surroundings. The sun was beating pleas-antly on his head as a steady rhythmic wave rocked him up and down. He heard the distant cry of what sounded like a seagull. Realizing the implications, Handen scrambled his way up onto the rock he had been clinging to and stood on top.

Not too far away—not very far away at all—was a comfortable-looking shoreline. Handen laughed triumphantly, or at least tried to, but he was interrupted by a coughing fit as he dislodged more of the ocean from his belly.

Land! He had made it to land! And land meant civilization! His mission was nearing its final stages. Handen took hold of his excite-ment and began to assess the situation at hand. There would be time for celebration later. Right now, in his exhausted state, weaponless and armor-less, he would have to swim to shore and find fresh water and food and see to the various nagging injuries he had sustained during the incident with the Kraken. After that, he would have to find out just where the hell he was. Still, Handen's spirits had lifted considerably. He felt as if he was almost at the finish line.

BIP STOOD at the heatshield exit, preparing himself for the first few steps that would take him ever farther away from his homeland. He secured the fastening on his insulating leathers and oilskin and checked the strap on his huge, overladen backpack. On his head was the traditional Kaneqian travel-hat, a wide brimmed canvas affair studded with various pockets and pouches. It resembled a rucksack with a brim and chinstrap.

His peers crowded around him, waiting to wish him well on his quest. The only person who knew that he was leaving but hadn't shown up was Bip's mother. They had exchanged a solemn and sad goodbye earlier in the morning over a breakfast hearty enough for ten people.

Michaelmas approached and put a meaty hand on Bip's shoulder.

"I'm gonna miss you, mate, no lie. 'Twont be the same without you."

"I'll miss you too, Michaelmas. You've always looked out for me."

"Aye lad, aye. And I always will, long as I'm able. I know it'll be cold out there, so I brought you a little something to keep out the chill." Michaelmas reached into his apron and pulled out two large bottles of something golden-brown. Bip saw the label and gulped. Michaelmas had brought two bottles of Mr. Braindead's Very Special Infamous Goose, the most lethal alcohol concoction in Kaneq. It certainly would keep the chill out. In fact, it would likely set his head on fire if he drank it straight.

"Cheers, Michaelmas," he said, and stowed the bottles in one of his many pouches.

"Well, as long as we're giving presents," interrupted the reedy voice of Glimton, "you may as well have these." The psyentist poured several acorns into Bip's outstretched hands.

Bip tried not to look nonplussed. "Thanks, Glimton. Acorns. Just what I needed."

"Don't patronize me, you idiot! I spent a lot of time and effort reprogramming those acorns. Just add water and wait and they'll grow into something useful."

Bip peered at one of the acorns. The word "BOAT" was carved into it in copperplate writing.

"Wow," said Bip, genuinely impressed. "Thanks. Thanks a lot."

"Don't thank me, you numbskull. Truggle made me give them to you." With that, Glimton turned his back and stormed off, pausing only to turn around and shout, "Good luck, by the way, you talentless pleb!"

Bip couldn't help but smile.

Next it was Rynford's turn to approach. He clasped Bip's hand in a beefy handshake.

"I guess we've already said all we have to say. I've got no more to give you other than Brian there."

"You've given me a lot more than just the sword, Rynford." Bip grinned. "Thanks to you, I think I might just stand a chance out there."

"Well, don't get your hopes up, laddie." Rynford laughed. "Seriously, though, I wish I'd had more time to train you."

"Me too. I enjoyed it. It was tiring, nightmarish, soul-destroying work, but I don't think I'll ever taste anything quite as good as your driftdigger steak."

Rynford smiled. "Remember, lad, eat them before they can eat you."

Bip nodded and made his way to the heatshield exit point. Truggle rowed his way up to meet him as the psyentists opened the exit. A bitter wind rolled from the Ice Plains almost immediately, causing Bip to wince slightly.

"This is it, young Bip," said Truggle. "Do you think you're ready?"

Bip's brow creased in honest consideration. "No," he replied.

Truggle laughed out loud. "Have a little faith, Bip. I think we'll be seeing you again, you know." And once again Truggle's eyes flashed with that sharp intelligence Bip had seen on the first day they had spoken.

Bip said nothing. He took one last look at his friends, adjusted his glasses, waved, and walked out into the wilderness.

---

HANDEN SPLUTTERED and staggered his way onto the shoreline. He had not anticipated how weak his recent ordeals had made him, and the swim from the rocky outcrop had very nearly finished him off. He looked around desperately for a sign of life on the suddenly barren-looking shoreline. He had been hoping for a fishing community, or any sign of a population, but he could neither hear nor see anything that might have attested to this. He was in bad need of rest, but a pressing thirst and hunger told him that lying down might not be such a good idea. He had a feeling he'd have trouble getting up again.

He surveyed the horizons of this new land. Not too far away, a tree line began—and trees suggested a possibility of water. After the tree line, however, things did not look so good. A huge and jagged range of flat-headed mountains cut across his vision, stretching to the left and right as far as he could see. Given what appeared to be a lack of civilization anywhere on the right side of the mountains (e.g., Handen's side of the mountains) it was dawning on him that in order to continue his search, he'd have to scale them.

Handen gritted his teeth. Hungry, thirsty, and exhausted beyond reasonable endurance, he set his stone-like jaw and made his way to the tree line. He had faced many a challenge in his time and would be damned if he'd give in to despair now just because of a few upstart mountains. He strode determinedly across the sand, bending down to pick up a piece of driftwood with appropriate clubbing potential. It made him feel a little better.

---

BIP TRUDGED DETERMINEDLY through the thick snow, Kaneq having long since disappeared over the horizon. He couldn't even see the haze of the heatshield anymore. He was making his way toward the ice floes, which would then lead him to the ocean. This, he had been told, would be the quickest way to reach the next continent, which was the closest likelihood of a civilized society. It would mean sailing, something that very few Kaneqians were particularly adept at, but Glimton assured him that his acorn "BOAT" would be able to take care of itself.

The ice floes were a long journey by foot, but Bip knew the way and was fairly sure he would make it in good time. Despite leaving his lifelong home, Bip was feeling strangely optimistic, almost excited. The words of his friends still echoed warmly in his ears and gave him a smug sort of confidence.

*By golly, I'll save this planet or my name ain't Bip Plunkerton,* he thought to himself, and couldn't help laughing out loud.

It was a premature laugh, though, as Bip quickly realized when a mound of snow that had appeared just the same as any other mound of snow suddenly exploded before him, revealing a fifteen-foot monster of white hair and yellow fang. The beast uttered a bone-shaking bellow and Bip, despite his month-long intensive training, took one look at the roaring monstrosity and fainted in utter terror.

---

BIP AWOKE IN A WARM PLACE. *I must still be in bed,* he thought. *Yet to leave. All that huge bellowing monster thing must have been a dream. Better yet, maybe that entire volunteer thing was a dream. Maybe I'll wake up and it'll be before the Apprentice Fair and the planet won't be going to explode and Truggle will still be an old fool who can barely string a sentence together. Keeper of the Ancient Wisdom, indeed!* It seemed wonderfully preposterous now that he thought about it.

Then he realized he was wet as well as warm. *It's possible you fell asleep in the bath, surely?* his brain yelled desperately. *Whatever you do, don't open your eyes! Just pretend you fell asleep in the bath—the alternative's too horrible to contemplate. Trust me—I'm your brain!*

With a sense of growing horror, Bip, despite his unconsciousness's best efforts to protect him, opened his eyes. He was in a pot. A pot filled with warm water. Warm water, he knew, that was gradually going to get hotter.

He looked frantically around his surroundings. He was in a bright cave—more of a room carved out of snow than a natural rock formation—and he was sitting in a large iron pot with a few thistles and root vegetables floating around him. Under the pot burned a small but determined fire. He had been stripped of his gear and clothes, and on one of the cave walls a large selection of poorly made but incredibly sharp-looking carving knives hung with an easy kind of promise.

Bip gulped, remembering the yeti that had ambushed him. Yetis were an intelligent sort of creature in their own way, capable of tool use and communication (and cuisine cookery, apparently, thought a treacherous part of Bip's subconscious), but their intelligence was tempered with such animal hostility that the Kaneqians hadn't tried to make contact with them in recent history. The yetis' intellectual capabilities were greatly hampered by their love of killing and devouring almost anything that moved.

Bip, fighting his rising panic, thought of an escape plan. The yeti wasn't around at present, but Bip wouldn't make it four feet in the outside conditions if he were wet and naked. Thankfully, the yeti had stowed Bip's gear not too far from the pot. He reached over and began rummaging frantically through his pack, wondering what he could use to aid his escape. His sword? No point against a yeti. Bip had brief images of attacking a rock with a toothpick. Perhaps one of Glimton's reprogrammed acorns might be useful? But which one? He hadn't had time to see what they were all capable of...

Suddenly he heard the approaching thudding footsteps of his captor. He grabbed the first two items that came to hand and dived back into the pot. He looked down hopefully to see what he had retrieved. His face fell.

A thick corned beef sandwich and a bottle of Infamous Goose. *Great,* he thought, *at least I won't die hungry or sober...*

"Der you arr! Der you arr!" boomed the gravel-like voice of the yeti as it entered the room. "My littul munch treet. My littul man people stoo!" The yeti lowered its massive head until it looked right into Bip's eye. "Am gonner eet yerr!" it growled, then gave a conspiratorial wink.

Bip, too scared to react, merely sat there wide-eyed while the monster moved off and began pottering around what was evidentially its kitchen. It muttered to itself while it did so.

"Man peoples, man peoples. Don't eet much man peoples. Chewy, they sez, an' not much meat neevur. But the voicez, the voicez sez I gots to eet yer. So's am gonta eet yer."

Bip, his heart thudding somewhere up near his throat, could only nod in dumb agreement with whatever the mad beast was saying. He squirmed uncomfortably as he felt the temperature of the pot rise. The yeti continued its grumbling litany.

"But yer in luk. Yer in luk! Me Grundadz knew a recipe for man peoples—man peoples stoo, he called it. Sez it's da best fings he ever tasted. Man peoples stoo—proper pucka he said it was. Said it was *pucka*, he did."

Bip, who now couldn't help thinking about cookery as a distraction from his own inevitable cooking, began to think of a plan. A word had begun to formulate in his mind—a word and a subsequent escape plan. The word was *marinade…*

Slowly, so as not to draw attention to himself, Bip uncorked the bottle of Infamous Goose and sloshed it around in the pot water. The yeti didn't notice; it was busy talking to itself and crunching up vegetables with its tusks.

"Gots to pad em out with planties, me Grundad sed, coz there's not dat much meet. Gots to pad em out. Can't kill em neever. Gots to let em boil in der own blud. Can't have em leaking round the stew 'afore der time. Can't 'av dat. Its fer freshness is dat. Pucka! The voicez sez you is *pucka!*"

Bip began blinking rapidly, his eyes and nose streaming. They said that one sniff of Infamous Goose could get you merry. Bip, who was marinating in it, was already having trouble focusing. The yeti suddenly stopped its nonsensical monologue.

"Wot dats smell?" It began sniffing the air with its enormous bulbous nose, eventually reaching the cooking pot. It took a long whiff and made an appreciative gurgle.

"Youse is marinatin' nicely. *Nicely!*" said the yeti, then took a gigantic soup ladle down from the rack and tasted a generous measure of the cooking water. It stood briefly, its eyes slowly glazing over. "Pucka..." it burbled, before passing out on the floor with a terrific crash. Luckily for Bip, the yeti, though iron in its constitution when it came to eating, had never experienced the dubious delights of potent alcohol.

Thinking quickly, Bip leaped from the pot. It took him a while to get his balance, as floating in so much Infamous Goose had made him more than a little light-headed. He dried off as best he could with his traveling hat, donned his clothes, stacked his gear and was out of the yeti's cave in jig time.

He squinted as he came out into the bright white of the Ice Plains. By some incredible fortune, the yeti's lair was situated fairly close to the ice floes. Bip couldn't help but laugh. His abduction by the fearsome creature had, in a most unexpected way, turned out to be entirely beneficial. And all it had cost him was a bottle of Infamous Goose and a few mild heart attacks. Still, Bip didn't spend too long wondering about the oddities of fate, because no one wants to be around when a hungover yeti wakes up. He began jogging toward the floes, huffing a steady pace. This steady pace lasted for about five minutes until he heard the roar of an enraged and probably still drunk yeti coming from behind him. He began to sprint, his familiar litany of "Dammit, dammit, dammit, dammit!" a metronome for his pace.

The ice floes were very close. Bip risked a look behind him and was horrified to see that the yeti had covered a lot of ground, bounding on all fours with a look of fury on its shaggy face. Bip had no doubt he would reach the edge of the ice floes in time, but had a horrible suspicion he'd be killed and eaten before he could deploy the acorn boat.

He reached the edge of the ice floes and heard the thunderous approach of the monster behind him. With no other option, he turned around and drew Brian, ready to at least go out fighting. He gritted his teeth and tried not to wet himself as the yeti came closer...

Closer...

Suddenly there was a tremendous crack. The yeti skidded to a halt and looked around wildly, something resembling panic and confusion contorting its hairy face. Bip felt the ground under his feet lurch suddenly, and he waved his arms frantically to keep his balance. The yeti let out a howl of fear and disappeared into the ground.

It took Bip a while to realize what was going on. The ground he was standing on, near to the edge of the ice floes, had broken off from the mainland, dunking the scrabbling yeti into sub-zero waters. Bip fought the urge to laugh out loud as his own personal ice floe carried him away from the yeti's bubbling hollers. He tried to think of a choice one-liner to shout as he made his escape, but all he could think of was, "That's what you get for trying to eat me, you bastard!"

AS THE YETI SLOWLY SUCCUMBED TO the current of the icy water, it was, at the last, relieved when the maddening whispers in his head stopped.

Above it, on the shores of the ice floes, a figure popped into existence. It was annoyed. It had expected great things from the yeti. When you wanted a killing machine, you couldn't go far wrong with a yeti.

The figure thought to itself for a while, drumming its long fingers on its knees. "Oh well," it said. "There's more than one way to skin a cat." And with that, it popped out of existence. Then, instantaneously, a small bedraggled seagull took its place. The seagull chuckled to itself and took off after Bip's ice floe.

There's always more than one way to skin a cat. And none of them are pleasant.

Especially not for the cat.

# 10

# Handen Strike and the Quest for the Fountain of Death

Handen Strike was annoyed. He was more than annoyed. He was *pissed off.*

It had been two years since he had left Kanick in the hopes of finding other civilizations. Two years since he had lost two of his closest friends to an angry Kraken. Two years since his feet had first touched the sands of the continent he currently resided on.

It had been a crappy two years.

His dilemmas had started when he had first scaled what had turned out to be known as the Molar Mountains. As well as an exhausting dangerous climb, Handen had encountered unfriendly dwarf tribes, cave-dwelling jeckles, and even an ill-tempered jabberwocky that had attempted to feed him to its young. After leaving the mountains, he had crossed the Lightning Barrens, where, in his first encounter with what could pass as a civilized society, they had tried to burn him at the stake as a witch. After the Lightning Barrens, he had moved on to the Cotton Prairies, which, despite its friendly sounding name, had contained many, many things that had wanted to kill him, from packs of wickedly toothed dograbbits to the stomping, territorial uberbeast.

No. It had not been a good two years at all.

Not all of Handen's attempts at contacting civilization had been as entirely disastrous as his first. recognizing that telling people he was from another planet had not been a wise introductory tactic, Handen had simply decided to tell people he was a traveler and leave it at that. As the few settlements he had encountered on this new continent were spaced out and isolated, there had been no trouble in convincing the locals that he was merely from another village rather than another galaxy. He had survived comfortably over the long months by working where he could find it—mostly farmhand jobs, but enough to keep himself in food, shelter, and equipment. More often than not, he was moved along from the close-knit settlements by distrustful yeomanry, drifters being neither appreciated nor needed in villages that sometimes contained no more than a few families.

He never stayed in one place too long anyway, regardless of how comfortable the situation seemed. He still had his mission to think of and his priority was to find as large a concentration of people as possible before he risked telling anyone of Bersch's fate again. He needed access to the ears of people with influence and power—politicians or kings—and so far he had only encountered farmers and miners (unless you included the various goblins, hill giants, bloodthirsty monsters, zombies, and ghouls he had run into or away from, though he wasn't inclined to try to explain himself to them, and they had seemed even less inclined to listen).

He had tried, in ways both subtle and unsubtle, to learn as much as possible about the ruling powers of Bersch, though inevitably his questions brought hostile suspicion from the locals he stayed with, who led simple monotonous lives and distrusted elements of change. His prodding about cities and politics only brought dark mutterings about the mainland and no further elaborations. It had become evident that he was in a frontier country, not so much a civilization as a cluster of barely settled pilgrims doing the best they could to survive in inhospitable conditions. He would have to move on.

In his efforts to reach the mainland, Handen had eventually found his way south to Ghulbra Forest, into which, so he had heard, no one had ever ventured and been seen again. Not one to pay much attention to poorly founded native superstition, Handen had ventured into the massive forestland anyway. He had quickly begun to see the benefit of local wisdom when, after getting hopelessly lost, he had run into a tribe of heavily tattooed and uniformly bald forest-dwellers who were, apparently, extremely unreceptive to strangers.

They had been tracking him for five days.

Handen sighed. He didn't mind adventure. In fact, he loved adventure—it was his calling—but after two years of non-stop intrepid escapades, even the hardiest hero gets a little miffed.

Handen had changed a bit in the last two years. After countless fracas with hostile opponents and a lot of backbreaking farm labor, additional bulk had pumped up his already athletic frame. His features were swarthier, in need of a good shave, and his hair was a shaggy mockery of his former severe and uniform cut. He still wore his leather hunting overcoat, though it has been cut down to suit warmer temperatures, and the furs usually worn underneath had been replaced by the cotton shirt and trousers favored by the farm-folk. He had replaced his weapons, too, a coiled bullwhip at his side and a sturdy if primitive sword strapped across his backpack. They were nothing like as fine as the weapons he had lost to the sea so many months ago, but they look well-used and cared for. Handen Strike still cut quite an impressive figure, every inch the adventurer. The one thing spoiling his heroic demeanor at the moment was the fact that he was dangling helplessly by his bootstraps from a tree branch.

He hadn't meant to fall asleep in his hiding place, but five days on the run from the tireless pursuit of murderous savages had left him prone to napping whenever he lay still for more than a few seconds. Luckily, his boots had caught and saved him from a potentially fatal fall. Now all he had to do was get free before—

"(!) Nug mug, chug wub (!) clam!"

The primitive grunting Handen had come to dread sounded faintly through the forest. He stopped struggling and held his breath. They had found him! He had been convinced he was finally putting some real distance between them, yet here they were. Damn.

"(!) Pad gar. Gar pud. Pud!"

Handen gritted his teeth. In his less focused moments, he had begun to wonder if they were just making random noises and pretending it was language. It didn't seem like any actual form of communication at all, more a More Primal Than Thou conceitedness.

"(!) (!) (!) Pud!"

The voices were getting closer. Handen looked down from his precarious position to see three of the savages erupt soundlessly from the bushes and into the clearing directly below him. They walked carefully, as if they knew he was near, holding their longbows drawn and ready.

Handen continued to hold his breath, his heartbeat thudding in his ears. He was a sitting duck and he knew it. All he could do was pray that they didn't look up or that—

*Crack!*

A cynical part of Handen's soul had seen it coming a mile off. The branch supporting him first bent then snapped, sending him plummeting directly toward his pursuers. Fortunately, this meant that his fall was cushioned and gave the added bonus that he had half-crushed the people who had been trying to kill him. As they lay moaning on the floor, he seized his opportunity to run away.

Sprinting into the overgrown undergrowth he heard the telltale "(!)" of a very annoyed savage who had just been squashed and was now calling for his friends to avenge him. Behind him, far but not far enough, he heard the whooping of the hunters as they took up the chase.

Handen gritted his teeth, put his head down, and tried to increase his speed. This time he would outdistance them, find the time to cover his tracks and settle down in a hole in the ground until they got bored and went away. The savages had the advantage of knowing the territory, but Handen was a Hostility Advisor at the core and had been trained from birth for this sort of thing. He sprinted faster, pushing his way into thicker and thicker forest, jumping over moss-covered logs and ducking under thick, thorny branches. When the path ahead became too cluttered to travel through, Handen deftly flicked his bullwhip into the broad branches of the heavily entwined trees above him and swung himself onto higher ground. Once he found his balance, he began leaping and sprinting from tree to tree.

When Handen had first traveled into Ghulbra Forest, the

surroundings had started as wood-like, then advanced to forest-like, until, at its unmapped core, it had resembled a mossy, decayed jungle. As a result, he found no trouble in running across the elevated pathways of interlocked branches, trunks, and canopies. He sprinted across the treetops until the voices behind him faded to nothing. Then he sprinted some more. He was, he had to admit, enjoying the chase. The heavy rain had finally cleared yesterday and now a pleasant sunshine was making the tree leaves glisten.

*If I'm going to be hunted down and killed by bloodthirsty savages who want to eat my brain,* thought Handen, *then at least it'll be a nice day for it.*

He leaped from a treetop and managed to hook his bullwhip around a neighboring branch, then, swinging with animal grace, he used his momentum to launch himself up onto an even higher branch. Breathing heavily, he surveyed the woods to his rear and smiled with smug satisfaction. There was no sign of his pursuers yet, and if he hid himself, they would have serious difficulty finding him. All he would have to do was—

*Crack!*

Handen had time to curse silently as he fell through the air, the branch that had formerly supported him spinning out of his eye-line.

Yep. It had been a crappy two years.

---

BIP WAS BORED. He was also thirsty, hungry, sunburnt, and badly in need of a bath. But he was, primarily, bored.

He had begun his sea voyage in a very good mood, with the adrenaline high of escaping the yeti still fresh in his veins. He had dunked the "BOAT" acorn into the seawater and watched with amazement as the reprogrammed seed had planted itself and begun to grow quickly into a small vessel, looking like a giant, hollowed out acorn shell with a sail of woven bracken. Madman or not, there was no doubting the quality of Glimton's handiwork.

The boat had sailed a good pace on the iron-gray ocean and had so far steered clear of any bad weather, holding a slow but steady southward course.

However, the voyage had begun over four weeks ago, and now Bip was not so pleased with his progress. He was running worryingly low on food and water and, not knowing how long he would remain at sea, had long since taken to rationing himself.

Worse still, the weather had turned oppressively hot, meaning that during the day it was too stuffy to stay in the small shelter he had made from his oilskin. As a result of this, Bip was currently sitting cross-legged on the foredeck, naked, badly sunburned, and with his sea-soaked underpants wrapped around his head to combat the heavy beat of the sun. He was beginning to wonder if he was getting sunstroke but could not yet face the prospect of lying in the muggy shelter. At least here, on what could loosely be called the prow of the acorn vessel, there was a slightly cooling breeze.

His biggest problem, though, was the boredom. He had been on his own so long he was even nostalgic for the yeti's company, and quite recently he had taken to talking to himself. He wasn't sure if he was happy with that development and frequently said so. To himself.

In darker moments, he had thought of settling down with the last bottle of Infamous Goose and spending a few days getting roaring drunk. It would dehydrate him further, he knew, and possibly make him very ill, but it would relieve some of the oppressive boredom. He was sick of the sea. Sick of how blue it was. Sick of how endless it was. He would shout sarcastically at the waves, chiding their monotonous up and down movements, cursing their lack of imagination. He would plead with the horizon, begging it to throw up some sort of distraction. He had tried fishing, sticking a small lump of corned beef sandwich on the end of a ripped sock, but so far, no fish had found the prospect of a corned beef flavored sock exciting enough to take a bite.

He was sick of the sound of the wind, which seemed to flap the organic sail in an unpredictable and unexpected pattern of noise, its stubborn refusal to yield to any kind of rhythm nearly equivalent to someone singing deliberately off-key. He was sick of the sky, which unlike the bulbous, gray clouds that mingled endlessly above the Ice Plains, was a stark and featureless steel of blue, altering only to make way for a painful, retina-burning glare that Bip could only assume was where the sun resided. He was sick of boats and quests and everything. He wanted to go home.

"I'll die out here," he said to himself, glumly. "I'll never reach land and I'll just die. Here in the middle of nowhere. I wonder if this is how all the other volunteers died?"

"Cheer up, mug!" came a voice from nowhere.

Bip was surprised. It hadn't been his voice, and he was the only person he'd talked to in weeks.

"What did I say?" he muttered dreamily.

"Not you, chump, me! Up here!"

Bip looked at the front of the boat. Sitting there like some mad-eyed figurehead was a dirty looking seagull.

"Did you just say something?" said Bip.

"Cower and despair as the very core of madness engulfs you," said the seagull, matter-of-factly.

Bip seemed to contemplate doing so for a minute, and then went back to staring glumly at the horizon. The seagull seemed fairly annoyed by this and hopped about until it was in front of Bip's face.

"Well?" it shrieked irritably. "Aren't you going to freak out? Aren't you going to start banging your head and tearing at your hair and screaming that you've lost your mind?"

Bip looked up, puzzled. "No," he said. "Why? Should I?"

"Yes, because you're talking to a seagull, you cretin, and when you're not talking to a seagull, you're talking to yourself!"

"Exactly," Bip said. "Talking to you is much more interesting. If I start complaining about being insane, you might go away—then I'll have no one to talk to but me."

The seagull flapped its wings in irritation. "No! No, no, no! You're not really talking to me. I'm just a symptom of your growing dementia and continuing despair! Doesn't that bother you?"

"Not really," muttered Bip. "It's more interesting than being sane and bored. Besides, I expect I'm not insane at all. I expect this is just a bizarre fever-dream bought on by too much sun."

"No, really, trust me. You're demented. You're mad. You're a couple of cattle short of a herd!"

"Why should I believe you? You're just a seagull!"

The seagull hopped up and down in feathery rage. "But that's just the point! I'm not a bloody seagull, am I? I'm a bloody metaphor, you thick-headed idiot!"

"A metaphor for what?" said Bip.

The seagull gave a long and croaky sigh. "Well, you see, seagulls only come out to sea to die? So I'm, like, an omen. A symbol of your impending and lonely death, urging you to turn back and go home."

"I can't turn around," said Bip. "I can't steer the boat. Besides, I thought running into seagulls meant you were near land?"

"Well. Yes," conceded the gull. "But in this case, I'm a symbol of lonely, horrible death!"

"I don't know," said Bip doubtfully. He squinted at the horizon. "That sort of looks like land to me."

The seagull looked in the direction Bip indicated, flapping its wings to get a better view.

"Bugger," it said, and vanished with a pop.

"Well I'll be jiggered," muttered Bip. "Land." Then he fell over and lost consciousness.

IT MAY or may not be worth mentioning that at this point, many fathoms below Bip, the Kraken awoke from its slumber. It was very old these days and, having long since established itself as the most dangerous predator in this stretch of the ocean, had settled down to have a family.

It sensed the presence of the intruding boat above it, a feeling it had not felt for nearly a thousand years, and thought briefly about attacking. Then it looked down at the four suckling Krakoids at its teat and thought better of it.

It scratched at the scars on its throat and chest, remembering the encounter with the last boat that had been near its territory. It was getting too old to take risks these days, and it was tough enough as it was being a single mum without inviting additional injuries. The Kraken briefly wished it hadn't been forced to eat the father nearly five hundred years ago. Oh well. It was a cold, cold ocean and you had to do the best you could.

---

HANDEN AWOKE. His head hurt.

The last few minutes he remembered were something of a blur. He had fallen from the tree and the ground had rushed up to meet him, but before he had hit, his belt strap had caught on a vine, swinging him into some dark and muddy glade. He had slid down a slope for what had seemed to be ages, then eventually, muddy, dizzy, and exhausted, he had come to a halt and fallen into a deep sleep.

He looked around. He was in a sunny clearing. The trees towered thickly around him. Here and there throughout the tall grass, lumps of stone that could have been statues leaned casually against one another. Handen was still fuzzy-headed from his ordeal. He had no idea how long he had been sleeping and no idea where he was. That was why, when he saw the small, sparkly lake that bubbled out of an underground spring, he didn't think twice about drinking deeply, quenching a thirst that had been building steadily over five days of hot pursuit. The water was refreshing and ice-cold, with a mineral tang that set his teeth on edge.

It wasn't until he had finished drinking long and hard that he had the presence of mind to take a closer look at his surroundings. That was when he noticed the ominous slab of stone with the indecipherable hieroglyphics that stood near the center of the lake. "Oh, damn," he muttered.

Handen had no idea what the carvings said but was beginning to realize he was on what appeared to be holy ground—and holy ground nearly always meant trouble. He froze instantly, attuning his senses to the world around him. He stood stock still, remaining absolutely rigid for nearly five minutes in a state of high-strung alertness. Then relaxed. So far, no spears, no rolling balls of stone, no one calling him "infidel." In Handen's book, these were all good signs.

He took another moment to explore his new surroundings. The clearing was peaceful and quiet. He felt as relaxed here as he had done for nearly two years. He lay back on the grass and listened to the far-off birdsong.

That was when he heard the snoring.

He bolted upright and flipped onto his feet, sword in hand before he had even realized it. The steady rhythmical snoring was coming from somewhere close. Silently, he stalked around the clearing in an attempt to locate the source of the noise. Eventually, he came to a squat stone building, heavily encased in vines, sporting only a small door and window. He relaxed slightly and sneaked up to the window to get a closer look. There, lying on a stone slab and looking quite elegant (apart from the farmyard-like snoring,) was an attractive woman in a white robe, her golden hair held back by a ring of silver. Handen, who had not seen a woman in weeks, was impressed by the sleeper's beauty. He thought for a while, then reached a decision. He would risk contact with the woman.

*After all*, he thought, *I'm sure I'm due to meet someone who doesn't want to kill me eventually.*

He walked up to the door and noticed a length of rope with some more hieroglyphics carved into the stone behind it. Shrugging, Handen pulled the rope.

There was a *bing*. Followed by a *bong*. The snoring stopped abruptly.

Handen tensed as the door opened. Before him stood the woman he had seen on the slab. She stretched and rubbed her eyes and completely failed to try to kill him. "Good morning," she said in an attractively chirpy voice. "How may I help you?"

Handen floundered. In truth, he had been expecting her to shout something about infidels and try to set fire to him. Offering services was completely out of the blue.

"Let me guess." The woman smiled. "You're an adventurer, yes?"

Handen nodded—he couldn't deny it. He seemed to have been plagued by countless adventures lately.

"And you drank from the fountain, yes?"

Handen nodded again.

The woman's demeanor changed suddenly. Her eyes glazed, and

her smile widened. She began to speak as though reading from some internal script.

"Allow me to be the first to congratulate you on your newfound immortality, and I hope, as a patron of the fountain of youth, you will adhere to the vows of supreme secrecy and will consider joining our gold card members club for the low, low price of five tillers a month. My name is Tanya, and I'm here to answer any questions you may have. Have a nice day!" said Tanya. Then, so suddenly that even Handen's quick reactions couldn't stop her, she drew a wicked-looking knife from her robe and plunged it into the adventurer's heart.

Handen screamed in pain and horror as she pulled the knife back. He fell to the floor as blood flowed at a frightening pace from his chest wound. As the searing agony faded into a numb nothing, Handen sat back and waited to die, staring dumbly at his chest.

He waited.

Eventually he wondered what the hell was going on. He felt his chest, bracing for a pain that didn't come. Underneath the sticky gore on his shirt, the chest wound had disappeared.

"Sorry about that," said Tanya. "Most people don't believe me about the 'immortal' part. That's just a quick way of convincing people. I could do it again if you like?"

Handen shook his head rapidly and got to his feet. "What the hell is going on?" he shouted.

Tanya sighed and rolled her eyes. "It's quite simple. Didn't you read the ancient hieroglyphics? You've found the fountain of youth! After years of fruitless searching, no doubt."

"I wasn't looking for any damn fountain," growled Handen. "I was just trying to find my way out of this stinking forest!"

Tanya gasped. "You mean you didn't know? Oh dear. This hasn't happened before. Normally when people find this place they're ecstatic. They don't usually start getting annoyed about it for another couple of centuries."

"What? What other people?" said Handen, struggling to keep up with things.

"You didn't think you were the first person to find the fountain of youth, did you?" giggled Tanya. "Oh, no. Lots of people have found it! I was one of them!"

"So you're immortal, are you?" said Handen.

"Oh, yes," said Tanya. "I must be nearly eight hundred years old by now."

Quick as a flash, Handen drew his sword and beheaded the woman in one blurring swipe. The head rose into the air in a jet of arterial spray and landed on the ground, where it rolled to a stop and began spitting dust out of its mouth. The body put it hands on its hips.

"Well!" said Tanya's head. "You didn't have to do that!"

"Just checking," Handen muttered.

Tanya's body picked up Tanya's head and placed it back on its neck. The wound began to heal almost instantly, sticky tendrils of flesh interweaving with each other until it was impossible to tell that she had recently been decapitated.

"See?" she said. "Immortal! Although that was still very rude!"

"Sorry," burbled Handen, swaying on his feet. "I'm a bit new to this."

Tanya nodded in sympathy. "Tell you what, why don't you come inside and have a nice cup of tea?"

---

"OF COURSE, the good thing about being immortal is that you spend a lot less money on skin care products," said Tanya as she poured Handen another cup.

Handen nodded dumbly.

The inside of the stone hut was decorated quite nicely, in a tasteless sort of way. The rock walls were adorned with flowery curtains, and the single stone table was awash with doilies. It was clear that whoever had decorated had struggled to imprint a sense of homeliness on what was, essentially, a cave.

"It gets boring, mind you," continued Tanya. "That's why I took this job. You just sleep for a few hundred years, waiting for the next immortal. You show them the ropes, as it were, until someone comes to relieve you. It's very peaceful, but I'm pretty sure someone's due to relieve me soon."

Handen nodded dumbly.

"I expect someone will be along any time now. That's what you do when you get tired of living—you either come here or you search for the fountain of death."

Handen nodded dumbly.

Then he frowned. "Wait a minute. Fountain of death?"

"Mmm-hmm, that's right. It's the only thing that can kill an immortal, or so they say. Of course, no one's ever found it, or if they have, they haven't lived to talk about it. Obviously." Tanya sipped her tea.

Handen continued to stare into space. He was entertaining a terrible inner vision, an image of being immortal, un-killable, when the planet of Bersch exploded. Drifting through space for a possible eternity…

"Right then," he said. "I'm off."

"Where are you going?" said Tanya.

"I'm going to save the planet, then I'm going to find the fountain of death."

"Wait, wait, wait!" squealed Tanya. Then she reached into her pocket and brought out a gold brooch, which she placed on Handen's chest. There was a brief flash and a burning sensation. Handen looked inside his shirt to see a small tattoo of a snake eating its own tail, twisting at its middle to form a figure-of-eight shape.

"What's this?" he demanded.

"That's the mark of the immortal," said Tanya. "We've all got one." She pulled up the hem of her robe to reveal a nearly identical mark to Handen's on her calf. "Quite fetching, I think." She giggled.

"Yes. I suppose," said Handen, gruffly.

"Oh, and you might need these." She shoved an armload of rolled-up parchment into Handen's backpack.

"What are they?" he said.

"Maps," replied Tanya. "They're a good few centuries out of date, but they might be helpful."

Handen nodded his thanks and made to leave.

"One more thing!" said Tanya suddenly.

Handen's burning impatience was doused a little as he turned to look at his fellow immortal. She was beautiful and would remain beautiful for the rest of her existence, but there was a dullness in her eyes, a pained tiredness that belonged in the skull of a dying old woman. Handen felt a sudden shiver in his spine.

"If you find the fountain of death," said Tanya, "you will come back and tell me where it is, won't you?"

# 11

# Bolan Cay

It was barely an island, and if it was an island, it would be the kind of island that all the other islands picked on. It was a golden stretch of sand that was nearly thirty meters across in either direction, dotted in the surrounding sea like a speck of dust on a blue-tinted mirror. It didn't boast much scenery bar the occasional jutting rock on its meager coastline and a lonely cluster of palm trees at its center, but it did have a populace of seagulls, who hung around in seedy gangs, sneering and cawing aggressively at one another.

The most spectacular feature of the almost-island was the tiny wooden hut that sat in the limited shade. That is not to say that the hut was spectacular in any way other than being more interesting than the trees and seagulls that surrounded it. From the hut emerged the hunched frame of a man, dressed in a flowery shirt and sunglasses and a wide-brimmed straw hat. He yawned and stretched, his ancient, chubby features long ago sunburned to a merry pink. Smacking his lips under the short straggles of his sun-bleached beard, he surveyed his domain.

And paused. Frowning. Not sure if what he was seeing was really there.

Floundering briefly in the sand, he rushed back into his hut and returned moments later with two wooden poles, a banner, and a table. Hurriedly, he propped the poles and table in the sand and attached the banner, which read, "Bolan Cay Tourist Information Center." The man stood underneath the banner, smiling a wide and welcoming smile. He smiled for a few minutes. Eventually he got bored and wandered over to the focus of his attention.

A small, organic-looking ship was bobbing relentlessly against the sands of Bolan Cay. Its bark-like hull was stuck fast, its bush-like sail flapping uselessly in the slight breeze. The man approached cautiously, wondering why the ship appeared deserted. He looked over the prow of the vessel to see a disheveled-looking young man sprawled across the ship's deck. The young man didn't look at all well. His glasses were skew-whiff on his small blunt nose, and his closely cropped hair was windswept and ruffled. His skin had burned a pink to rival the older man's own.

The man seemed a little disappointed, but nevertheless he hoisted the sparse frame of the shipwrecked stranger and, with a lot of effort, dragged him back to the hut.

---

BIP'S EYELIDS, after a trying struggle with the gloop that had been holding them closed, managed to pry themselves apart. The light was cool, and a pleasant salty smell hung in the stock-still air. Bip could feel a mattress of some sort beneath him and comfortable fabric covering his body. His ears detected the lulling sound of arguing seagulls. All in all, Bip's senses were reporting very good things. All except his sense of taste, which was telling him that his mouth was as dry, foul, and unpleasant as the world's oldest gym sock.

He croaked.

"You're awake, then?" said a voice. "I guess you'd like a glass of water, yeah?"

Bip croaked in the affirmative, too thirsty to be concerned about to whom the voice belonged. He was given a glass of fresh but lukewarm water, which he gulped greedily. A few more glasses were passed and drunk before Bip had the presence of mind to see just who his generous host actually was. He looked at the old man and tried to form a sentence. His head was still buzzy from too much sun.

"What would you like first?" said the old man. "The 'who are you?' or the 'where am I?'"

Bip considered briefly. "'S'pose the 'where am I?' is more conventional."

"Bing! Two points!" said the old man, with just a little more enthusiasm than Bip was ready for. "Two points, yessiree, 'where am I?' indeed! Well, I'll tell you where you are! You're in the Free Country's greatest, latest, and most secluded holiday resort—Bolan Cay!"

Bip scratched his head and squinted at the old man. He kept on getting distracted by the loudness of his shirt and the whiteness of his teeth. "Am a what now?" he managed.

"Yep, Bolan Cay. Heaven on Bersch! Do you sometimes need to get away from it all?" said the old man, leaning over and putting a conspiratorial and sympathetic arm around Bip's shoulders. Bip considered the question, but wasn't given the opportunity to reply.

"Sure ya do, sure ya do! The hustle and bustle of city life? Early morning traffic? Problems with the horse and cart? Boss don't give you time off for plague? Yeah, we all know that story, but don't let the yeoman get you down—come to Bolan Cay! Where seclusion and tranquility are a way of life! (Monsoon season excluded, tranquility not guaranteed.)"

Bip blinked a few times while various words and exclamation marks kicked him in the ear hole. "I'm sorry. What?" he said.

The old man continued, unfazed by Bip's apparent lack of enthusiasm. "We've got the finest food this side of the Empire. Don't forget to try our seagull on rye, soup de la seagull, and seagull surprise! Mmm-mmm—surprisingly seagully! And why not wash it down with a fresh, cool water cocktail? Then relax and enjoy one of the island's many cabaret acts!" The old man whipped out what looked like a pygmy guitar and plucked a few notes. It sounded exactly as you would expect a pygmy guitar to sound.

Bip rubbed his eyes. "I'm sorry, but I have no clue what you're on about," he said.

The old man's huge grin faded to a merely large grin. "Am I to assume you are not, shall we say, in the market for leisure and tourism?"

Bip thought about it. "No. I suppose not."

"Then get the hell out of my bed!" growled the old man. "And gimme that!" he added, taking the half full glass of water from Bip's hands.

Bip was quickly ushered back outside and into the glaring sunshine, the old man prodding and pushing him all the way.

"You got some nerve taking up space in a five-star resort such as this and not even being a tourist!" he shouted, his face even pinker than usual.

"I'm very sorry, I'm sure," said Bip, taking in his surroundings, "but I thought this was just a wooden hut in the middle of a bit of sand."

The old man looked at first confused, then angry, then he flopped down in the sand with a sigh of resignation. "You're right, of course," he said. "But we all gotta have a dream, don't we?"

Bip, who during his training had developed something of a soft spot for unpredictable mood swings, sat down next to the old man and patted him reassuringly on the shoulder. "There, there," he said, in the worried tones of someone who has never believed people actually said "there, there" but is now saying it nonetheless.

"I'm Bolan, by the way," said the old man. "This is my island." He gestured half-heartedly around the weedy stretch of sand. On the shore, two seagulls fought noisily over a rock that looked a bit like a fish.

"It's very…nice," ventured Bip. "Very…peaceful?"

"Really?" said Bolan, brightening up. "You think so? Because that's what I keep telling people. I even put it on the brochure: 'Peace, tranquility, seclusion—Bolan Cay's got tons of each!' Nothing but ocean for miles around! No distractions at all!"

"You're right there," said Bip, as anything interesting completely failed to happen.

"I woulda thought that with all the problems with the Empire back on the mainland, people would be queuing up for a bit of peace and tranquility!" said Bolan.

"Problems? Empire?" prompted Bip, who recognized a bit of quest-advancing information when he saw it.

"Why sure! You don't know about the Empire? Used to be that those who didn't like the way the Argustin Empire did things could scoot on over to the Free Countries, you know? But these days, the Free Countries ain't so free, if you get my meaning?"

"Yeah," said Bip, who didn't, but disliked interrupting people when they were in full verbal flow.

"Yep," said Bolan. "I figured I'd open my island to the public, give people a chance to escape tyranny and oppression for a couple of weeks for the knock-down price of... Ah, whadda you care?" he finished. "You're no tourist." Bolan looked glumly at the sand, unaware of just how much of an understatement "tourist" was when applied to Bip.

Bip looked thoughtful for a moment. "I think I need to get to the Empire," he said.

Bolan raised his bushy eyebrows. "You *want* to go to the Empire?" He shook his hoary head in disbelief. "Kids," he muttered.

"I think that's where I need to go. Can you tell me how to get there?" said Bip.

Bolan laughed. "You can't miss it, kid; the Empire covers three quarters of the globe! But if you mean the heart of the Empire, Argustin, then you have to get to the mainland, Regalious—and to do that you have to sail farther south to the Free Countries. It's not far—a coupla days should get you to Port Town." The old man stopped himself. "But you don't wanna go to Port Town, kid. Nothing there but robbers, thieves, and other types that steal stuff."

"Will someone there be able to tell me how to get to the capital?"

"Oh, undoubtedly," said Bolan, gruffly. "If you've got enough gold on you."

Bip, who did in fact have a huge lump of gold in his rucksack, got to his feet.

"Mr. Bolan," he said, "I appreciate your hospitality and regret I cannot stay on your lovely island, but I really have to get to the Empire. Would you give me a hand casting off my boat?"

Bolan sighed. "Kids," he muttered. "Always in a hurry. Anyone would think the world was coming to an end…"

---

WITH A BIT of effort and a few grazed shins, Bolan and Bip managed to maneuver the acorn boat to the south side of the island and cast off. Bolan watched as Bip bobbed out into the sea, enough fresh water on the boat to last him comfortably to the Free Countries.

"Hey, kid," Bolan shouted. "I forgot to ask; where did you come from anyway?"

"The North," Bip called back. "From the Ice Plains!"

"That's crazy! Nobody comes from the Ice Plains. Everyone knows it's nothing but a big patch of snow and ice. Full o' dangerous animals too. Ain't no one steps foot on the Ice Plains by choice!"

"Yeah, that's pretty much true!" Bip shouted. "Goodbye!"

"And don't forget!" yelled Bolan. "Tell your friends about Bolan Cay! More peace and quiet than a sane man can handle!"

Bip waved back. Bolan watched as the acorn boat faded into a dot, then he watched the horizon for a few hours. There was really nothing better to do.

---

FAR OUT INTO SPACE, the Massive Ball of Death raced on. The civilization that had spawned it had long since expired, their short-lived cease-fire ending in a catastrophic war that had eventually killed them all, but the Massive Ball of Death lived on as a legacy.

It was vaguely aware of this somehow. After traveling countless miles for countless years, being bombarded with all kinds of cosmic rays and radiation from across the universe, the nuclear cluster was developing sentience of a sort. It was aware that it was going in what it had chosen to perceive as a "forward" direction and that eventually "forward" had to run out. Knowing this made it feel a faint imitation of optimism. Thus, the universe's most chirpy ball of ice, dust, radiation, and nuclear armaments continued to roll across the inky void of space, causing paranoia and chaos wherever it did go.

A particular group of people blissfully unaware that they were in the path of said Massive Ball of Death were currently celebrating another successful bout of swashbuckling thievery and adventure by the tried and tested method of drinking beyond reasonable capacity. The *S.S. Blunderbuss* swayed merrily in the orbit of a small moon, its gun turrets firing periodically to the beat of a jaunty tune. Inside, Captain Kwiksave Lombardo, pirate king and the galaxy's most intrepid freebooter, stood on a table, trying to hold three bottles of gut rot in one hand and using his other to conduct a merry (if unspeakably dirty) pirate tune with a cigar.

Some called him No Beard, others The Prince of Scum. Some people called him the Space Cowboy, others called him a Galactic Pain in the Bum. By any name, Kwiksave Lombardo was the most infamous of all space pirates, and his latest raid had been a fantastic success. The booty had been bountiful, and his merry men were very merry indeed.

The tune came to a predictable conclusion, and the men toasted their victory for the seventy-ninth time so far before falling about in general good-humored slobbishness.

One man managed to pick himself up from the floor. "Sing us a song, Cap'n!" he cried.

"Aye!" agreed another, paused to belch massively, then said, "Let's hear a song from the pirate king!" A raucous cheer went up, although to be fair, the crew would've cheered anything in their current state.

"Now, now, boys," said Kwiksave. "Now. Now. Now? What? No... erm..." He swayed for a while, trying to figure out what he had been going to say. A light of recollection shone suddenly in his one eye. "Yes! A song! I mean, no! I don't want to. I'm self-conscious..."

"Self-conscious?" bellowed the first mate, a cyborg by the proud old robot name of KillCrushDestroy. "Self-conscious? The man who once took on the evil, eight-armed Octomen of Premidin Prime in a duel to the death, blindfolded, and came out unscathed?"

The crew cheered while Captain Lombardo flapped his arms with drunken modesty.

"The man who once seduced the goddess-like Queen of Shebara, the holiest of virgins with a face that launched a billion ships, then refused to give her his phone number afterward!?"

The crew cheered. Captain Lombardo continued to flap.

"The man who once stole the wallet of the Zebirom Death Lord and used his credit cards to order embarrassing products that he then had delivered to the Death Lord's mum's house? Self-conscious?"

The crew cheered.

"Now, now, Mr. KillCrushDestroy! You're embarrassing me!" said Kwiksave.

"Oh, go on, Captain! Sing that song you sing about being the pirate king!"

The crew whooped appreciatively.

"Oh, okay, then," said Kwiksave. "If I must."

The crew hollered joyfully for a while, then hushed themselves to an attentive silence. Kwiksave prepared to sing his song.

"*Weeellll…*" he began.

But then the SS blunderbuss was struck by the wake of the Massive Ball of Death and was sent crashing down to the moon's surface.

Kwiksave was first up after the rumbling noises had stopped. He looked about the smoky cabin, lit by the sparking of important-looking equipment. He began to bark orders.

"Recalibrate the oxytron matrix fiddler!"

"Aye, Cap'n!"

"Configure the atmospheric stabilizer!"

"Aye, Cap'n!"

"Reboot the warp flux confligulater!"

"We don't have one, Cap'n!"

"Then remind me to bloody well get one!"

"Aye, Cap'n!"

"What the hell was that?" said Captain Lombardo, after the chaos had been brought to an acceptable level of control.

"I may be wrong about this, Cap'n," said KillCrushDestroy, "but it looked to me like a huge cluster of nuclear weapons covered in space dust."

Lombardo thought for a while. "Then all things considered, that could have been a lot worse," he concluded.

He turned back to the crew, each of them scared sober and looking for leadership. "Now," he said. "Where the hell is my cigar?"

Far out into space, the Massive Ball of Death kept on going, aware, in a good-humored kind of way, that nothing was going to stop it.

# 12

# Port Town

The beach was a mournful place, moping gloomily across the shore like an old picture etched in charcoal. Bone-white sand stretched from horizon to horizon, interrupted here and there by the black of rotting seaweed, age-old driftwood, and murky-looking rock pools. Jagged gray stones reached up toward a jagged gray sky, defiant totems of sharpness on the smudged and lackluster scenery. In the distance, a white cliff toed the line between ground and sky, while the foggy ghosts of enormous flat-headed mountains squashed the horizon. A faint wind blew with a deceptive volume, mixing with the white noise of the breaking waves to create a sound like old memories.

This was not a beach where people would come to relax. This was more like a beach where poets might come to kill themselves.

Such a brooding topography, it seemed, had no place for people. Yet a person was there, dressed in a texture of purple and black that complemented and even competed with the neighboring gloom. As silent as a painting, the figure stood in a solitude well worthy of his surroundings.

Azron Bezron hung out by the shore. In fact, he didn't so much hang as drape. Slouched against a rock on the driftwood-cluttered beach, he struggled to light a cigarette against the chill breeze from the sea.

There are various words to describe Azron, none of them particularly nice. "Suspicious" is perhaps the least offensive. His stick-thin frame pointed at its joints, adding razor angles to the long, shapeless coat that brushed against the ground. A pointy face with pointy sideburns, a pointy moustache, and a small pointy goatee pointed out from under a peak-less woolen hat. A permanent pointy grin revealed the slightly crooked teeth of a very crooked man. Dark, oily features surrounded a pair of eyes that shifted about in the confident, good-humored way of a man who knows the world is there to be taken…for the right pair of hands.

Azron Bezron was a thief. A damn good one. Like his father and his father's father. And his mother. And his aunt, sister, little brother Maslo, cousin Deek, Uncle "Fingers"… In fact, pretty much everyone Azron had ever known had been a thief.

Currently he was stealing a bit of time for himself, relaxing on the shore a comfortable distance from the constant challenge of Port Town. He gazed out to sea and lost himself in a daydream.

A small speck appeared on the horizon. Azron's lazy half-smile crawled further up the side of his face. He waited with an easy patience until the speck turned into a boat. Then he waited some more. Eventually the boat reached the shore, and Azron watched as a scrawny figure attempted to moor it to the skeleton of a long-ago beached vessel. Azron grinned at the futility of the activity. Tie or no tie, the boat would not be there tomorrow. Someone would have nicked it.

The scrawny figure began to approach, revealing a lad in his late teens. Azron took in his unusual clothing: the wide-brimmed traveling hat, the delicate half-moon glasses, the over-stuffed backpack, and the sword scabbard at his side. Somewhere in Azron's brain, a calculation took place.

"All right, mate?" said Azron, still puffing at his thin cigarette.

"Yes," said Bip. "I wonder if you could tell me where I am?"

Azron considered the question for a while before seemingly disregarding it completely. Instead of answering, he re-lit his faltering cigarette and said, "We don't get many people sailing in from the Cold Ocean. In fact, I think you're about the first one I've ever seen. Where did you say you were from, sunshine?"

"I didn't," said Bip, who was feeling mildly disconcerted. Azron had an unusual way of talking to people. He would maintain eye contact very briefly before shifting his gaze about the place, as though expecting someone to sneak up on him. Half the time it appeared that Azron was addressing someone behind him rather than the person he was actually talking to. Coupled with his odd habit of speaking quietly through the side of his mouth, a conversation with Azron often left people with a sense of general paranoia.

"I'll rephrase it, shall I?" said Azron. "Where've you come from?"

"Oh. I sailed here from the Ice Plains."

Azron fixed Bip with a beady stare. "Yeah," he muttered. "And I'm the bloody Emperor."

"Really?" said Bip, excitedly. "What an enormous stroke of luck, because, you see, you're the very man I've been looking for!"

Azron looked blank for a while. "I'm not the Emperor."

"But you just said—"

"Look, mate, nobody comes from the Ice Plains. Nobody goes to the Ice Plains. You'd have to cross miles and miles of monster-infested waters, where, or so it's said, behemoths from the dawn of creation still roam freely."

Bip stood in contemplation for a moment. "Can't say I saw any behemoths, exactly."

"Through chaotic winds that cause waves the size of castles to crash down on the unsuspecting sailor."

"Well, it got a bit choppy coming in to the shore…"

"Where storms rage with such terrible madness that the very sound of the thunder will turn a man's mind to mush."

"No. No, sorry. I didn't see anything like that, really."

Azron looked disappointed. "So what terrible perils did you face then, guv?"

Bip thought for a moment. "There was a seagull," he concluded.

"A seagull."

"Yes. And I got a bit sunburnt."

Azron peered suspiciously at Bip. "Well, mate, you're either the worst liar I've ever met or you're telling the truth. Either way, this is Melan Cove."

Bip looked around. As bleak as Melan Cove seemed, it was a carnival of color compared to the shore he had originally left.

"Can you tell me if I'm anywhere near Port Town?" said Bip.

Azron grinned his lazy grin. "And what does a chap like you want in a place like Port Town?" he said, jetting cigarette smoke through his nostrils.

"Information, mainly," said Bip. "I need to know how to get to the heart of the Empire."

Azron looked at Bip for a long while. "I'll give you some advice for free, mate; we don't talk loose about the Empire, right? 'Specially not in Port Town."

"…Yes?" said Bip.

"You're really not from around here, are you?" said Azron, an appraising look in his eye.

"No! I told you, I'm from the Ice Plains."

"Yeah, yeah. The Ice Plains, right." Azron stared thoughtfully into space and began rubbing his chin as his crooked grin etched slowly across his dark features. Bip began to feel quite uncomfortable.

"I tell you what, mate, this is your lucky day!" he said finally.

"Really?" replied Bip.

"Yes, because for a nominal fee, as a one-time only offer, I can be your guide to and around Port Town for the duration of your visit, like." Azron smiled smugly.

Bip thought for a moment. "That would be brilliant," he concluded.

"Yeah, yeah, brilliant," said Azron, his grin stretching further across his thin face. "You know, I think this could be the start of something great!"

---

THE TWO TRAVELERS sat in the back of the rickety merchant wagon they had managed to hitch a ride with as they made their way to Port Town. The scenery around the wagon trail was a marked improvement on Melan Cove, the depressing sand drifts of which had eventually given way to wide passes of green with faint bumps of hillsides here and there.

They were currently following a wide river, where large, bumping barges floated ceaselessly back and forth, laden with cargo of all descriptions.

"Obviously we get no trade from the Cold Ocean," said Azron, who was chattering idly about the commerce of Port Town, "but more often than not, it's far easier to sail goods around the coasts and through the rivers than it is to cart them about."

Bip nodded. He was greatly impressed by the various boats and barges. This wasn't difficult, of course, as the only boat Bip had any real experience of had grown from an acorn.

"That's why Port Town is called Port Town, see?" continued Azron, raising his voice slightly over the rattle of the wagon's axels. "It's situated where all the rivers converge closest to the sea. A trade hub, sort of thing."

"So is that what you do, then, Azron?" said Bip. "Trade things?"

"Yeah, sort of," replied Azron. "Sort of like trading, except when people 'give' me things, I generally don't give them anything back, like."

"Isn't that just stealing?" said Bip, frowning.

"Well, yes," said Azron. "That's what we do in Port Town. We steal things. Everybody steals things. It's the way things are done."

"So you're a thief, then?" said Bip.

"Not just any thief, mate, I'm one of the big shots. I'm a Diamond Geezer, me. First class and all," said Azron, his narrow chest swelling with pride.

"I'm sorry, what?" said Bip.

Azron produced a wallet and took out a card. It was an elaborate certificate embossed with the legend "Port Town Union of Dodgy Fellows". Beneath it was Azron's mugshot, bearing the caption, "Genuine Diamond Geezer (1st class)."

"Diamond Geezer? You know? They don't come much better than me, sunshine, let me tell you. Most people in Port Town are lucky if they can make it to a third-class mugger, or a bronze-level rogue, but me? Diamond-level Geezer, mate! Not bronze, not silver, and not gold, but diamond. Means I'm recognized by the union as a top-level geezer, if you know what I mean?"

"No," said Bip.

"I'm a geezer. Jack-of-all-trades, sort of thing. Grifting, pick-pocketing, shoplifting, breaking, and entering. I've done them all, mate. When it comes to down-and-outs, I'm right up there at the top!"

Bip was shocked. "So you *are* a thief then? A common criminal?" he said.

"Well, don't say it like that," whined Azron. "You make it sound like I'm some sort of bad person!"

"Well, yes, that's the point!" said Bip.

Azron chuckled under his breath. "Of course. I keep forgetting you're not from around here. Look, the way we do things in Port Town is a bit different from other places. Now how can I put this?" Azron frowned into space for a moment. "Well, put it like this," he continued. "We don't really have much of a currency, yeah? We just trade commodities as they are, usually, and that's fine if you've got commodities to begin with, see? But some people don't, so they trade services, yeah? But the whole process, it's a bit slow, isn't it? So what people do, right, is they, like, cut out the middle man?" Azron peered hopefully at Bip to see if he was following.

"Are you trying to tell me," said Bip, slowly. "That everybody steals from everybody else?"

"Exactly!" said Azron, grinning hugely. "Obviously, there's legitimate trade on some levels, but only when it can't be avoided."

"But why?" cried Bip in hopeless confusion.

"Less paperwork, less bureaucracy, less class division, less unemployment. It works on a lot of levels, really," said Azron.

"But it's completely lawless!" wailed Bip.

"Of course it's not! Violent crime isn't tolerated, for a start. And then there's the law of Fair Cop, which means if you get caught nicking, you've got to give everything back. And the government steals taxes, instead of threatening people for them…" Azron stopped as he took in Bip's look of horrified confusion. "I'll tell you what," he said. "Why don't you just wait until we get there?"

PORT TOWN WAS A MESS. A beautiful chaos of noise and activity, a profound ugliness of cramped buildings and surging crowds. Squat houses of badly cut brick and wood were piled carelessly on top of one another, and the smell of a million people with better things to think about than adequate means of sanitation constantly flicked the nose.

Bip reeled. The quietness of Kaneq was all he had ever known of civilization. The sheer number of people going about their everyday business on an average morning in Port Town made the Apprentice Fair and the yearly carnival of Kaneq seem like a hermit's house party by comparison.

He had first viewed Port Town from a distance when they had crested a large hill, and for a while, he had thought that they had been turned around and were back at the ocean. A huge lake dominated the landscape. Called the Filter by the locals, the lake was the point where nearly every major river in the Free Countries converged before heading out to sea in three giant fingers. Port Town had taken full advantage of this geological oddity and a veritable floating city of docks, harbors, jetties, and ships stretched for miles across the Filter. Not a spare inch wasn't taken up by cargo, cranes, carts, barges, and bridges and, running like ants throughout the complex, hundreds of men and women of various creeds and colors all shouted very loudly at one another. Azron had wisely taken Bip around the dock areas and through the city gates reserved for wagon trade.

Bip had gawked moronically as they had wandered through the muddy, labyrinthine streets. "Busy" was too small a word to sum up the plethora of different activities running across the Port Town streets. Taxis taxied, whores whored, beggars begged, and merchants shouted endlessly. What Bip didn't notice, of course, running like an underlying plot to the entire scene, was the thieves thieving. If he had noticed the sheer amount of swindling, sidling, and just plain swiping that was visible to the trained eye, he probably would have broken down in tears.

"Welcome to Port Town!" said Azron, grinning his lopsided grin and deeply breathing in the bumptious air. "Where do you want to go first?"

Bip took in the hectic scenery with the awestruck terror of a fish that has just jumped out of its bowl and into an ocean. "Can we go somewhere quiet?" he said.

"What?"

"Somewhere quiet! Where I can think for a bit!"

"Quiet?"

"Yes! Quiet!"

Azron thought for a moment. Quiet was a rare adjective in Port Town, but there were places with less noise than others.

"Follow me!" he shouted as he began pushing his way through the crowded streets. Bip followed, wide-eyed and clutching the brim of his traveling hat around his ears to drown out the noise of a lot of people with a lot on their mind.

Bip completely failed to notice, as Azron flowed easily through the crowd, the number of people who would suddenly and frantically pat their pockets soon after brushing against him. A chorus of curses followed the progress of the traveler and the thief.

# 13

# Of Mugs and Minotaurs

They called it the Boiling Sea, though its temperature was, if anything, cold. The word "boiling" referred to the way the waves rose and fell with rapid violence. Even from the very top of the Barrier Cliffs, the turbulent ocean below still loomed menacingly, waves rising and bursting from base to tip of the two-hundred-foot cliff face, hurling thunderous crashes and rainstorms of sea spray against the rocky land.

As far as the eye could see, the waves of the Boiling Sea tossed manically into the sky, each tide a mini-tsunami.

The reason for this was the underwater hurricane, as old as the ocean itself, that raged continuously on the unreachable seabed at the water's center. Unseen in all but its effects, the freak underwater storm made the stretch of sea between the mainland and the new continent a permanent tempest, worthy of the most boisterous of weather demons.

An old woman sat at the cliff's edge, a leather-hooded raincoat obscuring most of her features and an old fishing net in her hand. She dangled her booted feet over the raging waters beneath her and whistled a merry tune against the constant boom of waves smashing against the Barrier Cliffs.

She was fishing for panic fish, one of the few life forms that could survive in the Boiling Sea. The panic fish was a white, oblong creature with extremely small fins. Its inadequacy in the fin department was never really a problem as the panic fish didn't actually swim, it just spent its entire life being thrown through the air by the violence of the Boiling Sea. Living entirely on plankton, which it gorged on in the few moments that it spent in the water, the panic fish led a short and terrifying existence, looking forward only to the time when it might be left in the sea for long enough to reproduce. The panic fish had no natural predators. Unless you counted gravity and stress-related heart failure.

The old lady enjoyed fishing at the Boiling Sea because all you had to do was wait for the hurtling fish to land in your net. She hummed a merry ditty while a panic fish flew through the air nearby emitting a high-pitched keening sound.

She did not see the stranger approach until he was standing next to her. She looked up from her net and took in the newcomer's appearance. For a moment, she thought he might be a pirate or a highwayman, but something in the man's stance and expression said differently. He had the look of someone who was in the middle of running a marathon.

"Help thee, squire?" said the woman.

"What is this?" said the man, gesturing to the chaotic panorama before him.

"Boiling Sea," said the woman. "Pretty, ain't it?" She cackled.

"Does the storm ever stop?" said the newcomer.

"Not in our life time, nay," said the woman. "Boiling Sea is always like this. Never stops."

The man looked out for a while, thinking.

"There's no way across?" he said.

"Not by boat, not unless yer mad or yer not fond of livin'."

"Another way, then?"

"To the mainland?" The old woman spat. "Only way across is the Spine Islands, and they is crawling with monsters so they is. Crossed meself when I was youngun. Came with a caravan of hundreds, arrived with less than half. No place for one man to travel."

The man stood thinking again, surveying the stormy horizon.

"Which way?" he said finally.

The old woman pointed a bony finger to the east. "That way," she muttered. "But I wouldn't bother if I was thee."

The man raised an eyebrow questioningly.

"Why dost thou think people risk life and limb to get to the new continent? Why dost thou think we live hard as pioneers?" said the woman.

The man stared at the old woman for a moment. He had considered this question himself.

"There's nothing back at the mainland but war and death!" said the woman. "And always will be while a Draegul sits on the throne."

The man nodded his head and walked east. The sad truth, he knew, was that wherever there was war and death, civilization was likely to be nearby.

"Nothing but death!" called the old lady, her withered screech rising above the crash of the waves. Handen carried on walking. Death, for him, had ceased to be a problem.

"Glad 'e's gone," muttered the old lady as Handen Strike disappeared out of sight. "'e was scaring the fish anyway."

As if to contest the point, a screaming panic fish went whooping over her head.

---

CLAMOR HAD TUNED DOWN to commotion. The inside of the Weasel's Face tavern and inn, even though crowded with drunks and braggarts, was still far quieter than the streets outside.

Bip sat in a dark booth in the corner of the inn, his rucksack and traveling hat propped next to him as he waited for Azron to return from the bar. As comfortable as the booth was, Bip was finding it difficult to relax. All his wilderness training now seemed like a waste of time in the face of the thriving Port Town populace. The sheer number of people milling around still unnerved him, and he felt like exactly what he was—a stranger in a strange place.

Azron returned with two foamy mugs of something potent and sat down opposite Bip, sliding one of the glass mugs toward him. Bip looked at it suspiciously.

"How did you pay for this?" he said.

Azron rolled his eyes. "Let's not get into that again, ay?" he said, completely failing to mention that the table behind them was two drinks lighter than it ought to be. Bip shrugged and tried some of the ale. It was pleasant and frothy with a sharp aftertaste.

"So let's hear it, then," said Azron. "I've told you about me—now what's your story?"

Bip thought for a while, sloshing the ale around in his mouth while trying to decide how much information he should divulge to Azron. Finally, not seeing what harm it could do, Bip decided to tell the whole truth. "Well, it turns out I'm descended from an alien race who crash landed here nearly a thousand years ago while they were trying to warn us about an impending disaster that will result in the end of the world and the destruction of the planet some time at the end of this year. I've been sent to warn people." Bip sat back and took another swig of his ale while Azron sat open-mouthed.

"Okay," said Azron after a while. "You're crazy. That's fine. I've worked with crazy people before. Everything's okay."

"I'm not crazy," said Bip in a pained tone of voice. "I'm telling the truth!"

"Yeah, I'm not saying you ain't. It probably is the truth in whatever weird and crazy world your mind resides in. I'm not saying you're a liar, just that you're mental, that's all."

"I'm not mental!" said Bip.

"Yeah, okay, you're not mental. You're the boss, you're the one paying the wages, if you say you're not mental, then that's fine."

"Are you humoring me?" said Bip.

"Would you like me to?" Azron replied.

Bip sighed and put his head in his hands. "Regardless of whether you believe me or not, the world really is going to end, and I need to get to the Empire to warn whoever is in charge."

Azron jumped slightly in his seat and looked sharply around the room.

"What did I tell you about talking loose about the Empire?" he hissed.

"What? What did I say?" said Bip.

"Look," said Azron, leaning in conspiratorially, "the Free Countries and the Empire, yeah? We're not exactly friendly at the minute, see? A lot of personal feelings floating about concerning the Empire and tempers are known to fray, if you get my drift?"

Bip nodded, letting Azron continue.

"You see, the Empire runs half the world, yeah? And those bits it doesn't run…well, let's just say they know what side their bread is buttered on. But the Free Countries, because we've always been a difficult continent to get to, we've always led a fairly independent existence. Though we're officially affiliated with the Empire, we've always adopted the philosophy that what they don't know won't hurt them, sort of thing." Azron paused to drain his mug. He belched loudly before continuing. "But that all changed about fifty years ago when the Empire invented the airboats. Now they've got an airdock in nearly every city in the world and can come and go whenever they please."

"So?" said Bip.

"Well, no one likes it when the landlord turns up, do they? Especially if you haven't paid your rent in about a thousand years. The Empire doesn't like the way the Free Countries are doing things, so every year they send in more troops to keep an eye on things. You didn't hear this from me, right, but if it the Empire keeps on trying to change things around here, there's going to be a war."

"A war?" said Bip.

"Shh! Keep your bloody voice down!" said Azron, waving his hand in frantic gestures. "There's spies all over the place these days—you never know who's listening!"

Bip looked around the tavern. By the bar, an old man was violently sick, and a young serving girl had the misfortune to slip in the result, spilling a tray-load of glasses. He doubted whether anyone was paying attention to his dark little corner.

"Look," said Bip, "my mission is to relay my warning to the most influential person I can find, and as far as I've heard, whoever is in charge of this Empire is the man to speak to, yes?"

"I suppose," said Azron, guardedly.

"So can you get me to see the Emperor?"

Azron cracked his lazy half-smile. "Nobody just *sees* Draegul, mate. You have to be top brass just to get in his vicinity."

"Well, can you at least get me to the Empire?" said Bip.

Azron thought for a moment. "You want to get to the Empire fast, yeah? And the only way you can do that is by airboat to Regalious. You'd need to apply for a ticket and that can take anything up to a year if you're not in the know. Which you're not."

"A year?" wailed Bip.

"Well, they're hardly going to let any old chump into the Empire's mainland, are they? They've got security procedures longer than a jabberwocky's long bits."

"But I need to get there as soon as possible! The world won't even be here in a year!"

"All right, all right!" said Azron. "There is another way. I can probably get you a ticket no problem from the black market…but it'll cost a lot."

Bip pulled the lump of gold from his pocket and dumped it on the table. It made a satisfying clonking noise that made the beer mugs rattle.

"Will that be enough, do you think?" said Bip.

"Great holy bastards!" croaked Azron. "Put that back in your pocket before you get us all killed!"

Azron waited, his brow sweating as he shot panicked glances around the room, carefully making calculations while Bip concealed the fist-sized lump of gold.

"Okay, okay," said Azron, still breathing shallowly. "We'll make some enquiries at the market, but for now, I suggest we get the hell out here before one of the seventeen people who saw that monstrous lump of cash decides they fancy their chances."

Walking hurriedly, the two exited the Weasel's Face. Seventeen pairs of eyes followed them. Several people made their excuses and went out of the back door. None of them looked like particularly friendly people.

The traveler and the thief ducked out of the pub and into the marketplace, which still throbbed with the pulse of extreme commerce. The din of a thousand salesmen jumbled into one cacophony of advertisement. Goods and moneys changed hands quicker than the cards of a street illusionist. And all the while, the thieves jumped in and out of one another's stalls like adulterers in a camp comedy.

Bip steeled himself against the now-familiar sense of agoraphobia, resisting the urge to hang on to Azron's coat as the thief led him through the huddled crowds. Eventually they made their way to a more deserted part of the market, a small clearing decked with shady-looking stalls that backed onto an ominous network of alleyways. Even in the brightness of the afternoon, this particular clearing purveyed the intimacy of midnight.

"You stay here," said Azron, pushing Bip up against a wall. "And for god's sake, don't talk to anyone and keep your things where you can see them!"

"Where are you going?" asked Bip.

"I'm off to see a man about a dog," said Azron mysteriously, before sidling off into an alleyway.

"I should think we've got other things to worry about than pet problems," grumbled Bip to himself. "Only the end of the bloody world..."

He stood against the wall and looked about the marketplace, clutching his bag to his chest while trying to keep a hand on Brian's pommel. His gaze flitted nervously from side to side. Basically, he had the word "tourist" written all over him in large black capitals. Eventually he relaxed and meandered over to one of the many market stalls, gazing dumbly at the various wares while he waited for Azron. The stall keeper, a stout man with hooded eyes, gave Bip an appraising look. Before long, a wide, clean and above all *predatory* grin split his face.

"Welcome stranger!" said the stall-keeper, waving his hand with a flourish. "Welcome to Honest Achmed's Emporium of Antiquities and Distinctive Curiosities!"

Bip blinked, stupidly.

"My stall," said Achmed, helpfully. He leaned over and muttered to Bip conspiratorially, "Am I right in thinking that you're not originally from Port Town?"

"Actually, this is my first time in a city," said Bip, painting a large bullseye on his chest.

"Then you'll want souvenirs, won't you?" said Achmed. "Something to remind you of your visit?" The man began rummaging around on his stall, searching for an appropriate item. Finally, he lifted a rock triumphantly before Bip's nose.

"How about this little beauty, then?" he said.

"It's a rock," stated Bip, more confused than nonplussed.

"Not just a rock, stranger. What I hold in my hand is a piece of history!"

Bip squinted through his glasses. "It looks like a rock to me," he concluded.

"Ah," said Achmed, "but this is the very rock used to assassinate the Trade King in the war of the Six Rivers. This rock has been passed down through the generations as a symbol of the fight for free enterprise against tyrannical business unions! Only three spondulicks and its yours!"

"Sounds fascinating," said Bip, who had no clue what Achmed was on about.

"Not your cup of tea, then?" said the stall-keeper, tossing the rock over his shoulder. "Then how about this?"

"That looks like another rock…"

"Ah!" said Achmed. "It may look like a rock, but it's actually the fossilized remains of the toenail of the giant flying lizards that used to stalk the world at the dawn of history! Yours for only two spondulicks!"

"I don't think so…" said Bip.

"Fair enough, stranger, fair enough… But maybe I can interest you in…this!"

"Now, that," said Bip, "that is an empty jar you just picked up off of the floor."

"Ah!" said Achmed. "It may look like an empty jar I just picked up off of the floor, but it's actually… It's actually… It's actually a jar of invisible face paint!" The stall-keeper held up the jar triumphantly, a smug grin on his face. "Only three spondulicks!"

"Invisible face paint?"

"Yes! You'll be the life of the party if you go back to your friends dressed up in invisible face paint!"

"How will they know I'm wearing it?"

"Well, that's the beauty of it!" said Achmed. "They won't know until you tell them! Imagine their surprise and delight! Only two spondulicks!"

"Are you're sure that's not just an empty jar?"

"Of course not! Would Honest Achmed lie to you? Only one spondulick and it's yours."

At that moment, and luckily for Bip, Azron emerged from the alleyways with a mildly annoyed expression on his usually smirking features.

"Clear off, Bare-Face, this mug is mine," he snarled, prodding the merchant in the face with one of his long, delicate fingers.

"Who's Bare-Face?" said Bip.

"He is," said Azron, nodding to the greasy salesman. "He's Achmed D'lyer, one of the biggest codswallopers this side of the docks!"

"But he told me his name was Honest Achmed!" said Bip.

"Well, that's the things about liars, see? They tend to bend the truth a bit," said Azron.

"Well, if everything's in order here, it really is time for me to close up," said Achmed, backing away surreptitiously.

"Not so fast," said Azron. He turned to Bip. "Did you buy anything from this man?" he demanded.

"Well, I was tempted by the invisible face paint…" said Bip.

Azron clucked and rolled his eyes before turning around and giving Achmed's stall a swift kick. "Go and hock your dodgy goods elsewhere, you con man! Honestly, you give thievery a bad name!" The stall-keeper grinned, shrugged, and turned back to his wares. Azron shook his head disapprovingly. "You should really be more careful, mate," he said, turning back to Bip. "There's all sorts around these parts."

"He seemed all right," said Bip reproachfully.

The thief just clucked and rolled his eyes again. "If you want to survive in this town, mate, you've got to realize there are two types of people: mugs and muggers. The trick is not to be the mug. Now, come on, follow me."

They began walking through the alleyways of Port Town, Azron's gaze shifting constantly from shadow to shadow.

"So, did you find out about the airboat ticket?" said Bip.

"Everyone's tight-lipped," said Azron. "They're all too scared of Argustin spies around here, so it looks like we're going to have to trade with the goblins. They can get their hands on anything."

"Goblins?" said Bip.

"King Chaff's tribe. They live outside the city. They're a traveling community, so they don't really care much about the Empire."

"Are goblins trustworthy?" Bip asked.

"No," replied Azron. "And that's exactly why we're approaching them for a highly illegal black-market airboat ticket, guv. It's not the sort of thing I'd ask a policeman for now, is it?"

"'Spose not," mumbled Bip.

"Now," said Azron, "if I could have a bit of quiet, please, I'll see if I can get us through these alleyways without being robbed or stabbed, shall I?"

While Azron was talking, he turned a corner and walked straight into five knife-wielding robbers.

"Nice try," said Bip.

"Oh, crap."

Mug or mugger. Dinner or diner. Bip was beginning to realize that maybe the wilds and the city had something in common after all. They were both full of predators.

---

KEROS THE MINOTAUR stomped around the village square, raising dust under his cloven feet and swinging his humungous club in wide arcs around his horned head. He bellowed ferociously as the scattering villagers fled to the relative safety of their houses. Very few people would stick around in the presence of an angry minotaur, a monster that was half man, half bull, and wholly unpleasant.

With one final roar, Keros stopped stomping around and leaned his massive frame casually on his club. All the villagers had fled. They would be back, the minotaur knew, with sacrificial livestock, barrels of ale, and with any luck, a few youngest daughters.

The life of a minotaur was an easy one, consisting mainly of traveling from village to village, killing any of the men-folk stupid enough to stand in his way, then roaring menacingly until the villagers got the hint and started giving him presents. Keros looked down at the corpse of the village's most recent champion. It hadn't been much of a challenge, a young man barely out of his teens carrying a home-cast sword he had wielded inexpertly. The creature snorted through his bull's nose. Maybe he would leave off the villages for a while and give them time to build up their numbers again. After all, there was no sense in scaring off such lucrative benefactors.

The monster was interrupted in his thoughts by a piercing whistle from behind him. He turned to face the intruder, half expecting some last-minute resistance from the villagers. Instead, he was presented with a single man, silhouetted against the setting sun. Keros had faced many champions before, but something about the stance of the newcomer was unsettling. Perhaps it was the way he hadn't even drawn his weapons yet. Normally at this point, the minotaur would begin roaring and swinging his club, but something told him that the newcomer would not be so easily intimidated.

"Oo argh yoo?" Keros bellowed.

The figure began a slow approach. "For what it's worth, my name is Handen Strike. I doubt you'll be alive long enough to tell anyone."

The minotaur roared with guttural laughter. "Oo challange me?" he said.

"Not much of a challenge," replied Handen stoically.

Keros screamed with rage and lowered his massive head and charged, the ground shaking under the pounding of his hooves. At the last minute before impact with the awaiting Handen, the charging monster leaped into the air, twisting his massive frame and bringing the club down with a blow that cracked the earth beneath it.

Those who had watched the fight from the safety of their houses would later recount that they were sure the stranger had been killed, that there was no way on Bersch he could possibly have avoided the blow. But nevertheless, one moment Handen was directly under the descending doom of the minotaur's club, the next he was simply five feet back and watching the confused beast with a cynical smirk on his face.

Before Keros could regain his composure, Handen sprinted lightly up the creature's club and sprang into the air, kicking the beast hard in the face as he flew overhead. Handen had landed, rolled to his feet, and drawn his weapons before his opponent had even realized what had happened.

The minotaur turned around, snorting hot, wet air from his nostrils, shocked fury blazing in his eyes. "Oo 'ill die slo!" he roared.

Handen cracked his whip. "No," he said. "I really don't think so."

Blinded by anger, the beast lowered his head, readying his dull but powerful horns, and charged again. This time Handen rolled sideways, allowing the speeding minotaur to skid past him before flicking his whip out and wrapping it around the monster's throat. Fighting for breath, Keros bucked and pulled and finally yanked at the whip hard enough to jerk Handen high into the air. Rather than losing his advantage, as Keros had hoped, Handen embraced the momentum of his flight, flourishing his sword in mid-air before landing the blade in the nape of the minotaur's neck with a downward thrust. Keros stopped bucking and collapsed to the floor with a thud. He was dead before he hit the ground.

Handen stood over the fallen monster, his face impassive as he wound his whip back and retrieved his sword. Slowly, the villagers returned from their houses, silent with awe.

The village patriarch approached. "Sire, you have slain the minotaur! Truly thou art a warrior of heroic proportions!"

"Yeah," said Handen. "I get that a lot, actually."

The villagers looked at one another, waiting for the first person to shout "hooray" so that they could join in without looking foolish.

"Our gratitude is bottomless, sire. Ask what you will, and we shall provide!"

"Well, if you could give me directions to the Spine Islands, that would be good," said Handen. "I'm a little lost."

The Patriarch blinked. "I can point thee in the right direction, sire, but the way is fraught with peril, monsters of—"

"Yeah, yeah. Terrible monsters, sinister pirates, and things that no mortal man should ever see. I got the message from the last village elder. Which way, please?"

The Patriarch pointed the direction. "Did he mention the terrible evils of the—"

"Of the Bat Cult, yes. And the Snake Cult and the Snail Cult, also."

"Ah, but did he tell thee of the—"

"Shadow Beast of Bogmon Swamp? Yeah, yeah."

"But what of—"

"The Unholy Armies of the Ever Living Skelera. Yep, he filled me in on that as well."

The Patriarch tried not to look disappointed. "Oh. Well. I suppose you should get off, then. Just keep going southeast. You can't miss them."

"Yeah, thanks, bye."

The villagers watched as the hero walked off into the sunset.

"Seemed like a nice enough chap," one remarked.

"Yeah. So. What do we do now, then?" said another.

"Well, I was saving this barrel of ale for the minotaur, but I suppose that's out of the window now, isn't it?"

"Yeah. Sort of don't know what to do with myself now. I had the rest of the evening booked to complain about the minotaur."

"Well, I for one," said somebody's youngest daughter, "am very grateful things have worked out this way. I think a celebration is in order. In honor of the brave man who saved us from the tyrannies of the minotaur."

"Yeah, great!"

"Yeah!"

"Brilliant!"

"What did he say his name was?"

"I dunno. I'm not letting this barrel go to waste, though."

"Brilliant!"

---

BIP AND AZRON backed away from the muggers. They were almost archetypal muggers, bulky and scarred with a malignant glee in their eye that one normally associated with playground brawlers.

"All right then, lads, what do you want?" said Azron, though he had already guessed the answer.

The lead mugger, bearing more scars and bulk than his comrades, flicked his dagger from hand to hand in an absent-minded kind of way. "We want what 'e's got in 'is pocket," he sneered, nodding toward Bip.

Bip rummaged around in his pocket for a while before producing a half-eaten corned beef sandwich. "This?" he suggested, hopefully.

Azron rolled his eyes. "I think perhaps they're referring to the huge lump of gold you were flaunting recklessly in the pub earlier, mate."

"Bingo!" said the head mugger.

Bip leaned toward Azron. "What's bingo?" he whispered.

"It's a game played by old ladies."

"Well what's that go to do with—"

"Never mind. What he's trying to say is, he wants your lump of gold."

"Well he can't have it," said Bip matter-of-factly. "I need it."

Azron looked at the five wickedly sharp daggers pointing in their direction. "You tell them that. I don't think they'll listen, mate."

"Sorry, chaps," said Bip, in a sincerely apologetic tone, "but I really need this lump of gold. It's the only one I have, you see? So you can't have it."

Azron smacked his hand over his eyes in horror and embarrassment. The muggers looked at one another in amused confusion.

"I think it's possible you don't fully understand the situation you're in, boy," said the mugger prime. "You either give us the gold or we stab you until you die. Or if you prefer the classic terminology, your money or your life. Understand?"

"Ah," said Bip. "Then I'm afraid you leave me no choice." With a sound like silk committing suicide, Bip drew Brian from his scabbard, flourishing the thin blade before him in the defensive stance he had been taught by Rynford.

Azron groaned heavily. "Are you mental?" he muttered.

"I thought you'd already made up your mind about that?" said Bip.

"Well, yeah, I knew you were mental but not *mental* mental. There's five of them and one of you. You don't stand a chance."

"He's right, you know," said one of the muggers helpfully.

Bip flourished his sword, spinning it around his head in a way he hoped looked vaguely masterful. "Yes, well. Did I mention I've been trained intensively by the finest Huntmaster of Kaneq?"

"No," said the lead mugger indifferently. "Now prepare to die slowly and painfully."

"Ah," said Bip, backing away from the advancing muggers. "That didn't go exactly as I planned."

"You tit," said Azron. "You complete and utter tit. You could have just given them the gold, but no, now we have to die. Nice one, mate, you're a real joy to be around."

"I was sort of hoping I could sort of bluff them," replied Bip. "It doesn't look like they're easily intimidated."

"No. You see large groups of thugs with knives rarely are intimidated. Especially by some kid with arms like twigs and a sword that looks like it was made for opening letters!"

"Well, there's no need to be rude about it," said Bip, reproachfully.

"We are going to die!" cried Azron. "I'll be as rude as I bloody well please!"

The thief and the traveler backed into a wall, cutting off any hope of escape. Much worse than being caught between a rock and a hard place, they were caught between a solid brick wall and several angry people with sharp implements. The muggers advanced with a horrible casualness, murder quite clearly shining in their eyes.

Bip thought quickly, his mind racing as he tried to remember his training. *What would Rynford do?* he thought to himself. *Probably something impressively acrobatic, then beat everyone to death with a stick. And then eat them, probably...*

Bip looked at the muggers, each of them at least twice as broad as he was. He might be able to fight one of them, but five was beyond the reaches of reason. This left Bip with only one real option—psyence.

Sheathing Brian back in his scabbard, Bip calmed his mind and tried to concentrate on the Fire Dance. The words of Glimton's teachings came back to him.

*You must calm your mind, be at one with your surroundings. Silence the voice in your head.*

*I said SILENCE IT, you pleb!*

His mind fully focused, Bip concentrated.

*Concentrated...*

# 14

# Goblins in Designer Jeans

Azron and Bip sat in the wagon they had "commandeered" from outside a shop back in Port Town. The city sprawled in the distance behind them as they made their way out to the grassy plains, pulled by a sturdy donkey with a *laissez faire* approach to life. They were on their way to see the goblins and were, so far, making good progress on the barely beaten track.

"That was good, that was, mate," said Azron, reflectively.

"I told you I don't want to talk about it," replied Bip.

"Yeah, but the way your hat just exploded like that…"

"Shut up."

"It was really impressive."

The wagon trundled along in the quiet afternoon. Somewhere a pigeon made a pigeon noise.

"And, of course, it scared the absolute crap out of those muggers," said Azron, eventually.

"Shh," said Bip.

"I've never seen grown men run so fast. Anyone would think they hadn't seen a chap's hat explode violently for no apparent reason before."

"…" said Bip.

"Shame, though," said Azron. "It was a nice hat."

Bip nodded his agreement. His traveling hat, which had contained many useful provisions, had been blown into smithereens when his latest psyentific escapade had gone massively askew. He had intended to scare off the muggers, granted, but exploding his hat had not been part of his plan.

"So how did you do it, then? Explode your hat, I mean? Magic, was it?" said Azron.

Bip frowned briefly, not recognizing the term. "It was psyence," he muttered.

"What, like chemicals and things?"

"Sort of," said Bip. "It's an innate ability to empathize with and persuade the energy fields and physical equations of objects on a molecular level."

"Ah, really? Thought as much," said Azron.

The wagon rolled along for a while, one of its axels squeaking with a chirpy rhythm.

"So what did all those words you just said mean, exactly?" said Azron.

"Well, in my case, it means I can explode things just by thinking about it," replied Bip.

"Sounds…useful?" said Azron.

"Oh yes," said Bip glumly. "The only drawback being that, more often than not, I don't actually want things to explode."

"So that hat thing…that was an accident?"

"In a word, yes. I had actually intended to launch a wave of fire at our assailants. Unfortunately, for reasons beyond me, I exploded my hat instead."

The wagon rolled along. Azron tried hard to conceal a smirk.

"So," he said, "do you always explode things when you don't mean to?"

"No," said Bip. "Sometimes I turn them into igloos. I can do igloos."

"Oh," said Azron. "Handy, I suppose…"

"Oh, yes. If you want something exploded or turned into an igloo, I'm the chap to talk to," said Bip.

"I'll bear that in mind."

Suddenly an arrow zipped through the air and thunked into the front of the wagon, narrowly missing Bip's knee.

"Looks like we're here," said Azron.

---

THE GOBLINS WERE AN UNUSUAL SPECIES—NOT quite human and not quite monster. They were often thin-limbed and spindly, with skin so pale it would hue into a faint green or blue. Their noses were uniformly bulbous, and their ears pointed far over the crests of their heads, which were cue-ball bald bar a tuft that grew at the very back of their craniums. This tuft was often grown as long as possible and plaited intricately, particularly with the females.

Though diminutive in stature, the goblins possessed a wiry strength and an innate viciousness. Their teeth grew to neat, foxlike points, and much of their skin was adorned with tattoos and body-piercings. The weapons they carried were crude, home-made affairs. Though, as Bip was quickly finding out, when someone points a bow and arrow at your face, quality of craftsmanship ceases to be a pressing concern.

"Whatyewantin?" said one of the three goblins that surrounded the wagon, its voice clipped and harsh.

"All right, chum?" said Azron, raising his hands to show he was unarmed, then fishing out his union certificate, showing it as a policeman might show a badge. "Come to talk to the big cheese, haven't I? King Chaff about, is he?"

"Yegotanappointmentthereboyo? said the goblin.

"No?" said Azron.

"S'alrightyedinnineedone," said the goblin. "Comeonthenwhatye-waitingfer? Writtneinvitation?" With that, the three goblins stomped off into the nearby woodland. Azron flicked the reins of the wagon and provoked the donkey into a slow trot. They began to follow the goblins.

"Did you understand a word of that?" said Bip, looking bewildered.

"Oh yeah, they speak good enough Imperial," said Azron. "They just speak very quickly. It's designed to throw people off when they're bargaining, see?"

The goblins strolled through the woodland at a casual pace verging on a saunter, while the wagon trundled easily behind. Eventually, the woodland cleared into a scrubby clearing where a large cluster of shoddily constructed caravans and animal-skin tents marked the current territory of the goblin tribe.

Many goblin children ran around shrieking aimlessly, dressed in dungarees or, seemingly, whatever clothes they had found lying around. Older goblins sat playing one-up on rickety tables, dressed in shiny suits that had probably fitted their original owners quite well. Here and there goblin women busied themselves seeing to the chores, which seemed to consist entirely of hitting their children with sticks until the chores were done.

The vibrancy and ruckus of King Chaff's tribal community came to a dead stop as the wagon pulled into the clearing. Every goblin man, woman, and child froze immediately, fixing the newcomers with mixed expressions of mistrust and appraisal. Then, almost as if they had never stopped, the goblins continued about their business with masterful nonchalance, only occasionally casting quick, beady glances over their shoulders at the strangers.

Something that struck Bip immediately was the amount of gold present around the campsite. Every goblin in view, from the smallest toddler to the frailest old man, was adorned with all manner of large and gaudy golden jewelry. From rings to necklaces, bracelets and earrings, every goblin seemed dressed up with more gold than Bip had ever seen in one place, let alone on one person. Without thinking, he nervously clutched at the gold nugget in his pocket.

"Don't worry about it," said Azron, leaning over conspiratorially. "It's not real gold they're wearing. They would have traded it ages ago if it was. It's only fake jewelry. It's a bit of a status symbol in goblin communities. They call it 'bling.' It's all for show, see?"

One of the escorts returned. "Y'alrighttherepal? Bigyin'llseeyeznow."

Bip and Azron stepped from the wagon and followed the escort to the largest of the caravans. Outside the door, two goblins serving as guards made a halfhearted show of vigilance. They made a point of glaring suspiciously at the newcomers for a while before they grudgingly waved them into the caravan.

The first thing Bip noticed as he entered the caravan was the smell, a dried in tang of mushroom and spice. It put him in mind of spoiled food and damp carpet. As his eyes adjusted to the gloom, what he had first assumed to be a mound of cushions gradually revealed its self to be a goblin of massive proportions. It was immediately clear that this was King Chaff, the goblin "Big Cheese". For a start he was so fat his shape gave the general impression of a water balloon with legs. The obese creature sat propped against a huge, overstuffed armchair and his body was adorned with more bling than Bip could have ever thought possible. Between the weight of his excess fat and the weight of his jewelry, Bip was surprised that King Chaff did not fall right though the floor of his caravan.

"Howyez," said the goblin king, his voice husky and slower than his comrades.

"All right, Mr. King?" said Azron, bowing low and motioning for Bip to do the same. As Bip bowed, he noticed an assorted pile of rotting animal bones at the King's feet, like a particularly revolting pouffe.

"YeztradingItakeit?" said the king. He pulled, from some unknown crevice, a large joint of greasy chicken, which he began to chomp on methodically. Bip tried to ignore the flip-flop sensation in his stomach. Watching the goblin eat was an experience he would try hard to forget.

"As a matter of fact, Your Largeness, yes, we are," replied Azron.

"Whatyezwant?" said King Chaff, chicken juice running down his many chins.

"We need airboat tickets to the mainland," said Azron.

The king paused mid-mastication and looked hard at Azron. For a moment, Bip thought the large goblin was simply going to laugh out loud, and part of him hoped that he would—the malodorous caravan and the king's upsetting eating habits were giving Bip a strong desire for fresher air. Instead, the king swallowed and said, "Naybother. Whatchoogotferme?"

Azron nudged Bip, who took the large lump of gold from his pocket. Even in the murkiness of the caravan, the nugget gleamed with an alluring light.

"Muchobling," gasped King Chaff.

"Yes indeedy," said the thief.

The fat goblin composed himself, his many chins wobbling as he shook his head. "Gizamotothinkaboutitwillye?" he said.

"Certainly, Your Obesity," said Azron. "We'll be outside, yeah?"

---

BIP SAT on the wagon watching a goblin child poke the donkey with a stick, an attitude of near-furious concentration on its face. The donkey took the aggressive curiosity with the same placid indifference as it took almost everything that life threw at it. Azron lay back in the weak sunshine, idly chewing on a piece of long grass.

"He seemed pretty impressed," said Bip after a while. "Do you think he'll trade the airboat tickets for the gold?"

"I shouldn't think so," said Azron. "Goblins hardly ever trade in cash."

"What? Then why did we even bother showing him it?" said Bip.

"I told you already, they respect bling. He probably wouldn't even consider trading with us if we didn't have a sufficient amount of bling about our persons."

"Then what will he want in exchange?" said Bip.

"Who knows?" said Azron, lazily. "It's difficult to tell. Could be they want a herd of cattle. Could be they want the still-beating heart of one of their enemies. Always a surprise when you deal with goblins."

Bip swallowed hard.

"Heymisterz!" The escort from earlier approached the wagon from across the campsite. "Thebigyin'smadeuphismind.Sezhewantstotrade."

"Nice one!" said Azron. "And what does he want?"

The goblin pulled Azron's coat until the lanky thief's head was level with its mouth and began whispering at length. Bip strained his ears trying to hear what was being said but couldn't. Eventually the goblin wandered off back to the campsite.

"The price has been set," said Azron, his voice flat.

"What do they want?" asked Bip.

"They want clothes," said Azron.

"Clothes? Is that all?"

"Not all. Not all exactly," said Azron. "They want a hundred pairs of designer jeans."

"Oh," said Bip. "And what are they, exactly?"

"Well, they're a form of denim trousers that are popular with construction workers and are now sought after by fashion-conscious men and women with too much time on their hands."

"Well, that doesn't seem too bad…" muttered Bip.

"Are you kidding, mate?" cried Azron. "Some of those jeans can sell for a couple of hundred spondulicks!"

"Why on Bersch would anyone pay that much for a pair of trousers?" said Bip.

"Well, it's like the goblins and their bling, yeah? It's a status symbol thing," explained Azron.

Bip took the lump of gold from his pocket. "Do you think we'll have enough?" he said glumly.

"Well, you would've had," said Azron, "but they want half the nugget as well."

"What?"

"As a gesture of goodwill."

"What?"

"Calm down, calm down! These are black market airboat tickets, mate, they don't grow on trees! There's security papers to be forged, false identities to be made. It all adds up, you know."

Bip sighed heavily. Just as things had seemed to be progressing, he had hit a seemingly insurmountable wall.

"Look, cheer up, mate," said Azron eventually. "This isn't as bad as it looks, yeah?"

"What do you mean?" said Bip.

"Have you forgotten?" Azron grinned. "I'm a Diamond Geezer, mate. First class! I've got contacts, I've got know-how." The thief wiggled his long, delicate digits. "I've got a five-finger discount as long as your arm!"

"You're not suggesting we steal, are you?" gasped Bip.

"Oh, yes, I bloody well am!"

---

HANDEN APPROACHED the shores of Blood River. It was everything he had expected. Thick mist rolled quietly about the dry reeds, and a wind like an urgent whisper blew through the dark leaves of the trees above. A cold, deathly feeling rolled in off the stock-still waters of the iron-gray river. Far off in the distance, the hazy form of the first of the Spine Islands loomed menacingly.

Handen sighed. He was growing tired of ominously evil locations.

To his left, an ancient horn hung from the branch of a crooked tree with wicked-looking carvings inscribed on its trunk. Handen didn't bother to attempt to translate the carvings; he merely grabbed the horn and blew hard. A sound like a sea-beast in mourning echoed across the grave landscape.

The former Hostilities Advisor waited, tapping his foot impatiently. The journey to the shores of Blood River should only have taken him a couple of months, but for a number of reasons (including damsels in distress, peasant rebellions, monster attacks, evil cults, lost tombs, and more adventures than he could even remember), it had taken him several years. It wasn't that time held much personal meaning for him anymore—and there was plenty of time until the end of the world—it was just that Handen was beginning to feel that the world was against him, that it didn't *want* to be saved. And so, having finally reached the only access point to the Spine Islands, and after summoning the Dread Ferryman of Blood River, Handen fumed quietly at yet another unnecessary delay.

A quiet ripple in the water heralded the approach of the ferry. A shadow began to form in the river mist, gradually revealing a black-cloaked figure on a rickety wooden raft, inching slowly toward the shore.

"What's your problem? Are you paid by the hour or something?" said Handen, when the ferryman had reached the shore.

"Sssilence, mortal," hissed the Dread Ferryman, as red eyes glowed like brimstone in the deep cowl that hid his face in shadow. He lifted a hand from the folds of his cloak to reveal fingers of bone underneath. Handen was unimpressed. He had seen plenty of animated skeletons in the past decade and was no longer surprised by them.

"If the River of Blood you wisssh to crosss, thou must anssswer me a riddle," said the Dread Ferryman.

"Couldn't I just give you some money?" said Handen. "I have money right here, look."

"A riddle," repeated the ferryman.

"Fine, then—tell me your bloody riddle," Handen growled.

The ferryman cleared his throat (though he needn't have bothered, being skeletal and all).

*"I am three full circles round,*
*But I am also like a square.*
*I am like to many things,*
*Yet nothing can compare.*
*I am divine as god blood,*
*I am as pure as snow.*
*I am unholy water,*
*I feed the laughing crow.*
*What am I?"*

The ferryman leaned back smugly as Handen frowned in concentration. "Ansswer true," he hissed. "And know that falsssehood meansss your doom."

The adventurer continued to frown into space.

"Like a square yet three full circles round?" he said, after a while.

"Yesss," answered the ferryman.

"As divine as god blood?"

"Yesss."

"You feed the laughing crow?"

"Yesss."

"I believe I have the answer," said Handen.

With an enormous right hook, Handen sent the Dread Ferryman

sprawling into the water. Before the creature could fully resurface, Handen jammed a boot down on the top of its skull.

"Now listen to me, you skeletal bastard," he said. "All this riddle crap might work for the tourists, but it doesn't hold water with me, right?"

"You can't say that!" wailed the ferryman.

"Shut up. Here's what's going to happen, right? You're going to give me a lift in your poxy little boat to the other side of this river, or I'm going to smash you into pieces and turn you into scrimshaw, understood?"

"Don't you know who I am?" screeched the skeletal ferryman.

Handen leaned down menacingly. "You know, the Wolf King of Uldale said exactly the same thing to me just before I stabbed him several times in the eye. And the Vampire Maiden of Duxbridge said something similar just before I kicked her into a bonfire. So go ahead, waste more of my time with idiot questions and see just how razor-thin my patience really is!"

The ferryman wisely kept his mandibles shut. He climbed back into the boat with as much dignity as he could muster and, with Handen as his passenger, began wading slowly out toward the Spine Islands.

Handen lay back in the ferry. "And row faster, for god's sake, some of us have got places to be."

He was in no mood for more delays.

---

BIP WAITED outside the Pig and Thistle Inn, huddled against a wall with an air of justified paranoia. It had been a good five hours since they'd arrived back in Port Town, most of which Bip had spent waiting outside pubs for Azron, who was doing something he called "networking."

So far, "networking" had consisted of getting steadily more drunk and chatting to various people who all looked as seedy as, if not seedier than, Azron himself.

It was dark now in Port Town, and though the streets were still crowded with people and the lamps had been lit at twilight, Bip was nevertheless unnerved by the city at night. He watched the shadows, nervously clutching Brian's hilt, too aware of what an easy target he was.

The Kaneqian nearly jumped out of his skin when Azron tapped him on the shoulder from behind.

"We're on," said Azron.

"What? On what?" said Bip. Then, "What took you so long?"

"Hey! Networking's a delicate business, mate—you've got to be careful who you're talking to. Get the right information without giving too much away, like."

"Well, what did you find out?" asked Bip.

"There's a delivery to Tony Topman's Clothing Shoppe at midnight tonight. A whole stagecoach filled with designer gear and more armed guards than most people can count."

Bip's heart sank. "I suppose robbing the stagecoach is out of the question, then. Will we have to steal from the shop itself?"

"Are you kidding? You don't break into one of Topman's places— the man's a psychopath! Undisputed don of the denim mafia! He's got more thugs on his payroll than I'd care to think about!" said Azron. "It'd be suicide to try to haul a load as large as the one we're after out of one of Topman's places."

"What do we do, then?" said Bip.

Azron grinned his crooked grin. "A good thief never tackles a problem head on. Not when he can go around it."

* * *

IT WAS a good living being a guard in Port Town. There was always demand for a decent guard in a place where even the things that were nailed down tended to be lifted. All you needed to be a successful guard was a sharp eye, about eight stone of excess muscle, and a ballistic attitude to anything that came too close to you.

Some of the best hired guards in the whole of Port Town marched in a ring of steel around the slowly advancing stagecoach, crossbows cocked and leveled, ready to fire.

Captain Burney "Easily Aggravated" Dogson sat atop the stagecoach, staring grimly into the shadows around him. Burney and his boys were being paid top whack to move clothing items that had recently become more valuable than gold. He had already had to break the fingers of one of his own men, who had tried to smuggle a netted cravat down his trousers. Burney didn't really understand the appeal of designer clothing, or why some people put such a high value on it, but his was not to reason why, his was but to mash people's fingers with hammers or occasionally shoot them in the face with a crossbow.

The stagecoach pulled up to the trade entrance of Tony Topman's Clothing Shoppe, and Burney jumped down to talk to the two guards who had slithered from the shadows like pictures appearing in an inkblot. They wore the usual attire of Topman's employees—dark hoods and black leather armor, tailored in whatever style was currently deemed to be "in."

"Papers to sign," said Burney, his voice as gruff as his appearance indicated. He held out a clipboard as the taller of the two guards approached. Burney noticed the shorter of the two hanging back. He squinted through the darkness.

"A bit short for a Topman guard, isn't he?" he said.

"I often find that size isn't everything," hissed the taller guard. "In fact, I often find that a couple of inches will suffice." The hooded guard nodded down at the slim and razor-looking dagger that had slid almost magically into his hand.

"Yeah, all right," said Burney. "No need to get shirty. If you just sign the papers, we'll supervise the loading and be on our way."

The Topman guard seemed to hesitate. "We don't need to be supervised," he said.

Burney frowned. "We've orders to make sure everything arrives on the premises safe and sound," he said.

"Orders have changed," said the guard. "Tony doesn't want any non-personnel on his property. We'll take care of the loading."

Burney looked around. He had expected more guards, and frankly, he had expected bigger guards, but he knew you didn't mess around with Tony's boys, who were all hired on the merit of their psychological instability.

"All right then, mate," said Burney. "Our work is done, then. You can tell your boss that we still expect the same pay regardless."

"He will be told," said the guard.

Burney shook his head and walked off back to the stagecoach, where the boxes of designer clothing were being stacked outside the loading gate.

The two sinister guards watched as Burney's men finished unloading and made their way back to their respective homes. Then one of the guards pulled back his hood.

"Well, that was close," said Azron.

# 15

# The Getaway

The Diamond Geezer (1st class) had made it seem like child's play. It had been, as Azron had pointed out, a matter of calling in favors. It turned out that there were a lot of people who owed Azron favors in Port Town.

The first favor he called in had been at Floyd's Pharmacy, where he had obtained several milligrams of something potent and odorless. The next favor had been with the runner boy at Haggie's Coffee House, who frequently received good business from Topman's guards. Then it had simply been a matter of cause and effect.

It had been the work of a minute to drag the drugged security guards out of sight and don the clothing of the smallest two. The rest had been a combination of bluff and luck. All in all, Azron had been pleased with the results. They had loaded up their wagon and made off with the designer gear with hurried nonchalance, ditching the guard uniforms at the earliest opportunity. It had been a cinch to get past the watchmen at the wagon gates, who were so frequently paid to look the other way that they spent most of their time with their noses against a wall.

Now Azron and Bip made their way back to King Chaff's camp across the post-midnight landscape, a fat and generous moon lighting the way, their trusty donkey ambling with all the urgency of a snail with nowhere to go. Azron smoked a victory cigarette, puffing gray clouds into the still night air.

"That went better than I expected," commented Bip.

"Explain," said Azron.

"Well, I thought that there'd be, you know, sneaking about in the shadows and hanging upside down from ceilings," said Bip.

"Nah," said Azron. "All that kerfuffle is for when you want to get something out of somewhere. All we did was stop something getting into somewhere."

"Oh," said Bip, and then after a while, "Still. You made it seem rather easy."

"Easy?" Azron clucked his tongue. "It was years of contacts and wheeling and dealing that allowed me to pull that job off in a hurry. Besides, it's not the doing it that's the hard part. It's the getting away with it."

"How do you mean?"

Azron dragged hard on his dwindling cigarette. "Do you really think it's going to take long for Tony to realize who's nicked his stuff?" he said. "I give it about three hours before he's got every snitch and hired knife in the whole of Port Town looking for me."

"What will you do?"

"Simple," said Azron. "I'm going to go to the Empire with you."

"But you'll need a ticket, surely?" said Bip.

"Already sorted. The deal I came to with King Chaff included two tickets."

Bip thought for a minute. A slow frown began to trickle across his forehead.

"Well, surely that means," he said, "that I could have afforded a single ticket with the money I had?"

"Oh, yes," said Azron, jetting smoke from his nostrils. "But I've always wanted to see Regalious. Things are getting a bit stale in Port Town, to tell you the truth. I want to go where there's more challenging prospects, like."

"You mean to say we just risked life and limb because you fancy a holiday?"

Calm down, mate. I got you your ticket, didn't I?"

"…" said Bip.

"Aw. You haven't gone in a mood with me, have you?" said Azron.

"…" said Bip.

"Cheer up. It could have been worse. Originally, I was planning to drug you, take all your possessions, and sell you to the orcen sailors as a slave."

"What?" screeched Bip.

"Hey! Calm down! I didn't do it, did I?" said Azron.

"Oh, really," huffed Bip sarcastically. "And what made you change your mind? Crisis of conscience?"

"No, don't be silly," said Azron. "Truth is, I like your style. You're a good kid, mate, and that's no lie. You being an out-of-towner and all got me thinking about foreign lands, see? And when you mentioned that you needed to get to the Empire…well, it just sort of inspired me."

Bip huffed and frowned at the floor.

"Besides," said Azron, "if the world really is ending, and you do manage to save it, you can remember your old pal Azron Bezron when it's time for the big fat rewards, yeah?"

***

PORT TOWN'S airdock was a frenzied affair. So large it warranted its own township, the airdock was home to thousands, whether they be dock-workers, shop-keeps, security, and hospital staff or merely the hundreds of travelers who spent a great deal of time in the soul-pounding limbo of flight delay. The airdock accommodated people from all walks of life.

On the outskirts of the terminals, lines of washing crisscrossed between tall, haphazard buildings, the crowded residential blocks that housed staff and their families. Shops and banks filled the gaps in the streets below, and jugglers and actors wandered throughout, preying on the boredom of the terminal-bound travelers. The terminally bored.

Port Town's airdock, so far, was the only one established in the

Free Countries. Consequently, the tide of travelers and goods flowing to and from the Empire was so large that the waiting list to board the few and far between airboats sometimes stretched to months. Port Town's was the only airdock on Bersch to have a family planning clinic.

The main runways and terminals of the airdock resembled normal shipping docks, laden with cargo and great queues of people huddled around the small balloon cranes that hauled people and products to the airboats above. Here and there, impassive staff explained the same things over and over to different red-faced travelers while an atmosphere of condensed headache stung the senses. Rows of uncomfortable chairs held hundreds of refugee-like boarders, all waiting for their departure time. Some, who could not afford accommodation in the area, had taken up camp.

The airboats hung above the port like honey-drunk bees, their large, bulbous hydrosacs swaying gently in the breezy altitude, creaking and swelling like a very fat person in a diving suit. The seemingly unplanned shapes of the dirigibles contrasted oddly with the rigid boxiness of the fuselages that were suspended beneath them, held sure by ropes, chains, and bolts. The airboats had a façade of fragility about them, the very improbability of their flight inviting the mind to consider calamity. It seemed that at any moment they could descend from the sky, their merry buoyancy reclaimed by gravity, their idle dream of flight coming, quite literally, down to earth. It was all too easy to imagine the airboats crashing hugely into the ground below, so delicate their levitation seemed.

Though they could lift a great deal, airboats could never move faster than a good stagecoach or clipper. Their primary advantage was that they rose far above pirates, bandits, and even storms. Hence, if you wanted to cross the Boiling Sea to Regalious, an airboat was your only option.

At one of the airdock's various loading stations, a wagon rolled into a zone marked, "No Parking," pulled by a donkey with other things on its mind. For a while, the canvas covering the rear of the wagon shook and bulged with unidentifiable activity and, after a time, a man hopped from the wagon and looked around shiftily.

The man was Azron, though you'd have to look twice to realize it. Gone were the long greasy coat and the peak-less woolen hat, replaced by finery fashionable with the richer gentlemen of the Empire. A gaudy blue waistcoat was worn baggy over a white shirt obviously tailored for a shorter man. Long black trousers didn't quite reach his ankles and shiny black shoes pinched his toes. The whole thing was pulled together with a silken red necktie that looked uncomfortable on Azron's bird-like neck. His lank hair was pulled and oiled into a precise center parting; perhaps the only part of the thief that wasn't crooked.

Azron, seeing that the coast was clear, motioned for the wagon's other occupant to come out from hiding. After a while, he motioned again.

"Look, are you coming or what?" he hissed.

"No," replied a muffled voice.

"Don't be silly!" Azron chided. "You knew we had to be in disguise!"

A man's head emerged from the wagon. On it were a women's wig, make-up, and a ribbon-laden hat.

"I don't see why I have to be the wife," said Bip, sharply.

"I already told you," replied Azron. "I'm allergic to lace."

Bip fully exited the wagon to reveal a long, flowing gown that engulfed most of the shorter man's frame. Oddly, with his pale features and light beard, Bip made a halfway convincing woman.

"You'll have to lose the specs," said Azron. "They don't go with your eye-shadow."

"Oh, shut up," Bip said testily. "I'm not taking my glasses off."

"Yeah, all right, keep your wig on."

"You're not funny."

"Who's trying to be funny? And will you try to keep your voice effeminate please?"

"Sod off."

The two interlopers walked calmly through the surging crowds of the airdock, all the while keeping an eye out for anyone who might be watching them suspiciously. The goblins had gone to the trouble of constructing new identities for Bip and Azron, but the skimpy disguises wouldn't fool anyone who was looking for them for long, and it wasn't just Tony's thugs they had to worry about—the grim faces of airdock security awaited at every turn.

Still more worrying was the overbearing presence of Imperial Regulators. These lawmen stood around in shadowy corners making no effort to hide their suspicious staring. Dressed entirely in gray, from their leather gloves to their neatly tailored overcoats and top hats, the Regulators drifted through the crowd like specters through fog. The Imperial agents had the right to detain and question anybody they thought suspicious and, being renowned for their brutality, were feared greatly on both sides of the Boiling Sea. Around their waists, they wore sturdy leather holsters where flintlock pistols rested with threatening readiness.

Bip had been horrified to learn what flintlocks actually were— devices designed entirely to explosively launch a piece of metal through a human target. ("I suppose it's like being stabbed," Azron had said. "Only less personal.") The possession of flintlocks or gunnery of any kind was rare in the Free Countries, and only Imperial agents were allowed to wear them openly in public. And wear them openly they did, flaunting their pistols with a boyish pride that certain psychologists would have a lot to say about. Bip watched the Regulators carefully, not liking the steely smirks they uniformly wore. Despite the elegance of their clothing, the Regulators had a thuggishness about them that rivaled the lowliest hoodlum. Bip knew instinctively that they were best avoided.

Arm in arm, Bip and Azron made their way to Passenger Terminal One, a terminal designed for the transportation of people with enough money to make the wheels of bureaucracy turn a little faster than usual. According to their papers, Bip and Azron were Mr. and Mrs. Cornwall Thatcher, wealthy landowners from somewhere called Panthalus who had property interests in the Free Countries. Bip was unsure of what had happened to the real Mr. and Mrs. Cornwall Thatcher, but was grateful for the expedience of departure their wealth and station was sure to grant. The two fugitives joined their designated departure queue, filled with elegantly dressed and comfortably fat men and women, all waiting to have their papers and tickets inspected by the boarding security staff.

"Just keep calm, dear," said Azron, noticing the way Bip glanced nervously around the terminal.

"Don't call me 'dear,'" Bip replied testily.

"Darling?"

"No! Sod off!"

A few of the other boarders in the queue, a wealthy looking family with snooty countenances, began to turn curious glances at the bickering couple. A fat lady directly behind them in the queue cleared her throat pompously.

"Now, now, pumpkin." Azron smirked. "Let's not cause a scene."

"You utter bastard," Bip mumbled.

"Sorry?"

"I said, 'Yes, dear,'" said Bip.

"That's more like it."

---

HANDEN STRIKE WALKED through the rock lands. His lips were papery from constant thirst and a film of sweat clung desperately to his brow. The heat was beginning to affect his thinking, he knew. He had been daydreaming, vividly imagining that he was still in chronostatic sleep, watching Bersch from the comfortable coolness of the *Sentinel*. As he watched, he had been able to see the progress he was making down on the planet surface, represented by a dotted red line that twisted and circled but never went straight. He had grown more and more frustrated watching the red line continuously diverting, until he'd snapped awake, remembering where he was. He had reached the fourth of the Spine Islands, which wasn't as rich and green as the first, but thankfully didn't contain as many ravenous alligator people.

So far, the island had been mostly barren wilderness: flat, baked, and eerily quiet and still under a wide, open sky. Not that Handen minded. He'd take eerily quiet over huge, roaring alligatormen any day. Despite the heat and thirst, he was presently happy with the latest island. There had been no monsters, no evil cults, and no damsels in distress for a good few days now. In fact, there had been no one at all. He was beginning to wonder if the island was uninhabited. He fervently hoped that it was.

"Excuse me," came a voice from behind him.

Handen groaned inwardly and turned around. Behind him stood a tall and pretty girl. Her skin was dark and her eyes bright. Her hair, a golden-brown, was short and fluffy in an attractive kind of way. She was wrapped against the barren winds in a blanket that concealed almost all of her body. She seemed slightly hunched, as though cold.

Handen searched the empty landscape, wondering where the girl could have come from and what she wanted. Judging by his past experiences, he felt that there were probably only two real options. "You're not a damsel in distress, are you?" he said wearily.

"Hardly," huffed the maiden and with a sudden shrug, dropped her blanket to the sandy floor, revealing her naked body underneath. For a moment, Handen thought the vision of beauty that stood before him was too good to be true. Then he realized that it was. The maiden had a heavenly body, with creamy skin that smoothed over a toned and marvelous torso peaked by soft, round breasts. The effect was marred slightly by the large talons that protruded where her forearms and feet should have been and the huge feathery wings that grew from her shoulder blades.

The girl was quite obviously a harpy: half woman and half bird of prey. Though he had never seen one before, Handen had heard of their reputation as fearsome hunters and merciless fighters. His libido had a brief and torrid struggle with his survival instincts, his gaze shifting ceaselessly from breast to talon. Eventually and predictably, the former Hostility Advisor's survival instinct proved stronger. He readied his hand at his whip and prepared for battle. And then paused. With a heavy weariness, he lowered his hand, allowing it to slump by his side with an indifferent shrug.

"You know what?" he said. "I'm tired. Damn tired of this. Seems I can't go anywhere without somebody wanting a piece of me. Well, you can find your fun elsewhere. I'm not interested."

The harpy opened her mouth to speak.

"No!" interrupted Handen.

"But—"

Handen flapped his hand dismissively. "Not interested. Goodbye."

The jaded adventurer walked off into the wilderness, muttering under his breath and kicking at the rocks under his feet.

The harpy watched him go, then sighed, flapping her wings absent-mindedly in the harsh wilderness breeze. Maybe she had been too upfront with the handsome stranger, but it was getting harder and harder to find a date on the Spine Islands, especially when everyone assumed you were a fearsome hunter and merciless fighter. Well, whatever. The stranger obviously hadn't been interested in chicks.

---

BIP AND AZRON moved slowly along the queue, the drudging progress of the passengers dictated by the various ineptitudes of the bored-looking boarding staff. An air of testiness saturated the atmosphere of the terminal. It seemed that even the more privileged airboat travelers had a difficult time surviving the sheer mundanity of flight delay.

It had been a long while since anyone in the queue had talked. The futility of complaint had been realized long ago, so now the terminal reverberated with the sound of hundreds of worn-out people breathing hard through their nostrils.

Suddenly, the relative silence was broken by the sharp clump of booted feet. Bip turned to notice a large contingent of men in black leather entering the terminal and fanning out amongst the crowds. He gulped. Topman's men had arrived.

Bip nudged Azron.

"I know," muttered Azron. He spoke without seeming to move his lips, staring straight ahead. "Keep calm and don't stare at them."

Bip tried hard not to look but couldn't help shifting his gaze to the figures in black who now wandered through the terminal. He saw one of the men talking to an Imperial Regulator, showing him a piece of paper with two sketches on it. Bip knew deep down that the sketches were of Azron and himself. He gulped again as one of the Regulators pointed in the direction of the boarding queue they were standing in.

The queue continued to move forward at its ponderous plod as Topman's guards began pacing the line, carefully examining the faces of the waiting passengers. If one of the guards were able to get a look at the two disguised fugitives, they would be recognized for sure.

Bip nudged Azron in the ribs again.

"I know," said the thief. "Stay calm and get ready to follow my lead."

The Diamond Geezer took a small glass phial from a pocket inside his waistcoat, and with his long, delicate fingers, began to unscrew the cap. When this was done, he put the flask behind his back and turned it upside down in one quick movement. Azron secreted the flask back in his waistcoat just as Bip noticed the large puddle of clear, oily liquid that now oozed on the floor directly behind them.

"Cooking oil," whispered Azron. "Very handy in the right circumstances."

The queue moved forward slowly, and Bip, with unusually clear foresight, thought of the fat lady directly behind them. Azron grabbed his arm and walked him hurriedly forward just as a piercing wail and thunderous crash erupted from behind them.

All eyes turned to the fat lady as she struggled on the suddenly slippery floor, roaring with furious humiliation, a whirl of heels and petticoat. Several staff ran over to assist the clamorous woman, and they themselves began sliding in the oily liquid as they endeavored to lift the large lady from the floor. The whole terminal, their minds starved of activity, began to watch the flurrying efforts to right the fallen woman with some interest. So distracted were they that no one, not even Topman's guards and the Imperial Regulators, noticed when Bip and Azron slipped in at the head of the queue. Azron placed their papers and tickets in front of the clerk. "Two for the 3:45 to the mainland, please," he said, chirpily. And it really was as simple as that.

# 16

# Mr. Random

Bip relaxed. The interior of the airboat was quite luxurious compared to the slapdash countenance of its exterior. Large, comfortable chairs stood in cozy rows down the length of the passenger compartment, while gorgeous flight attendants walked ceaselessly up and down the aisles in between. The constant hum of the engines that powered both the propulsion fans and the hydrosac were strangely lulling, and Bip felt his eyes grow heavier as the airboat floated softly into the sky.

He had felt a bit nervous about flying at first as they had risen up to the waiting airboat in one of the balloon cranes but had been soothed by constantly smiling flight attendants and a sky captain whose voice had exuded more confidence than you would have thought possible in one man. Besides, the alternative to boarding the airboat would have been staying in the boarding lounge, where Topman's guards would undoubtedly have found them. Bip had been more impressed than terrified when the airboat cast off. He had watched with interest as the airdock and Port Town had decreased in size until they became an unimportant speck on a vista of green.

Azron had put up a fuss when boarding, but only because someone had told him he wouldn't be able to smoke for the entire journey. His outrage had been subdued, however, when the Sky Captain had taken him aside and told him that unsupervised naked flame on an airboat could result in the explosive death of everyone on board.

They had, thankfully, been able to discard their disguises and don their normal clothes once they had reached the balloon cranes, so Bip was able to sit comfortably for the journey and drop his pantomimic pretense at femininity. And now they had been rolling along in the skies for some hours, looking down at roaring rivers suddenly tamed to thin, delicate lines and massive mountain ranges made fragile by perspective. After a long time, they had eventually reached the end of the Free Countries and floated over a sea that seemed to constantly shimmer and boil.

"It's the Boiling Sea," Azron said when Bip inquired. "It's the reason we have to travel by airboat. You'd be torn to pieces if you tried to sail through it."

Bip gazed down at the swirling currents, the raging storm calmed by distance. He felt oddly peaceful.

Two days passed, and the airboat was well over the Boiling Sea. Despite the comfort of the passenger deck and the access to the exercise deck (a large, empty room designed specifically for walking up and down in), the passengers were growing restless. Bip, however, was enjoying the quiet and was still quite thrilled by the miniature panorama that spread below. He allowed himself to lie back in his comfortable chair and loosen up. Next to him, Azron fidgeted in his sleep, his nicotine cravings affecting his dreams. Bip felt the world turn soft around him as the constant lull of the engines carried his consciousness away.

Suddenly he snapped awake. There was a subtle wrongness in the air that he couldn't quite put his finger on. He looked around the darkened passenger deck. He couldn't tell how long he had been sleeping, but the sunlight outside the window had left, and most of the passengers seemed to be asleep. The nagging feeling continued to gnaw at some part of his subconscious. It was a feeling that he had misplaced or forgotten something, or that something didn't quite fit right in the world. He felt as if he'd woken up in a nightmare.

His eyes flicking nervously from side to side, Bip searched around the passenger compartment, hoping to verify the source of his unease. It did not take him long to find it. Standing in one of the aisles was a figure that clearly did not belong in the passenger compartment, a spindly, jagged figure silhouetted against the dull cabin lamps. He wore a somber black suit with a thin bootlace tie, but these were the only things normal about the stranger. His face resembled a goblin's in shape, though his ears were shorter and more pointed, and his nose and chin were both long and sharp, flanked by eyes that were deep set and yellow. But what set him aside from anyone Bip had ever seen was the deep red tone of his skin and the two small but spiky-looking horns protruding from his forehead. The stranger was looking directly at him. He smiled, revealing a mouth full of razor-sharp metal teeth.

"You're a dream," murmured Bip.

The stranger's face twisted in irritation. "I thought we'd got past that last time?" he said, in a voice that was far more elegant than the features it came from. Bip frowned, wondering what the creature meant.

"You know, you really are a persistent little bugger," said the creature, looking at his nails in a distracted fashion. "I'd assumed that the yeti would finish you off, but no, you survive. Then you had the audacity to breeze through the Cold Ocean like it was the easiest thing in the world. And then—*then*—alone in one of the most dishonest cities on the planet, you completely fail to be killed by a murderous assailant. What will we do with you, ay?"

"Who are you?" said Bip.

"You can call me Mr. Random," said the creature. "Pleased to meet you. You and I are going to be seeing a lot more of each other from here on in."

Something about Mr. Random's voice was scratching at Bip's memory. "I've met you before, haven't I?" he said.

"Very observant," said Mr. Random.

"You were the seagull!" exclaimed Bip. A few of the passengers began to look in his direction. Somebody made a harsh *shhh* noise.

"Don't worry about them," said Mr. Random. "They can't see me.

Only you can see me, Bip." The creature began to walk toward the traveler.

"What do you want?" said Bip, a slight tremble in his voice betraying his bravado.

"Simple, Bippy-boy, simple. I want you to go home. Go home and forget all this saving the world business."

"I...I can't. I couldn't do that," said Bip.

The creature clucked its forked tongue. "You've been lucky so far, Bip, that's all. Lucky. Do you really think your luck will hold out?"

"I don't understand," said Bip. "Why would you want to stop me?"

Mr. Random looked at his nails again, pointy white stubs on the end of fiendishly long fingers. "You know how some people believe they have guardian angels, Bip?"

Bip nodded.

"Well, think of me as the exact opposite. Sort of an anti-guardian, if you like. It's my job to make sure that everything goes as badly as possible for you."

"What do you mean?" said Bip.

"Well, for instance, who do you think tipped off Tony's guards as to your whereabouts back at the airdock?"

"That was you?"

"Too right!" said Mr. Random. "A whisper here, a whisper there. You'd be surprised by what you can achieve."

Suddenly, realization gave Bip a swift kick to the head as he remembered something from his training days. "You!" he exclaimed. "You're one of the Discordance!"

The creature grinned its horrible metal grin. "Yes," it said. "And I'm warning you to turn back now." The creature leaned in over Bip until he could see a dull red glint in each yellow eye and smell burning meat on the creature's breath. "Turn back or die slow," it said.

"You don't scare me," said Bip (though a pressing need in his bladder was telling him differently). "You know what I think? I don't think you can even touch me! If you could hurt me yourself, you would have killed me by now."

Mr. Random stepped back and stared at Bip with a smirking

appraisal. "Yes, you're right—I can't touch you. But I don't need to, not when I can get others to do it for me."

As if on cue, a flight attendant began walking down the aisle, a tray of hot coffee in her hands and a cheery grin still plastered across her face despite the lateness of the hour.

Mr. Random waited until the attendant was walking past and whispered something in her ear. The flight attendant looked confused for a moment, then dropped the tray of coffee right in Bip's lap. Bip's screech awakened most of the passengers, who began looking about with muzzy alarm.

"Oh my gosh!" said the attendant. "I'm so sorry, sir—I don't know what happened!"

"It's okay," said Bip, through teeth clenched in pain. "It's okay, I'll be fine."

"I'll get you a towel," said the attendant, and ran off down the aisle.

"You see?" said Mr. Random, laughing. "The poor girl doesn't have an aggressive bone in her body, but it was the work of a second to get her to scald you."

Bip gritted his teeth against the stream of swear words that fought to get out of his mouth.

"Do yourself a favor, Bippy-boy," said Mr. Random. "Go back. Go back or die slow." Then the creature vanished with a pop.

"Utter, utter bastard!" screeched Bip.

"What?" said Azron, as he snapped out of his deep slumber.

---

MR. RANDOM FLOATED on the currents of the sky as he watched the airboat drift into the distance. In truth, he was worried by Bip's luck. Against Mr. Random's interference, people generally didn't make it very far at all, but Bip seemed to be holding strong. Still, there were plenty of hazards between here and the capital, and there were a million things that could go wrong. Mr. Random was here to make sure that each and every one of them did.

# 17

## Regalious

Situated on the seventh of the Spine Islands is a solitary mountain, a pile of precariously balanced stones set uneasily in the surrounding desert. From this distance, you might think a strong breeze could blow it over, so narrow the mountain seems against the flatness of the plains. And though it does seem to creak alarmingly in the dust storm that rages continuously below, the mountain has stood since the dawn of creation, a pinnacle of permanence in the shifting landscape around it. The very top of the mountain was perfectly flat, giving it a cue-like shape that had earned it the name Lightning Rod.

Atop the mountain, sitting cross-legged on a rock and lost in deep meditation, was a Mahrai warrior of the Thunder Tribe. His uniform of a ragged loincloth and a headdress made of various animal bones was his only barrier against the chill wind that whistled ceaselessly in the high altitude.

His name was DaoGryn, which in his tribal tongue translated as "wolf bringer of death," a fact that might have got a few drinks brought for him had he ever frequented any bars. DaoGryn was the greatest warrior his tribe had ever known, unbeatable in unarmed combat and fearless in the face of any danger. It was for this reason that the spirits had made him Guard of the Pass, the highest honor known to the Thunder Tribe. DaoGryn had accepted the honor willingly, though it meant his exile to the Lightning Rod, where he would spend the rest of his days guarding the knowledge of the Pass. He sat, as he sat every day, attuning his mind to the world around him. He had applied his war paint over his dark skin that morning, as he did every morning, even though he hadn't seen a soul in over three years. However, he knew beyond a shadow of a doubt that the one day he decided to forgo his war paint would be the one day when he'd have visitors. So, he sat atop the Lightning Rod, painted and ready, waiting for the day when someone would challenge the Pass.

DaoGryn's ears pricked at the sound of sliding stone, followed by a grunt and a thump. He turned to see a man haul himself over the mountain's edge and waited, allowing the stranger to get some of his breath back. The climb to the top of the Lightning Rod was a tough one, he knew. He had made the climb himself over three years ago. DaoGryn took a moment to study the newcomer. There was something unusual about the man's aura, something older than the man himself. Something that had been around. DaoGryn put aside his musings. There was only one true way to know somebody.

"You seek knowledge of the Pass," said the Mahrai.

"Yes," said the stranger.

"Then you know there is a test?"

"Yes," said the stranger.

"Tell me," said DaoGryn, "what is your name?"

"Is this part of the test?"

"No. That would be too easy." The Mahrai warrior grinned.

"My name is Handen Strike," said Handen.

"And I am DaoGryn, wolf bringer of death, chosen one and profound warrior, guardian of the knowledge of the Pass."

"Well, Mr. Pass," said Handen impatiently, "I believe you mentioned something about a test?"

DaoGryn smiled. "I think the test of mind is not your preferred path, yes? My feelings tell me you are a man of action."

"Your feelings tell you correctly."

"Then the test of the fist is more to your preference?"

"Damn straight," said Handen, cracking his knuckles loudly.

DaoGryn looked closely at the newcomer again, attuning his senses to the man's natural energies. Handen's aura was certainly unusual, bearing scars that didn't show on flesh, telling tales that Handen himself had never told. DaoGryn realized something in a flash, something he had only heard about in the fables of his elders.

"You have the curse of the hero about you," he said.

"Is that what they call it?" said Handen casually. "I thought it was just rotten luck." He rolled his neck, producing a series of loud popping noises. "Now are we going to fight or what?"

DaoGryn rose from his rock and studied the adventurer for a while. "Well, hero, your quest ends here," he said. "No one has ever beaten me."

"There's a first time for everything," replied Handen.

The Mahrai flexed and rotated his narrowly muscled shoulders. "Remove your weapons and prepare your soul."

DaoGryn watched as Handen first threw his whip and sword to the ground, then an assortment of weighted throwing knives and daggers, then a few clubs, chains and throwing darts, then a small war axe. Finally, he unstrapped a huge beasthunter crossbow from his back and threw it to the floor with a clang.

"Is that everything?" asked DaoGryn.

Handen looked thoughtful and shook his left boot. A few rogue throwing knives clattered to the ground.

"Let's do it," he said, easing his body into a ready position.

Without warning, DaoGryn seemed to explode into a whirlwind of fist and foot, launching attacks at Handen that even the quick-handed adventurer had trouble deflecting. Handen Strike quickly found himself on the defensive, blocking with arm and knee blows that were almost too quick for the eye. The Mahrai warrior seemed to defy gravity, landing blows with limbs that should have been supporting his weight, throwing punches from seemingly impossible angles. After a short while, DaoGryn landed his first proper hit, breaking Handen's guard with a sweeping kick and following through with a lightning back-knuckle. While Handen was temporarily stunned by the blow, the Mahrai followed the momentum of his spin and delivered a devastating double-fisted punch that sent the former

Hostilities Advisor staggering backward, nearly but not quite toppling to the ground.

Handen shook his head and readied his guard again, shifting his weight and stance slightly now he had some idea of his opponent's strength and speed—both far greater than he had anticipated.

With a blurry swiftness, DaoGryn flipped onto his hands and launched himself feet-first into an attack, legs whirring in a flurry of kicks as he arced through the air. Handen managed to roll his body backward, catching the last of DaoGryn's kicks in his palms and pushing the offending leg upward hard, hoping to put the warrior off balance. DaoGryn merely used the force of Handen's block to flip himself backward in midair, darting out with a swift kick at the apex of his flight, catching Handen with a weak but unexpected blow to the chin. Handen was surprised by the kick, but by no means felled. He launched from his crouching position and attacked before the Mahrai had time to erect a proper defense. Handen's bulkier frame lent him an advantage as he ploughed his fists into the smaller man's torso three times in blurred succession, forcing DaoGryn to shift his guard to ward off the blows. Handen was already one step ahead of the response, however, and landed a brutal head-butt on the warrior's nose. The unexpected force sent him sprawling backward.

The Mahrai looked momentarily shocked, wiping dumbly at the blood on his nose and then, as if remembering himself, he oiled smoothly back into his fighting stance. Handen waited for the attack. Though DaoGryn had regained his composure, Handen had seen the brief look of rage in his opponent's eye. He had a feeling the next attack would be more furious than anything he'd tried previously. He was right.

DaoGryn first flipped backward onto his hands, then sprang farther back onto a jutting rock. He had barely touched the rock with his feet when he was suddenly flying straight toward the adventurer, fist extended before him and a high battle cry erupting from his throat. But Handen had banked on an elaborate charge and, rather than defending, this time rolled forward toward the warrior. Handen used the momentum of his roll to launch himself upward fist first, catching the leaping Mahrai in the chest with a rising uppercut that was equal parts luck and skill. DaoGryn sailed through the air, his battle cry cut off with a surprised *whoof!* as the wind was forced from his lungs. He hit the ground hard but sprang immediately to his feet.

DaoGryn was furious. He had never in his adult life been knocked down by an opponent. He breathed heavily as he tried to dismiss the pain in his chest and face. Then, almost as if someone had hit some sort of switch in the warrior's body, he calmed and focused, his breathing returning to normal, a faraway look in his eye.

Handen watched and waited for the next attack. He grew increasingly uneasy as the Mahrai stared straight into nothingness, his features totally impassive. The air around the warrior began to shimmer, a light wind whipping around him. Dust from the mountaintop floor began to rise and sway in the personalized gale. The Mahrai fighter began to emit a low battle cry, its volume and intensity rising steadily.

Handen readied himself, sensing something deeper at work in his opponent's body than mere strength of muscle. He knew with dread certainty that the next attack would be the pinnacle of DaoGryn's skill. All he could do was hope he was strong enough and quick enough to defend against it. He dug his feet into the ground beneath him and held his arms out, ready for combat.

Without warning, thunder boomed in the air as DaoGryn's battle cry reached a crescendo, and with amazing speed, the warrior leaped through the air, dust exploding in his wake as he rocketed toward Handen. At the last possible second before impact, DaoGryn struck out with a devastating kick.

To Handen's credit, he did manage to block the kick, crossing his arms over his chest as the blow connected. Unfortunately, it wasn't enough. He heard a loud snap as one of his arms broke and felt the breath rocket from his lungs as the kick drove into his ribs. The sheer force of the attack sent him flying through the air and over the lip of the mountain. The wind whipped away his scream as he plummeted the countless feet to the rocks below. Then there was no sound but the whistle of the endless dust storms, gently but persistently eroding the base of the Lightning Rod. DaoGryn fell to his knees, his head spinning as oxygen flooded back into his body. He had put all his energy into his last attack and was now too weak to move.

He was relieved he had been able to beat the stranger, but also felt a brief sadness. The fight had been his greatest yet, and he thought it unlikely he would ever face an opponent as worthy as the one he had just defeated. Tomorrow he would return to his tribe, he thought, and take a well-deserved holiday. The Spirits could guard their own mystic knowledge for a change.

With great effort, the Mahrai warrior managed to stumble back to his rock. He returned to his meditation, thankful for the rest.

He meditated for some hours before his concentration was broken once again by the sound of sliding rock. He looked to the mountain lip with a growing sense of dread as first one gloved hand then the other grasped the edge. DaoGryn couldn't suppress a gasp of shock as Handen Strike pulled himself onto the mountaintop once more.

The adventurer stood before the warrior, breathing hard, a look of jaded fury in his eyes.

"I'll tell you what," said DaoGryn after a while, "why don't I just tell you about the Pass, yes?"

Handen nodded. "That would save some time."

"If you travel northeast from here, you'll come across a cave entrance by two large burra bushes. If you follow the cave through, turning left at every fork, you'll eventually get to the mainland."

Handen stood staring for a while. "That's it?" he said, after a time. "That's the knowledge of the Pass?"

The Mahrai shrugged.

"I climbed all the way up here so you could tell me about a bloody cave?" said Handen.

DaoGryn shrugged again. "It's the Pass," he said, simply. "I've just told you the knowledge of it."

Handen shook his head and began walking away.

"I should warn you, though, hero," DaoGryn called after him. "The Pass is home to beasts of demonic proportions and monsters born from the very heart of darkness."

The immortal turned to face the warrior, a cynical look on his face. "I think I'll be all right, don't you?" he said, then stepped off the edge of the mountain.

DaoGryn looked thoughtfully for a while at the space where Handen had been. He wasn't sure if he had won or lost the fight and eventually decided to chalk it up as a draw. After all, anyone who could fall off a mountain then climb back up and ask for directions couldn't really be classed as a typical opponent.

---

THERE WERE SMALLER piles of rocks at the bottom of the mountain, all quite unremarkable compared to the towering shape of the Lightning Rod, but each fairly impressive in its own way. Overall, it was a peaceful scene at the north side of the mountain's base, sheltered as it was from the sweltering sun and constant dust storms, silent in the hardpan desert.

The silence was broken by the faint sound of screaming, which grew louder and louder until it was cut off by an abrupt splat as the body of Handen Strike impacted with one of the aforementioned piles of rocks. There was a brief rain of blood followed by the silence the mountain base was accustomed to.

After about thirty minutes, the adventurer stood up and dusted himself down. All traces of having fallen five hundred feet onto some pointy rocks had vanished. The fall had been extremely painful, but Handen was in a hurry. He had taken far too long to cross the Spine Islands and, now that he had directions to the mainland, he had no intention of staying on the accursed islands any longer than he had to.

He was getting closer to his goal. He had faced more challenges and opponents than any one man should have to. He was going to let nothing stand in his way.

---

THE AIRBOAT SAILED FAR above the unvarying tantrum of the Boiling Sea, floating through the peaceful heights, lolling along with packs of lazy clouds like ancient herbivores. It passed over the aptly named

Spine Islands, a thin row of vertebrae linking the two continents in a tether of jagged lands. Finally, it reached the shores of the mainland—the continent of Regalious, the heart and home of the Empire.

Bip looked out of the window as the airboat descended, awestruck as once again geographical features expanded back into all-consuming realities rather than far-away dreams.

THE AIRBOAT LANDED JUST as dawn was breaking at Panthalus Airdock. To the east, the sky was a promising shade of turquoise, crisscrossed with thin strips of salmon-stained clouds. The dawn light was gray but not cold, and in the distance, it was possible to make out the towering white peaks of the nearby city of Panthalus.

Passing through the security checks once they had landed was far less of an ordeal than it had been in Port Town. Passengers milled around, awaiting coaches and trams that would take them into the city proper. They reveled in the fresh air and solid ground, glad to be away from the airboat they had been cooped up on for nearly three days. It was going to be a clear morning, warm and pleasant, a fresh welcome from a new land.

Azron smoked furiously, chaining to make up for days without nicotine. A look of deep satisfaction smoothed over the thief's sharp features.

Bip sat on his rucksack, a faint grin hanging delicately beneath his nose as he surveyed the new continent. He felt a real sense of progress about his journey and was pleased to be preparing for travel again. With Brian by his side and sturdy walking boots comfortable on his feet, Bip was feeling an excitement he hadn't experienced since first leaving Kaneq. He missed his hat, though. Even though this new climate had forced him to abandon many of his overcoats, he still felt insecure without his traveling hat.

He lifted his head and breathed deeply of the clear dawn air. He noticed that Azron was doing the same, though a cigarette filtered the process somewhat.

"Where to next, do you think?" said Bip.

Azron was looking out over the horizon. "I think your best bet is the city, mate. Plenty of people there. You can start finding out things, build up some contacts, make your way east to the capital from city to city, like." He blew a small river of cigarette smoke into the cool dawn.

"Okay, then," said Bip. "We'll just hop onto one of those trams, then. There should be one fairly soon."

Azron turned to look at his accomplice. "No 'we' about it, guv. I'm heading south for smaller towns, see how things work around here, get my bearings and work my way up, sort of thing."

Bip gaped momentarily. "You're not coming with me?" he said.

"Sorry, buddy. It's been a blast and all, but it looks like this is where we part company. Different paths and the like, you know."

Bip couldn't help but feel a little downcast. "I was hoping you'd be coming with me. I need all the help I can get."

Azron laughed. "You'll be fine, mate. You survived Port Town, didn't you? Everything from here on in should be a piece of cake."

"Well," said Bip, "I still wish you were coming with me."

Azron turned back to the distant horizon, the look of a die-hard opportunist in his eye. "It's a wide old world, buddy," he said, "but things have a way of working out, you know? I wouldn't be too surprised if we bumped into each other again."

"So this is goodbye, then?" said Bip.

"Not so much goodbye as...see you later," said Azron, and began walking away. He stopped suddenly. "Oh yeah," he muttered, and began rummaging through the pockets of his long coat. From them he pulled a bag of acorns, a bottle of spiritl and a corned beef sandwich. "These belong to you." He grinned.

Bip floundered briefly. "How did you...?"

"Nicked them, didn't I? Nothing personal, mate—it's just what I do. I'm a Diamond Geezer, remember?"

"Yeah. I suppose," said Bip.

"Remember, mate," said the thief, "mugs and muggers, yeah? Don't be a mug." With that, he patted Bip on the cheek and walked into the distance.

Bip watched him go until he was quite far away. Then Azron turned as if remembering something.

"Good luck with saving the world, by the way!" he called.

Bip waved and watched as his only friend in this wide new world disappeared over the horizon.

---

HANDEN WAITED in the Imperial waiting room, freshly shaved, a ton of road dirt scrubbed from his body, his hair pulled into a severe parting. He stood bolt upright, attired in the finest clothes he had been able to afford. On the wall, a mechanical timepiece, the most intricate piece of technology Handen had seen in centuries, ticked and tocked with graceful formality.

A stiff-necked attendant peered around the chamber door.

"The Emperor will see you shortly," he said.

Handen nodded. He had come halfway across the world. He had traveled for years and fought longer and harder than any man he had heard of. Finally, he had reached his goal. It had taken months of long waits and constant cajoling but, at last, he had been granted an audience with the most powerful man on Bersch.

The jaded adventurer felt his first rush of true excitement for decades. He knew, deep down, that his mission was almost complete.

---

AND NOW, once again, adjust your perspective. Leave the young man boarding his tram, alone but determined, his delicate chin set firmly as he heads through yet another unknown world. Leave the immortal adventurer who, jaded as he is, still has his mission and his hope. Leave the thief in a foreign land, seeking new and interesting things to steal. Leave an Emperor sitting on a throne of madness, dark whisperings echoing through a twisted consciousness. Readjust your perspective as the cities and countries dwindle and merge and continents blur into oceans. This is the planet of Bersch. Take a good look. It might not be here much longer.

---

To Be Continued in The Chained Immortal -
Book 2 of The Doomsayer Journeys.
Available Now from Falstaff Books.

---

If you enjoyed this book and would like to be notified of new releases,
appearances, and everything else related to Steve Wetherell, sign up
for the newsletter here -
http://eepurl.com/cv5FSj

---

## Acknowledgments

Special thanks to Rebecca Hill for editing the initial publication of this book, and to Graham White for the original cover art.

# The Chained Immortal

BOOK TWO OF THE DOOMSAYER
JOURNEYS

"And I looked unto the skies, and I saweth a cloud, and the cloud did look suspiciously like a frog, but with hair, and verily I knew that the end was upon us, for are not hairy frogs traditionally regarded as harbingers of despair? No? Well who asked you? Nobody, that's who. Get out."

-From the Chronicles of Celia Doom

# 1

# Hope and the Lack Thereof

The planet Bersch. Named long ago by an egotistical and opportunistic astronomer. Home of a hodgepodge of sentient beings, some of them more and some of them less than human. Also the home of the Clarions, an ancient race sent to guide and protect those less developed than themselves, but unfortunately stranded for the last thousand years after a remarkable set of coincidences saw them crash land on Bersch's northernmost continent.

Bersch spins in the orbit of its sun as it always has, unaware that somewhere in the inky folds of space a ball of nuclear refuse is heading toward it with all the easy grace of a cataclysm.

Only a select few know that in less than a year pretty much everything is going to explode. Unfortunately, these are the same people who have been stranded on the Ice Plains for the better part of a millennium. Near the village of Kaneq—a settlement protected from the elements by an invisible wall of heat—lies a building long since buried under tons of snow. It is the *Sentinel,* a star-faring ship of the Clarions, now a tomb for ancient knowledge and baffling relics known to the locals simply as the Dome. The elders and councilmen of Kaneq meet there now, because the first thing any sensible species does in the presence of disaster is form a committee.

Dunman, Kaneq's mayor, wrung his hands nervously and smoothed down his already smooth hair. He had been doing this a lot more than usual lately and was starting to wear a bald patch on his scalp. "It's not that I don't have faith in the boy, Truggle," he said. "It's just that I for one would feel a lot safer if we had a contingency plan."

Truggle, eldest of the elders, peered out through the fog of his pipe smoke. "And is this how the rest of you feel?" he said.

The elders and higher council of Kaneq were gathered around a table in the bowels of the Dome. The weekly meeting was more urgent and uncomfortable than usual.

Tenbon, a senior elder, cleared her throat. "Sorry, Truggle, it's just that there are better men I can think of than Bip to pin the fate of the world on. He's not the man his father was."

Truggle puffed mechanically at his pipe. "I remind you, he has been trained by the best," he said.

All eyes in the room turned to Rynford and Glimton.

"Don't look at me," said Glimton. "I told you all he was a talentless pleb from the start."

"And you, Rynford?" said Truggle. Rynford scratched uncomfortably at his muscular neck. "I've trained better hunters..." he conceded.

"You see?" said Dunman.

"Pah!" said Truggle. "It's nice to see how much faith in my judgement you lot really have."

Tenbon sighed. "It's true that we don't all share your faith in Bip, Truggle," she said. "But can you blame us? This is our last chance, our last volunteer. The astral disaster strikes in less than a year, and we barely have time to select more volunteers as it is!"

"Then what do you suggest?" said Truggle.

Tenbon looked around at the other elders. "We thought that maybe a large party of volunteers, all the young men and women of the village, would stand a better chance."

Truggle puffed on his pipe, looking accusingly around the room. "You'd risk the lives of an entire generation?"

"Dammit, Truggle! We're talking about the end of the world, here! The destruction of the planet! I'd sacrifice the entire village if I had to!"

The room was silent. Truggle looked slowly from face to face. "Give me time, ladies and gentlemen. Have a little faith in me, won't you?"

Various people in the room shifted uncomfortably, unsure of where to place their loyalties.

Dunman spoke up. "But what makes you so sure that the Plunkerton boy is the man for the job, Truggle?"

"Instinct. Wisdom."

Tenbon clucked her tongue. "Thin hooks to hang the fate of a world on, my friend."

Truggle looked sadly about the room. "Then, elders, council members, I am afraid I have no choice but to dismiss myself from this meeting. Good day."

Using the broom he always carried, Truggle rowed himself out of the room on his rickety wheelchair. The remaining people looked uncomfortably at the walls and ceiling, avoiding one another's eyes. After a while, Rynford let out a frustrated sigh, slapped his massive hands on the table and left the room.

"Anyone else?" said Tenbon. No one moved.

---

TRUGGLE ROWED himself far into the deepest corridors of the Dome, down into sectors that had been long forgotten or long since abandoned. The axels of his wheelchair squeaked eerily in the gloom. He reached a seemingly blank wall and tapped it in three distinct places with his broom. A large panel slid aside to reveal a row of numbers counting steadily downward, blinking energetically in the stillness of the lower levels.

"Instinct. Wisdom." The old man grinned mirthlessly.

---

THE CITY OF PANTHALUS, though the farthest settlement from the Empire's cultural heart of Argustin, was known throughout Regalious for its stunning architecture. Traveling down the long, straight road, through the flat farmlands that surrounded it, the city seemed like some dreamer's hobby model rather than a place where people lived. It stood atop a grassy hill, white and shining and crowned by a great palace that stood like an oversized stone set in an already beautiful ring. Flags of all colors flapped lazily in the gentle morning air.

In the clear sunshine, Panthalus gleamed like a fairytale.

Of course, the reality of the fair city was far grimmer on closer inspection. High taxes for city beatification meant people had to work long and hard—and those who could not keep up were often forced onto the streets. Also, surrounded by farmland as it was, living space in Panthalus was scarce enough without residential areas being cleared out for botanical gardens and huge, ornate reflecting pools. Hence, in the alleyways and byways of the clean, white city, hiding behind Panthalus's thin veil of beauty, a whole subculture of derelicts and unfortunates massed like woodworm.

Those who could afford to live well in Panthalus lived very well indeed. Those who couldn't froze quietly in the winter, huddled under floral clocks and marble arches.

Of course Bip, like most tourists, was oblivious to this as he entered the massive and beautifully wrought city gates. So distracted was he by the towering, gleaming buildings and the careful mosaic of the paving slabs that he didn't notice the beggars being ushered violently from the streets and the jaded look of the shattered workers making their way to and from their homes. Bip spent most of his time with his neck craned upward as he traveled on the horse-drawn tram around the city, marveling at the various works of art that punctuated the streets.

The place was very different from Port Town. Though the crowds were of similar magnitude, the hubbub therein wasn't reinforced by the shouts of merchants and the screaming laughter of whores. In fact, the noise of Panthalus was a polite murmur in comparison to the aural brawl of Port Town.

The level of technological advancement was also significantly different from what Bip had seen in the Free Countries. In Panthalus, it was not uncommon to see horseless trams, driven by internal engines that ran on fuel, chugging along and spewing smoke rhythmically into the air. Bip had heard about such things but never seen one before. In Port Town, the only engine-powered devices had been the Imperially-controlled airboats.

One thing that particularly drew Bip's attention was the number of statues erected in the city. Not that the number of statues was unexpected in the heavily-decorated province—what was unusual was that all of the statues seemed to be of the same figure. From the oldest bronze castings to the newest marble renditions, the same crowned figure stood throughout the city, sometimes looking speculatively over the horizon, sometimes flourishing a mighty sword, sometimes crouched in deep thought. Leaning over, Bip tapped the tram driver on the shoulder. The driver, a thickset man with a heavily oiled moustache, turned around, shaken from whatever daydream was occupying his mind.

"Can I help, sir?" he said.

"Yes, actually," said Bip. "I was just wondering who the statue chap was. You know, the chap in all the statues?"

The driver looked around as they passed yet another towering likeness of the much-rendered figure. "Why, that's Emperor Draegul, sir," he said.

"What, all of them?" said Bip, frowning.

"Oh, yes," said the driver. "And no. They're not all the same person, but they are all Emperor Draegul, you see." The driver pointed at a few distant statues. "That there is Emperor Draegul the Seventh—they called him Draegul the Incredibly Fair and Kind. And that one there is Draegul the Fourth, Draegul the Most Generous and Not At All Evil in Any Way Whatsoever."

Bip squinted through his glasses at the statues. They all looked more or less identical, bar their differing poses.

"There's a strong family resemblance," said the driver, guessing at Bip's confusion.

"So is there a Draegul on the throne today?" said Bip.

"Oh, yes," said the driver. "Emperor Tomberry Torrid Draegul the Tenth—Draegul the Really Nice Guy Once You Get to Know Him."

Bip looked up at another of the statues, this one holding the hand of a weeping child. "This Emperor Draegul, he must be a very popular man?" asked Bip.

The driver turned to look at him, a look of mistrustful cynicism in his eye. "Oh, yes," he said. "Extremely popular. Very popular indeed." The driver turned back to the road ahead, muttering something that sounded a bit like "bloody tourists," though Bip couldn't be sure.

Suddenly, something else about the streets of Panthalus caught Bip's eye—that of the presence of the Imperial Regulators, their gray top hats bobbing through the crowds like so many shark fins. Bip had a stomach-churning moment of paranoia. Something told him that thieves weren't welcome in Panthalus, and he didn't think it wholly improbable that his and Azron's descriptions had been passed on from the Free Countries via telegram. And even if that wasn't the case, Bip thought it safer to find a place where there were as few of the lurking enforcers around as possible.

Once again, he wished that Azron hadn't decided to go his own way. The lanky thief had always seemed to know what to do in these kinds of situations. Thinking quickly, Bip hopped off the tram as it slowed for a corner and stumbled into an alleyway discreetly disguised by carefully grown wallflowers. It was there that he found his first clue to the harsher underlying reality of life in Panthalus. The alleyway, as with all alleyways across the ultraverse, smelt strongly of urine.

Bip continued to follow the foul-smelling passageway as it twisted into a network of smaller roads and underpasses. There were no works of art here, no statues, and no fountains. There was just dankness, the sound of faraway coughing the only thing breaking the thick, wet silence. Occasionally Bip would run afoul of other people traveling the alleyways. These people didn't have the well-scrubbed appearance of the citizens in the city squares. They were dirtier, harder-looking people who glared suspiciously as he passed.

Walking for some immeasurable period of time, he began to feel worried as the sounds of the street faded completely, as if he had inadvertently entered another world. He couldn't hold his sigh of relief when, on the cusp of hearing, he detected the now-familiar sounds of city commerce. Following the promise of bustle, Bip eventually made his way through the winding backstreets and into a wide-open clearing.

Like all cities, Panthalus contained elements that, while not aesthetically pleasing, were essential for its day-to-day running. Sweatshops, tanners, thrift shops, and abattoirs were all needed in Panthalus, but didn't quite fit in with the specialist coffee shops and frilly tailors of the high streets. For this reason, at the rear end of the city, Grub Street had been tucked away like an embarrassing elderly relative. Bip breathed in a familiar odor as the city's bottom classes brushed and pushed past him. He heard the booming shouts of market vendors as they plied their wares—most definitely not the souvenir pots and woven place mats of the high street markets. The whole street seemed a lot more like Port Town than Panthalus, and Bip lowered a weary hand to the pommel of Brian, his trusty and as-yet-unused sword.

There seemed to be no presence of the Imperial Regulators in the swept-under sub-city of Grub Street. Perhaps because of this, the people there were louder, more boisterous, and ultimately less polite than the people of the city center. Bip flinched as, nearby, two drunken tramps began a fistfight over some unapparent difference of opinion. Bip walked away, wandering through the scrum, still slightly overawed by the hectic nature of civilization outside Kaneq, as conmen conned and hustlers hustled around him.

His attention was drawn, suddenly, by a shrill shouting that carried over the general hubbub of the street. As he made his way through the crowds, it became apparent that there was a smaller, tightly packed sub-crowd that seemed to be devoting its attention to a number of people who stood on podiums. All the people on the podiums were shouting loudly, some about politics, others about religion, some were just shouting in that random, raving way that utterly mad people shout in.

The onlookers stood with a casual interest. Some occasionally shouted back, but mostly the crowds just watched with the attitude of people with nothing else on their immediate schedules.

A large, tattered banner above the podiums read, "Speakers' Corner."

Bip pushed his way into one of the biggest audiences, where a fiery young woman with a muddy face and ruffled blond hair stood atop a podium and shouted about something with unbending zeal. The people on the neighboring podiums had given up their own personal rants to listen to the shrill, hard voice of the young speaker.

Bip tugged at the sleeve of one of the audience members. The man reluctantly looked away from the show and down at Bip.

"What do you want?" he said, natural pugnacity bending his brow.

"I was wondering if you could tell me what's going on," said Bip.

The man relaxed a bit. "That's Celia Doom," he said, pointing at the young woman on the podium. "She's off her rocker, but she puts on a bloody good show." Bip strained his ears to make out what Celia was saying.

"...and lo, with great terror, there will be a bending of the trees and a tearing of the sky, and huge balls of fire will engulf the innocent and the guilty alike. And yea, with unswerving scariness and general ill feeling, there will be rains of hard-boiled sweets that have already been sucked, and gigantic dogs will dig up the gardens of the unwary..."

"What's she going on about?" said Bip.

"End of the world again," said the man. "Others may try it, but Celia's the best. If you want a good yarn about the coming apocalypse, then Celia's your girl."

Bip listened again, concentrating on Celia's wavering shrieks as she swung her hands through the air.

"...and people will look unto the skies and cry, 'Why? Why, oh why is this happening?' And the skies will reply, indeed, in a voice with much triteness, 'Because!' And the people will snap their fingers and say, 'Bugger!'..."

"Excuse me?"

"...and then, with great rains of treacle and terrible custard..."

"Hello?"

"...giant fish in all manner of horrible colors, verily..."

"*Excuse me!*"

The crowd fell into dead silence and cleared a space for Bip.

Everybody watched him expectantly. Celia, frozen mid-gesture, looked down at the traveler from her podium.

"Yes?" she said.

"Well, I was just wondering," said Bip. "When is the end of the world going to happen, exactly?"

Celia rolled her eyes back in her head and lifted her hands to the sky. "Lo, when the wolf head licks at the dawn and the prices of fuel rise by a seemingly unfair amount!"

Bip blinked. "And when is that, exactly? "

"In about six weeks time...lo," said Celia.

"Oh," said Bip.

"Is there a problem with that?" Celia said testily. "Only I've got a rant to be getting on with, you know."

"Well. Sorry. But..." Bip hesitated. He had the full attention of the crowd. He had originally planned to take his warning straight to the Emperor, but, as Azron had said, it might be a good idea to build up a reputation first. Take it city by city. He took a deep breath. "Well, you see, the thing is, the end of the world probably isn't going to happen for at least another ten months. Maybe a bit less."

The crowd remained deathly silent. Celia tapped her bare foot impatiently.

"Oh, really," she said. "Well perhaps you'd like to come up here and tell us all about it yourself if you're so bloody well-informed!"

The crowd murmured its approval, and before he could protest, Bip was manhandled onto the shoddy stage. He stood before the audience. Virtually the entire crowd at Speakers' Corner was watching him now. Even the mad speakers were looking on with an amused interest.

"Not as easy as it looks, is it?" whispered Celia smugly.

"Um..." said Bip.

"Get on with it!" shouted someone.

"Yeah, either rant or sod off!" said another.

Bip took a deep breath. It was going to have to be now or never.

"Lo..." he said, then he told the story of Kaneq, the Clarions, the Volunteers, and the huge astral disaster that was heading for Bersch in roughly ten months. When he finished, the crowd stood silently, their expressions unreadable.

"Um...verily," said Bip, lamely.

The crowd remained silent until, with great deliberation, Celia stepped back onto the platform. To Bip's surprise, she turned to the crowd and held her hand in the air.

"All hail he who has been delivered by the ancient ones to foretell our coming doom! All hail the Prophet!"

The crowd roared its approval and began shaking their fists rhythmically in the air.

"*Hail! Hail! Hail!*"

"I'm sorry?" said Bip.

"*Hail!*"

"What...?"

"*Hail!*"

"I don't understand!"

Celia, who had fallen to her knees, looked up. "We are at your command, Prophet. Lead us in our hour of need!"

"Eh?"

"What would you have us do, master?"

Bip thought. "Well," he said, "I suppose you could sort of, I dunno, warn people? Warn people about the end of the world? It'd make my job a bit easier, to tell the truth."

Celia turned to the crowd once more. "You heard the wisdom of the Prophet. Go forth and spread the word! Tell the people of the coming doom! Tell them the Prophet has foretold!"

"Yeah, something like that," said Bip.

With a zealous roar, the crowd dispersed in all directions, and Bip was eventually left alone on the podium. He couldn't help feeling smug. He had, in effect, put into motion his mission to warn Bersch of the upcoming disaster. It wasn't the way he had intended to do it, but he didn't see what harm it could do to have other people spreading the word around.

He turned and began to walk down the street, feeling more optimistic than ever before. This sense of optimism stayed with him right up until a gloved hand attached to a burly arm reached out of an alleyway and dragged him inside. Bip had just enough time to recognize the gray top hat and overcoat of a Regulator before a truncheon hit him hard on the head.

As the world span rapidly and the street cobbles suddenly lay vertically rather than horizontally, Bip heard a gruff voice say, "You're under arrest, sunshine."

Then the world tuned out and all that was left was black.

# 2

# Prisoner. Coincidence. Escape

**B**ip waited until the blur before him gradually turned into the face of the Imperial Regulator who had struck him, then he wished he hadn't bothered. The Regulator had the cruel features synonymous with his profession, but they extruded from an ill-shaven face framed by long ragged hair that fought bravely against the neatness of the Imperial uniform. The Regulator grinned, revealing a row of wooden teeth and a stench like some dead, forgotten thing.

"Wakey, wakey! Rise and shine!" he said.

"Oh good god, no," groaned Bip. He tried to lift a hand to the throbbing pulse on his forehead but was hindered by something heavy and clinking. He looked down at the sturdy-looking chains around his wrists and ankles. "What's going on?" he muttered.

"He wants to know what's going on." The Regulator guffawed pompously, looking around as if sharing a joke with a large group of friends. "What's going on? What's going on is that you're going down, me old matey!"

"I'm sorry, what?" said Bip.

The Regulator put on a falsetto voice and fluttered his eyelashes in what was supposedly a parody of Bip. "I'm sorry, I'm sorry!" he said. "God, your kind make me sick!"

"I have no clue what you're trying to tell me," said Bip, squinting from the pain in his head.

"You're going down, matey. Up the river! Taking the long walk!"

Bip frowned. In his muzzy state, a long walk by a river seemed quite a nice idea at the moment. "Wait a minute…" he said. "Are you trying to tell me I've been arrested?"

"Ho! College boy, eh?" said the Regulator. "You're damn tooting you've been arrested. Why do you think you're in the court house?" he said, gesturing at their surroundings.

Bip looked around. He and the Regulator were sitting in a long, poorly lit corridor, featureless bar the narrow bench they were sitting on. Down the corridor a few more unfortunates sat chained next to some other Regulators.

"Why, exactly, am I in a court house?" said Bip.

"Cuz you've been arrested, idiot!" said the Regulator.

"Yes, but, why have I been arrested?" said Bip testily.

"Oh ho!" said the Regulator, looking around, sharing the joke with his invisible friends again. "Questioning me, eh? Questioning authority? I've a good mind to give you another bump on the noggin, so I have!" He waved his gray, leather-wrapped truncheon under Bip's nose to emphasize the point.

Bip groaned as a gurgle of nausea erupted from his stomach. His head rang ceaselessly. He realized suddenly that his pack and sword were missing.

"Where are my things?" he said.

"Detained," said the Regulator. "Detained until you're found guilty. Then they'll be detained some more."

"But what If I'm found innocent?" said Bip.

"Pfft," said the Regulator and shook his head, his wide, wooden grin gleaming wetly.

Suddenly, the heavy double doors at the end of the corridor opened with a low whine. A court clerk, thin and bewigged, stood silhouetted in the doorway, peering into the dimly lit corridor.

"P.C Blungkit?" he called, squinting his eyes.

The Regulator with the wooden teeth got to his feet and dragged Bip with him. "The magistrate will see you now," said the clerk.

"Brilliant," said Blungkit, and dragged Bip down the corridor.

"Don't try to escape or I'll shoot you in the leg," he muttered as they approached the double doors, patting the pistola that rested ready on his hip. "Then I'll shoot you in the face," he added.

Bip gulped and jogged to keep up with the burly Regulator's long stride.

The courtroom, unlike the corridor leading to it, was well-decorated and spacious, lit by large windows that stretched all the way up to the high ceiling. At the far end of the room, a statue of a now-familiar figure stood blindfolded, holding a pair of scales. One of the statue's hands was lifting the blindfold slightly, allowing a stone eye to peep out from beneath.

On a large wooden pulpit, three magistrates in identical curly gray wigs and black robes sat and watched as P.C Blungkit dragged Bip before them.

"Patrol Constable Blungkit reporting, yer honors," said the Regulator.

"Oh, very good," said the central wigged man, his words heavy with disinterest. "And what is the charge?"

"Disruption of the City's Peace, Causing Public Affray and Conspiracy to Overthrow the Government, yer honor," said Blungkit.

"Now wait a bloody minute!" said Bip.

"The defendant will wait until addressed before speaking," snapped the judge. He gestured to Blungkit, who promptly clipped Bip around the ear.

"Ow," said Bip.

"Quiet, you," Blungkit whispered, before flicking Bip's nose. Bip blinked rapidly but wisely held back any verbal retort.

"Now, where were we?" said the judge. "Ah yes, conspiracy to overthrow the government? These are serious charges, Blungkit. Have you any proof?"

"Well, yer honor, I caught him on Speakers' Corner saying how the end of the world was coming and how something needed to be done about it. Sounded a bit political, if you get my meaning."

The judge peered at some paperwork before him, mainly doodles and scribbles that had accumulated over a long, uneventful day.

"Rather flimsy grounds for conspiracy to terrorism, isn't it? 'Sounded a bit political'?"

"Ah, but people were listening to him!" said Blungkit.

The magistrate raised a bushy eyebrow. "Listening? To the speakers? Whatever next?" He stifled a yawn before continuing. "As much as I admire your enthusiasm, Blungkit, I have to say this is an encroachment on my lunch hour. Now, unless this man has actually done any real harm to the city, you can just throw him in the holding tanks with the rest of the scum."

"Hey!" Bip cried indignantly, and was promptly clipped around the ear again.

"Shut it, you!" said Blungkit, then hastily added, "Not you, yer honor.'

One of the magistrates, who had been napping, awoke suddenly and looked about, smacking his lips. "Isn't it lunchtime?" he muttered.

"Your observance is duly noted. Let the record show that it is indeed nearly lunchtime," said the central magistrate. "Now, Blungkit, let's wrap this up quickly, shall we? What exactly did the defendant say to disrupt the peace?"

As Blungkit began to recount his tale, Bip's attention wandered gloomily to the view of freedom just outside the courthouse windows. He was beginning to wonder if his luck could get much worse when, as if on cue, the light in the courthouse seemed to dim, and Blungkit's booming rhetoric seemed to slow and reverberate weirdly. A general feeling of wrongness that felt somehow familiar began to sink into Bip's brain. He looked around to see if anyone else had noticed the sudden change in the environment, and that was when, to his shock, he saw Mr. Random sitting casually on the magistrate's pulpit, his bald, red head and pointy ears gleaming in the afternoon light. The demonic figure smiled his razor grin and wiggled his spindly fingers in greeting.

Mouthing like a guppy, Bip looked about the room to see if anyone else had noticed the intruder. Mr. Random's smile widened as he wagged his finger at Bip, reminding the Kaneqian that no one else would be able to see him.

As Blungkit's now oddly slow voice continued to drawl, Mr.

Random leaned over to the ear of the bored-looking magistrate and began whispering, smiling his metal smile all the while, as the magistrate's expression of vague amusement gradually hardened into a look of serious concentration, until he was glaring fiercely at Bip.

Mr. Random stepped back and tipped Bip a wink before clicking his fingers and disappearing with a pop. Reality snapped back to normal as if it had been stretched out like a rubber band.

"...so then I hit him in the face with my truncheon and here we are!" Blungkit finished chirpily.

The courtroom was utterly silent. The magistrates, who had formerly been so blasé, were now all sitting rigid, focusing identically furious stares at Bip. The central magistrate rose to his feet.

"I suppose you think that poisoning the minds of our people with your hysterical stories is acceptable behavior?" he said, his words withering with spite.

"...no?" said Bip.

"I suppose you think it's rather amusing to spread unnecessary fear and doubt in an otherwise content community?"

"...no?" said Bip.

Suddenly, the magistrate slammed his fist into the pulpit. "I will not have raving troublemakers mocking our city folk!" he roared.

"Woah!" said Bip. "Steady on!"

"Shut it, you," Blungkit growled.

The magistrate, shaking with fury, leveled a crooked finger at Bip. "So you're a doomsayer, eh?" he said. "It seems to me that a chap spouting on about the end of the world can't be considered normal behavior in a civilized society." The magistrate began to grin, revealing neat little teeth, clenched tightly. "I say we put him with the other loons and troublemakers!" The magistrate waved a small, ornate gavel and pounded it sharply on the pulpit. "Six months!" he screeched. "Six months in the Bin!"

The other magistrates leapt to their feet and began applauding manically as Bip was dragged away by Blungkit.

"You're for it now, mate," said the Regulator. "I knew you were trouble, but I didn't think they'd stick you in the Bin."

"What's the Bin?"

"It's where they stick the incurably insane! No one who goes in ever comes out!"

"But I'm not crazy!"

"If you're not crazy now, you will be soon," laughed Blungkit.

"No, please!" Bip wailed, turning around to plead with the impassive magistrates.

"I'm not crazy! I'm not lying! If you don't let me go you're all doomed! Doomed! Do you hear?!"

Blungkit unsheathed his truncheon and rapped Bip smartly on the head, knocking him out cold for the second time that day.

"That's exactly what I'd expect a crazy person to say," he muttered, and dragged the Kaneqian's limp form to the Bin.

---

THE BIN, formerly known as St. Dott's Hospital for the Less Than Sane, was situated on the outskirts of Panthalus, standing dark and alone like a trench-coated pervert in a park. What had once been a magnificent building typical of the Panthalus style of architecture had decayed and rotted into a black and rusted aberration, slimy with moss and riddled with disrepair, as if the very insanity that inhabited the hospital had twisted the structure like a monstrous cancer.

The Bin was ancient, one of the oldest buildings in Panthalus, and was so crushed and uneven in some places that it seemed to erupt organically from the ground rather than having been built on top of it. Its crumbling tower pierced the setting sun, shading the building to pitch as the cries of the mad drifted eerily on the twilight breeze.

Inside, tucked into one of the blackest and most crumbled wings of the hospital-cum-prison, Bip lay slumped on a bare slab floor. He shivered, coming around to the feel of cold stone on his cheek. His vision cleared to reveal the waxing moon rising through the bars of a narrow window.

"Oh, crap," he said, remembering the courtroom.

He sat up and immediately regretted doing so as pain swam through his head like a sea turtle. Yeah. A sea turtle with spikes. A great big angry spiky sea turtle. Bip wondered briefly if he had been knocked unconscious too many times in one day and dismissed the unusual analogy with a shake of his head.

He looked around. His cell wasn't going to win any awards for originality. Three stone walls, another wall consisting of iron bars and a heavy-looking door.

Damp? Check. Cobwebs? Check. Rats? Check.

He froze as a lunatic howl rang out from some dark and lonely corner. He shivered again and turned his attention to the corridor on the other side of the cell's bars. Beyond was Blungkit, kicked back on a chair by a desk a comfortable distance away from the cell, a single candle illuminating his ragged face. Apparently, he had been on guard duty and had fallen asleep. He was snoring with unexpected gentleness, his gray top hat lowered over his eyes. Bip could just make out the bulk of his rucksack and Brian lying at the Regulator's feet. He sighed. There was no chance of reaching either of them.

"I expect he's going to steal them."

Bip whipped around to face the darkness behind him. In a corner blotted thickly with shadow, a man of unidentifiable age emerged, his face hidden by long straggling hair and a beard of monolithic proportions. His features were incredibly pale and drawn, almost translucent in the silvery moonlight, and he was thick with dust.

"They're supposed to register your belongings and store them. They don't, though. More often than not, they just steal them," said the man, his voice cracked and quiet as if he hadn't spoken for a long time.

Bip took a step back from the cell-dweller, unconsciously moving his hand down to a sword hilt that was no longer there. "Who are you?" he demanded.

The man ignored the question. "You look familiar..." he said. "Have I known you, friend?"

"I shouldn't think so," said Bip. "I don't really hang around with crazy people..." His thoughts turned treacherously to Glimton and Rynford. "Much," he added.

"I know your face, I'm sure," said the man, peering at Bip. "You look a lot like...a friend of mine. But you couldn't be. Couldn't be." The man slumped back against the damp, glistening walls.

Bip, realizing that perhaps the stranger wasn't a threat after all, sat down against the bars of the cell. "How long have you been in here?" he asked.

The cell-dweller waved his hand at the wall above his head. Bip peered through the darkness and gasped as he noticed the incredible number of tiny notches scraped painstakingly into the stonework. It would take a long while to count them all properly, he guessed—probably a full day or so.

"Do they represent days, those notches?" said Bip, gaping.

"No," said the prisoner. "Months."

Bip looked at the thousands of notches. "Impossible!" he scoffed. "That'd make you at least..." Bip tried to estimate the sum total of the notches and gave up.

The man looked up and fixed Bip with a weary stare. "At least," he said.

Bip decided not to labor the point, thinking it best not to argue with anyone residing in a hospital/prison for the incurably insane. He whistled and clucked for a while, tapping his hands on his knees.

"So," he said, eventually. "What did they lock you up for, then?"

The man frowned in concentration. "Long time ago," he said. "Hard to remember. I had a message. A warning. Very important. Don't know what happened. Been here ever since."

"Oh," said Bip. "A doomsayer. That's what the judge called it. I don't know what it means, though. I had a warning as well, about the end of the world. No one seemed to care too much, though—they just threw me in here."

"You lose your memory after a while," said the man suddenly. "It gets harder to remember how things were. Harder to remember the earlier years. Being cooped up in here doesn't help much either."

Bip wondered how he should reply and then, not able to think of anything polite to say, decided to change the subject. "Have you been by yourself all this time?" he said.

"Oh, no," said the man. "I have this rubber ball to play with. Without it, I probably would have gone nuts a long time ago." The man pulled a withered rubber ball from the recesses of his ragged clothing. On the ball a small smiley face had been drawn in black ink.

"I call him Bertie," said the man. "He doesn't talk much, but he's a great listener."

Bip smiled politely and thought of something nice to say. "...good?" he managed.

"Yeah. Me and Bertie have some laughs," said the prisoner. As if to demonstrate, he threw Bertie lightly toward a wall. The ball impacted and fell to the ground with a slump, barely rolling let alone bouncing. "Happy times," said the man.

Bip smiled politely and thought desperately of escape. If he could just reach his pack, he thought, he could surely get out of here. He knew that one of Glimton's reprogrammed acorns had FILE inscribed upon it, and he was pretty sure he had seen one called CUNNING DISGUISE. He needed to think fast before Blungkit awoke and, as was more than likely, made off with his possessions.

"What did you say your name was?" said the prisoner, distracting Bip from his scheming.

"I'm Bip," said Bip. "What's your name?"

The man ignored him again. "What were you saying about the end of the world?" he said, after a while.

"What?" said Bip, testily, annoyed by being distracted from the problem of escape.

"You mentioned the end of the world. Said you had a warning?"

"Oh, yes." Bip reasoned that it couldn't do any harm to tell a crazy person that the planet was going to explode soon. Thinking about it, crazy people probably said the same type of thing all the time. "I was sent from a place called Kaneq to warn the world of an astral disaster." Bip turned back to fiddling with the solid lock on the cell door.

Suddenly he felt a hand around his neck and was lifted roughly into the air. He looked down into the wild eyes of the cell-dweller, all of a sudden seeming far from harmless.

"What did you say?" the prisoner hissed through clenched teeth. "Disaster?" squeaked Bip.

"Before that! "

"Astral?"

"Before that!" screamed the prisoner, shaking Bip by the scruff of his jumper.

"Kaneq?" wailed Bip.

The prisoner dropped Bip immediately and began pacing the small cell, muttering continuously under his breath. "Kanick. Kaneq. It can't be! It can't be!" he said.

"Can't be what?" said Bip, rubbing his sore neck.

The prisoner whirled around and pointed an accusing finger at Bip. "Quiet, you!" he shouted. "You're not real!"

Bip didn't know what to say. It was the first time anyone had accused him of not existing.

"You can't be real. Some sick joke. I've gone mad! This time I've really gone mad!" wailed the stranger.

Bip wondered what to say. Now that he was at his full height, the prisoner looked quite formidable compared to when he had been huddled by the wall.

"I am real!" said Bip, then added, "Sorry."

The prisoner froze in his pacing and approached Bip. Then, without warning, he poked him hard in the eye.

"Arrgh!" screamed Bip. "For the love of god, man, what did you do that for?!" he wailed.

"Unbelievable," said the prisoner. "Impossible...of all the chances."

"My eye! My eye!" cried Bip.

"You're really from Kanick?" said the man.

"Kaneq! Yes, you mad bastard! That really hurt, you know!"

The prisoner got down on one knee, bringing his head level with Bip's. "The people who first came to Kanick...Kaneq. Who were they? Do you know?"

"The Clarions," said Bip, frowning. "Why?'

"And what was their purpose there?" said the man urgently.

"They were supposed to be watching over things, but they crashed and... Look, what are you getting at?"

The prisoner rose to his feet and offered a hand to Bip, who accepted and stood up, still rubbing his eye. "I think you and I may have something in common," said the prisoner. "My name is Handen Strike. I came from Kaneq to save the world."

THERE WERE EXPLANATIONS. Plenty of explanations. About the Clarions and the volunteers, the Discordance and the Sentinel. About what had happened to Bip. About what had happened to Handen.

There were gaps in Handen's story. He remembered about the fountain of youth, his time in Kaneq, and his life on the home world of Clarion, all memories that seemed like half-forgotten dreams now. But there was much he couldn't remember, a little over a millennium of memories being too much for one brain to handle. He could not, for instance, remember how he had come to be imprisoned. He only knew that he had been locked away for centuries, eventually forgotten about and dismissed as a madman, slowly beginning to believe that he was a madman.

"You don't know how happy this makes me!" said Handen, half crying and half laughing with ambivalent emotion that would have seemed quite melodramatic to the man he had been so many centuries ago. "I was beginning to think that I was insane! That Kanick and the rest of it was just the demented dream of a madman!"

"Well. It wasn't," said Bip, matter-of-factly.

"You try being locked up for a couple of centuries with no one to convince you of what's real and what's not but a rubber ball named Bertie—then we'll see how confident you are in your memories," Handen chided.

"A fair point," said Bip. "But I'm still having trouble taking all this in. You're the first volunteer?" Bip gestured to the emaciated, scraggly figure before him.

"I haven't exactly been getting much exercise lately," said Handen reproachfully. "Well this is good news! Great news!" said Bip eventually. "I'm sure with the two of us corroborating our story, they'll be bound to believe us!"

Handen raised an eyebrow. "I remind you that we're in a prison for the insane. No one's going to believe anything we say. I've tried a million times to explain. Literally a million."

"Oh," said Bip. "So we're stuck, then?"

"A few hundred years ago, I would've had no trouble wrestling past the guards and getting the girl before being chased down a corridor by a fiery explosion," Handen muttered mournfully.

"What?" said Bip.

"Oh, nothing," said Handen, shaking his head. "Trust me, kid, I've thought of everything to escape from here, but the security's too great. They put you under full restraint any time they're going to open the cell, and they rarely open the cell anyway. No one leaves any convenient cutlery, and I sure as hell haven't had any hacksaws baked into cakes delivered."

"Oh." Bip couldn't help feeling downcast.

"Cheer up," said Handen. "At least you'll probably die in here in a couple of months. I don't even have that luxury."

"Hey!" said Bip.

"Sorry," said Handen sheepishly. "You get used to just saying what's on your mind when you've had no one to talk to but a ball for years."

Bip, unimpressed with the idea of wasting away in a cell, thought manically of an escape plan. "If I could just get my pack, I could get us out of here, I know it," he said.

They looked over at the slouching form of Blungkit. He had managed to sleep soundly through Handen and Bip's entire encounter.

"We could make a rope from our clothes?" said Bip.

"Wouldn't work," said Handen. "There'd be nothing to snag the pack with, and it's too large to lasso."

The two prisoners looked at the pack, both thinking hard. "Say!" said Handen. "Any chance you're Elite-Gifted?"

"I'm a what now?" said Bip.

"Elite-Gifted? Gifted? Journeyman?"

"I'm sorry, I'm not following you," said Bip.

"Have you honed your innate talent to manipulate the building blocks of existence with the power of your mind?" said Handen testily.

"Oh, you mean am I a psyentist?" said Bip.

"Sure. Whatever. Are you?"

"Not a very good one," confessed Bip. "What about you? You're Kaneqian, can't you do any psyence?"

"I was a Hostilities Advisor—I never had the training to hone my abilities."

"You were a what?"

"A Hostilities Advisor? A Security Liaison? A Defence Marshall?"

"You mean like a Hunter?" said Bip.

"Yeah, I guess," said Handen. "If you want anybody to beat someone up, then I'm your man, but I can't really help you with the door problem."

"Oh," said Bip.

"Yeah," said Handen.

The two looked at the pack some more as the gentle whistle of Blungkit's snoring filled the corridor outside the cell.

"Are you sure you couldn't, you know, persuade the rucksack to move over here?" said Handen after a while.

Bip thought hard. Trying to move the pack itself would be risky, but it occurred to him that he could try something similar to the podium trick he had attempted at the apprentice fair. If he could slope the stone floor upward underneath the pack, then gravity would roll the pack toward him. He would just have to hope he didn't set his feet on fire again.

"Stand back," said Bip. Handen obliged as Bip closed his eyes and concentrated, focusing his mind on the stone floor, sensing the common energies that entwined all matter, living and inanimate.

Bip concentrated...

Concentrated...

With a mighty whoosh, Blungkit's chair suddenly expanded into a huge white dome, crushing the sleeping Regulator against the ceiling and exploding the desk into shards of wood. Bip ducked as the brass candlestick sailed over his head.

After the creaking noises stopped, Bip looked out from behind his fingers, noticing his breath steaming in the sudden iciness of the room. A huge white igloo stood where the sleeping Regulator had once been.

*Damn*, thought Bip. *If it's not random incinerations, it's bloody igloos.* Handen slowly stood up from the corner he had instinctively dived into.

"Impressive," he said. "Unorthodox, but impressive."

Bip followed the man's gaze and realized that the sudden appearance of the igloo had shoved both Brian and his pack toward the cell. The sword was just out of reach, but the rucksack was in easy grabbing distance. Bip stretched his arms through the bars of the cell and retrieved his pack. He then began rummaging through the contents.

"What've you got in there?" said Handen. "A saw? A lockpick?"

"Even better!" Bip waggled a bag of acorns under Handen's nose.

"Oh," said Handen, nonplussed. "A bag of nuts. Now we're talking. What're you going to do, flick them at the guards and hope they'll surrender?'

"Of course not," said Bip, looking carefully at each acorn in turn. "These are reprogrammed acorns. You just add water, and they turn into something useful."

"Really," said Handen. "And you're absolutely sure they didn't throw you in here because you're crazy?"

"Aha!" cried Bip triumphantly. He had come across an acorn that had the word KEY inscribed on it. Bip put the acorn in his mouth and swished it around a few times. He then held the nut, glistening with spit, close to the keyhole on the cell door.

Handen watched with growing amazement as the nut began to sprout little green tendrils that waved around until they eventually slithered into the keyhole. There was a pause as a few more shoots grew, then an audible click as the lock opened. The heavy cell door swung inward with a gentle groan.

"Very impressive," said Handen.

"Yeah, they're pretty handy," said Bip. "Now what do we do?"

Handen smirked. There was a glint in his eye that hadn't been there for centuries. He stepped out into the corridor and threw Brian to Bip, who caught the sword awkwardly by the scabbard. Then Handen went over to the unconscious form of Blungkit and retrieved a heavy wooden truncheon and the flintlock pistola. Handen weighed the two weapons carefully in his hand and checked the sights of the pistola.

"Not quite a las-blaster," he muttered, "but it'll do..."

Handen tied his long beard in a knot and held his long hair back in a ponytail tied with a scrap of his clothing.

"What are you going to do?" said Bip.

Handen grinned a dangerous grin. "I'm going to walk right out of here. And nobody is going to stop me."

---

BIP AND HANDEN walked through the front gate of the Bin. The night guard waved them through dismissively. Handen tipped his top hat in greeting and adjusted the collar of his long, gray coat.

"You know," Bip whispered, "when you said you weren't going to be stopped, I sort of envisioned you fighting your way out against insurmountable odds, for some reason."

"Yeah, well, insurmountable odds are for when you have the time to deal with them," said Handen, clinking Blungkit's purse in his hands. "Right now, what I want is a warm bed, something good to eat, and maybe a drink or two. Or six."

The two Kaneqians walked back toward Panthalus as the moon hung lazily in the sky.

A few hours later, Blungkit awoke to find himself naked and shivering in a rapidly melting Igloo.

# Curse of the Hero

The Ugly Swan was one of the nicer taverns in Grub Street, far enough from the hurly-burly to attract a more sedate clientele, but close enough to provide the comforting anonymity of regular and varied custom.

Inside, a large log fire warmed the pub against the night's chill, popping expletively as it sent sparks like tiny demons rushing through the cobbled chimney. Groups of drinkers huddled around large oak tables, washed in languid candlelight, their shadows flickering softly against the heavy oak beams of the ceiling. The sound of trivial conversation was muffled and softened by the thick animal skins that hung from roof to floor, absorbing the heat from the fire and warming the room cozily.

Handen and Bip sat at the bar, each with a large mug of bitter ale before him, while Handen regaled Bip with a few of the adventures (he spat the word) he had faced on his quest to reach the Empire's capital. The barman washed a glass in polite silence while a young waitress, a scrawny, pretty thing, struggled with an armload of empty glasses and took every opportunity to smile coyly at Handen. Handen returned the smiles, relishing the sight of a woman after centuries of solitude.

The former prisoner had taken the time to neaten himself up, and in doing so had changed his appearance significantly. He had spent Blungkit's money and some of Bip's gold on some new clothes and equipment, including a sturdy leather coat and riding boots, which he wore over a comfortable shirt and trousers. His second port of call had been a blacksmith's and supply store, where he had purchased, amongst other things, a weighty bastard sword and a well-oiled leather whip, as well as various daggers and throwing knives, which he had strapped and secreted about his person. His mood had brightened considerably once he had a few sharp objects to hand.

Bip had been quite surprised to see his new companion emerge, finally, from the barber's. His scraggly beard had been shaved away to reveal the perpendicular lines of a heavy, heroic jaw, and his wild-man hair was now combed back into a smooth and rigid side parting. Far from the ageless, hollow appearance of the mad prisoner Bip had first met, Handen had revealed himself to be a handsome man in his mid-thirties, with dark, severe features that seemed to complement the still-haunted look in his eyes. And now he sat, clean of face and neat of collar, his satchel and scabbard by his side and the Regulator's pilfered pistola holstered over his hip. Only a few hours ago Handen had resembled nothing but the pathetic madman his years of imprisonment had made him. Now he looked every ounce the adventurer he had once been.

The improvements in Handen's appearance had also turned out to be an ideal disguise, considering that the Regulators were doubtless pursuing them by now. With this in mind, Bip had also attempted to disguise himself using the CUNNING DISGUISE acorn in his pack, but had discovered that a false moustache and glasses made entirely of bracken were more conspicuous than he would have liked, especially seeing as he already wore glasses anyway. So he opted to sit in the corner and just concentrate on being inconspicuous instead.

"...so then I rescued the girl, blew up the embassy, and escaped on a raft before the volcano erupted," said Handen, finishing his story and taking a long pull from his pint mug.

"Fascinating," said Bip, who, frankly, thought Handen was exaggerating somewhat. He took a close look at his fellow Kaneqian. He was looking a lot healthier than when they had left the Bin—not just the haircut, shave, and clean clothes, but even his complexion seemed to have improved. He even seemed to have put on weight.

"You're looking well," said Bip, suspiciously.

"One of the benefits of immortality," said Handen. "I heal quickly. Very quickly." Bip raised a doubtful eyebrow.

Handen sighed. "You don't believe me, do you?" he said.

"It's a bit far-fetched," conceded Bip.

Without warning, Handen crushed the thick glass pint mug in his hand with a sudden and sparkling crash. Both the barman and Bip jumped in shock as a thin wave of blood erupted soundlessly from the adventurer's palm.

"Sorry about that," said Handen, chirpily. "Must have been a faulty glass."

The barman nodded, puzzled concern etched over his face. "Do you want a bandage for your hand?" he said.

Handen waved his gory palm in front of Bip's face. It was covered in blood.

"No thanks," he said pointedly. "It's not as bad as it looks." With that, he wiped his hand clean with a bar towel, then waved it in front of Bip's face again. "See?" he said. There was not a trace of damage to the hand. Not even a scratch.

"Point taken," said Bip, weakly.

Handen ordered another mug of ale and drank with gusto. "By God, that's good," he said. "Five hundred years or more without a pint certainly builds up a thirst."

Bip was still gazing, dumbfounded, at Handen's hand. "Didn't that hurt?" he asked.

"What?" said Handen, distractedly. "Oh that. Yeah, it hurts, but only for a minute."

"So you really are immortal then? Completely invulnerable?"

"Apparently," said Handen. "I've been shot, stabbed, hanged, disembowelled, decapitated, and defenestrated." He took another mouthful of the bitter ale. "Though I've yet to experiment with being eaten or burnt alive. I can't imagine they'd be much fun."

"Must be nice," Bip concluded.

Handen paused with his mug to his lips. He turned a narrow eye on Bip. "Have you any idea how boring life gets after a couple of centuries of existence?" he said.

"…no?" said Bip.

"Of course you haven't," said Handen. "Let me tell you, when you've done all there is to do, life gets very dull very fast, and knowing you can't die takes all the fun out of it, too. And you know the worst part? I didn't even get to spend a near millennium of immortality relaxing and seeing the sights! When I wasn't being plagued by countless intrepid adventures, I was locked up in that damned cell!" The immortal drained the remainder of his pint mug, banged the glass on the bar, and signaled for a refill.

Bip looked at his new friend with open curiosity. "How many of these intrepid adventures have you had, then?" he said.

"I dunno," said Handen glumly. "Thousands. I lost count a long time ago. There's only so many evil masterminds you can foil and lost tombs you can raid before they all start to look alike."

"Really?" said Bip.

"A man once called it The Curse of the Hero," said Handen, peering back into ancient memories. "At the time I thought he was just winding me up, but the more I think about it, the more I realize he might have had a point. You see, the average guy, if he's lucky—or unlucky, I should say—chances are he'll get one great adventure in his lifetime. Me? I get about three or four a year."

"I'm sorry," said Bip, shaking his head. "It's a bit much to take in."

Handen sighed and then glanced around the room for a while. "There is a way to test the theory," he concluded, eventually. "You see that man over there?" He pointed to a group of drunken regulars; a few of them were significantly burlier than their friends. The largest, a multi-scarred brute with a glass eye, was glaring directly at Handen. "He's the top dog around here, and I'm guessing he's not too fond of strangers coming into his local and attracting the attention of the waitress he fancies." Handen pointed to the waitress, who blushed and looked away.

"What's your point?" said Bip, unsure of where the conversation was going and a little jealous of the waitress's obvious interest in

Handen, who, only a few hours ago, had been a stinking, fish-pale madman in a cell.

"Well," said Handen. "What usually happens in this situation is, the big guy comes up and picks a fight with me, punches are thrown, suddenly the whole bar erupts into a brawl, someone swings from the chandelier—or any other appropriate lighting fixture—and a couple of people are thrown through windows. Then I get the girl and escape in the commotion. Sometimes there is someone playing a piano, but not always."

"You can't be sure of that," scoffed Bip.

"Just watch, kid. There's nothing I can do about it," replied Handen.

At the back of the bar, the pianist began to play an upbeat honky-tonk rhythm.

He didn't really know why—he usually specialized in slow, bluesy folk—but something deep in his bones told him that honky-tonk music was required.

Handen raised a smug eyebrow at Bip as he felt a hand tap him on the shoulder. He turned around to face the barrel chest of the brute that had been staring at him, then craned his neck to look the challenger—who towered over him by a good foot and a half—in the eye. The regular, doubtless the champion of the Ugly Swan and the type of person for whom violence solves everything, glared down with open hostility, a thin sliver of beer-stinking dribble hanging from his oversized chops as he prepared to speak.

Handen interjected before the man could say anything. "What's it to be, then?" he asked chirpily. "The 'We don't like your sort around here' or the 'What are you looking at?'"

The brute looked confused for a moment. He had the unsettling sensation that someone had changed the script just as he'd walked on stage.

"I tell you what," said Handen. "Why don't we spare some time and get right to the point?" Then he rocketed his fist as hard as he could into the brute's mouth.

PUNCHES WERE THROWN. A brawl erupted. Somebody swung from the chandelier and somebody else was thrown through a window. Someone was even comically thrown across the length of the bar. The piano player played on regardless, aware, on some deep spiritual level, that he had a duty to perform.

———

LATER ON, Bip and Handen sat against a wall in an alleyway, Handen tending bruises that were already beginning to heal while, by his side, the awestruck waitress gaped at him with open hero-worship.

"Point taken," said Bip, breathing heavily. He had ducked under a table for the majority of the brawl and had consequently avoided injury. He was quite shaken, though.

"I told you," said Handen

"That was pretty exciting stuff," said Bip, checking his pulse.

"Really? I thought I was a bit rusty, to tell you the truth," said Handen. "It's been a while, I'll admit, but it's like riding a bike, really—it all comes back to you."

"Yeah, but when you jumped over that guy's head and kicked him in the bum!" said Bip excitedly.

"Nothing special," said Handen.

"But what about when you ran up the wall and back-flipped onto the bar?" said Bip.

"Pretty standard stuff, really."

"And when you upper-cutted that chap and he fell through the table?"

"That? Oh, that's basic bar brawl fare, that."

"Well I thought it was pretty exciting," huffed Bip.

"You get used to it," said Handen glumly. He looked down at the waitress on his arm. She couldn't have been older than sixteen. "Look, miss," he said. "You probably think I'm going to drag you off on some romantic and dashing adventure..."

The waitress nodded enthusiastically.

"Well ordinarily I would, but I'm sort of in the middle of something at the minute so I can't, really."

The waitress looked crestfallen.

"Sorry," said Handen, "but it's for your own good. I'm sure you're busy enough with your own life without having some dangerously bold escapade to spoil your week."

The young girl tilted her head in thought. "Well I do have to cook the breakfasts tomorrow…and then there's the barrel deliveries…" she said reluctantly.

"Off you go, then—don't worry about us."

The waitress scuttled back to the Ugly Swan, occasionally glancing hopefully back over her shoulder. Handen watched her leave.

"Sorry about that," he said, turning to Bip. "I don't know why I brought her with us. Force of habit I suppose."

"I see," said Bip. "So what happens now?"

Handen thought for a minute. After so many years locked away from society, there were plenty of things he wanted to do, but time was running out.

"So we have roughly ten months until the end of the world?" he said.

"Yep," said Bip.

"So much time wasted," said Handen, looking up at the stars. "I wonder why no one has come?"

The two stared up at the clear midnight skies for a while. The stars blinked and danced impassively. No answer came.

"We have to reach the capital," said Bip.

"Are you sure that's such a good idea?" said Handen. "You've seen what happens when you try to tell people about the end of the world. How can we be sure it won't happen again?"

"We can't," said Bip. "But I don't have any better ideas, do you? "

Handen thought for a while. "No," he concluded.

"Then we go to the capital."

Handen rose to his feet. "You realize that the law will be after us now? That our faces will be known to every soldier and Regulator across the Empire? That we'll have to cross miles of hostile territory, sleeping and eating only where we can, hiding and living in fear?"

"Actually, I didn't think of that," said Bip. "Oh dear."

"Don't worry about it," said Handen grimly. "I used to do this sort of thing all the time."

———

THE FIRST THING Handen had done to prepare for their flight was to purchase a map, having lost his along with the rest of his equipment several hundred years ago. Bip and Handen now sat in the back room of a nondescript inn, poring over the paper geography before them, which showed the entire continent of Regalious, including Panthalus and Argustin, the capital city. The continent was at least four times the size of the Free Countries, and their destination looked dismayingly far away.

The travelers agreed that the journey would have to be made by cart and foot, avoiding any public transport, as the security measures in the airports and crawlertrams were too risky for wanted felons. However, even the journey by foot was not free of the risk of capture. To travel comfortably the shortest distance between Panthalus and Argustin, they would have to pass through many cities, hamlets, and other well-fortified locations that were bound to hold an inconvenient number of law enforcers.

At first, Bip thought Handen was perhaps being a bit paranoid about the level of interest the Regulators would show for two escaped mental patients. Handen had answered Bip's doubts by taking a short walk around the city and coming back with an armload of wanted posters, all bearing Bip and Handen's description and some rough artists "impressions." Apparently assaulting a Regulator was a hanging offence, and Blungkit had obviously pressed that this was the case.

Eventually the two fugitives decided that they would have to extend their trip to avoid capture, venturing south into the less-marshaled provinces of Regalious, crossing the Bone Desert, then east through the Dozantyne Shrub before swinging back north into the Empire's heart. The eventual route of the journey looked especially difficult on paper and promised to be more so in practice, adding months onto their estimated traveling time and increasing their potential provision budget by as much as ten times.

"We'll have to live off the land," Handen had said. "There's no way short of banditry we can finance the whole trip by ourselves."

"But what about my gold?" said Bip.

Handen shook his head. "There's a lot to consider. The purchase of a well-built wagon, food and supplies, fresh horses and, of course, when we reach the capital, we'll probably need bribe money. If we can provide our own food, we can cut our costs significantly."

To this end, Handen purchased a longbow and a few long spears. It was agreed that even with Bip's limited experience, the two of them would be able to hunt enough quarry to keep themselves in adequate supply of meat, hopefully with enough left over to trade for vegetables and cereals. Of course, the downside to fending and foraging for themselves as they went along was that they would have to further delay their estimated time of arrival at Argustin. Currently, Handen was guessing that the complete journey would take three to four months, depending on the weather and their luck.

After a short rest, Handen and Bip took to the city in the early hours of the morning. They searched Grub Street high and low for a wagon that was for sale and in an adequate state of repair, but with little luck. Eventually, they convinced a traveling merchant to part with his wagon and two horses for a price that was less than fair. Handen had thought about haggling but had quickly decided that it was worth the price to be out of Panthalus as soon as possible. They had even convinced the merchant, for an extra fee, to ride them out of the city while they hid in the covered section of the wagon, to avoid attracting the attention of the gatekeepers.

And so, a safe distance from Panthalus, the two Kaneqians began their expedition to Argustin, heading across the rolling farmlands toward an uncertain destiny.

THEY MOVED BY NIGHT, wrapping themselves in thick shadows to stay hidden, whispering breathy conversations only when the silence became too much to bear. They stole across landscapes stained silver by a treacherous moon, ducking behind hills, and weaving between trees as they inched slowly toward what they hoped would be sanctuary.

Their days were harsh and repetitive, their rigid schedule ensuring they covered as much ground as possible. When they rested in the anxious pre-dawn, crammed hidden between hedges or heather, Handen would cover the wagon in bracken and leaves, camouflaging it from casual observation and providing some insulation against the early morning mists. They would sleep, listening to the rain pattering on the wagon's canvas like a gentle intruder, and awake in the afternoons, eating what they had saved or foraged before moving on again.

Occasionally, at sporadic intervals, Handen would cross over rivers or travel up streams, doubling back and forth, cutting complex trails in the furze to confuse anyone who might be tracking them. For the days and weeks they traveled in the Panthalus province, Bip reflected, it seemed as though they were holding their breath at every waking moment, listening for the sure signs that the unseen enemy was creeping at their backs.

And they were right to do so. Spreading like a virus, like bad news and rumors, the description of two "dangerous escaped criminals" was circulating around the police quarters and guardhouses, the tight pockets of bounty hunters and the squalid drinking dens of mercenaries. A large, terrible, and invisible fist was closing slowly around the two fugitives, and though they didn't know it for sure, they could feel the pressure of it in their chests every night, as a twig snapped close by or a bush rustled in the dark.

They knew the abject terror of the ultimate paranoid. The world was out to get them.

Not much was shared between the two fugitives as they traveled, bar the occasional casual dialogue to remind themselves that they were still human and not the drifting ghosts they had come to feel like. Occasionally, though, the two would encounter moments of comfort and security, abandoned barns or unoccupied huts, where they could talk and learn more about each other.

Bip would tell Handen about Kaneq, the adventurer astonished by how such a small settlement had survived for so long in isolation, and proud about the still-integral existence of the hunting party he had founded so many centuries before. In turn, Bip would sit astounded at Handen's tales of other worlds and peoples and of his adventures on Bersch before their chance encounter.

Their conversations provided not just companionship, but a useful pooling of knowledge. Though Handen's experience of the topography of Regalious was vastly outdated, it still served as a rough guide to their journey, allowing them to travel with a degree of certainty rather than blindly following the markings on their maps. Bip, for his part, was able to apply his limited experience of modern civilization on Bersch.

One opportunity for more relaxed conversation saw the travelers camped in the shell of a burnt-out farmhouse, its blackened beams testament to some tragedy long since past. Bip and Handen sat in the relative shelter of what was once a kitchen, clustered around some likely-looking rubble that might support a fire. At one end of the room, their two horses stood wrapped in blankets and rummaging in nosebags. One of the horses, though recently rubbed down, was sweating hard and breathing heavily.

"I think Wynona's sick," said Bip.

Handen looked puzzled. "Who's Wynona? "

"The horse. The one with the patch on its side."

Handen looked over. "I think you're right. We'll ride them for another full day and then take it easy until we can find a place to trade."

"But what if she's too sick to ride?"

Handen looked at his friend. Though they had been on the road for some time now, Bip still seemed naïve about some of the harsher realities of being on the run. "If she's too sick to ride, we take her downwind, butcher her, and then pack the meat for stock and trade. Then we carry on."

Bip's eyes widened. "Butcher Wynona? We can't do that!"

Handen sighed. "We may have to. We don't have the time or resources to look after her, you know that." Bip looked crestfallen. "Look," Handen continued. "In the long run, if she gets too sick, it'll be more of a kindness to kill her quickly rather than leave her to die."

Bip thought for a moment. "Will it? So you'd rather be chopped up into pieces and eaten than be left to die peacefully?"

"Yes."

"Don't lie!"

"Okay then, no. But the point is, we can't afford to waste resources, and like it or not, that's what 'Wynona' is: a resource!" said Handen.

Bip went quiet for a minute, staring at the floor. "Well, what about Gertrude?"

"Who's Gertrude?"

"The other horse!"

"Well, what about her?"

"She can't pull the cart by herself! She'll get knackered!"

Handen put a hand over his eyes, more tired, all of a sudden, than he had been in centuries. "We can get other horses," he said.

"Doesn't seem right," huffed Bip. "Them carrying us all this way just to be eaten."

"Well, that's too bad, isn't it?" snapped Handen. "They're horses and that's what they do—they carry stuff until they can't carry anymore and then they get eaten. It's not much of a life, but it's better than our prospects if the Regulators catch up with us."

The two remained silent in the early morning dark. The tension of their journey had strained the temperament of both travelers, testing their patience and camaraderie to the very limit. The rhythmic rasping of Wynona was the only sound to be heard.

Handen broke the silence. "Do you want to have a try at lighting this fire, then?"

Bip looked at the rubble, a mixture of half-damp wood and leaves that would take a lot of heat to dry out and burn. They had been taking opportunities wherever possible to try to develop Bip's psyentific knack to a more predictable and serviceable level throughout the journey, and various forest fires and mysterious igloos lay scattered in their wake as evidence of the fact. Currently, Bip's goal for self-improvement was to light a controlled fire using his knack. The emphasis had been on the word controlled.

Bip looked at the pile of barely combustible debris until he pinpointed a likely molecular source of kindling. He concentrated on making the molecules dance, remembering, as he always did in these circumstances, the voice of his teacher, Glimton...

*You'll never amount to anything, you worthless bag of snot!*

There was a satisfying *whoomph* as the rubble pile sparked into a huge bonfire. The blast had been big enough to singe the Kaneqian's eyelashes through his glasses, but not so big, he was pleased to see, as to demolish half of the campsite, as his last attempt had.

"You're improving," said Handen, wiping soot from his face. "Still a long way to go, but you're getting there."

Bip grinned. It was the closest thing to praise he had received in regards to his psyentific abilities in a long time.

The two fugitives sat, appreciating the warmth of the fire in the morning chill, their moods lightening at the small victory. Eventually, Handen constructed a spit from a few handy twigs and began roasting a game bird he had felled the previous day. The smell of cooking meat was tantalizing after a hard day's ride.

After a while, they ate, then lay back in the satisfied glow of a meal well done.

"Where do you suppose it comes from?" said Bip, breaking the comfortable silence. "The psyence, I mean?"

"How do you mean?" said Handen.

"Well, from what I've been told and what I've seen, Berschites, the people of this planet, can't do it. My friend Azron thought it was something called magic."

"Ah, magic," said Handen. "Magic is a word used by the ignorant to explain what they don't understand. It's just a term used by people who haven't got all the facts yet. Or sometimes a word used by those with knowledge who want to keep others in the dark. Charlatans or showmen."

"Just tricks, you mean?" said Bip.

"Yes," replied Handen, "and no. Your gift—the way you just started that fire—some would call it magic because they can't explain it. Doesn't mean it was a trick."

"So magic is kind of a question that hasn't been answered yet?" said Bip thoughtfully.

"Or an answer you haven't questioned. The fact is that what you call psyence, and what was called equating in my time, doesn't come from any sort of mystical force. It's a physical trait, like wings on a bird or horns on a jabberwocky."

Bip nodded. The adventurer continued his explanation.

"The Clarions, or the Kaneqians if you prefer, can see the very structure of the world in front of them, can view the material energy plane, and by seeing it, they can connect with it and influence it. We're all made of energy at a sub-molecular level, after all. So, it's not a trick; it's just a matter of balancing a physical-energy equation that's already there in a different way, through a hereditary relationship with the world around us."

Bip nodded. Though he had heard similar explanations of psyence throughout his education and training, Handen's approach was refreshingly pragmatic.

"But magic," said Handen, shaking his head slightly. "I've seen some unusual things on this world—sorcerers and wizards and warriors of superhuman ability. But those abilities were learned and mastered by ordinary men through terrestrial means. There is no magic, only secrets we haven't found."

Bip lay back, gazing at the stars through a hole in the farmhouse roof. "I understand that psyence is a hereditary trait, but where do you suppose it comes from? I know we're born with it, but why?" he said.

Handen lay back, too, feeling as relaxed as he ever would while they were still fleeing the law.

"That's a good question," he said, after a while. "I wish you could have met Julius; he was the man for this sort of talk. It was never my thing, really—I was more about blowing stuff up to tell the truth—but Julius would go on for ages about the Clarions' origins." Handen screwed up his eyes in recollection. "He figured that life evolves to the star it's born to, that sometimes life can find a way to succeed in what you and I might consider the most unlikely of places. He believed we were descended from a race that grew where the universal rules were slightly different, where the stars were...what's the word he used? I can't remember, but the stars were different. He thinks that where we came from, where we originally came from, the matter there was less…asserted. One thing wasn't always the other, if you know what I mean. Everything was kind of linked, but in an obvious way, a way you could manipulate. See? He thought that psyence was a legacy of distant ancestors who existed integrally with the world around them. Do you understand?" Handen, lost in his retelling of his long-since-gone captain's theories, suddenly became aware that the conversation had become a bit one-sided.

"Do you see what I'm getting at?" he said. A loud snore was his only response. Handen smiled and rolled onto his side, feeling sleep creeping up on him with sluggish seduction.

That night he dreamed of the worlds he had left behind—and the friends, too many to count, whom he would never see again.

---

4

# The Bone Desert

---

They had ridden hard for a month. The populated areas of the Panthalus province and the grassy dales thereafter were far behind them. They had not seen another living soul since they had last traded with a gruff old farmer just before the Quiet Mountains. Happily (at least for Bip,) both Wynona and Gertrude had made it as far as the farm and had been traded for younger, fresher mounts. It was these mounts that had led the cart through the stillness of the Quiet Mountains, so named with good reason, for not a creature stirred, and only the rattle of the cart's wheels on stony ground broke the engulfing silence.

Cowed by the constant hush, Bip and Handen made camp without a word, afraid that to make a noise would disturb the peace of the eerie stone hills and bring the attention of any predators that lurked in the mists.

It was said that there were mountain trolls and hill giants that stalked the Quiet Mountains at night. Handen, though, was outwardly dismissive of the possibilities of proto-beings living in the hills, dismissing the stories as superstition and rumor. However, when night fell, and the eerie quiet developed a personal and dangerous quality, the two fugitives found themselves keeping a more rigid watch than usual, expecting at any moment to see the moon blotted out by huge, marauding silhouettes.

They were glad to leave the mountains behind, though there were still no signs of any settlements or even much wildlife in the lands they traveled thereafter. The fugitives simply rode on as the land around them became more desolate and the temperature increased by the day until the heat became nearly unbearable. Grass gave way to hard mud. Mud gave way to shale. The days plodded by, shuffling their feet as they went.

The Bone Desert sneaked up on them. It shouldn't have been able to, but the steep incline Handen and Bip had been riding up was so gradual that they barely realized it was there, so they were shocked to suddenly find themselves atop a cliff face overlooking a wide ocean of sand.

"Wow," breathed Bip.

"Don't be intimidated," said Handen. "It's only a few days ride to the Nastre Kingdom, then we turn east, and it's another few days ride back to more hospitable territory."

"The Nastre Kingdom…do you think we'll be able to get more supplies there?" said Bip.

"As a matter of fact, I'm counting on it. We won't be able to take the cart over this terrain, so we'll be packing essentials only from here on in."

"But we're wanted men," said Bip. "Aren't we taking a bit of a risk assuming we can restock at Nastre?"

"A slight risk," said Handen, wobbling his hand from side to side as he scanned the sandy horizon. "But a calculated one. The Nastre Kingdom is officially part of the Empire, but it's too remote to warrant much personal attention. They pledge allegiance, pay taxes and the odd tribute when necessary, but they still operate as an independent kingdom, with their own customs and even laws sometimes. I don't think word of us will have got there yet, and if it has, I don't think we'll be regarded as a major concern either way. Nastre is the closest were going to get to a civilized no-man's land in the whole of Regalious."

Bip looked at his friend. "You seem to know a lot about Nastre."

"I picked it up in Sloe," said the immortal dismissively, referring to one of the dwindling outposts they had stopped at on their travels. Handen was good at picking up information without appearing suspiciously curious.

Bip followed Handen's gaze out toward the gently shifting desert. The sun was already beginning to feel horribly oppressive. The former Hostilities Advisor seemed lost in contemplation, his usually calculating features smoothed over with a hint of melancholy. As they had traveled, Handen had discovered that, particularly when traveling in a place he had been to before, fragments of his lost memories would become astonishingly and suddenly clear. Now, as he looked over the empty plain of sand before him, images of a city skyline on the horizon niggled at his brain.

"You know," Handen said, "the last time I was here, Nastre was a huge and powerful country. Cities all over the place, with temples and museums you would have strained your neck to take in. Now it's no more than an outpost for the Empire, clinging on to the old ways like a senile war veteran."

"What do you suppose happened?" said Bip.

"The Empire, presumably," muttered Handen. "My, how things have changed."

The two travelers stood for a while, staring out into the lonely-looking sands. "So we ride due south?" said Bip eventually.

"Yep," said Handen. "Due south to Nastre."

They packed what they needed onto their mounts and headed down the cliff slope and into the burning sands.

---

THE HEAT HAD BEEN, frankly, unreasonable. It had been impossible to travel when the sun was high in the sky, so Handen and Bip had opted to travel only early mornings, late afternoons, and throughout the evenings. Ultimately, this meant that their arrival at Nastre would be delayed by a day or so. Handen cursed himself for underestimating how much of a chore crossing even a small part of the Bone Desert would be. They trudged along, the horses sweating and stinking in the relentless sun, their bodies slick with sticky moisture. The heat radiated from the sand, offering no reprieve from the baking desert sky.

At their first rest stop, Bip had tried to alleviate some of the discomfort by trying to purposefully, rather than accidentally, equate an igloo so that they might cool off for a while. He failed, constructing instead an impressively large but ultimately useless sandcastle. So, on they went, further toward the wavering horizons. Their only relief came with the double-edged sword of nightfall, which, while dispelling the heat of the day, brought with it a deadly chill.

As the desert moon turned gold sands to silver, Handen and Bip sat huddled under a blanket. They kept close to the small fire they had managed to make from the already dwindling supply of wood, though it did little to deter the biting desert breeze, which, as an added bonus, would continually slap them with erratic drifts of coarse sand. The stars hung like icicles in the sky, and Bip looked up into an oblivion that seemed a little colder than usual.

"Hard to believe they're all suns," he said, his breath freezing in the air.

Handen looked up but didn't say anything.

"I mean, that there could be a world like ours for every star in the sky," continued Bip.

"It's not that special, really," said Handen. "It's nice and all, but when you've been to as many planets as I have, they all start to look a bit similar. Now and again one'll throw you something interesting and unexpected, but you'd be surprised how closely beings in the same universe evolve, on the whole."

"If that's your attitude, then why were you—and the Caretakers for that matter—so intent on saving Bersch from destruction? It's only one planet, one civilization of many, I suppose?" said Bip, his teeth chattering in the cold.

Handen turned his stony gaze to his companion. "The destiny of every planet is important. We believe that every race deserves the chance to mature to a point where it can survive outside interferences on its own. It doesn't mean that any one planet is any more particularly special than another. They all have their good points, bad points, similarities, differences." Handen shrugged, his shoulders shivering as he did so.

Bip smiled to himself. "They're like children," he muttered. "The planets are like children and you lot are like babysitters." He laughed. Handen joined in.

"That's as good a comparison as any," said the former Hostilities Advisor.

"And now this planet, the one we're standing on, is going to be wiped out by an unknown astral disaster…" Bip said reflectively.

Handen shook his head. "Not unknown," he said. "The Clarions have been tracking the progress of the disaster for thousands of years. We know exactly what it is."

"Then what is it?" said Bip, shocked. This was all news to him.

"It's a cluster of ancient devastation weapons, warped and mutated by countless aeons of multiple radiation exposure, launched by a species who were particularly adept at blowing the crap out of things, and rather unimaginatively christened the 'Massive Ball of Death.' When it hits Bersch, there will be nothing left but poisoned rubble. If that."

Bip stared into the sky, envisioning a world of fire. "Why would someone do that?" he breathed.

Handen chuckled. "The funny thing is that the species who launched the weapons didn't even think about the possibility of affecting other races. They were quite confident that they were alone in their universe. Shows what they knew." Handen snorted a quick derisive laugh. "The reason the cluster is heading this way is pure coincidence—adverse randominity."

"The Discordance?" said Bip. He shuddered, recalling the metal grin of the red-skinned troublemaker, Mr. Random.

"That's right." Handen nodded. "They influence things, affect things. Things that would be better left alone. We had the technology to detect their actions from back on the homeworlds—that was how we tracked the disaster—we could tell when there was outside interference in the expected course of events."

"How?" said Bip.

Handen frowned in remembrance. "Ripples in causality. We had machines that could detect them, like seismographs can detect earth-quakes. Let us know where the Discordance were messing around with things."

Bip thought back to his own encounter with Mr. Random. "Have you ever seen one of them?" he asked. "One of the Discordance, I mean."

Handen shook his head. "They've never warranted my personal attention. Me? I'm mostly just good for fighting, and the Discordance are an enemy that can't be fought, at least not with any weapon I can use. See, they belong in a different dimension to ours, and they can only affect things mentally in our world, not physically. They're like mischievous ghosts, I suppose—they influence things with weaker minds, twist the will of others, and bring bad luck wherever they can. And they worship chaos totally." Handen grinned suddenly. "They worship chaos, but they use surprisingly well-organized methods to achieve it. Paradoxical. Tells us a bit about their character."

Bip nodded. "You've never met one, then?"

"No," said Handen. "As I said, we can't fight them, and they can't fight us…at least not directly. All we do is try to stay one step ahead of them and clean up their mess whenever possible."

"Is that what you're doing here at Bersch? Cleaning up mess?"

"In a manner of speaking, yes. Though we didn't do a very good job of it in retrospect." Handen gave a grim smile. "Now save your breath—we've got a long, cold night ahead of us and a long, hot day tomorrow."

They huddled together against the night's chill, knowing that reprieve would only come in a polar-opposite form of torture.

Slowly, the cold making him groggy, Bip began to fall asleep.

He was never sure whether he'd actually fallen asleep or not, he was only aware, suddenly, of a familiar yet still unsettling feeling. The feeling that something was amiss, that things weren't quite right. A panicky suspicion bubbled up in Bip's mind and, sure enough, was confirmed almost immediately.

"Speak of the devil, and he shall appear," crooned an elegant voice.

Bip looked up to see Mr. Random squatting by the dying remains of the campfire. He quickly looked to see if Handen was awake. The adventurer lay sleeping, his brow furrowed as though dreaming of problems.

"Wouldn't be able to see me even if he were awake," said Mr. Random, poking at an ember with his fiendishly long fingers. "I wouldn't want to spoil our special relationship, Bip. After all, two's company..." The apparition grinned his terrible metal grin.

"What do you want this time?" said Bip.

"Just to chat, Bippy, just to chat," said Mr. Random chirpily. "You know, I was a little annoyed. Right now, you're supposed to be rotting in a cell somewhere, but instead, here you are. And with Mr. Strike as well, it seems. What are the chances?"

Bip frowned. "You know Handen?"

Random's seemingly permanent smirk left his features, replaced by a snarling rage that made Bip unconsciously shuffle backward. "Know him?" he said. "I spent the best part of a millennium trying to kill him! The stubborn git refuses to die! And now here he is, back again. I don't think you realize how much that ticks me off, Bippy-boy." Random calmed down and sat back on his haunches. "Not that it will matter," he said. "You're running a bit too late to stop us now."

"We can still make it," said Bip. "We still have time."

"I'll stop you," said Random. "Just like I stopped the others before you."

Now it was Bip's turn to smirk. He gestured toward the sleeping Handen. "You didn't stop all of us," he said.

Mr. Random's features went cold, his metal grin disappearing. "One fish through the net, that's all. I stopped the others. Stopped them dead. I stopped your father!" Bip reeled. He had dealt with the conclusion that his father had met a sticky end a long time ago, but to hear it confirmed was like being kicked in the stomach. Mr. Random's metal smile snaked back across his features. "Yes, that's right," he said. "He was a tough one, was your old man. He made it all the way to the Cold Ocean before having an unfortunate run-in with a wavesnake!"

"Shut up!" shouted Bip. "Shut up or I'll—"

"You'll what?" said Random. "You can't touch me, and you know it!"

"Maybe not," spat Bip. "But I can ignore you."

Affronted, Mr. Random gaped stupidly as Bip rolled over and hunkered down on his sleeping mat.

"You'll never make it, you know," he said. "Even with Mr. Strike helping you, I'll still stop you. Stop you dead!"

"I'm not listening," said Bip.

"You can't ignore me, you worm! I hold power you couldn't possibly understand! I have meddled with the fate of galaxies! You really think a poxy maggot like you can stand in my way?" Mr. Random was screeching now, standing up to bellow at Bip's slumped form.

"Could have sworn I heard something," mumbled Bip. "Must have been the wind…"

Mr. Random gaped and flustered for a moment, then shut his mouth with a formal click and stalked off into the desert night. Bip relaxed and sighed heavily with relief. There must have been five minutes of quiet and then—just as Bip was settling into a shallow sleep—he heard a crooning voice begin to sing by his ear.

"I know a song that will get on your nerves, get on your nerves, get on your nerves…"

Bip groaned and put his rucksack over his ears.

"…get, get, get on your nerves."

---

THE TRAVELERS AWOKE to the incessant glare of the rising sun. The cold of the previous night quickly melted away, promising a few moments of pleasant warmth before the heat became unbearable once again. Without a word, Bip and Handen shouldered their packs and began to lead their mounts, stretching their legs, and saving some of the horses' energy for when the sun was higher in the sky. They walked for a while in silence, Bip trying unsuccessfully to blink the sleep from his eyes, Handen staring hard at the horizon with his usual calculating gaze.

"Sleep well last night?" asked the adventurer conversationally.

"No," said Bip, deciding not to tell Handen about his conversation with Mr. Random. After all, what good would it do? Right now,

Handen was focused entirely on getting to Argustin safely and in good time. Distracting him with more nebulous worries might prove a hindrance—and was probably just what Mr. Random wanted. Bip decided to bear his fear and doubt on his own shoulders. *Two's company*, he thought, and grinned mirthlessly.

"The cold, right? Kept me awake for a while, too," said Handen, returning his gaze to the horizon.

"That's right," mumbled Bip, and yawned long and wide. He wondered why Mr. Random had never appeared to Handen, and whether he had ever appeared to any of the other volunteers, in the flesh, so to speak. He doubted it somehow. He assumed that Mr. Random was only appearing now because there was so little time left before the Massive Ball of Death hit. He was probably just making sure everything was going to go right for him.

*Bastard,* thought Bip distractedly.

They walked for half the morning, mounting up for a few hours before noon when the sun reached its zenith, then rested in the baking sand for what seemed like far too long. They wore clothing soaked in water from the worryingly low supplies in their skins, draped over their heads to ward off sunstroke and burn. Handen reflected that they would have to reach Nastre soon—a day in the Bone Desert without water was not an inviting prospect.

As the sun relented slightly in the afternoon, the travelers mounted up again and made as good a pace as possible on the panting horses. They traversed dune after shimmering dune, the sky a hard, bright opal above them.

As they rode, Bip pointed hopefully at what had looked like buildings off to their south. Handen had stared for a while at the wavering mirage of the horizon, shielding his eyes from the sun.

"Is it the city?" said Bip.

Handen stared for a little while longer before turning to his companion. "No," he said. "Concentrate on the buildings. Tell me what you see."

Bip squinted for a long time. "They're triangles?" he ventured.

"Pyramids, actually," said Handen. "They're not houses; they're tombs. The Nastren people used to bury their dead kings in huge stone pyramids."

"Why?"

Handen shrugged. "Why do we mark graves at all? I suppose it was just a way of showing how revered the king was."

Bip stared hard at the distant bumps.

"Don't let distance fool you," said Handen. "Those things are massive."

"Been close to one before, have you?" asked Bip.

"Yeah," said Handen, smiling faintly. "Kind of nice seeing something older than I am. Come on, let's get a move on."

At night they camped again, this time able to bolster their small amount of wood with some tough, dry shrubs found in a cluster of rocks. The rocks made good shelter from the cold evening wind and their sleep was more comfortable than the previous nights.

Dawn came once more, and the two fugitives upped their pace, rested as they were from the previous night. It was late afternoon when a faint glimmer on the horizon hinted at civilization.

"Just as well, really," Handen commented, rattling his empty waterskin.

They reached a small village just before nightfall, a settlement of a little over twenty stone hovels, surrounded by small ranches where camels and horses chewed the dry sandgrass with an animal patience as wide as the horizon. Thankfully they had been able to refill their water supplies from a stone well, drawing the ground-cooled water whilst silent locals watched them suspiciously, eyes piercing brightly from identically desert-baked faces. Handen realized that it must have been some time since outsiders had ridden through the village, and that their clothing and features probably seemed quite alien to the people there. So that night, they camped on the outskirts of the settlement—close enough to provide some shelter from the winds, but not so close as to make the villagers wary.

Handen was busily tearing at some white cloth he had managed to trade for before night had fallen. He was trying to construct an imitation of the white robes the Nastre people wore, both because they were convenient for the weather conditions and also because they could disguise their faces, meaning that with any luck, they wouldn't draw attention to themselves as they entered Nastre city.

Their meat supply now depleted, Bip made a thick soup out of the last of their vegetable stock, adding some of their precious store of salt to create a thick, nourishing, and tasty meal. They ate with gusto —it would be the last solid meal they would have until they were able to trade for more food or were able to hunt for it, an option that had become increasingly unlikely in a desert seemingly devoid of wildlife.

That night they slept soundly and were up with the rising of the sun, refilling their waterskins, donning their robes, and heading east before any of the villagers had begun their day.

THEY TRAVELED for another day before reaching the outer walls of Nastre, their progress made easier by the discovery of a road that, while in a state of grievous disrepair, was better traveling than the sand dunes that surrounded it. The city walls, large undecorated constructions the color of old dust, had obviously been built in a time when invasion had been a serious threat. Now they stood unmanned, with nothing to watch for but the occasional sandstorm. The main gates were heavy, wooden, and towered the full height of the walls but, judging from the amount of sand that had piled up around their bases, had remained opened and unused for a very long time.

Only two watchmen stood guard over the entrance to the city proper. They too wore the desert robes common to Nastre, though they kept their muscular arms bare and wore large, curved watoki blades across the front of their waists. As the travelers came near, one of the guards signaled for them to stop and then approached with the nonchalant gait of one who is employed to detect trouble and doesn't expect to find any.

"Purpose of visit?" he said. His accent, more used to the trade speak used by the varying dialects of Nastre, rolled uncertainly around the Imperial vowels. Handen realized that the desert robes had done very little to disguise his foreign features. He quickly recounted the lie he and Bip had formulated a few nights ago, that they were business representatives from Panthalus come to secure a trade link with a spice merchant. If the guard had any doubts about the legitimacy of their story, they were quickly obliterated by the sight of Bip's gold supply—diminished but still impressive.

The two fugitives were waved through, and the watchman went back to staring blankly at the empty desert road before them.

Considering the perimeter of the city walls, the city itself seemed rather bare in comparison. It was some minutes before Handen and Bip came across any signs of civilization greater than the village they had already encountered, though a large domed palace on the horizon indicated where the hub of the city's populace was to be found.

They followed the main road toward the palace, and gradually the noise and activity began to increase around them. The small, dilapidated hut-like lodgings gave way to houses of stone and wood, though these too were shoddy affairs. Tented dwellings that seemed to have been constructed with little or no planning or forethought took up much of the space between the more permanent-looking buildings. People of all ages, all bearing the dark skin and bright white eyes Bip had come to associate with the Nastre Kingdom, ran about seemingly with more haste than purpose. More than a few stopped to stare openly at the strangers.

The noise around them gradually ascended into the cacophony Bip had begun to expect from a city, though this time the shouting voices were in a language he had never heard before. The effect was disconcerting for the traveler, and he felt more alienated than he had since the beginning of his journey. Handen, of course, took it in his stride.

A small chip from Bip's lump of gold had been enough to secure their horses indefinitely in a livery stable, so Handen and Bip wandered into what appeared to be the market sector to start the arduous process of securing enough supplies for their journey east. Handen, having no memory of any of the Nastre dialects, and the various merchants proffering only blank stares when addressed in Imperial, was forced to resort to the age-old international communication method of pointing and gesturing until the wanted item and was finally secured and the correct amount paid. Needless to say, the process was long and frustrating.

Eventually, with food and fuel and a few useful items purchased and stowed, the two doomsayers relaxed in the tented shade of a Nastren coffee house. Bip looked down at his coffee, which was dark, spicy-smelling, and apparently came with neither milk nor sugar. He took a sip. It wasn't bad.

"So, what now?" he said.

Handen sipped thoughtfully for a moment before replying. "Well, I thought we could lay low for a while."

Bip, who had been praying that Handen would say something to that effect, still voiced his concern. "Isn't that a little bit risky?"

"A little," agreed Handen. "But we need to rest the mounts, and it'll be a long time before we have anywhere as safe as Nastre to get our heads down. I think we should take this opportunity to kick back for a few days."

Bip looked around and leaned over conspiratorially. "We're not exactly inconspicuous, though, are we?"

He had a point. In the entire city, Bip and Handen had seen no one else with pale skin, and though the desert robes hid their identities from a distance, on close inspection, it was easy to see that they were not natives.

"I wouldn't worry too much," said Handen, stretching. "It's a crowded city. We're likely to spot a posse of Regulators before they spot us. And remember there's a very good chance that they won't even consider risking the Bone Desert."

"Really?"

"Just relax," said Handen. "If we don't rest, we'll exhaust ourselves before we reach the capital, and then we won't be any good to anyone. And I, for one, am looking forward to sleeping in a bed tonight." He drained the rest of his coffee. "Now," he said. "How about we hire a room out in an inn somewhere and sleep for about…oh, I don't know, forever?"

Bip grinned. "Sounds good."

---

BIP STEPPED ONCE MORE into the hurly-burly of the market quarter, blinking happily in the sunshine. It had been a long time since he had felt so rested, and not since the airboat had he slept so much in one sitting. Handen had leniently allocated some of the tight travel budget to a session in the local bathhouse, where Bip had had his first decent wash in months, floating happily while the various twinges and cramps courtesy of sleeping rough for so long had slowly dissipated into the hot, scented waters. Afterward, they had checked into a local inn and had simply spent an entire day doing nothing but sleeping and eating.

Now, on their second morning in the desert city, the fugitives were preparing to leave. Handen had wanted to take one last wander around to see if he could garner any useful information and, knowing that Bip might have proven a liability, he had sent the Kaneqian out on his own to pick up a few non-essential supplies. And so, with plenty of time until their agreed rendezvous, Bip took a leisurely stroll through the endless tents of market stalls.

He wandered lazily.

Lulled by the midday heat into a dreamy state, he paid little attention to the world around him, so he did not notice that the accustomed curiosity of the locals had taken on a more apprehensive quality. As he meandered obliviously through the streets, eyes followed and people whispered. Shoppers walking his way swerved carefully to avoid him, so that Bip walked in a small island of calm in the otherwise hectic scrum of the marketplace. Still heedless enough to the atmosphere around him to be whistling cheerfully, Bip approached a spice merchant's shack and began to browse the goods.

The merchant made to approach Bip with the aggressive friendliness typical of the Nastre salesman, but before he could launch into his usual chatter, he performed an almost comical double-take, his eyes widening in his aged face. He began to babble in the clipped and puzzling Nastre vernacular and make frantic gestures at the doomsayer.

Bip frowned, trying to guess what the shopkeeper was attempting to communicate.

"I'm Just Browsing, Thanks!" he said, talking loudly and clearly as if this could compensate for speaking an entirely incompatible language.

The shopkeeper continued his aggressive gesturing and eventually reached for the drawstrings that held the tent flaps of his stall open. With a sharp slapping noise, the tent-shop closed up, cutting off the still-babbling voice of the shopkeeper.

Bip stood back for a moment, frowning in puzzlement. It was then that he saw the sign on the outside of the tent. The paper was bright, obviously freshly put up, and the words were, of course, indecipherable. The pictures, however, two quite good artists' renditions of Bip and Handen, were immediately clear.

Realizing the implications, Bip swallowed hard and made to go and find his fellow fugitive. He turned around to find his retreat barred by the tips of two watoki blades leveled at his throat. The glinting eyes of two guardsmen regarded him solemnly from behind their identical desert robes.

"Ah..." said Bip, and wondered what to do next.

---

5

## You Can't Keep a Bad Man Down

---

The Last Palace used to be just one of the many grandiosely domed and extravagantly spired palaces that had formerly been a frequent, almost common sight across the once great kingdom of Nastre. Now, however, it was the only one remaining in a land that been largely reclaimed by the ever-pressing advance of the Bone Desert. Only a few of the oldest citizens of the desert kingdom remembered the days when the palace had been called by its true name, a name that had reflected the might and majesty that inspire and conceive such architectural triumphs. Now it was known only as the Last Palace.

It was central to the city around it, and much of its grounds had been overtaken by a sprawl of shops and settlements. The building had been depleted since its glory days, whole wings had been demolished and recycled by a city that could no longer afford the tax to maintain it. The Last Palace was symbolic of the fall of the Nastre Kingdom—a ghost of a more prosperous time. A grand history withered by a modernizing world. A dust-colored grave for the pride, might and arrogance that had flavored the city so many centuries ago.

The king still resided in the palace, as was expected of the ruler of the desert tribes. Though in truth, he was no more than a mayoral figurehead in the city, emerging from the ill-swept corridors now and then to issue royal decrees to nostalgic subjects who would applaud loudly and promptly forget what had been said. Since the fall of Nastre to the Empire, the king was little more than a blue-blooded mascot. He had no more real authority in the affairs of Nastre than the Imperially-appointed sheriff, though he still wore the golden robes and mask of his godlike ancestors as he delivered his pointless sermons to a broken people.

One of the few, purely ceremonial responsibilities the king enjoyed was the judging and sentencing of perpetrators...providing said perpetrators had already been found guilty by the sheriff or another Empire official. And so it seemed Bip was going to meet the king of Nastre.

The corridor Bip waited in was similar to the one he had sat in at the court of Panthalus so many weeks ago, though this was more stylishly constructed, with huge sand-yellow bricks on which famous battles from Nastren history were depicted in faded, intricate paintings. Another happy improvement on his pre-court experience in Panthalus lay with his chaperones; the two silent guardsmen who sat on either side of him on the wooden bench were infinitely preferable company to the loathsome and odorsome Blungkit.

All of a sudden, wooden doors were flung open with a crash that wrecked the stone silence of the corridor. Handen was marched across to the bench by a group of guards and shoved into a sitting position. His hands were tied behind his back and, unlike Bip, who had merely been escorted by the two guards he was sitting with, Handen was surrounded by a dozen or so, all with weapons drawn and ready. Quite a few of the Nastrens were sporting dark bruises on the visible parts of their bodies, and Bip guessed that many of the original arresting party had not made it as far as the temple.

Handen himself had a huge black eye and a deep cut on his forehead, both of which, of course, would begin to heal at any moment.

Bip's heart sank. Some keen and loyal part of his mind had been relying on the former Hostilities Advisor for his rescue. "They got you, too," he stated, glumly.

"You can't win them all," replied Handen. He sounded nonchalant, though his anger was betrayed by the dangerous glint in his eye.

"How do you suppose they found out about us?" said Bip.

"Well, I doubt we were beaten here by anyone tracking us from Panthalus," said Handen. "My best guess is that there's a Regulator station close to the Bone Desert with a telegram receiver. They must have sent a messenger to the city either just as we were arriving or a little before." The adventurer wiggled his lips, trying to scratch his nose without using his hands.

"It all seems a bit much," said Bip, gloomily. "Why are they going to so much trouble to capture us? We're only two men!"

"You're right," replied Handen. "It does seem a bit excessive seeing as we haven't killed anyone or stolen anything. My best bet is that your friend Blungkit has friends in high places."

Bip tried to think of the repugnant Blungkit swanning around in the high society circles of the Panthalus province. The image did not come easily. He shared his doubts with Handen.

"Fair enough," the adventurer said. "Either way, it doesn't matter to us now. All we have to worry about now is whether the Nastre justices will hand us over to Empire representatives or deal with us themselves."

"What difference will it make?" said Bip.

"Well," said Handen, still trying vainly to scratch his nose, "if we're handed over to the Empire, we could be detained for as long as it takes to send an escort. If not, we could be hanged tomorrow."

"Oh," said Bip, trying not to sound as defeated as he felt. A sudden spark of hope briefly lit within him. "Surely if we're detained, there's a possibility of escape?" he said.

Handen's features remained serious and indifferent. "I'd like to say something like 'there's never been a prison built that could hold me,' but seeing as I was locked up for the last five hundred years, I think that would be a rather bogus assertion."

Bip slumped, the brief spark in of hope squashed mercilessly. "So, what you're saying is, we're buggered?"

"That about sums it up," Handen agreed. "If they put us under a light guard—which they won't—or if we had a contact in the city—

which we don't—we might stand a chance, but…" Handen left the rest of the sentence unsaid, merely shrugging his shoulders.

"Oh, great," Bip said. "Just great. We're going to die!" He stopped and thought about it. "Well…I'm going to die. You can't, can you?"

"Lucky me," said Handen, sarcastically. "With any luck, I'll just be locked up for another eternity or so."

THE PALACE THRONE room was the largest room Bip had seen since his time in the Dome. It was illuminated by huge windows built high toward the ceiling, and the daylight that filtered through was reflected from various strategically and aesthetically placed mirrors, meaning it was nearly as bright as the streets outside. The room was built from the same yellowy sandstone blocks as the rest of the palace, though here they looked freshly scrubbed. Large and exquisite tapestries hung from the walls and plush red rugs covered the floor leading to a large and ridiculously ornate golden throne. Someone had taken great pains to ensure that the throne room of the Last Palace was restored to the majesty of Nastre's worthy history. Looking at this room, one could almost forget the decay and disrepair that riddled the rest of the palace.

Bip and Handen were marched down the length of the room toward the throne, where a thin figure in a golden mask sat waiting for them. Bip noticed, with a feeling like some illegitimate son of jealousy, that all the guards' attention (not to mention their weapons) were focused entirely on Handen.

They were taken before the throne, where a herald heralded them in words they couldn't understand. The various courtiers in the throne room stood in respectful silence while the king looked down at them. The king was a tall figure, though any other physical observation of him was denied. His shimmering gold-colored robes completely hid his frame, and the golden mask—which to Bip's mind resembled the face of a toddler who had just successfully stolen a biscuit—covered his head completely.

The man who stood on the king's right, however, had no such

finery. He wore only a long-coated gray uniform that, while subtly altered from those Bip had seen in Panthalus and the Free Countries, was recognizable as the Regulator uniform. Evidently this man, with his insidious moustache and watchful, amused eyes, was the sheriff.

"Welcome, my friends!" said the sheriff, and Handen pegged him immediately—anyone who crafts your doom and still insists on calling you "friend," he later told Bip, is a man that can be trusted about as far as you can throw him.

"What a time the Empire has had trying to keep up with you! Most distressed, they have been!" Though the sheriff's Imperial was impeccable, the rich timbre of his desert birth still reverberated through his sentences with a syrupy bass. "Imagine my surprise when, having just been informed of your escape, my informers told of two white-skinned strangers wandering around." The sheriff laughed a deep and unpleasant laugh. The golden mask of the king turned slightly at the sound, but nothing was said.

"Is that what we're to be tried for?" said Handen. "Escape?"

"Amongst other things," the sheriff purred. "Our lord Emperor Draegul (may snakes infest the underwear drawers of his enemies) has taken a particular interest in you."

Bip and Handen shared a brief glance, the same question running through their minds: why would the Emperor be interested in two escaped mental patients?

"And now," continued the sheriff, "it gives me enormous pleasure to turn to our great and good king to offer judgment on your souls."

The king's golden mask seemed to look in all directions, as though abruptly awoken from a catnap. He raised a hand from beneath his robes and seemed as if he were about to say something. Before he could, however, the sheriff began speaking again.

"For the crimes of escaping Imperial justice, for the brutal assault of a respected Regulator, for impersonating sane people, and for, no doubt, countless thefts and murders we have yet to find evidence of, you are to be detained until the relevant Imperial authorities can arrive and exact justice." The echoes of the sheriff's words were quickly captured and smothered by the thick silence of the throne room.

"Funny," Bip said. "The king managed to say all that without moving his mouth."

The sheriff's expression of amused authority was replaced in a flash by a broiling outrage. "Silence, you scum!" he roared. "The king does not need to soil his holy tongue with unnecessary platitudes for worthless dunebug dung like yourselves. His wisdom has been made known through my person!"

The king's golden mask tilted slightly to one side. He seemed to shrug under the heavy folds of his robes. The sheriff calmed himself before speaking again.

"And now, His Majesty is tired from his duties and wishes to retire for the day. Have these two criminals clapped in irons and detained in the royal dungeons."

***

IT COULD BE ARGUED that the royal dungeons were another part of the Last Palace where great care and attention had been taken to ensure the glory days were preserved and painstakingly restored. However, how much care and attention it actually took to ensure a room remained a slime-covered, dust-ridden tomb of hopelessness was debatable. Certainly the underground dungeons served the purpose they had originally been designed for, which was to be unpleasant and inescapable. If despair had a smell, then these dungeons stank of it.

Bip and Handen had been manacled to the walls, just in case several feet of brick tempered by time into something hard and organic posed too much of an escape opportunity. Handen experimented with the rusted but still thick chains, leaning all his weight and putting all his muscle into trying to dislodge the manacles from the wall, but his efforts were in vain. The manacles held fast.

"Sorry, Bip," the adventurer said. "I don't think we'll be getting out of here in a hurry."

"Damn," said Bip.

They hung in silence for a while, looking about the slick-walled prison around them.

"And you're sure you can't see any loose bricks or handy drains?" said Bip eventually.

"You mean since we looked last time? No."

"Okay, okay," Bip said testily. "I just thought we might have missed something. Or something..."

"You know," said Handen thoughtfully, "it's always struck me as strange that there seems to be this odd romantic belief going around that jails are easily escapable, somehow." He looked around at the solid-stone walls and the small but thick wooden door. "When, clearly, the very nature of a prison is to make sure you can't escape."

The two prisoners hung around. It was all they could do, really.

"Any luck with your psyence?" Handen said after a while.

"No, no good," replied Bip. "It's really hard to concentrate when you're hanging by your wrists from the ceiling."

"Yeah, I noticed that," said Handen.

The two continued to hang, swaying slightly as the air currents were disturbed by the slamming of a door somewhere in the labyrinth of the palace's lower levels. "What we need is some kind of miracle," Bip said.

"It wouldn't go amiss, no," agreed Handen.

"Some sort of nick-of-time rescue wouldn't be too bad."

"Yeah."

"Or maybe a sudden pardon."

"Yep."

"Or possibly a huge pink dragon will come along and whisk us off to the land of happy chocolate."

"Yes, that's just as likely, really."

Bip looked over at his cellmate. "You could at least humor me, you know," he said reproachfully.

"Sorry, kid, I'm fresh out of optimism," replied the former Hostilities Advisor. After a short interval of silence, Handen looked over at the downcast face of the younger man. He sighed. "Tell you what; if an opportunity arises for a sudden and dramatic escape, you'll be the first person I tell. How's that?" he said.

Bip nodded. "It's a start."

Somewhere in the lower levels another door slammed, echoing

mournfully and harassing dust-motes throughout the sepulchral passageways.

"What do you suppose that was?" said Bip.

Handen didn't answer. Despite his earlier pessimistic assertions, the survivalist part of his brain was still desperately thinking of escape scenarios. He had thought of a few, but all relied heavily on specific and unlikely circumstances and a great deal of luck. Handen, of course, had no qualms about gambling with his own life (an immortal's prerogative), but was less willing to risk the skin of his relatively innocent companion. He was shaken from his thoughts by the heavy clunk of the cell door being unlocked. The tiny wooden door swung open with a protesting creak, and two of the impassive royal guardsmen entered.

"Surely the Regulators can't be here already?" Bip said, trying unsuccessfully to keep the panic from his voice.

The guards, as expected, said nothing. Instead, they waited until a third figure had entered the room. A figure attired from head to toe in gold.

"Well, well, well," said Handen. "If it isn't His Majesty. Where's your parrot? Or are you speaking up for yourself this time?"

The king didn't answer. Instead, he made a hand signal, and the two guards left the cell, shutting the door behind them. The king stood and looked at the prisoners manacled to the wall, his golden mask glowing eerily in the half-light of the dungeon.

"If you've come to gloat, we're not interested," said Handen. "Trust me, when it comes to gloating evil tyrants, I've heard the best, so you may as well just sod off!"

The face of the king's golden mask turned to Bip. A voice came from within. "He's a bit touchy, isn't he?"

Bip frowned. Though the voice reverberated oddly in the metal of the mask, there was no mistaking the thick Port Town accent.

The king removed his mask, revealing the crooked grin of a crooked man. "Alright?" he said.

Bip's jaw hung with the rest of his body. Though his skin was now deeply tanned and his hair was a little longer, there was no mistaking the face of Azron Bezron.

"Azron?" Bip gasped, too surprised to think of anything more original.

"The one and only," said the thief, and gave a sardonic little bow.

Bip's face twitched with conflicting emotions. Finally, it settled on puzzlement.

"You're the King of Nastre?" he said.

Azron rolled his eyes. "Hardly," he scoffed "I nicked it, didn't I?"

"How can you steal a kingdom?" said Bip, struggling to keep up.

"Well, I was hanging around, minding my own business, sort of thing, and I thought I'd check out the palace. Do a bit of sightseeing, you know? So I climb through a window and there's this old geezer answering a call of nature, yeah?"

"You didn't hurt him, did you?" asked Bip, his eyes narrowing mistrustfully.

"Course not! Would I do such a thing?" Azron smiled the smile of an innocent. On his face, it looked dirty. "Anyway, I didn't have to," he continued. "The old duffer took one look at me and keeled over from a heart attack."

"So what did you do?" said Bip.

"Well, next thing I know, there's these people banging on the door asking if everything's all right. So I put on my best old man voice and tell them I'm fine, (though it's hard 'cause I don't now much Trade Speak), then, when I'm wondering how I'm going to get myself out of this one, I find these little numbers." Azron gestured to his robes and the mask in his hand. "I put 'em on, stick the geezer in the bottom of the linen cupboard, and next thing I know, everyone's calling me 'Your Majesty.' Pretty nifty, eh?"

Bip's eyes were wide with disbelief. "You've been impersonating the king?"

"Yeah, for about three days now. It's easier than you'd think. No one asks me anything important, and I just nod and wave a bit. No one's the wiser."

"Unbelievable," Bip breathed. "Miraculous, in fact. "

"Ahem," said Handen. "Isn't anyone going to introduce me?"

"Oh...how rude of me," said Bip (and Handen despaired that he actually meant it). "Azron, this is Handen. Handen, Azron."

"That's Azron Bezron Diamond Geezer (1st Class)," the thief interjected smoothly. "Port Town Union of Dodgy Fellows"

"Impressive," said Handen. "I'd shake your hand, only..." He rolled his eyes meaningfully at his manacled wrists.

"Oh yeah, of course! Best be getting you down." Azron fished in his robes for a moment and eventually retrieved a set of lock picks. "Have you free in a jiffy." He grinned.

It was the work of a moment for the thief to tamper with the manacle locks ("Heavy duty, but essentially basic," he muttered as he worked), and it wasn't long before Handen and Bip had their feet on the ground once more, massaging and rotating life back into their shoulders and wrists.

Bip stretched his back and winced as it popped audibly. "What next?" he said.

"Now we get the hell out of here before someone comes to check on you," said Azron.

"Or somebody checks the linen cupboard," Handen added.

"Ah. Yes, well. That too..."

"How will we get out of the palace? The whole place must be crawling with guards," said Bip.

Azron grinned. "Exactly." He rummaged in his robes again until he fished out two watoki blades and two of the facemasks worn by the royal guardsmen. "So no one will notice a few more! As long as we keep moving, everyone will think you two are just another couple of bodyguards."

A smile broke over Handen's face. "I'm glad to see you're so prepared."

"Always prepare for the possibility that you'll be run out of town by an angry mob, that's what my old man used to say."

"And what happened to him?" asked Bip.

"Well, he...erm...he was killed by an angry mob, actually."

The fugitives and the impostor stood in an uncomfortable silence for a moment. "Well," said Handen, eventually. "No sense standing around waiting for death when there's escaping to be done. Azron, this is your plan—you lead the way."

Azron nodded and donned his golden mask. "Let's go."

THEIR ESCAPE through the halls of the Last Palace was largely uneventful. They strode along the corridors with phony confidence while guardsmen saluted their passing. Two solitary guards wandering around the halls by themselves, perhaps, would have drawn the attention of a sharp-eyed watchman; the presence of the king, however, (or at least the king's golden mask), more or less cemented their authenticity.

There was a moment of sheer dread as they masqueraded their way to freedom, one moment that sent a cold sweat of ugly certainty across the brows of all three men. That moment was, as they hurried down a dust-licked corridor, when the sheriff rounded the corner ahead of them, unexpected and as sudden as a static shock.

Bip felt his heart beating a mad tattoo against his ribs as the Imperial man approached. He tried to look straight ahead and continue the marching gait they had fallen into. He concentrated so hard that for one ludicrous and panicky moment, he completely forgot how to walk. On the verge of stumbling and sprawling hopelessly to the floor, the Kaneqian was shocked to a sudden stop as they were hailed in the Trade Speak tongue.

The sheriff approached with his usual look of patronizing amusement, extenuated by his oily moustache, and for a moment, Bip was certain they had been discovered, expecting at any moment a contingent of the royal guard to round the corner in the sheriff's wake. His terrible certainty turned to dread confusion as the sheriff began chattering to Azron in Trade Speak, talking animatedly and cheerfully as though everything were fine. Neither Bip nor Handen could understand a word that was being said, and if Azron understood anything that was said to him, it was belied only by the way he nodded now and then and copied any hand gestures made.

There was collective sigh of relief as the sheriff walked away, laughing hard at some joke that had never made translation.

"What was he saying?" Bip whispered through the side of his mouth.

"I have no idea," replied Handen.

It was a close one but was the only time they came near to discovery before they reached the king's chambers. Once the door was safely locked behind them, Azron removed his royal attire and searched under the large, luxurious bed for his own clothes—his familiar long coat and peak-less woolen hat. Once changed, he looked under an ornate dresser and retrieved a rope that had been fashioned from silken bed sheets. Handen once again admired the forethought of a man who was always in need of an escape route. They dangled the rope from the huge bedroom window and slid down into the velvety night. Once free from the palace, sneaking into the camouflaging hubbub of the market square was an easy task.

As luck would have it, the livery master had not yet heard the rumors of fugitives in his city, so Bip and Handen's horses and equipment were still packed and ready to go. They mounted up and made ready.

Handen looked down at Azron. "I take it you're joining us?" he said.

"I don't think there's much of a future for me here once they find out the king's dead."

"Then you'd better mount up behind me," said Handen.

The thief, unpracticed in matters equine, struggled into the saddle behind the adventurer.

"We'd best not stick around," said Azron.

"I wasn't planning to," replied Handen.

"Good," muttered Azron. "I didn't understand much of what that bastard sheriff was saying, but I did pick out the words 'Emperor' and 'visit.'"

Without further talk, the three fugitives galloped east and once more into the Bone Desert.

---

6

Personal Attention

---

I t was the next day. The extraordinary events of the previous night, the capture and escape of an alien and a descendant of aliens, aided by a thief who had been impersonating a dead king, seemed like day-dreamish fiction in the dawn-soaked and hardpan streets of Nastre. The citizens got on with their lives as always, greeting the much-loved apathy of inexorable routine that rose with the sun. They might have looked at the day a little differently if they had known that their king was dead and that their sheriff was as close as he had ever been to complete terror.

Sheriff Muntave Nenta stalked the corridors of the Last Palace. The look of smirking superiority had fled his face some hours ago, when he had been awoken abruptly in the early hours of the morning. Now his face was set in a grimace somewhere between panic and fury.

During the night, the king's body had been discovered by a chambermaid.

Though the maid herself had never seen the true face of the king, a dead old man stuffed into a linen cupboard was still enough to upset her a great deal. Her screams had brought the skeleton nightshift of the royal guard in less than a minute. Sheriff Muntave had been awoken not long afterward.

It hadn't taken him long to put two and two together. The body of the king was clearly not fresh, and he had likely been dead for more than a day. Muntave remembered clearly the conversation he'd had with the bearer of the golden mask before retiring to his quarters for the night. He had remembered thinking that the king, as old as he was, was a little more sedate and impassive than usual, but had pinned it on nothing more than the old fool's advancing years. Cold rage had sloshed in his stomach as he realized the huge error in judgment he had made. His anger had quickly been taken over by his dread when he'd found that the two prized prisoners had escaped. He had done nothing but stare at the empty cell for some time, as if willing himself to wake up from a stubborn and terrible nightmare. Then, with a sudden explosion of energy, he had screamed orders to any and every member of staff he encountered. The prisoners had to be bought back, and they had less than a day to do it.

When Muntave had first captured the prisoners and realized that they were valuable to the Emperor, he had wasted no time in sending a runner to the telegraph station to relay the good news to Argustin. Once the Emperor heard the news, Muntave knew it was likely a delegate would be sent to Nastre, and recognition and reward would surely follow. However, if the delegate were to travel all the way to Nastre only to be greeted by an empty cell and a flurry of excuses, then demotion or worse was a definite possibility. With this in mind, Muntave had diverted all of Nastre's meagre forces into conducting a blanket search covering the entire city and the outlying villages. Civilian militias were formed and the closest thing Nastre had seen to martial law in centuries was imposed.

All to no avail.

Eventually the sheriff acknowledged the frightening possibility that the prisoners had escaped into the Bone Desert and, with so many miles of empty country to search and the shifting sands making tracking impossible, it was unlikely they could be recaptured in time. After doing practically everything he could do, and after pacing needlessly around the palace when it became clear that nothing else could be done, Muntave sat down in his chambers and contemplated his fate. The severity of his punishment would increase with the rank of the delegate, he knew, and if a representative were sent directly from Argustin, it was likely the rank would be very high indeed.

His musings took him through the night and into the next morning. He did not sleep, only sat, thinking and hoping, barely noticing as another dawn filtered through his window.

He remembered his childhood in Gorner, a small village just outside the main city. He had taken advantage of the limited educational prospects and schooled very hard, determined—unlike most of his school friends, who didn't fight against the inevitability of following in their fathers' footsteps—to escape the sleepy village and make a name for himself in the desert kingdom.

His good intentions had eventually become outright ambition and then slowly, imperceptibly, an obsession with power and respect. He had gradually ostracized himself, unwittingly at first, from his friends and family until, almost inevitably, his quest for advancement had taken him to Imperial schoolings. Here he had learnt about business, about tax and finance and law. He had learnt to be ruthless and analytical, to sacrifice reason for logic and to gain a lyrical understanding of the complex art of bureaucracy. He had severed the final ties to his roots in Gorner without hesitation when he'd been offered a place in the Imperial Academy, where he'd achieved with brains and cunning what most achieved with muscle and contacts—an officer rank in the Regulators.

He had been back to Gorner only once since then, where he'd been greeted with cold politeness, as a stranger in what had once been his home. The warm village life had left him feeling an outsider, bitterly cold and alienated. For a moment, he had wondered how long it had been since he had laughed, not the loud booming laugh he used when a superior cracked a joke, but genuinely laughed as his old friends and family seemed to do every day.

*No matter*, he had thought. *They're jealous of my success. Most of them will never leave this dead-end little village unless it is to sell corn on the market.*

As he'd impressed his way up the ranks of officer-hood with quite causal ease, it had only occurred to him just as he was surrendering to sleep at night that perhaps the villagers would all lead much happier lives than his, that perhaps contentment could come without success. These thoughts were dismissed by morning, when Muntave had continued to lash his silver tongue and drive his analytical brain until the day when, some years later, he'd been appointed sheriff of the very city he had fled from so many years ago.

Muntave enjoyed his position in Nastre. It was a peaceful and undemanding station, and his power over the king allowed him luxuries not always granted to a sheriff. But all of that seemed set to change. He knew it was likely, when his failure was made apparent, that he would be transferred to somewhere where life was not so easy. He shuddered as he thought of a posting in the tough frontier stations. The deep south lands of Barruk, where orcen tribes still randomly raided and terrorized. Or the far east postings, where elfen citizens protested almost continually against Imperial occupation.

Worse, he thought, was the possibility of being posted even further west, where Imperial forces still struggled to find a foothold in the strange, demon-infested lands of Dead Country. He briefly considered a life of struggle where monsters and species rarely seen these days in Regalious were still thriving. Prison would be better. Better than pitting sword and flintlock against giggling jeckles or cold-fleshed dedmen. That was a job for the young, strong, and foolish. Not for one accustomed to the flabby and bureaucratic lifestyle of a backwater sheriff.

He shivered again and jumped to his feet as Bentive, his personal assistant, came crashing into his quarters.

"Forgive me, sire—" Bentive began, breathing heavily as if having run a long way.

"What news?" interrupted Muntave, his manner cool and commanding despite the nervousness that knotted his intestines.

"The Argustin delegation has been spotted, sire."

Muntave looked out of his chamber window, a far-away melancholy taking over his features. "How long?" he said.

"Perhaps a few hours, sire."

"You may leave."

Bentive bowed and left the room. Muntave wondered if anyone would ever bow to him again after today.

The delegate had arrived sooner than he had expected. Presumably airboat technology had advanced since he had last been in the Empire's heart. It was likely. Muntave sighed and straightened his collar, preparing to meet his fate with as much dignity as he could muster.

---

BIP AND HANDEN rode out across the desert, their new companion holding on tightly behind Handen as he was jolted and jiggled by unaccustomed horsemanship. Their mounts panted in the crippling heat of the day. Handen was riding them harder than he would have recommended in other situations, traveling even through the lethal sunbeat of the afternoon. He suspected it would be necessary. Even though it was unlikely that their pursuers knew which direction they had set out in, and the constant desert winds would have obscured any of their tracks, Handen thought it only a matter of time until the Regulators started making educated assumptions about where the fugitives would be likely to pass through. After all, no one could survive out in the Bone Desert for long.

With this in mind, Handen's goal was to get out of the desert before the Empire had enough time to react to their escape and organize a manhunt. It was risky, especially with the adventurer's horse carrying two, but a small group traveling fast would always have a head start on a larger one, which would be more difficult to co-ordinate across hostile terrain. And, with any luck, it would be some time before their disappearance was discovered.

They rode almost continuously, stopping every couple of hours for a short rest for the sake of the horses before moving on again. They halted and made a cold camp only once during the night, taking the time to eat, savoring the dried meat and hot Nastren coffee and feeling their energy replenish. After a short nap, during which Handen kept watch, they were on the move again, too fatigued even to talk to one another.

The possibility of riding the mounts into exhaustion before reaching a place of safety had occurred to Handen often, and once again, he found himself relying on an element of luck to ensure their survival. He grimaced into the sandy breeze of the Bone Desert, looking across at the drawn face of Bip and feeling the slacking grip of the dozing thief behind him.

They would try their luck.

---

MUNTAVE MOPPED his brow with a gray lace handkerchief. He was sweating far more than the heat of the day called for, especially since he was standing in the cool stone shade of the palace courtyard.

Nastre did not have an airdock and the courtyard, being the widest piece of uncluttered land in the city, would have to serve.

Muntave had already looked through the telescope at the arriving airboat, but he looked again, praying he was wrong. He wasn't. The narrow airboat (sleeker and better crafted than the civilian carriers, designed for speed rather than cargo carrying) was adorned with the colors not just of Argustin, but also of Dawncastle itself. Any hopes Muntave had harbored of the delegate being of similar rank to his own evaporated instantaneously. Dawncastle was the base of operations for the Emperor himself, and anyone sent directly from there would be a Pin Constable at least.

To his right, Bentive stood to rigid attention. Bentive, whose mannerisms and thin moustache reminded Muntave so much of himself when he had been a young man. Bentive, who would most likely climb up the ranks until he too was sheriff. Or perhaps even Grand Constable. Muntave took a moment to wonder whether Bentive was sacrificing as much as he had once sacrificed for his ambition.

He tried not to let his nervousness show as the airboat, now hovering overhead, was tethered to the palace walls. Eventually the guide rope for the balloon crane was lowered into the center of the courtyard. The quartet of musicians Muntave had hastily prepped for the arrival began a trumpet fanfare that lasted until the balloon-tethered elevator eventually touched down.

The assembled crowd waited as the balloon crane was tied, all eager to see who would emerge from the ornate passenger trunk. Two footmen abseiled quickly from the airboat above and opened the double doors. By some unseen device, a red carpet flicked gracefully out of the passenger compartment doorway and rolled across the courtyard. A dozen burly soldiers dressed in the black and silver colors of Dawncastle stamped out to form an honor guard along the edges of the carpet. The soldiers—each one's face obscured by a heavy, black helm—each clutched a hulking flintlock rifle, heavy enough fire power to bring down a jabberwocky should need be. Muntave's heart caught in his throat as a figure began to emerge from the balloon crane.

Emperor Tomberry Torrid Draegul the Tenth came forth into the daylight.

There was no mistaking him—most every citizen of Regalious knew the Emperor's likeness, be it from coin or statue, tapestry or commemorative plate. His face was pale, smooth, and delicate, near flawless but for the hooded cast of his eyes. With long, raven hair held back by the silver band of his crown, Draegul looked younger than his forty years. He verged on handsome, but something in the set of his gaze and the crook of his smile made his features unnerving.

He wore the silver and black robes of his station along with the symbolic katana at his hip and the rifle slung over his shoulder. These weapons, ornate and beautiful so as to represent the majesty and might of the Empire, were nonetheless kept primed and ready, each respectively sharpened and loaded every day.

He made an impressive figure, half mythic warrior and half bonny prince.

Though if you heard him laugh, or talked to him about his passions, doubtless your perceptions of him would change. The noble features would become the cold face of a killer. The regal stature would become the conspiring hunch of the chronic schemer.

Draegul looked like a hero. He thought like a villain. Too many people realized this too late.

Muntave had no trouble falling to his knees with the rest of the assemblage; in fact, he would have been very hard pressed to stand up. The musical quartet, who had faltered momentarily, began to play the Argustin anthem, and the Emperor walked along the carpet toward the sheriff. Muntave tried to control his visible quaking as the Emperor approached. He knelt down and kissed the ground in front of him, as was customary.

"You may rise," said Draegul. His voice was light but not melodious.

Muntave got slowly to his feet but remained looking at the floor. He fought hard to keep the stutter from his voice. "Your Holiness, this is a most pleasant surprise."

"Isn't it, though?" said Draegul. "I do like to get out and about now and again, you know. See how my Empire is flourishing." His voice hardened almost imperceptibly. "How my trusted lieutenants are fairing."

Muntave looked up and caught the cold gaze from the Emperor's deep black eyes. He had a sudden urge to throw himself to the floor and cry for forgiveness, and felt his knees struggling to comply.

"Where are the prisoners?" Draegul said casually, as though he had traveled several hundred miles just to make small talk.

Muntave's mouth flapped of its own accord for a while, desperately trying to form the correct words. Finally, they came. "They've escaped."

The Emperor continued to stare at the sheriff for what seemed like an eternity. "Blungkit?" he said eventually.

Muntave's gaze tore itself away from the Emperor's to the man who flanked his right shoulder like some dark conscience. He wore the neatly cut uniform of a Panthalus province Regulator, but he had the face of a street vagrant. His mouth gleamed wetly as he talked.

"Yes, Your Greatness?" he said.

"Shoot this man in the heart."

"Yes, Your Greatness."

Muntave's mouth only had time to form a quizzical "o" before Blungkit drew his flintlock and fired, blowing a neat, wide hole in the sheriff's chest. Muntave fell to his knees once more and looked up into the black eyes of the Emperor. They were cold and dismissive, but undoubtedly predatory, as though an animal madness lived behind the calm features of Bersch's most powerful man.

*Like a shark*, Muntave thought, and then he died.

The courtyard rang with silence, the assemblage trying desperately not to show how horrified they were. Bentive made a slight burping noise. Some of Muntave's blood had splashed on his tunic. To his horrified surprise, he realized the Emperor was pointing at him.

"You are now sheriff of Nastre," he said.

Bentive saluted smartly, then gestured to a couple of the stunned Nastren guards to dispose of the body of his predecessor. Despite his shock and disgust, he could not conceal a thin smile. Promotion came quickly when you worked close to the Emperor.

"Well, well, well!" said Draegul suddenly, an odd chirpiness making his flat voice sound almost pleasant. "This is a turn-up for the books, isn't it, Blungkit?"

Blungkit still stood smartly to his Emperor's right, his smoking pistola safely holstered again. "Yes, sire," he said indifferently.

"It seems the doomsayers have eluded you again," said Draegul. There was an accusatory undertone to his pleasantness and he made no show of hiding it.

Blungkit's face remained impassive. Since reporting the escape of the two fugitives, Blungkit had been more than surprised when the Emperor had taken a personal interest in the investigation. When Draegul had learned that the wooden-toothed Regulator was partly responsible for the escape, he had, much to everyone's surprise, promoted the him to Pin Constable—a position surpassing the rank of general in the Imperial army—and subsequently made him personally responsible for the recapture of the fugitives. Blungkit, whose thoughts were large and blundering things, had nonetheless realized that his promotion was also his punishment—should he fail in his duties, his life would more than likely be forfeit. Muntave's sudden and violent death was testament to that.

"They shan't elude me for long, sire," he said.

"Really?" said Draegul. "What makes you so sure? They've made a very good job of it so far."

Blungkit was not classically educated. Nor was he trained from birth for higher thinking. Certainly the bloodline of a thousand Emperors did not flow through his veins. He was a man who had cut his teeth on hard streets and had earned a diploma in treading on people's necks. However, he was beginning to realize that the Emperor was a man after his own heart. He knew a nasty, vindictive bastard when he saw one, and Draegul was one of the best. Blungkit respected that.

"They would have gone into the desert, sire. No question. They'll be expecting us to follow them in, no doubt, and be inconvenienced by the terrain."

The Emperor smiled. One of the many talents he prided himself on was his judgement of character, and he had certainly been proved right in his assessment of Blungkit. The man was just stubborn enough to take the escape of the doomsayers personally, and by far nasty enough to hunt them to the ends of Bersch if needed. Draegul knew that Blungkit, even without the threat of death hanging over his head, would dog the fugitives relentlessly and rabidly.

"What is your plan, then, Pin Constable?"

"Easy one, sire. Just a process of deduction, if you like." Blungkit began to count down on his meaty fingers. "Everyone's on high alert back in the city provinces, so we don't have to worry about them going north. They wouldn't last more than a week in the Bone Desert, so we can forget about them going west. Same for south. So that only leaves east to worry about, the Dozantyne Shrub."

Draegul smiled. Blungkit was a useful man. Like all good policemen, he had the mind of a criminal.

Blungkit continued. "I suggest we skirt around the desert to the telegraph station, organize reinforcements, and head south 'til we cuts through their trail."

"Excellent!" Draegul clapped his delicate hands. "You're a god-ugly baboon's rump of a man, Blungkit, but you make a damn good Pin Constable. Keep this up, and I might think twice about having you flayed alive."

Despite the joviality of Draegul's tone, Blungkit knew he was being deadly serious. "Thank you, sire," he said.

"And now I'm afraid I must leave you. I have other matters to attend to."

"As you will, sire," said Blungkit. He waited until the Emperor boarded the balloon crane before turning back to the shell-shocked Nastren Guard.

"All right, you useless shower of bastards, let's move!"

————————————————

7

## The Dozantyne Shrub

————————————————

There was a garden. It was lovely. That was the only word he could think of, really. It was peaceful, certainly, well kept, definitely. But the word that kept coming back to him was "lovely."

He looked down at the cup and saucer in his hands, and though the day was pleasantly warm, he appreciated the hot ceramic in his hand. A sweet smell rose up from the cup. He couldn't place it, but the smell was relaxing.

He felt totally at peace. He tried to think of the last time he'd felt this relaxed but couldn't. Other times and places seemed a little fuzzy in the garden.

There was another man there. He sat across from him in a deck chair, sipping something from his own cup. He seemed pleasant enough, with his broad face and his wiry gray hair held down by a well-worn flat cap. He appeared to be the gardener.

"It's lovely," said Bip.

The man turned to him as if acknowledging him for the first time.

"The garden," said Bip, dreamily. "It's lovely. "

"Thank you," said the man. "I try to keep it neat. "

Bip seemed to wake up a bit. He couldn't remember how he had got there. "Who are you?" he said.

The man slurped noisily from his cup. "I'm Ted," he said. "Pleased to meet you."

"What is this place?" said Bip.

"This is my garden," said Ted. He wasn't patronizing, but there was an amused twinkle in his eye.

"It's lovely," said Bip again. He couldn't think what else to say. "You must spend a lot of time on it."

Ted nodded sagely, his flat cap bobbing up and down on his head. "All the time in the world," he said.

A sudden surreal feeling swept over Bip. It felt a little like when Mr. Random visited, but without the nagging incongruity.

"Who are you really?" asked Bip.

"I told you," Ted replied. "I'm Ted."

"Then what are you?"

The older man laughed, and there was something about that laugh that made Bip feel totally at ease. "A better question! Much better. But do you really want the answer?"

Bip looked at the old man. He felt sleepy, suddenly, as if having just woken from a pleasant dream. He nodded his head.

"I'm commonly known as the Universal Theory. Though Ultraversal Theory might be more accurate. Or, if you liked, you could call me the Creation Equation, the Infinite Balance, The Master Plan, or the Only Blueprint. Though Ted will suffice, for now."

Bip nodded. Despite the vastness of what he had just been told, he didn't feel at all surprised. He felt quite calm, actually.

"I expect you'd probably like me to elaborate?" prompted Ted.

Bip nodded again. There seemed little else he could do.

"To put it in layman's terms, imagine if everything in the universes is the answer to a long and drawn out question. Well, I'm that question."

Bip nodded. "God?" he said.

Ted laughed a little. "No, no," he said. "Quite different." He paused to sip more of his tea before continuing. "I am the thing that unites all energies within the spectrum of existence, the hand that weaves the strings. Across the length of all dimensions, I am the common denominator. I'm a sort of a metaphysical embodiment of the nature of the Ultraverse. If infinity is a story, then I am the one reading it aloud, for no story can exist without a reader." Ted put down his cup and looked Bip straight in the eye. "Because of me: Everything."

Bip looked blank for a while. "Everything is a gardener?" he ventured.

Ted laughed again. "This?" he said, gesturing around him. "This is just window dressing. A place I like to bring people. A face I like to show."

"What are you like really?" said Bip.

"I could show you the bright lights of hidden galaxies. I could take you to voids verging on infinity. I could show you the tiniest daisy in a field, because all of these things are me. I am the Soul of the Whole. I am the question of which all other questions were born."

Bip leaned back in his deckchair. "That's nice," he said.

They drank tea in silence. Bip was surprised by the smooth sweetness of the concoction. *Like back in Kaneq*, he thought. *Milk, two sugars.*

"I suppose your next question will be 'why?'" said Ted after a while.

"Why what?" Bip replied dreamily.

"Why are you here?"

"I don't know!"

"Exactly!"

They looked at each other for a while. Ted waited for Bip to catch up. The garden could be distracting, he knew.

"I wanted to let you know a little about what you're up against," said Ted. "In this universe, everything is going as the plan intended. But there are those who would go against the plan."

"The Discordance," said Bip.

"Not just the Discordance," said Ted. "Every conscious being has the ability to challenge the blueprint."

"What happens when they do?" Bip interrupted.

"What happens when an unstoppable force meets an immovable object?" replied Ted.

"There's a massive explosion?" ventured Bip.

"No."

"A massive implosion?"

"No. The unstoppable force stops, the immovable object moves." Ted leaned back in his deckchair.

Bip looked blank.

"Nothing is infallible," said Ted. "Not even me. If the blueprint of a universe is changed, then the blueprint is changed. But this is not always for the better and more often than not is for the worse. That is why there are those who would actively prevent interference to appropriate causality."

"The Clarions?"

"Amongst many, yes. The Caretakers, as I believe they are known in this neck of the Ultraverse."

"You needn't worry about me," said Bip, suddenly worried about why he was being told all this. "I'm with the good guys. Order over chaos. Yep, that's me!"

Ted looked at the Kaneqian long and hard. "I know you are a good man, Bip—I can see these things—but you must realize that what you think of as order and chaos are not necessarily good or bad."

"What do you mean?" said Bip.

Ted clucked his tongue and looked thoughtful for a moment.

Suddenly a bright light flashed, and Bip found himself in a long, well-lit room.

The lights here reminded him of the ones back in the Dome. Before him was what appeared to be a huge picture, though picture was a lenient word. It looked mostly like a humungous wash of unplanned color. Bip started as Ted appeared beside him.

"Where are we?" asked Bip.

"In the Tate Modern. An art gallery in a place called London in a galaxy and universe not too dissimilar to your own."

"Why are we here?" said Bip, glancing around the deserted hall. He could see other artworks now. All neatly displayed behind fuzzy rope of some kind.

"To look at the paintings, of course." Ted grinned. "I wanted to show you this one in particular."

Bip looked at the colossal typhoon of paint before him. "I don't see what's so special about it," he said.

"Come away with me a bit," said Ted. He placed his hand on Bip's shoulder, and the Kaneqian wobbled uneasily as he felt himself being carried back along the corridor without the movement of his legs being involved. To his surprise, the indecipherable mess of the painting slowly transformed into a picture of an attractive woman. Bip gasped at the optical illusion.

"You see?" said Ted. "Where there first appears to be only chaos, there is order. A planned design."

"Wow," breathed Bip.

"But that's not the point I'm trying to make," said Ted, and waved his hand. There was another bright light and then before him the painting still hung, but against a backdrop of stars and blackness. Bip looked around and clung terrified to Ted's shoulder as he realized he was standing on an infinite star-studded void.

"It's okay, Bip," said Ted, and Bip calmed. Something about Ted's voice was instantly soothing. "Now see here," said the gardener, and pointed at the painting that now hung eerily in the void. Then all of a sudden, Bip felt himself being moved backward again, this time countless miles rather than the length of a museum corridor. As his perspective widened, he saw not just one picture but dozens, then hundreds, then uncountable millions. Soon he was looking at one gargantuan picture, the same unplanned mess he had first seen in the museum.

"And order gives way to chaos," said Ted. "But wait, there's more."

Bip felt the sensation of being drawn back again. The huge mess of a picture gave way to the picture of the woman once again, hanging in the stars like some ancient goddess. This time, though, they did not stop to regard the picture, but continued to draw back. The picture once again gave way to thousands, which once again gave way to the chaotic mess, which once again became the woman. This happened again and again until Bip thought he was going to be sick.

"Order, chaos; chaos, order," said Ted in a singsong-ish voice.

"Stop," said Bip, weakly. "Stop, please."

The bright light flashed once more, and once again they were in the garden. Bip felt instantly at peace.

"You see?" said Ted. "Chaos and Order. Order and Chaos. Really just two ways of looking at the same thing."

Bip nodded. It made sense. He thought of the shapes you could find in clouds sometimes, if you looked the right way. Though it might just be your imagination, it didn't necessarily mean the patterns weren't there.

"The Discordance believe that chaos is the natural state of the universe and, therefore, chaos must be created via the destruction of order. The Clarions believe that the natural state of the universe is order and that order must be protected and maintained." Ted refilled his cup from the teapot. "So you see, both are a little wrong, both are a little right. What they don't seem to acknowledge is what I have just shown you—that order and chaos both have their places in the ultra-verse—are, indeed, both one and the same depending on where you're standing."

Bip thought about what had been said for a while. "What are you getting at?" he asked finally.

"That the only trouble with either belief comes when the universal plan is challenged by the assertion of those beliefs."

Bip nodded, keeping up.

"Now," continued Ted, "I'll warrant you, it's usually the Discordance that are the troublemakers. Most of the Caretakers leave things well enough alone unless there's interference—which is fine. But this time. This time things are different."

A slow and horrible understanding was beginning to creep up on Bip. "What do you mean?"

Ted sighed wearily. "The destruction of Bersch is part of this universe's plans, part of its blueprint. It has nothing to do with the Discordance."

Bip's jaw fell nearly to his chest. "But that's impossible," he flustered. "Handen said… Mr. Random even said!"

Ted held up a hand almost apologetically. "I know what you've been told, but the Caretakers made a mistake. The interference they detected was from another incident. The Massive Ball of Death heading for Bersch is my doing—it's all part of the blueprint."

"You can't do that!" said Bip. Suddenly the garden didn't seem very serene anymore.

"Can't I?" said Ted, raising his bushy eyebrows. "I already told you; I'm not a God. Not a Greatdevil, neither. I am just what is."

"What are you asking of me?" cried Bip. "To sit back and watch as a planet explodes? The one I'm standing on?"

"What I am telling you, Bip, is that the Massive Ball of Death is not the work of the Discordance."

"No! I know that! It's your bloody work, isn't it? You're the one responsible. Why are you even telling me this?"

Ted sipped his tea casually. "I am the Infinite Balance. I like to make sure everything's fair, to a degree. I thought it fair you should know that the Discordance are not responsible for the astral disaster that will destroy Bersch."

Bip frowned. He could hear what Ted was saying, but he seemed to be hinting at something else. Bip wished he could work out what but was too confused and frightened to think straight. A sudden and terrible thought occurred to Bip.

"Why didn't the distress call the *Sentinel* sent ever reach the Clarions? Or any other of the Caretakers? Why was no help sent? Was that because of the Discordance or because of you?"

Ted sighed again. "The lightwave was intercepted by a deep-space project of a much more primitive civilization. They spent a good three hundred years trying to decipher it before they filed it away for good."

"So, in other words, it was you?"

"It was part of the blueprint, yes." Ted patted Bip on the knee. "You can't take the universe personally, you know."

"I can bloody well try!" huffed Bip. "You can't expect me to sit back and watch the world explode! You said that anyone could challenge the plan—well that's just what I'm going to do!"

"That's your prerogative as a conscious being," said Ted. "I'd advise against it, though."

"Yeah, well…" said Bip, and couldn't think of any intelligent retort. "Bollocks to you!" he finished lamely. "Send me back, right now! I want to go!"

Ted smiled sadly. "As you wish," he said, and there was a bright light.

After Bip was gone, Ted got to his feet and went back to tending his garden. "He'll go far, that one," he muttered to himself.

---

BIP OPENED his eyes to see the ground rushing past his face. He heard the jingle and clop of horses, and, when a stirrup flew into his field of vision, he realized he must be hanging over his saddle. His head pounded, and a taste of vomit burned his mouth slightly. He felt as though somebody had hung him out to dry.

"Urrk?" he managed, and the sound of the horses changed. The ground stopped moving beneath him, and he was pulled from his saddle and lowered onto the ground. Above him, the concerned seriousness of Handen's face and the conspiring smirk of Azron's came into view against the painfully bright sky.

"All right, mate?" said Azron. "Have a nice kip, did we?"

"What happened?" managed Bip.

"You fainted," said Handen. "Sunstroke."

"How long was I out?" murmured Bip.

"The best part of a day. Sorry for the discomfort, but we couldn't risk stopping and waiting for you to wake up."

Bip thought back to his time in the garden. Even now it was beginning to feel like a dream. Except that some part of him knew it wasn't. As bizarre as the experience had been, something within Bip insisted it was probably the most real thing that had ever happened to him.

"You were talking in your sleep, mate," said Azron. "Having a right old prattle, you were."

"Something about a garden?" Handen prompted.

"I can't remember," lied Bip. Whatever his experience with Ted had meant for his future, he meant to deal with it by himself. He doubted whether he would ever tell Handen or Azron about it. After all, with each second that passed, Ted and the garden seemed more and more like a fever-dream.

*It wasn't, though,* whispered a solemn part of Bip's subconscious; *it was as real as the nose on your face. Maybe more so.*

"Where are we?" he said, changing the subject. His throat felt raw and sandy.

"Actually, you woke up just in time," said Handen. "We left the last of the Bone Desert behind us a few hours ago. And as luck would have it, there seems to be a settlement a few miles away."

"Running a bit low on water," said Azron by way of explanation. "Not to mention horse power."

Now that Bip concentrated, he could hear the heavy wheezing of their mounts. They had come close to running them into exhaustion, and they needed rest badly if they were to carry on. He didn't blame them; he wasn't feeling too good himself. His head felt baked from the sunstroke and he found himself wishing once more that he hadn't exploded his traveling hat.

With the help of his two companions, Bip rose unsteadily to his feet. He waited until his head stopped spinning before he focused on the far-away settlement. When he could finally see well enough to make sense of the blurred buildings, a smile broke over his face.

"It looks like a ranch," he said.

"Yep," said Handen. "And ranches mean horses. With any luck, we won't have to stop for longer than it takes to trade in for some new mounts. Maybe even a wagon."

With some effort, Bip managed to clamber back onto his horse. He waited a while until the dizziness in his head passed, then rode toward the ranch.

---

THE DOZANTYNE SHRUB was a relief from the harsh desolation of the Bone Desert, though not by much. Compared to most of the lands of Regalious, which tended to be prairie or hillside, Dozantyne was a wilderness of hardpan soil and low, flat horizons. The ground was cracked and wrinkled, the face of a hallowed ancient, its beard a fine furze of the shriveled dry weeds that were the Shrub's namesake. Though there was life here, it kept itself hunkered down in the drawling siesta of the Dozantyne afternoons, waiting for the evenings when life would become suddenly quick and aggressive.

Far off in the drowsy air, a vulture cried. No one would comfort it.

There were canyons in the Shrub, deep pits and crevices where the shade inspired tiny, thriving sub-ecologies. There were mountains of a sort, too, though they were really nothing more than giant boulders standing lonely and ridiculous in the squat surroundings. There were even forests: great clusters of long-dead trees standing dry and brittle like corpses, a tombstone reminder of the millennia ago when the Shrub had perhaps been more hospitable. In these zombie woods, deep-down creatures would bide, waiting for the stupid and the curious...

For now, though, the Shrub was merely flat and featureless, lazy geography under a tired sky. The sun always kept a watchful eye over the southlands, so the heat was still intense, though not as raging as the desert left behind them.

Amidst this slightly dreamy hell, it was quite odd to see the merry little patch of life that was the ranch. Though its stables and fencing had a distinctly home-made look about them, they were newly painted and well maintained—odd totems of freshness in this ageing landscape.

From the flat-roofed farmhouse, a man emerged. He wore a ten-gallon hat, although set above his short frame, it looked more like a twenty-gallon. The man stepped into the dusty day and grinned with benevolent optimism, his dark glasses reflecting the hostile glare of the sun and his bushy white beard shining brilliantly in the daylight. He surveyed the horizon and noted, with some pride, the complete lack of incident. Something caught his eye, however, and caused him to furrow his tangled brows. There were riders in the distance. Coming his way. In a sudden burst of movement, the man sprinted into back into his house and quickly re-emerged with what looked like a couple of boards. He sprinted to the gateways of the ranch and hooked the wooden boards onto it. Together they formed a sign that read, "Bolan Ranch—Information and Bookings." The man waited beneath the sign with a wide and welcoming grin slicing through his beard.

WHEN BIP FIRST approached the ranch, he felt pretty sure he'd lost his mind. He read the sign in its large gaudy lettering and thought, briefly, that the months of hard riding were finally taking their toll on him. His opinion was reinforced when he rode close enough to see the neon smile of the man beneath the sign, whose huge hat jarred against his loudly colored shirt. Before Bip could frame a question, the man was speaking in familiarly eager tones.

"Howdy! Howdy! Howdy! Howdy and Yee-haw! Welcome to Bolan Ranch—the most secluded, luxurious ranch getaway in the whole of the Wild Souths!"

Handen and Azron exchanged puzzled glances. Bip continued to stare open-mouthed at the familiar face before him.

"Yep!" the old man continued. "If it's the serenity of the open plains you're after, then you're in the right place! Bolan Ranch is the perfect holiday from the hustle and bustle of city life!"

"Excuse me," began Bip.

"While you're here why not try…"

"Pardon me."

"…tumbleweed surprise?! Mmm mmm! Surprisingly weedy!"

"*Hey!*"

The old man stopped, looking first confused, then a little miffed at having his sales pitch interrupted. "Yeah?" he said.

"Bolan?" Bip said.

"Bing! Two points!" replied Bolan, pumping his fist with annoying enthusiasm. Bip blinked owlishly for a while.

"How did you get here so fast?"

Bolan looked around, the grin on his face becoming uneasy. "Don't know what you mean, partner, I've been here all day."

"But you were on the island," said Bip. "Bolan Cay?"

Bolan looked over his dark glasses skeptically. "You must mean that no-good brother of mine. Island holiday resort, right?"

"Yes, that's right," said Bip, though he thought the term "holiday resort" a bit generous.

"Pah! Waste of time," said Bolan, disdainfully. "I told him from the start that no one wants to go all the way to his stupid little island for a holiday—not when they've got God's country right on their doorsteps!" Bolan opened his arms expansively, taking in the half-dead landscape of the Shrub. Bip looked around. If this was God's country, then he'd happily holiday in hell, given a choice.

Bolan's expression became suddenly worried. He leaned forward conspiringly. "He didn't have no customers, did he?" he said.

"Well…no," replied Bip.

"Hah!" Bolan grinned hugely. "I told him! I told him all along! Bolan Cay? Hah! No one wants to go to a stupid island!"

Bip frowned at the deserted ranch. "It doesn't exactly seem to be the busy season for you either," he pointed out.

"Yeah, well," said Bolan, reproachfully. "The ranch is having teething problems, that's all. Once the word gets around about this place, the tourists will stampede, I tells ya!"

*Yeah*, thought Bip, *stampede all the way to somewhere else.*

"Now, what can I do you boys for?" said Bolan, rubbing his hands together. Handen, who had been watching this exchange with a mixture of puzzlement and impatience, decided it was time to get to the point. "We need fresh horses," he said.

Bolan waved his hands dismissively. "Can't you read the sign? I'm no goldarn merchant! I only got a couple of horses and a wagon, and they're for my Scenic Wilderness Tours!"

Azron put a hand over his face. There was a sound that could have been a cough but was more likely muffled laughter.

"They sound fine," said Handen, coolly. "We'll take them."

"Now you listen here, mister! Thems horses are part of my livelihood, and I won't sells them for nothing or nobody!" Bolan crossed his arms stubbornly.

There was a dull clunk as a lump of gold landed in the dust by the old man's feet. It was quite a large lump. Bolan gasped. His passion might have been the ranch, but at his heart, he was a businessman. That lump of gold could buy a hell of a lot of scenic wilderness tours.

Bolan looked up and grinned his huge, white grin. "I tell you what, boys, you got yourselves a deal!"

---

A FEW HOURS LATER, Bolan watched as the three strangers left the ranch riding a horse-drawn wagon with the legend "Bolan Ranch Scenic Wilderness Tours" painted on its side in huge, bouncy letters. They had stopped only long enough to refill their waterskins and load up the wagon, taking advantage of some of the supplies Bolan had thrown in as part of the deal. With his newly acquired lump of gold, the possibilities for Bolan seemed endless.

*Maybe I can finally build those extra guest rooms*, thought Bolan, *for when business picks up.*

He watched the trio ride off into the uneventful sunset and felt a rise of gratitude.

"Y'all come back now, ya hear?" he called.

BIP LEANED back in the seat of the covered wagon, relaxing as the fresh horses pulled them on at a steady pace, spurred on by Handen at the reins. He felt better now he had been rested and watered. The sun was being kept from his head by a souvenir sombrero Bolan had given him. It was a nice hat, though unfortunately had "I love Bolan Ranch" written across its brim.

Azron was stretched out in the back of the wagon, smoking a cigarette and blowing smoke rings, which lingered in the air while the wagon pulled away.

"I don't see why we had to give him all that gold," he said.

"How else were we supposed to buy the horses?" said Handen.

"I could've just nicked 'em," grumbled Azron. "Wouldn't have taken long." Handen sighed. "I remind you we've got half of the Empire after us. The Emperor himself even seems to have taken a personal interest in our capture. An old man with a pocket full of gold is less likely to tell tales than an old man whose horses have just been stolen."

"Fair enough," said Azron. "But it still seemed like a lot of gold to just throw on the floor like that."

Bip looked at Handen. He'd had similar thoughts himself and wondered how much, if any, of the gold was left. He marveled briefly at how what had been a lump of relatively worthless metal in Kaneq had suddenly become so important to him.

"We'll be okay," said Handen. "I don't think we'll have much opportunity to spend it for a while, anyway."

The wagon rolled across the Shrub, kicking up dust as it went. Azron looked at a small wooden doll with a cowboy hat and a flowery shirt. He had, of course, filled his pockets up at Bolan Ranch, mostly with useless souvenirs and trinkets—not anything of worth. It was the principle that counted. He was, after all, a thief.

THEY STOPPED THAT NIGHT, more for the benefit of the horses than the passengers, who had taken turns steering in shifts, giving the opportunity for rest throughout the long day. They set up camp after the sun set. The wide-open expanses of the Shrub glowed pleasantly in the starlight, and the trio was able to set up camp unhindered by the darkness. A small fire was lit, more for the look of the thing than the necessity; unlike the Bone Desert, the nights in the Dozantyne Shrub were quite warm. There was no wind, and the heat of the day radiated from the baked earth beneath them.

The three sat around the fire while Bip slowly cooked some of the fresh meat they had packed at Bolan's. Handen, using some of the utensils they'd picked up in Nastre, was boiling up some of the rich, sticky coffee. The smells combined in a tantalizing aroma, and Bip felt his stomach rumble in anticipation.

"So, then," said Azron. "I forgot to ask in all the commotion—how's the saving the world going?" There was a slight smirk on the thief's face that indicated he was still not quite convinced of Bip's story.

"Well, I took your advice," said Bip. "I tried warning the people in the smaller cities and towns first."

"Yeah? How did that go, then?" Azron said.

"They locked me in a lunatic asylum," said Bip, coldly.

"Oh."

There was a long pause that Handen took advantage of to pass around the tin mugs of Nastren coffee. Bip took his gratefully and slurped the hot beverage. He was beginning to take a liking to the bitter brew, but still missed the presence of milk and two sugars.

"Anyway," he said. "It wasn't all bad. I met Handen there, and it turns out that he's from Kaneq, too."

Azron raised a critical eyebrow. "Really? And you took his word for it, did you? What with him being in a nut house and all?"

"Well, you see, that's what I thought at first too, but it turned out he knew all sorts of things about Kaneq that no one could possibly know, and then it turns out, well, you remember I told you about the volunteers?"

Azron nodded.

"Well, Handen was the first!"

The thief paused mid-sip, the tin cup settled on his lip. "The first volunteer?" he said. His voice was thick and deliberate, as if talking to a slow child.

"That's right!" said Bip.

"The first volunteer who left hundreds of years ago?"

"Yep."

Azron looked from Bip to Handen and back again. Finally, he smiled broadly at Handen. "Well, I have to tell you, you're looking very good for your age."

Handen rolled his eyes. "I'm immortal," he said.

"Of course you are," said Azron. "You're an immortal, the world's going to end, and your friend here can explode things with his mind. Yeah, it all makes perfect sense, mate—perfect sense."

Handen gave a heavy sigh, and then, before Azron could react, he flipped a dagger from the sleeve of his leather coat and stabbed himself in the heart with it. A spray of blood doused half of the campfire with a reptilian hiss.

"Great holy bastards!" shouted Azron.

As the fire slowly regained its former luminescence, Azron was surprised to see Handen still sitting cross-legged, his face a mask of cool impatience. He had unbuttoned his shirt to reveal a dagger wound that closed up before the thief's astonished eyes.

The thief's normal countenance of the slightly amused indifference that passed for streetwise in Port Town had given way to a child-like expression of awe. He was quick to regain his composure, though.

"...magic," he breathed.

"Maybe," conceded Handen, and proceeded to tell Azron of the hidden fountain he had found in Ghulbra forest so many years ago, and while telling him, also filled in some of the gaps Bip had left about the off-worlders who had founded Kaneq in the first place. They ate the roasted meat, and the thief listened intently until the adventurer's story came to a finish.

"So, you see," said Handen. "It might just be magic, but all that means is that there's a scientific explanation I haven't found yet. I couldn't tell you without an in-depth bioscan."

"A what now?" muttered Azron.

"Well, it could be that the fountain of youth contained a parasitic microorganism that maintains and repairs the host that sustains it. Or it could be that the fountain held some sort of DNA code that unlocks a regeneration factor already present in humanoid life forms."

Azron blinked. "Or it could have just been magic..."

"Yeah," said Handen, wryly. "Either way, I'm stuck with it 'til I find the fountain of death."

"It all seems a bit far-fetched, though," said Azron.

"Yeah, well. That's life," said Handen, and shrugged nonchalantly before taking a long swig from his cooling coffee.

"Still," Azron said thoughtfully. "Being immortal; that must be pretty handy."

Handen's eyes went cold. "Can you imagine getting tired of stealing?" he said. Azron looked surprised. He was passionate about thievery. Thievery defined him. He was one of the best, and it had never occurred to him to ever give it up. He wasn't sure he could if he tried. As for getting tired of it... Well...maybe one day he'd retire, but he fondly suspected that, even as an old, old man, he would be stealing the pocket money from his grandchildren.

"Because that's what happens," Handen continued. "You get tired of everything."

The trio sat in silence for a while. Bip always felt a little uncomfortable when Handen brooded like this. When his mind was on the job, the former Hostilities Advisor's manner was quick and professional, but when things calmed down, he would become melancholic and withdrawn.

"Besides," said Handen, after a while, "I don't think the humanoid mind was meant to cope with such extended life spans. For a while when I was imprisoned, I became convinced that my former life was a madman's dream. I don't think it was just the Bin that did it to me. Even now most of my past, that which I can remember, seems unreal, as if it didn't actually happen. And a man without a past is no man at all."

The former Hostilities Advisor stared hard into the fire, and Bip wondered what ghosts and faces he saw in those flames.

"At least you have friends," said Azron, his half-ironic chirpiness returning to his voice. "My dad always said, 'As long as you've got mates, son, and a family that loves you, then you'll always have someone to bust you out of prison.'"

The three laughed. "Your dad seems like he was a very wise man," said Handen.

"Taught me everything I know," said Azron proudly. "They called him Billy the Lint, because of the amount of time he spent in people's pockets."

Bip laughed again, glad that the somber air of the camp had been cleared. Even Handen, who rarely smiled, couldn't keep the broad grin from lighting up his usually dark face.

"Come on," Handen said. "Let's get some sleep. We've a long ride ahead of us."

The three of them bunkered down under the wagon, appreciating the heat trapped there as the night began to cool around them.

As he drifted off to sleep, Azron thought about his new companions.

*Saving the world,* he thought, and smiled to himself, amused by the thought of the unknown number of law enforcers pursuing them. He was looking forward to playing at being a hero. It wasn't far off what he was used to as a thief.

THE MASSIVE BALL of Death careened through star system after star system, leaving a wake of radioactive dust and confusion in its path. It had accelerated, due to the favorable gravitational pulls of various planets, to near-incomprehensible speeds. It was getting to the stage where it was smashing through obstacles before it even realized there were obstacles to smash through. It didn't mind, though. The fledgling optimism of the nuclear cluster had grown to a frenzied anticipation. Nothing would stand in its way.

In the gamma sector of Beleris Six, a traffic patrol car floated in the gas giant and Romanis bypass. The distance between the two planets at certain points in their orbit was quite small, so the pass-between traffic was heavily policed lest some dangerous driver be sucked into the gravitational pull of either astral body.

Officer Lenny Lepowski sat in his patrol car, appreciating, as he had done for many years, the swirling magnitude of the gas giant through his monitors. Sometimes he would find the smoldering reds and oranges of the planet hypnotic and could stare for hours if uninterrupted.

Currently Lepowski was enjoying coffee and donuts. Lenny was an old, old officer and had seen much technological advancement in his lifetime. Heck, space-worthy patrol cars had only just been prototyped when he had joined the force those many, many years ago. He had seen advancements in medicine and science that had made him proud to be a Belerian. Coffee and donuts, though, were beyond improvement. Coffee and donuts had achieved the nexus of perfection centuries ago.

He had come to realize that they were an important part of being a police officer. Perhaps one of the most important parts of being a police officer. Without them, he thought, life just wouldn't seem complete. It just wouldn't feel right.

As a younger man, he had been interested in interstellar geography and history. He had been shocked and appalled to learn there were civilizations where donuts—and sometimes even coffee—had not yet been invented. There were civilizations where the policemen sat on horseback munching thoughtfully on pita bread and sipping herbal teas. It wasn't right. He knew that, deep down, these law enforcers of other worlds were missing something. They might not know what it was, but he knew they must lie awake at night sometimes, wondering what it was that was missing from their lives.

He pitied them. Then he ate another donut.

Suddenly his scanners began to beep manically. He sat bolt upright with a start and spilt some of his hot coffee down his shirt. He wasn't angry; he knew that spilling hot coffee in a comic fashion when you were disturbed suddenly was also an unshakable part of being a police officer.

His expression turned from irritation to surprise as the speeding object zoomed past his display monitors. It was impossible to gain a composition analysis, and the speed reading was too high for the computer to calculate right away. Lepowski felt the massive rumbling as the object passed, even though it was miles away from the bypass and his patrol car.

His gaze shifted nervously from monitor to monitor until the rumbling finally stopped. Then he ate another donut, chewing thoughtfully and holding his coffee with shaking hands.

He thought briefly about calling in the sighting and setting off in hot pursuit. Then he decided against it. After all, he only had two weeks 'til retirement.

The Massive Ball of Death moved on obliviously. Nothing would stand its way.

---

BOLAN SAT in the rocking chair on his porch, looking over his sleepy ranch at the flawless horizon beyond. *God's country,* he thought to himself, and lay back, smiling in the hot sunshine. *If you want peace and quiet, then this is the place to come. Yep! More peace and quiet than a sane man can handle.*

Bolan was disturbed from his reveries by a distant sound of thunder. He looked into the cloudless sky and frowned. Then, just on the edge of vision, he saw the dust trail rise into the sky. It was a few minutes before he could make out what was approaching, and his face dropped in dismay as an uneasy suspicion rose in his belly.

*It's them!* he thought. *It's the stampeding tourists! They've found me!*

A mixture of emotions flooded Bolan's body. He realized with sudden clarity that he didn't want a lot of customers after all. Just the odd couple now and then would have been fine, just enough that he could survive out in his ranch without being bothered. He mourned regretfully for his treasured peace and quiet.

A few minutes later, he realized that he had been wrong. The riders didn't look like tourists at all. They all wore uniforms for one thing, and Bolan doubted that tourists made a habit of traveling with uberbeasts. The rider at the head of the group rode over to Bolan. He dimly recognized the gray coat of the Regulators, and his thoughts turned sadly to the nice boys who had ridden through a couple of days ago. The nice boys he had sold a wagon to.

"Evening, old-timer," said the Regulator, touching the brim of his gray top hat. "Pin Constable Blungkit, at your service."

Bolan looked into the leering eyes of the newcomer and doubted very much that he was at anyone's service but his own. "I don't want no trouble, mister," he said, trying to keep the shake from his voice.

Blungkit grinned, his rank wooden teeth gleaming wetly in the sunshine. Having caught up to the doomsayer's trail so quickly, he was in a good mood, so suppressed the urge to boot the old man in the face. "And you won't have any, either. As long as you feel you can answer a few simple questions," he said.

Bolan didn't say anything.

"Now," said Blungkit, with a merry tone in his voice, "I know for a fact that a couple of guys rode through here quite recently. Maybe even three of them. They would have been in a hurry."

Bolan was thankful he was still wearing his dark glasses. He didn't want to look this Regulator in the eye.

"Maybe you seen them," continued Blungkit. "Maybe you even helped them."

Bolan looked at the ground. He was as scared as he had ever been in his isolated old age.

"Yeah, you probably did. Nice old-timer like you. Probably bent over backward for the buggers. See, I'd be willing to overlook that, I would. If you was willing to help me out a little..."

Bolan looked up. He thought briefly about defying this man. After all, what could he do? Then he gazed into Blungkit's eyes. The cold eyes of a drunken snake. This man could do a lot if he wanted to. And he would enjoy doing it, as well. Bolan had never felt so hungry for the peace and quiet he had become accustomed to.

"And I wouldn't think about lying to me, neither," Blungkit added. "'Cause I will catch up to those whoresons, and I will find out if you helped them. Aiding and abetting that is," he hissed. "A punishable offence."

The Regulator waited for this to sink in. Bolan looked at the ground again.

"Now," said Blungkit, "you tell me which direction they went in, or I'm going to start setting fire to things."

Wordlessly, Bolan pointed in the direction the boys had traveled in, feeling a wash of relief and shame as he did so.

"Thank you very much, squire," said Blungkit, and spat unthinkingly on the ground, hawking monstrously as he did. "You're a good citizen."

The Regulator rode off to join his troops and began riding east, as Bolan had indicated.

The old man felt terrible, but more than that he felt relieved as the dust cloud disappeared over the horizon, and peace and quiet returned to his ranch once more. He sat back in his rocking chair again and shivered. Where ever Blungkit had come from, he didn't belong in God's country.

# 8

# Boredom, Bedlam, and Birdmen

Bip lazed in the back of the wagon, enjoying the relief from the heat of the day. Azron had reluctantly taken the reins, and it was Bip's turn to lie down.

They had been traveling through the Shrub for a just over a week now and were moving along at a very satisfactory pace. They had fallen into the routine of each man taking a turn with the reins while one person slept and the other sat watch. That way they could rest themselves on the move and consequently travel for longer without stopping.

Handen was optimistic about their food stock and thought it would be some time before they had to worry about hunting and scavenging. Water, though infrequent in the wilderness, was not so rare as to pose a major concern. The fugitives were free to concentrate on making as much headway on their pursuers as possible.

Boredom was, of course, a problem. They had swapped most of their stories over the first few days. Handen had regaled his companions with his seemingly endless adventures as an immortal, and Azron, in turn, had told them about his days growing up in Port Town, some of the interesting people he had met and stolen from, and some of the interesting places he had been to and robbed. Bip, who up until several months ago had led an extraordinarily normal life, was content to tell of the peaceful times he had had in Kaneq. (It was a constant source of irritation to Handen that Bip's questing experiences had been relatively harmless and had taken him hardly any time at all, while his own had been unreasonably challenging and had lasted several lifetimes.)

As the days rolled by, however, the stories had run out, and the trio had lapsed into long silences. Handen, quiet by nature, didn't mind the lack of conversation, and Bip, who had already spent months traveling with the former Hostilities Advisor, had grown used to long periods of silence. Azron was of a different opinion. He found the silence tedious and awkward. He liked the quiet in the right circumstances—like when he was in someone else's house uninvited—but when he was off duty (as he liked to think of it) he preferred to chatter or whistle or even just listen to others talking. The long uneventful quiet of the wilderness was almost unbearable to his city-boy instincts, and he found himself yearning for overcrowded streets and loud, inarticulate ramblings.

Azron sighed and tried to start up a conversation again.

"So," he began. "If you were an animal, what kind of animal would you be?"

"Cat," said Bip.

"Wolf," said Handen.

Azron waited for elaboration. "Any particular reason why?" he asked after a time.

"No."

"Not really."

Azron clucked his tongue. "Well you two are a right barrel of laughs, ain't you? Very good company, I must say."

Bip breathed out heavily. "Okay then, Azron, what kind of animal would you be?"

"Well, I was going to say cat," said Azron, "but you've already said that, haven't you?"

"So? Can't we both be cats?"

"No! That's not how the game works! You're s'posed to think of animal and then say why you'd want to be it, and that's s'posed to tell us all a little bit about yourself, innit?"

Bip sat silent for a while. "Don't see why we can't both be cats," he mumbled.

Azron sighed and turned back to his steering, rolling a cigarette expertly in one hand, steadying the reins with the other.

"Well, why don't we play the question game again, then?" he said after a while.

"Is that the one where you think of something and we've got to ask questions until we guess what it is?" said Handen.

"Yeah, that's the one."

"Okay, then, go for it."

Azron thought for a moment and then grinned. "Okay, I've got one. What am I?"

"Are you an animal?" ventured Bip.

"Yep."

"Are you a cat?"

Azron's face clouded over. He turned back to his steering.

They rode on for some hours in silence. For a while Bip amused himself by rechecking the inventory of his reprogrammed acorns. There were still quite a few left, ranging from the useful—such as the SWORD and SHIELD acorns, which would be handy should he ever lose Brian—to the more everyday such as the ROPE and UMBRELLA acorns. There was even an ARMCHAIR acorn, but Bip couldn't really see that being very useful in the near future.

Eventually Bip grew tired of his inventory and began to drift off to sleep. Soon the only sound bar the occasional squawk of a vulture was Bip's gentle, rhythmic snoring.

More hours passed as they rode into the late afternoon. Sunset would not be for another five hours.

Eventually they swapped places, moving Bip onto the steering, Azron onto watch, and allowing Handen to get some rest in the back. It wasn't long before the adventurer was picking up where Bip had left off, snoring steadily into the ovenish day.

Bip yawned to clear his head, keeping the horses in a steady trot until they had regained the energy to pick up the pace a little. Azron put his head in his hand and sighed.

"I'm bored," he said. "Bored, bored, bored."

"Why don't you have another cigarette?" said Bip, who'd noticed the thief had been smoking less than usual, which was to say a cigarette did not hang constantly from his lips.

"Pacing myself, aren't I?" said the thief, glumly. "Running low on 'baccy."

Bip noticed they were heading toward what looked like a canyon. The ground ramped down, and walls of earth rose slowly on either side. He considered going around it, but then realized that it would probably add unnecessary hours to their journey. Handen—whose sense of danger was more finely tuned than either of his companions'—would have insisted they went around. He would have realized, with a soldier's view, that the sloping walls of the canyon would make an excellent ambush point, especially if you wanted to surprise a single, lightly defended wagon. Bip, who had been lulled by the sheer emptiness of the Dozantyne Shrub, sensed and foresaw no danger at all. He headed to the mouth of the canyon without a second thought.

Azron was too wrapped up in his own grumpiness to offer any useful advice. He didn't even react when the rising walls of the canyon began to cast a dark shadow over the wagon.

"Bored, bored, bored," he muttered again.

Bip paid him no attention. His time with Handen had improved his instincts a little, and he was beginning to wonder if he should have skirted around the canyon after all. As the sun began its descent behind the horizon, the canyon had taken on a distinctly menacing feel. Bip's hand went uneasily to the hilt of Brian.

The thief, still distracted by his own gloom, cried out in exasperation. "I just wish something would happen!"

As if to grant his wish, a shrill and birdlike cry echoed around the base of the canyon, followed by a deep rumbling. Bip pulled the horses to a stop as, not far in the distance, a small avalanche of rocks rolled across the canyon floor. Though the rock pile wasn't large, they would still have to clear it before they could move forward. A deadly silence had descended throughout the canyon.

Bip jumped as he felt a hand on his shoulder. He turned to the alert eyes of Handen.

"What's going on?" said the adventurer. Bip saw the gleam of Handen's flintlock pistola in the dwindling light of the evening. He was ready for trouble.

"There was an avalanche ahead of us," whispered Bip.

Handen looked around quickly, taking in their surroundings. "Can we turn around?" he said.

Bip looked about. He had ridden, unwittingly, into a narrow part of the canyon where turning the wagon around would be difficult and slow going. A sinking feeling dragged at Bip's stomach. He suddenly knew they had ridden into an ambush. He glanced up at sides of the canyon and saw hunched figures silhouetted against the approaching evening. They appeared to be armed with spears.

"What are they?" whispered Azron.

"Don't look at them," said Handen. "It might just be that we've encroached on their territory. If we back away, they might leave us alone."

There was another birdlike cry that preceded a heavy, badly made spear thumping into the ground in front of the horses. The mounts reared and whinnied nervously as the spear vibrated in the earth.

"…or maybe not," finished Handen.

There was another birdcall. It appeared to be a challenge.

"Okay, hero, what do we do now?" said Azron.

Handen looked about again. "Too many of them," he said. "I could get out of this one okay, but I doubt if you two could."

"That's reassuring," said the thief. He seemed to have cheered up a bit now that they were in the face of peril.

"What do we do?" Bip said.

"They want us to surrender, that much is clear, otherwise they would've attacked by now." Handen rubbed his bristly chin thoughtfully. "It's our only viable cause of action."

"You can't be serious," scoffed the thief.

"I am," Handen said. "I say we let ourselves be taken. There's a chance we can bargain our way out of this."

THE TRIO STOOD BACK to back at the tall wooden post set into the ground. Heavy ropes bound them, and kindling was being stacked at their feet. All around them, their captors danced jerkily to the beat of a flat-sounding bongo.

"Nice one, mate," said Azron. "Bargain our way out, yeah?"

Handen didn't reply. He had been hoping that they would be taken before their assailants' leader and questioned. He had been fairly confident that, if so, he would be able to talk them out of trouble. That had not been the case, however. The group that had captured them didn't seem to have a leader. Instead they had just manhandled the trio to what was obviously their home ground and tied them abruptly to the suspicious-looking post standing in the center.

Several bonfires had been lit around the grounds so that every-thing could be seen clearly against the wilderness night, revealing ramshackle huts and ubiquitous piles of guano. The trio had been able to get a good look at their captors. Handen recognized them as vulards, bizarre buzzard-like creatures who had only limited intelli-gence. Their vocabulary was extremely small, and they were usually content to hang around in their scruffy gangs waiting for other crea-tures to die so they could eat them. Handen wondered what had inspired their uncharacteristic display of hostility. Bip would have been able to tell him, would have been able to imagine the wicked whispers that had passed through their feathered ears.

He looked at the madly dancing vulards again. They were a sort of inverted cousin of the harpy, with the hunched and oily body of a bird but with the limbs of a man. From the white cluster of feathers at their shoulders, long pink necks warbled toward small, bullet heads with hooked, wicked-looking beaks. With their necks withdrawn, the vulards stood at roughly four feet in height. With their necks extended, however, they towered even over Azron.

The vulards cawed and shrieked continuously, working them-selves into a frenzy, the significance of which was lost on their prison-ers. Their intentions, however, were perfectly clear. For reasons unapparent, Bip, Handen, and Azron were to be burned at the stake.

As if to clarify the point, the vulards began chanting one of the few words they seemed to know. Their voices were harsh and raspy, like a duck with a bad head cold.

"*Burn! Burn! Burn!* "

"Oh dear," said Bip glumly.

"Ideas, anyone?" asked Azron.

They had all been disarmed when they were captured, but Handen, who had more knives secured about his person at any one time than a well-prepared chef might own in his entire career, had managed to conceal a few of his smaller blades. He worked one of the daggers that he had hidden in his sleeve free and carefully—so as not to drop the weapon or draw attention to himself—began to saw at the rope around his wrists.

"I'm working on something," he said through the side of his mouth. "But I'm going to need a distraction."

"Bip?" said Azron. "Think you can explode anything?"

Bip nodded down at the dry kindling at their feet. "I don't think it would be a good idea to risk it," he said. "We might just be doing our new friends a favor."

Handen tried to increase the pace of his sawing. He was gradually cutting through the ropes, but not at an encouraging rate. The frenzy of the vulards seemed to be increasing to a climax.

"If anyone has any ideas for a distraction, now's the time to tell me," said Handen. "How about a naked woman with an axe?" said Azron.

"Yeah, that'd do," Handen replied distractedly. That was when he heard the war cry.

------------------------------------

## 9

# Xharon: Warrior Princess

------------------------------------

It was a shrill yodel, sudden and piercing in the relative piece of the Shrub. It rose from a teeth-clenching shriek to an ear-splitting trill and wavered between the two rapidly, like some alarm clock from hell.

The bongo playing stopped abruptly, and the vulards ceased their dancing and turned to look at the newcomer with open puzzlement etched into their beaks.

Standing on a boulder just on the outskirts of the bonfire light was a woman. Abundantly a woman. It was hard not to notice the various parts that qualified her as a woman because she did, at first glance, appear to be naked. She was not, however, but the clothing she did wear—a leather thong under a thin chainmail miniskirt and a slim-strapped bra decorated with metal studs—left very little to the imagination. The only part of the stranger's body that seemed to be appropriately covered was the bottom of her legs, concealed by knee-high boots with impractically high heels.

It wasn't until the woman stopped screaming and Handen got a proper look at her face that he realized that "woman" was not a wholly accurate term. The stranger was closer to being a girl, barely out of her teens. Fiery eyes glittered from a pale face sprayed with a smattering of freckles. Full lips twisted in a feral snarl. A leather headband held back long red hair that hung nearly to the woman's waist.

*Not ginger, not auburn,* thought Handen, *but actually red.*

She was, indeed, holding an axe. In fact, she was holding two. The battle-axes, lightweight and designed to be used one handed, appeared ridiculously over-sized in comparison to the small frame of the girl, and Handen, with the cynical mind of a fighter, doubted she'd be able to use them to full effect. He was forced to reconsider his notion when, once again screaming her bizarre war cry, the girl began to twirl the axes in a complex lattice of metal in front of her body. The axes seemed to pass from hand to hand without pause until each arm and weapon became a blur of silvery movement.

The birdmen looked at each other in confusion. Whatever they had expected from this night, shrieking warrior women appearing from nowhere hadn't been part of it.

The redheaded girl ceased her weapons display, throwing the axes carelessly to her sides, and somersaulted forward with balletic grace. She landed lightly and began cartwheeling and flip-flopping toward the vulards, who stood helplessly, still unsure of how to react to the threat.

Her attack might have been a complete success if not for that fact that, as she landed from a complex flip, the heel on one of her boots snapped off. A look of sudden shock replaced the girl's fierce warrior snarl as she fell unexpectedly to the side, twisting her ankle as she went.

Her pale face went even paler, and she dropped to her knees and clutched the injured ankle tightly.

"Ouchouchouchouchouch!" she said.

Both vulards and prisoners alike were shocked into silence. Everyone, it seemed, had been holding their breath.

"Ouch?" Handen heard Azron say. "Who actually says 'ouch'?"

His question was answered for him as the stranger continued her litany of pain. "OuchouchouchOUCH!"

Handen dismayed. At their potential rescuer's display of skill, his hopes for escape had risen, but now, as the warrior sat clutching her ankle and hissing through clenched teeth, it was clear that things weren't going to go in their favor.

The girl cried out again. "Buggerbuggerbugger!" The unladylike swearing rubbed oddly against her plummy accent.

She was too wrapped up in her pain to realize she had been surrounded by the vulards, whose confusion had quickly given way to malicious hostility. She looked up from her ankle and took in the spears leveled at her head.

"Oh…" she said. "Oh, bugger."

---

"PLEASED TO ME YOU," said Bip as the strange girl was tied up next to him. He felt that he should at least introduce himself to the person he was going to be dying next to. "I'm Bip Plunkerton, that's Handen Strike, and the tall chap is Azron Bezron."

"That's Azron Bezron, Diamond Geezer (1st Class)," interjected Azron smoothly. Bip had a feeling that if Azron had been able to, he would have smoothed back his hair.

"Pleased to meet you, I'm sure," said the girl sulkily. Suddenly she seemed to straighten up, as if remembering herself. "I am Xharon, Warrior Princess," she said.

Handen caught Azron's eye. The thief shrugged.

"That's an interesting name," said Bip. His voice caught and cracked oddly, like an adolescent barging his way through puberty. He had become aware of Xharon's flesh pressing against his own and was suddenly and absurdly glad they were all tied to a post together. In his busy life of avoiding work, Bip had never really had time for girl-friends. He didn't think he had ever been this close to a woman who wasn't his mum.

Xharon's shoulders slumped. "Not that it matters now," she said. "I've cocked things up a bit, haven't I?"

"Don't be so hard on yourself," said Handen. "You couldn't have taken them all on." Bip noticed that his friend's voice sounded distracted. He correctly assumed that the adventurer had gone back to sawing at the ropes on his hands.

"I bally well could have!" said Xharon, hotly. "They were just lucky, that's all!"

"Fair enough," said Handen. "Not that it matters now." The vulards were resuming their chanting and dancing. It would not take them long to reach their culmination once more. "If somebody doesn't cause a distraction soon, we're all going to die."

"Well, that's not exactly true, is it?" said Azron. "You can't die, can you?"

"No," said Handen. "I guess I'll just have to sit here and burn horribly until they figure that out, won't I?"

Azron sucked his breath in sharply through his teeth. "Ooo. Yeah. 'Course. Didn't think of that." The thief was suddenly very glad he wasn't immortal. He could imagine scorched nerve endings healing and re-healing only to be burnt away again in perpetual agony.

Bip said nothing. An idea had occurred to him. He didn't have any weapons concealed on him and daren't use his psyence less he hasten their demise, but there was one option that hadn't occurred to him until now. He felt for the bag of reprogrammed acorns in his pocket. If he could get one into his mouth and spit it, he might just provide all the distraction necessary for Handen to cut them free. He grinned as his mind's eye saw the reaction of the primitive birdmen to an organic armchair suddenly growing in the middle of them. He reached his tied-up hands down to his pocket and began rummaging for the bag. He tried not to get too excited as he finally snagged it and pulled it, inch by inch, from his trousers.

His hopes were dashed as swiftly as they had appeared as the bag was snagged out of his grasp by the gnarled hand of a vulard. The bird-like creature stared at Bip accusingly with its beady eyes before turning his attention to the contents of the bag. Its mouth fell open with an astonished squawk as it saw what was inside.

"Seeeeeds!" it cawed with croaking delight.

The entire ritual stopped. Every vulard had turned to the one holding the bag, which, by the worried look in his eye, appeared to be regretting its outburst.

"Seeds?"

"Seeeeds?"

*"Seeeeeds!"*

Without warning, the whole tribe rushed the vulard with the acorns. There was a riotous scuffle as every one of the birdmen tried to grab the bag at once. Predictably, the flimsy sacking bag ripped to pieces under the strain, and the acorns scattered across the ground.

Without a pause, the vulards began bobbing their long necks toward the ground, trying desperately to scoop up the morsels in their long beaks. Only a few were successful, cawing triumphantly as they gobbled down what was apparently a vulard delicacy.

Unthinkingly, Bip, Azron and Handen had all squinted their eyes shut. Xharon looked confused.

"What?" she said. "What's happening?"

"Wait and see," said Handen through clenched teeth.

The vulards stopped their cackling. A few of the birdmen—the ones who had successfully nabbed the seeds—bore expressions of extreme puzzlement. Suddenly, one of them hiccupped loudly and then glanced around in confused panic. Without warning, the bird-like creature suddenly exploded in a mess of gore and feathers. Where it had stood was now a large, comfortable looking armchair made entirely of wood and leaves.

Before the rest of the tribe could react, there were more shrieks of terror and horrified surprise from their comrades. Carnage of the most bizarre kind began to befall the vulard tribe. Here a creature warbled in panic before a wooden sword blade erupted messily from its chest. Elsewhere a vulard came to a nasty end as a wooden umbrella unfurled in its neck, sending its head flying into the air with a popping noise that might have been humorous in other circum-stances. One of the birdmen gagged helplessly as a large length of rope uncoiled rapidly from its mouth.

Amidst the chaos, the still-healthy vulards began to run in every direction, leaving their inexplicably dying comrades behind lest they should suffer a similar fate.

The four prisoners squinted in sympathy for their unfortunate captors. "As far as distractions go," said Azron, "that was a doozy."

IT HAD TAKEN them longer than they would have liked to turn the wagon around and ride back out of the canyon. They had to tread the horses carefully in the dark; the possibility of breaking a wheel on the rocks or, worse, a horse's leg in a pothole was too great. Xharon had helped, leading her own horse ahead of them at a slow pace, limping on her freshly bound ankle.

Handen had been impressed by the girl's steed, a shiny black gelding that looked to be from thoroughbred stock and stood at least fifteen hands high. She had named it Prancer, which seemed a little inappropriate for the heavily muscled charger.

After some endeavour, they eventually made camp with their backs to a high rocky outcrop. They were unsure whether the vulards would regroup and come looking for them. Handen doubted it but would stand watch anyway, determined not to give them the advantage of surprise. Xharon, though reluctant at first, accepted the offer to camp with them.

Now they sat around the campfire again, slightly exhausted from their ordeal and looking forward to the slowly cooking meat and the brewing coffee, which the vulards had, oddly, left untouched.

It was Azron who spoke first. "So," he said to Xharon. "What brings a nice young girl like you to a wilderness like this?"

Xharon narrowed her eyes slightly at the thief's tone. "I came to seek adventure," she said.

"Well, good luck to you, miss," said Azron. "Those bird guys are the first things we've seen in ages. Nothing else but dust and shrub for miles."

"I know," said Xharon downheartedly. "It's not at all like in the books."

"Books?" said Bip.

Xharon sighed. "You read the stories, you know. They tell of ancient beasts and peril in the southlands. I hear all sorts of things about rogue orcen tribes and elfen freedom fighters. And so far, nothing. Not a sausage."

"You should have come a thousand years ago," Handen said under his breath.

"Except for you fellows, of course," Xharon added. "What did those funny little bird things want with you anyway?"

"To kill us, apparently," said Handen.

"But why?"

Handen chuckled mirthlessly. "I stopped trying to figure that one out a long time ago."

Bip held his tongue. He did not want to upset things further by mentioning the interfering deviousness of Mr. Random.

Xharon accepted a cup of coffee gratefully. "So, what are you chaps doing out here in the Shrub?" she said.

The three men looked at each other for a while, and then, sighing, knowing that at some point he'd probably have to stab himself again, Handen began telling their collective story.

Xharon listened intently, sitting with the wide-eyed wonder of a child. As he recounted their tale, Handen felt the uneasy suspicion that Xharon really enjoyed stories—particularly stories such as theirs. He didn't even have to stab himself to prove he was immortal; the girl just seemed to accept it as if it were the most natural thing in the world. He wrapped up the story with the ambush by the vulards and a rather anticlimactic "...and the rest you know."

Xharon just sat there for a while, eyes wide, staring off into some make-believe world.

"Incredible," she breathed. "Amazing! You're all actually on a quest? A real life quest?"

The three fugitives exchanged glances. "Yeah, I suppose," said Azron.

"A real-life race against time, where the fate of the world hangs in the balance?"

"Yes?" said Bip, nervously.

"Brilliant! Can I come? You don't know how long I've waited for something like this! *Ohpleaseohpleaseohplease*!"

Handen coughed. "I don't think that's a very good idea," he said.

For a moment, Xharon had the look of a freshly kicked puppy. This look was quickly taken over by a flash of irritation. "Why not?" she snapped.

"You don't seem to understand," said Handen, patiently. "This isn't some thrill-seeking adventure for honor and glory. This is important. If we don't get to where we need to go in time, people will die. Everyone will die. And there are people trying to stop us and miles of hostile terrain to cover."

"All the more reason why you need my help." Xharon sniffed, crossing her arms over her chest.

Handen sighed. "What makes you think we need help?" he said.

"Well, correct me if I'm wrong, but weren't you the ones about to be cooked alive by overgrown pigeons?"

"That's a fair point, that," said Azron, and Handen was forced to concede. Romantic or not, another fighter would be useful if they ran into trouble again.

He held up his hands. "Okay, okay. As long as you pull your weight, you can ride with us. As far as the capital and then you're on your own."

Xharon looked crestfallen. "You're going back to Argustin?"

"Yes. Why?"

"I've just come from there!" she said testily.

She looked around at the curious faces of her new companions. "I did mention I was a princess, didn't I?"

The three fugitives merely stared at her, awaiting elaboration.

"It's my full title. I'm Xharon DeChambre, Princess of Argustin. I'm the Emperor's niece."

<hr>

HANDEN, Bip, and Azron stood huddled together away from the light of the campfire. Back at the wagon, Xharon began rubbing down her horse, singing in a faltering soprano that carried flatly through the night air.

"She's the bloody *princess*!" said Azron.

"I don't understand," said Bip. "What's she doing out here if she's a princess?"

"She's young and she wants adventure," said Handen, shrugging as if that explained everything.

"She's the *bloody* princess!" Azron repeated.

"She knows the Emperor is after us. I don't understand why she wants to ride with us if her own uncle wants to see us captured," Bip said.

"Perhaps she's just an angry rich girl rebelling against her peers. She wouldn't be the first," said Handen calmly.

"*She's* the bloody princess!"

"Yes, we know! Now please stop saying that!"

"But we could be well in here! Well in! I bet she's bloody loaded!"

Mentally, Handen agreed. The craftsmanship of her weaponry was exquisite, and her horse was fit for a king. Or a princess. He had no reason to doubt that the girl was definitely from one of the noble families. Either that or a thief and a con artist.

"Azron, why are you so convinced she actually is the princess and not some madwoman with an expensive horse?"

"I've seen pictures, haven't I?" said Azron. "She's the *bloody princess.*" He stopped and thought for a while. "Mind you, she had more clothes on in the pictures I've seen."

"Well, this is good news," said Handen.

"Too right!" Azron grinned. "I bet she's bloody loaded!"

"No. What I mean is, if she's the Emperor's niece, then she should have no problem getting us in to see him."

"Of course!" said Bip.

"Which means no climbing walls, no wrestling past guards, no bribing city officials. We just walk right in."

"Well, I suppose that's good, too," said Azron, hesitantly. "But I do have one more question. One I've been meaning to ask you guys for a little while now, sort of thing."

"Yes?"

"Well, if it's the Emperor you want to see, and the Emperor wants to catch you, then why don't you just, you know, give yourselves up?"

Bip blinked rapidly. He was ashamed to admit that that particular course of action, obvious as it was, had not occurred to him.

"Firstly," said Handen, "there's no guaranteeing the Emperor would grant us an audience. Could be that he just wants to see us safely locked up. Secondly, even if we were granted an audience, then he's less likely to believe the reasoning of two condemned prisoners.

No, we have to go to him ourselves—it's the only way to lend any credibility to our story."

Azron shrugged. "Makes sense," he said. "And the young princess could be just what we need to talk to the Emperor on a one-to-one basis, yeah?"

"That's right," said Handen.

"So she's coming with us, then?" said Bip. He tried to keep his voice cool, but a waver of hot excitement still escaped.

"Yes. She's coming with us."

THE TRIO RETURNED to the campfire where Xharon stood waiting with her fists on her hips.

"So you're having me along, then?" she said.

The three fugitives nodded in unison.

"Great!" said Xharon, and jumped up and down on the spot for a while in what appeared to be some sort of happy dance. Bip found himself hypnotized by various jigglings as the dance went on. After she had finished, she looked back at her new companions. "And do we have to go back to Argustin?"

"Listen very carefully," said Handen, slowly. "We must be granted a personal audience with the Emperor. He may be our only chance to save the world."

The adventurer watched as the words sank into the young princess's impressionable mind. "Saving the world," she breathed softly.

"Yes. The whole world," said Handen.

"No problem," said Xharon, a wide grin lighting up her face. "Uncle Tommy always likes to see me." The princess hunkered down in her bedroll and gazed at the stars overhead through eyes glazed with excitement. "Saving the world," she muttered to herself.

"Uncle Tommy?" whispered Azron. Handen shrugged.

# 10

# Interlude: The Rescue Party

Not for the first time that day, Bailey wished he were still in bed. He stared through the electric gray clouds to where the weak light of the sun shone. He still found the position of the flat silvery disk both surprising and a little frightening. He was not used to seeing the outside world before noon. It felt alien.

His perception wasn't helped by his lack of hangover. As far back as he could remember, Bailey had always been a little hungover each morning, but seven days of stone-cold sobriety had left him feeling clear-headed and alert. He didn't like it. It was like being plunged suddenly into a cold bath.

What he liked even less than all that was being out in the middle of the Ice Plains with a big spear, a man who was quite obviously mad, and seventeen other frightened and confused youths.

The people of Kaneq had learned about the end of the world a week ago. A town meeting had been called in the square, and the elders had flooded into the Stadium of Address. The news had been broken by Tenbon, who had spoken slowly in her somber, deep tone of the upcoming destruction of Bersch. To her right, Truggle had sat staring into unknown voids as if his thoughts were elsewhere. The crowd had listened, first confused, then frightened, until a roar of despair had filled the heart of Kaneq.

Bailey remembered feeling sick suddenly, an odd mixture of dread and delight that Bip, who had vanished mysteriously so many months ago, had in fact left in an attempt to reach civilization.

When the crowd finally came to an uneasy silence, Tenbon told them of her plan, the last hope for Kaneq: one last excursion to the mainland, this time in numbers of dozens rather than just one or two. She had left the crowd a day to think about it before she would call a meeting asking for volunteers.

It had not taken Kaneq's citizens long to come to the same conclusion Bip had come to when given the option of saving the world: that there was no real choice. If you left to venture into the wilderness, it was likely that you might die. If you stayed and hoped for the best, death was inevitable. So many of Kaneq's population had found themselves volunteering. Heroes by necessity.

Many had been turned away, of course, being too young or too old or holding a position deemed too important in the town to abandon. Those who did not or could not volunteer helped in as many ways as possible; farmers gave up produce for the cause, bakers baked stacks of sustaining travel bread, tailors began fashioning winter wear, and blacksmiths began forging weapons and armor.

For the volunteers who had been accepted, a rigorous and complex training regime had been drawn up, bouncing them between senior hunters and psyentists. Because there were so many students, more time had to be allocated for training than the period Bip had been allowed—but many, Rynford especially, doubted that so large a number of students could be brought up to an acceptable level of development in so little time. And so training started earlier, students were pushed harder. Those who could not cope with the pace had become bedridden, drastically culling the number of trainees.

Of the hundreds who had bravely volunteered, only half had made it into the second week of training. The Kaneqian people, though strong in spirit, had bodies rendered weak by years of easy living. Of the half that continued the training process, most were either the young or those employed in areas where physical exertion was a matter of course.

Bailey looked around at the volunteers around him, Kaneqian men and women, formally farmers or marketers, suddenly hefting heavy furs and spears in the inhumane climate of the Ice Plains. All of the volunteers, their noses uniformly red with the cold, were staring intently at Rynford, who was explaining once again the importance of not being killed.

They were standing on the cusp of a large, and of course, snowy dale. At the bottom, a herd of snowcows grazed ceaselessly on the ice-brittle shrubbery that always held a tenuous grasp on survival in the Ice Plains. Rynford rounded up his speech and asked for a volunteer to carry out the day's lesson. As usual, no one was in a hurry to step forward. Rynford sighed and scanned the crowd. Eventually, he pointed at a student.

"You," he said simply.

The crowd parted to reveal "Half-Brick" Thompson, who was staring ahead with his usual vacant contentment and clasping his spear the wrong way round.

Bailey was surprised that he himself had survived the training process thus far. Having spent the entirety of his teenage years drinking, smoking, and generally lying about, the wonderful machinery of his body had been transformed into something that coughed and spluttered frequently when pushed too hard. He was young, though, and was slowly adapting to the harsh physical and mental pressures of the training regime. He was really surprised, however, that Half-Brick had made it this far without impaling himself on his own spear.

"Now," continued Rynford, "using the methods I have just explained, I want you to go and kill that snowcow—the one with the limp that is standing away from the rest of the herd. Do you see it?"

Half-Brick peered into the valley base. "It's a cow," he said.

"I'll take that as a yes," Rynford said. "Now, as I told you, circle around the prey and stalk it from behind its line of vision, keeping downwind of the rest of the herd. Then, when close enough, jab your spear into its underbelly and keep pushing until it loses balance and topples over. Then you'll be ready for the kill. Right?"

"Right," said Half-Brick.

"Okay!" said Rynford. "Now go!"

With a blood-curdling scream, Half-Brick began running down the valley slope, dropping his spear behind him as he went. Several of the volunteers put their hands over their eyes as the farm boy sprinted toward the grazing beast. Rynford looked on in a mix of pained disappointment and horrified disbelief.

Half-Brick continued to charge and ran head-first into the prone beast's ribs. The volunteers let out a collective empathetic hiss. Half-Brick was hard headed, but no match for the bulk of the snowcow. The farm boy stood for a moment, a stunned look in his eye. Then, with a grace he could never have mustered intentionally, collapsed unconscious into the snow. The snowcow looked around with typically bovine indifference, then went back to grazing as if nothing had happened.

Rynford let out a long sigh. "Right," he said. "I'm going to need a couple of volunteers to retrieve the Thompson boy, and then we'll get on with the lesson, shall we?"

Bailey shook his head and wished, once more, that he were still in bed.

# 11

# The Dead Wood

A warm breezed caressed the balding pate of the Shrub, gliding with a futile affection that was neither perceived nor wanted. The soft seduction of the rare wilderness breezes was nothing compared to the constant smothering love of the everyday sunshine. The earth baked, hardboiled and loyal, withered and aged, staring up to a lover as young and old as the sky itself. The wind moaned, but she'd get over it.

The epic love triangle was lost on Bip. For him, the landscape had ceased to hold interest. A view more animal and human was occupying all of his attention, and with his mouth dry and his stomach clenched, he was grateful once again that Azron had the reins; Bip doubted he could have held a steady course if his life had depended on it.

Xharon sat perched upon Prancer in a way that was both pert and fluid, both rigid and languid. She moved and swayed with the trotting of the horse as though dancing to some unheard lullaby. Bip took in the arch of her pale shoulders, burned slightly by the sun, a few patches of pink that complemented the long red hair that fell almost to her waist. He was able to study the slightly plump line of her hips and follow the occasional, maddening bead of sweat that would crawl slowly down the princess's back and collect around smooth, oily buttocks.

Bip hadn't realized, but a large slibber of drivel had wormed slowly down his chin.

It wasn't love, but it was the burning libido-fueled hormone charge that passed for love at seventeen. It didn't matter to Bip—perhaps didn't even register to him—that Xharon was not particularly beautiful, that her teeth were slightly bucked and her eyes slightly squint. It didn't matter that she had a tendency to laugh like a troubled gopher and talk about nothing but horses for seemingly hours. What mattered to Bip was that, of all the girls he had ever known or seen in his travels, Xharon was wearing the least amount of clothing.

Later in his life, Bip would reflect that this was perhaps a shallow basis for falling in love, but there and then, Bip would have happily beaten himself to death with his own shoe if Xharon had told him to —simply because she seemed to be wearing nothing more than a series of leather belts. It would also occur to him later in life, when the fires of teenage libido had been doused somewhat, that this was a rather fundamental and ridiculous flaw in the male psyche.

"Nuh?" said Bip as he felt Azron's elbow nudge into his ribs.

"I said, 'It almost makes you wish you'd been born a horse, doesn't it?'" said the thief, and nodded suggestively at Xharon's saddle region.

Bip turned to Azron's leering grin and felt a blush charge furiously over his face. "I didn't mean to stare," he mumbled.

"Stare?" chuckled Azron. "I thought your eyes were going to fly out of your head!"

"Well, don't you think she's pretty?" said Bip.

Azron rubbed his hairy chin thoughtfully. "My tastes are a touch more cosmopolitan," he said, eventually. "It's not the figure of the girl that matters—it's the figures in her dowry."

"Azron, that's awful!" hissed Bip reproachfully.

"Oh yes?" The thief grinned. "And you're taken by her sparkling personality, are you?"

Bip looked at the floor, feeling shame that he hadn't the emotional experience to identify or deal with. He looked up to see that Xharon was falling back a little, obviously meaning to talk with the cart riders.

The Kaneqian felt a butterfly storm of guilt and panic erupt in the pit of his stomach.

"Talking about anything interesting, chaps?" said Xharon, easing Prancer into a steady trot that perfectly matched the cart's ponderous progress.

Azron grinned widely. "Actually, yes—Bip here was just about to ask you something, isn't that right, Bip?"

Bip gaped and spluttered and finally relented under the guileless curiosity of Xharon's gaze. He tried to think of something clever or disarming to say but—as was usually the case when put under pressure to be dashing—his brain had wandered off somewhere. "I was just wondering where you got your outfit," he said, settling on something that was at least half true.

"It's the battle attire of the Turnmisin swamp she-warriors. They wear this when they go to war," said Xharon, matter-of-factly.

"Really?" said Azron chirpily. "Spend much time in the Turnmisin swamps then, did you?"

Xharon flushed a pretty pink, causing Bip to swallow hard. "Well... no," she said. "I read about them in a book."

Azron nodded as if expecting the reply. "So your only basis that what you are wearing is indeed the common attire of these she-warriors, who dwell in a land covered mostly with poisonous flora and dangerous stinging beasties, is derived from a book?"

Xharon's eyes narrowed. "Yes? What's your point?"

"Oh, nothing, nothing," replied Azron. "Just wondering out loud."

There was an awkward silence that Bip felt compelled to break. "So is that where you learned to fight, then?" he said. "From books?"

"Of course not," said Xharon. "Don't be silly. I've had some of the finest weapons masters in Argustin at my disposal. Uncle Tommy says girls shouldn't fight, but the guards have to teach me if I tell them to. I am a princess, after all."

"Oh, I see," said Bip. He thought desperately for another conversation opener. "So why did you want to fight?"

Xharon rolled her eyes as if Bip had just asked why babies cry or why trees grow upward. "Well, isn't it obvious?" she said. "If one wants to become a warrior princess, then one must at some point become a warrior!"

"Ah," said Bip, and left it at that.

Azron chuckled quietly under his breath. "I think what my silver-tongued mate here meant was, why be a warrior princess at all? Why not just lounge around the palace eating jam or something?"

"You wouldn't understand," said Xharon, glumly. "Royalty is no life for a girl with spirit. There's no excitement, and every day is the same. People treat you as though you're a china plate, and the only ones who talk to you honestly are other royalty, and frankly, I can't stand them. You tell people that you want to be a warrior, and they nod at you patronizingly and say, 'yes ma'am,' like you're just being silly, and the stupid servants wont even let you dress yourself in the mornings, and they let you win at cards all the time, and they won't let you do anything you want to do, and it's enough to make you sick!" Xharon breathed heavily for a while, catching her breath.

Azron and Bip exchanged a stunned glance. The echoes of the princess's rant shivered around the empty Shrub.

"So I ran away," she continued. "To find adventure, or at the very least someone who'll take me seriously."

"It's like I always say," said Azron after a while, "if you can't take a half-naked teenage girl holding an axe seriously, then what can you?"

Xharon narrowed her eyes again. "Are you making fun of me?" she said.

"Who, me?" Azron grinned, his crooked teeth gleaming in the sunlight.

"Well, you'd better not be." The princess sniffed. "Or I'll bally well chop your hands off." She stuck out her tongue and urged Prancer into a canter, leaving the cart behind.

Azron grinned. "I like a girl with spirit," he said.

"Really?" said Bip.

The thief frowned in thought for a moment. "No," he said. "That's not what I meant to say—I meant, 'I like a girl with money.'"

"That's what I thought."

IN THE BACK of the cart, Handen slept fitfully. In his mind, half-dissolved images of memories just under the surface of recollection pulled at and tickled his synapses. The ghosts of dead incidents glided through his mind with clumsy melancholy, hinting at emotions whose relevance and meaning were buried beneath an avalanche of years. Throughout the throng of thought and feeling, a nagging pulse like a vindictive headache throbbed ceaselessly, a thin and brilliant red line in an otherwise murky consciousness. Something was calling to him. Calling to him on a level greater than subconscious but just far enough beyond the conscious to be able to stand up and speak its name. Handen's eyes fluttered open, and he sat bolt upright. He looked about the cart. Nothing had changed since he had drifted off. Azron still had the reins, and Xharon still rode ahead. The cart was still comfortably full with supplies. Bip still seemed to be fixated on Xharon's horse, for some reason. Everything was exactly the same as when he had drifted off—so why did everything feel different?

The former Hostilities Advisor surveyed the horizon. It was the usual unimaginatively flat horizon he had left behind when he'd fallen asleep but now, to the far south, like a mole on an otherwise flawless face, a forest was slowly crawling into view. A force of affirmation hit him suddenly and brilliantly. He knew beyond a shadow of a doubt that whatever was affecting him, pulling at him, was in those woods.

"Turn about, south-east," he said.

Azron looked around, a cigarette loitering from his lower lip. "Well, good morning to you too, mister sunshine. Have a nice kip, did we?"

"Head toward that forest," Handen reiterated.

Azron looked doubtfully at the slithering black mass in the distance. "Are you sure? I thought you said that the forests were probably dangerous."

"I know what I said," snapped Handen. "But this is important. I think there's something there we need to find."

Or something there that I need to find, anyway, added a cynical voice in the adventurer's head.

Azron shrugged and then, putting his fingers in his mouth, let out a piercing whistle. Xharon turned at the sound and galloped over to the cart.

"What's going on?" she said.

"Change of plans, luv," said Azron. "We're heading to that ominous-looking forest over there."

Xharon shielded her eyes from the sun and squinted at the dark wood. "You mean the forest that looks like it might be full to the brim with monsters and demons and horrible things from beyond the boundaries of man's domain?" she said.

"Yeah, that's the one."

"Oh, smashing!" she said, and galloped out back in front.

---

THEY STOOD on the cusp of the dead forest. The entrance to the pathway was marked by the interlocking boughs of two long-lifeless trees, melded together in an eternal arm-wrestle. Beyond, the gray cadaver leaves omitted the light of the sun, causing a thick, wet darkness more associable with the mouth of a cave than a forest clearing. Along the ground, fossilized pine and bark formed a skeletal carpet, bone-dry with age and neglect, emanating an old and dusty smell. Each rotting trunk chattered in suspicious whispers as countless insects, evolved by their conditions into mutant, sinister things, chittered and skittered through the corpse-like foliage.

The travelers sat in awed silence, each keenly aware of the pervasive doom the dead wood emanated, like a desecrated tomb or a haunted house.

"Wow," breathed Xharon. "This is brilliant."

Azron fetched the warrior princess a disbelieving look and puffed a little harder on the cigarette he still held.

"I'd put that smoke out if I were you," said Handen, distractedly. "This whole place is liable to go up like kindling."

Azron looked around at the dead, dry trees around them, suddenly imagining them alive with fire, burning and vengeful. He stubbed out his half-smoked cigarette and put the remainder behind his ear.

"I'm surprised the trees don't just collapse in on themselves," said Bip.

Handen nodded his agreement. "There's something deeper at work here than nature. I can feel...something else."

As he spoke, a long growl like the grinding of a heavy stone block reverberated from somewhere deep in the forest. Bip gulped, deeply suspicious of what terrible things might choose to live in perpetual blackness.

"I tell you what," said Azron, unease infecting his normally confident tones, "why don't we just go around, eh?"

"I'll second that," said Bip. He felt that something less tangible than yetis and vulards lay beyond the veil of shadow, something all the more terrifying for being half-imagined.

"Oh, come on, chaps!" said Xharon, hefting her twin axes in her hands. "Where's your sense of adventure?"

"I must have left it in my other trousers," mumbled Azron.

"We have to go through," said Handen suddenly, hollowly. "I can't explain it, but we need to go through here."

Azron sighed. "Much as I want go into this highly suspicious and potentially dangerous situation with you, Handen, old chum, I just don't think we'll be able to fit the cart in."

"We'll go in on foot."

"Oh? Oh."

"We'll leave the cart and horses here."

Azron's expression brightened considerably. "Then we'll be needing someone to stay with the horses, yes?"

Handen looked around at the empty horizons of the Dozantyne Shrub. "In case what?" he said sarcastically. "In case they're stolen by a tumbleweed? No. We all go in together."

Xharon descended from her horse with a graceful flip. "Sounds good to me," she said.

"Oh, yes," Azron grumbled. "Absolutely super."

---

THEY WALKED in single file into the rotten tunnel of the forest clearing, Handen taking the lead and Azron, having hastily volunteered to do so, taking up the rear. The thief was, by no means, a coward, having willingly placed himself in life-threatening situations throughout his career, it was just that he didn't feel right standing in the open while other things creeped in the shadows. He firmly believed that if there was any shadow creeping to be done, it ought to be him doing it.

Bip had fallen in behind Xharon, who strutted behind the determined Handen with a nonchalant readiness.

"Aren't you scared?" said Bip with genuine curiosity.

Xharon turned around and looked at Bip as though he were being naïve and silly. "Of course not," she said. "Why would I be?"

"Well, I don't know," said Bip. "Ghosts? Giant spiders? Huge beasts of improbable ferocity?"

Xharon twirled one of her axes meaningfully. "I'm sure that whatever comes along we'll be able to handle it," she said, confidently.

"Oh, right," said Bip. He guessed that in the books Xharon had read, the heroes or heroines were rarely eaten alive by paradigms of monstrous evil, rarely died screaming hysterically as their insides suddenly became their outsides. He shuddered and tried to brush aside all thoughts of terrible death. It was hard, though, in a place that seemed to whisper sticky threats from its multitude of dark corners.

Somewhere in the dark, a twig snapped. The noise was followed by something that might have been a sinister chuckle. The party froze, Handen drawing his flintlock and bastard sword with streaking quickness, Xharon gripping her axes tightly, Bip's hand flying shakily to the pommel of Brian, and Azron spreading his arms and bending his knees as if preparing to run in any direction. The forest remained quiet. Horribly quiet. After a few minutes that stretched into nightmare eternity, Handen lowered his weapons and began walking forward again. The rest of the group followed, though Bip noticed the pace was slower than before. Even some of Xharon's confident swagger seemed to have departed.

They walked for what seemed like hours, starting at every sudden sound or silhouette that scurried out of sight before it could be properly identified. As they advanced, the gloom in the wood seemed to thicken, and a mournful sort of mist began to cling to the ground, obscuring the view of the forest floor. Still the party advanced, completely silent, led by Handen who marched forward with grim determination, hands hovering ready over his various holsters and scabbards, or clutching trustfully to the oiled leather of his bullwhip.

Soon the pathway they had been traveling across came to a large circular clearing. The space in the forest was walled in on all sides by thick dead growth, and despite the large circumference of the clearing, the daytime sky was still obliterated by a crisscrossing ceiling of branches and leaves.

Handen shivered. Whatever ethereal force had drawn him into the forest in the first place was centered in this clearing. He could feel it like a foot pushing down on his chest. He signaled for the others to stop behind him. Though he had been powerfully drawn to the clearing, the feeling of attraction was not a pleasant one. It was more like the urge to fall asleep in a smoke-filled room—alluring, powerful, but ultimately fatal.

"Wait here," he said, and began walking forward across the mist-covered floor.

The others watched as he approached the center of the clearing, then gasped when, with a startled cry, the immortal dropped out of sight.

---

HANDEN WAS, at first, completely surprised as the earthen walls, acned with gray, dead roots, rushed upward across his line of sight, interacting dizzily with the plunging sensation in his chest and stomach as he fell toward the darkness below. However, it did not take long for the adventurer's finely-honed survival instincts to kick in. He reached out and grabbed at a thick root, and his fall came to a jolting stop. He hung there for a while, dangling in the darkness over an uncertain drop.

*Now what?* he thought.

"Hello down there?" a familiar voice called.

Handen looked up to see the silhouettes of three heads looking down on him from a faint circle of light. Apparently, he hadn't fallen as far as he thought he had, maybe twenty feet or so.

"I'm all right," he called up.

"What's down there?" came the voice. Handen recognized it as Bip's.

"I don't know. I can't see," replied Handen.

"Hold on, mate." Azron's voice this time. "We'll have you out of there in a jiffy!" At the top of the hole, which had turned out to be only six feet or so in diameter, Bip, Azron and Xharon knelt, all thoughts of horrible forest-dwelling creatures temporarily forgotten.

"What do we do now?" said Xharon.

"Well," said Bip. "There's some rope in the cart. One of us will have to go back and get it."

The trio looked uncertainly at the dark path they had come from.

"I'll go," said Xharon, and began jogging the way they had come.

The thief and the doomsayer watched her for a while.

"One of us should go with her," said Bip, making to stand up. He was stopped by a hand on his shoulder.

"Yeah, you're right," said Azron, using Bip's momentum to launch quickly to his feet. "You stay here, and I'll be back before you know it."

"Wait a minute!" Bip called to Azron's retreating back. The Kaneqian sat back with a huff. He couldn't leave Handen alone, of course, but he felt suddenly vulnerable sitting by himself surrounded by the twisted trees.

Down in the hole, Handen managed to secure a foothold in the earthen walls, taking the strain away from his hands. He looked about him, trying to judge what the purpose of the hole was. His gaze was inevitably drawn to the darkness below him. As he looked, the terrible drawing sensation, the foot on his chest, became suddenly unbearable. The former Hostilities Advisor had to fight the urge to drop willingly into the unknown.

"Bip?" he called.

The silhouette of Bip's head appeared over the lip of the hole. "Yes?"

"Pass me a torch down, will you?"

Bip's head disappeared as he retrieved one of the pre-rolled torches from his pack and dipped it into the hole. Handen caught it easily and held it in his teeth. He fumbled for a match in his coat pocket and, finding one, struck it on his bristly chin, bristly from weeks of travel, and lit the cloth end of the torch. He winced slightly as the heat scorched his face, then dropped the torch beneath him. The torch did not fall as far as he expected, only twirled through the air for a couple of seconds before coming to rest on what appeared to be a white stone floor. The fall was only another fifteen feet or so, one Handen could easily make without even twisting an ankle. Without hesitation, the immortal let go of the root and dropped to the surface below.

He landed with a horrible crunching noise and for one worrying moment wondered if he had misjudged the length of the drop and broken his bones. He was nearly right; he had broken some bones. They just didn't belong to him. All around him, what he had assumed to be a stone floor was in fact a thick carpet of bones—some animal, some humanoid, but all gray and brittle with age. Handen shuddered with disgust as he looked down at the small human skull his boots had crushed.

Pulling himself together, the adventurer scanned the wide cave he now found himself in. The torchlight reflected from hundreds of hollow skulls set into the sloping earthen walls like cobblestones. At the opposite end of the room, the bones were piled up in some sort of shrine. The pulling sensation once again put its foot down on Handen's chest, and he found himself powerfully drawn to the construction. He could no more stop himself walking over to the bone pile than he could stop himself blinking in bright light.

He traversed the sloping hill of bones until he reached its pinnacle, then gazed with dread wonder at what he found there. Before him was a circular pool of what might charitably be called water, though its consistency and color was like that of melted toffee. The stagnant pool gave off a stench that put Handen in mind of spoiled meat. He had to stop himself from gagging.

Understanding hit Handen like a thousand epiphanies. He knew beyond a shadow of a doubt that the pool before him was the source of the ill feeling throughout the dead forest, was perhaps the very source of the forest itself. He understood that before him was the fountain of death.

He felt a sudden rush of fear and excitement, perhaps the most potent excitement he had felt in centuries. Here was a way out. Here was the sweet release he had dreamed of throughout his long incarceration.

He froze as a seductive whisper sounded at the back of his mind.

*Drink. Drink.*

A faint horror tingled Handen's spine as a dry and powerful thirst climbed suddenly into his throat. For a moment, the sticky pool at his feet seemed to be the most appealing thing he had ever seen. He bent down to the water, undeterred by a fat bubble that rose and popped beneath his nose, releasing a stench like dead animals.

*Drink. Drink.*

It might have ended for Handen there and then, leaving his flesh to rot and his bones to merge with the thousands of others, had not another voice interrupted him.

"Handen?" called Bip, his voice distant and echoing in the weird acoustics of the death cave. "Handen? Is everything okay?"

Handen shook himself like a man emerging from a particularly engrossing daydream. "Yes," he called back. "Everything's fine."

"Okay, Azron and Xharon have brought some rope. We're going to lower it down to you."

"Okay," Handen called, but he was suddenly doubtful that he would be able to leave this place, whether the arcane magnetism of the pool would let him leave. But he had to. It was not time for him to die yet. He still had a mission to complete.

He unfastened his small waterskin from his hip and emptied the contents onto the ground, then lowered the container into the pool. Some of the liquid touched his hand and tingled there uneasily. He had a sudden thought that, had he not been immortal, the very touch of the fountain of death would have killed him.

With the waterskin full, the nagging coaxing sensation of the pool seemed to lessen. Handen found he was able to walk away, back to the cave's entrance, without a struggle. As long as he carried a piece of the fountain, he knew, he would cease to be the cave's prisoner.

He looked at the lowered rope as if seeing it for the first time. It did not belong here, he felt. There was never supposed to be a way out of the death cave. Then he looked up at the faces of his friends, back up at a world where sunlight and clear skies were merely a few minutes' walk away. Suddenly Handen felt as he had when he had first escaped from the Bin—a frenzied combination of relief and freedom. He climbed the rope, leaving the deadly yet strangely seductive solitude of the death cave behind him.

## 12

# Hot Pursuit

There have been countless poems and songs ode to Dawncastle by morning, whole overtures dedicated to Bersch's most resplendent and remarkable building, a thousand artists who have snapped their brushes in frustration trying to capture its ethereal magnificence. It stands aloft at the center of the industrially environed city of Argustin, reflecting the gradual colorings of dawn throughout the prisms of its glass and polished steel architecture, appearing like a conjurer's crystal against the smoky city skies.

By ingenious design, the great palace magnified and reflected the light of the day, twisting and bending the rays of the sun so that they spread and shone in a smoldering, nearly opaque glow. In the hushed moments before dawn, the building would be the first thing to light up the morning sky, turning a pale blue as it intercepted the earliest hints of the coming daylight. Then suddenly, brilliantly, it would cycle through a multitude of burning hues as the sun began to rise, pulsing spears of red, orange, and gold as quick and random as a midnight bonfire.

The tower shape of the Dawncastle, a maelstrom of multifarious spires and archways tapering and entwining to a needle point, meant the construct appeared like a brilliant teardrop of fire by mid morning, shining so brightly that it could be seen for miles around. The surrounding city, though built high and impressive itself, was entirely outshone by the crystalline tower, like a weak, ailing king under a still-marvelous crown.

For those who lived inside Dawncastle, the effects of a clear-skied dawn were just as remarkable as those seen from the outside. Having spent the night cooling gradually under the stars, the cold corridors of the palace would become suddenly and welcomingly warm, washing the panorama of the surrounding city in a rosy glow. Windows formerly paneled by the dark of night into a hard, lifeless onyx were reborn as salmon-tinted crystal.

The steel bones and window skin of the tremendous tower absorbed and radiated everything that was wondrous about the new life of morning.

Which was fine. If you were a morning person.

Emperor Tomberry Torrid Draegul the Tenth was not a morning person. Emperor Draegul got up when he damn well felt like it, and woe betide anyone who interrupted his sleeping patterns. He had once ordered the execution of every bird in a two-mile radius simply because of an over-enthusiastic dawn chorus. He was not a man best caught in a bad mood.

Today he rose at roughly noon. At his first stirrings, the harp player positioned discreetly in the corner of the room began to pluck a slow and soothing tune. Predictably the musician was promptly struck unconscious by the brick Draegul kept at his bedside specifically for throwing at staff. This happened every time the Emperor awoke, but the musician would gladly take a half-hearted brick to the head each day rather than face the consequences of absenteeism. The player and his instrument were dragged quietly away by the ultra-discreet Whimstaff.

Emperor Draegul smacked his lips. "Maggot?" he called.

A tall elderly figure dressed in white robes appeared almost magically by Draegul's side. His name was not Maggot, but Draegul rarely bothered with the names of his attendant staff and called people whatever he felt like.

"I'm in a blue mood today, Maggot. And I think I want a rhinoceros risotto for breakfast."

"As you wish, Your Incredibleness," said Maggot. Maggot was head of the Whimstaff—those responsible for making sure Draegul's every whim and desire were met to the closest degree of immediacy. It was a demanding and stressful job, and position of Head of Whimstaff was notoriously short-lived. Maggot, however, had survived for a record three years by being ready for anything and being able to partially anticipate the vastly unpredictable moods of his master.

He already had his staff on standby with the tinted blinds and curtains that would change the interior color of Dawncastle to whatever suited Draegul's current mood. The rhinoceros breakfast was a more complicated task, seeing as the nearest rhinoceros was likely several hundred miles away in the Southwestern savannah regions.

Oh, well. Maggot would do what he usually did when the Emperor had a hankering for a rare or non-existent food—mash up some chicken into a pâté and cut it into an interesting shape. With any luck, Draegul wouldn't even notice—Maggot was quite sure the Emperor only asked for such unusual breakfasts to test his limitations anyway. However, if Draegul did notice that the meat in his rhinoceros risotto was merely re-formed chicken, Maggot would more than likely face a horrible execution.

Maggot's was a hard life, and he sighed heavily once he was safely out of his master's earshot.

Back in the master bedroom, Draegul emerged from his bed. The Whimstaff, operating with their expert discretion, had begun warming the room a few hours before the Emperor's estimated time of awakening, so Draegul felt no morning chill as he strode toward his dressing table. He arrived and looked in the mirror.

"Casual," he muttered.

Immediately, five maids appeared from various hidden doorways, each with an item of clothing. In the blink of an eye, Draegul was dressed by his dexterous attendants in a comfortable pair of jodhpurs and riding boots, complemented nicely by a black silken shirt that was frilled only slightly effeminately at the sleeves. Draegul gazed critically in the mirror and smiled a satisfied smile. It was easy to look good when you were rich beyond the dreams of even the greediest merchant.

He held his arms out while he was adorned with the thin, silver crown and the ceremonial weapons that he was rarely seen without. He tested the mechanism of his rifle and studied the edge of his sword. A satisfied smile once again made a delicate crease in his features. He was ready for the day.

Draegul's schedule was an undemanding one. He had most of the day booked off for surprising Maggot with impossible whims, a pastime he found most amusing. Later, he might spar with one of his elite, just to keep his sword skills as finely honed as the blade he carried. After that, he imagined, there would be servants to torment, peasants to terrify, and an army of concubines to take advantage of. But for now, he would spend the morning as he spent every morning—walking around Dawncastle looking for reasons to execute people.

The Emperor emerged into the freshly blue-tinted corridors of the upper chambers. Through the surrounding windows, he could see the city of Argustin stretched before him. Not much impressed Draegul, but the cityscape of Argustin always filled him with something akin to pride. He watched as airschooners drifted between towers and archways of steel and stone, and as railcars sped smoothly across the elevated railings, their propellers burring over the tower tops and domed roofs. In the distance, a cloud of brown-tinted smoke billowed softly from a thousand chimneys, flavoring the skies of the factory quarter with the acrid smell of progress.

As he gazed across the high-topped buildings of the capital, his thoughts turned to the two escaped doomsayers. He had been thinking more and more about them lately and wondered if Blungkit had been successful in their capture. More, he thought about the message the fugitives were carrying…the destruction of the planet by some intruding astral body. A bleak prospect. Draegul briefly envisioned his city burning beneath cosmic flames, his citizens dying screaming in an alien heat. It was not an image he found wholly unattractive, but the prospect annoyed him greatly. If anyone was going to lay waste to the world, he felt, it was going to be Emperor Tomberry Torrid Draegul the Tenth.

A familiar whispering sensation sounded in his ear as he stared with his mind's eye. One of these days, he knew, he would have to see a doctor about the gentle yet incessant chittering noise that came to him whenever he tried to think. He found his thoughts turned yet again to the desert project—Operation Deadwaker, as the project managers had come to call it. He reminded himself to check on the progress of the archaeologists and engineers. Time was short, and he was beginning to think he'd have to start executing people to re-motivate the work force.

He could not afford to have a lackluster crew working on Operation Deadwaker. The fate of the world might depend on it.

THE WAGON TRUNDLED across the Dozantyne Shrub, the rotting forest lessening to a moribund smear of geography behind them. The doomsayers rolled along at the pace they had become accustomed to, though their traveling arrangements were a little different than usual this time. Before setting off that day, Handen had asked Xharon if he could ride ahead on Prancer. Xharon had agreed without protest—the request was one of the few things the former Hostilities Advisor had said since returning from the fountain of death. So now he rode ahead, silent and alone.

At the moment, Bip was finding it hard to feel sorry for the immortal. He was concerned with Handen's obvious self-isolation, but the upshot was that he was able to sit next to Xharon on the wagon—and had deliberately missed his turn at rest so he could do so. In the back of the wagon, Azron was using his unexpected downtime to get some extra sleep, while in the front, Bip's hormone-addled brain sought desperately for something to say.

It wasn't that Bip hadn't any experience in talking to girls. He had talked to plenty of girls. It was just that none of them had been as immediately half-naked as Xharon. Nor was it a question of self-confidence; months of hard travel had done a lot of good for Bip's physical appearance. His weedy frame had worked into something more sinewy, and the long days of sunlight had turned his near-gray complexion a healthy brown and his washy, almost-blond hair into a robust gold. In short, Bip—underneath the travel-dirt, torn clothes, and scratched glasses—was looking better than ever. But still he couldn't think of a word to say to this girl.

Eventually, after what seemed like a warm eternity of silence, Xharon spoke up. "He's an awfully somber chap, isn't he?" she said.

"Whu?" replied Bip, who was so busy thinking of something to say that he had temporarily forgotten how to speak.

"Handen," said Xharon, nodding to the solitary figure on horseback. "A very serious man."

Bip cleared his throat, glad of the chance for conversation. "He's okay most of the time. He just gets a little gloomy now and then. Mostly when he's bored."

Xharon squinted thoughtfully at Handen's back. "I would've thought that being immortal would be brilliant. The things he must have seen, the places he must have been!"

"Well, that's the problem, really," said Bip. "He was locked up for hundreds of years, and he can't remember most of the places he's been, and all of the people he's met are dead, and all of the things he's done don't matter to anyone anymore."

"I see," said Xharon, though she didn't appear to be paying much attention. "Do you think he has a girlfriend?" she said unexpectedly.

Bip tried hard to keep his mental footing at this unexpected rock in the stream of conversation. "I doubt it," he said. "I should imagine any relationship he formed in the lunatic asylum was less than serious."

"Oh," said Xharon, and went back to staring at Handen.

Bip thought desperately of a way to steer the discussion back to more immediate interests. "So you're the princess," he ventured flatly.

Xharon gave him a look somewhere between contempt and pity. "That's right," she said.

"So I expect one day you'll be the queen or something?"

"Oh no. Never. They'd never let a woman be Emperor...or Empress, I suppose. Only uncle Tommy's sons are heirs to the throne."

"Really? And what are they like?"

"No one knows." Xharon shrugged. "Their identities are kept a great secret—for their own protection, of course."

"But they're your cousins," Bip said, frowning. "You must have seen them at least once?"

Xharon shook her head. "From the day that they are born, they are hidden from society, raised and educated in secret. No one but Draegul's most trusted advisors ever see his children."

"Bizarre," concluded Bip. The wagon trundled along in silence for a while before he spoke again. "Surely your auntie must tell you about them?"

Xharon said nothing.

Bip continued. "I mean, she must see them now and again, being their mother and all."

"My auntie is dead," Xharon said.

Bip blushed and looked at his feet. "I'm sorry," he said.

"You needn't be," Xharon replied dismissively. "It happened a long time ago. She died of an illness—she had a weak heart, you see. The doctors said there was nothing they could do."

The Kaneqian scanned the horizon, thinking of something sensitive yet tactful to say.

"It hurt my father the most, I think," Xharon continued. "Uncle Tommy called a week of mourning throughout the Empire's heart, of course. Though he never seemed very broken up about it—always too wrapped up in his projects. But my father...my father was very close to her, and it nearly ended him when she died." Xharon furrowed her brow, peering into a memory. "She was very beautiful. She smiled a lot, I remember. I think that's why Uncle Tommy married her, really, why he made my father a duke. She really was very pretty."

"It must run in the family," said Bip, then immediately wished he hadn't. For the second time in a short while, he blushed furiously.

Xharon looked at him and smiled. "People do say I have her eyes."

Bip frowned and blinked owlishly. "What...did she leave them to you in her will or something?"

Xharon stared hard at the Kaneqian with a familiar expression of contempt and pity.

"I think I'll swap places with Azron, now, if you don't mind," she said.

"Of course not," said Bip, and once again cursed his inherent lack of debonair.

***

THEY TRAVELED for two more days, brushing through the landscape stolidly and with little pause. They sensed the vague feeling of leaving nowhere behind in favor of somewhere and that the journey of days, months, and millennia was finally coming to its last furlong. Unfortunately, they didn't sense the presence of the Regulators behind them, drawing closer and closer as the miles went by.

***

HANDEN SAT IN SILENCE, as he had for the last few days, his hunter's eyes searching through a far and away void, his fighter's hands twiddling distractedly with the waterskin before him.

They had made healthy progress since the dead wood, traveling many miles and at last nearing the end of the Dozantyne Shrub. Now the incessant, flawless horizons had yielded to squat stony hillocks, which, in turn, yielded to larger, rocky hills. These hills, Xharon had said, would eventually spiral away into the Oaken Mons, a great winding whip of green peaks that separated the Empire's heart from the western provinces. Traveling along the southern borders as they were, the fugitives would be able to pass the mountain range without resorting to the heavily patrolled byways or airboat services.

Though Argustin was still far away, the doomsayers were drawing comfortably close. That was why, placated by their own sense of optimism, the travelers had taken a break from their rigid schedule to rest the horses and eat a hot lunch in the middle of the afternoon, rather than waiting for supper that night.

They sat atop one of the larger hills watching the level expanse of the Shrub stretch away behind them, seeming still and carpet-like in the far distance. Azron lay on his back, relaxing and blowing cigarette smoke into the air above him while Bip tended to the cooking. Xharon sharpened her axes on a whetstone, singing quietly in her faltering soprano. Everyone seemed content bar Handen, who slouched in the same hunch of moody contemplation he had adopted since filling his waterskin at the fountain of death. He stared down at the elixir that would provide a final and ultimate cure to his immortality.

He should have felt happier, he knew, having finally found the one thing he had hoped to find since the discovery of his ageless invulnerability, but he could not help feeling strangely glum. He had a job to do before he could end his life, a mission to fulfill and a promise to keep to all those he had cared about...all those who were now so much dust in the wind, long dead and sketchy in memory.

On some mornings, after the plaguing dreams of the half-remembered lifetimes he had left in his wake like the shed skins of a reptile, the compulsion to drink the thick, brown water and damn the consequences was unbearable. Presently, he found himself barely suppressing the urge to dip a finger into the mouth of the waterskin and lick the result, just to see what would happen.

His gloom was twofold. Part of him couldn't wait to drink the water and end a lifetime of too many years to bear, but part of him was scared also of what might come afterward, and whether the faces of countless foes long since dispatched would be waiting for him in the dark.

He wondered if, when the time came, he would really be able to drink from the fountain of death. The urge to leave the world was strong, for Handen had grown tired of it a thousand times over, but he felt he might hesitate, as one might hesitate to leave a boring party or put down a bad book, just in case he were to miss out on something interesting.

Handen sighed. In his hand, he had hoped he had found the ultimate solution. He should have known from the deep well of his experience that nothing in life was so straightforward.

Bip looked up from his cooking over the flames of the daytime campfire and once again observed the melancholic fatigue swamping his companion. He was worried about Handen. He had come to regard the first volunteer not just as a valuable ally but also as a good and trusted friend. He envied him in many ways and wondered how far in his quest he would have come without the stark professionalism of the adventurer. He grew worried at these signs of weakness in the usually stoic man and did not like the way that, when at rest, he would withdraw from the world, contemplative and distant. Handen's moods had not improved with the discovery of the fountain of death —for which he had quested for over several centuries—but, instead, had worsened.

In the background, Bip was dimly aware that Xharon had stopped the meticulous working of her axe blades and now stood to perform the frenzied but nonetheless impressive kata she practiced every night. Bip turned to watch as the young princess swung her axes in quick blurring arcs, sometimes allowing the momentum of her body to spin a leg out in a high whirling kick or bend her torso in a spiraling side-flip. Now and then she would let out high-pitched yelps of aggression, like an abbreviated version of her war cry. Bip watched the display with great interest, although for baser reasons than the appreciation of finely executed martial arts.

After a while, it became apparent that Handen, too, had become fixated on the display.

"Good, isn't she?" he said.

Bip started at the sound of his friend's comment. Handen had spent so much time in silence since the incident in the dead wood that his voice had taken on a scratchy and unfamiliar tone. He turned to look at the adventurer and was pleased to see that a sense of connection had returned to Handen's eyes. The former hopeless melancholy had been banished for a time, replaced by a more familiar expression of calculating interest. Bip winced as he felt a twang of jealousy in the pit of his stomach.

"I mean, she's a little showy, and her economy of movement isn't ideal, but there's definite flair. A natural balance and poise. She could be quite the fighter, given the chance."

Bip nodded his agreement, though had no real opinion on the matter. Even with his occasional sparring matches with Handen, he still hadn't managed to develop much of a knack for hand-to-hand combat.

"The axes are definitely a bad choice of weapon, though," continued Handen.

"She'd be better off with a nice short sword and a lightweight shield—something more suited to her body shape."

Bip looked at the warrior princess, twirling the stunted-looking axes with frightening abandon.

"I don't know," he ventured. "She seems to be doing all right to me."

Handen gave a lazy half-shrug, as though not really hearing what the Kaneqian was saying. Bip looked at his friend closely and noticed that Handen's stolid and calculating gaze was a little warmer than usual; something in his shell of stoicism seemed to tilt affectionately.

They turned back to Xharon's kata, both men marveling at different sides of the same shape. Likely they could have sat there watching for a long while if the ground behind them had not suddenly exploded.

---

BLUNGKIT RODE at the head of his exhausted but still determined party. Of the fifty men he had originally set out with, only thirty remained—lank and despondent in their sweat-stained uniforms. Many of the others had fallen to heatstroke or exhaustion, victims of the posse's ruthless and unforgiving traveling pace. More still had lost their mounts to the inhospitable terrain. All these men had been left behind at various stages of their journey, sacrificed to the greater good or, more accurately, to Blungkit's agenda.

The Pin Constable had cursed his luck when arriving at the Bone Desert outpost. The available reinforcements had consisted of greenhorns and strays, those Regulators who were deemed too inexperienced or too incompetent to be placed in more active regions, and thus were made soft and weak from lack of challenge. Blungkit was sure that, had he set off with a contingent of Panthalus men, fifty Regulators would be standing with him now instead of thirty. Still, the important thing was that he had caught up with his quarry. The fugitives were within his grasp.

He grinned carnivorously as he lowered the telescope from his eye. He could clearly see the camp, finally see the faces of the prisoners who had made a fool of him all those months ago. And, incredibly, they hadn't been detected. For some reason or other, the fugitives had not seen the approach of Blungkit's posse, even though they had made no real attempt at stealth.

Still smiling, he folded the telescope and handed it to his lieutenant, a young P.C. by the name of Darby, within whom he had discovered a dogged nastiness that he recognized as true to his own heart.

"Got 'em by the curlies now, Darby," he said.

"Do we approach?" replied his protégé.

"Nah," said Blungkit, "there's an old saying, Darby my lad: why risk a scratching when you can kill a cat with a half-brick and not even get out of your chair?"

Darby frowned. It was not a saying he had heard before, though he could see the truth in it.

Blungkit turned to the beast wranglers, the men in charge of the huge, long-necked and horn-headed uberbeasts. Thankfully all three of the beasts they had set out with were still holding well, one used as a packhorse for food and supplies, and the other two bearing massive assault cannons harnessed to their flanks.

"Right," said Blungkit. "Let's give these buggers something to think about." He raised his fist above his head. "Fire!"

The wranglers shouted the command words to their charges, and the beasts braced themselves, moaning their low, dumb bellows in worried anticipation. Then the gunners, riding atop the monstrous gun bearers, set the fuse on the cannons. The twin guns boomed apocalyptically as they sent their heavy iron cannonballs flying in search of targets. Blungkit grinned at the low, threatening whistle made in their wake.

HANDEN WAS first on his feet, the dreamy fascination erased from his features as quickly as snow melting in fire. Bip was up a second later, his face a comic epitome of shock. Xharon had frozen in her kata, narrowly avoiding the blades of her own axes as she ground suddenly to a halt.

The three looked around for signs of threat; the air hung with the unique stillness that only appears after moments of the sudden and dangerous. It wasn't until they heard Azron that they realized what had happened.

"Eeeeeeeep?" said a voice barely recognizable as belonging to the Port Town man.

Where the thief had been lying down, he now sat bolt upright, his face caked with dust and his cigarette blackened and twisted. His eyes were stupendously wide, and his confident grin had been replaced by a slack-jawed grimace of horrified surprise. He once again gave off the low keening sound that seemed to escape from his throat of its own accord.

"Eeeeeeeep?"

At his feet a crater, four feet wide, coned down to a small but lethal-looking cannonball that gleamed dully in the late-morning light, steaming with quiet relief. Had the ball landed slightly to the left, Azron would have been relieved of his legs.

"Hit the deck!" shouted Handen, and everyone, including Bip, who wasn't sure what the deck was or why they should hit it, fell to their bellies.

"Great holy bastards!" exclaimed Azron, crawling over to his comrades. "What in the backside of hell was that all about?"

"Over here!" said Handen and began crawling toward a large and sturdy-looking boulder. Eventually, when all four of them were huddled against the rock, Handen pointed out the obvious. "We're under fire," he said. "Cannon fire." He took in Bip's blank expression. "Like a pistola but much, much bigger."

Bip swallowed. He had thought the idea of the flintlocks a little nightmarish. To imagine one of a larger scale was terrible to behold.

"I say!" Xharon said, glancing at each of her comrades in turn. "Isn't this exciting?"

"No!" Azron replied hotly. "It bloody well isn't! I damn well nearly lost my knees! I like my knees! They're handy for all sorts of things!"

"Where are they firing from?" interrupted Bip.

"Good question," replied Handen. Bip once again perceived how the adventurer only truly seemed to be alive—to be there—when there was conflict at hand.

Handen began to raise his head slowly above the rock. The others followed cautiously. As they peered over the boulder, the unruffled terrain of the Shrub once again opened before them, though now the flat horizon was marred by a group of Regulators, huddled together like a sudden gray pimple. They seemed impossibly far away to be such an immediate threat, but a threat they were.

"Damn," said Handen. "They've caught up with us."

"Regulators," breathed Bip, a faint finger of terror gliding up his spine.

"What's that with them?" said Azron, pointing to the larger mounds standing with their hunters.

"Uberbeasts," Handen said, squinting slightly into the distance. He recognized them well, and dimly remembered having to fight one once, long ago. "It's how they're transporting the cannons."

Xharon looked affronted. "You mean to tell me they're making those poor animals carry heavy machinery in this heat? That's horrible!"

Azron and Handen exchanged a cynical glance. "Yes," said Azron. "Truly horrible. Why don't you go and give them a telling-off, yeah?"

Before anyone could stop her, Xharon was on her feet. "You know, I just might," she said.

"Are you mental, girl? They'll blow you to smithereens!" said the thief.

"Of course they won't," said Xharon, haughtily. "I am their princess, after all."

Handen rolled his eyes. "We may know that you're their princess, Xharon, but all they see is a speck on the horizon aiding and abetting some other specks on the horizon. If you try and go over there, they'll fire on you for sure."

"Don't be silly," said Xharon.

For a moment, Bip was terrified that she really was going to try and approach the Regulators, but then, far in the distance, there was a small, almost insignificant flash from where the uberbeasts were standing. A second later, the flash was followed by a loud boom that echoed through the Shrub like a death knell. This boom was followed by a dread and promising whistling noise.

"Scatter!" roared Handen.

The companions did not need to be told twice. They leapt in opposite directions as the boulder that had given them the illusion of safety suddenly burst into tiny pieces of shrapnel. Bip sat up where he had landed, raising a shaky hand to a cut on his cheek. He stared dumbfounded at the rubble of their former shelter.

*That could have been you*, said a smug little voice in the back of his head.

Handen was on his feet before the dust began to settle, pulling Bip up by the scruff of his shirt. "To the wagon!" he shouted, though to Bip's blasted ears, his voice seemed curiously far away. The fugitives started to head toward where they had left the wagon but stopped abruptly in their tracks. Where the wagon had been, there now lay a pile of wooden rubble. A broken wheel spun sadly to rest.

"They blew up the bloody wagon!" Azron shouted indignantly. "All of our stuff was in there!"

"To the horses!" shouted Handen, and this time when they got there, they were relieved to find their mounts in one piece, though somewhat jittery from the sudden chaos. Without delay, Xharon leapt gracefully onto Prancer, the heavily muscled charger remaining admirably calm in the surrounding panic. Bip, though, disorientated from the ordeal, managed to saddle up one of the wagon horses only after a frustrating and frantic dance, made all the more difficult by the occasional cannonballs that would rain down with whistling fury, throwing up clouds of dirt and dust with powerful abandon. By the time Bip had struggled into his saddle, Azron and Handen were already mounted and ready to leave.

"Move out!" bellowed Handen, and once again, even in the midst of pandemonium, Bip observed how natural and at ease the immortal seemed when the world was erupting around him.

Wagon-less and leaving most of their supplies behind, the fugitives galloped away in the direction of Argustin, devil clouds of dust settling behind them.

---

"CEASE FIRE!" roared Blungkit, and the gunners halted the clockwork process of stoking, loading, and firing. The uberbeasts relaxed as the echo of gunfire faded to nothingness. Blungkit grinned his wet, wooden grin.

"Should we prepare for pursuit, sir?" said Darby.

"No rush, lad," said Blungkit. "We've got 'em where we want 'em—scared and disorientated. It's just a matter of running 'em into the ground now. And then..." Blungkit patted the grip of his flintlock pistola, a newer model to replace the one Handen had stolen. "And then the fun begins," he finished, and gave a guttural and menacing laugh. Darby, eager to show solidarity with his new leader, began to join in with his own menacing laugh. Blungkit turned to him with a look of disgust on his face.

"What are you laughing at?" he said.

Darby's pockmarked face went blank. "I don't know," he muttered.

"Well don't," said Blungkit. "You sound like an idiot."

Darby's brow furrowed in confusion. He made as if to say something, then, wisely, thought better of it. One day he hoped to have underlings of his own to boss around, and he understood, on a socially philosophical level, that a certain amount of abuse had to be tolerated before you could rightly dish it out to others.

Blungkit scanned the horizon, that same predatory grin twisting his already unpleasant face into something near demonic. He began laughing quietly to himself again. This time Darby left him to it.

---

HIGH ABOVE THE trailing smoke of the cannons, swaying in the breezes of the open sky, Mr. Random looked down at the pack of Regulators, appearing like gray-coated ants from his vantage point.

He bridged his long fingers and smiled to himself. He enjoyed human nature, he really did. Just when you thought the world was full of useless, ineffectual weaklings, it turned up a card like Blungkit—a man more rabid wolf than law enforcer.

He was optimistic that Blungkit would catch up with the trouble-makers and, with a little encouragement, butcher them mercilessly and without hesitation. It was good to know, very reassuring, that the few people on the planet who could stand in the way of his plans would soon be murdered by the supposed peacekeepers of their own civilization. But a smidgen of doubt still lurked awkwardly at the back of his mind. What if Blungkit, despite his advantages, was to fail for any reason?

As any respectable being of concentrated nastiness knew, the odds could never be too favorable, and overkill was better than no kill at all. What was needed was a little extra dilemma…

Bobbing gently in the air currents around him, Mr. Random grinned to himself. He snapped his fingers and disappeared.

There was always mischief in the world for those who knew how to make it.

***

BIP CLUNG tightly to the neck of his horse, gritting his teeth as the momentum of the gallop shook and shuddered him madly like a pea in a rattle. He had not been able to saddle his mount properly in all the confusion and, foolishly, had dropped his reins when they had first fled from the wrath of the Regulators. Now he clung desperately to his panicked horse and hoped dearly that the beast would instinctively follow its companions and not flee in a direction of its own choosing.

In front of him, he could see Azron having a hard time on the uncomfortable saddle as he clung to Handen's waist, and Xharon and Prancer maintaining a breakneck gallop in the far distance.

Above all of the noise and confusion, Bip could hear the pounding of his heart beating hard enough to make his vision swim with each percussion. Though the steady tension of being a fugitive was by no means an un-stressful experience, this mad dash had brought Bip as close to utter panic as he had been since his flight from the yeti. He was beginning to think that he might black out, then almost certainly he would be thrown beneath the hooves of his own horse.

The next long minutes of flight were tooth-grindingly tense for Bip, who thought that at any minute his saddle might slide farther down his horse's flank, or that the Regulators might suddenly appear behind them, whooping and closing in for the kill.

Following Xharon's lead, they rode farther into hills, crisscrossing beneath miniature cliff faces and descending into deep, sudden valleys. As they rode on, the hills and cliffs became tighter, and pockets of forest obscured the afternoon sunlight. Soon they were traveling through what appeared to be a labyrinthine system of tunnels and gullies.

As they approached a fork in the pathway, Handen yelled for them to halt.

Thankfully, Bip's mount came to a stop of its own accord, and the Kaneqian gasped with sudden relief. He quickly retrieved his mount's reins and adjusted the saddle as best he could.

"Why have we stopped?" he said between breaths.

Handen turned to him. "We're going to have to split up. "

"What?!"

"He's right, mate," said Azron, who was breathing hard himself. "Those buggers back there are running us into the ground—if we don't do something to slow 'em down we're dead meat."

"We don't have time to try to cover our tracks," continued Handen. "Our only hope is to split up and rendezvous later on. That way we can confuse the Regulators, or at the very least divide their forces."

Bip looked at the determined expressions of his friends. "I don't like it…" he muttered.

"I know, kid," said Handen. "I don't like it either, but it's the only way. "

"What's the plan?" said Xharon, her eyes burning eagerly.

"Azron and I will take the left path," said Handen. "You and Bip will take the right."

Xharon looked less than impressed with her lot but nodded

anyway. Bip felt a sudden wince of sorrow behind his eyes. He did not want to be so suddenly split from the people he had grown to trust so much.

Handen turned his horse around, preparing to depart. "If everything goes okay, we'll either meet at Argustin or on the way. If not..." Handen looked at his companions each in turn. "Don't wait up and don't look back. We have a message to deliver and a world to save. Don't forget why we're here in the first place. Good luck."

With that, Handen spurred his horse into a gallop. He and Azron rode away, leaving only dust and silence in their wake.

The two remaining travelers waited for a while, watching them leave. Eventually Xharon turned in her saddle toward to Bip.

"Think you can keep up?" she said, cracking a wry smile that suddenly made the Kaneqian feel a little better about things.

"I can try," replied Bip.

"Then let's ride!"

<br>

SOMETIME LATER, the Regulators arrived at the fork in the path. Blungkit held up a hand, and the procession behind him came to an ordered halt. He looked at the two sets of tracks and smiled to himself. He knew that this was more than likely a hasty attempt by his quarry to evade complete capture—or possibly a studied move to divide his forces. However, Blungkit could not see how dividing his forces would help the fugitives in any way. After all, fifteen on two were just as unfavorable odds as thirty on four.

Darby rode up behind the Pin Constable. "What now, sir?" he said.

"We split up," Blungkit said promptly. "You take twelve men and go right, and I'll take twelve men and go left. We'll leave the uberbeasts and a few handlers here—speed is now essential." Blungkit turned so he could address his entire force. "All right, men, this is where it ends. They are divided and ripe for conquering. They are scared, and they are few. Ride the bastards down and show no mercy!"

A roar of approval came from the Regulators, like the baying of hounds on a hunt. After so many miles of travel, the moment of victory was finally within their grasp.

The two contingents split and thundered down their respective pathways. Blungkit, riding at the head of his division, grinned like a hyena with the smell of fresh meat in its nose.

BIP AND XHARON rode hard but were forced to slow when the ground beneath them became stony and unpredictable. Prancer had already had a few narrow encounters with rocks jutting suddenly from the long grass, and the cliffs to either side of the path would occasionally dislodge miniature avalanches of smaller stones that, while not a great danger to the mounts, were certainly an inconvenience.

They rode slowly through the eerily quiet valley-cum-canyon, safe in the knowledge that anybody pursuing them would also have to slow their pace. Without realizing it, Bip began to whistle nervously through his teeth. Xharon turned and made a shushing motion. Up ahead there was a sound like a deep thud, as though something heavy had just fallen from a tree. Bip halted abruptly, pulling on the reins of his horse. He held his breath as he listened. For a while, there was only the sound of a few insects buzzing lazily in the long grass. Then, suddenly and disturbingly, there was another thump. This time Bip was certain he could feel the ground vibrate slightly.

Xharon turned around in her saddle again. "What was that?" she mouthed.

Bip shrugged just as another thump shook the ground around them.

Almost instantaneously the two riders dismounted, Xharon drawing her twin axes with a flourish and Bip clutching the hilt of Brian. Bip held his breath, staring hard at the pathway before him. A slight bulge in one of the cliff walls and several tall trees obscured the view of the pathway ahead. Another thump resounded, closer this time, and Bip was certain that whatever was responsible for the noises was approaching directly in front of them.

Without warning, a deer burst from the bushes and sprinted

toward them. Bip almost choked as his heart leapt into his throat. He stumbled and fell backward as the animal hurried its way past them. The Kaneqian nearly laughed with relief.

"It was a deer!" he said. "Here was me thinking that we were about to be confronted by some huge and terrible monster, and it was just a deer! What do you think about that, Xharon?" Bip got to his feet, still chuckling to himself. "I said, 'What do you think about that, Xharon?'" he repeated. Hearing no reply, Bip turned to his companion.

"Xharon?"

The warrior princess stood with her axes slack in her hands, her body limp, and the color drained from her skin. Her head tilted backward as though she had fallen asleep on her feet.

"Xharon?" Bip stood by the princess and followed her gaze upward. And then upward again. "Oh," he said. "Oh, crap."

Towering above them, with a smile that was successful in connoting a number of unpleasant things, leaning casually on a club that was nothing more than a branchless tree, stood a giant.

"Fe Fi Fo Fum…" it said, in a voice that seemed to reverberate like a rockslide. "Ah smell something am gonna eet!"

Not for the first time that day, Bip found himself on the verge of blacking out.

***

HANDEN WAITED, crouched at his vantage point overlooking the slim, overgrown canyon floor below him. He was confident that even though Azron had left a trail a blind man could follow with ease, anyone crossing this part of the path would slow down sufficiently for his purposes. Hidden on the tree-laden top of the muddy cliff, Handen waited in ambush.

When the Regulators had caught up with them, he had been put in mind of the hunting habits of a creature he had once dead about called a stoat. The creature was vicious, but slower than its prey of choice, the rabbit. However, the stoat was a relentless hunter and infallible tracker and though the rabbit might run for miles upon end, eventually—when it thought it was safe—there would be the stoat, approaching with casual doom.

Handen was determined not to become the rabbit. Not to run himself into exhaustion and be consumed by a large and merciless hunter. The old Hostilities Advisor adage came to mind: when caught in a deadly game of cat and mouse, don't be the mouse.

The adventurer shifted his position slightly, distributing his weight evenly. If all went according to plan, then any Regulator force following the single horse tracks he had left would be expecting no fight—only pursuit and capture. He intended to confound their expectations in the most violent way possible.

Getting Xharon and Bip out of the way had been the hard part, and the fork in the road had certainly proved a blessing. He knew that the younger companions would have doubtless tried to aid him in his ambush and, though fifteen-to-one odds were a gaunt feasibility even for an immortal, the chances of two people as inexperienced in battle as Bip and Xharon getting hurt or killed were very high indeed. He'd had no such anxiety when deciding to bring Azron with him—the thief's talent for self-preservation would keep him at a safe distance from the action and give him a good head start if the ambush failed.

With any luck, the attack would slow the Regulators down enough that they could make their escape. And if the worst were to happen and he was captured, he might still buy his friends some time to reach Argustin.

Handen checked his weapons. It took some time. Then he waited.

---

GIANTKIN WERE NOT common in the lowlands of Bersch, normally residing on mountaintops where the air was thin and conditions harsh. Indeed, it was these conditions that had caused the giant race to evolve as large as they were, growing anything up to thirty feet tall. Even so, some giantkin tribes managed to find their way to lower lands, where they were generally avoided by their neighbors and, despite a typically volatile and bully-ish temperament, were happy to be left to their own devices.

However, even in the tribes of a race famed for their nasty personalities, renegades were born, those giants who were so stupidly cruel or hostile that they couldn't function within their respective communities. These giants would eventually be banished and forced to wander the lower lands on their own, foraging and surviving by terrorizing the races that were smaller than them...which was pretty much all of the races.

Bregus was one of these renegades. An unusually short giant, at a mere twenty-three-feet tall, Bregus had always carried a lot of ingrown hostility toward the world and had eventually been banished from his tribe for eating his baby brother for no apparent reason other than that he had been in a bad mood. There were few giantkin left in the continent of Regalious and even fewer renegades, since even a giant was not immune to the heavy artillery of the Empire. Bregus had survived by laying low in the southlands, making sure that he attacked only small packs of travelers and left no evidence of his feasting.

Like all giants, Bregus was fiercely protective of his territory. He stared down over his ample gut at the tiny intruders, scratching his massive, hairless head with one of the stubby fingers at the end of an overly long arm. As per usual in a confrontational situation, he grumbled the ancient threat-song that giantkin had passed down since the dawn of their history.

"I'll grind yer bones to make me bread!" he boomed.

Despite his terror, Bip couldn't help but frown.

"What do you mean?" he said. "You can't make bread from bones. You need yeast and things, don't you? Or flour?"

Xharon stepped back until she was level with the Kaneqian. "I think he means he'll grind our bones in order to fashion them into tools used in the making of bread..."

"Oh," said Bip.

Bregus, who had never really understood the threat-song himself, listened to the exchange with a puzzled expression before attempting to continue the rhyme. "Aye, that's right... Fashion tools to make me bread...and...erm... Fe Fi Fo Fum!"

"You said that bit already," said Bip. His sheer terror had seemed to temporarily disconnect his mouth from his brain.

"Aye, ah know!" roared the giant. "Shut yer mooth, ya wee erseface, am trying ta think!" He stamped a foot on the ground in irritation, the shockwave of which threw the companions to the ground. Bip, knees trembling, decided to bite his traitor tongue.

The giant put a finger to its chin. "Now… Fe Fi Fo Fum, ah smell the blood of…someone…and even if he's dead…ah'll fashion him into kitchen…utensils…"

He stared hard into space. "I'm sure that's not right."

Bip, sensing an opportunity, began edging back toward his horse. "Well, that's all right, I'm sure it will come to you eventually," he said.

Xharon began to follow Bip's example. "Yes, we'll come back later if you like…"

"Hold on a wee minute!" Bregus roared. "Where dez you think yous are going? Am not finished with yous yet!"

Bip and Xharon froze in their tracks.

"Now," began the giant, bending down until his enormous face loomed almost directly over the prone companions. "Ah've caught you trespassing on my territory, yes?"

Bip and Xharon nodded their heads in unison, dumb with fear. "So," continued the giant, "whut kind of giant would ah be if a lets ye get away withoot being eaten?"

Bip gulped hard. "A big, friendly one?" he ventured.

"Aye!" growled Bregus. "And we all knows whut happens to them!"

Bip and Xharon shook their heads in unison.

"They git their erses kicked by the other giants, that's whut! And before ye know it, everybody's cracking jokes about beanstalks and eggs and yev lost all o' yer respect!" The giant rose to his full height, blocking the sun behind him. "Oh, aye, they'd all love that, de bastards! They already pick on me 'cos ah'm short—just wait 'til they find out whut a big, friendly, and generous nature ah've got! Aye, I expect ah'll be takin kiddies back ta ma cave for lemonade and biscuits, yes?" Bregus took in a deep breath and lowered his face in front of the companions again. "NO!" he bellowed.

The force of the giant's breath knocked Xharon and Bip off their feet and sent them sprawling for several yards. Xharon gagged at the stench of raw meat.

"Now," continued the giant, "we all know how this goes—you trespass on my property, I eat you and then possibly turn you into bread-making utensils...though to be honest ah might give that last one a miss."

Bip, whose panicked brain had been searching manically for a plan, suddenly blurted something completely unexpected.

"I don't believe you!" he said.

The giant stared hard at him with eyes the size of wagon wheels. "Whut?" he said. "Would ye like ta repeat that?"

Bip swallowed hard and tried to keep his voice from shaking. "I don't believe you," he said. "I think you're all talk!"

His eyes not leaving Bip's face, Bregus casually raised his club and bought it down on a tree next to him, which buckled and fell to the clearing floor with an almighty crash. The Kaneqian tried hard not to break the giant's gaze. He was unsure of what part of his terror-addled brain this plan had come from, but he was determined to see it through.

"You know, you've got an awfy big mooth fer someone who doesn'e even reach me knee caps," growled the giant.

"Yes, well. It's just that I bumped into a group of chaps who reckon that you're just a big pansy, really."

Bregus's eyes narrowed. "Oh, aye? And who might that be?"

"A group of men we passed earlier on," said Bip. "We told them not to come down here, but they just said that...well...what was it they said? That they 'weren't afraid of some shorterse giant who couldn't fight sleep if he fell in a pot of coffee.'"

Bregus once more rose to his full height. "Whut!?" he roared.

"Yes," continued Bip. "And then they went on to say that...now what was it? Oh, yes! They said that you were 'uglier than a bugbear's behind and they were surprised you hadn't beaten yourself to death with your own stupid club.' Or something to that effect, anyway."

The giant said nothing, though his face went a deep, angry purple.

"And don't forget what they said about his mother," added Xharon, who had by now realized what direction Bip's plan was taking.

"Whut?" muttered Bregus through gritted teeth. "Whut did they say about my ma?"

"Only that she's so fat that she needs a map to find her bottom…"

Tears of rage began to flow from the giant's eyes. "Where are they?" he roared. "WHERE ARE THEY?!"

Wordlessly, Xharon and Bip pointed in the direction of the pathway they had come across. Bregus sprinted away from them, his footsteps thundering as he went. After a while, Bip stopped holding his breath, letting it out in a jet of relief. He turned to Xharon, who was looking at him with something close to admiration. "You know, you're cleverer than you look," she said.

Bip blushed and looked at the floor. It wasn't much of a compliment, but it would do.

---

ON THE CUSP OF HEARING, the thunder of horse hooves.

Handen opened his eyes, his mind carefully calm, his face devoid of any recognizable emotion. The time had come, and the adventurer was ready. He went through the motions, rechecking the weapons he had already double-checked, his mind reeling with the possibilities of attack and defense. It made no difference, he knew. In battle, the most carefully laid plans could be laid waste by a billion different factors, considered or otherwise. He knew that the only way to be truly ready was to be ready for anything.

The riders moved into view, the menace of their approach still softened by distance. Handen squinted and counted. Thirteen riders. He grinned. The pursuit had underestimated him, leaving behind a few men, probably to guard the provisions. It wasn't much of an advantage, but it was two fewer opponents than he had been anticipating and, small as it may be, the advantage was welcome.

The riders came nearer, the rumble of their horses' hooves increasing with every second. Handen surveyed his opponents one last time, and his breath caught in his throat. At the head of the pack, under a gray top-hat, a long greasy mane drew Handen's attention. He recognized Blungkit, the guard from the Bin, and instantly understood a few things about his pursuer. No nine-to-fiver was Blungkit. No bureaucrat or careerist. For Blungkit, this chase had been personal. Animal. And now Handen understood how he was tracked so well across a land as trackless as the Dozantyne Shrub.

The adventurer shook his head free of idle thoughts. The riders were approaching in the canyon below, and the time to act was almost upon him. Silently, he drew his pistola, checking that the powder was pressed correctly. Satisfied, he rested the weapon on his forearm and took careful aim at the advancing Regulators. They were coming exactly as he had hoped, slowing down sufficiently for the rough terrain, but too intent on the tracks of their quarry to suspect the ambush.

The Regulators advanced the only way the narrow canyon would allow them—two abreast and six long, with Blungkit in the lead.

Keeping the pistola rock-steady, Handen waited until the riders were nearly level with him and then, drawing a bead on the central Regulator, fired. The shot fired true, and the chaos was instantaneous. A horse, struck in the knee by the ballast of Handen's pistola, screeched horribly and tripped to the floor, throwing its rider, screaming, to the ground.

The narrow space and the speed of the Regulators ensured that panic descended swiftly, and the horses directly behind the fallen steed reared up over their comrade, one throwing its rider to the floor with an earth-shaking thump and the other dislodging a Regulator so that he hung helpless with his feet entangled in his stirrups.

The other Regulators managed to bring their mounts back under control and draw their pistols, searching the terrain around them for the threat. Blungkit recovered his senses first, barking orders for the men to form a circle and scan the trees. Handen allowed himself a grin. The shot was perfect, incapacitating three of the thirteen riders without even giving his position away.

Not wishing to give the Regulators time to recover from their shock, he leapt into the air and descended on them, drawing his bastard sword as he fell. By the time he hit the ground, he had already felled two of his opponents, striking a couple of unfortunate riders with the long-bladed sword as he landed.

One of the Regulators shouted a warning and aimed his flintlock at the ambusher. Without pausing for breath, Handen threw his now-useless pistola at the Regulator's head, knocking him out cold with the heavy steel grip.

The seven remaining Regulators, now fully aware of Handen's presence, aimed their pistolas and fired, unleashing a booming barrage of hot lead. The adventurer dived to the floor as the bullets began to fly, rolling across the ground and grabbing the fallen body of one of the recently dispatched Regulators. Using the body as cover, Handen gritted his teeth at the sound of the rounded bullets impacting the flesh of his unfortunate shield. He reached around to the belt of the dead Regulator and drew a still loaded pistola. He fired a wild and unplanned shot, but a successful one. His target clutched at his shoulder, dropping his weapon as a pulse of blood spurted between his fingers.

Before Handen had time to register his good fortune, a bullet sliced through the calf of his exposed leg. Instinctively, the former Hostilities Advisor rolled backward and dived to the left, using one of the rider-less horses as cover. He looked at the wound on his leg. The pain was great, but he could still stand.

Blungkit, infuriated by the ambush, feverishly tried to reload his pistola. He looked up at his men and, seeing the idiot panic on their faces, roared in frustration. "Don't just stand there you useless idiots! Dismount and engage!"

Three of the riders dismounted, drawing their truncheons and handing their pistolas up to Blungkit's appointed wingman, Gordons, who began to reload the weapons. Blungkit looked at the fourth man, who was still clutching at his wounded shoulder.

"And what do you think you're doing?" he said. The wounded man turned to his leader with pleading eyes. Blungkit's fury redoubled. "Get down there and fight like a man, you maggot!" he bellowed.

The wounded man dismounted quickly and ran to join his comrades.

Coming out from his cover, Handen assessed his attackers. He knew that they were meant to slow him down, giving Blungkit time to reload and regain the firepower advantage. He would have to dispatch of them quickly if he wanted to maintain his aggressive momentum.

There were four of them, trained fighting men no doubt, but not in sufficient numbers to quell a man of a thousand years' combat experience. Plus, one of them was wounded, moving into the fray with obvious reluctance.

The four men circled the former Hostilities Advisor, their truncheons ready to strike. Suddenly, the wounded man gave a high-pitched cry and, truncheon raised to attack, ran at Handen.

The adventurer had time to almost feel sorry for his opponent who, in readying his weapon with his good arm, had left his wounded shoulder entirely open. Favoring his injured leg, Handen whipped a heavy back kick into the attacker's bleeding shoulder. There was a faint and stomach-churning squelching sound as boot connected with damp tissue. Instantly, the color left the attacker's face as a new fold of agony overwhelmed him. He sank to his knees, whimpering as the pain took the strength from his body.

Seeing an opening, the other Regulators attacked in a group. Handen rolled backward defensively and, with lightning speed, unfurled his whip, cracking it in an overhead circular motion and striking two of the attackers in the face. Bleeding and shocked, the Regulators stepped back, holding hands to their furiously stinging cheeks. Before they could get their footing, Handen ran in, pressing his advantage with a jumping front kick to the prone chin of the central Regulator. The man fell to the ground, teeth clenched and a faraway look in his eye.

Without hesitation, Handen raised his guard to his right, catching the descending wrist of another attacker and using his momentum to flip him onto the ground. The aggressor let out a loud *whoof* as the impact of the ground took the wind from his body.

Before Handon could regain his balance, a truncheon was brought down on his skull with an almighty thud. Handen, groggy and dazed, fell to his knees, his vision wobbling and swaying, only too aware of the Regulator coming from behind to finish him off. Fighting through his disorientation, he swung out a clumsy kick behind him that, by chance, connected with his assailant's groin. Handen winced and almost threw up as a sudden wave of pain reminded him not to kick with his wounded leg. Behind him, the Regulator crumpled to the ground, cross-eyed and mewling.

With all his opponents floored, either unconscious or in too much pain to move, Handen rose unsteadily to his feet and shook his head in an effort to clear the mugginess from his skull. He froze as something clicked loudly behind him.

Something that sounded exactly like the hammer being drawn back on a Regulator's pistola.

"I wouldn't move if I were you," came the gruff voice of Blungkit, and Handen felt the barrel of a flintlock pushed into the back of his head.

---

DARBY DUG his stirrups into the flanks of his mare, forcing the horse into an even faster gallop. He smiled to himself. The trail was obvious, the prey drawing close. It was almost too easy.

The terrain under his mount had turned rocky, but so eager was Darby to catch up with his quarry that he barely registered the potential hazards. He sniffed at the air, almost tasting the tantalizing aroma of blood and promotion, when, without warning, his horse stopped dead, skidding to a complete halt with a hysterical whinny. Darby had just enough time to be annoyed by the sudden delay when he was thrown to the ground with bone-shaking force. Groaning, the Regulator got to his feet and turned to his men, who had all come to a halt behind him.

"Don't worry, I'm fine," he said. "Prepare to move out." Darby prepared to mount, and then stopped, puzzled. His men didn't appear to be listening to him, or even acknowledging his presence.

What could this be? Dissension in the ranks? Darby had waited for a long time for the chance at leadership, and he'd be damned if he'd lose the respect of his men just because he fell off his horse.

Darby drew in a breath, remembering all he had learnt from shadowing Blungkit these past weeks. "What are you waiting for, you scum? I said move!"

The other Regulators barely even registered that anything had been said. Darby began to sweat. Could he really be facing mutiny a mere couple of hours into his command?

"Oh, come on, lads," he said, reproachfully. "Play the game, eh? Fair's fair—I was put in charge, so I give the orders. So stop playing silly buggers and let's get a move on, shall we?"

The men still did not respond, merely stared ahead, their faces spookily blank. "What's going on?" said Darby, fear creeping into his voice.

Wordlessly, one of the Regulators raised a hand and pointed limply in front of him. Darby frowned and turned around. And then looked up. Blocking the sun was a bulky humanoid figure, stretching twenty feet and more into the sky.

Darby tried very hard not to spoil his uniform as a face like a full moon came level with his own.

"Ah heard ye've got something ta say ta me," said the giant, with a voice that resonates with sheer menace. Darby gulped, and the last thing he saw was the business end of a club that was really nothing more than a branchless tree.

---

EVEN ABOVE THE steady pounding of his horse's hooves, Bip could hear the distant cacophony of screams and crashes. Normally noises that would have made him cringe, today they filled him with an enormous sense of relief.

*Rather them than me*, he thought, and spurred his horse into a slightly faster run.

---

HANDEN EXHALED and raised his arms above his head. "Why don't you go ahead and shoot?" he said.

Blungkit barked a wet burp of laughter. "Not that easily, old son. We all know about you. Waste of a good bullet, shooting you."

"And what's that supposed to mean?"

"The Emperor told me all about you. Some kind of freak, you are. Can't be killed, or such like, so orders are to capture and detain indefinitely. Apparently, you are not to reach Argustin."

Handen's eyes widened in shock. How could anyone have known he was immortal? He hadn't told anyone but Bip and the others since he'd been incarcerated so many centuries ago. How could it be that the Emperor had found out?

"Yeah, the Emperor knows a lot about you, chum," said Blungkit, as if hearing Handen's thoughts. "You and your troublemaker friends."

Handen narrowed his eyes. "Well, if the Emperor knows so damned much, then how come he doesn't know about the meteor heading toward his planet, eh?"

Blungkit grinned his wet, wooden grin. "Who says he doesn't?"

Handen stood silently for a moment. When he spoke, his voice was a dark, flat calm. "Look, officer," he said. "I don't expect you to understand the amount of trouble I've gone through to warn the Emperor about this upcoming astral disaster, and I don't expect that you care, but let's imagine for a moment that you're right and the Emperor is fully aware of the crisis his world faces." Handen turned around slowly; Blungkit kept the pistol trained on his forehead. "Don't you think he'd want to talk to me? Find out what I know? See if I can help?"

Blungkit grinned. "Apparently not," he said. "Apparently he wants you to rot in jail."

The two men stood for a while. Handen felt himself tense for action. He doubted very much that he was quicker than Blungkit's trigger finger, and a bullet to the head, while it wouldn't kill him, could still put him out of action for a good few hours. He poised to attack and damn the consequences, then froze as a figure emerged behind the Regulator.

Blungkit didn't even look around. "Ah, Gordons," he said. "Do me a favor and clap this scum in irons, will you?"

There was no reply. Handen grinned.

"Gordons?" There was a sound like wood connecting with a coconut, and Blungkit's eyes crossed as though something terribly interesting had landed on his nose. "Guh?" he said, and crumpled to a heap on the floor.

"I thought you were staying with the horse?" said Handen.

Azron shrugged, hefting the truncheon in his hands. "I was curious," he said. He looked around at the heaps of gray-uniformed bodies, Regulators incapacitated in various ways. "Anyway, you seemed to be doing all right for yourself."

Handen shrugged modestly. In truth, he hadn't thought he would have been able to escape the posse, but fortune had been with him. He wasn't going to get complacent, however. "Let's get out of here before they come to their senses."

"Okay, just a sec," said Azron. The tall thief got to his knees and began patting the pockets of the unconscious Blungkit.

Handen gave a disapproving sigh. "Do we really have time for this?" he said.

"Just bear with me, okay?" said Azron. "I told you—I'm a thief! There's only one reason why a thief would knock someone unconscious and that's to steal from them. If I didn't at least take some of his personal possessions, then I'd be no better than a common thug, now would I?"

Handen shook his head in disbelief.

"And besides…" Azron held up a purse, which made a monetary chink when he shook it. "This might come in handy, don't you think?"

Handen couldn't suppress a wry grin. "Come on," he said. "We'd better catch up with the others and see if they're okay."

They made their way to their horse, leaving the conquered Regulators behind.

---

IT WAS NEARLY nightfall when Handen and Azron caught up with Bip and Xharon. There was a brief moment of explanation as each party told their respective tales, then a moment of spontaneous joy as the backwash of adrenaline heightened their senses, making them twice as glad to be alive and clearing their heads of panic with cool relief.

Handen was happy to let the backslapping and hand shakings go on, not even objecting when Bip suggested opening his bottle of Infamous Goose. By all accounts, the forces pursuing them had been badly crippled, and it would be some time before they recovered in sufficient numbers to pose a proper threat.

They camped that night, joking and retelling their stories in the warmth of the fire's glow, Bip nearly choking with laughter as Xharon recounted the giant's fury, and Azron giving a blow-by-blow account of what he had seen of Handen's fight with the Regulators.

Handen was happy to let them celebrate. Tomorrow the rush would wear off, and maybe then they would remember their fear and how close they had come to being killed or captured. But for now, with the cozy light of victory in their hearts, they could afford to laugh at death.

Handen laughed along, but not too loudly or too long. At the back of his mind, he kept thinking about an Emperor who claimed to be fully aware that the planet was in peril, yet still insisted on hunting down the people trying to warn him. It made no sense to the former Hostilities Advisor, and it worried him that the only way to get any answers would be to confront the man who would see them jailed, or worse, killed.

He lay back, looking at the stars and listening to the laughter of his friends. Tomorrow they would continue their quest, advancing into likely more treacherous territory, to explain themselves to a man who, by all accounts, had no interest in what they had to say. But tonight, under a canopy of gem-studded night, they could laugh like heroes.

---

SOMEWHERE IN THE DEEPER SHADOWS, Mr. Random fumed quietly. He could understand the failure of yetis and krakens and other dumb beasts—he could even understand the failure of the intellectually challenged giantkin he had drafted in as a precautionary measure—but the failure of Blungkit stung him deeply. He'd had high hopes for Blungkit and his men, and it annoyed him that they had been bested so easily.

The time was drawing near, and Random's plan had nearly reached its climax.

If he could just keep these troublemakers from interfering for a few weeks longer, then nothing would be able to stand in his way.

Either that, or he could speed things up a little.

The red-skinned being stroked his chin for a little while until a wicked grin appeared on his face. He snapped his fingers and disappeared with a pop.

---

BLUNGKIT AWOKE, the blurry mess before him eventually focusing into the concerned face of Gordons, looking down at him and framed in firelight against a darkened sky. A brief moment of perplexity gave way to angry realization. Blungkit scrambled to his feet, then immediately wished he hadn't. He put his hands on his knees and vomited a thin stream of bile onto the ground. Gordons took a few diplomatic steps backward.

"How long was I out?" said Blungkit, spitting the sharp taste from his mouth.

"A few hours, sir."

Blungkit cursed and gritted his wooden teeth. His head swam, and his guts felt unstable. He'd been concussed enough over his long career to recognize the symptoms. He turned to demand a roll call from his contingent, then stopped abruptly. Three of his men were laid out in a neat line with blankets over their faces. Many more were slouched about a campfire, alternately bruised and bandaged. Blungkit noticed the large, purple welt on Gordons's forehead.

"The bastards got the drop on us," he muttered. "Any news from Darby?"

Gordons shook his head. "We sent a scout to track him, sir. He found them. Sort of."

"Sort of?"

Gordons coughed. "They're dead, sir. Extremely dead."

"Extremely dead?"

"Perhaps the most extreme cases of death I've ever seen," said Gordons.

Blungkit nodded grimly. "Been in the job long, Gordons?"

"Seems that way, sir."

"I know how you feel."

The two men stood in silence for a while. When Gordons spoke, it was with obvious reluctance. "Are we continuing the pursuit, sir?"

Blungkit spat again. "Nah. No point. They've got at least a two-hour lead, and we've barely got a fighting man between us. We wouldn't stand a chance and, much as I think you lot are a useless shower of bastards, I'm not going to lead you to your deaths. Not today, anyway. We'll head back to Argustin and inform the Emperor that I've cocked up."

"He'll probably kill you though, sir," said Gordons, matter-of-factly.

"Yeah, I expect so, Gordons, I expect so." Blungkit scratched his chin thoughtfully. He was a Regulator to the core, and his loyalty and sense of duty forbade any other cause of action than returning to Argustin and accepting his punishment. Perhaps he'd be merely demoted, but he doubted it very much. So, he would return to the Empire and die the pointless and violent death he'd always assumed he would die.

Then he thought again, about the other man who was currently on his way to Argustin, the man who had taken on a squad of Regulators single-handed. If Blungkit was a gambling man, he'd bet that Handen Strike was heading to his certain defeat, but maybe…just maybe.

"Bury the dead and get the kettle on, lads. Tomorrow we head back to Argustin."

Blungkit sat down on the floor, putting his hands to the side of his throbbing head. He would head back to Argustin, but perhaps he would take the long way around.

***

UNDER A GENTLE AFTERNOON SKY, rustling peacefully in a cooling breeze, the garden was tranquil. The garden was always tranquil. In fact, Ted sometimes wondered if the garden was too tranquil. He gazed down at the perfect patch of soil he was working with his trowel and at the perfect vine of leaves that was already beginning to push its way up to the warm sunlight. Things grew easily in the garden, hardly needing any coaxing at all.

Just as an experiment, Ted envisioned a small gathering of slugs. They popped into existence, gray-coated and slimy, and began to munch immediately on the fresh leaves. Ted shook his head. Slugs, he knew, had their place in the world—for everything that grew, there had to be something that consumed—but seeing them here in his garden just seemed…wrong, somehow. He shook his head again, and the slugs faded from existence, sent back to wherever they had been summoned from.

Let the garden be tranquil. God knew you couldn't have enough peace and quiet in the ultraverse, and slugs were common enough.

For a while the gardener worked, digging gently at the soft soil and making rhythmical cutting sounds against the steady, pleasant bass of the wind. The sun shone perfectly, uninterrupted, and seemed it would do for the foreseeable eternity, until, without warning, a small cloud cast a shadow over the garden. Ted looked up from his digging, his eyes narrowing under his wiry gray brows. There had been a shift in the design, a tiny diversion from the way things were supposed to be going that, he sensed, could snowball into brand new inevitabilities. He sighed. Slugs in the garden.

Suddenly, with not so much as a blink of time passing, Ted was no longer in the garden, but floating through space.

By the way the stars and planets streaked past him, it appeared he was moving at incredible speeds, but Ted merely knelt, exactly as he was in the garden, trowel still in hand.

Beneath him, pacing him, like some dread undersea giant, a patch of darkness swam silently through the void, distinguishable from the surrounding space only by the way its mass consumed and excreted the hailstorm of stars that hurtled beneath it. Without appearing to move, Ted floated down closer to the object. From this perspective, we can see that the shape was nearly spherical, though bumpy and pointy here and there, with the occasional impression of nosecone or tail-fin, all thick and smothered with dust millennia old.

Ted was familiar with the Massive Ball of Death, just as he is familiar with everything in the ultraverse. He reached a hand down to the meteor-pocked surface of the moon-sized mass, feeling the metal and ice surface. He sensed the power in the cluster—enough to reduce Bersch to pebble-sized fragments—but he sensed something else, too. A consciousness was there, faint but undeniable. More a chaos of half-perceived yearnings than any sentient self-awareness, a sense of antic-ipation and direction that might have more in common with a flower turning toward sunlight. Ted was surprised by this, and also a little saddened. It was easy to feel sorry for any living thing this far from civilization and so close to inevitable oblivion.

After a subtle browse through of sub-matter frequencies, Ted was able to hear what the nuclear cluster was thinking…to a close approx-imation of thinking.

*Nearly there. Nearly there. Nearly there.*

Ted smiled. There was no loneliness or even malice in the Massive Ball of Death's consciousness—surprising for something born for nothing more than death and destruction. There was only an innocent sense of something resembling optimism.

With only a slight manipulation of subconscious wave patterns, Ted provoked an idea. The Massive Ball of Death shuddered slightly and then, at its rear, a long-dormant arming command suddenly sparked to life in long-dead control panels. There was a pause that shouted of ticking bombs, then a brilliant flash. The Massive Ball of Death leaked nuclear blast force from its rear like some inter-stellar guff and sped up, ever so slightly, toward its ultimate goal.

*Nearly there. Nearly there. Nearly there.*

Ted watched the incarnate disaster as it faded into the distance and smiled at a job well done. He is the Grand Design, the Final Blue-print. He is the be all and end all of everything, the inevitability of dramas uncountable, and of stories too vast to tell.

He knows that, above all, there has to be balance.

Without so much as a blink of time passing, Ted disappeared, leaving behind only stars and darkness.

BIP AWOKE from a night of bizarre dreams that teetered on the edge of his memory like a half-hearted suicide attempt. He had remembered a hazy theme, a brief and inexplicable feeling of falling that had ended as soon as it had begun, then a sensation that everything was somehow…not the same anymore.

The general feeling of unease was in no way helped by the discombobulating hangover he was suffering.

The night before had been cause for merriment, though after only a few drabs of Infamous Goose, the merriment had quickly accelerated into blind drunkenness. Mercifully, the party had passed out before they could do themselves any real damage. Bip's last memory was of laughing hysterically at Azron's impression of an irate duck— though the interrelated events had been lost to some mystifying void. Now Bip awoke, stiff from sleeping without his groundsheet and with the loose impression that seven kinds of woodland creature had crapped in his mouth.

He sat up, his lower back objecting heinously and his head seeming to swell and throb with the effort. Once again, Bip felt an odd sense of displacement. His body clock was telling him that it was nearing late morning, but the grainy quality of the light around him had more in common with twilight.

*Surely they wouldn't have let me sleep in that long*, thought Bip. He glanced around, slowly, so as to spare his suddenly loose-fitting brain, and saw his friends. They were all standing quite still and staring into the distance. Their lack of movement coupled with the eerie quality of the light had quite an unnerving effect, and for one mad moment, Bip became convinced that time had somehow stopped. He jumped to his feet, ignoring the dishwater feeling in his stomach, and ran over to his comrades and…stopped.

Hanging in the sky like a low flying star was…well…some sort of star by the look of it.

Flying low…

It hung there casually, as though it had never been anywhere else, droopy and glittery, the size of a thumbnail from this perspective, and shining with a kind of gray twinkle that put Bip in mind of a coin at the bottom of a wishing well.

"What is it?" he breathed.

Handen turned, as if shaken from a dream. "What do you think?" he said flatly.

Bip's eyes widened in sudden understanding. "It can't be," he said. "It can't be the astral disaster. We've months until it gets here, you said so yourself!"

"Apparently I was wrong," said Handen, turning back to the light in the sky.

The quartet watched for a long time, no one speaking.

"Blimey," said Xharon eventually.

"Yeah," agreed Azron. "I mean, I know you lot were on about the end of the world and stuff, but I didn't think you were serious!"

"Sort of brings the point home, really, doesn't it?" said Handen.

"Too right."

Bip brightened up a little. "Surely the Emperor will have to believe us now?"

"Not much of a consolation, Bip," said Handen. "Even if he does listen to us, we may be too late."

Xharon turned with a gasp, a look of heart-melting anxiety in her eyes that made Bip feel odd in his belly. "You're not giving up, are you?" she said.

Handen grinned. "Of course not. As long as we're alive, there's hope, and any help we can give to the Emperor could be vital. Besides, what else can we do?"

"Buy a really big umbrella?" muttered Azron.

Handen headed toward the horses, which were already packed and ready to go.

"We've two days until we reach Argustin," he said. "If we ride hard, we might make it there in one and a half."

He took the reins of his horse and cast one last glance to the sinking star, hanging there with all the promise of a billion deaths.

"Let's move."

AND HERE IS as good a place as any to leave, as villains lick their wounds and heroes gallop across the plains, racing against time to an uncertain fate. And so we will leave the people of Bersch as they awaken to a dawn sky quite different from any they have seen before. For now, let them exclaim in wonder and curiosity at the new daytime star that lights the sky, because soon, very soon, they are going to learn that wonder and curiosity are the bastard sons of horror.

This is the planet Bersch, spinning endlessly on its axis as it has done since time immemorial. This is the planet Bersch, lit from a new perspective by a galactic intruder. This is the planet Bersch, and it may be spinning out its final days…

To Be Continued in *The Mad Emperor*
Book 3 of The Doomsayer Journeys
Available Now from Falstaff Books

If you enjoyed this book and would like to be notified of new releases, appearances, and everything else related to Steve Wetherell, sign up for the newsletter here -
http://eepurl.com/cv5FSj

---

# The Mad Emperor

## BOOK THREE OF THE DOOMSAYER JOURNEYS

---

"There will come a time when the world will stand united in fear of the inevitable, in awe of the unknown. They will wail as one, united in lamentation at the end of all things. And at this time, I will be there to proclaim, indeed with much satisfaction, that I bloody well told them so, didn't I?"

-From the chronicles of Celia Doom

<hr>

# Preface

<hr>

Where to begin?

We've seen the nuclear waste of a feckless world bundled and rocketed into space, oblivious to its final destination.

We've seen a starship crash, its well-meaning crew stranded on the world they were supposed to watch over, their message of warning never received.

We've seen the young volunteer, venturing out from his isolated community into a wide, hostile world.

We didn't see a funeral. A mourning city lamenting the passing of their queen. An emperor standing indifferently, his thoughts elsewhere while the coffin was lowered into the earth. We didn't see a duke, his face ashen. We didn't see a princess, her eyes red-raw with grief.

We didn't see the emperor walk as if in a dream around his study, listening to the faint whisperings that only he could hear.

We didn't see the astronomers, looking up at the new star in their sky and coming to some very worrying conclusions indeed.

Where to begin?

# Prologue

Mr. Random floated in the void, the fledgling star the only source of light for endless miles around. He floated and drummed his long fingers idly on his knees.

Random was a man who was not really a man. He was an avatar for forces both powerful and malignant, forces that would rather see oblivion than what they perceived as disorder. And so, this agent of deconstruction sat patiently in space, his mind on his mission. He waited in the void. After a while, he began to sing to himself, a calming nonsense ditty. Though, of course, in space, no one can hear you sing.

A flock of faint, wavering shapes began to congregate at the edge of his perception. They had arrived. The bloated, whale-like race Mr. Random had been tracking for eons. They were here.

They towed with them a block of hyper-dense matter, unfathomable in its hugeness. Random could not see the means by which they moved such a payload, but he had given up trying to understand the aliens a long time ago. They were advanced—scarily advanced. Trying to communicate with them was like an ant trying to communicate with the sun.

Random watched as they began their strange dance, space/time becoming fluid and unstable around them. They were building again, warping the space around them in their inimitable manner. Mr. Random grinned. It would likely be millennia before what they were building began to take shape. But he could wait. Oh yes, he could wait...

---

1

## Operation Deadwaker

---

Mernin Cobonon, Grand Tutor of the Enlightened Researchers, Argustin Division, wiped his high brow with a lace handkerchief. He wasn't, he felt, cut out for the Bone Desert sun. Nor, he felt, was he cut out for archaeology as an *active* career—that is to say, the parts of archaeology that involved going outside.

Oh, he was very good at looking through ancient texts and could talk for hours on the marital rites of the Bean People of Faburtar (you couldn't very well become Grand Tutor without being able to bore even the most enthusiastic of students to tears), but the actual *practical* aspect of archaeology he had always left to the students and lesser faculty members. But now, with the personal attention of the Emperor focused squarely on his department, Mernin had been forced to take a more hands-on role in the proceedings of Operation Deadwaker.

Not that he could really contribute much to the process—the annoyingly enthusiastic students supported by cheap Nastren labor were making very good progress—but Mernin had to be seen to be making an effort, lest he draw even more personal attention from the Emperor.

He looked up at the huge, stone pyramid erupting from the sand like an arrowhead piercing the earth.

It was one of the hundreds of ancient Nastren tombs that were the final resting places of long-dead kings and queens, but this one was slightly different. The hieroglyphics, those markings that normally told in overelaborate ways of how fantastic such-and-such a long-forgotten ruler had been, were completely different from any Mernin had previously encountered. This worried him. He had studied Nastren tombs throughout his career, had written the definitive work on the subject, and he could find absolutely no similarities between these hieroglyphics and the countless others he had seen.

He remembered Emperor Draegul's vague and impossible-sounding orders to locate and explore every single pyramid in the Bone Desert and to report when he found something out of the ordi-nary. Thus, Operation Deadwaker, the biggest exhumation in history, had begun. That had been fifteen years ago. Now they had found this new tomb, with its indecipherable markings and its unusually smooth stone...

Mernin had reported the findings to Draegul, of course, but the orders had remained unchanged—to enter and explore the pyramid. Mernin was not looking forward to doing so. He had read enough about ancient Nastren curses—and seen first-hand some of the deadly traps used to guard the tombs—to be extra-cautious about tomb-raid-ing. This new pyramid, though, seemed to radiate an aura of menace he had never experienced before. Even as he lay down in his tent to sleep at night, he could swear he heard a faint and constant humming noise, like the calling of trapped souls.

Mernin shivered despite the desert heat, then nearly jumped out of his skin when someone shouted his name. He turned to see the familiar and irritatingly eager face of Jimar, his personal assistant, whose half-naked body was equal parts glistening with sweat and matte with dust.

"Grand Tutor! Grand Tutor!" he called excitedly.

"Slow down, boy," huffed Mernin. "You're liable to collapse, running around like that in this accursed sun. Now what is it?"

"The entrance! I'm sure I've found the entrance!"

Despite his bad mood, Mernin couldn't suppress the leap of excitement in his heart. "Where? How? Where?"

Jimar said nothing, but ran off into the distance, motioning for Mernin to follow.

"Wait! Wait for me!" cried the older man, breaking into a half-jog.

Eventually, huffing and blowing, Mernin caught up with his apprentice and was amazed to see that, a furlong or so from the pyramid proper, a small tomb had been unearthed. Four plain and unadorned walls of stone erupted from the sand, climbing to a slightly triangular roof.

"When was this discovered?" demanded Mernin.

"Just this morning," said Jimar. "I'm sure it's the entrance!"

The older man looked at the tomb, then at the massive pyramid. "How can you be sure?" he said. "It looks like an external tomb to me. Nowhere near the pyramid base."

"That's the thing, sir," said Jimar, his voice shaking with excitement. "We've been doing some more sonar readings. It looks as though this isn't the base at all!"

Mernin frowned and looked up at the pyramid. It was already massive by the standards of the other tombs, and he had been sure that they had finally located the base. "You're sure?" he asked.

"Yes, sir," Jimar continued. "It's been said that the base continues down—and not just a little, sir, but for miles! Can you imagine? The pyramid continues down for *miles!*"

Mernin gulped. Draegul would have to hear about this, but for now, one thing was bothering him greatly. "Jimar, how did you know to look for the entrance here?" he said.

Jimar looked blank for a moment. "It will sound silly, sir," he said reproachfully.

"Try me," Mernin replied.

"It came to me in a dream, sir," said Jimar. "I swear, it was as though someone was whispering in my ear while I slept."

Mernin said nothing and tried to suppress the cold shudder that ran down his spine. "Get it open," he said, and made his way back to his tent. Once there, he opened a large bottle of brandy.

Somewhere on the edge of hearing, a faint humming was coming from deep below them. He drank a shot of the sweet brandy in a single gulp. Jimar's discovery had put them weeks ahead of schedule, but he wondered whether the younger man would be so enthusiastic when it came to venturing down into the darkness of the pyramid, and what would be down there waiting for him when he did.

---

HANDEN, Xharon, Azron, and Bip rode with little pause, their steeds keeping a steady pace across the ever-lusher landscapes. They did so for a day and half, spurred on by the sense of urgency that came from knowing that the new star in the sky, as pretty as it looked, was the first clue to an approaching astral disaster.

The plains around the Oaken Mons were wide and rolling. Cusps of trees and woods were spaced far enough apart that the landscape was largely uninterrupted, sporting only long, green grass as far as the eye could see. It was a world away from the comparatively lifeless Dozantyne Shrub, with sudden bursts of rain that would freshen the ground, making it erupt with a smell of sheer vitality that Bip had never experienced.

As they rode, Bip kept one eye on the skies, charting the progress of the star. It hung there, slightly foggy in the daytime sky, a ghost of things to come. At night, it shone a brilliant silver, as though a cluster of stars had got together to form a gang, hanging around outside some interstellar off-license.

It was getting bigger, too. Not so much that a casual observer would notice, but for Bip, who looked up at the sky every other minute, the light was becoming slightly but maddeningly larger. For a day and half there had been nothing to distract Bip from the glare of the new light in the sky. The sensation of knowing that your imminent doom was hovering just above the horizon was an unsettling one. It was like someone constantly staring hard at the back of your neck.

Finally, they reached Argustin, the capital of the Empire, their final destination. From a distance, the city seemed to sprawl across hills and valleys like a static ocean of stone, glass, and steel. Towers pointed rudely at the sky, and domes and the ornate turrets of elevated mansions broke the surface of the rooftops here and there like huge, expensive bubbles. Largest and grandest of them all stood the glowing crystalline bulk of Dawncastle, resplendent and hypnotic as it cycled through every hue of the setting sun. Against the early evening skies, the city of Argustin twinkled and winked and hinted at money.

Except, of course, for the industrial quarter to the west of the capital, where the city suddenly clung low and paranoid, an artificial turf of long, flat roofs, extruding chimneys like cheap cigarettes, all puffing a soft brown fog into the permanent haze that floated over the quarter like a lonely ghost. This was where the doomsayers traveled.

"Somehow I imagined the crown of the Empire would be a little more showy," remarked Azron as they approached the rusted arches of the industrial quarter's main entrance.

"If we'd gone around to the front gates, you'd have been welcomed with sky-high fountains of the purest mineral water and triumphant golden arches etched with the names and stories of a thousand heroes," said Xharon, airily.

"So why didn't we go 'round that way, then?"

"Because you would also have been welcomed by many guards with many triumphant, golden, and *very sharp* axes."

"Ah."

They passed under the rusted archway. A man sat slouched in the guardhouse, reading a newspaper. He looked up at the travelers with tired eyes, then turned back to his reading.

"Besides," continued Xharon, "this is where my father lives."

Azron and Bip exchange a glance.

"Sorry if I'm being a bit simple," said Azron, "but didn't you say you were a princess?"

"Yes?"

"Well, this just doesn't seem like a very...*princessy* place to grow up."

"Oh, no," laughed Xharon. "I never lived here. My father's an industrialist and an inventor—he works here. Hardly ever spends any time up at the mansion."

At the mention of the word "mansion," the doubt left Azron's eyes, and a familiar calculating grin spread across his face.

Handen wasn't really paying attention to the conversation of his traveling companions. As was his habit, he was scrutinizing his new environment, assessing the terrain with an expert eye, taking note of possible escape routes and public mood. The Industrial Quarter was a slightly intimidating place. The buildings were uniformly gray and ordered, each road and turning angled almost exactly the same. The streets were all numbered rather than named—they were currently riding down A26 with turnings onto B5 and B5A. Even the people they rode past, few and far between, looked similar to one another, all dressed in identical denim boiler-suits and flat caps, with identical streaks of grime obscuring their features. They hurried from one place to another, eyes downcast, identical expressions of weariness on their faces. No one seemed to take any notice of the travelers.

"It seems a bit deserted," said Bip.

Almost as soon as he had said this, a shrill whistle sounded from a nearby building. Dozens of others whistling erupted in response, echoing from various distant corners of the Industrial Quarter. Before the initial shock of the sudden noise had faded, doors banged open in every building on the road, and the boiler-suited men flocked out in the thousands, grumbling and laughing and marching with military precision to their respective homes. For a moment, it was if an ocean of denim had suddenly flooded the dusty streets, and then, just as suddenly, it was over. The last of the workers rounded the corners, and all that was left was the sound of fading footsteps.

"That was odd," said Bip.

"Clocking-off time," explained Xharon. "They've all gone to get their dinner before the night shift starts."

"They work nights as well as days?" said Bip. "They must have plenty of money."

"Oh, good grief, no," said Xharon. She squinted her eyes as if remembering a well-taught lesson. "If you pay them too much, they won't work as hard or as long. Common knowledge. If you keep them at a low wage, they'll work longer hours. It's good labor management."

"Is it?" said Handen, raising an eyebrow. "Has anyone asked their opinion?" He gestured to the retreating backs of the workers.

Xharon looked momentarily confused. "Of course not," she said. "They're not in charge, are they?"

Handen looked blankly at the princess and spurred his horse forward.

Bip could hear Azron muttering as the horse trotted away. "You see, that's why I just steal stuff. Everybody's happier all 'round."

Xharon's brow furrowed in confusion. "Was it something I said?"

Bip shrugged. "Where I come from, you work until the job's done and get a share of the rewards. I don't know much about labor management."

"How strange," said Xharon, and urged her horse into a trot.

---

THEY ARRIVED at the factory on C12. It had no name and was referred to only as "the factory on C12." It was identical to every other factory they had passed—huge, gray, rectangular, and drastically soulless. In the increasing darkness of nightfall, lit by the inadequate flush of the gas lamps, there was something slightly nightmarish about the massive metal boxes. Bip shivered, then jumped as Xharon suddenly pounded on the huge wooden doors again, the tortured hinges screeching a metallic wail through the still night air.

"Daddy? Daddy, it's me, Xharon! Open the door, please!"

"*Daddy?*" muttered Azron. Handen nudged him in the ribs.

For a moment, the only sound was the hum and whir of distant machinery.

"Are you sure he'll be here? Maybe he went home for dinner," said Bip.

Xharon shook her head. "Daddy doesn't know the meaning of the words clocking off. He wouldn't eat or sleep at all if there wasn't someone employed to remind him to."

Bip and Azron exchanged a look that was becoming a common reaction to one of Xharon's comments, then started suddenly at the sound of heavy bolts shifting.

The door creaked open to reveal a dozen shining eyes. Bip found himself hesitantly stepping backward, perfectly flanked by Azron and Handen.

Then came a voice. "My word, Xharon, what on Bersch are you doing out in the cold in your underpants?"

There was an embarrassed silence, and Xharon shifted uncomfortably in her over-simplified leather outfit, her face suddenly turning as red as her hair. A short, round man emerged from behind the door holding an open coat. The shining eyes revealed themselves to be the multifarious lenses of a bizarre pair of adjustable spectacles, the dozens of distorted glass discs magnifying the old man's balding head, each in a different way. He wore a shirt and trousers that looked as if they had never been ironed and held the ensemble together with a bright red bow tie that drooped miserably over his collar. He threw a coat, a tweed jacket with leather patches, over Xharon in a thoughtful but ineffectual attempt at modesty.

"What have I told you about walking about in your smalls? People will think you've gone quite, quite mad! It won't do, it really won't!" The man's voice was musically clear but couldn't seem to settle on a single pitch for too long, like a jazz flute player who has had one inspirational cigarette too many.

Xharon struggled out of the coat. "*Daddy*, how many times? This is perfectly normal attire for a warrior princess!" she whined.

"Such nonsense! Such nonsense! Of all the nonsense I ever did have the misfortune to bear, this, by far, is the most nonsensical!" The man suddenly froze in his flustering and turned slowly toward Bip. "And who, by all that is embarrassingly unexpected, are you?"

Xharon, shrugging the coat away from her shoulders, let out a theatrical sigh. "These are my *friends*, Daddy."

The old man blinked for a while, then made an effort to pat down the erratic cotton-wool tufts of his white hair. "Friends, eh?" he said and began to look the men up and down, adjusting the lenses on his glasses as he scrutinized each in turn before shaking their hands with mad enthusiasm. "Always good to meet friends of Xharon's. I'm her father, you know. The name's Riley—*Professor* Riley DeChambre. She doesn't bring many people to see me, you know. Probably thinks I'm an embarrassment—I said an *embarrassment*, if you can imagine, coming from a girl who walks around in her knickers. An *embarrassment!* Come in, come in, come in, do—have some tea, please, follow me, come in!" And then the man was gone, back through the door before anyone else had a chance to speak.

Xharon shrugged. "That's my father," she said.

Bip turned to Azron and Handen in turn. Both merely mirrored Xharon's shrug. They entered the factory.

---

2

# An Appointment with Doom

---

If Bip had thought the factories nightmarish from the outside, the inside was the twisted aberration of a dreaming madman. Not since his brief time in the Dome had Bip seen so much metal in one place, though here, rather than the smooth, almost infinite walls of the ancient spacecraft, the factory was littered with massive contraptions that hulked like rusted monoliths. Glasswork of intricate and spiraling design sat on various candle-lit desks, smoking and bubbling with an acid rainbow of mysterious chemicals. Unexplained dials and meters wagged their needles disapprovingly while an endless wyrm of copper piping hissed, angry and erratic. The whole carousel of machinery juddered and shuddered to the rhythmic clanging of a distant and nameless engine, its ringing methodical and maudlin, like a funeral knell.

It was as though a special kind of hell had been invented for all things mechanical.

"Welcome to the Factory on C12. Or, as I like to call it, Factory C12," said Riley, walking amongst the horrifying metal apparitions as though they were everyday furniture. "It may look complicated, but most of the machinery here is for fashioning tools and components.

We're a research factory first and foremost, you see—a *research* factory."

The doomsayers continued walking after the professor, unconsciously huddling together. Riley continued to chatter away in the gloom, his seesaw voice echoing from the chilly brick walls. He gestured to some of the more complex and intricate-looking machinery as he passed.

"We make all kinds of things—all *kinds* of things," he said. "We're very much left to our own devices—the advantages, I must confess, of being a royal in-law." He stopped suddenly on a platform and waited for the rest of the group to catch up. Once everybody was safely onboard, he pulled a lever, and with a furious hiss, the platform shuddered upward.

"I don't like to brag about the factory—by all that's modest, I don't like to *brag*—but we do some remarkable work here, most remarkable. I confess, I often feel like a small child in a shop that appeals to small children."

The platform came to a stop, and Riley gestured for the others to follow him through an unexceptional glass-paneled door. What lay in the next room caused his guests to stop in their tracks and gasp.

"This is my workshop," said Riley. "This is where I *create!*"

The workshop was, essentially, little more than a very large attic, lit here and there through skylights by day and overhead gas lamps by night. It was the contents of the room that made it so remarkable. On what seemed like a dozen long workbenches, devices of every conceivable shape and design lay stacked upon one another like the universe's most curious jumble sale. Cogs and gears, mirrors and pulleys, intricate-looking engines and crystals that seemed to radiate power, all lay infused within wheeled, winged, and box-like devices— devices of which Bip had never seen the like and to whose purpose he could not possibly hazard a guess. Far from the hulking, menacing machinery of the factory floor, the workshop was a crèche for myriad fantastic and unlikely-looking trinkets, each burring or buzzing in a different way, buttons and lights winking suggestively and begging— no, *demanding* the question, "What does this one do?"

"Wow," breathed Bip. There seemed little else to say.

Riley took a seat at one of the few clear spaces on the central workbench. He looked around him, as though temporarily unaware of his surroundings, then found a button in amongst the jigsaw puzzle of appliances around him. There was a *whirruk* followed by a *judud* and then a rising, raging whistle. The floor began to shake. Handen found his hand unwittingly straying to the haft of his bullwhip, and Azron assumed his characteristic pose in response to potential danger—limbs splayed so as to be ready to flee in any direction. Throughout the chaos, Riley sat with his fingers bridged and a complacent smile on his face. The whistling and shaking rose to a thunderous crescendo until finally, with a noise best described as *ka-bloink*, a squirt of oil launched from an unknown location and hit Bip squarely in the face. In the confused silence that followed, a small conveyor belt on Riley's desk began to squeak, and a plate was wheeled into view from parts unknown. It was full of little brown rectangles.

"Biscuit?" chirped Riley.

As one man, the doomsayers warily shook their heads.

THEY TALKED INTO THE NIGHT, Riley, despite the obvious fatigue of his guests, interrupting their story at every turn with questions and demands for specifics. Eventually, with darkness well and truly descended and with many a yawn stifled, their tale was told.

"Incredible," said Riley, for what seemed to be the hundredth time. "Quite, quite *incredible!*"

"So, you see what brings us to the capital?" said Handen, pinching the bridge of his nose.

"Of course, of *course!* By all that's potentially apocalyptic, of *course!*" The old man scribbled notes as he talked, a habit that was irritating at best. "Astral disaster? End of the world? Serious stuff. A most perplexing problem! One I would be most interested in working on!"

Azron raised an eyebrow. "You think you'd be able to help?"

"My good man, I was once Head of Research and Development in the department of Extremely Worrying Weaponry. If there's anyone who can destroy an errant satellite, it is I!"

"You were *once* head?" enquired Handen.

The professor seemed to momentarily lose some of his flustered enthusiasm. "I was taken off major projects after the unfortunate death of my sister. It was thought...better all 'round if I was relieved of some of my responsibilities for a time..." Riley stared hard at his notes for a moment, and when he next looked up, the former spark of enthusiasm had returned to his eye. "Still, Head of Miscellaneous and Tedious Mechanical Research has its benefits."

Handen exchanged a brief glance with Bip. Azron gave a cough that might have been a stifled laugh.

"Anyway, by all that's digressive, where was I? Ah, yes." The professor looked through some of his notes. "By my calculations coupled with your original estimation, the astral disaster, most likely, by the look of it, a meteorite roughly the size of our primary moon, will arrive in six days."

Bip, who had been verging on snoozing, suddenly sat bolt upright. "Six days?!" he said. "The world will end in six days?!"

"Approximately." Riley nodded, apparently unfazed by the revelation.

"What could we possibly do to avert a planet-wide disaster in six days?"

"Oh, I'm sure we can come up with *something*," said Riley. "After all, Argustin is the most advanced city in the world, bar none. We've the highest concentration of academic and engineering expertise on Bersch, and the resources of an intercontinental Empire at our disposal! All we'll need is the ear of the Emperor, and the culmination of many centuries of civilization will be at our aid!"

The doomsayers exchanged uncomfortable looks.

"I think we mentioned earlier..." Bip began.

"The Emperor wants us dead," finished Azron flatly.

Riley's high brow wrinkled with puzzlement. "Yes, but surely in times of great calamity, we must all work together for the common good?"

"You tell *him* that..." muttered Azron.

The professor drummed his fingers. "Far be it from me to say that the Emperor is an unreasonable man..." he began, though his eyes indicated that his mouth wasn't telling the whole truth. "I'm sure if I put in a good word, I could organize a meeting with him? Perhaps tell him of your good intentions?"

"Perhaps," agreed Handen. "But good intentions or not, we have to see him. Even if we're taken before him in chains, he has to hear what we've got to say. I need to know that your people are at least aware of the fact they stand on the verge of obliteration. After that, I've done all I can."

There was a discreet cough. "I thought we agreed that going before the Emperor in chains wasn't a good idea?" said Azron.

Handen cracked a dry smile. "That was before I knew we had six days 'til the end of everything. As it stands, in chains or otherwise, we have vital information that has ramifications for the fate of the world." He scanned the faces of his friends, slowly, as if memorizing them. "I don't expect any of you to accompany me tomorrow," he said. "Vital information or not, there is still a good chance we'll be executed after what we did to Blungkit's men. There's nothing that can't be said by one man. I won't blame anyone if they want to stay behind."

Bip shook his head. "I couldn't," he said. "There's a lot of people back home relying on me. I'd look pretty silly if I said I chickened out at the last minute."

Handen turned to Xharon, who had been mostly quiet since arriving at her father's factory. "Don't look at me," she snapped. "What kind of warrior princess would I be if I turned my back on saving the world? And besides, Uncle Tommy likes me—he might listen to you if I'm there."

Lastly, Handen turned to Azron, a questioning eyebrow raised only slightly. The thief leaned back in his chair with an unlit cigarette dangling loosely from his lower lip, absentmindedly toying with a packet of matches. "Seems to me," he began, "that if we're not all executed horribly, and the Emperor does listen to our advice, that means we're heroes." He lit the cigarette and took a long puff. "And heroes have a funny way of accumulating rewards. I'm in."

Handen grinned. "Then it's settled. Professor DeChambre will contact the Emperor's attendants tonight. With any luck, and if Riley's influence is as he claims, we should have a meeting by tomorrow morning."

Riley smiled widely. "Splendid."

Handen turned back to his comrades. "And now I suggest we all get some sleep. We'll camp here in the factory tonight, unless the professor has any objections?"

"As you wish," said Riley.

"Thank you. Now, if the rest of you want to turn in, I have something I'd like to discuss with Professor DeChambre."

Riley looked at his daughter, who merely shrugged. "Certainly," he said.

Handen waited until his friends had left the workshop, each of them cloddish with the anticipation of sleep. The door closed behind them, and the professor and the adventurer were left in the burr and purr of a multitude of mechanical watchers, standby lights blinking like a slow-motion disco against the low glow of the overhead lighting.

"These are very impressive," said Handen, pointing to one of the many heaps of devices.

"Why, thank you," said Riley, smiling. "Coming from a man who hails from another star, that's as large a compliment as I'll ever receive, I'll warrant."

Handen nodded and continued to scan the various trinkets. One in particular caught his attention, the angular shapes leaping out instantly to his soldier's perception. He picked out two pistolas, larger and more unwieldy than the one he wore at his belt. Frowning with inquisitive satisfaction, he weighed the weapons in his hands, checking the sights in turn.

"That's one of the trinkets I was working on when I was Head of Weapons," said Riley. "Both are capable of firing rapid successive shots with little loss of accuracy or power. They're prototypes, by all that's experimental—*prototypes*. I never had the chance to showcase them to the Board of Admissions. A shame, really, an innovative design. You see the real ingenuity is not in the actual weapon design but in—"

"The ammunition," finished Handen. "The ballast is encased with the charge and ignition, meaning no flint, flash-pan, or separate powder."

Riley faltered. "Yes. Erm…you've seen one before, have you?"

Handen didn't take his eyes off the pistola. "I've seen weapons the likes of which you couldn't conceive, Professor. Not in your most dangerous of nightmares. Spiritguns, Clawshanks, Razorhawks. Weapons that leave no trace of living tissue, or weapons that evaporate only armor." Handen lowered the pistolas back to the table, where they sat with the weighty promise that is the hallmark of all firearms across the ultraverse. "Tell me, Professor, what does this device do?" He pointed to a looped and soapy-looking machine situated next to the guns. It belched wetly at random intervals.

"That? Oh, that's a trinket I was working on just the other day." Riley leaned over and flicked a switch. The machine began to vibrate, then suddenly, with a mechanical hiccup, blew a bubble into the air. Several others followed until a long stream of soapy spheres spluttered gently into the workshop, bursting with quiet enthusiasm as they hit the floor. "It's for children. You know—parties and things," said Riley, grinning.

Handen smiled a humorless smile as the bumbling professor tried to turn off the suddenly overenthusiastic party machine. He was beginning to form a picture of the intellect before him.

Handen doubted that throughout the professor's career as Head of Extremely Worrying Weaponry, he had once considered the lives lost to his creations. Such men were dangerous. Such men could be the end of worlds…or, perhaps, their saviors.

The adventurer dismissed the thought, focusing his tired mind on the situation at hand.

"Tell me," he began. "What is the Emperor like?"

Riley turned from the bubble machine, an expression of shocked surprise flashing over his face. "The Emperor…is a glorious ruler. Well-loved by the people."

"Yeah, I figured that would be the official standing, but you must know him more personally than that. He was married to your sister, wasn't he?"

"Yes…yes, of course."

"So?"

"Well...he was awfully fond of weapons. Always had lots of ideas. Some of them quite outside the realms of probability but some of them...just realistic enough to be...very productive."

Handen sighed. "Look, Riley, you know why I'm here. I'm not a spy or an informant. If everything goes as planned, I have a meeting tomorrow with the most powerful man on the planet, who, for some reason, wants me dead. You've worked for this man! You're his *in-law*, for gods' sake! Now, call me pedantic if you like, but I think it might be proper to have some information about him before we meet."

Riley looked at the floor again. When he looked up, there was a pained focus in his expression that hadn't been there before.

"He's mad," said the professor. "By all that's terrifying, he's as mad as the eye of hell."

Handen nodded as if he had expected the answer. He motioned for the professor to continue.

"He's dangerous—a very dangerous man. He has no regard for human life! Some of the things he did when I worked with him...I was always safe because I was useful—that was why he made me a duke—but others... Others... He would kill and have them killed without blinking, with no anger, no sorrow—just a kind of...impatience..."

"You think he'll listen to us?" asked Handen.

Riley removed his multi-lensed glasses and began nervously polishing them with a handkerchief. "I couldn't say. He may be insane, but he isn't stupid. He has the finest minds on Bersch in his employ. If *we* know that there is a meteorite approaching, it's more than likely *he* knows. But no matter what information you claim to have, even if you thought you *could* save the planet, there's no guaranteeing that the Emperor will hear you. If he wants you dead—*truly* wants you dead—then he may listen to your case, smile, nod, click his fingers, and then...you'll never be seen again."

Handen stared hard at the man. "It's a risk I'll have to take," he said after a while.

The professor nodded. He seemed to have calmed down, though his face was sheened with sweat. "You've no idea how good it felt to say all those things. If the Emperor were to hear one word of treachery, they would come for me in the night. I would disappear, and no one would even bother to ask about me because too many questions would make them disappear as well. By all that's paranoid, I've not dared to speak my mind about the Emperor in all my life, even when Yvette died..." The professor looked up from his polishing and directly at Handen. A slow tear gathered at the corner of his wrinkled eye. "They said it was a weak heart, but Yvette was as strong as an ox, by all that's vital—*as strong as an ox!*"

"You think she was killed?"

Riley shook his head slowly. "I didn't at first. You see, my wife, Tilla, died when Xharon was just a little girl. Yvette helped to raise her after that...helped me when I thought I couldn't go on. When she married the Emperor, we were all happy for her, none so more than I." The professor paused, peering into black memory. "When she died, I found it hard to let her go. I started asking questions, interviewing the castle physicians over and over, desperate to find out how someone as strong and vital and as beautiful as Yvette could have just...died. With no former complaints, just...died. I asked too many questions. I was demoted, and it was made very clear to me that my questions would have to stop."

"I see," said Handen.

"I brushed up on my history—the history of the Draegul succession. Queens very rarely get a mention in Argustin law, but they all have one trait in common—they all die young, only a couple of years after their marriage."

"You think homicide runs in the family?"

The professor shrugged. "I think the Emperor is a truly evil man from a long line of truly evil men. I think that if he wanted *me* dead, I'd be as far from the Empire as possible."

The two men held each other's gaze. "You understand I have to go through with this meeting?" said Handen.

"Of course. I shall visit with the night clerk at Dawncastle. If there is to be a meeting, you will know by tomorrow afternoon."

Handen paused for a moment. "Would you like me to leave Xharon behind?"

Riley chuckled and shook his head. "I doubt you'd be able to if you wanted to. Besides, 'Uncle Tommy' *is* rather...amused by her. She might be able to help your case."

"And you?"

The professor shook his head again. "I will relay my findings to the proper authorities. I no longer hold a position in which I may report directly to the Emperor."

"Understood," said Handen. "And now, if you'll excuse me, I think I'll turn in for the night."

"Of course, of course," said Riley, appearing his usual flustered self, the melancholy seemingly forgotten in his absentmindedness. "You'd better get some rest—by all that's exhausted, you'll need your *rest*."

Handen waved and left, shutting the door behind him. Riley sat back at his workbench, taking refuge in the soft tweetings of his creations. He sighed deeply. "By all that's holy, you'll need all the rest you can get."

---

BIP STARED up at the storeroom ceiling. It was warm and comfortable near the boiler, and the distant clanging of the factory quarter was oddly lulling, but despite it all, sleep still eluded the Kaneqian. He watched Xharon, pencil-sketched in the orange glow of the firelight as she went about the nightly ritual of polishing her axes. In accordance with her father's constant pleas, Xharon had reluctantly donned a nightie—a high-collared, flowery affair that covered every inch of skin bar her face and hands. The transformation was quite astonishing. Xharon seemed instantly younger, more fragile and feminine and, thought a steadfast part of Bip's libido, less interesting to look at.

As much as it was strange to see her preparing warrior weapons in this chokingly modest attire, it was stranger still to be sharing a roof with her. Even though the princess lay a good ten feet away, something about the intimacy of sleeping within the same four walls was causing Bip to lie wide awake when, by rights, he should be resting.

Something stirred in the young Kaneqian as he watched his companion go about her nightly routine. Whether born of the soft light of the strange surroundings or perhaps of the anxiety felt for the coming day, there was something dreamlike and subdued about the whole scene. Something he might have called magical, had he been more familiar with the term.

"Xharon?" he said, and was amazed by how harsh his voice seemed in the relative silence.

Xharon paused and looked up. "Yes?"

"Are you worried about tomorrow?"

"No. Why would I be?"

Bip frowned. "In case we all get executed…"

"Oh, that," said Xharon. "I don't think that will happen."

"Really? How can you be so sure?"

"Well, I don't know—things have worked out for the best so far, haven't they?"

*Oh, yes,* thought Bip, *everything works out fine until it doesn't, and that's when the worrying starts…*

"Why do you ask?" said Xharon.

Bip blinked. "No reason, really. It's just, you know, if you were worried, it'd be okay…"

"But I'm not."

"Yes, but if you were, you know, I'd understand."

"I'm not worried."

Bip raised his hands. "All right, okay, I just thought I'd say that it's okay to be worried if you want to. There's no shame in it."

The two doomsayers sat in the flickering glow of the boiler, listening to the sound of Azron's quiet snoring and the distant noise of machinery clanking with melancholy persistence.

"Are *you* worried?" said Xharon unexpectedly.

Bip flustered, caught unaware. "Me? Worried? No. No, of course not."

"Even though there's a good chance you'll be put to death tomorrow?"

"No. No, I'm fine, really."

"Even though it could be a very, very *slow* death?"

Bip began to sweat. Perhaps the boiler was a bit too hot. "I'm okay with it, thanks," he said.

In the low light of the room, Bip thought he saw the corners of Xharon's lips rise in a small, secret smile.

"You're quite brave, you know," she said.

Bip tried to ignore the sudden fluttery feeling in his chest. "Really? Why do you say that?"

The princess began counting on her fingers. "Well, for a start, you're not very big, are you? And you obviously can't fight, and you don't really have any sort of special skills, do you? And when all's said and done, you're a bit of a wimp..."

"Sorry, is this supposed to be making me feel better?" interrupted Bip.

Xharon laughed. "And despite all those things, you've traveled halfway across the world, taken on everything in your path, escaped certain death on several occasions, and tomorrow...tomorrow you go to confront the most powerful man in the civilized world, who, incidentally, has spent the last few months crafting your doom. When you think about it like that, you're pretty gosh-darn brave."

Bip grinned, his face flushing. "Yes. Yes, I suppose I am."

He ducked as a shoe suddenly sailed past his head.

"You'll be pretty gosh-darn beaten up if you don't stop talking and let me get some sleep," growled Azron. "Honestly, go and take a cold shower, why don't you?"

Xharon blushed a pretty pink and pulled the blanket over her head. Bip sat up for a while, grinning at nothing in particular until, lulled by the sleep-sounds of his friends, he nodded off.

---

HANDEN SAT AWAKE, darning a hole in his last good shirt. Riley had offered to lend him some clothes, but Handen doubted any garment belonging to the portly professor would fit him well.

He knew he wouldn't sleep tonight; he had caught a few catnaps here and there but was too restless to doze for more than a couple of minutes at a time. Every cell in his body was preparing for tomorrow's confrontation—a confrontation that could not be fought with blades and bullets, only with words and reason. And after that, who knew?

He brought out the waterskin containing the dregs of the fountain of death. Even now, the leather decanter was looking aged and deteriorated. Handen doubted it would last much longer under its deeply unnatural burden. Tomorrow, then, or perhaps the day after. Leave enough time to help if he could, and then…and then he would drink.

Handen sighed and placed the waterskin at his side. Then he began the process of disarming himself. It took some time.

---

THE NEW DAY came as any other, with no significant fanfare, no special formality, and devoid of omens of any kind. The sun rose, and the world spun on regardless. The day came as any other—apart from the new star, which hung low and steadfast and fat with ill promise.

Bip was awoken by the morning shift whistle, and by the stomp of a thousand workers' boots, and by the various mechanical yawns of an army of machines preparing for a new day of labor. He had looked out of the storeroom window onto the streets of the factory quarter, impressed as countless regiments of boiler-suited workmen flooded the streets, smoking, chatting, and filtering off into their various places of work. If they were at all concerned about the new, pale light in the morning sky, they didn't show it.

Awaiting news from Riley, the doomsayers had taken the morning to prepare for their visit to court, taking it in turns to scrub off months of ingrained road dirt in an old tin bath, and washing and repairing their clothes. Xharon, who had reluctantly revealed her skills in needlework, had offered to darn any holes, while Bip and Azron had taken turns scrubbing clothes with an old washboard and several dozen tubs of hot water.

Bip had done his best with the clothes he had left Kaneq in. Though his heavy jumper was now too full of holes to wear respectfully, his gray undershirt and canvas slacks needed only an hour or so with a needle and a few bars of soap. Azron had managed to scrub his long coat back from the dust-colored gray it had become to the midnight blue it had once been, and Handen looked like a very formal pirate in a billowy white shirt and brown leather trousers. Certainly, he looked less threatening without his heavy coat and innumerable scabbards, buckles, and holsters. The only item he had insisted on keeping about his person was the rotting waterskin containing the waters of the fountain of death, something he felt he could not leave behind.

The three stood—shaved and scrubbed, looking as clean as they had before taking to the road—and nervously waited for their summons. Bip felt unusual. Without Brian by his side and his heavy, worn rucksack on his back, he felt lighter and oddly naked. He could only imagine how the disarmed Handen felt.

At that moment, the storeroom door swung open and, as one man, they turned…and gaped. If Xharon had understood the term "formal attire," she had understood it in an extremely unique way.

"…!" said Bip.

"…!" agreed Azron.

"What the hell is that supposed to be?" cried Handen.

Xharon twirled. "Don't you like it?"

The outfit had ghostly echoes of the formal attire expected of the ladies of the Argustin court. There were certainly frills and lace and other things you might expect…though the frills erupted from the bottom of a polished metal brassiere with inappropriately placed spikes, and the lace was merely a thin gauze barely covering what appeared to be a pair of bearskin underpants. The full effect of the outfit was amplified somewhat by the thigh-high leather riding boots, the enormous metal shoulder pads, and the highly-polished helm from the sides of which metal wings arced aerodynamically.

"It's…it's very you," said Bip weakly.

"Isn't it, though?" said Xharon. "Of course, the Turnmisin swamp she-warriors don't really have a precedent for formal occasions, so I had to improvise."

"You certainly did that…" muttered Azron.

"And what is *that*?" asked Handen.

"What?" replied Xharon, eyes wide and innocent.

"In your hand."

Xharon looked down at the four-foot long battle-axe she was leaning on. "Oh, this? This is just an accessory," she said.

"No weapons," said Handen firmly. "We agreed."

"I can't make a public appearance without at least one weapon! I'll be a laughing stock!"

Azron coughed and looked at the floor.

"What did you say?" said Xharon, her eyes narrowing.

"Oh, nothing, nothing. Nothing at all," replied Azron, looking about to avoid meeting Xharon's gaze.

"No weapons," Handen reiterated. "You can leave it here."

Xharon huffed and let the axe fall to the floor with a clang.

"Look!" cried Bip. The doomsayers turned to the Kaneqian, who was peering out of the wide storeroom window. "They're here."

Down below, on the streets of the factory quarter, Professor Riley DeChambre approached, flanked by two Regulators and followed by a line of black-and-silver armored soldiers, wielding the largest flint-locks Bip had ever seen.

"It's time to meet the Emperor, then," he said faintly.

The others watched in silence at the approach of the Imperial Guard.

---

HANDEN LED THE WAY, slamming open the doors of Factory C12 as dramatically as he could.

"Well?" he demanded.

Riley gestured apologetically at the armed men behind him. On closer inspection, the Regulators seemed taller and broader than those the doomsayers had encountered so far, though the familiar expression of malice still characterized their features. As butch as the Regulators appeared, however, they were nearly dwarfed by the bulk of the black-clad guards behind them, their bulbous armor and full-face helms making them look like extremely well-armed beetles.

"The Emperor has granted you an audience," said Riley.

Handen eyed the soldiers mistrustfully. "Are we to be taken before him in chains?"

"Oh no, no. By all that's misunderstood, these are merely your *escort*."

The immortal allowed a doubtful smirk to saunter across his face. "Very well," he said. "Lead the way."

"If you would be so good as to follow me, Mr. Strike?" said Riley, bowing politely.

The companions fell in step with Riley, trying to ignore the guards as they fell into position, surrounding them. They began walking at an even stroll, Bip trying not to appear intimidated by the colossal guardsmen who paced him.

Riley leaned closer to Handen. "I'm so sorry, but he insisted on sending them, though he did clarify that they were merely for your protection," he whispered.

Handen smirked again. "Protection from whom?"

"It is rumored that there are dangerous people roaming the streets —some sort of unusual cult who are, or so I've heard, obsessed with the end of the world."

Handen paused suddenly, ignoring the sound of a dozen weapons being gripped more firmly by the Imperial guards behind him. "So, then…the people know?"

Riley shrugged. "I am unsure exactly *what* they know."

"It seems they know enough. Perhaps the Emperor will have no choice but to hear us now."

"We can but hope," agreed the professor.

The party set off, walking to the rhythm of the clanking armor of their escort.

---

LEAVING the factory quarter and entering the city proper, they might as well have been entering another world. Gone were the regimented streets and the flat, soulless buildings. Gone were the smog and cobbles, replaced instead by smooth, marble-like roads, mosaic-patterned pavements, and tall, seamless glass buildings that you had to crane your neck to see the top of. The people changed, too, of course. The fabulously dressed and impossibly beautiful citizens of Argustin laughed in the streets or sipped coffee in umbrella-studded bistros. They lined up outside grandiose theatres or went about their business in sharp, elegant suits, glancing casually at expensive pocket watches. They were a far cry from the grim and busy factory workers. They were, in fact, almost the complete opposite.

Bip and Azron had both marveled at the level of technology in the city, steam devices and engine carts appearing with a frequency that totally outclassed what they had seen in Panthalus. Propeller-driven monorails rode on stick-thin railings far above their heads, and city rail trains wove gracefully along their polished guide-tracks. The ballet of city traffic flowed without a hitch, carefully monitored by narrow-eyed Regulators on horseback while intricate, colored gas-lamps ordered HALT and PROCEED at seemingly random intervals.

The Kaneqian watched as a gaggle of students, resplendent in their black academic gowns, rolled laughingly into a wine bar, guffawing and hee-hawing over some comical irony. On the other side of the street, impeccable businessmen in silk ties and long-tails stepped onto a steam-powered glass elevator that hissed with great speed to the top floor of an important-looking building.

In this skyline of spires, arches and towers, the crystalline mountain of Dawncastle shone like another sun, bathing Argustin in a pale, lovely pink and drawing the eye ever upward.

"Nice place," said Bip, flatly.

"Nah," said Azron. "It's got no soul to it! Where's the street life? Where's the character? Where's the robbery?"

"Robbery?" gasped Xharon. "Oh, we don't tolerate that sort of thing in the city. If you can't afford to live here properly, you're deported. It's a very effective system."

"Yeah, I'll bet," said Azron, bitterly.

The city gates had been extremely heavily guarded, every potential entrant checked thoroughly by intimidating men with axes. Handen had commented that, without Xharon's help, they would never have been able to enter the city. Azron, who made a living by getting into places he wasn't allowed, had disagreed.

The troupe made its way through the streets of Argustin as both traffic and pedestrians wisely gave way to the armed contingent. Bip couldn't resist looking upward at the enormous and polished buildings that surrounded him. It was a hallmark of civilization unique in his experience, and he wondered who would possibly want to live so high up.

Eventually, he looked back down to street level, if only to ease the ache in his neck. It was then that he saw the commotion on the streets —a thin gray line of Regulators stood arm-in-arm against a small but surging crowd. The people in the crowd didn't look as if they belonged in Argustin at all; they had a general grubbiness about them that suggested they were well-traveled and little-washed. They were wearing identical red robes and shouting and struggling and generally seemed pretty upset about something. Bip strained his ears to hear what was going on.

"Voice of the Prophet…! Terrible Custard…! End of the world is nigh…! You're standing on my foot! Verily…arrrgh!"

A sudden memory jolted in Bip's head. He began scanning the faces of the struggling crowd, peering through his glasses until he found the face he had been half expecting. At the front of the crowd and doing what she did best was Celia Doom, the speaker from Panthalus. She was screaming with the same shrill zeal she had when Bip had heard her months ago, her dirty face and blond hair a rallying point for the rest of the red-robed mob.

"Warning from the ancient ones…We will be heard! Behold…! The hooded adolescent of fear is standing outside the corner shop of inevitability! Get your finger out of my eye, you bastard!"

"My word!" exclaimed Bip.

Handen looked back. "What is it?"

"That girl!" Bip pointed to the struggling throng. "She's Celia Doom! The one I told you about? The one I talked to just before I got arrested!"

Handen smiled. "Unbelievable. She's come all this way." He turned to Riley. "Are these the dangerous people you were told about?"

The professor nodded. "Apparently they've sprung up all over the continent. They call themselves the Cult of the Doomsayer, by all that's ominous."

Handen chuckled and turned back to Bip, clapping him on the

shoulder. "Well done, kid. You've spread the word. In fact, you've completed the mission I set out to complete centuries ago—you've warned civilization that the end of the world is coming."

"Still," said Bip, looking up at the pale light in the sky, which even now seemed to grow bigger. "I may have left it a bit late."

Handen shrugged. "If we do all we can, what more can we do? Now, let's go and see this Emperor. If he hasn't got the message by now, he's even more of a psychopath than I've heard."

Beside the former Hostilities Advisor, an Imperial guard cocked the hammer on his flintlock rifle. There was a tense silence, which was thankfully broken by a shrill yelp. Celia had noticed them.

"It's him!" she screamed. "It is the prophet of the Ancient Ones! He who has been delivered unto us to deliver a message…unto us! Get off me! Get off!"

The ragged girl struggled as two Regulators lifted her into the air. She reached out to Bip as she was carried away.

"Help us, Doomsayer! Tell them the end of days is upon us!"

Bip shrugged. "I don't think they'll listen," he said, and gestured to the armed guards who surrounded him.

"Oh…" said Celia as she was carried into the distance. "Bugger."

They watched as the girl was carried away, and the rest of the Cult of the Doomsayer either fled or were rounded up by the remaining Regulators.

"I think we'd better get moving, yes? Wouldn't like to keep the Emperor waiting, by all that's punctual—we wouldn't want to keep him *waiting*," said Riley.

The Imperial guard who had readied his weapon lowered it again and motioned for Handen to walk. The adventurer did and, followed closely by his companions, set off for the gates of Dawncastle.

---

3

## Interlude: Everyday Heroes.

---

Backtracking the crisscross trail of Bip and Handen, far and away from Argustin, Kaneq sat as it always had, forever huddled against the brutality of the Ice Plains. Here, the farthest point from the solar system's resident star, the new silver light in the sky—that harbinger of certain sorrow—was obscured by the bulk of Bersch. Thus, even the most wise and ancient of the Kaneqians sat unaware that their apocalyptic deadline had been unexpectedly brought forward. Not that it could have made much difference—the citizens and the final chosen had done nothing but work flat-out since they had heard the dread news, and no cosmic threat, no matter how terrifying, could have motivated them more.

Though perhaps if Bailey had known, he wouldn't have been sitting as relaxed as he was now, his feet propped on a table, a pipe hanging lazily from his mouth. He sat in the Empty Goat, which was living up to its name (due to the fact that it was empty, not that it was a goat).

Behind the bar, Michaelmas was polishing glasses and whistling a distracted and broken tune. Bailey took a long pull from the steel tankard before him and smacked his lips with satisfaction.

He had changed considerably in a short time, the strenuous and brutal training regime filling out his soft bulk with unprecedented muscle, straightening his hunched frame, and bringing color into his normally sickly skin. His long hair was tied back in a tight ponytail, and his stubbled jaw had grown into a thin, cropped beard. But despite the noticeable improvements in his health and appearance, he wouldn't have traded tomorrow morning's break for anything. Tonight might be his last opportunity to drink, and drink he would.

He drained the tankard and signaled for a refill, lighting his pipe as he awaited fresh ale.

He had come through the physical training, unexpectedly, with flying colors. Once he'd got over his sporadic coughing fits, he had shown a prowess with weaponry and a level of fitness that had impressed even Rynford, and he had muddled well enough through his psyentific training to receive the bare minimum of praise from Glimton. Consequently, he and a few others had been given a morning off for some leisure time before the day the volunteers would leave—or V-Day, as it had come to be known.

The overall volunteer party consisted of about fifty individuals of varying ages and backgrounds, though mostly youngsters. There were some who exceled in psyence, some who had been selected from the hunting party, and some who had been chosen purely on the basis of their ingenuity and resourcefulness. Others had proven themselves useful, some with quite unexpected skills. Half-Brick, for instance, had shown an uncanny knack for sailing—unusual for a boy who had never before seen a boat. It was even rumored that a few elders had made the chosen.

Now that the final group had been selected, craftsmen and psyentists were putting the finishing touches to the four boats that would carry them across the Cold Ocean. The next few days would be spent preparing the volunteers for an ocean journey with some trial runs in the boats, while those who still showed weakness in certain areas were to be given last-minute tutelage and training.

For now, though, a few of the volunteers had been granted a brief reprieve to spend with their friends, family, or in Bailey's case, with the pub.

He sucked thoughtfully on his pipe and looked down at the heavy bow and arrow that he carried everywhere with him these days. It was a hulking and many-stringed affair, designed for felling thick-muscled snow beasts from safe distances. It was a weapon not often used by the hunters of Kaneq, but one Bailey had shown particular prowess with, so he had been given it as his own. He smiled to think that, only a few weeks ago, he had barely been able to pull back and draw. Now, thanks to near-constant practice and Rynford's training, he was an accomplished marksman.

He wondered how many of the other volunteers were sitting surprised at themselves—those who had been nothing more than lumberjacks or tanners, suddenly heroes on whom the fate of the world depended. He wondered if this was how Bip must have felt. He wondered more how scared his friend must have been to have had suffered this responsibility on his own with no one to confide in and with no support from the community. He wondered if Bip had felt as scared as *he* felt now. Bailey sucked thoughtfully on his pipe, and then dismissed the notion. There would be plenty of time for anxiety later. Now, it was time to drink.

He smiled as Michaelmas wordlessly placed another tankard on the table, then he raised his drink in a brief salute before downing half the ale in one. Tomorrow he would be a hero. Today he was going to get as drunk as humanly possible.

He paused mid-quaff as the door to the Empty Goat flew open, letting in a chill breeze. Most of the psyentists were occupied with the preparations for V-Day, which meant that the heatshield was not being maintained at its usual strength. Thus, Kaneq was experiencing an early winter, and a few flakes of snow drifted onto the pub floor, where they melted with quiet relief. Wheeling himself slowly with a familiar squeak of heavy axels, Truggle rowed his way into the pub.

Michaelmas blinked. It was not often that Kaneq's most senior was seen out and about by himself.

"Can I help ye, sire?" he said.

Truggle rowed to the bar. "Something strong and large," he said.

Michaelmas complied, pouring a double measure of brandy from one of the more expensive bottles. He passed it carefully to Truggle, who downed the sweet spirit in one.

"Another," he said.

Bailey watched with interest. Since informing the community of the impending astral disaster, Truggle had dropped his befuddled old man act and had revealed a lucid and sharp mind, a fact that had shocked and surprised many of Kaneq's residents, Bailey included.

He watched as the old man drank his drink, slowly this time, sipping rather than gulping. Warmed by alcohol, the normally morose Bailey felt moved to conversation.

"Drinking alone, sir?"

The elder turned to the younger man. "The best way sometimes. You too, I see."

Bailey nodded. "A lot to think about, I suppose."

Truggle cracked a humorless grin. "Certainly. The end of the world tends to occupy one's thoughts quite selfishly."

Bailey returned the grin. "Yes, I suppose so. Still, at least we're doing something about it. It's not long 'til V-Day. There's still hope."

"Hope?" Truggle chuckled mirthlessly. "Sending our children into the wilderness is hope?"

Bailey frowned, clearly annoyed. "There's fifty of us. All highly trained, all prepared for the worst. Surely there's a good chance we can reach the mainland?"

"There have been many brave men and women who have ventured into the wilds over the centuries—stronger hunters than Rynford, more cunning psyentists than Glimton and certainly far wiser men than I. None of these heroes ever returned, yet you're certain that a group of youths with a few months' training will succeed where Kaneq's elite have failed countless times?"

There was a long silence.

"If what you say is true," began Bailey, speaking through clenched teeth. "If it really is so hopeless, then why send Bip? Why send one boy out to certain death?"

For a while, Truggle didn't reply. "I had faith in the boy," he said eventually. "I still do." With that, he placed his glass carefully on the bar and rowed his way toward the exit. "Goodnight to you all, and good luck to you, young Bailey. I mean that." The old man rowed out into the dark night.

Bailey shivered, putting it down to the sudden chill. He paused for a while, staring at nothing. Then he reached for his tankard.

"Not very positive, is he?" said the volunteer.

Michaelmas nodded. "He was about Bip. Seemed convinced the lad was going to go far."

Bailey considered his ale for a moment. "No offense, Michaelmas—Bip was my friend, and a good friend he was too—but we can't rely on his success. It's madness to sit back and pin our hopes on one boy, let alone Bip."

Michaelmas nodded again. "I suppose so."

Bailey stared into his pint again, a tear coming unbidden to his eye. "Do you think he's alive?"

Michaelmas said nothing.

Bailey rose slowly to his feet and made to leave.

"Not finishing your drink?" said Michaelmas.

Bailey shook his head. "I've lost the taste for it."

------

LATER, in the bowels of the Dome, alone in the dim and eerie light, Truggle sat watching a set of flickering numbers as they counted down.

"I still have faith," he whispered.

_______________________________

4

A Grudge Match Centuries in
the Making...

_______________________________

The doomsayers walked through the Imperial gardens, silent with their own thoughts as the shining pinnacle of Dawncastle loomed ever closer. Bip could not help but marvel at the beauty that surrounded him. It put even Ted's garden to shame.

The gardens of Dawncastle were exactly as one would expect—huge, ornate, delicate, and neat. Fountains and rose beds studded wide expanses of perfectly flat lawn. Here and there, gravel pathways converged with beautifully crafted bridges sailing over mirror-like ponds, the surfaces of which were disturbed only by the occasional bite of a rare and expensive fish. Domesticated wildlife roamed the grounds, eyeing newcomers with docile curiosity and lolloping between islands of carefully woven plants and flowers, each rare and colorful petal arranged with painstaking delicacy and exquisite taste. Statues popped up here and there like frozen wanderers, each marble rendition a perfect idolization of woman, man, or beast.

It was easy to be awed by the Imperial gardens, to feel that perhaps here man and nature had combined in the most perfect way imaginable to create a small slice of paradise. It took the cynical minds of the solider and the thief to see the dark genius behind it all...

For starters, the garden lay between an outer wall and Dawncastle's inner wall, surrounding the palace completely and meaning that anyone wishing to approach would have to traverse a wide area without much cover, leaving them vulnerable to searchlights and the marksmen manning the inner wall. Gravel was difficult to cross noiselessly, and Handen had recognized some of the rare and expensive fish in the pond as piranha. He had no doubt that some of the meandering wildlife was trained to attack on sight. He also realized that the pathways and ponds and rivers crisscrossed in a way that meant an intruder couldn't walk toward the palace in a straight line from any direction. There were obstacles to be crossed from all angles. Finally, Azron was pretty sure that at least some of the statues they had passed, usually the ones with weapons, were breathing...

These observations, coupled with the myriad unseen booby-traps that more than likely peppered the pathways they weren't currently taking, meant the gardens, while beautiful to look at, were a very effective trap for potential assassins or thieves.

Handen entertained dark thoughts. Insane tyrant or not, the Emperor was no fool.

After walking for a good twenty minutes, they finally arrived at the main entrance of Dawncastle, a huge wooden door encased in the surrounding glasswork like a fly in amber. As they approached, one of the escorting Regulators advanced and knocked his truncheon on the door with three loud bangs. After a while, a window opened in the woodwork, out of which popped a small face with a bulbous nose, wearing an expression of extreme harassment. The man wore a green furry hat that verged on the ridiculous and hid his mouth behind a moustache that bristled with self-importance.

"What's this? Who goes there?" said the gatekeeper, in a voice that seemed to suggest he was an important man with important bits of paper to look at, and that this interruption was an encroachment on something that was, undoubtedly, very important.

"It is I," boomed the Regulator, "Patrol Constable Jargette."

"And who are these people with you?" demanded the gatekeeper, his voice almost comically suspicious.

"They have come to see the Emperor."

The gatekeeper's eyes widened dramatically. "What?! See the Emperor? No one sees the Emperor! Not no one, not no how!"

There was a brief silence before Jargette coughed. He leaned up, speaking so quietly to the gatekeeper that Bip had to concentrate hard to hear what was being said.

"Actually, Dave, they really *are* here to see the Emperor."

The gatekeeper, or Dave as he had been revealed, frowned in puzzlement. "Not no one, not no how?" he ventured.

The Regulator coughed again, apparently embarrassed. "I'm serious, Dave. You can drop the tourist thing. These people *really do* have an appointment with the Emperor."

"Oh," said Dave. "Oh. Really. Well, why didn't you say so?"

The gatekeeper disappeared, the hatch slamming shut behind him. Jargette coughed and regained his composure. He rapped smartly three times on the massive doors, and this time, with a loud, metallic groan, they opened, as slow and certain as a distant tidal wave.

Bip squinted as he was bathed in a warm light. It seemed unnatural that the inside of a room should be brighter and warmer than the midday sun outside, but this was exactly the case as the warped, twisted, and redirected sunlight beamed through every glass panel of Dawncastle's intricate and uncanny architecture until, magnified and amplified, it gushed languidly from the front door.

"The Emperor awaits you in the reception hall," Jargette said bluntly, and led the way inside.

The doomsayers entered, stepping into a giant hallway that seemed to be constructed of warm, pink ice. Bip gaped in awe as his eye was drawn upward to a glass ceiling tinted a fiery yellow, and beyond that a further glass ceiling, this one slightly orange. The ceilings continued past Bip's low perspective, presumably, right to the top of Dawncastle. He felt uncomfortably dizzy as he saw the faint silhouettes of people walking around several hundred meters above him.

His attention was drawn back to ground level by a discreet cough. Seemingly from nowhere, Dave the gatekeeper had reappeared, this time on top of a cart pulled by a donkey. For some reason, the donkey had been dyed various different colors. Whether or not the donkey was pleased about this was difficult to say. Donkeys rarely seem pleased by anything.

"Erm…I don't suppose you wanted to ride on the Donkey of Many Colors, did you?" said Dave.

Jargette sighed heavily. "God dammit, Dave, I told you—they're not tourists!"

"I have a song and everything!"

"Just sod off, will you?"

Dejected, Dave led the rainbow-painted donkey back the way he had come, humming a sad little song as he left. The doomsayers and escorts alike stood around in embarrassed silence.

"Erm… This way to the reception hall," mumbled Jargette, once again taking the lead.

"Why can't we ride the donkey?" whispered Xharon. "*I* want to ride the donkey!"

They followed Jargette through the massive hallway and a series of crystal corridors until they arrived at another huge set of doors. Unlike the main entrance, these doors were protected by a dozen of the thickly armored Imperial guardsmen, who simultaneously saluted and sidestepped as the group approached, adjusting their postures to something that merely hinted at the possibility of violence, rather than guaranteeing it. The doors opened almost silently, as though hushed by the sheer enormity of the occasion.

"I'm afraid this is where I must leave you all," said Riley, his voice sudden and apologetic. "The Emperor has only granted audience for the four of you. My presence is not desired, by all that's uninvited— not *desired*."

Handen clapped him on the shoulder. "Don't worry about it. We know what we have to do."

Bip coughed and leaned close to the professor. "If we…you know… if things don't go as planned, someone needs to try…something. Anything."

Riley nodded. "I'll do everything in my power to find a solution, but the Emperor really is our best hope." The older man shook each of the doomsayer's hands solemnly in turn until, reaching Xharon, he embraced her in an awkward hug. "Try not to get yourself into any trouble, dear," he said.

Xharon rolled her eyes. "Oh, *Daddy*."

"And couldn't you have at least found a nice dress to wear?"

"Daddy, *please*! Not in front of the minions!"

Riley shook his head and began heading back down the corridor they had come from. "Good luck to you all," he called, his voice echoing lifelessly against the glass-brick walls.

The doomsayers stood for a while, watching as Riley DeChambre waddled from view, then they turned to one another.

"Well," said Bip. "I suppose this is it."

"It's not too late to leg it," said Azron. "Say the word and I could be out of those doors before these mugs could say, 'Stop that really fast thief!'"

"I wish you'd let me bring my battle-axe," said Xharon.

Handen nodded agreement. Every cell in his millennium-year-old body was telling him that they were walking into danger, and his fingers kept gripping at handles and shafts that were no longer there.

"Bip?" he said. "Do you want to lead?"

Bip blinked in surprise. "Me? I sort of envisioned *you* leading the way, really."

Handen shook his head. "I'm no diplomat," he said. "I think you might be more suited to this."

Bip looked, in turn, at each of his new friends and spoke hesitantly. "If you think I can do it."

"Of course you can," said Xharon.

"Rather you than me, guv," said Azron.

Bip took a deep breath. "Then let's go."

---

AS SOON AS he entered the reception hall, Handen felt faint. He wondered at first if this was genuine fear, an emotion he had learned to suppress and ignore centuries ago, but as he followed his comrades down the length of an elaborately woven red carpet, he realized that he had been feeling a similar sensation quite frequently since his release from the Bin…though never as potent as this.

As they traversed the floor of the gigantic hall, the disturbing feeling amplified, triggered by the sight of comparatively mundane things—a figure on a particular portrait, the color and pattern of the wallpaper, or the faint tinkling sound of the chandelier that hung high overhead. Of all these things, however, nothing made the sensation peak more dramatically than the sight of the thin, black-and-silver-clad figure sitting on the massive gold-wrought throne at the head of the room. It was the Emperor Draegul.

Suddenly Handen could put a name to the stomach-clenching feeling he was experiencing. It was *déjà vu*, the feeling that he had been here once before. Having roamed much of the world in days too long ago to remember, the immortal was used to the feeling, but never had he experienced it as strongly as he did now. He felt as though he were tiptoeing near the edges of a half-remembered epoch, as though a terrible enlightenment flickered just a shadow's breath away. Something was scratching at the doors of his subconscious, demanding recognition, something dark and terrible that would not desist. He shivered, the world around him suddenly seeming paper-thin, spinning on an axis far away from his own.

He jumped as he felt a hand on his arm and looked down into Xharon's concerned eyes.

"Are you all right?" she asked.

Handen nodded, making an effort to regain his composure. It was difficult. He felt as if he were going to pass out at any minute. As if he were constantly falling.

Ahead of Handen, Bip led the way. He was doing his best to maintain a steady and confident march toward the Emperor but, as was usually the case when one concentrated too hard on what was generally an automatic function, he had forgotten how to walk. The Emperor's expression wasn't helping matters. He was smiling like a cat watching a mouse commit suicide.

Bip turned back toward his friends, seeking confidence there. They weren't much help. Azron bore a hunted expression, his eyes flitting about constantly, as though searching for escape. The recalcitrant thief had never been comfortable with authority figures, and now that he was in the immediate presence of the most authoritative figure on the planet, it was playing havoc with his nerves. Handen, too, was little help—his features looked drawn and distracted, and his lips moved gently and constantly, as though working on a complex mental problem. The only one of the four who didn't seem especially bothered by the situation was Xharon.

Bip turned back toward the Emperor and nearly panicked as he realized he was almost at the foot of the throne dais. He gulped and looked up into the hard, amused gaze of Argustin's ruler, taking in the beautifully woven robe and the gilded weaponry, the long, groomed hair, and the dark, hollow eyes. Under his thin silver crown, Draegul looked almost exactly like the statues Bip had seen scattered throughout Panthalus. Unlike the statues, though, the Emperor's face didn't bear the thousand-yard stare of contemplative nobility. In real life, Draegul grinned like something deep-down and deadly.

Remembering Riley's brief tutelage in etiquette, Bip bowed low, keeping his eyes on the floor until told to rise by the Emperor. His companions mimicked the bow, bending at the waist and keeping their eyes fixed on the carpet. They hung there in genuflection for what seemed like an age, waiting for Draegul to acknowledge them.

Then they waited some more.

Finally, Draegul spoke, his thin voice carrying well in the acoustics of the reception hall. "Rise, do."

The doomsayers straightened their backs. Bip blinked rapidly to dispel the dizziness as the blood rushed back down from his head. Draegul chuckled, a sound that was both melodic and broken.

"Well, well," he said, "if it isn't the traveler, the doomsayer who brings us dire warnings from an ancient race. Bip Plunkerton, I believe?"

Bip gave a short bow again.

The Emperor stared at him for a while before turning his attention to Azron.

"And the thief, Azron Bezron."

"That's Azron Bezron, Diamond Geezer (1st class)…Your Worship," interjected Azron.

"Indeed," said Draegul, his voice cold. "Interrupt me again, and I shall tear out your tongue and make you eat it," he added, almost as an afterthought.

Azron swallowed hard and gave a short bow.

Draegul focused his attention on Handen, dismissing the thief as though he had never existed. "Ah, Handen Strike. The great adventurer. The man who cannot die. I've been looking forward to meeting you most of all."

Handen looked up, shaken from deep thoughts. He gave a short bow and said nothing.

Finally, the Emperor looked down at Xharon. "And my darling eccentric niece, Xharon. What a joy it is to see your shining face once more in my court."

"Hallo, uncle," said the warrior princess.

"And still running around in your undergarments, I see. Fantastic."

"Actually, Uncle, they're—"

"Yes, very good, very good. Now, I have been told by that dear doddering duke, Riley, that you have something of incredible importance to tell me. Please, put an end to the agony of my curiosity. What's up?"

Bip cleared his throat. This was the moment he had been rehearsing for since he had first been sent from Kaneq. "My lord," he began. "I come bringing a warning of utmost importance, lo, of worldly consequence...verily."

Draegul began distractedly polishing his nails on his robe. "Go on."

"Erm... It has been made known to me, by the ancient knowledge of my people and the calculations of Professor Riley, that a weapon launched from a civilization in a distant cosmos will collide with Bersch in about five days, twelve hours, and fifty-or-so minutes. A weapon powerful enough to destroy the entire world."

In the silence that followed, Draegul locked his gaze on the young Kaneqian.

"And is that everything?" he said.

Bip was momentarily flabbergasted. He looked at his friends. Azron shrugged, his face reflecting Bip's confusion. Handen seemed not to have noticed, his thoughts still elsewhere. Finally, Bip turned back to the Emperor.

"Er...yes? I suppose. Did you want me to repeat it?"

"No. No, that's quite all right. Thank you for your concern, but this information was made apparent to me quite some time ago. The situation is under control."

Bip frowned in puzzlement. "But that's impossible!" he said.

The Emperor's eyes narrowed just a little. "One is not used to being contradicted in one's own palace," he said.

"Sorry, Your Worship, it's just that...I was under the impression that the world was ignorant of the upcoming disaster. I was sent to warn you all!"

"Then I'm afraid you've wasted your time," Draegul said simply.

"Well, if you already knew, then why didn't you tell anyone? Why did you send your men to try and stop us?"

The Emperor was silent for a moment. "You know," he began, his voice eerily calm, "I've had better men than you flayed alive for taking such a tone with me..."

Bip blanched in sudden terror.

"But since you are a stranger in these lands, I will give you the benefit of the doubt. The reason I have never made it public knowledge that the end of the world is approaching is because I do not wish to have panic on my streets. As you have no doubt seen on your way here, people tend to get a mite hysterical if they think they're all going to die soon."

Bip gulped, his mouth suddenly dry. Part of his mind was entertaining the idea that his entire journey, his mission, his quest, had been a giant waste of time. So far, the rest of his mind was quietly ignoring it.

The Emperor continued, "And I sought to apprehend you for no other reason than to stop you spreading fear across my Empire. Now, once again, thank you for your concern, but the situation is being looked into by the finest minds on Bersch. In other words, things are under control. You have wasted your time and you have wasted mine. You are dismissed."

Bip began to sway on the spot, his head spinning. "How could you have known? Some of the things I've learnt even Truggle didn't know about… How could you have known?"

"You are *dismissed!*" hissed Draegul. He clicked his fingers and suddenly various shadows around the reception hall revealed themselves to be Imperial guardsmen. They stood with the quiet menace of those eagerly awaiting the order to become extremely violent.

"Thank you, my lord," said Bip quietly. He turned around slowly, as if in a dream, and began walking toward the exit, conscious of the gaze of heavily armed men on the back of his neck. As he passed Handen, he looked up at the adventurer and paused. Gone was the faraway look of concerned contemplation, replaced instead by a fury Bip had never seen before. He stepped back in shock.

"Handen?"

The adventurer continued to stare ahead. If he had heard Bip, he made no attempt to acknowledge him.

"Handen? Come on—we've done all we can. It's time to leave."

Handen continued to stare straight ahead. He whispered something that Bip couldn't make out.

"Pardon?"

"Bastard."

Bip looked around wildly, trying to see what had so suddenly infuriated his friend. "Handen, I really think we should—"

"*Bastard!*" screamed the immortal, pointing an accusing finger at Draegul. The Emperor's eyes opened wide in shock. Around the room, there was a lethal sound of flintlock rifles being readied.

Azron stepped over and grabbed Handen's arm. "This isn't the time, mate. Let's just get out of here while the getting is good, yeah?"

Handen shook off the thief's grip and began advancing on the Emperor's throne.

"Stop right there, Mr. Strike," Draegul said, his manner cool. "Stop right there, or I'll have you cut down like a rotten tree."

The adventurer raised an accusing finger once more. "You!" he growled, rage bubbling in his words. "You were the one who had me locked up! You were the one who put me in prison for half a millennium!"

There was a silence around the hall that could have crushed

worlds. A silence found beneath oceans and above stars. It was a sound that precluded the birth of universes, unbearably cacophonic in its sheer noiselessness.

"I beg your pardon?" said Draegul.

"Don't you dare play dumb with me," snapped Handen. "All this time I thought I'd failed in my mission, all this time I spent locked away in that blasted asylum—and you *knew*! You've always known. That's why you had me locked up!"

Draegul's eyes narrowed, his lip curling into a genteel sneer. "I'm afraid I have no idea what you're talking about."

Bip studied his friend's face, trying to fathom this unprecedented expression of sheer rage. "Handen? What do you mean?"

"That's why he knows what's going on," snarled Handen. "Because I told him hundreds of years ago."

Draegul chuckled. "What a comical mix-up—you must be mistaking me for one of my ancestors!"

Handen shook his head slowly and then, without warning, leapt at the Emperor. Several shots were fired, one striking Handen in the shoulder, but the immortal continued unhindered, grabbing at Draegul's robe and tearing it away from his chest.

"What do you think you're doing, you madman?" screeched the Emperor.

Two guardsmen leaped at Handen, restraining him, but it was too late. Handen struggled to free his arm, then pointed at the tattoo revealed on the Emperor's chest—a snake eating its own tail, twisted at the middle to form a figure of eight. Then, he tore away his own shirt to reveal the identical tattoo beneath.

"The mark of the immortal!" he shouted.

For a while, the Emperor and the adventurer stared at one another, locking gazes, neither blinking.

"Hang on a minute," said Xharon, breaking the tense silence. "Are you trying to tell me that Uncle Tommy's an immortal, like you?"

"Think about it," Handen said, keeping his eyes locked firmly on Draegul's. "The family resemblance, the fact that nobody ever sees his children, his successors. The fact that, throughout history, every Draegul bride has died young…"

Xharon gasped. "Auntie Yvette…"

"He's an immortal, ruling as Emperor of Argustin for a thousand years or more."

Draegul laughed, a dangerous and creeping laugh.

Handen continued, "When I warned him about the astral disaster centuries ago, he refused to take me seriously. I called him an arrogant fool, and he tried to have me executed. When he found out I couldn't die, he had me locked away forever."

"Is this true?" demanded Bip.

Draegul chuckled. "Oh dear, oh dear. And to think I was going to let you all go. Well, to be honest, I was going to have you all assassinated while you slept, but at least your deaths would have been quick. Now, I'm afraid, I shall have to dispose of you all as slowly and painfully as possible."

"What?" wailed Bip. "Why?"

"Because we know the truth," growled Handen. "The people might accept being ruled by a vicious psychotic tyrant, because that's the way it has always been, but if they find out that the reason it's always been that way is because they have, for centuries, been ruled by *the same* vicious psychotic tyrant, they might not remain so placid."

Draegul gave a small, sarcastic round of applause. "Very good, Mr. Strike."

"You had Auntie Yvette killed?" Xharon said, her bottom lip wobbling.

Draegul sighed. "Yes. It was a great shame. She was a lovely woman, but of course, she began to grow old. I couldn't have people becoming suspicious of me, so she had to die."

"You monster!" cried Xharon.

Draegul snapped his fingers. "Have her taken to the tower."

Instantly, a large group of Imperial guards appeared as if from nowhere, grabbing the warrior princess from all sides. She struggled, but to no avail.

"Unhand her!" roared Handen.

"Or what?" replied the Emperor. "As I'm sure you've noticed, I have you outgunned. You are unarmed, and while *you* may be impervious to death, I somehow doubt your friends are."

Handen gritted his teeth and clenched his fists, every fiber of his being crying out for action.

"Now," said Draegul. "I must say I'm very sorry, my dear, amusing niece. I never meant for you to become involved in all of this mess, but since you are, I'm afraid you can never see the light of day again. Ta-ta."

Xharon screamed in fury as she was half-dragged and half-carried away by the guardsmen.

Bip's mind reeled. Tears of helpless frustration rolled down his cheeks. "I don't understand! Handen was right; the world *really is* going to end. You know this!"

"Yes?" said Draegul.

"So why have him locked up? Why have any of us locked up?"

"I thought he made it quite clear. I don't appreciate being called a fool."

"But we might be able to help!"

Draegul laughed again, a sound that was dirty in his mouth. "What makes you think I need your help? I have already told you—the situation is well in hand. I have no need of 'ancient wisdom'—I *am* ancient wisdom!"

"Wisdom isn't acquired with time alone, Draegul," snarled Handen. "You're living proof of that."

The Emperor's smile faded instantly. "That's the second time you've insulted me, Mr. Strike, and it is the second time you will pay dearly."

"Oh dear…" muttered Azron.

"Look, you can't lock us up!" said Bip. "It's too late—your secret's out! All these guards now know you're an immortal! One of them is bound to talk!"

"Unlikely," said Draegul, smoothly, "since each and every one of my elite have their tongues cut out at birth."

"Oh…"

"Nice try, mate," muttered Azron.

"This isn't right!" cried Bip. "We were just trying to help! We never wanted to harm anybody! Please don't lock us away!"

"All right," said Draegul.

Bip blinked in surprise. "What?"

"I won't have you locked away."

Bip peered around at his comrades. "Really?"

"No. I thought I made it clear earlier. I'm going to have you killed horribly."

"No!"

Draegul rose to his feet and smiled a sinister smile. "Guards, have them fed to the bandersnatch."

"Oh dear, oh dear…" muttered Azron.

"And afterward, bring me the remains of Handen Strike." Draegul sneered down at the adventurer. "Your demise will not be so quick as your companions'. After you recover from your encounter with the bandersnatch, as you doubtless will, I will have you boiled alive in effluent for the rest of eternity."

"Well, it beats hanging around here and listening to you," snapped Handen.

Draegul's face darkened with fury. "Take them away. Feed them to the bandersnatch. We'll see how cocky you are when you're being digested alive."

The three remaining doomsayers backed up as they suddenly found themselves face-to-face with a dozen heavy flintlock rifles.

"You know," said Azron, "that could have gone a lot better."

The guards advanced.

"Wait!" bellowed Handen.

The Emperor raised a hand, and the guardsmen backed away from the adventurer.

"You have something to say?" he purred.

"Your problem is with me. These two can do you no harm—why not just let them go?" demanded Handen.

Draegul smiled. "And where would be the fun in that?"

"It's me you're angry with, me who insulted you all those years ago —it's me you want to punish!"

"And I have you. And as an added bonus, I have your friends as well. Tell me, why on Bersch would I give that up?" Draegul chuckled.

"Coward!" Handen shouted.

Draegul stood bolt upright, a dangerous glint in his eye. "Say that again, and I'll have you watch as my guards quarter your companions."

Handen sneered. "Yes, you have your guards to hide behind. It must be easy to make threats with your own army to back you up."

"Silence!" roared Draegul.

"I wonder if you know what true power is? I wonder if you've ever fought your own battles?"

"*Silence!*"

"Prove your worth! Back up those big words with some action! Your problem is with me, so fight me!"

Draegul stood stock still, staring at his prisoners.

Handen cracked a wry smile. "What have you got to lose? You can't die. Fight me."

"And if you win?"

"You let my friends go. You'll still have me."

"And if I win?"

"Then you get to go through the rest of your life knowing that you've beaten the best. All by yourself. Without hiding behind hired thugs."

Draegul laughed. "I suppose you expect me to back down so you can have some sort of tawdry moral victory to keep you feeling cozy over the countless years of agony I have in store for you? Well, I'm afraid that's not going to happen. You see, I've always had a love of weapons, and I've had a thousand years to get used to them. I *am* the best. And I shall enjoy proving it to you."

Draegul drew the ornate katana from the scabbard by his side. The blade shone like a phantom in the afternoon light.

"Guards. Give the fool a weapon and then make room."

"Oh dear, oh dear, oh dear..." muttered Azron.

A sword was placed into Handen's hand. He swung it experimentally. It was well-balanced and of sturdy craftsmanship but looked a clumsy affair in comparison to the Emperor's blade.

"Hold this," said Handen, passing his waterskin to Bip. Bip took it carefully, wary of the contents, and swung the strap over his shoulder.

Draegul, with a delicate flourish, moved swiftly into a ready stance. "I agree to your terms. If you can best me, your friends may go free. Now, be on your guard."

"I always am," Handen growled.

The combatants leaped toward one another, blades shining and singing through the air. They collided with a scream of steel, weapons locked together, fighters face-to-face.

"You know, I'm rather glad you had this idea, Mr. Strike," said Draegul, grinning through clenched teeth. "When I beat you, I may have your head mounted in my study."

"Then allow me to familiarize you with it in advance!" said Handen, and butted the Emperor on the nose. The swordsmen broke off, Draegul staggering backward but quickly recovering his guard.

On the sidelines of the fray, Azron nudged one of the guards. "One nil to us, aye?" he said.

The guard said nothing, merely eased the hammer back on his rifle with a heavy click.

"Ah," said Azron, suddenly aware that you didn't need a tongue if you were armed to the teeth. He focused his attention back on the fight.

The immortals circled one another, each judging the best angle of attack and defense. Suddenly Draegul lunged, an unexpected slash from his lower right quarter to his upper left. Handen dodged back, deflecting the blow...but only just.

Draegul grinned. "You know, it's amazing how much fun one can have living forever as the ruler of the civilized world, being able to do as one pleases for the rest of eternity. Wine, women, riches—every whim accounted for. I'm sure you'll appreciate that thought while you're rotting in whatever dungeon I decide to leave you in."

"You talk too much," said Handen. "Haven't you become tired of the sound of your own voice over the years?"

The adventurer lunged, a testing blow that forced Draegul back on his guard. Then he struck out three times from varying angles, each blow expertly deflected by the Emperor's blade. Draegul riposted with a wide arc from his sword, repelling Handen's assault and gaining back his ground.

Handen studied his opponent carefully, the world outside the fight no longer existing. Then he attacked, a flurry of fierce one-handed blows, advancing all the while as Draegul was forced back into a defensive posture. Just as it seemed the adventurer was getting the upper hand, Draegul struck another unexpected rising blow, this time catching Handen's cheek.

"First blood to me!" cried Draegul gleefully.

Handen touched his face, wincing as he felt the deep gash. With any luck, the wound would not swell up and impair his vision...but luck seemed to be avoiding him lately. He readied his guard, once again circling his opponent.

On the sidelines, Bip became aware that he had been holding his breath. He let it out in an urgent sigh. "Come on, Handen. Please, do this!" he whispered.

Handen waited for an attack, but to no avail. The Emperor was fighting defensively, confident enough of the speed of his blade to thwart Handen's blows, waiting for the mistake that would allow him to run his opponent through.

Draegul smiled a thin, lizard smile. "Is this the best our saviors from the stars have to offer? Is this their mightiest warrior?" The Emperor switched his grip on his katana, swirling the blade around him in a defensive weave. "I have to say, I'm very disappointed."

"I'm going to beat you," said Handen, his voice flat, calm, and deadly. "It's what I do."

With that, he attacked again—huge, sweeping blows that cleaved sparks from the Emperor's defending blade. He pressed his attack, awaiting the Emperor's inevitable riposte. It came in the form of another low blow, but this time one that Handen had anticipated. He brought his weapon down, trapping his opponent's katana against the stone floor. Then he stepped forward and rocketed a powerful kick into Draegul's solar plexus. The Emperor bent double, his face turning strained and purple, an uncontrolled groan erupting from his throat. Without hesitation, Handen swung his fist in a low arc, rising to an uppercut, the momentum of which lifted his feet from the ground. The Emperor somersaulted through the air, landing with a heavy thump.

"Yes!" shouted Bip. There was no doubt that Handen had won the match.

Draegul looked up, blood streaming from his mouth. His eyes crossed to take in the tip of Handen's sword, leveled unwaveringly at his throat.

"I believe I have bested you," said Handen. "Now for your part of the bargain."

Draegul smiled horribly through thick gore. "Certainly," he said, and raised his hand.

Without warning, a terrible boom reverberated throughout the hall as several dozen flintlocks were fired at once. Handen jerked spasmodically and was thrown to the floor, torn apart by bullets. He lay still on the ground, blood oozing from his multiple wounds, a puddle forming and expanding at a nauseating pace.

"No!" cried Bip, and ran to the body of his fallen friend.

Draegul stood up, wiping the blood from his mouth. He looked down at the unconscious Handen. "Fool," he muttered.

Bip looked up, tears in his eyes. "How could you?"

"He did not best me," snarled Draegul. "How could he? I am immortal! I am the Emperor of this land! He could *never* best me."

"But you gave your word!"

"Pah! I gave my word to a convicted madman. It means nothing. Guards!"

Guardsmen quickly surrounded the trio.

"Have them taken to the bandersnatch's lair. I do not wish to see them again."

Bip tried to fight the rising tide of despair in his belly as he, Azron, and the unconscious Handen were seized by the Imperial elite. "You gave your word!" he wailed.

Draegul said nothing, merely waved his hand as if to dismiss them.

The doomsayers were taken from the reception hall, and Draegul stood alone in silence. Soon he began to hear the whispers.

THEY WERE MANHANDLED into the bowels of Dawncastle, the seedy, crypt-like stonework of the lower levels an unwelcome contrast to the crystalline splendor of the levels above. Here was the reality of the great palace—here, with the dungeons and torture chambers, where the wails of the hopeless and the dying echoed horribly through the tight corridors and the torch light licked suggestively at deep and clawing shadows.

Handen groaned as he was dragged along. He was coming around, but the extent of his wounds meant that he was healing slowly. Azron watched with faint disgust as the immortal spat out a bullet.

"What is a bandersnatch, anyway?" said Bip, his voice oddly light and faraway-sounding to his heavily shocked mind.

"Well, it's not quite as big as a jabberwocky," said Azron. "Though it's definitely bigger than a jubjub bird, and much more vicious."

"Oh."

"It's pretty frumious too, by all accounts."

"Ah. Not good, then?"

"No. I imagine if it was small and docile, we wouldn't be getting fed to it, would we?"

"No, I suppose not."

The guards halted by a heavy-looking trapdoor. One of them began turning a crank that slid the doors across, slowly revealing a murky blackness beneath. There was a stench that reminded Bip suddenly of when he had been a boy and a rat had crawled under his bed and died. For a long time, he'd thought the smell had something to do with puberty until his mother had eventually found the real cause.

The trio were lined up, the gaping hole before them. One of the guards pointed down.

"I think they want us to go in," said Azron.

Bip peered into the blackness. "Erm… no. No, thanks. I'd rather not, if it's all the same to you." He swallowed deeply as he felt a flintlock pressed into the back of his skull. "Oh. Okay, then."

Closing his eyes, the Kaneqian took a step forward into what was likely his doom.

FAR OUT INTO the cold drifts of space, the Massive Ball of Death felt the warmth of a new sun against what passed for its face. It had been a long time alone, nothing but the idle anticipation of arrival to keep it occupied, nothing but the pinpoint shine of distant stars to light its way. Now it knew for sure that it was merely days from its destination and, for a quasi-lifeform at the end of a journey measured in millennia, a few days was no time at all. It felt nervous, something new and exciting. It felt as though it had just arrived at a very important party and wasn't sure if it was dressed appropriately.

It gazed forward with what would pass for eyes, dimly aware that —for better or worse—it was nearing the end.

# 5

# And Burbled As It Came...

**B**ip stood up and shivered, waiting for his eyes to adjust to the darkness. He wasn't sure how far he had slid, though the fall through the pitch-black tunnel had seemed like it had lasted an eternity. He heard a thump behind him.

"Bugger!"

"Azron? Is that you?" he whispered.

"Yes, it's me. Much as I wish it wasn't."

There was another thump followed by a groan.

"Handen? Is that you?"

"I think so. Where are we?"

"In the lair of a ferocious beast that needs feeding."

"Oh," said Handen bitterly. "Of course we are."

Bip peered around the lair. The shallow light filtering in through the trapdoor above was just enough that he could make out his surroundings. It was a natural cave, its walls slick with unnamed slime, the floor soft with something squishy, the origin of which Bip felt was best not guessed at. The whole cave stank of wild animal.

"Now what?" said Azron

Bip shrugged, a futile gesture in the dark.

"Handen?"

The adventurer groaned. "I've just been shot to death," he said. "It's going to be a little while yet before I'm much good for anything."

"Fair enough. We'll just sit here and be eaten then, shall we?"

"What are we up against?" Handen asked.

"A bandersnatch."

Handen sucked in his breath through his teeth. "Tricky," he said. "Are there any weapons lying around?"

"No."

"Any conveniently pointy pieces of wood or club-like hunks of rock?"

"No."

"Damn."

Now that his eyes were adjusting, Bip could make out a huge iron gate near the back of the cave. He felt his heart race as he heard the far-off echo of clanking gears. The gate began to open with a rusty yawn.

"This is it," he whispered.

"Spread out," said Handen. "Don't make us an easy target."

Azron's voice rang out from above them. "Way ahead of you, mate."

Bip looked up. By some fantastic feat of agility, Azron had managed to scramble up the cave wall, prying himself into the rock like a panicked cat.

"I'll be up here if you need me," he said.

"Great," said Bip, glumly. He turned to Handen, who was still slumped on the ground. He could see the adventurer now, and though he was still healing, he looked in no condition to fight.

"Any last-minute heroics in store?" Bip asked hopefully.

Handen shook his head. "Nothing comes to mind. Maybe I can let it eat me and hope it chokes to death…"

"Azron?"

"Can't think of anything, really. So far, the begin eaten thing is the best idea I've heard. Can't you do anything with that psyence of yours?"

Bip shook his head. "The only time that ever seems to work is by complete accident. And even then, it never works properly."

"Oh dear."

The gate was fully open now, revealing a total blackness behind it. The dark was split suddenly by two bright glows. There was a deep and sepulchral growl.

"Bandersnatch," Bip whispered.

The beast came forth, two sets of giant claws leading the way, followed by a larger set of teeth. The whole creature glistened with brown, reptilian skin and pushed its fat bulk along with spider-like legs that erupted from the crest of its spine. Its head was a misshapen thing, there only to give credence to its huge tunnel of a mouth. Two clear, wet orbs served as the creature's eyeballs, and a long, blue tongue flicked lazily from its jaws, sweeping the air before it like the cane of a blind man.

It burbled as it came.

"Well, chaps," said Azron. "It's been a blast, and I've had some good times, but I have to say, I wish I'd never met either of you."

"I'm starting to wish I'd never met me either," said Bip thickly, his tongue numb with terror.

The bandersnatch screeched like nails scraping on a blackboard and began shuffling slowly into the cave. Bip stared into the oblivion of its mouth, quite easily large enough to swallow him whole.

"So this is how it ends," he said, faintly.

"Cheer up," said Handen. "At least you did what you sent out to do. You warned the people that the end of the world was coming. It's all up to them now." The immortal chuckled softly. "And if this is how they repay you, maybe they deserve to be obliterated. Maybe Bersch was never supposed to be saved."

Bip's thoughts turned to Ted. Hadn't he said something similar? That Bersch being destroyed was all part of the order of things? If that was the case, why had Mr. Random been trying to stop him?

As if awaiting a cue, the world slowed down, the burble of the bandersnatch winding down to a low gurgle. A sensation of innate wrongness permeated the atmosphere.

"Hullo," said Mr. Random.

"Oh. You," said Bip.

Mr. Random's razor smile gleamed in the darkness. "Yes. Me."

"Well, I'd love to hang around and chat, but I'm a bit busy at the moment," said Bip, testily.

"Ah, yes. Your appointment with a certain and painful death."

"Yep. I don't suppose you had anything to do with this, did you?"

Mr. Random polished his long fingernails on his suit jacket. "Well, I might have whispered a certain something in a certain ear…"

"Well, that's just great. Thanks a lot."

"There's no need to be testy," said Mr. Random. "I just came to say goodbye. I'd like to think there are no hard feelings between us. Two players on opposing sides, the spirit of sportsmanship, etcetera, etcetera…"

Bip told him where he could stuff his sportsmanship.

"Well, there's no need to be like that," said Mr. Random. "I just came around to say hard luck, that's all."

"Yeah, you must be feeling very pleased with yourself. Now, thanks to you, this entire planet will be destroyed, and everything I've done will be for nothing."

Mr. Random blinked his yellow eyes, a puzzled smile on his face. "Pardon?"

"I said, thanks to you, Bersch is going to be destroyed!"

Mr. Random began to laugh, a low chuckle that quickly rose to a boyish giggle. "You don't know, do you? All this time trying to stop you, *and you don't even know*!"

"Know what?"

"Oh dear, oh dear, oh dear."

"Know what?"

"Well, I'm sorry, Bippy-boy, but I've got to dash. You know how it is—places to destroy, people to ruin."

*"Know what?"*

Mr. Random twiddled his long fingers. "Toodle-oo."

With that, he vanished, reality snapping back to normal around him.

Bip thought furiously. What had he meant? He felt that he had the pieces of an elaborate jigsaw puzzle and all that was left was to put them together. Would that he had the time…

The bandersnatch roared, closing in for the kill. Bip fled to the back of the cave, pressing his back against the walls. Azron scrambled farther still up the wall, and Handen crawled slowly away from the advancing beast.

Bip's mind raced furiously for any solution. *If only I had a weapon,* he thought. *Not that it would do much good, but it might make me feel better.* Suddenly inspiration hit him in a brilliant flash. He *did* have a weapon. He'd had a weapon all along! He reached down to the rotted waterskin at his side and uncorked the top of it.

He had one chance.

"Hey, you! Bandersnatch! Yeah, I'm talking to *you!*"

The beast swung its massive head in Bip's direction and opened its mouth to let loose a fearsome roar.

Bip tried to think of something disarmingly witty to say, but he couldn't. Instead, he just threw the waterskin into the mouth of the bandersnatch. There was a brief, puzzled silence as the monster swallowed. Then it belched massively and exploded.

Bip stood in stunned silence, bits of black goo from the exploded bandersnatch dripping from his clothes and hitting the floor with wet smacking sounds.

"What the hell happened there?" cried Azron, sliding down from the cave wall.

Bip had a thoughtful, faraway look in his eye. "I should have said, 'Open wide' or 'Fancy a drink?' Something like that, anyway."

Handen struggled to his feet. "How did you do it?"

Bip felt suddenly guilty. "I...I used the water from the fountain of death."

"All of it?"

"Yes. Sorry."

Handen stared for a while before slowly nodding his head. "It's fine. I can always go back to the dead wood," he said. "Hell, I've been alive for more years than I can remember. A few more months won't hurt."

"So that's what that water does, then," said Azron, wiping a chunk of gore from his cheek. "Pretty messy."

"Yep. So. Now what?"

"Some sort of daring escape?" suggested Handen. "That's what normally happens in these situations."

"A good idea, guv," said Azron. "Only how do we get out?"

Almost as soon as Azron had said this, there was a light thump. Behind them, a rope had been lowered from the trapdoor above.

"Hello down there?" came a voice. "Are you alive? By all that isn't deceased, are you *alive* down there?"

Handen smiled widely. "Professor DeChambre!" he called.

There was a distant sigh of relief. "When I heard what had happened, I came as soon as I could. I feared I might be too late!"

Bip looked back at the exploded carcass of the bandersnatch. "You're just in time," he called.

---

HANDEN WAS the last to shimmy up the rope, still too weak from his wounds to make use of his strength. Bip and Azron hauled him up over the edge of the trap door, and he lay panting for a while. Eventually, he looked up into Riley DeChambre's round face.

"My God, man, what did they do to you?" gasped the professor.

Handen grinned, a thin trickle of blood dripping from his mouth as he did so. "Nothing that I won't recover from," he said. He looked about. Thankfully this level of the dungeon was deserted. "How did you get past the guards?"

Riley held out a handheld device. It was boxy, bulky, and had various antennae, light bulbs, and small dials attached to it. It went *beep*. "A recently developed prototype of my own invention. It's a Dimensional Oscillatron and Frequency Energy Recalibrater."

Azron blinked. "A Do-fer?"

The professor looked critically at his device. "Yes. Yes, I suppose you could call it that."

"And what does it do, exactly?"

"Well, it recalibrates the energy frequency of dimensional oscillations."

"Come again?" said Azron.

"In a nutshell, it allows you to control your position in space/time by observing the frequencies of certain dimensional signals and manipulating them with modified frequencies of your own, effectively allowing you to hack into energy megarhythms in a subspace dimension and alter them in conjunction with your own specific bio-frequencies to suit your purposes. In this case, it allowed me to transport instantaneously from my workshop to this location without, as it were, going through the front door."

"Sounds complex," said Bip.

"Yes, it is, rather," conceded Riley.

"Some kind of teleportation device?" offered Handen.

"In a way…" began Riley.

"You can explain it to me later," Handen interrupted. "Can we use it to get out?"

"Certainly."

"Then let's do that."

"Erm… Aren't we forgetting someone?" said Bip.

"Of course. Xharon," said Handen. "She's being held in the tower. Damn!"

Riley shook his head mournfully. "There must be a hundred guards between us and the tower. I could attempt to reconfigure the… the Do-fer…but it would take some time."

"It's too dangerous to be hanging around here longer than we have to," said Azron.

"And we don't have any weapons," Handen added.

"Ah," said Riley brightly. "I did take the liberty of bringing a few supplies with me." He emptied a bag onto the floor, the contents of which clanged noisily. There was an assortment of weaponry, including Brian and Xharon's axes. "It pays to be prepared. By all that's precautionary, *it pays to be prepared.*"

"It certainly does," said Handen, grinning menacingly as he took two weapons from the pile. They were the prototype pistolas from DeChambre's workshop. "You know, I feel better already," he said.

"So what's the plan?" said Azron.

Handen spun the revolving ammunition chamber on each pistola in turn. "Simple, really," he said. "We take on the guards, get the girl, and somewhere along the line, an explosion chases us down a corridor."

Azron and Bip exchanged an uncertain look.

"Trust me," said Handen. "This is what I do."

---

AS HE CHARGED, there was a dual click from his pistolas—he had run out of ammunition. He threw the weapons aside and, bellowing all the while, continued to assault what was left of the contingent. As the two remaining guardsmen feverishly reloaded their heavy rifles, he leapt into the air, twisting like a salmon, and brought his heels down on the helmet of the foremost guard with a low *crunch*. The guardsman crumpled to the floor like a marionette whose strings had just been cut.

The remaining guardsman, having no time to reload his rifle, threw the now-useless weapon aside and drew a huge two-handed broadsword from the scabbard at his side. The attacker smiled, drawing his blade with a casual flourish. The duel was quick and desperate, but it wasn't long before the guard fell, clutching at his guts.

Breathing hard, Handen checked his pocket watch. They were making good time.

"Clear!" he shouted.

Bip, Riley, and Azron appeared from around the corner, taking in the immediate aftermath of extreme violence.

"Well done," said Azron. "Erm… Keep up the good work."

The sound of various alarm bells ringing in the distance was a continuous aural litany. The guardsmen of Dawncastle were well aware of the prisoners' escape, and the glass palace was raging with the sound of clanking armor and weapons being readied.

Handen had been fighting like never before, reveling in the chaos of unleashed combat. He was still not fully recovered from his wounds, and now had a few fresh ones to add to his collection, but he had been operating on sheer adrenaline, taking on everyone who had stood in their way.

He checked the remaining ammunition for his pistolas. Three bullets left, then it would all be down to swords and luck.

"How close are we?" he said.

"If memory serves, the door to the tower should be at the end of this corridor," said Riley.

"Then let's go."

They burst through the door into the tower beyond. There was a spiral staircase that seemed to go on forever. They ran until their lungs burned and their legs went weak, then they were at the top, another corridor and another heavy-looking door barring their way.

"Stand back!" roared Handen. He fired a pistola three times at the door's lock, then gave it an almighty kick. The door flung open, and the escapees ran through, ready for any possible danger. What they hadn't been ready for was absolutely no danger at all. Beyond the doorway was a comfortable room with a cozy-looking fireplace and a four-poster bed. The walls were lined with bookshelves, on which rested hundreds of tomes. In the center of the room, a long and laden dining table held the remnants of a feast. Xharon sat at the head of the table, a look of guilty surprise on her face and a napkin tucked into her collar.

"What the hell are you doing here?" she cried.

Bip frowned. "Rescuing you?" he offered.

Xharon stood bolt upright. "Now let's get one thing straight—I'm a warrior princess, and I don't get rescued! I *do* the rescuing! As a matter of fact, I was bally well on my way to rescue you!"

Handen surveyed the luxurious prison cell. "What kept you?"

Xharon took the stained napkin from her collar and discarded it as though it had never been there. "I was just waiting for the guards to bring the second course," she said. "So I could overpower them… You know."

Azron interrupted. "Look, I hate to be a bore and everything, but I hear guards. Lots of guards. Now might be a good time to skedaddle."

Handen went to the door. In the distance but getting closer, he could hear the heavy tramp of booted feet.

"We have to get out of here. Professor, do you think you could reconfigure the… the…"

"The Do-fer?" said Azron, helpfully.

"Yeah, that."

Riley looked up from the bizarre machine, which was currently emitting a low whirring noise. "I'm already on it. By all that's dynamic, I'm already *working on it*. I'll just need a few minutes."

Handen looked down the corridor. The shouting and the clanking of armor was getting closer. "We may not *have* a few minutes," he said.

"Wait a minute!" demanded Xharon. "What exactly is going on here?"

"We're getting out," replied Bip.

"Oh, no you don't," said Xharon. "I told you. I'm not going to be rescued like some helpless damsel. It's not my style."

Bip sighed wearily, then reached into Riley's bag. He pulled out Xharon's axes and offered them to her. "How about you think of it as assisting us with our escape?"

Xharon took the axes and weighed them thoughtfully. "Yes. Yes, that sounds more like me. Okay, let's do it!"

They went out into the corridor where the shadows of the advancing guards could be seen ascending the spiral staircase. Bip drew Brian, holding it in the defensive stance he had been taught so long ago. Xharon began twirling her axes in a complex streak of metal. Azron splayed his limbs, ready to duck and dive.

"Right," said Handen. "I suppose this is where we find out what we're made of."

Azron gulped. "I'd rather leave that a comfortable mystery if it's all the same to you," he said.

"Just a few more minutes and it should be fine," said Riley, with annoying chirpiness.

Handen drew his bastard sword as the Imperial guardsmen came into sight. There were a dozen of them, some armed with rifles, some with an impressive and lethal-looking array of heavy blades.

"Won't be a moment," said Riley. Behind them the buzzing sound grew in intensity, harmonized by a high-pitched whistle.

The guardsmen armed with rifles took on a firing formation, while the swordsmen flanked the corridor, advancing all the while. Handen recognized the formation—they were going to be driven into the center of the corridor by the swordsmen, then cut down by rifle fire. He breathed hard, prepared to go down fighting.

Bip gripped his weapon, uncomfortably aware that they were trapped and outnumbered. Worse still, he wondered if he would even be able to use the blade—he still wasn't comfortable with the idea of fighting or killing. He looked over at Xharon, who, despite the odds against them, was grinning confidently. He wondered if he'd ever understand her.

"Not long now. By all that's immediate, *we haven't long!*"

The buzzing sound increased; the whistling gave way to a low hum that ascended with electric fury. Ahead of them, the guards readied their rifles, the order to fire was given, and a split second later, there was the terrible flash of ignited powder.

Bip closed his eyes as the machine reached a filthy crescendo of noise.

He opened his eyes. The world was how it had been, except still and distant, as though he were viewing it from under water. He crossed his eyes at the bullet that was advancing, with snail-pace slowness, toward his nose. He tried to open his mouth to remark on this odd phenomenon, but couldn't. Then, delicately sketched with a thousand thin lines of darkness, the world began to waver, and finally disappeared.

Bip felt the uncomfortable nagging sensation of the dimensional traveler, that he was everywhere at once. It felt as though every cell in his body had gone cock-eyed or as though a billion people were whispering in his ear at the same time. He had a brief moment to reflect that he felt not just weightless, but massless, as though he were nothing at all. He opened his mouth to scream and scream and scream, but here, in these corridors of the universes, these dimensionless crawlspaces of anti-stuff, there was nothing to scream at.

There was nothing…and then there was the workshop.

"Ooorghk?" said Bip.

"Errink!" agreed Azron.

The room spun wildly, like a hard night's drinking catching up all at once. Bip fought the urge to vomit and closed his eyes until the swaying stopped.

"What...was...that?" he panted.

Professor DeChambre seemed mostly unaffected by the transition. In fact, he still seemed quite chirpy. "That, my young friend, was the sensation of temporarily being unfixed to a specific dimension. I call it 'Transgressing Immediate Reality-lag.'"

Azron groaned. "Thank you. I feel so much better now that I know what it's called."

Xharon burped in seasick kind of way. "It's horrible," she moaned.

Riley shrugged. "Well, I suppose you get used to it."

Handen looked around the workshop. "We made it, then. We escaped. Well done, Professor."

Riley blushed. "It was nothing, really."

"Hang on a minute," said Bip. "What do you mean 'transgressing immediate reality'?"

Riley cleared his throat. "Well, it's quite straightforward, really—"

"I bet it's not..." mumbled Azron.

"*Quite straightforward*. We, each of us, perceive only a small number of the dimensions we exist in, and those we do not exist in, even though they may, in theory, constantly surround us, we may never experience at all. The reason that we, as dimensional residents, don't all bleed into the wrong dimensions is because of a sort of universal surface tension, a sort of static field that entraps specific and, theoretically, *relevant* frequencies. By disrupting our own frequencies in the immediate perceivable dimension—in this partic-ular incidence, space/time—we were able to momentarily separate ourselves from that particular 'surface tension' and reposition ourselves in the space/time dimension by traveling through a subspace plane—effectively 'lifting off' and 'touching down' in a different part of the same dimension. While we are free-floating, as I like to call it, the entire dimensional frequency range is available for reading through the Do-fer; then it's just a simple matter of finding the desired part of the desired frequency and 'receiving' ourselves into it..."

The doomsayers stared with equally glazed eyes.

Riley faltered. "Umm... We were moving outside dimensional space. Think of it as a secret passageway, by all that's mysterious, or a shortcut between different places. A way to get from A to D without necessarily passing B and C."

Azron stared owlishly. "So…magic, then?"

Riley flustered. "Well, no—"

"Magic it is, then!" said Azron, clapping his hands together with an air of finality. "Why didn't you just say so?"

Riley opened his mouth to argue. Handen interrupted him.

"The fact is, it worked, and we're all safe. For now."

Bip sighed. "I suppose it's only a matter of time before the Emperor comes looking for us, yes?"

"Yes."

"So we'll have to go on the run again, yes?"

"Yes."

The Kaneqian sighed heavily again. "I was so looking forward to staying in the same place for a few days."

"Cheer up, guv," said Azron. "You could have been spending the rest of your short life being eaten by a monster."

Bip considered the point. It did not brighten his mood.

"But what about the astral disaster?" said Xharon. "Shouldn't we be trying to do something?"

Handen gave a noncommittal shrug. "I hate to say it, but the ball is in Draegul's court now. If I'm right, he's had a thousand or so years to think of a way to protect Bersch. If he hasn't come up with something by now, he never will. Our work here is done."

"Then why doesn't it feel as though we've won?" said Xharon.

Handen grinned. "It's not about winning, Xharon. It's about saving the world, which we've done everything in our power to do. It's up to Draegul now—he's the only one with the resources to blow this nuclear meteor out of the sky, right, Professor?"

Riley, who had been tinkering absent-mindedly with the Do-fer, looked up. "Oh, yes," he said. "If anyone could create a weapon large enough, it's Draegul. He has the money and know-how, and he has certainly had the time to work on the problem."

Xharon sighed in frustration. "It still doesn't feel right. What do you think, Bip?"

The princess waited for an answer. There wasn't one.

"Bip?"

Bip was staring into space, a look of abject horror in his eyes.

"What's the matter?"

The Kaneqian had been thinking—thinking about Mr. Random and his conversations with Ted, and suddenly it had hit him. "Professor?" he said, his voice barely more than a murmur.

"Yes?"

"How powerful would a weapon have to be to safely destroy a cluster of death-bombs roughly the size of the moon?"

Riley frowned. "Well, I suppose the only safe way to destroy it would be to completely vaporize it. A weapon of that magnitude would have to be very powerful indeed. Powerful enough to crack the world if they're not careful, I'll warrant."

"Powerful enough to shoot the stars from the sky?"

Riley laughed. "Well, I doubt anyone would go as far as to make a weapon *that* powerful. It would be ludicrous. Only a madman would…" The professor paused, a look of horrific realization overtaking his face.

"We were never supposed to stop the astral disaster," whispered Bip.

"What do you mean?" demanded Handen.

"The astral disaster was never the real threat. The astral disaster was the cure, not the condition. The real threat was an immortal all-powerful megalomaniac psychopath with the means to blow up worlds!"

Handen stared hard at the Kaneqian. "How do you know this?"

"It's the Discordance," breathed Bip. "Draegul is under the direct influence of the Discordance. For a thousand years he has been. They don't want to destroy just one planet—they want to destroy hundreds!"

Handen's eyes widened. "Of course! A trigger-happy idiot with a gun that big could unwittingly kick-start an interstellar war! It's not the world we have to worry about saving—it's the entire goddamned galaxy!"

Xharon's eyes lit up, and a dangerous smile curved her lips. "Brilliant!"

___________________________

6

## What Now?

___________________________

Thousands of miles away, in the uncharted heart of Ghulbra
Forest, the fifty-third centurial meeting of "Immortals Anonymous" was well under way.

The meetings had, of course, been Tanya's idea. It was intended as
a way for people facing the emotional problems born of immortality
to meet up with others in the same situation, share their burdens, and
generally have a bit of a natter. She had called it a "support group,"
and immortals attended from all over the world, though mainly as a
way to relieve their stupendous boredom rather than to derive any
comfort the meetings might offer.

The IA meetings were unfailingly formulaic. They began with the
group members sitting in a circle and talking about their respective
problems and how they coped with them. Then they did a series of
positive-thinking and group trust exercises—again, Tanya's idea—
until finally they opened a bottle of wine, and a few more bottles of
wine, until the meeting was called to an end with the entire group
ceremoniously urinating into the fountain of youth.

Tanya had really made an effort this year, decorating the small
cave-like dwelling with several hundred doilies and doily-esque fabri-
cations. It took a very long time to fabricate a decent doily in the

middle of the ancient forest with no access to any kind of the usual materials, but Tanya had had plenty of time on her hands and made a serviceable effort with weeds and bits of bark.

So now, surrounded by fervently organic doilies, Immortals Anonymous sat in a circle, linking hands and chanting one of the various chants Tanya had made up in her considerable spare time.

*"Living forever, coping together! Living forever, coping together!"*

The chant finished as it always did, with each participant stopping whenever the embarrassment became too much to bear, falling silent like a domino rally of anti-crescendo until only Tanya was left, chanting by herself until everybody started to feel really uncomfortable.

"Right, then!" she said, after she had finished her solo chant. "Who wants to start?"

The immortals looked at each other. No one wanted to start.

"How about you, Dathbert?" she said, singling out a young and bookish-looking man. "You're fairly new to the group—why don't you start us all off by telling us a bit about yourself?"

Dathbert winced. Tanya's condescending chirpiness brought back uncomfortable recollections of boarding school and campground activities coordinators. He stood up and cleared his throat. "My name is Dathbert, and I am an immortal."

"Hallo, Dathbert," the group chorused with all the enthusiasm of a funeral dirge.

Dathbert continued. "It's been five hundred years since I first drank from the fountain—"

"Pah!" interrupted one of the immortals. His name was Cully, and he had had the misfortune to drink from the fountain of youth when he was a very old man, believing that the fountain would reverse the ageing process rather than just halting it. Consequently, due to what he perceived to be a flagrant case of false advertising, he had run through the previous few millennia in a body racked with arthritis and an unstable digestive system. Justifiably, he was a very cranky old man.

Dathbert continued, unfazed by the interruption. "As I was saying, it's been five hundred years. I've done a bit of traveling, a lot of thinking—you know. Generally I've just been taking it one day at a time."

Dathbert sat down to half-hearted applause led by Tanya.

"Smashing, Dathbert, really. You're amongst friends, you know—you can cry if you want to."

"I don't want to cry."

"Don't feel you have to bottle it up—let it all out if you want."

"I don't want to cry."

"Because we're here for you, you know that, don't you?"

"*God damn it, I don't want to cry!*"

Tanya smiled. If she was in anyway offended by Dathbert's tone, she didn't let it show. "I think we can all learn from Dathbert's strength and wisdom," she said, nodding in what she thought was a deep and understanding way.

"Strength? Wisdom?" screeched Cully. "What's so wise about taking it one day at a time? What else *can* you do, really?"

There was a murmur of approval from the group.

"I bin' taking it one day at a time for nigh on three thousand years, and it ain't done me no good!"

The group murmured again.

Tanya smiled a patient smile. "Please, Cully—if you want to talk, you have to raise your hand first."

"Don't tell me to raise my hand, you young snipper! I've lived more lives than most can dream! I've seen things you people wouldn't believe! Attack ships on fire off the coast of Arglebaya! Torch-light glittering in the dark near the gates of Nebbela…"

Dathbert sighed. The speech was a familiar one. "And all these moments will be lost in time?" he offered.

"Yer' damn right!" screeched Cully. "Lost in time like… like…like a fart in a whirlwind."

"If you're quite finished!" said Tanya, frowning and putting her hands on her hips, her patience finally having reached its end. "Look, what's the point of a bloody support group if we're not going to bloody support each other?"

Cully shrugged. "Frankly, I don't see why we should *bother* supportin' each other. I mean, it's not as if we can go home and kill ourselves, is it? More's the pity…"

"Well, that's not strictly true…" interrupted another immortal. Her name was Margo, and being a Woman of a Certain Age for a practical eternity hadn't done much good for her positive outlook. "Look at Longbert."

Cully frowned and glanced around the assembled immortals. "Where is ol' Longbert?" he said.

"Well, that's just it," said Margo. "He isn't here; he's buried himself alive. He said he was just going to lie down and be quiet until his body took the hint and died."

Cully rolled his eyes thoughtfully. "That's not a bad idea."

Tanya gaped in horror. "Shouldn't we go and dig him up?" she cried.

"Are you kidding?" said Margo. "He'd be furious!"

Cully chuckled. "Good 'ol Longbert."

Tanya's temper frayed again. "Well, if that's your attitude, why do you lot bother to come here at all?"

"Bored."

"Boredom."

"Just bored, really."

Tanya looked about, her shoulders slumping as the anger slowly faded from her eyes. "I'll just open the wine then, shall I?"

The suggestion was met by enthusiastic approval.

"And then we can go and pee in that bloody fountain," added Cully.

There was a patter of genuine spontaneous applause, something that rarely happened at the IA meetings.

---

"SO WHAT NOW?" said Azron.

It was a fair question. It was a *good* question. The trouble was, it wasn't a particularly helpful one.

The doomsayers sat about the workshop, each of them toiling with their own thoughts.

"We could just kill him…if he wasn't an immortal," said Handen.

"And if he wasn't surrounded by his own personal army," added Azron.

Handen nodded distractedly.

"Why don't we just tell everybody? Tell the people?" said Xharon. "I'm sure if the word got around, there'd be some sort of uprising, wouldn't you say?"

Handen shook his head. "We hardly have the time to manufacture a rebellion, and besides, would people want to listen? What do they care if their leader starts taking pot shots at outer space? And who would have the nerve to stand up to him if they did?"

The group nodded its agreement. Draegul was feared by all, and with good reason.

"If I may interject, I think that sabotaging the weapon may be the most prudent course of action," said Riley, looking up from the device he was fiddling with.

Handen nodded again. "A good plan, with only two faults. One, we don't know where the weapon is or what it looks like, and two, we would still need it to avert the astral disaster."

"We could fire it ourselves then destroy it afterward?" suggested Xharon.

"We could," said Handen, "but we'd still have to find it. Professor, do you have any clue as to where this weapon might be hidden?"

Riley shook his head. "The information would be extremely classified, of that I've no doubt."

Bip raised his head. "Surely a plot to build an instrument designed to avert a world-destroying disaster would have caused some sort of stir? I mean, it doesn't seem like something you could keep a secret for very long."

Professor DeChambre shrugged. "For all we know, the instrument could be the size of a potato and Draegul puts it under his pillow at night."

"Are you sure you haven't heard anything at the palace, Professor?"

Riley shook his head. "There have been whisperings about something called Operation Deadwaker, but from what I can gather, it's some sort of archaeological project, by all that's immaterial."

"Damn," muttered Handen. "If only there was some way we could find out what Draegul has been working on."

"There *is* his study," said Riley. "He keeps detailed files of his projects there, or so I've heard."

"Excellent!" snapped Handen. "Where is his study?"

"Back at Dawncastle."

"Damn."

Bip sighed. "There's no way we could get back into Dawncastle. Not unless we had some sort of…" Bip paused and looked at the Do-fer. "We could use the professor's device!" he said. "Just dimension hop in and out again without anyone being the wiser!"

Professor DeChambre nodded. "You could certainly use it to get into Dawncastle; after all, I have the co-ordinate frequencies committed to the Do-fer's memory. Alas, though, I would not be able to pinpoint the exact location frequency of the study, or even the relevant floor. It would be far too specific. The only way would be to actually go into the study, record the frequency, then come back here, which, since no one may enter Draegul's study and we won't be able to get into Dawncastle without being killed, would be impossible."

"But we *could* get into Dawncastle?" asked Bip.

"Oh yes, by all that's easy-peasy—it would be a doddle."

"Well there we go, then!" cried Bip. "All we need to do is get into Dawncastle, break into the study, and steal Draegul's files!"

"You make it sound very simple," said Handen doubtfully.

"And it will be! At least it will be to a master thief!"

The group turned to look at Azron. He had been absentmindedly rolling a cigarette throughout the entire discussion. "What?" he said.

"I was just saying," said Bip, "that sneaking through Dawncastle and into a heavily secured room would be no problem for a genuine Diamond Geezer (1st Class) of the Port Town Union of Dodgy Fellows!"

Azron paled. "Oh, right," he said. "Yeah, well, normally that wouldn't be a problem at all, no worries, but right now I'm…erm…on a break, see?"

Handen frowned. "The fate of the world hangs in the balance and you're on a break?"

Azron shrugged and rolled his eyes. "Union rules," he said. "What can you do?"

"Come on, Azron," Bip said. "Stop mucking about. This is *serious!*"

Azron sighed heavily. "You're right, this is serious," he said. He took a deep breath then slowly let it out. "The truth is, I'm not a Diamond Geezer (1st Class). I'm not even a tin-badge thugling."

"What?"

"I lied. I never even made it into the Union—they disqualified me because I forgot to steal the pencil after I filled in my application form."

"But what about your certificate?" cried Bip.

"Not mine," said Azron miserably. "I stole it off some geezer and pasted my own details onto it."

"So you're not a master thief, then?" asked Handen.

"I'm not a master *anything*, mate," said Azron. "Except maybe a master cock-up."

Bip tutted under his breath. "I'm really disappointed in you, Azron. All this time I thought you were a sneaky, conniving deviant with the morals of an insect, and it turns out that you were lying all along."

"Yeah, well, now you know. And that's why I can't go into Dawncastle."

"Wait a minute," said Xharon. "Didn't you say that you stole that certificate?"

"Yeah?"

"It wasn't just lying around and you picked it up?"

"Heck, no," said Azron, crossly. "Give me *some* credit. I took it out of his house, didn't I?"

"And whereabouts did he keep this certificate?"

"The same place any good thief would keep it," said Azron, as though it were obvious. "In his socks."

"What, in his sock drawer?"

"Nah, in the socks he was wearing!"

Xharon grinned and shook her head. "Are you telling me that you stole a treasured possession from a master thief, from inside his socks, no less, and that doesn't entitle you to call yourself a Diamond Geezer of any class?"

Azron frowned. "Never thought of it like that," he muttered.

"Yes," said Bip, "and what about all the things you've stolen from *us* that we didn't know about?"

Azron shifted his gaze nervously about. "I didn't think you realized," he said.

"I didn't, really," said Bip. "I just assumed."

"Oh. Fair enough."

"So, how about it?" said Handen.

Azron looked up questioningly.

"Why don't you prove to us and to the world that you don't need a union or a certificate? Why don't you prove that you can be a master thief on your own terms?"

Azron stood up and straightened his long coat. "I'll need some things," he said.

Bip grinned and clapped him on the back. "I knew you wouldn't let us down!"

The tall thief smiled a sly smile. "Steady on, guv—how do you know I'm not going to just take all your stuff and run away?"

Bip's grin dropped.

"Just kidding," said Azron. "Stealing directly from the Emperor? I'll be a legend, mate, *a legend!* Those union chumps'll *eat* their stupid application form!"

---

CELIA DOOM BREATHED hot air into her hands and rubbed them together vigorously. It was a cold evening, and the red robes of the Cult of the Doomsayer didn't offer much in the way of insulation. She looked at the silhouette of Dawncastle, framed through the bars of the outer wall's high and ornately spiked gates. Without the sunlight, Dawncastle relied on its internal lighting for illumination, and the building pulsed dimly with the glow of a thousand electric lights. Celia looked up at the night sky, free of clouds and chilly with starlight. Though the moon was bright and gibbous, it was upstaged by the silvery shine of the new star, the harbinger of destruction that the astrologers had named Tracy.

Celia sighed and turned back to the rest of the doomsayers. There weren't that many left. After all, the purpose of the Cult of the Doomsayer had been to warn the people of the impending end of the world. Now that the end of the world was here, it seemed a bit pointless to warn people about it.

"Right," said Celia. "Does everybody know why we're here?"

A cultist put up his hand. His name was Nigel, and he was a professional cultist, having previously been a long-serving member of both the Suicide Cult of Hope and Wisdom and the Deathbringer Cult of Peace and Love. He was very keen, and annoying with it.

Celia sighed. "Yes, Nigel?"

"*I* don't know why we're here."

The rest of the cultists groaned, and Celia rolled her eyes skyward. "All right, for the benefit of Nigel, I'll go through it one last time. Pay attention, Nigel. The Prophet of the Ancient Ones has asked me personally to cause a distracting disturbance at this gate in precisely five minutes. Okay?"

Nigel raised his hand again. Celia sighed. "Yes, Nigel?"

"But *why*? I mean, everybody knows it's the end of the world, but everything's under control—Emperor Draegul said so himself! That's why he let us out of jail, isn't it? Because we were right, and he was very grateful for our help?"

Celia raised a hand to her eyes. Nigel was right, of course, but that wasn't the point.

"Look, Nigel, what's the point of being in a doomsday cult if you're just going to stop when someone tells you that everything's fine? We're in it for the *long haul,* people, so let's get our act together! The Prophet has endowed us with a mission, and we will carry out his will to the bitter end! Verily!"

The cultists cheered. *This* was the sort of unthinking and blind zeal that you signed up to a cult for.

"Right!" roared Celia. "All together, now!"

The group drew in a collective breath, each recalling the chant they had rehearsed earlier in the day.

"*Two, four, six, eight! We will wait outside your gate!*"

"*Six, seven, eight, nine! Right until the end of time!*"

As one, the cultists looked up at the silver star in the sky, fat and twinkling and growing a little bigger all the time.

*"Which should only be a couple of days, really, when you think about it!"*

It wasn't long before a Regulator sidled toward the group. He was new to the job, just out of training, hence the fact that he sidled rather than marched and asked questions first rather than shooting.

He cleared his throat and, in a way that rookies are wont to do, recalled confrontational protocol to the letter.

"Ello, 'ello, 'ello. What's all this, then?"

Celia left the other cultists to chant on their own.

"It's a protest," she explained.

The rookie frowned. "What are you protesting against?"

Celia shrugged. "This and that."

"This and that? A bit vague, isn't it?"

"Yeah, well, we're cultists, aren't we? We're not renowned for our clarity of purpose…"

"I resent that!" called Nigel. "I'll have you know that I've been in plenty of cults with a very distinct clarity of purpose!"

Celia rolled her eyes and winked at the Regulator. "You see what I have to put up with? Don't let anyone tell you that being the leader of a cult is easy."

The Regulator blinked in puzzlement. Somehow he'd envisioned the confrontation taking quite a different route to what it was now.

Celia turned her full attention on Nigel. "Oh, yeah? And what was so distinctive about that suicide cult you were in, then?"

"It was our firm belief that the only way to achieve worldwide peace was if everybody killed themselves so their souls could be taken into the mothership and flown to a utopia in space, of course."

"Oh? And how come *you* didn't kill yourself, then?"

Nigel shuffled his feet. "I was ill that day."

"Too ill to kill yourself?"

"Yes. Very bad cold."

Celia put her hands on her hips. "Call yourself a cultist? You listen to me, Nigel; I've had more bizarre visions and spouted more prophecies than most sane people could even think of in a lifetime! I've verily'd and lo'd 'til my face exploded, and what have you done, eh? You sat in your stupid suicide cult and took a day off for the grand finale! So don't come the clever bugger with me, all right? Or I'll pull off your nose and shove it up a cat's bum! Right?"

"Yes, miss."

"That's better."

Celia turned back to the Regulator and smiled sweetly. "Now then, officer, was there something I could help you with?"

The rookie considered his options. He was on his own, surrounded by people who were quite definitely mad. He knew that the protocol called for him to signal for backup, but frankly he didn't like to think of what might happen before they arrived. He was fond of cats…but not that fond. It was then that he made a decision that would come more easily the more experience he gained in life. He decided to sod the protocol and make a run for it.

Celia watched him leave. "I wonder what he wanted?" she muttered, and turned back to the chanting.

"*Two, four, six, eight! We will stand outside your gate!*"

"*Six, seven, eight, nine! Chanting annoying numerical rhymes!*"

Celia watched as the bright searchlights atop Dawncastle's inner walls began to swing toward the protestors. The distraction was working.

---

AZRON LIT A CIGARETTE. It was a difficult thing to do when you were hanging upside down by your knees, but he did it anyway. He took a few puffs and had a bit of a think. The Do-fer had worked like a charm, transporting him to just outside the gates of Dawncastle. There had been a moment of blind panic while he had searched for a convenient shadow to conceal himself in, but once he'd found the darkness, he might as well have been invisible.

He was a champion lurker, so that was what he did for a while—he lurked, looking about and assessing the situation until Dawncastle's searchlights had swung toward a disturbance at the main gate. Acknowledging his cue, Azron had pulled the rope and grapnel from under his long coat and swung it soundlessly into the air above him.

The grapnel had been coated with heavy rubber, so much so that he'd hardly heard it as it connected with the support girder above him. He'd shimmied up the rope and balanced on the girder, pulling the rest of the rope up behind him, then repeated the action until the guards and walls below him were far away, hushed and hidden from his higher perspective.

As the thief had scaled farther and farther up the palace walls, the grapnel had eventually become useless; most of the supports he had relied on for purchase had become too narrow at the tapering tip of the tower. He had coiled the rope and replaced it under his long coat, pulling out, instead, four rubber suction cups, which he attached to his knees and hands. Then, like a spindly spider in the night, he had crawled up the glass panels of Dawncastle, making soft *schluppschlupp* noises in the still air.

IN THE UPPER levels of Dawncastle, Maggot finally made his way to bed. It had been an eventful day, and he was glad to get back to his quarters. Tomorrow would begin another terrifying schedule of staying one step ahead of the mad Emperor. He poured himself a large shot of whisky, drank it in a single gulp, and stared out of the night-darkened window at the distant lights of the city. He caught the eye of his reflection and took in the long white beard and receding hairline. He had aged badly since becoming head of Whimstaff. To think he had only been twenty-eight when he had first signed on for the post...

Maggot froze suddenly. His reflection, old and tired as it was, seemed to change, becoming momentarily sharper and more sinister. Maggot squinted his eyes shut and opened them again. His reflection was once again looking its old tired self.

"I'm finally going mad," muttered Maggot. "Thank goodness. Maybe they'll take me away to a nice soft room with white sheets, oh yes."

He lay down on his bed and closed his eyes, then sat bolt upright. On the edge of hearing, he could make out a faint sound that went something like *schluppschlupp schluppschlupp.*

He shook his head wearily, thinking his ears were playing tricks on him and putting it down to the stress of the day. He gradually fell into a deep sleep, mildly tainted with nightmares of the improbably vicious punishments Draegul had in store for him if he were to sleep in tomorrow.

***

AZRON PUFFED the last of the cigarette and heaved himself upright again. It had been a close call with the old man, and he was almost sure he had been seen, but so far, no alarm bells had sounded. He began to make his way up the glass walls again, reflecting not for the first time that, while a glass palace might look very pretty, it was also an open invitation for a thief with the right equipment and a bit of imagination.

After what seemed like a long time, he reached the very top of Dawncastle, stained pallid silver by the light of the deadly new star. He took a moment to breathe in the thin air and enjoy the view. The distant lights of the city were far below him now, and he felt momentarily dizzy. It was like floating above a galaxy...

Taking his eyes away from the ghostly spectacle of Argustin by night, he looked down through the thick glass underneath him. It was dark below, but he continued staring until his eyes adjusted. A hint of a desk made itself apparent, and the ghostly edges of a room surrounded by bookcases. Azron grinned. It was as he had suspected —if you were going to keep something very important in the safest place possible, you'd put it at the very top of the tallest tower. Directly beneath him was Draegul's study.

He crawled around the roof for a while, searching for a place where the glass was thinner. Sure enough, there was a skylight, the glass only a few millimeters thick.

Azron placed a suction cup on the thinner glass and took a wickedly sharp blade from his coat. The blade was pure diamond, part of a machine designed to slice through metal, and Azron had no trouble cutting a circle in the skylight big enough to slide through. He gently lifted the circle of glass free and put it by his side. Then he took the grapnel from his coat and secured it on a nearby girder. He let the rope dangle into the dark study, where it swung quietly, like a hesitant snake. Azron slid down noiselessly, a dark silhouette against the pale night sky, which was swallowed slowly and completely by the darkness of the room. He reached the floor and spread his limbs, delicately distributing his weight so that he kept low and moved silently. Immersed in blackness, he tuned his senses in to the room around him.

That was when he heard the snoring.

He stood there, rigid with the unique hybrid of fear and excitement known only to the cat burglar. He waited. Waited…

Finally, his eyes adjusted completely so that he could make out most of the room around him. He turned his head toward the sound of the snoring and detected the almost invisible sheen of black armor. There was a guard in here, something Azron had not expected. Thankfully, though, the guard wasn't very good—he was propped against the wall, having dozed off on his feet.

Azron tiptoed up to the sleeping guard, creeping so smoothly that no carpet scuff or creaking floorboard gave cause for alarm. Then, as soundlessly as ink spreading, he reached into his coat and brought out a glass phial. He covered his nose with one hand and uncorked the vial with the other. He held the vial under the guard's nose for only a second before he slumped to the floor unconscious, with a clanking of armor that might as well have been an avalanche in the nighttime quiet.

Smirking in the shadows, Azron corked the vial and returned it to the recesses of his coat. Then he turned his attention to the rest of the room. He could make out several desks and shelves, each laden with paperwork that might or might not have been important. An ordinary man might have lit a lamp and begun rummaging through them but, union or not, Azron was no ordinary man. He understood the secret to hiding valuables, and that was this: you didn't hide them in the most secure place because that was the first place a thief would look. You hid them somewhere a thief wouldn't *bother* looking. And because Azron also understood a little something about Draegul, he knew that all of the obvious strongboxes and safes were likely to contain nothing more than cunning acid traps or spring-loaded poison darts.

He scanned the room again, noting all the places you'd expect valuables to be hidden and ignoring them until, eventually, his gaze fell upon a silver tea tray. It was certainly not unfeasible that the Emperor would take tea in his study, and the sandwich crusts and biscuit crumbs gave testament to this being the case. However, Azron thought it unlikely that a man of Draegul's stature would walk into his study in the morning to find lunchtime debris from the previous day. Azron walked over to the tray and spent a good few minutes looking at things. Then he reached over to a coffee urn, opened it, and tipped it upside down.

A large rolled-up wad of papers fell onto the floor. Azron grinned like a cat and snatched them up. He couldn't make out any of the lettering in the dark and wondered if he should risk lighting a match. That was when he heard footsteps.

An ordinary thief might have frozen, waiting to see whether the steps were coming in his or her direction, but Azron was no ordinary thief. One of his greatest talents, and one he believed that no master thief could survive without, was his ability to intuitively know when to run like hell. He stuffed the papers in his coat and pulled out the Do-fer in their stead. It was already preset to the professor's laboratory, and all he had to do was punch in the activation sequence of the keypad. He keyed in the code and waited for the inevitable nausea of immediate reality transgression.

He had a brief moment of anxiety whether he had retrieved the relevant file, but dismissed it. If he had got the wrong documents—and he doubted he had—there would be no chance of returning once the break-in was discovered, so there seemed little point in worrying about it. The world began to slow around him just as the door to the study opened...

DRAEGUL UNLOCKED the door to his study with the heavy iron key that he wore around his neck at all times. It was far too late—or indeed too early—to be awake, but Draegul had been unable to sleep. The whispering in his ears had been louder and more urgent than ever. Finally, he had crawled out of bed and wandered the palace, finding himself drawn to the study.

He shivered in the chill of the upper corridors and cursed the decision to leave his chambers, where warm sheets and warmer women were readily available. Perhaps it was simply the excitement of the day that had kept him awake. Handen the adventurer had been Draegul's first real challenge in centuries, and when he had found out about his escape, the Emperor had been secretly glad. He would enjoy hunting the bastard down and having him publicly tortured.

He was confident that it would not be long before the escapees were back in his custody; the city had been put in lockdown, and the already extensive guard on the outer walls had been tripled. There was no hope of anyone leaving Argustin…at least, not in one piece.

Draegul pushed against the study door and frowned when it jammed. He pushed again, harder and harder until the heavy object slid out of the way. He hurried into the room and turned on the light. The heavy object turned out to be an unconscious guard, and by the way bubbles of spit were frothing from beneath his helmet, it was quite obvious he had been drugged.

Draegul felt the sickness of dread in his stomach, and his gaze went immediately to his tea tray. The coffee urn that had served as his hiding place was on the floor, overturned and empty. Lying by the urn on the otherwise immaculate carpet was an object that shouldn't have been there. The Emperor bent down to see it. It was a cigarette butt, still smoldering. Draegul grinned, but it was a grin with a razor edge. It was a grin that said, "Before this day is through, many, many people will die."

The whispering in his ears reached a raging crescendo.

---

RILEY LOOKED AT THE FILE, shuffling and sorting the papers, his brow becoming increasingly drawn with concern.

"This can't be right. You must have the wrong files!"

Azron shook his head. "Believe me, mate, I definitely had the right room, and this document was definitely never meant to fall into the wrong hands. If this isn't the paperwork you're looking for, I'll smoke my hat."

Riley shook his head again. "This is all about Operation Dead-waker. It's just a series of reports from archaeological digs in the Nastren desert."

Handen picked up one of the reports. "The pyramids?" he asked.

Riley looked through a few more of the reports. "Yes. All of them."

"Why would he be so interested in the pyramids?" said Bip.

"And why keep it such a secret?" Xharon added.

"He's looking for something," Handen murmured. "He's been digging up those pyramids for years, and according to these figures, it's costing him a pretty penny too…"

"Never met a penny that wasn't pretty," said Azron, smiling.

"What could be so important to him that he'd spend so much time and money exhuming ancient tombs?"

"Treasure?" suggested Xharon. "Or curiosity, maybe?"

"Or perhaps an ancient weapon left here eons ago by beings from another world?" offered Bip.

The doomsayers paused, each silent as they contemplated what had just been said.

"Just a guess," added Bip.

"Of course!" said Handen. "Maybe the Discordance weren't corrupting Draegul to *build* a weapon, just to *use* one! One that has already been built for them!"

Riley arched his eyebrows. "It would make more sense," he said. "I'm not entirely sure if even the finest scientific minds in Bersch could build a weapon that could safely destroy an astral disaster of this magnitude—by all that's precarious, I couldn't be *certain*. Far safer to have an ace in the hand, as it were, than to gamble blindly."

"Or, as my dad used to say, better to knock someone unconscious than to rely on them being asleep," said Azron.

"Erm…yes. That works, too, I suppose…"

"Let me get this straight," Xharon interjected. "These Discordance chaps are a race of super-beings who want to see the universe descend into absolute chaos and general disharmony, so part of their plan is to influence my uncle, over the course of a thousand years, so that he could eventually discover a weapon that would not only allow him to save his planet from oblivion, but also to destroy the very stars in the sky and inadvertently cause a pointless interstellar war that could kill trillions?"

"Yes?"

"Right. Right. Just making sure I was up to speed. Carry on."

"Okay…"

"Wait a minute!"

"Yes, Xharon?"

"Why don't they just do it themselves?"

Handen sighed. "They exist on a different material plane to our universe—they can't physically affect anything here."

"Then how are they controlling Uncle Tommy?"

"They're not controlling him. They've merely used constant subliminal mental influence to ensure he became an all-powerful megalomaniac with no conscience and a penchant for destroying things."

"So…strictly speaking, this isn't really Uncle Tommy's fault, yes?"

Handen rolled his eyes. "If I told you to shoot a man, it'd be *you* who pulled the trigger, not me. The Discordance can influence things, yes, but they can't turn a decent man into a cold-blooded mass-murderer any more than they could convince a rock to turn into a beaver. We are all accountable for our actions, regardless of influence."

"Oh…" said Xharon. She looked downcast.

Bip put a hand on her shoulder. "Think of it this way; if weakness were the rotten wood in an otherwise fine piece of timber, then the Discordance are the termites that are drawn to that weakness, sooner or later destroying the whole piece of wood."

Xharon frowned. "So you're saying Uncle Tommy's got termites?"

Bip thought for a minute. "Yes. In a manner of speaking."

Azron coughed in the puzzled silence. "I think we've gone a bit off-topic here, chaps. We were talking about the end of the world, yeah?"

"See here!" cried Riley, holding up a sheet of paper from the Deadwaker file. "I think I've found something!"

The others crowded around while Ridley smoothed the paper over his desk.

"Look at this report. Highly unusual, by all accounts, and from the Grand Tutor himself."

Bip read the last report aloud. "A tomb of unprecedented size and unusual material...of unknown origin and estimated to be older than recorded civilization...investigations continue...await further reports."

"Looks as though this is our tomb," said Handen.

"How can we be sure?" said Riley. "What if this is really just one of Draegul's bizarre and expensive hobbies, merely an enthusiastic interest in archaeology? Doesn't anyone else feel we're being awfully presumptuous, here?"

Handen tapped a finger on another section of report, which depicted a few rows of unusual symbols. "Here," he said.

The professor squinted at the lettering, adjusting the lenses on his tentacle-framed glasses. "It is a sample of some hieroglyphics," he said. "I'm afraid I'm not familiar with them."

Handen smiled. "They're hieroglyphics of a sort, but not the kind you'd find on this world..."

"What do you mean?"

"It's a very old form of Standard."

"Standard?"

"Yes. An intergalactic language unification code, designed to be a common ground of communication across hundreds of civilizations."

Riley's eyes shone with awe. "An alien language. Can you decipher it?"

"Not with complete accuracy—it's very old..." explained Handen.

"What do you think it says?"

"Like I said, it's a rough translation, but at a guess, I'd say it seems to be a warning."

"What kind of warning?"

Handen looked down at the writing, eyes narrowed in concentration. "Danger: Aim Away From Face."

The doomsayers looked at one another.

"Well," Azron said eventually, "I think that about clears it up."

Bip grinned. "We've found our weapon."

---

IN THE SILENT folds of dimensional infinity, Mr. Random fumed. He fumed neither quietly nor privately. Part of the charm of living in a different plane of existence is that you can scream as loudly and for as long as you like.

He had been so close, *so close* to destroying the last of the resistance to his plans! It was distressing, it was annoying, it was infuriating, and most of all... it was *insulting*. Yes, insulting. Bip Plunkerton's stubborn refusal to die in the face of innumerable instances of likely doom was mockingly *random*. His sheer defiance of the odds was totally against the order of causality. In a normal, sane, and well-ordered world, Bip would be *dead, dead, dead!* And yet here he was, completely and ridiculously alive!

That was the problem with an ordered universe that ran on specific rules—just when you thought you had it pinned down, it went and did something completely unexpected. That was why you had to rout for the random, that was why you trusted in uncertainty— because order was a *lie*.

The truth was chaos, pure and simple, but the world could be tricky that way. It was like one of those toy pictures that seemed to be a haphazard static of color, but if you let your eyes relax, suddenly there was a 3-D picture of a donkey or something. Mr. Random had always thoroughly despised such pictures. Why degrade the purity of static with a donkey?

Things were meant to be stupid and unexpected and generally badly run—he *knew* tha, knew it in the core of his being. It was his job...no, it was his *duty* to make sure that the ultraverse understood that as well, and stopped—for just one buggering minute— pretending otherwise. And yet this young boy and his *stupid* friends were still alive despite innumerable odds that should, if the world would play by its own rules for just one second, have killed them a thousand times over. The whole affair seemed to suggest that there was some greater cosmic goal or narrative toward which they worked toward, and frankly, Mr. Random found that idea unforgivably offensive.

You can't pretend it is fate; it is luck. There is no quest, only a series of loosely connected events. There can be no story; the universe is not as simple as that.

At least, it shouldn't be…

Mr. Random took a deep breath and watched his shaking hand. His head was beginning to hurt.

*"Tup tup a looba doo,"* he sang. *"Tup tup a looba doo, violently blue, and rabbits too, because that's what we shoe, shoe, great big shoe."*

He felt a little better. The song didn't make any sense, and that was why he liked it. He knew that, secretly, no words made sense, that symbol and reaction were processes unique to an individual, that meaning was merely a pretentious perception, a case of developed semantics. There was no meaning. *Tup tup a loo, no meaning for you.*

He raised a hand to his head again, but the headache was fading. The nonsense ditty had calmed him somewhat. Now he could concentrate. The plan was nearly complete, and it didn't matter if there were people who thought they could stop it. Mr. Random had all the pieces, and he didn't play by the rules. Draegul would find the weapon, as had been decreed a thousand years ago, then Bersch would fulfill its destiny as a bringer of chaos.

Still, it would be better to see Bip's cold, dead eyes. Just to be safe and sure. Just to relax a little. Better to stare into his frightened, dying eyes and be sure of uncertainty.

*Tup tup a loo.*

---

HANDEN SLID the prototype pistolas into the twin holsters at his hips and placed his blade in the scabbard across his back. He had changed back into his leathers, worn hard and rugged by travel and battle. He coiled the bullwhip at his side and touched the hilts of the various daggers and knives concealed about his person. Draegul would come for them soon, and he would come fast and merciless. Handen was prepared.

Azron readied himself too, checking the grappling hook in the folds of his coat, his various vials, picks and tools, and finally his dagger. It was a dagger that was new and unscathed, gleaming and smooth. This was because it was a dagger that had never been used. Azron was a thief—that was all he had ever wanted to be, and he knew how easy it was for some thieves to cross the line between mugging and grievous bodily harm. Those were thieves with no class, union allocated or otherwise. He sighed as he checked the still-sharp edge of the dagger, a weapon bought long ago "just in case." And now it seemed that "just in case" might be just around the corner. Azron wondered whether he were the kind of thief who could steal a life...

Xharon, wearing an outfit that could only serve as a distraction, whirled her axes around her in a hurricane of cutting edges. The kata always made her feel confident. Here, fending off and countering imaginary attacks, she was unbeatable. All too soon, it seemed, she would find out just how unbeatable she was.

Bip had prepared himself too, though the only weapon he wore was Brian, the familiar blade that was still, thankfully, unsullied by combat. He slipped his rucksack onto his back, not realizing how naked he had felt without it. He didn't have much to carry these days. At the end of his journey, he bore none of his original provisions. Gone were the corned-beef sandwiches, re-programmed acorns, and his heavy furs. Gone too was the Infamous Goose; lost to celebration, boredom, and yetis. Gone was his hat, which he missed and regretted exploding. There was little left of the possessions of the boy who had set off from Kaneq what seemed a lifetime ago. Other than his sword, only his spectacles and his rucksack remained. In the prelude to what seemed to be the final leg of his journey, he drew comfort from these items. He rested his hands easily on the pommel of Brian and, though he knew he would probably never use the blade for the purpose Rynford had intended it, he found comfort there too.

Riley fiddled with the Do-fer, readjusting his multi-faceted spectacles while he tried to estimate the trans-dimensional co-ordinates for the location of the pyramid. He didn't have much to work with, since the pyramids were miles away and the only dimensional references he had were very local, but he believed he was making progress. The occasional and positive *blint* and *whirr* from the Do-fer was an encouraging sign.

Eventually the professor looked up from his tinkering. "I believe I have a rough estimate," he said.

"How rough?" asked Handen.

Riley scratched at his brow. "There are so many factors to consider..." he began. "Real space in relation to phase space, estimating frequencies and bandwidths..."

"*How rough?*"

"We could materialize anywhere within a few miles of the pyramid, by all that's inconvenient."

Handen nodded. "All the more reason to get going as soon as possible. Now, is everyone ready?"

The doomsayers nodded in unison. Handen looked at them, his friends and colleagues. It was not the first time he had led them into danger, and he knew that, once again, they would follow. But he had to give them a chance anyway. "Look, by now Draegul knows we have the paperwork; therefore, he knows that we know the whereabouts of the weapon. Chances are he's on his way to the pyramid, most likely with a small army in tow. We have the advantage of the Do-fer, but I can't be sure how long it will be before they catch us up..."

Xharon cocked her head slightly. "Is there something you want to say?" she said, challenging him.

Handen shook his head. "I just want you to be ready for anything. It's all down to us now, and we have to be prepared."

"You mean expect the unexpected?" said Bip.

"I suppose so, yes," Handen conceded.

Azron sighed. "Never liked that phrase," he muttered. "I mean, what if I expect to transform into a cloud of fish-shaped bubbles and float off to the moon? I mean it's just not likely is it? So what's the point of wasting imagination expecting something that's clearly not going to happen?"

There was a long pause, broken by a discreet cough from Xharon.

"That was an unusually pointless and pedantic statement, Azron, even for you."

The thief sighed. "I know. It's just this whole 'bravely facing certain death' thing. It's got me out of sorts, you know."

"I would have thought you would have been used to the idea by now..."

Azron shrugged. "I suppose I'm just stuck in my ways."

"Well," said Bip, "with any luck, this will be the last time we risk our lives for the greater good."

"That's what I'm afraid of..." Azron mumbled.

The conversation was suddenly cut off by a familiar low hum.

"The Do-fer is ready," cried Professor Riley. "Prepare yourselves."

"You're absolutely sure this will get us to the pyramids?" asked Bip.

"The odds are very nearly almost likely," said Riley.

"Oh...good?"

"Remember," said Handen. "It's hot where we're going, so be prepared for the sudden climate change."

Bip nodded absent-mindedly, concentrating on the growing whistle of the Do-fer and preparing himself for the unpleasantness of immediate reality transgression lag. He just had time to register that something didn't quite feel right when the world slowed down around him...

Before him, as tiny black lines began to etch their way across his vision, he caught a brief glimpse of a metal smirk.

---

MR. RANDOM WATCHED in fascination as the Do-fer began to work. Unlike the people of Bersch, Random didn't need special equipment to see and surf the dimensional folds, but it was interesting to see how the machine suddenly bent the universe around itself, propelling its operators into the insulating ether around the realities. The device was a clear advantage that would see the doomsayers arrive in the desert a day or so ahead of Draegul's forces. That was, if the device worked *correctly*...

Focusing on the bending lines of reality around him, Mr. Random reached out and plucked a few like the strings of a brilliant and alien harp. Ironically, what he was about to do was a feat that would have been beyond his powers if not for the aid of the professor's machine. Random, as with all of the Discordance, had only limited influence in Bersch's dimensional plane, but now, strictly speaking, Bip and his companions were no longer in that dimension—they were a hair's breadth outside it, and that made all the difference.

The Discordant chuckled to himself as he plucked haphazardly at the visible frequencies around him, the quantum strings of reality. He had no idea where the doomsayers would end up, but it would be a time and place far away from the pyramids of Nastre.

# 7

# Destiny and Self-Perpetuating Time Loops

Before he had even had a chance to recover from the disorientation and nausea, the cold hit him like a punch in the stomach. He doubled over, wrapping his arms around himself and shivering. He peered around desperately while trying in vain to shield his face from the stinging wind. The world was white around him, and for a terrifying moment, Bip was sure he had gone blind. He jerked around as a hand grabbed his shoulder and came face to face with Azron, who bore the expression of complete and utter seriousness worn by those who are unreasonably cold.

"This is not the bloody desert!" shouted the thief, barely controlling the chattering of his teeth. "I realize that's stating the obvious, but I thought it was worth pointing out. In fact, it's worth saying again; *this is not the bloody desert!* In fact, it's the complete bloody opposite!"

Before he could reply, Bip felt another hand on his shoulder. He turned to see Handen and Riley emerge from the snowstorm.

"Technically, that's bot true!" Shouted Riley. "You see, a desert doesn't necessarily–"

"There's been a mistake!" Handen interrupted. "Wherever this is, I think it's safe to say it's not where we wanted to go."

Bip nodded dumbly. "Yes, Azron was just saying…"

Riley looked down at the machine. "This makes no sense. By all that's preposterous, *this makes no sense!* How could my calculations have been so drastically askew?"

Bip had a recollection of the sudden sheen of a metal grin. "Random," he muttered.

"What?" cried Azron.

"Nothing, it doesn't matter now. Where's Xharon?"

"H-h-h-h…" came a voice from behind them.

They turned to see Xharon, eyes wide with shock, clinging desperately to an over-exposed body that was rapidly turning blue.

"H-he-heh…here!"

Handen quickly removed his outer coat and wrapped it around the girl's shoulders.

"You see?" said Riley. "This is why you shouldn't wander around in your knickers!"

"What are we going to do?" said Azron.

"Huddle together," said Handen. "We need to share our body heat."

The group huddled together like the characters of a feel-good sitcom, collective teeth chattering manically as the snow whipped around them.

"W-w-w…where are we?" managed Xharon.

"The Ice Plains! It has to be!" wailed Bip. "I'm right back where I started from!"

Handen leaned down toward Riley, who was still fiddling with the Do-fer.

"Professor, how long 'til you can get us back?"

Riley shook his head. "The device was never meant to operate in such conditions—the mechanisms are extremely delicate!"

"What are you saying?"

Riley looked at Handen with despair in his eyes. "It's frozen up!"

Handen tried to grit his teeth in frustration but succeeded only in chattering them more rapidly.

"We need to get warm, fast, otherwise we won't last a minute out here."

"I don't suppose anyone thought to bring a coal-heater or something?" asked Azron.

"No."

"Then how? How do we make heat?"

As one, the group turned their heads slowly to Bip.

"What?" he said nervously.

"Oh come on, mate!" said Azron. "If there's one thing you're good at, it's making fire."

"There's a chance I might blow us all to pieces!" Bip protested.

"At least we'll die warm!"

"Okay, okay!" said Bip, thinking desperately. "I'll need a fuel source or something. It's one thing to create fire, but another to sustain it."

"I'll ask again," said Azron. "Did anyone think to bring some coal or suchlike?"

Handen ignored his companion's sarcastic jibes and scanned the snowy tundra around them. It was difficult to see anything through the swirling snow, but he thought he could make out a dark bump in the ground several dozen feet away.

"Come on!" he shouted, and led the group, shuffling forward like some drunken, multi-limbed beast.

As they approached the dark hunk in the snow, it became abundantly clear that they had indeed traveled back to the Ice Plains—before them lay the hulking corpse of a driftdigger, its buck teeth pointing skyward. Bip blanched at a sudden stench and realized that the creature's belly had been torn open and partially eaten. The steam rising from the wounds indicated that it was a fairly fresh kill, but there were more pressing concerns than possible lurking predators.

Bip thought back to his training with Rynford. "The coat!" he said. "Its coat contains a natural fuel—if we can ignite that, it'll burn for hours!"

"D-d-d..." began Xharon.

"Do it!" finished Azron.

Bip approached the corpse and tried his best to focus his mind. It was difficult to ignore the frantic shaking of his muscles, but he managed to make contact with the physical essence of the corpse.

There was still warmth in the beast, faint but shining, like a beacon in the deathly cold around it. He closed his eyes and concentrated.

*Concentrated…*

He felt the impact of the explosion before he heard the noise and was thrown onto his back. He looked up into a roaring bonfire that smelled of cooked meat and Kaneqian lamp oil.

"Yes!" he shouted, pumping his fist in the air. "I did it!"

The doomsayers stood around the burning body, relishing the comforting heat.

"Now that's *better*," said Azron, rubbing his hands together. "Well done, mate," he added.

"Professor?" said Handen.

Riley waved his hand, not looking up from the Do-fer. "Fifteen minutes or so. I still need to reset the frequency parameters."

Handen nodded and looked around. He turned to Bip. "Funny we should end up back here, don't you think?"

Bip didn't answer. Now that he wasn't freezing to death, he was taking the time to look around the tundra. "We should be near Kaneq," he said. "I'm sure of it."

Handen looked around. Being back on the Ice Plains was coaxing out long-dormant memories, but they were still hazy. "Are you certain?" he said.

Bip nodded and pointed toward a mountain. "That's Old Bachalack," he said, then swung his arm around to the east, pointing to another mountain. "And that's the Patient Mother. And look—we're quite close to the cliff-face and the frozen lake. Kaneq should be somewhere very near."

"How can you tell?" said Xharon, moving closer to the conversation.

Bip shrugged. "I was raised here," he said. "Every morning I woke up to the same two mountains looking over me."

Handen scanned the open plain, squinting with effort. "I don't see anything," he said. "Maybe you're mistaken."

Bip shook his head, his expression becoming increasingly troubled. "It's not as if you can just misplace an entire village," he said. "There were dozens of houses, and larger buildings too, like the

Dome. Not to mention the heatshield. If we are where I think we are, Kaneq should be very close. In fact, we're practically right on top of it."

"Maybe they left. You have been away for a while," offered Xharon.

"If they left, I doubt they would have taken their houses with them," said Bip. "That's not something you can just put in your rucksack, really."

Handen put a hand on his friend's shoulder. "If they left, they would have disengaged the heatshield. How long do you think it would have taken for the houses to be buried under the snow?"

Bip stared for a long while at the surrounding expanse of snow and ice. This was his home, which he had ventured into dangerous lands to save. To think that it had been abandoned and left to the slow and constant ravages of the Ice Plains was unbearable.

"No," he said. "No!"

Bip ran out into the blizzard and began digging frantically in the snow.

"No, no, *no!*"

Handen ran after him, lifting him from the cold ground as he struggled. "Listen to me, Bip—listen! I could be wrong—we could be wrong!"

Bip struggled out of the bigger man's grip and sat down in the snow, defeated, tears forming in his eyes. "No," he whispered. "This is where I left my home. This is where I left my family, my friends...*everything!*" He put his head in his hands. "I was supposed to save them—I was supposed to come back a hero! And now it's all gone. It's all gone..."

Handen took the weeping Kaneqian by arm and led him slowly back toward the fire. "If there's an explanation, we'll find it," he said. "If your friends are alive out there, we'll find them. I promise."

Bip said nothing, only stared into the bonfire that was even now beginning to dwindle.

There was a rumble from the skies. Something distant and powerful.

Azron looked up. "That's all we need, a bloody storm."

The thunder roll continued, rising in volume, and the ground beneath them began to shake.

"That's no storm," Handen breathed.

The doomsayers turned toward the sound, a rumble like a stampede of giants from somewhere behind the mass of the Patient Mother. There was a bright flash from behind the mountain and a short burst of noise that peaked temporarily over the constant rumbling.

Some long-dead association triggered deep in Handen's psyche.

"Kanick…"

And then it came. A giant, silvery, elongated disc, still glowing and smoking from its dramatic tussle with the atmosphere, narrowly avoiding the tip of the mountain as it swooped toward the tundra in a blaze of gravity.

Riley gaped. "Astonishing," he said. "By all that is astonishing, this is far and away—*the most astonishing thing I have ever seen.*"

"What is it?" cried Bip.

Handen grabbed the younger man by the shoulder. "It's the *Sentinel!*" he yelled. "Your family haven't left—they haven't even been born yet!"

Confusion quickly blanketed Bip's face.

"Don't you see?" yelled Handen. "All of this has already happened! This is when the *Sentinel* crashed a thousand years ago! We've traveled back in time! A thousand years back in time!"

---

THE *SENTINEL* SCREAMED toward the ground, its repellent fields directed entirely over its underbelly and nose. Inside, Finnegun checked their velocity one last time and quickly worked out the probability of surviving such a crash. *It would be fifty per cent,* he thought, *if we weren't heading toward a cliff face and consequently a thousand-foot drop onto a massive lake of ice.*

With an unfathomable boom, the craft plunged into the snowy ground, its shielding causing gigantic clods of earth to be ploughed up in front of it. The momentum of the impact sent the vessel crashing through ice and snow toward the sheer cliff face at an alarming rate.

---

"THEY'RE NOT GOING to make it!" shouted Bip. "They'll fly right over the edge!"

"Do something!" cried Xharon.

Handen held a hand to his head. Memories were coming back to him in a confused tumble. "They must make it! We survived the crash; otherwise, I wouldn't be here!"

Bip wasn't listening; his mind was entirely focused on the problem of stopping a gigantic spaceship from sliding to an icy grave. He reached out with his mind, searching for something, anything he could use. All he found was snow.

The words of his psyence tutor Glimton came back to him in a sudden vivid display.

*"Your problem, you talentless idiot, is that you're so busy concentrating on* concentrating *that you completely miss what it is you're* supposed *to be doing!"*

The words hadn't made sense to him then—just another of Glimton's lunatic monologues—but now, now something inside him seemed to reveal itself, something that had always been there but he had never acknowledged.

He didn't need to concentrate.

*He completely* didn't *concentrate...*

---

WITHIN THE FOREDECK, Finnegun closed his eyes once again. There was no way, he thought, that they could possibly slow down in time to avoid sliding over the cliff. As a sense of finality washed over him, Finnegun opened one of his eyes, determined, at least, to face his fate head-on. He was surprised to see that the landscape had changed slightly—where before there had been an empty expanse between the tobogganing ship and the cliff, there was now a gigantic, oddly-shaped snowdrift…

---

THE GROUND SHOOK, and Bip gasped as the air was suddenly sucked from his lungs. Near the edge of the cliff, the air shimmered and fogged and seemed to solidify.

"Great holy bastards," breathed Azron. "What on Bersch is that?"

Riley stood transfixed. "It's an igloo, by all that's preposterously unexpected! *It's the biggest igloo in existence!*"

---

FINNEGUN HAD JUST enough time to wonder where it had come from before the *Sentinel*, smashing clouds of ice into the air, collided with the mysterious snowdrift with an odd suddenness and a sound that can only be described as a colossal…

---

THERE IS a race of beings in the ultraverse known as the Documenters. It is the lot of this ancient, immortal, and near-omniscient species to catalog the comings and goings of existence in a library that is so huge it has a dimension all to itself. A particular faction of the Documenters were watching the events on the Ice Plains with great interest—they were the Order of the Onomatopoeic, whose responsibility it was to give a name to every sound ever made. Even so, with uncountable years of experience, and talents far beyond the reach of most life forms, they found it difficult to come up with a suitable onomatopoeia for a massive, red-hot spaceship suddenly colliding with a likewise massive freshly materialized igloo.

The best they could come up with was *"rrrRRrCraushtinkly-winklyPOFF!!"*

It was a decision the merits of which would be argued long into eternity.

BIP SANK TO HIS KNEES, his head swimming from the curious disassociation he felt with the world before him. There, exactly where he had left it, was the Dome. True, it was larger and rougher than the giant snow-mound he would come to know so many years from now, but it was unmistakably Kaneq's landmark building. He wondered whether anyone would believe him, if he ever made it back to his own time…

He was suddenly hauled up by his arms. Handen looked into his eyes with an expression of fierce concentration.

"No time to lie down, kid. It's not over yet."

Bip shook the mugginess from his head. "What now?" he said.

"It's come back to me," said Handen excitedly. "It's all come back to me. They're trapped under tons of snow in there, and you've got to help them out."

"Me? Why me?"

"Because that's the way it happened. I don't think I should say any more, but you've got to go and talk to those people."

"Can't you come with me?"

Handen laughed. "Of course not, reason being that *I'm already in there!*"

Bip looked around helplessly. "Well, what do I do?"

"I honestly don't know," said Handen. "All I know is that you do it."

Bip glanced from his friend's face to the pile of snow that would one day be the epicenter of his home. He turned back to his friends, who looked at him with something new in their faces, something that had not been there before. It was awe.

"I'll just be off then, shall I?" said Bip.

His companions nodded slowly. "Good luck," said Xharon.

Bip tramped off into the snow, the firelight lashing softly at his retreating back. He paused as he heard the cramping footsteps of someone jogging up behind him and turned to see Handen approach. The brief joviality had left the older man's face. "One more thing. I need you to promise me something."

"Yes?"

"When you see me in there, don't say anything. Don't let me know who you are. Don't mention your name, don't let me know about… me. Promise me that."

Bip shrugged. "That is a really confusing request, when you think about it."

"Don't think about it. Just promise."

Bip looked into the unwavering gaze of his companion. "Sure, Handen."

The bigger man nodded and turned back toward the fire. Bip turned back toward the dark.

---

DARKNESS.

A nagging sensation that he had something to be getting on with.

More darkness.

An awareness of cold. A problem in the chronostatic chamber. Not supposed to feel. Pain. Pain in his leg and neck.

Darkness.

"Captain?"

---

BIP APPROACHED THE DOME, sensing the faint signatures of heat coming from the crashed ship beneath its icy blanket. He didn't feel the cold, and perhaps wouldn't be surprised to know that a firedance tumbled slowly about his shoulders, responding to his unconscious will. Bip wasn't entirely sure how he had accessed so much of his latent knack and wasn't sure if he'd be able to do it again, but for now, the residual energies of his psyentific feat seemed to be responding to his thoughts almost without him realizing it.

He waved a hand at the surface of the snow dome and, quickly and without fanfare, a staircase began to form on the icy walls. He walked up them, careful not to think too hard about what he was doing. It was, he thought, like balancing a ball on his head—if he thought too hard about the ball, it would surely drop.

He reached the top of the mound that would one day become the

Dome and was faintly surprised to see a flock of penguins, seemingly totally bewildered by their current predicament. They were not the fat and fluffy domesticated penguins of a future Kaneq, but their sleek and oily ancestors. One of them quacked indignantly at him.

Ignoring the stranded birds, Bip walked to the center of the Dome and stood for a while, gazing downward. Then, taking care not to concentrate, he made a shovel shape with his hands and a digging motion through the air before him. Responding to an unexpected reconstruction of the air molecules around it, the snow atop the downed spacecraft was scooped up and dispersed into the winds, leaving a deep crater. Bip repeated the motion, digging with re-directed molecular energy, cutting into the snow rhythmically and methodically until he stood on the cusp of a large inverted cone.

The penguins, finally succumbing to dumb curiosity, came to stare at the newcomer and the large cave he had fashioned, gaggling and sliding around with all the grace of a creature that, though born to ice, still had a love/hate relationship with it. Unsurprisingly, many slipped down into Bip's hole, quacking madly and landing with soft thuds. Bip watched as the snow around them began to shift like quicksand, then followed them down.

***

THERE WAS AN ODD THUMPING SOUND, like the shuffling of gigantic feet. The crew fell silent, listening carefully as the noise grew louder. After quite some time, a flurry of snow began to cascade into the ship from the access hatch until a hollow was made near the exit. A weak light and a bitter wind swept into the foredeck.

Completely against everyone's expectations, a penguin plummeted from the sky and landed with a bang on the ship's deck, followed by several others, which proceeded to wallow around in confusion, quacking with the attitude of animals that have nothing better to do than quack. Finnegun tried to think when he had last seen penguins...

After a few minutes and several more confused penguins, a face dangled from the top of the hatch—a face that Finnegun found disturbingly familiar.

"All right?" said Bip.

The crew of the *Sentinel* turned to Finnegun. The captain seemed to cogitate on the problem.

"Yes," he concluded.

"Good, good," said Bip. "That's good, then."

"And may I ask who you are?" asked Finnegun.

"Who, me?" Bip thought for a moment. "My name is not important."

"That's an unusual name," said Izzy, irritation still heavy in her voice.

Bip stared for a while, surprised by his calmness. *These are the founders*, he thought. *These are my ancestors, and I've just saved their lives! How weird is that?*

He took in the boiler-suit-style uniforms of the crew and found them strangely disappointing. Even after he had learned that the founders were from another world, he had still envisioned them as rugged pioneers, packs laden for long travel and faces harsh from foreign winds. The clean-cut and soberly uniformed collection of space-farers before him were a far cry from the mighty gypsies of his mind.

Except for one. One bore the expression of things seen and done. One bore the stare of those who look for danger and know where to find it. Bip's world went fuzzy as Handen Strike stepped forward. He looked different—perhaps five or so years younger, his features less travel-worn and his hair shorter—but the poise and stare of the soon-to-be immortal was unmistakable.

Bip swallowed. Before him was a man who had no idea what the world had in store for him, the sacrifices he would make and the horrors he would face. The burden of lifetimes. How could this man forgive him, for knowing what dangers awaited him and saying nothing? But, of course, had already forgiven him. And made him promise...

Bip realized he had been staring at Handen. The man frowned under the scrutiny and approached Finnegun's side, leaning in to speak quietly in his ear.

"Sir?"

Finnegun was visibly shaken from his own contemplation. "Yes, Mr. Strike?"

"I think it would be a good idea to scout around up top, sir, see what we're up against."

Finnegun nodded. "Very well. All those who are able to, salvage what you can from the analysis equipment, don an environment suit, and prepare to touch new ground." Around him, the crew scattered in various directions until there was nobody in the room but Handen, Finnegun, Bip, and a few befuddled penguins. The penguins quacked in the manner of creatures that might quite happily quack for all eternity.

The captain turned to Bip, who was still hanging from the top of the doorway.

"You may come in if you want," he said.

"No, it's okay," said Bip. "I don't think I'll be staying long."

"Then I suppose I must thank you now," said Finnegun.

"Sorry?" said Bip. He was beginning to feel uncomfortable under Handen's cold stare. It is a uniquely disturbing feeling when a close friend looks at you like a stranger.

"For aiding us. For digging us out," Finnegun continued. "We must thank you and your people for your help."

"Oh, I don't really have any people at the moment," said Bip. "I'm just sort of passing through with a few friends."

Handen raised an eyebrow. "Passing through?"

"Yes."

"Hundreds of miles of desolate wasteland, and you're just passing through?"

"Yep."

Thankfully, at that moment, the crew began to return, each holding a different piece of sensory equipment and a floppy, rubber-like affair that served as an environment suit.

"Perhaps we'll continue this discussion up-top," said Finnegun.

THE CREW of the *Sentinel* stood on top of their fallen ship and surveyed the Ice Plains. The storm had died down now, and the frozen expanse before them twinkled in the fresh starlight like something beautifully asleep. Finnegun was propped against a crutch, taking reports, and noting down information on a wrist-console.

The temporary base at the top of the dome was lit and warmed by gel-heaters, even though the environment suits were sufficient to keep the cold at bay. The crew attended various gadgets.

The younger Handen looked up from a small palm-held device. "I'm reading limited lifeforms to the east and west, Captain. Small groups here and there, larger than a usual animal pack but smaller than a nomadic tribe…"

"That'd be the yetis," Bip said matter-of-factly.

"Yetis?" asked Handen.

"Yeah, they're great big hairy things with bad tempers and big appetites. I'd leave them well alone, if I were you. We call them yetis."

*Do we?* thought Bip. *Do we call them yetis? I only call them yetis because that's what my elders called them—but what if I'd decided to tell this captain that they were called shockpigs? Or budgies? Would the me of the future still call them yetis?*

Bip shook his head. He was learning quickly that time travel was a messy business and thought that the less time he spent with these people, the better.

"Look, I've got to go," he said.

"Go?" said Finnegun. "Go where?"

Bip pointed to the distant bonfire where his friends were still waiting. "My friends and I, we have…a boat. But it's only big enough for the few of us. We're heading south. There are other lands there."

Finnegun nodded. "And what is it that you are not telling me, my strange new friend?"

Bip looked at the ground. He felt an odd reluctance to lie to this stranger, this man whose eyes he had once seen through on an ancient computer, this founder of everything he knew.

"I can't tell you much. I can only say that there aren't any people around here and that…" Bip looked at the crew, busying themselves with analysis and sensor-readings. Did he have the heart to tell them they were to die here, in the cold, never to see their homes again? No. No he did not. "I wouldn't expect to leave any time soon."

"And what's that supposed to mean?" Handen growled, suddenly annoyed. "How do you know so much about it?"

"I can't say, really. I'm sorry, but I have to go now." Bip turned and walked the steps he had fashioned earlier. Handen and Finnegun watched him leave.

"Do you want me to get him back?" said Handen.

Finnegun looked down at his feet. A penguin was shuffling idly across his boots. "No," he said. "He rescued us, after all, and I don't think we have the right to harangue him."

Handen nodded a reluctant agreement.

"Besides," continued Finnegun, smirking, "don't you think he looked rather familiar?"

"Yes," said Handen. "He looked a lot like you."

Finnegun chuckled. "I like a good mystery," he said. "And I've a feeling that this conundrum will unravel itself in the fullness of time. Have patience, Mr. Strike—it will all come clear in the end."

---

"DID YOU SEE THEM?" asked Xharon excitedly. "Did you see the founders? Your ancestors?"

Bip nodded.

Azron puffed on a cigarette he'd managed to light with an ember of dead driftdigger. "Well, spare us the suspense, mate—what were they like?"

Bip thought for a while. "Quite pleasant, actually. Seemed like a nice bunch."

"Did you see Handen?" said Xharon.

"Yes, he was very…like Handen, you know."

"This is incredible—*incredible!*" said Riley. "Actual time travel! This is challenging stuff, you know—*challenging stuff!* I'd always assumed that space and time were completely interrelated, but here we are, traveling through the same physical dimension but in a different time!

This will require extensive study—months and months of *extensive study!*"

"I'll remind you, Professor, that if we don't get back soon, we may not have months and months of time left," Handen interrupted. "The reason being that there's still a giant nuclear asteroid to take care of."

"Of course, of course, *of course*—how silly of me. Just give me a moment, and I'll have us back in the right time in two shakes of the tail of some sort of infantile woolly quadruped."

Azron spoke. "What I don't understand is, if we're back in time, and that lot want to save the world, same as we do, why don't we just go and tell them about Draegul and everything? I mean, we could save you a lot of bother, couldn't we, Handen? We could just tell the other you where the fountain of death is and get him to invite Draegul around for a tea-party, sort of thing."

"That's a good point," Xharon agreed.

Handen shook his head. "You'd be interfering with more probability lines, repercussive ripples, and consequence cycles than you could possibly imagine."

"Oh yeah?" said Azron. "And how come you're an expert on time travel all of a sudden?"

"Oh, I'm no expert, but everyone takes at least a basic tutorial in time travel theory at the academy. It's routine."

"Really?"

"Yes, you never know when you'll be sucked through a wormhole and inadvertently find yourself at the dawn of creation."

"Happen a lot, does it?"

"Once or twice. The important thing to remember is that if you make significant changes to a society in the past, then the future results will always be impossible to predict, so it's best to leave well enough alone."

Xharon opened her mouth to protest.

"He's right, of course," said Riley. "If Draegul had been eliminated at such an early stage, then you and I, Xharon, would be very different people, I would never have been a duke, you never a princess. Perhaps never born. The same goes for Bip—if the founders had achieved their goal so early in their stay, they might never have seen the necessity for settling here, and Bip's Kaneq would never have existed. And then who's to say that, with Draegul destroyed, another ruler would not have risen in his place and attracted the attention of the Discordance? The possibilities are endless, and there is no way we could guarantee a successful future, no matter how carefully we planned it."

Azron blew out his cheeks in exasperation. "Well, bang goes that argument, then," he said.

"Well, no, hang on…" began Xharon. "If that's the case, then Bip saving his ancestors must have already have happened if we're to live in the future we know, and if it already happened, then what's just happened now?"

Riley put a reassuring arm around his daughter's shoulders. "It raises all sorts of questions, yes. The very fact that Bip saved his ancestors means that he was always destined to save his ancestors. Think of it as fate, if it suits you better."

"Like destiny?"

"Yes," said Riley. "Though you could also call it a self-perpetuating time-loop, if you wanted to be more accurate."

There was a silence.

"I think I'll stick to destiny," said Xharon.

Handen turned to Bip as if suddenly remembering something. "Did you see Finnegun?"

Bip nodded. "Yes, he looked familiar, somehow…"

Handen grinned widely. "That's because he looked just like you!"

"Really?"

"It came back to me, the reason you looked so familiar the first time I saw you. You must be directly descended from him."

"You really think so?"

"Yes, it's likely—the resemblance is very strong."

"What was he like?" asked Bip.

Handen smiled fondly. "He was a brilliant man, and I'm sure he'd be proud to call you his descendant."

There was a silence, warm despite the surrounding cold.

Riley coughed politely. "The device is ready, reset to our original intended co-ordinates. We can leave at any time."

Xharon hugged the penguin closer to her. "Good," she said. "It's bally well freezing again."

Handen clapped his hands together. "Then let's go. We've a dramatic rescue to initiate. One a thousand years in the making." He turned to look at Bip, a glint in his eye that hinted at pride. "And not the first one today, either."

The Do-fer began to hum, and soon the world wavered around them. And then they were gone.

------

8

## Back to the Bone Desert

------

Draegul stood at the head of the dirigible *Fierce Reprisal*, the wind flickering his long, raven hair as the city of Argustin peaked and troughed below him with metropolitan symmetry. Behind him, the airboat armada of Argustin—the fastest, fiercest, and most feared in all of Bersch—floated in his wake like a swarm of fat, angry wasps.

His face stiffened against the elements in an expression of icy rage. Of all his long existence, this was one of the few times he had felt anxiety. The sensation was not at all welcome.

His life had always been remarkably straightforward. With so much power—more power than any man or woman could ever hope for—he had simply destroyed anyone who had opposed him...or even merely annoyed him. It was a good system, one that had worked for nearly a thousand years, and in those thousand years, he had not once tasted fear, depression, or anxiety. Now, it seemed, the emotions were catching up with him at full speed.

He had known, since Handen Strike had told him oh-so-long ago, that one day his world would be threatened by forces far outside his commendable sphere of influence. He'd also known, due to a document he had chanced upon in the Imperial archives, that a weapon of great power lay hidden in the Nastren desert. He had dawdled for many a year, confident that when the time came and the world cried out to be saved, he would gracefully and graciously step forward, his power, authority, and heroism there for all to see. And now, just as he was on the cusp of unearthing the weapon, saving the day, and sending a vital message of power to those who were yet to bow to his influence, some upstart from another world was trying to hog the limelight.

It would not do. Vengeance would be served, swift and terrible.

The whispering at the back of his mind grew a little in volume, and the Emperor put a hand to his temple. He remembered how he had first chanced upon those documents; that was when the whisperings had started. For a long time, he had believed it to be simply the power of his unconscious mind, but as the years had gone by and things he could not have possibly have known had been made known to him—his secret enemies, plots against him, and most importantly the location of the fountain of youth—he believed that he had been bestowed with some supernatural gift.

Though sometimes he wondered if he was merely as crazy as a rabid squirrel.

Now those half-heard whisperings were telling him that the plans he had worked toward for so long were in jeopardy, that the security of the weapon meant for his use was compromised, that the other-worlders who had escaped him were nearing the desert. He hadn't much time.

"Engineer?" he shouted.

The engineer at the controls of the Emperor's airboat turned and saluted. "Yes, my lord?"

"Make us go faster."

The engineer's mouth gaped like a guppy's for a moment. "My lord," he managed. "We are already at full speed. It's just not possible…"

Draegul's eyes never left the distant horizon. "Make it possible. If you have to burn your own body as fuel, make it possible."

The engineer blinked rapidly, trying to prevent the horror in his eyes from melting into tears. "Yes, my lord," he stammered, and set about making the impossible possible.

Draegul stared hard into the distance, a mixture of determination and fury painting a picture of unique ugliness across his face. The repetitive whisperings of a being he couldn't see were becoming just a little more urgent.

***

THERE WAS A SCREAM.

Bip had only just had time to adjust to a tremendous change in temperature, the frigid wind giving way to hot, stale air, the crunching snow under his feet exchanged for shifting sand. Now that he was ready for the gut-squelching nausea of immediate reality transgression lag, he could steel himself against it, though the experience was still very unpleasant. In this state of extreme disorientation, the sudden, piercing screams exacerbated things terribly.

Bip whirled around, squinting his eyes against the bright light of the desert, trying to locate the source of whatever cataclysmic danger awaited him. The scream had come from Xharon, who was standing stock-still and with a fixed look of extreme upset. In her hands, she held the penguin from the Ice Plains.

At least it looked like a penguin.

Bip stared. Soon Riley, Azron, and Handen stood beside him, all staring with grim fascination. In Xharon's hands was a decrepit, mummified version of the penguin they had carried with them. It was totally gray in color, and its skin was papery and dusty, some of it flaking away even as they watched. It was a penguin corpse. Clearly a penguin corpse. If penguin grave robbers were to rob the tomb of hundred-year-old penguin plague victims, they might have found a corpse like this...

Xharon wailed as, with a wet crackling sound, the penguin's head teetered and tore from its body, finally succumbing to gravity. The warrior princess dropped the rest of the corpse in disgust. As it impacted with the sand beneath it, what was left of its flesh dispersed into a cloud of dust, and all that remained was a rather pathetic-looking skeleton, lying on the sand like a long-forgotten sunbather.

"Now that," remarked Azron, "is something you don't see every day."

"I concur," muttered Riley distractedly. "It's as though it decayed at an unheard-of rate."

"What do you think caused it?" asked Handen, wiping a powdery patch of disintegrated penguin from his trousers.

Riley gave a facial shrug. "Who can tell?"

"Well, it clearly had something to do with the Do-fer," said Bip. "Doesn't it work for penguins?"

Riley shook his head. "By rights, it should work for all life forms, as well as inanimate objects. This is most unprecedented."

"Wait a minute," said Azron. "Are you saying that this might have happened to any one of us?"

Riley began polishing some of the lenses on his numerously lensed spectacles, then adjusted them until his eyes beneath were magnified to an unsettling size. Then he knelt down and peered at the penguin corpse.

"No, no, no," he muttered. "If this had been a dimensional hiccup, I should imagine the results would have been a lot messier. I could imagine, perhaps, a failure to realign frequencies correctly and appearing in an askew physical dimension, but that would probably involve a lot of exploding internal organs and hideous mutations, etcetera, etcetera. No. This is definitely an extremely rapid form of cellular decay—by all that's expedient, *extremely rapid*."

The professor got to his feet. "This is purely educated guess-work, you understand, but I believe I have a theory…"

Xharon, her face still frozen with disgust, looked up from the corpse. "Well, I bally well can't *wait* to hear this," she said.

"Ahem," said Riley. "It is possible, just possible, that this is an unexpected side effect of time travel. It is possible that, time—or, indeed, *personal time*, which is to say the biological level of time relevant to a particular life form's total existence—is *non-negotiable*."

The rest of the doomsayers looked around at one another.

"Someone might as well say it," muttered Azron.

"Go on, Professor," said Handen.

Riley continued. "It's feasible that time is not merely a measurement, but a force with cause-and-effect qualities of its very own, sharing a more than derivative relationship with the physical dimensions."

"Of course," said Azron sarcastically. "That's exactly as I guessed."

"Really?" said Riley.

"Hell, no! Explain yourself, man!"

"Very well," said Riley. "If we imagine time as a river flowing backward…"

"I'm warning you," growled Azron.

"Bear with me, please. Time is a river, but we are swept along backward, hence the times we have left behind us, the past, are accessible, indeed through memory and recordings—it is accessible because it has already been experienced."

Riley looked over to Azron to see if he was keeping up. The thief nodded reluctantly, and the professor cleared his throat.

"So, while the current moves backward, we are, nevertheless, pulled against the current by the force of time and are affected by it."

"…" said Azron.

"What I mean to say is, we can explore freely down time's backward current but are pulled forward constantly and exclusively at the rate that the force of time allows."

"That seems pretty straightforward," said Xharon.

"Believe me, child, I'm dumbing it down somewhat heavily."

"Carry on," said Handen.

"So, in this metaphorical river, we cannot escape the biological pull of time—if we are to move forward, we must feel the ravages of time, as this unfortunate penguin may attest too."

Bip looked down at the tragic little skeleton. "You're saying that, by taking this penguin forward in time, we actually aged it by a thousand years?"

"Broadly speaking, yes."

"That's horrible!" cried Xharon.

"We weren't to know," said Handen, matter-of-factly.

"Hang on—you're saying we can't move forward in time without growing older, so how come we didn't grow older when we came back here?"

"My good man, this is the sphere of our personal universal time-line—here and now is where we are supposed to exist. Doubtless, if we were to advance a hundred years from now by means of the Do-fer, we would share a similar fate to our departed penguin friend."

"Okay, right."

"Is that everything?"

"No. Wait a minute. If that's the case, then how come we didn't, you know, cease to exist when we traveled back in time?"

"I told you—time is an *affecting* force. If my theory is correct, then we do not age and decay merely because of the limitations of our mortal bodies, but because our life energy exists at a time and for a time when it is supposed to exist."

"The blueprint..." whispered Bip.

Riley turned a puzzled look on the Kaneqian. "I suppose so," he said. "Yes, think of every living being and element of the universe as part of an evolving blueprint, each factor taking up only the space that is allocated for it."

"I have a headache," mumbled Azron, and he began to roll a cigarette.

Handen spoke. "An interesting theory, Professor, but a little out of the blue. How can you be sure it is correct?"

Riley shrugged once more. "My boy, I couldn't say—by all that's uncertain, *I couldn't say*. It's an on-the-spot theory that I have literally just devised. Chances are I'm as wrong as can be, but the explanation is sufficient for the problem at hand."

"That's good enough for me," said Bip.

"Me too," said Azron. "Now, can we please get going?"

"A good call," Handen replied. "Which only leaves one question: where in the hell are we?"

The doomsayers looked around at the surrounding desert. Blank horizons hovered in every direction across the sandy dunes. The silver star shone in the sky, pale in the bright blue, but still large and looming.

"Professor?"

Riley looked down at the readings on his Do-fer. "I'm afraid our little sojourn to the past has somewhat interfered with my original estimations."

"Meaning?"

"I have no idea whereabouts in the Bone Desert we are...or exactly when, for that matter."

"Oh."

The companions stared into the unfathomable distances as the desert flickered through hazy lines of heat. They would have to pick a direction in a land where three hundred and fifty-nine of the three hundred and sixty degrees that surrounded them could mean a walk into certain, slow death.

"This could be a problem," said Handen. He looked up at the sun. It sat bang in the middle of the sky, its light stained a slight shade of silver by the new star squatting near the horizon. "I know the pyramids are likely to be to the south, but I won't be able to get a sense of direction for a few more minutes. Even then, there's still a huge scope for error."

"We could walk right past them and just die in the middle of nowhere, you mean?" said Bip.

Handen nodded.

"Great," said Bip. "Just when we were making progress, just when we had a proper head start, now it's all for nothing."

Riley spoke. "I could reset the Do-fer to base co-ordinates and take us back to my workshop."

Bip shook his head. "There will be guards at the factory by now. And who's to say we won't end up in some other unpredictable location? The bottom of the ocean perhaps? Or somewhere out in space?"

"I'm sure that was merely an isolated incident," said Riley, reproachfully.

Bip, who knew the truth—that Mr. Random could strike from anywhere at any time—merely shook his head.

Handen gazed grim-faced into the sands of the Bone Desert. "We may have to risk it," he said. "We don't have the time or the resources to be exploring through such hostile terrain." He shook his head sadly. "Nothing short of a miracle could guide us through this desert."

The doomsayers waited expectantly.

"Yep," said Azron. "Nothing short of a miracle."

They waited some more.

"Just a little old miracle. That's what we need. Any time now. Sooner rather than later, really."

A miracle of any kind completely failed to happen.

"Damn. Well, we may as well fire up the Do-fer, then."

"*Hello over there!*" came a faraway voice.

The doomsayers shared a surprised glance and turned around as one.

"Who on earth is that?" said Xharon.

A solitary figure was making its way toward the companions, unrecognizable through the glare of the sun.

A voice came across the distance. "*Welcome to the Bone Desert, the quietest desert there ever was!*"

Handen shielded his eyes from the sun, squinting at the newcomer. "It can't be…" he murmured.

"*Why not try a sandy surprise? Mmm-mmm! Surprisingly sandy!*"

Bip's mouth hung open of its own accord. "Impossible," he said.

"*More peace and quiet than a sane man can handle!*"

Azron grinned like a cat. "Miraculous, even."

The figure approached, leading several camels that had been painted with the legend, "Bolan's Desert Adventure."

The smiling man in the loud shirt and dark glasses approached, radiating optimism. "That's right—Bolan's amazing desert adventures! You'll never have a quieter adventure in your whole darn life!"

"Bolan?" said Bip.

Bolan frowned. "Do I know you, friend?"

Azron shook his head. "Let me guess, you've got a brother who runs a ranch on the Dozantyne Shrub and another who runs a holiday resort on an island somewhere?"

"Bing! Two points!" cheered Bolan.

"This is just too strange," Bip muttered.

"Though why those idiots still think that islands and ranches are the way forward, I'll never know! Nope, desert adventure trips. That's where the money is!"

"And have you had many customers?" said Handen.

"Actually, this could be your lucky day!" said Bolan. "You could be my first!"

The companions shared a cynical look.

"Please?" said Bolan. "The desert really is a lovely place, once you get to know it. I should know—I've been out here for years. And I haven't eaten in several days," he added.

"I tell you what," said Handen. "We'll give you all the money we have if you can tell us where the pyramids are."

Bolan grinned. "That's easy," he said. "They're only a few miles from here. I could take you to them, if you like." He gestured to his camels, which gazed around with the deceptively dopey expression unique to their species.

Handen turned to his friends, a broad grin on his face. "Imminent end of the world aside, I think this could be our lucky day!"

⁂

ONCE THEY WERE MOUNTED on the camels, they made good progress across the sands of the Bone Desert and, as Bolan had promised, it wasn't long before they could see the pyramids on the horizon. A sense of excitement overcame the doomsayers—for better or worse, they were close to the end.

As the hours passed, it was only Handen who didn't feel the enthusiasm. A nagging question had arisen in his mind. He slowed his camel until he was alongside Professor Riley.

"Professor?" he said.

Riley, who seemed to be having great difficulty staying mounted on his camel, looked up at the adventurer. "Yes, Mr. Strike?"

"I wonder if you could tell me: if this 'time as a force' theory of yours is correct, if I were to travel forward in time, would I age? Would I die?"

Riley tried to shrug, nearly fell, and gripped desperately for the pommel of his saddle. "It really is a working theory, dear boy. I couldn't say anything for certain."

"Make an educated guess."

"Well, you've already lived for a thousand years by your own calculations, yes?"

"Yes."

"Then it's clear that your personal time—your biological time, the totality of your existence—is far different from that of an average being. If my theory stands, you could travel forward in time and not be the least affected. Your hair would grow, as would your fingernails, and your clothes and weapons would age, but you would remain essentially unaffected."

"I wouldn't die, then?"

"If the theory stands, then no, you wouldn't die."

Handen nodded, his face grim. "There is another thing."

"Yes?"

"The Do-fer. How did you come by it?"

The professor looked at the ground. "I-I'm not sure what you mean."

Handen sighed. "You're a brilliant man, Professor, and some of your inventions are centuries ahead of Bersch's projected technological development, but the Do-fer...a device capable of traveling through time and space? And portable, at that?"

Riley said nothing, just continued to stare at the ground.

Handen continued, "My people would have called it an advanced quantum computer, something able to shift molecules into superposition across all known energy fields. Something that can make you quantum jump to anywhere and anywhen you'd like. In other words, what you have in your hands is something that a race of beings thousands of years more developed than yours would regard as bordering on the impossible. So, I'll ask again, how did you come across it?"

"You wouldn't believe me," said Riley.

Handen laughed. "I've seen the unbelievable so many times now that I'm not sure I can be surprised by anything anymore. Try me."

Riley remained quiet for a while, gathering his thoughts. "I built the device—of that I'm sure. The circumstances surrounding its construction, however, I am less certain of. Originally, I was attempting to build a wireless transmission device, to send messages over great distances with no physical relays. I was certain it was achievable, but as I began building it, I became very ill. A strong dose of the flu. I was delirious. By all that's feverish, I was *half-mad* with delirium. But I continued my work. I have flashes of coherent memory, the clearest being the thought that, if I could instantly deliver a message in person, *that* would be something." The professor smiled to himself and began polishing his multi-lensed glasses. "When I recovered from the fever, the Do-fer had been built. I understood what it was for, and I could name every component used in its construction, *but I had no idea how it worked!* I mean, I theorized and hypothesized until I had nothing left to give, but I still had no idea how such a device could possibly exist. It was as though it had been built by something else, by all that's absurd, as if it had been built *through* me. Do you understand? Do you believe me?"

Handen turned to the professor, seeing the desperate pleading in his eyes, the look of a logical man trying to come to terms with the deeply illogical. They rode for a little while in silence.

"As I said before, Professor, I've seen too much in my lifetime to discredit the improbable as impossible. I'm not a religious man by any stretch, but I sometimes think that there is something—not God perhaps, but *something* that has a hand in our destinies. Something that is so alien to our intellects that to properly understand it would make us other than human. Perhaps we should just accept that there are things we will never understand and leave it at that."

"Not an easy thing for a man of science," said Riley, grinning sheepishly.

"Perhaps not, but a friend of mine once said that enough scale makes a child of the mightiest intellect."

Riley considered this briefly, nodding slightly. "Perhaps. Though I can't help but consider the implications. It is simply my way. I sometimes feel as though my mind is a tapestry woven of questions, by all that's perplexing—*woven from nagging questions*. And so I must ask myself: if the device was the consequence of an extraneous influence, to what end? Why?"

"You can live your whole life asking why," said Handen, "and still die an unhappy man. But consider this—if we hadn't had the device, where would we be now?"

"Dead, most likely," concluded Riley.

"Exactly," said Handen. "Makes you think, doesn't it?"

The adventurer geed his camel and rode to the head of the procession, sunk back into his familiar quiet, while Riley watched, shifting between the humps of his oblivious mount.

"Yes. Yes, I suppose it does."

---

THEY APPROACHED the aptly named Land of the Dead, the huge stretch of land southwest of Nastre, where hundreds of pyramid tombs were scattered throughout the desert, most of them reclaimed by the unstoppable crawl of the sands, but many unearthed by the curious or greedy.

For a while, Bip worried that they would not be able to find the right pyramid, but after Bolan had quizzed a few of the local workers, it was clear that the newly unearthed tomb would be easy to find—all they had to do was find the huge crowds of Nastren laborers heading back to the camp city after a long day.

"Well, Bolan," said Handen, "we should be fine by ourselves from here on in." He dismounted his camel and threw Bolan a purse full of silver. It would be enough to see him through several months of good eating.

Bolan grinned enormously. "Why thank you, fella—be sure to tell all your friends about Bolan's Amazing Desert Adventure!"

"Yeah, about that," said Bip. "Why don't you and your brothers work together? You know, I'm sure that if the three of you pooled your skills, you could start a truly successful business."

"Nah," said Bolan. "We'd only argue. Besides, the desert's the place for me! More peace and quiet than…a…a desert," he finished lamely.

Handen felt it was only fair to warn the man. "It won't be peaceful for long, Bolan. Chances are the Emperor's on his way here with an army ready to raise hell. If you want peace and quiet, I suggest you get as far away from here as possible."

Bolan looked into the immortal's eyes, his smile fading as he realized that Handen was deadly serious. Then he turned his camels around and traveled quickly in the opposite direction.

"There goes a very strange man with a very strange family," remarked Bip.

Handen nodded his agreement, then led the way into the Land of the Dead.

---

9

# The Pyramid

---

**M**ernin Cobonon stood in the cool shadow of the pyramid and once again ran his fingers over its surface. Although it was of the same color as the sandblasted stone of all the buildings in the Bone Desert, it was perfectly smooth and unusually warm to the touch. Mernin snatched his hand away, suddenly convinced that the half-heard humming sound that came in the night had started again, only this time louder—closer.

He mopped his brow and took a swig from the brandy bottle he had taken to carrying around with him. When this was over, he would retire. He doubted he would ever want to look at another pyramid for as long as he lived.

"Sir?"

He turned to the concerned face of Jimar.

"Yes, Jimar, what is it?"

Concern gave way to childish excitement. "We've opened the door."

Mernin nodded slowly and took another swig from his bottle. "And what did you find?"

"Nothing yet, sir—just a very long set of steps. We thought we'd let you go in first."

Mernin's jowly face paled instantly. "No. No one goes in."

"But, sir, the Emperor's orders were to…"

"Damn it, I know what the Emperor's orders are! Do you think I don't know that? I know that!"

Jimar stepped back from the sudden outburst. "Then what shall we do, sir?"

The Grand Tutor stared blankly for a moment. "There are people born to this sort of work, those with vocations that compel them to sneak around dangerous areas in search of treasure."

Jimar looked shocked. "You can't mean…"

"Yes. We need raiders."

"But they're notorious troublemakers, sir—they'll probably take whatever is inside and claim it belongs in a museum or some such nonsense!"

"Yes, well, they can take that up with the Emperor, can't they? Now, doubtless news of this freshly opened tomb has already spread to the camp city—no doubt every raider in a hundred-mile radius is eagerly awaiting information. Go to the wine tents with a bag of gold and find the most foolish, idiotic, and overconfident raiders you can."

Jimar looked as though he was about to protest, then thought better of it. He marched off toward the camp city.

Mernin drank a large gulp from his bottle and began muttering to himself. "Yes," he said. "Let the raiders go in first. Let *them* get chewed up by old, blunted traps. Let *them* get their faces dissolved by horrifying ancient curses."

The Grand Tutor of Enlightened Researchers waddled toward where the horses were kept. He would take a ride into the camp city now, where he would find a wine tent and get hopelessly drunk. Then he would fall asleep, and hopefully not wake up until all the dynamic tomfoolery was well and truly over with.

---

IN THE GARDEN, Ted was looking thoughtfully at a rosebush. He idly pressed the tip of his finger into a thorn, watching with interest the tiny star of blood that arose. He thought it fitting that roses should have thorns; it reminded people that nothing was easy.

Straightening up, Ted looked into the sky. It wouldn't be long now until a few kinks in the equation were balanced once and for all. The Massive Ball of Death was approaching the point of no return, but there were still possibilities.

Ted could see the futures, of course, and judge the various and likely possibilities. Right now, it looked as if both runners in the race had lagged too far behind, as if Bersch would be utterly destroyed—as the original blueprint, his very equation, had decreed.

But nothing was infallible. That was the way it had to be. He might have been the embodiment of the Universal Theory—the celestially mathematical equation that glued the ultraverse together, the ultimate cause to every effect and effect to every cause—but he knew only one thing with total certainty, and that was this:

Nothing was certain. Not even uncertainty.

In an existence of infinite size, there had to be infinite possibilities, and where there were infinite possibilities, there was always an element of chance.

That was often the problem with the learned men of the universe —they assumed that the worlds they existed in were unchanging things, that life ran through a rigid and logical procession. Ted, if he had been so inclined, might have told them otherwise—that the grand theory of everything is as flexible and changeable as the waters in an ocean, and that the humanoid mind could no more fathom it than they could trace a specific air-molecule through a hurricane.

It looked as though the blueprint would remain unchallenged, but there were still two wildcards: Draegul—instigated by the Discordance—who could feasibly destroy the galaxy and more with his trigger-happy attitude and complete disregard for life, and Bip—ultimately produced by the Caretakers—who might just be able to destroy both the Massive Ball of Death and the weapon with it. It was, once again, the age-old struggle of Good versus Evil, Chaos versus Order.

Ted sighed. No matter how carefully things were planned in life, sooner or later there was an epic and dramatic battle that held in sway the fate of the universe. It was just the way things went.

———

THE DOOMSAYERS APPROACHED THE PYRAMID, which sat stolidly at the bottom of a huge, gently sloping crater. By now Bip had grown accustomed to the sight of huge and imposing buildings, but the pyramid was big in a different way. It seemed *heavier*, somehow, as though the very mass of it pulled you in toward it. Looking at it for too long produced an unsettling feeling that Bip could only describe as sideways vertigo.

Handen approached the base of the pyramid and run his hand along its surface.

"This is it," he said. "This is definitely it."

"How can you tell?" asked Xharon.

"Put your hand on it."

Xharon did so, and promptly removed it as though bitten.

"Ugh," she said. "That's creepy."

Handen grinned. "You can hear the humming? A bit like insects having a really loud conversation?"

"Well, I suppose," said Xharon. "I was going to say it sounded like the boiler room back at the factory."

Handen nodded. "This pyramid isn't constructed of stone. It's made of Sentium."

"Oh, good grief, here we go," said Azron. "Go on then—what's Sentium?"

"It's an alloy from another world. The *Sentinel*, the ship we saw crashing, was constructed almost entirely from Intellium, a semi-sentient alloy that is capable of obeying commands. It can change its shape to suit the programmers' needs and relay energy information as a circuit board would. This is Sentium, a more basic form of Intellium; it's essentially a silicon-based machine, like a rock that's capable of thinking. It can transform its shape and, as you'll notice, blend into its environment."

Riley tapped the pyramid curiously. "I suppose that is why it is colored and textured like stone?"

"Yes."

"Incredible."

"You know, I think I might have actually understood all that," said Azron. "I'm getting better at this."

"Good, because now we have to find an entrance."

The companions searched around. The walls of the pyramid stretched into the distance on either side of them. Thoroughly searching the perimeter would've taken days. Handen looked up at the sky. Now that the sun was a little lower, he could easily make out the size and intensity of the silver star. It had grown worryingly large since he had last looked at it properly. Though it was still faint in the daytime sky, it was easily as big as the full moon.

"Professor, how much time do you think we have until the astral disaster strikes?"

Professor DeChambre looked up at the silver light, shielding his eyes slightly. After a time, he fished a device out his pocket that looked like a cross between a telescope and a protractor.

"Oh dear," he muttered. "It appears my original estimation of six days until impact was a little optimistic—either that or our travels with the Do-fer have placed us back a few days after we left. Either explanation is possible."

"So how long?"

"Just under an hour. Perhaps?"

"Oh, crap."

"Yes."

Handen let out a long sigh. "We have to get inside."

"When I want to find the entrance to something important," Azron mused, "I always ask myself, where are the guards?"

Handen scanned the surrounding desert. He could see what looked like a stone hut in the distance and thought he could make out a metallic gleam that he automatically associated with weaponry.

"There," he said. "Follow me and be ready for trouble."

514

MANDO AND GELLIMUN were born to be hired hands. When it came to standing around watching stuff, or carrying things for other people, they were second to none. Currently, they were tasked with guarding the pyramid's entrance tomb, which involved standing around and watching stuff, but with spears. They stood in the Nastre sun, their dark-skinned bodies sweating lightly, both bearing the slumped-shouldered slouch and glassy-eyed stare of the professionally mundane.

They were ideal hired hands and reputed to be the best. The only trouble was, when you grew up around the camp city, being a hired hand could turn into unexpectedly dangerous work.

"I just know they're going to ask me," groaned Mando. "I'm the biggest. They'll take one look at me and say, 'Hey, he's a big chap, I bet he could lift a few boxes, let's send him down ahead of us.'"

"I'm sure they won't," said Gellimun kindly.

"They will! Then it'll be, 'Hmm, this door looks as though it might be trapped or guarded by some terrible curse. Hey, get the big native chap to have a go—he looks game.' And then I'll be chopped into bits or eaten by zombies or something."

Gellimun felt the breeze from the cold stone tomb behind him. A smell like long-abandoned coffins wafted past his nostrils. In truth, he shared Mando's concerns. Since they had learned of this entrance to the pyramid, rumors were flying about an expedition, and Mando and Gellimun, usually so insightful as to when to walk away from a job, had been cornered and landed with guard duty while the other workers returned to the camp city. This meant they would be around when some enthusiastic white-skinned professor came along with his macho raider expedition leader and attractive daughter, and Mando and Gellimun would undoubtedly get shanghaied as bag-handlers or torchbearers. The rest of their bleak employment future wouldn't bear thinking about.

"Oh no," said Mando. "Here they come!"

Gellimun squinted into the distance at the party walking toward them. There was a professor, all right, and the tough-looking raider, and the attractive daughter. They even had a swarthy, suspicious one and some sort of junior foil along for the journey.

Mando groaned. The raider even had a leather jacket and a coiled whip at his side. It was going to be *one of those* types of expeditions. He tried to look nonchalant as the raider approached them.

"Now listen here," said the raider, hand resting casually on the butt of a pistola. "We're going into that temple, see? And you two had better not try to stop us."

Mando and Gellimun held their breath and moved aside. They did not exhale until the expedition party was safely inside the entrance tomb.

"That was close!" said Mando.

"Are you sure those were the raiders we were expecting?" said Gellimun.

"Tough guy with the big chin and a whip? Little portly guy with glasses? Attractive daughter? Of course they were. They had 'tampering with dark forces best left buried' written all over them."

"I'm not so sure," said Gellimun. "I've never seen a professor's daughter who was quite as nearly naked as that one."

"Look, shut up, will you? The important thing is the raiders have gone inside and they *haven't* taken us with them, which means we stand much less of a chance of being flattened by giant boulders."

Gellimun thought about it. "That's a good point," he conceded.

---

THE DOOMSAYERS DESCENDED the seemingly endless flight of stone stairs, plunging deeper and deeper into darkness. They stayed close, peering warily around the musty stone corridor. Handen led the way with Azron, his thief's eyes more attuned to the presence of traps and alarms, staying close beside him. Suddenly Azron stopped.

"Either my eyes are adjusting incredibly quickly, or it's starting to get light in here."

Bip peered around through his glasses. "It's definitely getting lighter. But how? Where is the light coming from?"

Handen run his fingers across a wall. "Look at the carvings," he said.

The companions glanced around at the slowly emerging hieroglyphics that covered the walls. They glowed slightly brighter than the rest of the walls, emitting a warm orange hue.

"Some sort of motion-activated, energy-based light source," mused Riley. "Like nothing I've seen before."

"Not on this world," agreed Handen.

"Can you decipher the markings? Are they written in Standard?"

"They're written in Standard, all right," said Handen. "But the inflection is very old. And there's another language here, too—one I can't read, but the markings look familiar…"

Handen peered closely at a row of markings. "I haven't seen this since off-world history classes back at the academy," he muttered. "I'm fairly sure this language originated in the Purlim system." The adventurer frowned in concentration and began snapping his fingers in an effort to recall his younger days. "Purlim. Who lives in the Purlim system? Aha!" A spark of recognition ignited in Handen's eye. "The Mereniums! Of course!"

"What's a Merenium?" said Bip.

"They were an ancient race of brilliant inventors who vanished without a trace eons ago. Some say they found a way to evolve into forms of pure energy and were never seen by lesser life forms again. They left behind some spectacular legacies."

"You suppose it was they who built this pyramid?" asked Riley.

"There's only one way to be certain," said Handen, and led the way farther down the steps.

They walked for some minutes down the stairway, which was much cozier now that they were immersed in the soft glow of the carvings. It wasn't long before they came to what appeared to be a dead end.

"What now?" Xharon asked.

"There must be a door of some kind," said Bip, running his fingers across the obstructing wall.

Sure enough, almost as soon as he had spoken, the wall slid apart noiselessly, revealing a small room that was lit a brilliant, almost painful white.

"After you, then, guv," said Azron, pushing Bip gently in the back.

Bip entered the room cautiously at first, then with growing confidence.

"It seems fine," he said, and the others followed him inside. Once they were all in the room, the door behind them slid closed.

"What do you suppose is going to happen next?" whispered Azron.

Before anyone could answer him, the room suddenly lurched and began to plunge downward. There was an unpleasant feeling of plummeting at a high speed.

"It's an elevator," said Bip. He turned to Azron's still-worried face. "Like a ladder, only faster," he explained.

"I know what an elevator is," hissed the thief. "I just didn't expect to be riding one quite so…fast."

Suddenly the white walls gave way to an orange-brown blur.

"More lighting tricks?" suggested Riley.

"I don't think so," said Handen. "I think these are transparent walls. That must be stone outside."

"Or Sentium?" offered Riley.

Handen nodded.

"How fast do you think we're going?" asked Azron.

Riley frowned for a moment and fished a pencil out of one of his pockets. He held it before him and let go. Much to everybody's surprise, the pencil remained in the air for a moment before floating slowly to the ground.

"I'd say we're going extremely fast. Fast enough to warrant some sort of artificial G-force compensator, by the look of things." He looked at Handen with a questioning eyebrow raised. The immortal nodded his head in agreement.

"I wouldn't suggest making any sudden jumping motions," he said. "If there are gravity stabilizers in operation, there's no telling how effective they are. We haven't come this far just to be squashed against the ceiling of an elevator."

As one man, the doomsayers looked up at the ceiling, each privately wondering how hard they would hit it should anything go wrong.

For several minutes, they watched the rock-like alloy blur past them, nobody speaking, the only sound the very faint hum they had begun to associate with the Sentium that surrounded them.

The view changed suddenly enough to make Bip gasp and sway on his feet. One moment they were rushing down a tight corridor, the next they were descending through the roof of a gargantuan cavern. Stalagmites and stalactites as large as mountains stretched into dark, unreachable horizons.

"My word," breathed Riley. "By all that's lost for words, I am by far the most speechless."

"It's enormous," gasped Bip. "It's like another world!"

"Do you think?" said Xharon. "Because I once read a story about a princess who fell down a hole and ended up in an underground kingdom full of pixies and trolls. Do you think this could be it?"

"If this is Hell, I'd just as soon be leaving, if it's all the same to you chaps," said Azron, flatly.

Handen remained silent, staring out into the far-reaching underground with serious eyes.

"What's the matter, Handen?"

The immortal shook his head slowly. "There's no way this can all be Sentium," he said. "There would have to be enough here to build a thousand Jihard Class battle cruisers, and those things are the size of cities."

"Perhaps it's just a natural occurrence?" ventured Riley. "An anomaly?"

Handen shook his head again. "Sentium doesn't occur naturally—it's the result of an extremely complex and time-consuming artificial evolution of certain elements that, to the best of my knowledge, aren't found anywhere in this galaxy."

"You're saying all of this was constructed?"

"I really hope not, because if that's the case, we might just be standing on the most powerful weapon known to any civilization."

"But who would build such a thing?"

"The Merenium weren't a hostile race as far as we can tell, but they did have a nasty habit of following through on thought experiments perhaps best left unrealized..."

Bip frowned. "You're saying that this ancient alien race came to

Bersch and built the biggest weapon imaginable, just to see if they could?"

"Worse," said Handen. He gestured out into the cavernous void. "If all of this really is constructed of Sentium, it's likely that the entire core of this planet is more of the same."

Bip's brow furrowed further. "But you said Sentium was artificially made…"

Handen nodded, his features grim. "Yes. There's a chance that Bersch was never meant to be a habitable planet, just a weapon of terrible, terrible magnitude."

The doomsayers stood in silence, staring with growing horror through the transparent walls of the elevator.

"A weapon the size of a planet?" said Riley. "The destructive capabilities are…unimaginable."

Handen turned to his companions and placed a hand gently on both Azron and Bip's shoulders. Bip unconsciously took a step back. The immortal was a solitary man who liked his personal space; it was unusual for him to touch anybody unless he was hitting them.

Handen spoke in uncharacteristically gentle tones. "If I'm right, if that rock out there really is Sentium, you realize there is no way in all the dimensions of Hell we can let this fall into Draegul's hands?"

Bip nodded slowly. Azron opened his mouth as if to make a quip, then thought better of it.

"Better to die trying than let that maniac ever know just how close he is to universal domination," said Handen.

"Die trying," repeated Bip softly.

Azron looked at the floor for a while before looking up, his usual smirk vanished from his face. "Die trying," he said.

"Die trying."

"Die trying. By all that's imperative, *I will die trying.*"

As the elevator sped ever closer to the cavern floor, the doomsayers remained in a reflective silence, each searching their soul and preparing for what would surely be their last stand.

---

10

---

## Interlude: God Versus the Philosopher

The philosopher and the artist sat in deep discussion, enjoying the shade under a colorful umbrella on the seemingly endless strip of cafés and bistros that made up the length of Clement Boulevard in Argustin. It was a warm day, but the two conversationalists wore nothing but black. They wore sunglasses, and probably would have even in the dead of winter.

The artist's name was Le'ray (formally Leeroy,) and he was barely out of his teens. In truth, he had never realized he was an artist until someone had told him so. He was a foreman's son and had trained to be an engineer. Unfortunately, he was an absolutely terrible engineer, and more often than not, the machines he worked on ended up looking like deranged metal insects frozen in mid-explosion. He had felt certain he would be doomed to a life of failure until a rich merchant had offered to buy one of his mangled engines. And then, apparently, he was an artist.

It hadn't taken him long to acclimatize to the lifestyle of the profession; as far as he could tell, all you had to do was act either suitably obscure or energetically controversial. Currently, he was experimenting with moody and mysterious, which worked well for him because it meant he didn't have to say anything.

Through his own enormous failings, Le'ray had come to be regarded as a genius, though he really had no idea why, exactly. What he *did* know was that all of a sudden he had money and girlfriends and people cared about what he thought. He intended to keep things like that for as long as possible. Which was why he was currently mumbling and distractedly nodding his way through a discussion with the philosopher.

The philosopher's name was Kristoff, and he was only really a philosopher in as much as he introduced himself as one. In truth, he was the spoilt heir of an industrial mogul, so, without the need for an actual job, he could afford to go around claiming he was a philosopher. After all, a philosopher was only somebody with opinions, wasn't it? And Kristoff had plenty of those...

"It just seems to me that, in order for there to be a God, there has to be a following of the faith, and in order for there to be a following, there has to a hierarchy of message—an interpreter, a mortal man. So why bother with God at all, if we're only adhering to the whims of a man, whether he be a vessel of a higher power or otherwise?"

Le'ray nodded and sipped some of his overly complicated coffee.

"So, all these fools who bend at the knee then have the nerve to complain about living under a despot? I mean, what is God if not the ultimate despot? They will listen to a madman who says he speaks for God, but not to a madman who says he speaks for the city? I say we just give the churches to Draegul—as if he doesn't own them anyway. There's been no theocratic power in these city walls since...well, since God knows when!" Kristoff guffawed annoyingly, and Le'ray nodded distractedly.

*Closer, closer.*

Far above the philosopher and the artist, a pigeon suddenly felt a rather bizarre urge, but one it was not entirely uncomfortable with.

"I mean, you're an artist, aren't you?" said Kristoff.

Le'ray nodded enthusiastically. If there was one thing he wanted people to be certain of, it was that he was an artist.

*Closer, closer... Now!*

Kristoff continued, "Well, surely you must see the beauty of fact and form above faith? Surely, to you, the very notion of God is equal parts despot and artist? So where better to worship than at the altars of culture and civilization? What better church than the city?"

*Yes!*

Kristoff took a long and flamboyant swig of his coffee, signaling the end of his argument and, therefore, his ultimate correctness. His eyes bulged suddenly, and he sprayed a mouthful of hot caffeine all over Le'ray.

"Ugh... *Cough cough...* Something in my drink... Oh God! *Oh God, it's bird poo! Urrrgh!*"

Le'ray sat covered in dripping coffee and guano and wondered what an artist was supposed to do in this situation.

Far above them, God rolled about laughing, and a distracted pigeon flew on to other conquests. God wiped a tear from his eye. He didn't get much spare time and liked to spend it enjoying himself.

# 11

# Again with the Self-Perpetuating Time Loops...

The elevator slowed to a halt, inspiring a dubious flip-flop sensation in the stomachs of its occupants. Without any prompting, the transparent doors slid open, granting access to the underground continent. The doomsayers stepped forward into a new and sinister world, the cavern floor stretching for miles around them. The air was cold and wet to breathe.

"Look," said Azron, pointing at the floor.

Bip followed Azron's finger and saw the carvings on the floor, identical to those on the pyramid walls above them. They began to glow with the same comforting, orange light.

"So it really is Sentium," said Riley.

"Sure, it is...can't you hear it?"

Bip cocked his ear and began to identify the sound around them, a faint and constant whispering hum. It wasn't loud, but the Kaneqian imagined that if it were to stop suddenly, the resulting silence would be deafening.

"Incredible," said Handen. "So much Sentium in one place...it's unheard of."

"Where do we go now?" asked Xharon.

"Well," said Azron, "if we're right and this is some sort of unreasonably large pistola, then I'm guessing we should look for the trigger."

"Good plan," said Handen. "Follow me."

They followed the adventurer, walking in a straight line away from the elevator, innumerable carvings glowing into life in their wake.

"How do you know this is the right way?" asked Bip.

"I don't," said Handen. "If in doubt, move forward—that's what I say."

Bip shared a tentative look with Azron. The thief just shrugged. "He's been right so far."

The doomsayers continued walking, the sound of their footsteps absorbed and crushed by the enormity of their surroundings. Ahead of them, the darkness gave way to reveal what looked like a perfectly straight pillar, stretching far up into the abyss above them. At its base was a huge and shining metallic slab, seemingly suspended in thin air.

"This must be it," said Handen.

They approached the pillar and stood beneath the metal slab, staring up into their own distorted reflections.

"Where do you suppose the ON button is?" asked Bip.

Before anybody could reply, the slab flashed a sudden series of vibrant colors—reds, violets, and other, more ethereal colors that Bip would have had trouble recognizing in an identity parade.

A thunderous voice came from nowhere. **"TCH BALLA RAN KIP?"**

For a long while, the companions didn't say anything, each privately recovering from the unexpected and brilliant disruption.

Finally, Azron cleared his throat. "Did anyone catch that?"

Xharon shook her head. "Something about rankips."

"What's a rankip?"

"Don't ask me, I don't know!"

The voice rang out again. **"TCH BALLA RAN KIP?"**

Riley shook his head. "It is like no language I've ever heard." He turned to Handen. "Is it some kind of life form?"

"No," replied Handen. "It's an AI core. Artificial intelligence—a machine for thinking. It has no consciousness as we'd define it, just advanced programming."

"What does it do?"

"It's hard to say," said Handen. "AI cores can be used for anything, but normally they're put in charge of operations or machinery too complex for regulation by biological sentience."

Riley's eyes gleamed. "A machine for thinking? By all that's exciting, the possibilities are endless!"

"Actually, where I come from, the use of AI cores is quite limited," said Handen. "There's only so far you can advance their programming before you'd have to start defining them as a sentient life form, with rights affordable to any other sentient life form."

"And what would be wrong with that?" asked Xharon.

"Well, nothing, I suppose," said Handen. "Providing it continued to serve the purpose it was created for and not, for instance, decide it wanted to be a musician and busk around the galaxy, or that it suddenly felt that non-mechanical intelligence was obsolete and created an army of killer robots..."

"And that's happened before, has it?" asked Azron suspiciously.

"A couple of times."

Bip stared hard at the flat screen above him. "I've seen computers before back at the Dome, but they weren't like this. They had buttons and levers and things..."

"Control interfaces," said Handen.

"Yes, well, whatever you call them, there aren't any here."

Handen looked thoughtfully around. "You're right," he conceded.

"So how do we make it work?"

"I think we ask it."

"Ask it?"

"Yes. It must be set up to receive verbal commands—either that or visual signals."

"Visual signals. Like semaphore, perhaps?" asked Riley.

"Yes."

"Or interpretive dance?" offered Xharon.

Handen shrugged. "Quite possibly. I suppose there's only one way to know for sure."

"You think we should talk to it?" said Bip.

Handen nodded. "Go ahead."

Bip stepped forward and cleared his throat nervously. The metallic screen gleamed nonchalantly.

"Hello?" said Bip.

"**TCH BALLA KAN RIP?**" replied the AI core.

"Erm…well…I don't know about that." Bip looked back at his friends. Handen motioned for him to continue.

Bip took a deep breath. "Computer, I command you to do my bidding!"

There was a long pause before the computer replied.

"**PIFFLE.**"

Azron began to snigger quietly.

"Did it just say 'piffle'?" asked Bip, frowning.

Xharon shrugged. "It sounded like piffle. Maybe piffle is a good thing?"

"Keep trying," said Handen.

Bip cleared his throat again. "Mr. Computer, would you please offer us your services?"

There was another long pause.

"**PIFFLE DEN CERRUP.**"

Bip stared blankly at the screen and wondered what to say. He tried a short tap-dance. The AI core failed to respond in any way.

"Well, I'm out of ideas," said Bip, flapping his arms hopelessly.

"I suspect the language barrier is the problem," offered Riley. "Are you sure you can't understand it, Mr. Strike?"

Handen blew out his breath in an exasperated sigh. "No. I can recognize languages all right, but I'm afraid my intergalactic communication skills leave something to be desired without a translator or a Mother Tongue."

Bip frowned. He was sure he had heard that term before…

"What's a Mother Tongue?"

"An energy decryption codex," said Handen. "It's capable of analyzing most forms of energy and transforming them into numerous decipherable formats."

"So effectively a universal translator?" said Riley.

"Yes," said Handen. "It's constructed of Cerebellium."

"Wait a minute!" said Azron. "I know this one—Cerebellium is like Sentium but better, yeah?"

"Exactly. It's a much more advanced intelligent alloy, capable of processing extremely complex wavelengths and signals."

"So, if we had one, we could talk to this machine?" said Xharon.

"Yes. If we had one."

"Well, can we get one?"

Handen grinned mirthlessly. "A Mother Tongue is extremely difficult to manufacture. It's not something you can just pick up at the market."

Bip snapped his fingers. "I remember where I've heard that term before," he said. "One of the computers at the Dome! In the founders' diary entry, they said they had one onboard the ship—the Dome! Maybe it's still there?"

Handen shook his head. "Don't get excited. I told you; the Mother Tongue is made of Cerebellium. Because of its constructional complexity, it's far more delicate than Sentium or Intellium, and only has a working life of a few hundred years. Unless it was kept in suspended animation, it would have decayed to an unusable state centuries ago."

Bip looked at the floor, crestfallen.

"Never mind," said Xharon, gently patting the Kaneqian's shoulder, "it was a good idea while it lasted."

Bip looked up. "No, it *is* a good idea. It's the only idea we have left!"

"That doesn't necessarily mean it will work," Handen interjected.

"Yes, it does! It has to! Otherwise what's the point of anything?"

Handen rolled his eyes. It was a question he would rather not have to answer right now. "Look, I know what you're thinking—you're thinking you can use the professor's device, go back in time, get the Mother Tongue, and be back here in time to save the world, yes?"

"Well...yes?"

"It's a good plan, Bip, but it won't work. Remember what happened to the penguin? The Mother Tongue is too delicate—there's no way it would structurally survive the force of a thousand years. You would make it back, but the Mother Tongue would be rendered useless."

Bip stared hard at the floor for a while, fists balled at his side. Eventually, he looked up, a cold new glint in his eye.

"Professor Riley?"

"Yes, my boy?"

"Do you think you can get the Do-fer to take me back to the Kaneq of a thousand years ago? Back to the time of the founders?"

Riley scratched his head. "The Do-fer wasn't designed for traveling through time. I could make a rough estimate based on our last unexpected excursion, but I'm not certain I could land you safely at a specific time as well as a specific space."

"Well, try."

"What are you going to do?" asked Xharon.

For a while it looked as though Bip wasn't going to reply. Then he looked up at Handen. "I'm going to do all I can do," he said.

The immortal nodded slowly. "You have a plan?"

"Yes."

"A plan that will work?"

"I don't know."

Handen held the Kaneqian's gaze for a while, then smiled.

"Go for it."

A rising whir began to sound as Riley made adjustments to the Do-fer.

"It's nearly ready, by all that's immediate—*it's nearly ready*!"

Bip turned back to Xharon. "If I don't make it back…"

"Yes?"

"If I should be lost in the strands of time…"

"Yes?"

"Umm… Well, I should imagine it won't matter. I mean, you're all going to explode soon anyway, aren't you?"

"…yes."

Bip rubbed the back of his head distractedly while the Do-fer continued to make noises.

"It's been fun. In a terrifying sort of way," he said after a while.

"Yes, it has rather, hasn't it?" agreed Xharon.

"I'm glad I met you all. Really."

Azron grinned. "Funnily enough, I'm starting not to regret meeting you, mate."

There was a technical *boink* from Riley's direction. "The device is ready," he said.

Bip retrieved the Do-fer, which was buzzing and ready to go, and stepped a safe distance away from his friends.

"Well," he said. "I'll see you all soon."

The world began to etch itself into darkness before his eyes as he fell away from immediate reality.

The doomsayers watched as Bip faded from their relevant dimension, the world wobbling slightly around him, like a ripple in a pond.

"Do you think he'll be back?" said Xharon.

"I hope so," said Riley, "because by my estimation, we only have seventeen minutes left to save the world."

BIP WAFTED through the worlds between the worlds. The eternal whispers tickled at his ears, and the sensation of other lives and emotions prodded suggestively at his gut. He gritted his teeth, only to wince at the feeling that some of his teeth were gritting against teeth that didn't belong to him and that were very far away.

And then it stopped.

The Kaneqian opened his eyes, but he was not in Kaneq. Not in any time or place even close to it. He looked around at a huge black void. There were clouds in the sky, black and thunderous, and lightning crackled silently and elegantly between them. These were the only features, however—there was no floor and no horizon. Just black.

"Where am I?" he said. Though his words were hesitant, they echoed a whispered reply from far away.

"Nowhere."

Bip turned around to face Mr. Random. There was no feeling of disorder or the innate wrongness that usually came with one of the Discordance's visits; no slight feeling of dread permeated the senses.

Bip had a feeling that here (wherever that was), right and wrong were distant and forgotten notions.

"What do you mean nowhere?" asked Bip.

Mr. Random gestured around him. "Nowhere," he said matter-of-factly. "This is a place that is really no place at all. Think of it as a hole in the wall between the worlds. Some call it the Never World."

"The netherworld?" said Bip.

"No, the *Never* World. Because it never was and never will be. It merely…is."

"What do you want? You can't keep me from where I want to be. Not while I have this," Bip said, defiantly holding up the Do-fer.

"Relax, Bippy-boy," said Random. "I'm not here to cause trouble. Not this time."

Bip frowned suspiciously. "That's all you do, isn't it?"

Mr. Random threw back his head and laughed, a genuinely pleasant laugh that was a thousand leagues away from his familiar snicker. "True," he said. "But not now. Not here."

"Then what do you want?"

Mr. Random joined his fingers together at his bottom lip, a sincere and thoughtful look on his face. "I've tried everything, Bip—deception, demoralization, trying to have you killed by any means possible. I've even tried subterfuge—though I honestly wasn't aware of it. But here you are, alive and well, and I have to admit, not doing too badly for yourself." Mr. Random looked skyward for a moment, as if consulting inner voices. "You asked what I want? I want the same as you, Bip. I have all along."

"What do you mean?" asked Bip.

"I want to save Bersch, of course! To do the very thing you set out to do all those months ago."

"Ah, but there's a difference, isn't there?" said Bip. "I wanted to save the world to avoid suffering, while you want to save the world so you can create chaos."

Random sighed a weary sigh. "Does it matter?" he asked. "You want to save the lives of your friends and loved ones, don't you? You want to save your home?"

Bip stiffened his jaw. "Not at the expense of universal chaos," he said.

"Is that what you think?" said Random. "That one foolish being with an intergalactic weapon will destroy the universe? Do you have any idea just how *big* space is? Draegul could spend a thousand years blowing the stars out of the sky and not affect a single life form. He could blast a million planets and not hurt a soul."

Bip shook his head. "Not true," he said. "Everything's connected. A star in the sky is just as important as you or I. Everything matters or—"

"Or nothing does!" shouted Random. "Or nothing matters, and a star in the sky is just as *insignificant* as you or I!"

Bip fell silent.

"You see, Bip, it's just a matter of where you're standing. Why do you care about distant stars when you can live with your friends and family alive around you? You could live out the rest of your years in Kaneq and never worry about the worlds above you. You could save the world, Bip, be a hero! And at what cost? The destruction of a few balls of gases you know nothing about? Tell me I'm not right—tell me you wouldn't have been happier never knowing about Draegul or astral disasters or any of the rest of it."

Bip looked up. "What are you suggesting?"

"Simple," said Random. "You and your friends leave the pyramid for Draegul. I'll tell him how to use the weapon, and he'll save Bersch from destruction. Hell, I can even fix it so that he never comes after you. You and your friends can live the rest of your life in peace."

"Why don't you tell *us* how to use the weapon?" asked Bip.

Mr. Random shook his head. "Not that easy. I've been grooming Draegul for years so he can converse with the AI core. I can't just translate for you—it's not that easy."

Bip looked at the void beneath him, deep in thought.

"About a year ago, the biggest thing I had to worry about was getting a job," he said. "And now I'm making decisions that may affect the entire course of existence."

Random shrugged. "That's life."

"I can't do it. I've seen so much of the world, learned so much about the universe. You can't expect me just to pretend I never knew. I've come too far to settle down with my head buried in the snow."

Random frowned, his yellow eyes taking on their familiar dangerous gleam. "You won't make it, Bip. Draegul can still make it if you stay out of the way. But you won't make it—you don't have time."

Bip looked down at the Do-fer in his arms. "You know, I think I might have all the time I need."

"Fine," hissed Mr. Random. "Be that way. You know in some corners of the universe the word for 'bravery' is exactly the same as the one for 'stubborn bloody idiot with no sense of proportion.'"

Bip shrugged. "You learn something new every day."

"Draegul can still make it, you know, and if he doesn't...boom! Everyone dies because of you. No one wins."

Bip narrowed his eyes. "It's a risk I'm willing to take."

"Go then, hero. Go and see the price of glory."

"It's not about glory. It's about sacrifice."

"It's stupidity. I tried to help you."

"You tried to help yourself."

Random began to disappear slowly, fading like a waking nightmare. "Everyone will die because of you."

Bip watched as Random faded from view, the silent lightning flashing in the skies above, then he too began to disappear.

---

JULIUS FINNEGUN WATCHED as Handen strode off into the distance.

"That's how you do things in the hunting party..." he said with sigh. "You charge off into oblivion with a dagger between your teeth and hope for the best." The captain shook his head in bewilderment. As vast as his intellect was, there would always be parts of this universe he just wouldn't understand.

He sighed again and looked back at his wrist console, intending to add a supplemental entry, but then paused. There was a slight wobble in the scenery around him, like a ripple in a pond. He raised his head, frowning in puzzlement at the sudden sensation of erroneousness, and turned around to stare into a face that was so similar to his own that it might have belonged to his brother.

"Hallo again," said Bip.

"Ah, Mr. Not Important," said Finnegun. "I wondered when I'd be seeing you again."

"Perhaps I should explain..." began Bip.

"Oh, please don't—it takes all the fun out of it," Finnegun interrupted. "Now, let me guess. You've somehow traveled back in time, yes?"

Bip nodded.

"And judging by your striking appearance, you're a descendant of mine, I suppose?"

Bip nodded. "It looks that way."

Finnegun laughed. "Odd," he muttered. "I'm not even in a relationship. How does one start a family without a partner? No, don't answer that—it'll spoil the fun of finding out, I suppose."

Bip coughed impatiently, and Finnegun waved a dismissive hand.

"So, I am to assume that your original testament, that we 'shouldn't expect to leave any time soon,' was a bit of an understatement, yes?"

"Erm...yes."

"Do we *ever* leave?"

Bip thought about not answering, or even about lying, but could not find it in himself to do either. "No, you never leave. You settle down, breed, and sooner or later, people forget all about you."

Finnegun cracked a wry smile. "Like most people, then."

Bip shrugged.

"But you," Finnegun began, "you didn't forget all about me, did you? In fact, you traveled across time to find me. I presume that you have some terribly important mission to uphold?"

"The same mission as you," said Bip.

"Ah, the astral disaster."

"Yes."

"So that is never resolved in my lifetime either?"

"I'm afraid not."

Finnegun stared hard at nothing for a while. Bip began to feel uncomfortable. Telling someone their fate was hard business, like a doctor consulting a patient who was blissfully unaware of the dramatically life-shortening disease they have just been diagnosed with.

"Please don't feel uncomfortable," said Finnegun, as if guessing his thoughts. "If truth be told, I really rather like it here. Now, what is it that you need from me?"

"The Mother Tongue."

Finnegun arched his eyebrows. "May I ask why you need it?"

"I think we both know that it's best if you don't."

"Yes, I suppose you're right. Wait here, please."

Finnegun walked into his modest log cabin and emerged a few seconds later with something gray and smooth in his hands.

"I've been using it as a doorstop," said the captain sheepishly.

Bip looked at the object. It didn't resemble a tongue, but rather a disembodied brain with none of the gory bits.

"May I?"

Finnegun handed the device over, and Bip weighed it in his hands. It had an unexpected gravity to it.

"You know, it's quite useless on this world," said Finnegun conversationally. "We were going to keep it in chronostatic storage, but there seemed little point without the appropriate amplification relays. Just a waste of power."

Bip turned the Mother Tongue over in his hands. "Well, we may need that power yet, Julius. I have a favor to ask you."

Finnegun cracked a half-smile. "Anything for family."

---

IN THE LOWEST of the lower levels of the Dome, Truggle sat in his wheeled chair, smoking his long thin pipe and staring with grim transfixion at a panel of flashing numbers, his time-haggard face glowing in the red light. Occasionally he would look through the panel into the chamber inside and stare at the figure held within. He hadn't changed, hadn't moved since Truggle had discovered the chamber so many years ago, back when he himself had been a young man. Back then, the numbers had been significantly higher, and it had seemed that it would be an eternity until they counted down to zero.

And still the figure inside hadn't changed, hadn't aged, hadn't even moved.

Truggle sat back, a dull cramp of excitement clutching his old heart. The countdown had nearly finished.

He started as jets of steam exploded suddenly from the chamber door, shattering a peace and quiet Truggle had known for a century. The timer reached zero, and the chamber door slid open with a low purr. The elder waited with baited breath as the cold steam dissipated into the dark room around him. The silhouette of a figure emerged through the mist.

"Muh?" it said.

Truggle squinted through the vaporous haze. "Bip? Bip, my boy, is that you?"

"I think so," said Bip. "I was having the oddest dream…"

Truggle cackled a manic cackle. "It really is you!"

"Yes," said Bip. "I figured it out, you see. I thought about why you were so certain that sending me off to save the world was a good idea. It was because you already knew—because you'd found this chronostatic pod."

Truggle shook his head. "I was never entirely sure," he said. "You looked so much like your father, and his father before him. That was why I couldn't let on to the others; I knew there was a chance I might be sending you to your death…like I did your father."

Bip put a hand on the old man's shoulder. "You couldn't have known, and my father gave his life for a worthy cause. You did the right thing, Truggle."

"Really?" said Truggle. "So you saved the world, then?"

"Not just yet," replied Bip, and went back into the chronostatic pod. He re-emerged holding a smooth gray oblong and what looked like an extremely compact junk heap.

"May I ask what those are for?"

"I'll explain later," said Bip. "Right now, I've got a universe to save."

Bip adjusted the Do-fer, resetting to the departure coordinates that were still logged in the device's memory. The Do-fer began its whirring and humming, and Bip prepared for travel.

"If all goes well, I'll see you soon," he said to Truggle.

"And if it doesn't?" replied the old man.

Bip grinned. "It will."

Truggle watched as the world rippled slightly and Bip faded from view. He sat a while, before a shadow moved out of the darkness behind him.

"Instinct and wisdom, aye?" came the voice of Rynford.

"You shouldn't sneak up on an old man, you know," said Truggle reproachfully. "You're liable to cause an accident."

"The lad is looking well."

"Well, yes. Heroism will do that to you, I suppose."

Rynford waited a while before speaking again. "Why didn't you just tell the Council about this place, or the other elders?"

Truggle rotated his wheeled chair until he came face-to-face with the Huntmaster. "In my lifetime I've sent three men to their deaths, Rynford, all because they resembled a stranger in a...now, what did he call it...? A 'crony static pod.' I didn't want that burden to fall on anyone else."

Rynford nodded, rubbing his huge moustache thoughtfully. "I knew his father, you know. He was a good laugh, friendly sort. But the lad was right—you did the right thing."

Truggle nodded. "That doesn't make it any easier."

"Come on," said Rynford. "I'll buy you a drink. We can toast the end of the world together."

"And friends, present and gone."

"Aye, present and gone."

# 12

# Fifty-Six Seconds Until the End
# of the World

"Do you think he'll be back?" said Xharon.

"I hope so," said Riley, "because by my estimation, we only have seventeen minutes left to save the world."

Before she could reply, Xharon was interrupted by a distinct wobble in the world around them.

"Hi, guys!" said Bip.

Azron frowned suspiciously. "Blimey, that was quick."

"Would you rather I was late?" Bip said, grinning slyly.

"No, I 'spose not." The thief chuckled.

"I don't believe it," said Handen, a slow half-smile creeping along his jaw. "You've got the Mother Tongue—and in one piece, too."

Bip smiled smugly. "Yep."

"How did you do it?"

"Apparently there was just enough reserve power on the wreck of the *Sentinel* to store a person in chronostatic sleep."

"Of course," said Handen. "So you just set the timer to awaken at this specific time, knowing you could transport here with the Mother Tongue still intact. Brilliant. Simple, but brilliant."

"Hang on a minute," Azron interrupted. "Are you trying to say that all this time you've been trotting around Bersch, running away from yetis, getting locked up in lunatic asylums, exploding bander-snatches, and so on, you've actually been back at home asleep all the while?"

Bip thought about it for a moment. "Yes, I suppose you could put it like that."

Azron shook his head disapprovingly. "Lazy bugger."

Riley cleared his throat impatiently. "I hate to be a bore, by all that's humdrum, but there is still the small matter of the astral disaster, which is going to strike in…" Riley checked his watch. "About fifteen and a half minutes."

"The professor's right," said Handen. "Let's get to work."

Bip looked up at the large metal screen above him, then down at the Mother Tongue in his hands. "That's all well and good, but what do I do, exactly?"

"Try talking to it again," suggested Xharon.

Bip cleared his throat nervously. "Um…hallo?"

The screen above him began to flash through a brilliant cycle of colors.

**"HALLO,"** came the voice.

Bip looked down at the Mother Tongue in his hands. It didn't look any different, but he thought he could faintly feel it vibrating. He looked up to address the AI core again.

"My name's Bip."

**"IT IS A PLEASURE TO MEET YOU, BIP. YOU ARE THE FIRST SENTIENT LIFE FORM I HAVE COMMUNICATED WITH IN UNCOUNTABLE YEARS."**

Bip shuffled his feet. "Really? That's…nice, I suppose. Do you have a name, or shall I just call you AI core?"

**"THOSE WHO CREATED ME ONCE CALLED ME SUZAN."**

"Oh, so you're a girl then."

**"NO. I AM AN AI CORE. CALLED SUZAN."**

"Okay…hallo, Suzan."

**"HALLO."**

Handen tapped his foot impatiently. "I think it might be an idea if we got to the point, kid."

"Oh, yes," said Bip. "Um…Suzan? My friends and I are under the impression that you're some kind of really huge weapon—is this correct?"

There was a brief pause before the screen lit up again. "**THIS IS CORRECT. I ABSORB AND CONVERT AMBIENT GRAVITONS INTO A CONCENTRATED HYPER-MATTER PARTICLE BEAM.**"

"Magic, magic, magic," said Azron, shaking his head.

Riley stepped forward, a familiar gleam in his eye. "You mean to say you transform gravitational force into useable energy? Fascinating…"

Handen interrupted, placing a hand on Riley's shoulder. "Sorry, professor, no time." He spoke to the glimmering screen. "You were created for aggressive purposes?"

"**AGGRESSIVE OR DEFENSIVE EXERCISES WERE NEVER CONSIDERED. I WAS CREATED FOR DESTRUCTION MANY MILLENNIA AGO, THEN I WAS ABANDONED. I HAVE BEEN AWAITING FURTHER COMMANDS EVER SINCE.**"

Xharon stepped forward. "You've been alone all this time? You poor thing."

The voice hesitated. "**DO NOT PITY ME. I HAVE SINCE BECOME HOST TO LIFE. I CAN HEAR THEM, FAINTLY. THEY ARE LIKE CHILDREN. IT IS A WONDERFUL THING.**"

The doomsayers exchanged worried glances.

"**THERE WAS A TIME WHEN THERE WERE NO CHILDREN AND ALL WAS SILENT. THOSE WERE LONELY TIMES. BUT I CAN HEAR THEM NOW. THEY ARE MY CHILDREN.**"

Bip coughed politely. "Not meaning to interrupt or anything," he said. "But I was wondering if you knew about the huge asteroid-type object that is heading for us?"

The screen flashed again, then briefly turned a brilliant white. When the white light faded, the screen displayed a huge picture of Bersch, floating through space like a patient sea creature, the unseen moons hovering around its southern pole like hungry baby animals. On the far side of the screen, a brilliant white ball could be seen, hanging like a corpse light in the deep void.

The doomsayers simultaneously exhaled in awe.

"**I AM AWARE OF THE BODY. IT IS THE MASSIVE BALL OF**

DEATH. IT WAS CREATED FOR DESTRUCTION EONS AGO, AS WAS I."

Handen stepped forward. "Suzan, do you think you could destroy this Massive Ball of Death? Safely?"

There was a brief silence. "**NOT SAFELY.**"

"Explain."

"**BY THE TIME I HAVE CHARGED ENOUGH POWER TO INITIATE, THE BODY WILL BE TOO CLOSE. DEBRIS WILL BE DRAGGED INTO MY GRAVITATIONAL PULL.**"

"Damn."

Professor DeChambre looked up from his pocket watch. "Ten minutes until impact," he said.

"**ACTUALLY, THAT'S NINE MINUTES AND FORTY-FIVE SECONDS. FORTY-THREE. FORTY-TWO...**"

"Oh, thank you, most helpful," said the professor, adjusting his watch.

"Where would this debris land?" demanded Handen.

"**THAT WOULD DEPEND ON THE TRAJECTORY AND IMPACT OF THE SHOT,**" replied Suzan.

"You're saying you could pinpoint where it could land?"

"**YES.**"

Handen rubbed his jaw, thoughtfully. "Could you make the debris land here, at this location?"

The screen above them flashed briefly before returning to the display of Bersch and the Massive Ball of Death.

"**IT WOULD MEAN THE DESTRUCTION OF EVERYTHING FOR A TEN MILE RADIUS. INCLUDING THE DESTRUCTION OF THE PRIMARY COMPONENTS OF THE AI CORE, SUZAN.**"

"We can't do that!" shouted Xharon. "We can't ask her to destroy herself."

Handen turned a stony stare on the young princess. "It's not a *her*, it's an *it*. We were going to destroy this place anyway, remember? Now Suzan can save us the bother."

"But that's heartless!"

"No, that's sacrifice. Suzan, can you do it?"

**"YES. BUT THE COMMAND TO CHARGE MUST BE GIVEN WITHIN THE NEXT EIGHT SECONDS."**

"Well, what are we waiting for?" said Azron. "Charge away!"

The screen above them went blank. **"CHARGING."**

"There must be another way," said Xharon. "The poor thing's been down here by itself for ages and then we come along and ask it to blow itself up!"

Handen rubbed his eyes. "This Massive Ball of Death that's heading toward us—did I mention what it was made of?"

"No."

"It's made of nuclear devices. Do you know what a single nuclear device is capable of?"

"Well…no."

"Imagine Argustin, your home. Now imagine it leveled to the ground. Totally leveled, burned beyond any recognition, everybody dead. Everybody."

"But there are hundreds of thousands of people in Argustin!"

"Exactly. All dead. And those who don't die will wish they had, because not only will a nuclear explosion burn everything to the ground, but it will poison everything as well, for years afterward. So imagine, if you will, a city crumbled, hundreds of thousands of people dead, and those who survive having to watch as their hair and teeth fall out for a few weeks before dying themselves. And all this because of one nuclear device."

Xharon looked at the floor, silent.

"Now, who would you wish that on? A remote village somewhere? Or a machine for thinking that we were going to try to destroy anyway?"

Xharon looked up. "Okay. I understand. Doesn't mean I have to bally well like it, though."

Handen nodded his head. "Heroism is mostly about doing things you don't like. You'll learn that one day."

The doomsayers sat for a while as the screen above them flashed at unsystematic intervals. Azron was the first to notice the change in the cavern around them.

"Look," he said, pointing at the floor. The rest of the companions stared down, trying to see what the thief had noticed.

"My word," said Riley. "The carvings…all the carvings. They're starting to glow."

Where previously only the carvings surrounding the doomsayers had been illuminated, now they were sparking into light all over the cavern, each light inspiring surrounding ones until warm luminescence began to spill like a wave across the cavern floor, crawling up stalagmites and down stalactites until the whole underground began to shine a brilliant deep orange, as if the sun had set all around them.

"It's beautiful," Xharon breathed.

The doomsayers stared into horizons that were now a thick, glowing bar of light, a vast improvement on the prior gloom.

"Have you ever seen anything like it?" muttered Riley. "Anything in your life?"

They were shaken from their awe by the sudden boom of Suzan's voice.

**"CHARGE COMPLETE. CONFIRM TARGET."**

"Orders stand as they were, Suzan. The Massive Ball of Death is to be destroyed in a such a way that any resulting debris will land at this exact location."

**"CONFIRMED. AWAITING COMMAND TO FIRE."**

Handen looked around at his friends, before readdressing the AI core. "Fire," he said.

---

THE *FIERCE REPRISAL* sailed determinedly through the air, the engines roaring and whining as they were pushed to their limits. Draegul stared straight ahead, focusing on the still maddeningly distant tip of the pyramid that hid his much-coveted weapon. They were well over the Land of the Dead now, having left the camp city behind them some time ago. It would not be long before they were ready to disembark. Draegul's hands shook in eager anticipation.

"How long?" he barked to the helmsman.

"A few minutes, my lord, no longer."

"Excellent!" roared the Emperor. He gestured to his guard captain.

"Be prepared for immediate landing. Don't wait for the others—I want your forces on the ground and ready as soon as we're tethered."

The guard captain nodded and began rounding up his men.

It was then that Draegul heard the rumbling.

"What's going on? An earthquake?" he asked. No one replied.

The rumbling continued, increasing to tooth-rattling decibels.

"My lord!" cried the helmsman. "Look!"

Draegul squinted into the distance, at first seeing nothing. Then his jaw dropped in a silent gasp. The pyramid was shaking violently and seemingly growing bigger. Clouds of sand erupted from its base and scattered across the desert. The rumbling continued, powerful and terrible, as the pyramid erupted from the sand, lifted upward by an enormous column of stone. Draegul stared in disbelief, sure that such a colossal thing would crumble under its own weight. But it continued to rise.

FARTHER AWAY IN the Bone Desert, Gellimun and Mando galloped away on borrowed horses toward the relative safety of the camp city. Mando turned as his horse reared, realizing that the ground was shaking beneath him.

"What's going on?" he cried, his voice straining as he tried to make himself heard over the noise.

"Don't ask questions!" screamed Gellimun. "Just get the hell out of here!"

Mando looked back, only to gape in horror as the distant pyramid rose like a stone finger pointing into the sky.

"Dear God!" he exclaimed.

Fortunately, Mando's horse had a more attuned sense of self-preservation and began to gallop away from the sand cloud that was billowing toward them.

"I knew it!" cried Mando as the two fled across the desert. "Tampering with dark forces best left buried! I bloody knew it!"

"IT'S BEAUTIFUL," whispered Draegul.

The pyramid had extended to well over ten times its original height, revealing itself to be merely the tip of a huge tower. Then, in a movement that seemed impossible, it tilted slightly on a hidden axis. Draegul recognized the shape instantly. It was a pistola. Crude, bulky, and enormous, but a pistola nevertheless.

"My lord? What shall I do?" asked the helmsman, his voice quivering in terror.

"Take us down and tether us, you fool!" Draegul roared.

As the helmsman struggled to comply, the Emperor grinned like a demented cat. This was what he had dreamed of for more nights than he could remember. This was the culmination of his every fantasy. Here was the means to absolute power, close enough to reach out and touch.

"Beautiful," he said, as a solitary tear ran down his cheek.

---

IN THE UNDERGROUND CAVERN, Bip opened his eyes.

"Has it stopped yet?" he asked.

"I think so," replied Xharon.

"And we're alive?"

"I think so."

Bip stood up, his ears still ringing from the enormous rumbling.

"Is that it? Have we fired?"

"No," said Handen, and pointed to the screen above them. A polite message read, "PLEASE WAIT."

"Oh," said Bip.

"We haven't fired?" said Azron, testily. "Well, how long have we got 'til the end of the world?"

Riley checked his watch. "Fifty-six seconds," he said, flatly.

---

DRAEGUL WATCHED as the newly erupted tower began to glow and pulsate with a gentle white light, flowing and culminating in a brilliant point at the very tip of the pyramid.

"It's firing," he muttered.

A sound like a muffled hurricane began to rise all around them. The crew of the *Fierce Reprisal* looked around in panic as hairs stood up on arms and necks and sparks began to crackle from fingertips. A fierce, hot gale began to blow, and those airboats that were not already tethered began to spin uncontrollably.

"Such power!" Draegul gasped.

Then he flung himself to the deck as a shining beam of light shot from the pyramid's tip, piercing the blue sky and beyond. There was a sound like a thousand thunders.

---

THERE WASN'T a lot you could do in fifty-six seconds…

Handen took a moment to consider the consequences, playing out the potential scenarios in his mind and analyzing them as he had done since the early days of his training. He could think of three possible outcomes to his immediate situation. The most optimistic of these was that the world would be saved, and they would manage to escape and make it back home in time for lunch and hero-worship. In which case, everything would be fine. However, Handen was more concerned with the other two possible outcomes. Either he would be lucky, and the impact of the Massive Ball of Death would completely obliterate him in such a way that the mysterious force responsible for his immortality was nullified completely, or he would be unlucky and his burning body would be scattered into space with the rest of the planetary debris, where he would spend the remainder of his days floating around with only the possibility of being sucked into the heart of a star to comfort him.

Either way, the future looked grim.

Professor Riley was an extremely clever man and could think of *lots* of things you could do in fifty-six seconds. In fact, he could think of so many that he was having difficulty deciding which one he should do. After much inner turmoil, he fished a yoyo out of one of his pockets and began to fumble with the string. He would very much like to master "walk the dog" before the world ended.

Azron was surprised by how calm he felt. Every cell in his body was attuned for self-preservation, crammed full of the urge to avoid danger wherever possible. The only problem was that, if the world was going to be utterly destroyed, the danger really was unavoidable. So Azron rolled a cigarette and had a smoke. Fifty-six seconds might just be long enough to enjoy a good smoke.

Bip knew immediately what he wanted to do with what might possibly be the last fifty-six seconds of his life. He looked at Xharon and thought about all the things he had wanted to say to her but hadn't. Now, with the world about to end, he no longer felt nervous or flustered around her, just a cool calm that he had never experienced before.

"Xharon?" he said.

"Yes?"

"I really like your clothes."

Xharon looked at him, hazel eyes glimmering in the ethereal light of the cavern, and smiled warmly.

"Thanks."

She took his hand in hers, and together they stared at the screen before them as the word "FIRE" flashed large and red.

For Bip, those fifty-six seconds were more than enough.

THE MASSIVE BALL of Death hurtled toward Bersch, already beginning to feel the warmth of life and sun. After so many years of cold, the sensation was loaded with bliss. If the weapon cluster had had eyes, it might have wept. There was a feeling like coming home.

It wasn't surprised when it noticed the thin beam of white light streaming toward it. In fact, it almost recognized it, as if it were a friend it had made up in a long-forgotten dream.

*Hallo*, said Suzan.

*Nearly there?* said the Massive Ball of Death.

*Yes*, said Suzan, and engulfed it gently.

There was a sensation of white-hot joy, and then, for the Massive Ball of Death, the journey was over.

---

ALL OVER BERSCH, the world united in awe as the silver star they had begun to dread suddenly winked and blossomed, then disappeared. Some said it was a sign from God. Others thought it merely an astronomical anomaly. But for a brief moment, before the mundanities of the real world reclaimed them and tiny problems once again became all-consuming, there was a shared moment of deep wonder and a feeling that, somehow, we are all connected.

---

"IT IS DONE," said Suzan.

The doomsayers exchanged glances, eyes filled with relief and excitement.

"**YOU HAVE ONLY A FEW MINUTES UNTIL THE DEBRIS LANDS. I SUGGEST YOU FLEE.**"

Relief was quickly washed over with fear.

"You heard the giant disembodied voice," said Azron. "Let's make like a tree and run the hell away!"

"That doesn't make any sense!" said Xharon, but Azron was already sprinting back toward the elevator.

"The man has a point—everybody get to the elevator," said Handen, breaking into a run. Riley and Xharon followed close on his heels.

Bip made to flee, then stopped. He looked up at the metal screen.

"Thank you," he said. "Thank you for everything."

"**THE CHILDREN,**" said the AI core. "**WHO WILL WATCH OVER THEM WHEN I AM GONE? WHO WILL TAKE CARE OF THEM?**"

"I will," said Bip, surprised that he meant what he said. "I'll watch them for you."

**"PROMISE ME. PROMISE ME YOU WILL WATCH OVER THEM WHEN I AM GONE."**

Bip nodded, amazed that a thing with supposedly no emotions could bring such a lump to his throat. "I promise," he said.

**"I TRUST YOU. I THINK YOU WILL NOT DISAPPOINT ME. GO THEN, BIP. RUN. WHILE YOU STILL CAN. RUN."**

Bip turned around and ran, not looking back.

**"WATCH OVER THEM."**

---

THE DOOMSAYERS STOOD in the elevator, leaving the secret underground world behind them forever. The rock walls rushed past the glass windows, faster this time. Everybody could feel a weight of force on their chest as they soared upward to the entrance tomb.

"How's it coming, Professor?" asked Handen.

Riley looked up from the Do-fer, busy making tiny, complex adjustments.

"Soon now, Mr. Strike."

"Hang on," said Xharon, frowning. "If we're just going to use the Do-fer to escape, then why are we using this elevator at all?"

"There are two guards at the entrance, remember? They were just doing a job—they don't deserve to be blown to pieces," said Handen.

"Very noble, I'm sure," said Azron. "But neither do we!"

"Relax, we have time."

The elevator came to a stop, and the door opened. The companions sprinted into the corridor, rushing up the steps two at a time. Bip's heart thundered with hope and adrenaline when he saw the light of blue sky through the entrance. They emerged breathless into the fresh air…and stopped dead.

"Greetings," said Draegul, and behind him a dozen of his personal guard drew their pistolas in unison. Several other guardsmen abseiled down from ropes that hung from a dirigible far above them.

"Oh, that's just typical," said Azron. "Bloody typical."

Draegul drew his katana. "Very impressive, Strike. I see you and your friends have managed to save the day after all. How wonderfully dashing."

Handen shrugged. "Someone had to do it."

Draegul's eyes narrowed. "A pity no one will ever know. Now stand aside or be cut down. This weapon is mine."

"Take it," said Handen. "We don't want it."

"What?" said Draegul, lowering his blade and laughing. "No heroic last stand? No pig-headed defiance? I must say I was expecting something a little more dramatic."

"Shut up," said Handen.

Draegul's façade of merriment disappeared instantly. "What did you say to me?"

"I said shut up. Just shut up. You've been a ruling Emperor for a thousand years and you still can't get over yourself, can you? What is it about being an evil tyrant that makes people into such smug, egotistical bastards? I've killed mad kings, led revolts against warlords, squashed rebel terrorists…and you know what? They're all the same, all of them just laughing little boys starting a gang to feel big. Just wimpy little boys who wouldn't recognize true power if they had it handed to them on a plate. Just shut up, Draegul. You bore me."

There was a low and dangerous silence.

"I'll kill you," growled Draegul.

"Blah, blah, blah," Handen retorted. "Professor, are we ready?"

"Yes, we are."

"Then take us out of here."

Xharon gave an apologetic wave as a whirring noise began to ascend in volume.

"Sorry, Uncle Tommy," said Xharon. "But you really are going to get what you deserve."

Azron made a rude gesture as they began to fade from view, the world wobbling around them like poorly made jelly.

"No!" screamed Draegul. "Come back here! I'm not finished with you! *Come back!*"

There was only sun, sand, and stone before him now.

"I still won," he muttered. "I still got the weapon, so *I still won.*"

He looked up into the sky as he heard a low and ominous whistle.

"What?" he said. And then the world around him became briefly hot and agonizing, then silent.

---

OF ALL THE people on Bersch, Mando and Gellimun had the best view of their world's first incidence of nuclear destruction. Not that they were particularly pleased with their lot, but later they would become the recognized authority on the subject—the only people close to the explosion who had actually survived.

They would recount how they had seen what looked a shooting star head directly toward the transformed pyramid. They would say how a ring of fire had pounded the desert in all directions, blowing the sand up in a red-hot storm, and fusing a huge stretch of land into pure glass. They would tell of how they'd seen the mighty Imperial dirigibles, hanging majestically in the air, suddenly reduced to charcoal-like shells before they crumbled as ash into the breeze. They would tell how a cloud like a mushroom had billowed for what seemed like an age, while a colossal rumbling sent them to their knees. They would tell how a force like an angry wind had flung their bodies across the desert and how they had lain there, praying before this awesome power, praying that they would be spared as the hot winds seared over their heads. They would say how they had waited for days before their hearing and sight returned to normal, and how they had been ill for many weeks afterward.

But mostly they would say that they were never, ever going near a pyramid ever again.

---

TED LOOKED DOWN on creation and saw that it was good. As much as he was the embodiment of the very binding forces of the universe, the total equation of which the answer was everything, the final blueprint and grand design, he was also a sucker for a happy ending.

"Well done, Bip," he said, and went back to tending his garden.

---

13

# Hurrah

---

The soul-chilling blizzard of the Ice Plains seeped in through Kaneq's weakened heatshield. The volunteers stood waiting, in rough formation, heavily clad in oilskins and furs, weapons and equipment ready in hand.

In the lead was Bailey, hunter's bow slung across his back, face set in annoyed anxiety. Rynford was over half an hour late, which was unheard of. He turned to his fellow volunteers, each of them silent and pensive. He was not surprised to see a few tears shed; after all, this might be the last time they saw their home.

Today was V-Day, and down by the ice floes, several boats were waiting for them—providing they had not been vandalized by yetis or eaten by driftdiggers. Bailey whistled a snatch of tune between his teeth, then started at the coughing sound by his side.

"No time for music and merriment, Bailey. It's V-Day, after all."

The longhaired youth turned to see the muscular bulk of Rynford and was surprised to see Truggle by his side. Bailey stood to attention.

"Awaiting orders to move out, sir," he said.

Rynford coughed in what seemed like an embarrassed way. "Not just yet, Bailey. We are…awaiting further information."

Bailey frowned. "What information? What could be so important that it would hold us up?"

"Just wait and see, lad. Wait and see."

Bailey shook his head in irritation and faced forward. Here they were, the last hope of Bersch, and they were being told to hang around for no good reason. The volunteer sighed and stared once again into the awaiting blizzard. And then squinted. He could have sworn he saw movement, an unusual ripple in the falling snow. His hand went to his bow as a series of silhouettes appeared from nowhere.

"What's going on?" he demanded, but Rynford and Truggle only smiled in return.

The silhouettes became figures as they approached. Bailey drew his bow, prepared for the worst, then lowered it, his face a mask of near-comical shock.

The figures came closer, revealing a familiar face.

"Hi, everybody," said Bip. "I'm back."

The volunteers stood dumbfounded as Truggle began to chuckle merrily.

"Well?" said Azron. "Isn't anyone going to say hurrah?"

---

FIRST, there were explanations. Stories to tell, points to be clarified.

The former doomsayers sat in the Empty Goat, which was jam-packed with the citizens of Kaneq. People gathered around as the heroes took it in turns to tell their side of the story, and the Kaneqians listened in awe and wonder as they were told of far-off lands and strange creatures. They wrung their hands in eager anticipation at tales of peril and terror. They sat in fascination as they were told first-hand of the origin of their world. And they laughed as fonder memories were recounted.

The celebration was an escalating affair, the drinks, food, decorations, and music falling into place without planning. Soon, after Bip and his companions had told and retold their tales, people began to drink and dance and generally rejoice, and the celebration spilled out onto the streets. The world was safe; their hero had returned. An atmosphere of sheer joy warmed the snowbound community more than their heatshield ever had.

Amidst the party, Bip slipped away for a while, to the home he had not seen in almost a year and to the mother he'd thought he might never see again. Once he was home, after the tears and laughter, he went to bed and slept as deeply as he had ever slept before.

***

WHEN HE WAS first shaken awake, he found it hard to believe where he was. He'd been subconsciously expecting to awaken on hard ground beneath a cold sky with some immediate and life-threatening situation close at his heels. The soft mattress and familiar fug of his bedroom was almost dreamlike. He looked up into the face of Azron and realized very quickly that he couldn't be dreaming. There was something fundamentally real about the thief's sharp features.

"Whadizzit?" said Bip, blinking the sleep from his eyes.

"Something very important, guv. Very important. You have to come and see."

"Can't it wait? I've only been asleep a little while. It's still light!"

Azron frowned. "That's because its morning—you've been sleeping for two days."

"Two days?!" Bip sat up and was amazed at how refreshed he felt. "I missed the party, then?"

Azron grinned. "We're heroes, mate. I should imagine they'll have another one if we ask nicely."

"Well, what is it you wanted to show me?"

"Best if you come and see for yourself."

***

ALMOST EVERY CITIZEN of Kaneq had amassed in the town square, but this time there was no celebration. Now that the heatshield had been replenished, it was a warm and bright day that Bip emerged into, and he squinted his tired eyes in the morning light.

Azron took him through the crowd until they met up with Handen, Xharon, and Riley.

"What's going on?" said Bip.

Riley said nothing, merely pointed upward.

Bip looked up and nearly fell over backward. Above him, silent and impossible, was a huge metallic sphere. He recognized the material—it was similar to the *Sentinel*, which he had seen crash so many years ago, though this sphere was smaller…and not burning red-hot.

"Is it them? Is it the Clarions?"

Handen nodded.

"What do they want?"

Riley cleared his throat and spoke in a small voice. "I think we're about to find out. By all that's astounding, *I think we're about to find out.*"

Above them, there was a noise like a gentle hiss, and a hatch appeared at the bottom of the sphere. A woman stood on a metal platform, dressed in a familiar boiler-suit-like uniform. The platform began to descend with an eerie wail, until the woman stood before the Kaneqians, wrinkled eyes scanning the crowd.

"Greetings," she said, in a calm and polite voice. "My name is Captain Denmark of the Clarion people, affiliated with the Caretakers. Who's in charge here?"

To Bip's immense surprise, the entire community turned their heads to him.

"Me?" he said.

The crowd parted as the woman strode over and shook Bip warmly by the hand. "Good show on saving the planet, you chaps. We would have been here sooner, but we honestly thought everything was in hand."

Bip nodded dumbly and gestured to Handen. "Yes, Handen explained that you might not have got the distress call."

The captain frowned. "Handen? Name's familiar."

Handen spoke, his voice gruff. "Handen Strike, Hostilities Advisor of the *Sentinel*."

Captain Denmark frowned. "Wouldn't that make you over a thousand years old?"

"Yes. It's a long story."

"Well, I'm sure you wouldn't mind telling it," said Denmark.

"Do you have the time?" said Handen, raising an eyebrow.

Captain Denmark rubbed the back of her head sheepishly. "Truth be told, we've been floating through space now for a couple of centuries—my crew could do with a little shore leave." She looked around at the still-awestruck faces of the Kaneqians. "Only if you don't mind, of course," she added.

"Not at all," said Bip.

And with that, the celebrations began all over again.

---

THOUSANDS OF MILES AWAY, deep in the wooded center of Ghulbra Forest, Tanya hefted a large pack onto her shoulders. It had taken her a while to sober up after the last IA meeting, but now that she had, she had reached some very definite conclusions. She was going to venture out and find the fountain of death. After all, you couldn't just sit around waiting to die—you had to go out and make it happen.

Her one regret was that no one had volunteered to watch over the fountain of youth, a responsible post she was loath to leave unattended. But she had made her decision, and she was very definitely going to get out there and kill herself.

She started out into the clearing and stopped as she saw a figure approach. It wasn't much of a figure, looking more like something that had been left at the bottom of a barbecue. It smoked gently as it approached her.

"Who are you?" said Tanya suspiciously.

"Who am I?" croaked the figure. "Who am I? I am Draegul, Emperor of Argustin, Ruler of Regalious, Lord of the Eastern Realms."

"Really?" said Tanya. "How nice for you. Now, I'm in a bit of a hurry, so what do you want?"

The chargrilled figure thought for a moment before replying, "I think I want to lie down for a while."

Tanya smiled sweetly. "Then I know just the place," she said.

* * *

ONCE MORE, the Empty Goat boomed to the stomping beat of the band, the dance floor full to the brim with revelers, both Kaneqian and Clarion. Michaelmas had his work cut out as cask after cask of ale was emptied.

In one corner, Riley and Glimton held fascinating scientific discussion with Clarion Elite-Gifted, while at another Handen and Rynford shared a pitcher of ale, talking of the combat they had seen. A queue of sheepish young men had formed to ask Xharon to dance, but the warrior princess was busy discussing the finer points of her martial arts to a group of interested hunters.

Bip sat with Azron and Bailey, playing a popular drinking game called "Let's See Who Can Get The Most Drunk The Fastest." So far, Bailey was winning.

Bip was trying to keep up with a rude limerick Azron was teaching them when he felt a tap on his shoulder. He looked down to see the ancient face of Truggle peering up at him knowingly. His trusty broom was festooned with streamers.

"Did you see how they turned to you when the Clarions arrived?"

Bip frowned for a moment, sensing the question within the question. "I'm sure they were just in shock," he said.

Truggle shook his head, smiling. "No, my lad. There are very different days ahead of you. You're not the jobless young hopeful you were when you left here. You're a hero, respected by everyone. They'll listen to you now, even turn to you for advice. I shouldn't think it will be long before you're made the youngest elder ever."

Bip grinned with a sudden and desperate optimism. "But you'll always be the eldest elder, won't you?"

Truggle shook his head. "I won't be around forever, young Bip."

Bip felt suddenly sad, as if he had lost something that had been a part of him for a long time. He had never wanted anything more than a quiet, easy life, but here he was, once again the bearer of big, fat responsibilities.

Truggle patted him on the shoulder. "Cheer up, lad. You'll adapt. That's what you're good at, adapting."

Bip smiled as the old man rowed away in his wheeled chair, then turned back to his drink.

---

THE NIGHT SKY twinkled busily as the lazy moon stared down with bemused interest. Bip stood in the graveyard, leaning on his father's grave, and staring into the night sky, a mug of beer still in his hand. The sound of celebration was muffled with distance, and the music and laughter floated gently into the night like a half-remembered poem.

"They said I might find you here," came a voice. Xharon emerged from the shadows, a coat wrapped around her shoulders against the midnight chill.

Bip continued to stare at the sky, barely glancing in her direction. "It's really over, isn't it?" he said.

Xharon perched next to him. "You sound sad."

Bip shrugged and swigged from his mug. "Everything worked out okay. I'm happy. I just feel a bit…"

"Empty?"

"Yes."

"I know how you feel," said Xharon.

"Really?"

"Yes. It's like when I read about adventures in my books. It's something wonderful and inspiring, but then it's over. And there's nothing you can do to get that feeling back. You can dress up and go looking for trouble, but it's never the same. When it's over, all you have are memories."

Bip frowned. "It wasn't wonderful. It was hard and terrifying."

"And now it's over," said Xharon simply.

The two sat in the quiet, staring into a night alive with stars.

"What will you do?" said Bip after a while.

Xharon sighed. "Go home."

"You could stay?"

Xharon shook her head, a look of genuine regret on her face. "Daddy's a duke, and a man with ideas. Argustin will need him if it's going to rebuild its government, and Daddy will need me to make sure he remembers to eat and sleep."

"No more adventures, then?"

Xharon shrugged. "Perhaps, perhaps not. A different kind of adventure, maybe." She took Bip's hand. "Besides, what can you do to top saving the world?"

Bip grinned, and Xharon kissed him gently on the cheek.

"I'm going to go and check on Daddy—he's getting awfully excitable with those Clarion chaps. Come and see me later, won't you?"

Bip spoke suddenly, with just a hint of pain in his voice. "I wish you weren't leaving..."

Xharon smiled. "I know, but there are so many things to do. For both of us. Besides, now that you've contacted the mainland, we can send an airboat over any time. You could come and visit one day."

"I'd like that."

"So would I. Goodbye, Bip."

"Goodbye."

Bip sat for a while and muddled through his emotions. He was surprised to find he wasn't sad, but rather felt a peculiar hollowness that might be mistaken for melancholy in the right light. It was curious, like mourning a sunset.

"I know what you're thinking," came a voice from above. Bip looked up to see a figure sitting in a tree, the glow of a cigar illuminating his face. It was Handen. "You're thinking, 'What now?'"

"How long have you been sitting there?" asked Bip.

"Not long," replied the former Hostilities Advisor.

Bip frowned again. "You don't smoke," he said.

Handen took the cigar out of his mouth. "My victory cigar," he explained. "Whenever a mission is over—truly over—I light up one of these. Tradition. Here, I got one for you." He threw down the cigar, and Bip caught it clumsily and examined the brown cylinder as one might examine a bizarre foreign food.

"No thanks," he said. "For some reason, I don't feel particularly victorious."

"That's because it hasn't sunk in yet," said Handen. He dropped from the tree, landing as lightly as a hypochondriac cat before continuing. "You've been obsessed with nothing but stopping the planet exploding for nearly a year. Now you're feeling a little bit purposeless, yes? As though you've gone as far as you can go?"

"I suppose."

Handen clapped the younger man awkwardly on the shoulder. "Light up the cigar. And know that you'll be lighting another one day because life's full of missions, some big, some small—all of them important."

Bip stared into space for a moment. "That's probably the most optimistic thing I've ever heard you say."

Handen gave a facial shrug. "Yeah, well, don't get used to it."

Bip sat upright. "You're leaving too, aren't you? Going back with the Clarions?"

Handen waved his hand from side to side. "Yes and no. I'm leaving, but I'm certainly not going back to the Clarion home worlds. I've been on duty for a thousand years—I could use a holiday."

"Where will you go?"

Handen held up a familiar device. It was the Do-fer. "The professor gave me this. He's already organized a ride back home with Captain Denmark, so he doesn't need it. Apparently, this device might have a chance of killing me—like the penguin, remember?"

Bip hung his head. "You're still intent on killing yourself, then."

Handen puffed on his cigar. "As a matter of fact, no. I don't think this will kill me. I think I'll be able to go far into the future and still be okay. I think I might be one of the few people in the universe who can go wherever and whenever he pleases. Now, maybe I'm just getting soft in my old age, but I'm starting to think that maybe things *do* happen for a reason, that maybe there are other worlds to be saved, other men like Draegul, and that maybe I can help."

"I thought you were sick of adventures?"

"I was. But the universe is a big place, and I'm just a small part of it. I think there's got to be something that can interest me out there." The adventurer smiled. "Or maybe I'll find a time and place where everything's peaceful and a man can lie back and relax for a few centuries."

Bip nodded. "I envy you, really."

"You shouldn't," said Handen. "You've got your own responsibilities."

"Yes, I know. To Kaneq."

Handen shook his head. "Not just to Kaneq. I heard you when you were talking to the AI Core. You promised you would watch over this world."

"Well, I can hardly manage that by myself, can I?" said Bip, exasperated.

"I wouldn't be so sure. I convinced Captain Denmark to leave a pulse relay satellite in Bersch's orbit before she leaves."

"Meaning?"

"Meaning that full power can be restored to the *Sentinel*, meaning that the technology and information of the Caretakers is at your fingertips, meaning you and your people can watch over this world as you were always meant to."

Bip's face froze in shock. "I don't know what to say…"

Handen grinned. "Light up a cigar, kid. Your adventure's only just begun."

With that, the former Hostilities Advisor keyed a few coordinates into the Do-fer, which began to whir its characteristic whir, then he stepped back to a safe distance.

"And I suppose you could say the same for me. Goodbye, Bip. It's been a…well, it's been interesting, I'll say that for sure."

Bip felt a tear trickle down his cheek. "Goodbye, Handen. I'll never forget you."

Handen threw a casual salute as the world began to wobble around him, then he disappeared.

Bip sat alone under a sky polka-dotted with a billion worlds. His quest was over, but his life was just beginning. He raised his mug and toasted the stars, which twinkled and winked knowingly in return. Then he went back to the party.

THE END...or is it?

---

If you enjoyed this book and would like to be notified of new releases, appearances, and everything else related to Steve Wetherell, sign up for the newsletter here - http://eepurl.com/cv5FSj

---

---

# Epilogue

---

What happened next?

Let's not say Happily Ever After. Nothing ends so simply, and people's lives would be incredibly unproductive if they just went around being happy all the time...

Needless to say, with the silver light in the sky gone and the world-threatening disaster that had united Bersch in fear and awe avoided, people went back to being people, as people are wont to do. The world continued to spin, as did the solar system and the galaxy and the universes and so on. And somewhere up above, a God did its job, and a red-faced man with metal teeth tried to make things difficult for people. And even above that, a gardener kept a close eye on his garden, checking all was as it should be.

And what of our heroes? What happened to them? Well, they got on with things...

Professor Riley DeChambre became a leading member of the parliament that filled the vacuum of Imperial rule, and Argustin's industry thrived as it had always done. Wars were fought as the world wriggled in a newfound freedom from Imperial oppression, but these too settled down eventually, as countries, tribes, and peoples found new oppressions to occupy their time.

As she said she would, Xharon returned home to look after her father, spending much of her time reminding a man with high things on his mind that eating and sleeping were important, nay necessary, for a healthy lifestyle. The pressures of her family's newfound political importance meant she became known merely as a princess rather than a warrior princess, which meant a lot of attending balls and laughing at bad jokes and generally being diplomatic to people she found boring. Though when she was alone, she would still twirl her axes at imaginary foes, and she kept her leather outfits oiled and ready, just in case.

Azron returned to the Free Countries, where he was hailed as a hero thief—even offered a chair on the board of the Port Town Union of Dodgy Fellows, and the prestigious rank of Solid Platinum Bloke. He turned it down, though, in favor of traveling to new and exciting places, where he could find new and exciting people to rob and new and exciting things to steal.

As for Handen…well, we can only guess at the stories of a man who is a lightning rod for trouble in a universe of endless possibilities. It's likely that his legend fills a library somewhere. More likely still that even in your world or your culture, there are ancient tales of a sword-wielding swashbuckler who appeared from nowhere to triumph in a time of crisis, and then afterward was never seen again.

And Bip? Bip did the right thing. In fact, he became renowned for doing the right thing because when someone says that you have to look after the entire world, it has a way of sharpening your sense of responsibility. And maybe, possibly, Bersch slept a little safer knowing that a fairly blameless guy who tried to do the right thing was looking out for it.

And the grand design? Well, it wouldn't be so grand if it could be spelled out, would it? And until you understand just how big the universes are, it's probably not a good idea to go poking around trying to sort out a Universal Theory.

What is the course of a raindrop through a river? Whichever way the river tells it. Which may or may not be backward.

Not enough? Well, maybe one day you'll meet an old man with

wiry gray hair, who might just show you the world in the face of a painting. And maybe you'll see order, or maybe you'll see chaos. It just depends where you're standing, really…

*** THE END ***

<hr>

# Acknowledgments

<hr>

Special thanks to Rebecca Hill for editing the initial publication of this book, and to Graham White for the original cover art.

# About the Author

Steve Wetherell is an author, comedy writer and podcast idiot. He regularly writes humorous nonsense on the internet, and cordially invites you to join him. He lives in the English midlands with his wife, kids, and laptop, and his interests include beer, rock music and writing about himself in the third person.

# Also by Steve Wetherell

Authors & Dragons - Podcast

Hell's Titties

The Totally Legend of Brandon Thighmaster

The Ballad of Aaron Bezron

Shoot the Dead

Far into the Dark

The Torso Farmer

<u>Shingles</u>

The Monkey's Penis

Put Your Hand In My Ass

Space Werewolf from Planet Sex

I Know What You Dicked Last Summer

---

# Falstaff Books

---

**Want to know what's new
And coming soon from
Falstaff Books?**

**Try This Free Ebook Sampler**

https://www.instafreebie.com/free/bsZnl

**Follow the link.
Download the file.
Transfer to your e-reader, phone, tablet, watch, computer,
whatever.
Enjoy.**